OF LOVE AND LIFE

OF LOVE AND LIFE

Three novels selected and condensed by Reader's Digest

CONDENSED BOOKS DIVISION

The Reader's Digest Association Limited, London

The Reader's Digest Association Limited
11 Westferry Circus, Canary Wharf, London E14 4HE

www.readersdigest.co.uk

ISBN 0-276-42733-5

For information as to ownership of copyright in the material of this book, and acknowledgments, see last page.

CONTENTS

Touching the Sky

Susan Madison

From an early age, Mel learned that love has the power to destroy. She vividly remembers the moment when, as a child, she asked her father if he loved her and he said that he did not. This painful rejection affects all her subsequent relationships with men: when she falls desperately in love with a talented sculptor who never wants children; when she marries a man twice her age who stifles her with his domineering demands. But Mel is a woman of great passion—a woman who needs to be awakened and to embrace all life has to offer.

Prologue

I AM WAITING FOR MY TRUE LOVE, Melissa Hart wrote in her journal on January 1st of the year she turned fifteen. The journal, leather-bound, its heavy cream pages edged with gold, was a Christmas present from her grandmother and, young though she was, she knew that what she held in her hands was exceptional, and required something of significance from her. But what? Bookish, lonely, she pondered the question for some time. What she really wished to say was *I want to be loved*, but the thought that her father might find and read the journal was too intimidating. Eventually, she pushed her heavy pale hair back behind her ears and, bending over the page, wrote in a careful italic script that she had practised beforehand: *I am waiting for my true love*.

She did not imagine that some day a prince would show up at the door with a glass slipper in his hand, or cut through a hedge of thorns to wake her with a kiss. But, as she listened to her father's cold voice in the living room below, her mother's subdued responses, she was possessed by the sustaining conviction that somewhere ahead of her lay choices, dreams, magical possibilities.

Somewhere . . . but not here. From an early age she had been aware of the sour currents that swirled between her parents. 'Do you love me, Daddy?' she had asked once, four years old, her hand on his knee.

He had put down his drink and stared at her without smiling. 'I'm afraid I don't,' he said.

Her mother had gasped. 'David . . . So cruel.' She caressed Melissa's thick mop of white-gold curls. '*I* love you, sweetheart.'

But it was her father's love she craved.

Years later, Melissa sometimes caught sight of what she expected true love to be. They were no more than brief glimpses, but they remained in her memory like a sip of champagne from someone else's glass.

After art school, she found a job in a New York gallery. She had discovered by then that she preferred to look rather than to do. Selling pictures, not painting them, she waited for her true love to appear. She had always assumed that when he did, other things would automatically follow: setting up house, having children, growing old together. A straightforward life, marked by recognisable milestones. But it had not been like that. From the first moment her lover walked into the gallery where they were showing his work, she had been captivated by the electricity that snapped and crackled around him. It was not until it was too late that she discovered she had fallen totally, hopelessly, in love with a man who did not believe in milestones.

His violent mood swings, the nightmares, the tempestuous scenes left her out of her depth. Gradually she pieced together some of his sad and bitter history—the death of his parents in Auschwitz, a childhood of being shunted between Red Cross centres and unloving relatives—but the knowledge did not make him any easier to deal with.

Remembering this now as they walked home through the midnight streets, she wondered wearily why nobody ever explained that the hard part was what came *after* you found your true love.

'Did you enjoy the party?' she said.

'Not at all. What shallow, artificial *poseurs* those people are.' He scowled. 'I felt as though I was being smothered.'

She laughed. 'You looked like you were having a ball.'

He did not answer.

After a while, she reached for his hand. 'Nice to hear that Rachel Friedkin's pregnant at last.'

'Why is it nice?'

'They've been trying for so long.'

'They are stupid people. Careless, unthinking . . .' He pulled away from her, and set off down the street at such a pace that she had to hurry to keep up with him.

'What's careless about it?'

'The world is already full of children,' he said. 'Starving children, diseased children, tortured children.' He shook his head. 'Terrible, terrible. Babies dying from lack of water, little kids going blind or being blown up by mines, teenagers forced into armies to kill other children. Why should these people wish to have more when there are already too many?' He swung round so fiercely that she stumbled into the gutter. 'Can you guarantee happiness for Rachel's child?'

'Of course not, but—'

'What if Rachel and Zeke should die in a car crash?' he demanded. 'What if Zeke abandons Rachel? Or Rachel falls in love with another man and runs away? Or the child is abducted by a madman.'

'Why should such things happen?'

'Look around you. Read the papers. They happen all the time.'

'You're being melodramatic,' she said. 'As usual.'

He suddenly smiled. 'You are right.' He took her by the shoulders and kissed the tip of her nose. 'You are always right, my darling.'

She leaned against him. His skin smelt of lemons and clay. To love, to be loved: there could be no greater happiness. 'I adore you,' she murmured, looking up at him. The streetlight above his head shone through the tight wildness of his curly hair.

He held her away from him, his expression serious. 'Melissa, my little honeybee,' he said. 'If you were to tell me you were pregnant, I would not be happy. I will not take the risk that any child of mine would have the kind of life I have lived.'

'But we'd do everything possible to make sure that it was happy and cared for.' We would, she thought, feeling slightly breathless, make sure it knew how much it was wanted. And, above all, loved.

'I'm sure my parents thought exactly the same as you,' he said. 'Unfortunately it doesn't work like that.' He let go of her and walked on.

'Why do you always have to be so cynical?' There were tears in her eyes now as she ran again to catch up with him.

'I mean it, Melissa,' he said. 'If you become pregnant, you will have to have the baby on your own because I *won't* have anything to do with it.'

'You'd think differently, I know you would, if it was yours.'

He stopped again. 'Think of it, Melissa. Think of the consequences. With a baby, we should have to find a bigger place to live, another studio for me to work in. There would be no sleep, no peace.'

'I see,' she said coldly. 'So all this about not bringing a child into a hostile world is just to disguise the fact that you're basically selfish. What if I want to be a mother?'

'Then you must find another man.'

Looking at the expression on his face, she realised that choices were being made for her, choices she had been attempting to avoid for the past few weeks. She tried again. 'What would you say if I *was* pregnant?'

'I would say you must get rid of this child, or go somewhere else. Do not tell me about it, don't try to persuade me to change my mind. I don't want to know.' He turned and took her into his arms, smoothing her hair away from her forehead. 'Oh, Melissa,' he murmured. 'Such hair. Like moonlight. Like melted pearls or silver water.' His voice was suddenly unsteady. 'Don't torment me with such talk. The sound of a child crying . . . I cannot stand to hear it. Not now. Not ever.'

With the heaviness of a stone sinking into a pond, she knew that he meant every word.

Two weeks later, having done what she had to do, she waited for an afternoon when he was absent, then walked out of their apartment for good. She did not even leave him a note. Heart raw with sorrow, she had packed a single bag: a few clothes, some books and photographs, three or four treasured possessions—the icon he had given her, a small wooden carving, an embroidered cloth.

For the last time she looked round the place where for three years she had been so happy. She was twenty-two years old; this part of her life was over. Stepping into the passage, she closed the door behind her.

Chapter One

PULLING INTO THE SHORT driveway that ran up one side of her house, Mel Sherman opened the car door. Instead of getting out, she sat for a moment, listening to the sounds of early summer: shouts from the schoolyard three blocks away, the swish, swish of a lawn sprinkler.

Her house gleamed in the late morning sun: strawberry-pink paintwork, white gingerbread trim, black shutters. The red japonica flowers glowed. Roses, lilacs, lavender poured fragrance into the air.

Every time she came home, she remembered her first sight of the house. She had driven into the historic little town of Butterfield searching for a coffee and a sandwich. Parking her car she had stepped out into a sense of time not just enclosed but cherished. Walking along the main street, past the porticoed town hall, the old schoolhouse, the bookstore and the Methodist church, she had begun to prowl the residential streets, recognising that this was a place where she might find sanctuary. And then, on Maple Street, she had seen the house—*this* house—with the FOR SALE sign half hidden by an overgrown hedge. Within an hour of that first glimpse, she was being shown round.

'Have you ever bought a property before?' the estate agent asked.

'No.' Mel was transfixed by the corniced ceilings, the cracked leaded lights, the brick fireplaces and scuffed wooden panelling.

'You couldn't live in this house without extensive modernisation.'

'I can see that, but I love it and I'm going to buy it.' She would use the money left to her by her grandmother. Then all of it would be hers: the semicircular porch, the rounded turrets on either corner of the house, the pink dogwood that matched what was left of the paintwork.

That was twenty-five years ago. Now the house stood ordered and serene. It had taken her nearly five therapeutic years, doing much of the work herself, to restore its former grace and make it into a home.

Getting out of the car, she crunched across the gravel towards the back porch and up the steps to the kitchen door. She put her shopping bags down on the table and turned on the heat under the coffeepot. There was a small stain on the stainless-steel draining board; she rubbed at it with a pad until it disappeared. She put away the groceries, then poured herself a cup of coffee and went upstairs to her bedroom. She took off her skirt and blouse and hung them in the closet before stretching out on the bed and closing her eyes. If she had had the slightest inkling of how exhausting the preparations for the Koslowski show would prove, she might never have embarked on the project. And yet, at the same time, it was the most exciting enterprise she had ever been involved with. Galen Koslowski, one of the leading contemporary sculptors, agreeing to display his work in a small art gallery in Vermont? *Her* gallery? Sometimes she could hardly believe it.

Eighteen months ago, she had been leafing idly through *Art Today* when his face had leapt at her from the pages of an article describing a retrospective of his work. In San Francisco. He looked older and almost respectable, almost Establishment, in a pale linen jacket worn over a dark T-shirt, his wild hair tamed. Reading the article and looking at Koslowski's photograph that day, she had been overwhelmed by nostalgia and struck by how much she missed the excitement of working close to the creative edge. And abruptly she had thought, Why not?

It seemed so outrageous that she had sucked in a sharp breath, then thought once more: Why not Vermont? *Why not the Vernon Gallery?*

She had called Koslowski's agent in New York and put the idea to him. The man had laughed. 'I'm sorry, Mrs Sherman, out of the question.'

'Why?'

'Vermont?' She could almost see the derisive expression on his face.

'I don't want to mount an all-embracing retrospective,' she said coldly. 'I'm talking about a selection of his work.'

'Are you, indeed?' His tone was sardonic. 'And what possible benefit is a well-known artist going to get out of a show in a—if you don't mind my saying—a one-horse provincial gallery like yours?'

'I do mind you saying,' Mel retorted. 'No contemporary artist can afford to turn down the chance to show his work. A smaller gallery like mine can often be more productive in the long run.' Mel's confidence increased as she talked. 'Mirja Kopler was my personal discovery. I was the one who gave her her first exhibition. I saw her work and recognised immediately that she was one to watch. And I've been proved right.'

'Only problem is,' the agent said, 'somebody already discovered Galen Koslowski.'

'This is true.' Mel took a deep breath. 'But the way I heard it, a lot of the major galleries won't show him any more.'

'Yeah.' There was a silence in which Mel could almost hear the agent's brain ticking over. 'He's a great guy,' he said finally. 'But when it comes to his work, he tries to impose all these conditions. Gotta display it in the right light, can't have anything else within ten feet of it, gotta choose the right background. I mean, these are wealthy collectors he's talking to. Some of them get sick of it and cancel their cheques.' He sighed. 'I'll put your proposal to him, Mrs Sherman. Just don't expect any miracles.'

I don't want miracles, she thought, putting down the phone, just *this* miracle.

Against all the odds, the difficult-to-please Koslowski had accepted her proposal and the event had been scheduled for the beginning of October. Ever since, she and Carla Payne, her assistant, had worked all hours, wooing the press and calling clients who would be interested. Now, with all the arrangements finally in place, Mel was taking some time off, leaving Carla to handle the day-to-day running of the gallery.

She finished her cooling coffee, then lay with her hands behind her head. In a while, she would go and pull a few therapeutic weeds in the garden and deadhead the roses, but for the moment she was content to absorb the quiet of this pale, peaceful room. Creamy Chinese rugs lay on the sanded pine floor. Bleached linen drapes hung at the windows that overlooked the rear of the house, the furniture was white-painted wicker. The only colour came from two big vases of flowers, and the icon that hung between the windows.

She napped for half an hour, then got up and pulled on jeans and a faded blue T-shirt. Downstairs, she ran her hand over the rounded contours of the small sculpture on her bureau, a curved column of polished rosewood no more than eighteen inches high, which only gradually revealed itself to the viewer as a virginal female torso, the breasts, buttocks and belly barely defined.

She went out onto the wooden porch that ran across the front of the house. A blue jay was clinging to the trunk of the big shade tree like a piece of jewellery, but it arrowed away as she came down the steps. In the still afternoon air, plunging her fingers into the earth, then reaching for the roses, she was aware of something very close to happiness.

Later, she went upstairs to shower and dress. In the bathroom, she examined the reflection of her unused body in the glass. Full breasts, rounded hips, small waist, strong and shapely legs. She touched the scar that ran below her left breast almost to her hip. Her arms were suntanned, the skin shiny where they flowed into the roundness of her shoulders. With her thick, silver-blonde hair, she did not look bad, she thought. Dispassionately she noted the way her stomach had begun to sag, however tightly she pulled it in. I am forty-seven, she told herself, smoothing her hands over her hips, how can I expect to look like a girl? More importantly, why should I want to?

Chapter Two

MEL HAD FIRST MET Lisa Andersen at the Mahoneys' spring party three months earlier, when Sarah had steered her across the room, saying, 'You *must* come and say hello to Lisa, our little newcomer.'

Mel had been reluctant. 'Why must I?'

'Oh now, Mel. Don't be so unsociable. You probably already know Lisa's husband,' she said. 'Ben Andersen? His family's had a house up by the lake for years.'

'The Andersens are my neighbours up there.' Mel was interested despite herself.

'Well, little Lisa and Ben have been living in New York until recently. Moved up here three or four months ago, renting the old Adams house. Lisa, dear . . .' Sarah's voice turned creamy, '. . . this is Melissa Sherman.'

'Lisa Tan.' The girl who held out her hand to Mel was as tiny and vivid as a hummingbird.

'I think you two are going to get along really well,' Sarah cooed. 'So much in common . . . both so artistic.' She faded away, leaving Mel and Lisa together.

'What do *you* think?' Lisa said. She wore a peacock-blue scarf and a yellow linen shift that glowed like sunshine.

'What about?'

'Us getting along.'

'If we're both *artistic*,' Mel said, 'not a chance.' She drank from the glass of wine she was holding.

Lisa grinned. 'I'm a potter.'

'Lisa Tan . . .' Mel said slowly. 'Hasn't Rita Bernhard got one of your pieces?'

'That's right.'

'I own the local art gallery.'

'That converted barn place on the way to Middlebury?'

'That's right.'

'From the road, it looks really interesting. All those weird stone sculptures out front. I keep meaning to stop and look at them more closely.'

'Come in when you've done that, and I'll give you a coffee.'

'It's a deal.' Lisa raised her glass of fruit punch, watching Mel over the rim. 'You wouldn't believe how many people I've been told since I got here that I'm going to get along fine with.'

'And have you?'

'Not so far.'

'Funny. You don't look like a social misfit.'

'I guess I just haven't developed a small-town mentality yet.' Lisa widened her eyes, which were so dark that it was difficult to distinguish the pupil. 'But perhaps I shouldn't be saying that.'

'Because I might have?'

Lisa put her head on one side. 'Nicole Farhi suit, Manolo Blahnik shoes—doesn't shriek small-town to me.'

'Good,' Mel said drily.

'I'm being way too personal. Ben's always telling me to watch what I say, in case I offend someone.'

'Which one is Ben?'

'The good-looking hunk over there, by the bookcase.'

The man she indicated was leaning against the wall at the far end of the room, looking through a book that he had obviously taken from the shelves behind him. One shoulder was hunched, as though he was trying to shut out the sight and sound of Sarah Mahoney's guests.

Mel realised that she had seen him many times before, up at the lake, rowing across the water, fishing from the dock in front of the Andersen house. 'He doesn't seem to be enjoying himself very much,' she said.

Lisa rolled her eyes. 'My poor husband. He's just come back from Peru so this is a bit of a contrast . . . And he hates parties anyway.'

As though he knew they were talking about him, he glanced up from his book. Despite Lisa's description, he was not particularly good-looking. His deeply tanned face was topped by short, untidy curls of an indeterminate colour, each one tipped with gold, as though bleached by exposure to the sun; his eyebrows were thick and so blond that they were almost white. But when he looked at his wife, a smile of extraordinary beauty lit up his face.

'Golly,' Mel said.

'I know!' Lisa laughed. 'From the very first time he did that to me, I was a goner.' She looked up at Mel. 'And which one of the dozens of guys standing round gawping at you is your husband?'

'I'm . . . My husband's dead.' Even after three years, Mel could not bring herself to use the word 'widow'.

'Oh . . .' Colour rushed into Lisa's face. 'I'm so sorry.'

'That's OK.' Mel changed the subject. 'Sarah said you'd been here for three or four months. How come I haven't seen you around before?'

'Ben's been away a lot. And I'm so scared of running into the folk I'm supposed to get along fine with that I stay home most of the time.' Lisa put a hand to her mouth. 'Oops! Probably shouldn't have said that either. Actually, I'm being unfair. I've met some really great people.' A grin spilled across her face. 'Most of them from my childbirth class.'

Mel's eyes dropped to Lisa's tiny waist. 'I'd never have guessed. When are you due?'

'October.'

'And it's March now.' Mel did the mental arithmetic.

'I know,' Lisa said. 'I'm just over two months. But I'm—*we're*—really excited about it.'

'What does Ben do?'

'He climbs mountains,' Lisa said, 'and a number of different things to fund his climbing. Odd jobs, mostly. Carpentry. Construction work. Rigging.' Lisa had smiled ruefully. 'Anything that'll give him enough money to go off again. Sometimes he leads walking tours. Guides people who want to go climbing. Mountains are what he does.'

Later, finding herself alongside him, Mel had introduced herself. Close to, she glimpsed in his deep-set eyes an almost chilling remoteness. 'I'm Melissa Sherman,' she said. 'My husband Eric and I bought our cabin by the lake from your mother.'

He did not smile, which disconcerted her. 'I've seen you up there.'

'Are you enjoying your move to Butterfield?'

He nodded. 'I don't like living in New York.'

'Nor do I,' she had said. And suddenly wondered if that was still true.

'Really?' He raised disbelieving eyebrows. 'You look like the sort who'd—'

'Do I?' She had turned away.

The Adams fruit farm had flourished for three generations, but the Adams sisters had been unable to keep the business going and now the original house, the barn beside it and a few scrawny apple trees were all that remained. In return for fixing it up a little, Ben and Lisa Andersen were able to rent the place for a nominal sum.

As Mel swept round the gravelled driveway, Lisa came to the doorway of the barn and waved. Despite being almost five months pregnant, she looked like a little girl, from the shiny black pigtails on either side of her head to the vivid colours of her clothes.

Mel stepped out of her car and handed Lisa a bag. 'I had to go to Burlington this morning and I simply couldn't resist this.'

'Another present? You're always bringing me stuff.'

Mel followed Lisa through the dark front half of the barn, which still contained the paraphernalia left behind by the Adams sisters: an ancient wooden cart, various farming implements, rusty window screens. But in the light-filled space beyond, sun streamed in through the back wall, its wooden planks now replaced by glass. A Mozart piano concerto spilled softly from speakers on the plain plaster walls, which Lisa had painted in muted shades of old rose, faded blue, dusky lavender.

Most of the studio was devoted to Lisa's wheels, her bins of clays, pails of slip and bowls of hand-mixed glaze, and the tools she used to shape and refine the pots she threw. Tables and shelving of matching maple lined the walls; the ceiling was wood too, set with large square skylights. Earthenware pots stood here and there, blue, green, turquoise. A couple of kilns stood against the far wall; the rest of the space was occupied by racks of paints and jars of brushes.

'Help yourself.' Lisa nodded at the long counter where a coffee-maker stood gently burping. 'There's cream in the fridge. I even made some of those butterscotch brownies you like.'

'A New York gal making cookies? Something's wrong somewhere.'

'Hey, when in Rome . . . Ben's brought me up here to live in the country so I gotta be a country wife.' Unwrapping tissue paper, Lisa pulled out a baby-sized pair of bib-fronted dungarees. 'Oh, Mel, so cute.'

'It was the gingham heart on the front of the bib that sold them to me,' said Mel.

'They're really sweet. Thanks so much.' Lisa reached upwards for Mel's cheek and kissed her. Suddenly shy, she rubbed the checked heart on the front of the dungarees. 'It's been really great, you know, having you as my surrogate mom.'

Mel could never have explained to Lisa how much the coming baby meant to her. She searched her friend's face. 'So . . . is everything OK?'

Lisa tapped her teeth with the end of a paintbrush as she stared at the small wilderness of trees and tangled undergrowth outside the window. 'Being alone so much sometimes gets me down. I knew when I married him that Ben would be off, climbing mountains, trekking.' She shook her head. 'It's just that now, with the baby and all, I wish he wouldn't.'

'Tell him how you feel.'

'I can't. Mountain-climbing is like a fix for him. The ultimate challenge. It's not for me to veto it.' She looked down at her coffee cup. 'The way Ben talks about it, the discomfort, the danger, I've realised that being scared shitless on a regular basis is what keeps him functioning. He lost a cousin when he was just a kid, in some kind of biking accident. I know he still blames himself, even though it wasn't his fault. So as far as I'm concerned, if climbing mountains is what Ben needs, then that's what he must do. It's just that sometimes I wish . . . this sounds so pathetic . . . I wish he wanted to be here with me, instead of out there.'

'It's not pathetic at all.' It was strange, Mel thought, that she had become so close to Lisa whereas Lisa's husband remained almost unknown, as inaccessible as the mountains he loved.

'And on top of that, I really miss New York and that exhilarating sense of living on the edge.' Lisa clasped her arms round her chest, staring out at the orchard with its unpruned fruit bushes and knobby-trunked apple trees. 'Trouble is, when he's away, I get so frightened. I lie in bed thinking what I'd do if something happened to him, how I'd cope.'

Mel felt suddenly cold. 'Come on, honey,' she said quickly. 'Nothing's going to happen to him.'

Lisa forced a smile. 'OK. That's enough griping. You won't want to see my latest *artistic* project, will you?'

'No,' Mel said firmly.

'Oh, go on. You'll love it.' Lisa grinned as she picked up a plate by the edges and showed it to Mel. 'It's a wedding gift, from the groom's parents, for a couple down in Texas. They want a dozen of everything—plates, soup bowls, side plates, dessert bowls. Plus serving dishes and platters. What do you think of that?'

'Great.' Mel's tone was deliberately noncommittal.

'The people are called Peacocke.'

'Which would explain all the darling blues and greens and feathers and stuff.' Mel gave an exasperated sigh. 'You know how much I admire what you've achieved, setting up your own business and all . . .'

'But . . .?'

'*But* you're an extremely talented potter. That's what you should be concentrating on. Not wasting time on crap like this.'

'At least it brings in good money while I wait for people to discover how extremely talented I am.'

'They will, Lisa. Be patient. There's been a lot of interest in those pieces of yours in the gallery.' Mel frowned at the plate. 'Think you'll be able to carry on working once the baby comes?'

'I've no idea. What I hear, it's unbelievable how much time one small human being can take up.'

'Only at the beginning. Listen, honey. If you get down again, don't keep it to yourself. Call me up and come round for a meal one evening.'

'I'll do that.' Lisa began jamming paintbrushes into a coffee jar that stood beside the sink. 'Mel . . . I didn't mean to badmouth Ben. I know you'd love him if you got to know him.'

'I'm sure I'd adore him. Pity he's not around long enough for me to find out.' She gathered her things together. 'I better get moving.'

Walking back with Mel to her car, Lisa put her head on one side. 'I hope you don't mind my asking, but why didn't you and Eric have kids?'

'I . . .' Her face flushing, Mel said, 'Eric felt he was too old to start a family.'

'I guess that's the way it goes, sometimes.'

But driving back to Maple Street, Mel felt a painful rush of guilt. She should have been honest. She should have admitted to Lisa that it was not Eric's fault there had been no children. But even after all these years, she still could not talk about, could scarcely think about the child she had once carried within her, and had then, quite deliberately, destroyed.

Night was beginning to drift across the mountains as Ben Andersen turned off the highway onto the road through the woods. However many times he drove these quiet lanes between the deep thickets of white birch and sugar maple, he always experienced a lift of the heart as the trees pushed close to the edge of the road and blotted out the sky.

Further along the dirt road, he pulled up. Turning off his engine, he got out and stretched. He'd set off early, driven all the way to Brattleboro, spent the day refitting a kitchen in a restored Victorian house up there. He enjoyed the challenge of fitting wood together, matching the grain, planing down the surfaces until they felt like silk under his fingers. And when he'd finished that, there would undoubtedly be more work. Kim Bernhard had asked him to drop by his house on his way home, to discuss a further project.

When he looked back at the years he had spent in New York, they now seemed like a punishment, a rite of passage, something to be endured. The money had been good, more than enough to subsidise his climbing: construction bosses were prepared to pay well for a good ironworker, a man who could walk the steel, work 800 feet up in the air.

He breathed in the good smells of leaf and earth and fresh air. God, he loved it here. The freedom, the space, the constantly changing beauty. If he was ever injured badly enough to stop him from serious climbing, then living in this place wouldn't be that much of a hardship.

The Bernhard house was big, built on the hill above the dam. Way below, the reservoir glittered among the surrounding trees, flat as a golden coin in the setting sun.

'What a view!' Ben said when Kim opened the door to him.

'We're lucky.' Kim was a big man with an attractively lined face. Ben usually saw him wearing a hard hat and a business suit, but today he was in corduroy trousers and a rollneck cashmere sweater. 'Come on in.' He led the way through a plant-filled atrium to a wide space that looked like a gallery. There were several velvet-covered couches in jewel colours: ruby, amethyst, topaz. The white walls were hung with paintings. 'You're looking well, Ben. Very fit.'

'I've been training,' Ben said. 'I'm off climbing again soon.'

'Where this time?'

'Alaska. Climbing Denali with a couple of friends.'

'Denali?'

'Mount McKinley.'

'Ah . . . I'm surprised you haven't climbed it before.'

'I have. Twice. But both times we had to turn back before we topped out. You can get some horrendous weather up there. Conditions are often worse than at the North Pole.'

Bernhard showed him into a large room that was part office, part studio. One end was cosily masculine, carpeted in dark blue, with a desk standing in front of a book-lined wall. Architectural prints hung on the walls, interspersed with photographs of buildings, which Ben guessed had been designed by Kim. At the other end of the long space, two drafting tables were set back-to-back in front of tall windows.

'So, third time lucky . . .' Kim waved Ben into a leather director's chair on one side of the large desk and folded himself into a high-backed padded chair on the other.

'I hope so. It could be good experience for the future.'

'Talking of which, how exactly do you see your future?' Kim laced his hands behind his head and leaned back.

As a lifetime of climbing, Ben thought. High peaks, adventure, the purity of striving. And Lisa to come home to. What else could there be? He lifted his shoulders in a shrug. 'Other mountains.'

'Right.' Bernhard stared at him with a slight smile then pushed over a roll of blueprints. 'Reason I asked you to drop by . . . these are some preliminary sketches for a winter sports centre that Bernhard Associates have been commissioned to build. Thing is, Ben, you're a sports-oriented guy. I'm not. You're an expert in your field.'

'Not really. Just a—'

'Come on, Ben. This last year, I've had to get into the specialist mountaineering and rock-climbing magazines in order to have some idea of what's going to be required for this project. Your name comes up all the time. Point is, I want to take advantage of your expertise.'

'Mountaineering? Is that what you're talking about?'

'That, and other things. What I'd like is to bring you in on this project by retaining you as our sports consultant. If this project goes well, there'll undoubtedly be others. You could carve out a very nice little niche for yourself. What do you say?'

Ben felt uneasy. This was exactly the kind of job Lisa had hoped he would find when they moved up here.

'Consultancy?' He couldn't help the chilly edge to his voice. 'I don't know. I'm a practical sort of person. I'm used to working with my hands. I'd have to think about it.'

Kim grinned at him. 'Meaning, in your head, you've already turned the idea down.'

Ben shifted in his chair. 'Not necessarily.'

'Think about it for a while before you decide, Ben. It could be a mutually beneficial arrangement.'

'I will give it some thought.' Ben pushed back his chair and stood up. 'I'd better get back.'

He drove home slowly. Lisa had told him that Mel Sherman was dropping by today and he wanted to be sure she was gone before he arrived. Women like that made him uneasy, all diamond rings and designer clothes. Not like Lisa, his gorgeous Lisa. His wife. God, he was lucky. As soon as he walked into the SoHo loft where he'd been invited to dinner, he'd noticed her, been mesmerised by the way her hair shone like water when she moved her head. Before he left that evening he'd obtained her phone number.

That first date, he'd picked her up from her apartment. She was wearing a turquoise silk dress with a high collar. Long turquoise earrings hung from her ears and jade bracelets circled her slim arms. It was a cold wet evening, the pavements slick with rain, wind gusting between the buildings. They'd ended up at a small Italian restaurant; with sudden clarity, he recalled opening the door from the dark street to warmth and light, ushering her into smells of garlic and rosemary and wine, still unable to believe his luck.

'I want to know everything about you,' he said, across the checked tablecloth. 'Absolutely everything.'

'How long have you got?' she asked.

He reached across and took her hand. 'The rest of my life.'

She smiled. Pulled her hand away from his. Looked down at the table. 'No, really.'

'Tell me about your family.'

She shrugged. 'Not much to tell. My mom had cancer and died when I was six. And my dad: he's Chinese, and he's blind.'

'I see,' he said, and was immediately mortified.

Then Lisa laughed. 'Which is more than Dad can do,' she said. 'Anyway, after my mom died, a cousin of my mother's came to live with us in Brooklyn. I was an only child, which made it even worse.' She lifted her head and stared at him, her eyes black and profound, and he thought he could see in their depths the confused little girl she must once have been. She shrugged. 'That's *my* family. What about yours?'

'A brother, two parents. Very dull, really.' As soon as he said it he felt guilty. 'No, I have a great family. I love them and I'm sure they love me back.' It wasn't quite true. Ever since the accident, he'd felt that he had forfeited the right to their love.

'But . . .?' she said.

'But what?'

'There's a skeleton in your cupboard, I can tell. What is it?'

He lifted his hands. 'No skeletons.'

'What does your father do?'

'He was a linguistics prof. He's retired. My mom's a pharmacist.'

'My dad is a piano tuner. He's very . . . I suppose distant is the word. Or self-sufficient. Perhaps he's had to be, being blind, having to fend for himself.' She put a finger on his hand so delicately it was like air blowing over his skin. 'You're an ironworker or something, aren't you?'

'Not in any permanent sense. I do it because it pays well, gives me the freedom to do what I really want to do.'

'And what's that?' When she looked at him, he was conscious of happiness swelling under his ribs.

He smiled at her and watched her face melt. 'Climb mountains.'

'What's it like, working up there above the city?'

'Great.' He wondered how much she would understand about a Manhattan construction site. 'It's like climbing. You get the same feeling of exhilaration.'

'Do you need special skills?'

'A head for heights mostly. A steady nerve. People do fall—I saw a man who fell forty storeys, once. Not good.' He turned his face away, remembering.

'I can imagine.' Lisa shuddered.

'Even so, even though you know there's always a chance of flying—falling—there's such a sense of freedom up there, such a terrific high.' He shook his head at her. 'I can't describe it.'

'That's something which, whatever else you do, nobody can ever take away from you,' she said quietly, and he realised that she had instinctively understood all the things he hadn't said. He knew in that moment that he had to spend the rest of his life with her.

He reached across the table and took her hand. 'Tell me three things you like.'

'Yellow roses. Silver spoons. Black coffee.'

'Coloured things.'

'How about you, what do you like?'

'Water. Rocks. Mountains, above everything.'

'Elemental things.'

'That's right.' He curled his hand round her small fingers. 'But I like you more than any of them.'

'Am I elemental?'

'Totally. Completely.' Laughing, he said, 'The five elements: earth, air, fire, water. And Lisa.'

Later, dropping her back at her apartment building, he said, 'Will you marry me?' He had never felt so reckless—or so sure.

She laughed. 'You don't know me.'

'I know enough.'

'I don't want to get married.'

'But if you did, would you consider me?'

He could see lights reflected in her dark eyes, and a tiny double image of himself. 'Maybe,' she said.

The next day he sent her a dozen yellow roses; the day after that, a bag of coffee beans; the following week, a pair of silver spoons he had found in an antique shop in the Village.

She sent him a bottle of Evian water. And a postcard of Mount Everest. She gave him a piece of rock studded with shining crystals. They surveyed each other's terrain like explorers.

She invited him round for supper at her apartment. Bone-white walls, black ash table and chairs, a black Flokati rug on white-painted boards, a single red rose in a glass vase.

'I warn you, I can't cook anything except pasta,' she said.

'My sister-in-law has this great recipe for pesto sauce. Want to try it?'

'Sure.'

'I should warn you that it's very, very sexy. One mouthful, and anything could happen.'

'I'm up for that,' she said, holding his gaze with her own.

Together they pounded up pine nuts and fresh basil, grated long strips of Parmesan cheese, added rough green oil. Watching her small, strong fingers peeling garlic, he was overcome with love.

'Mmm,' she said, dipping a spoon into the oily sauce and tasting it before pouring the mixture over the fettucini she had cooked for them. 'Oh, Ben, this is perfection. This is . . . orgasmic.'

'What did I tell you?'

Later, eyeing him over the rim of her wineglass, she said, 'I wonder what's going to happen.'

'How do you mean?'

'You said anything could, if we made this sauce.'

'Better believe it,' he said, his voice hoarse.

She had stuck candles into a rough stone bowl full of coloured glass beads. They sat at right angles to each other, gazing into each other's eyes, where reflections from the candles danced. She peeled him a pear, dipped it into her glass of white wine, held it delicately between her teeth. She moved towards him until their mouths met and he bit off the half she offered him, their lips brushing together. Juice ran from the corner of her mouth into the hollow at the base of her neck and he leaned forward to lick it away.

She arched her neck, closing her eyes. 'Ben,' she said faintly. 'Ben . . .'

He flicked his tongue over her lips, tasting garlic and pear juice. 'I love you.' He took her hand and pressed it to his heart. 'For always and for ever, I love you.'

Opening her eyes, she smiled. 'Shall we go to bed?'

Lying on the hard futon, which served as both couch and bed, Ben wrapped his arms round her and pulled her so hard against his chest that she gasped. 'Are you sure?' he said, lifting her little white T-shirt.

'Yes.' She fitted herself under him.

He had pressed his fingers against the tight bones of her back, so fragile, it seemed to him, that they would snap like breadsticks if he was too rough with her. Her hair smelt of coconut and garlic. He put his head between her small breasts and drew the scent of her deep into himself. Under his hand, her skin felt as soft as nectarines. She gazed at him with childlike seriousness when he entered her for the first time, catching her breath, holding him hard against her. 'Yes,' she said softly, when he came, when she came. Her smile was rapturous. 'Yes.'

He knew what she would say when he told her about Kim Bernhard's proposal. He smiled, thinking about it. She would launch herself at him, her face one big beam of delight. Fly into his arms, the bump of the baby keeping them apart, cover his face with kisses.

'Oh, darling, that's *marvellous*!' she would say. 'When do you start?'

He loved her so much. He wanted to make her happy. But he wouldn't tell her. Not yet. Not until he'd been up to the cabin and had a chance to think about the job and the loss of freedom that went along with it.

'Honey, I'm home,' he called in the deep voice that always made her laugh, coming in through the front door, leaving his keys in the hall. He could smell new paint, roasting chicken, fresh-baked cookies.

'Sweetie!' She stood for a moment at the door of the kitchen then ran into his arms.

There was a smudge of yellow paint on her cheek, a streak of it in her hair. He picked her up and whirled her round, then kissed her mouth. 'Oof!' he said, carefully setting her down again. 'I shan't be able to do that much longer. You weigh a ton.'

'I'm eating like a horse at the moment.' She took his hand and drew him behind her into the kitchen. She opened the refrigerator and removed a bottle of Coors. 'Here you are. Want a glass?'

He shook his head, removed the cap, raised the bottle to his lips. Pulling out a chair, he sat down at the table. 'So, how was your day?'

'Fine. I put a second coat on the baby's room. Had a nap. Made some cookies for Mel.'

'And how was she?' he asked, not really caring.

'Good. She brought this cute pair of overalls for the baby. Look . . .' She picked them up from the back of a chair and showed him.

'Very generous.'

'I know. She's almost as excited about the baby as we are. I guess—

poor Mel—this is as close to having a grandbaby as she'll ever get.'

'Her husband wasn't keen on kids, is that right?'

'Or maybe she just didn't want *his* children.'

'Can't say I blame her. I used to see her husband up at their cabin in the summer and he always seemed to be a bit of a jerk.' He reached behind him to the refrigerator and without getting up, hoicked out another Coors. 'And how are you feeling, darling?'

'Just peachy. The backache, the nausea, the heartburn—I *love* it.' She pressed her fists into the small of her back and arched her spine.

'Aren't there things to make all that easier?'

'Probably. Unless you happen to have a doctor who, whenever I mention any of that stuff, tells me it's a woman's lot.'

'Brad Patterson may be a bit old-fashioned but everybody says he's a good gynae man.'

'Yeah, well, I'll tell you right now that the second Andersen baby will be going to another doctor.'

'Next time . . . God, I hadn't thought beyond this one.'

'We want more than one, don't we?'

'Yes, but . . .' He wanted to savour this baby, this first child. 'As long as they look like you, we want dozens.' He tipped the bottle of beer towards his mouth. 'But let's get this one sorted out first, shall we?' He got up. 'What do you want me to do?'

'Make a salad. Everything else is ready.'

He kissed the top of her head. 'You are the cutest thing I've ever seen.'

'That's sweet of you, honey, but I caught sight of myself in the mirror and I know better. Swollen boobs and a huge belly. I look like a sow.'

Ben tore lettuce into a bowl. 'There's not the slightest resemblance.' He reached for oil and vinegar, garlic, mustard, then pretended to examine her face. 'Except maybe just a little round the nose.'

Lisa took plates out of the rack and found cutlery. 'Thanks a lot.' She put a bowl of cherry tomatoes in the centre of the table. 'The really great news, according to my childbirth group, is that after the baby arrives it takes weeks to get back into shape, and there's stretch marks and no sleep for years and years. I can't wait.'

'It'll be worth it.'

'I know that.' Lisa sighed. 'I can't imagine why I'm being such a grouch, when this is what I've looked forward to all my life. God, Ben, our first baby . . . it's the most exciting thing in the entire world.'

'And then some.'

'Someone to love. Someone who'll love me. I know I've got you, but that's different. A baby means absolute and unconditional love. And I so much want to do all the things with her—or him—that my mom never got to do with me. Play games, walk her to school, teach her to ride a bike, tell her I love her.' She bit her lip, smiling. 'I hope I'm not going to be one of those mothers who never stops talking about how brilliant their child is.' She pulled a pair of oven gloves over her hands and opened the oven door. 'If I start making the baby recite poems or play its little violin for visitors, bat me round the head, won't you?' She lifted out a roasting dish and put it on the table. 'Promise.'

'No way. I may even start looking out for a baby-sized instrument or a book of poems next time I'm in Burlington.'

'You're going to be as bad as me.'

'Much, much worse.' Ben smiled at her.

Later, they did the dishes. Lisa washed while Ben dried and put away. As the light faded from the sky, Ben could see their reflections in the darkening glass. A perfect domestic scene, he thought. A perfect marriage. We're set fair, the two of us. I am so damned lucky.

Chapter Three

ON HER WAY HOME from Lisa's place, Mel stopped by the Mayfields' house. 'Knock, knock,' she said loudly, walking into the untidy hallway, its once-polished broad-planked floor almost invisible beneath a layer of schoolbags and running shoes and piles of books. A row of hooks held coats and jackets, scarves, baseball caps, backpacks and a pair of binoculars. She paused at the doorway to the living room, which smelt of burnt toast, spaghetti sauce and old dog.

'Hi, Mel.' Twelve-year-old Jamie, Joanne's younger son, looked up from his book. Gargery, the family's ancient basset, lifted his head from Jamie's knee and gazed at her with mournful, red-rimmed eyes.

Mel planted a kiss on top of Jamie's head, and caressed the rough spikes of his hair. 'Before I go find your mom, bring me up to speed.'

'Lucy's in her bedroom having a fit 'cause Mom won't let her go to the Prom with some guy on the softball team. Tom's out in the garage making a bomb—'

'A bomb?'

'Not a real one, it's for the film he's making with Lee and Sam. And Mom's in the kitchen setting fire to everything.'

'So just another day in Paradise . . .'

'You got it.'

Mel had to restrain herself from putting her arms round him and hugging him until he squeaked. 'I think I'm too old for hugs,' he'd told her last time she had tried, looking very serious. 'Though I don't expect I'd mind too much on special occasions like Christmas or birthdays.'

'What're you reading?' she asked.

He held up his book. '*Lord of the Flies*.'

'Enjoying it?'

He pushed his round glasses further up his nose. 'I don't think enjoy is the right word,' he said. 'But it's very interesting.'

'*Lord* means you're at L again. What's next?'

He frowned, showing the dimple in his cheek. 'I can't decide. Mom suggested *Moby Dick* or *Mansfield Park*. Which would you go for?'

'*Moby Dick*. Save *Mansfield Park* for next time you get to M.'

'That's what I thought.' He looked down at the page. 'And before you ask, yes, I did lay the table for supper without even being told.'

'You're a star.' Mel went down the short passage that led to the kitchen at the back of the house. Joanne Mayfield, her closest friend, had lived in this big old house for the past fifteen years, ten of them without Gordon, her husband, who had moved out when Jamie was two and had gone to live in Connecticut with his then personal assistant. Mel rapped at the open door and went in.

'Oh God,' groaned Joanne. 'Look at you. Thin, tanned, gorgeous. Now I feel even worse.'

Mel held out the chilled bottle of Chardonnay she had brought.

'On the other hand, maybe I feel better.' Joanne indicated a bottle standing on the counter. 'That one's already half empty.'

'Or still half full.'

'I'm in a half-empty mood,' said Joanne sourly.

The big old-fashioned room had such a pall of blue smoke that Mel's eyes began to water. 'What happened?' she said.

'That damn toaster. I put a couple of slices of bread in and the thing wouldn't turn off, wouldn't pop up.' Joanne wiped an arm across her forehead. 'And I've just had a row with Lucy about the jerk who wants to take her to the Junior Prom. I said no way, not with the reputation he's got. So now, of course, I've ruined my daughter's life for ever and she might as well slit her wrists since there's nothing left worth living for.'

'And I hear Tom's making a bomb in the garage.'

'That movie!' Joanne said. 'What idiot gave Sam a camcorder for his birthday? If they don't hurry up and put it to bed or can it or whatever it is they do with films, I'll be slitting my wrists too.'

Mel put the wine she had brought in the refrigerator and found herself a glass. 'Sit down for a while,' she said. 'The kids can wait for supper. And darling Jamie's laid the table for you.'

'Lucy made a salad, too. I think she was hoping to soften me up before she mentioned Hank.'

Joanne was three years older than Mel but today, in her loose shirt, worn over a droopy denim skirt, she seemed younger. Refilling her glass, she pressed her fingers against her temples. 'What a day. This morning Jamie snuck into Lucy's room to play some stupid game on her computer and managed to wipe out the assignment she'd been working on. Plus it's been one of those days at the bookstore.' Joanne shook her head. 'First Wendy took sick and couldn't come in this morning. Then there was a Grade A fuck-up over a delivery of books for the high school. And on top of that, it turned into Dissatisfied Customer Day. I had three of them ranting at me at different times.' She looked at Mel over the rim of her glass. 'Do you realise it's nearly ten years since I took over the bookstore from Don Cunningham?'

'My God, so it is. I can hardly believe it.'

'I always meant to have a party, invite everyone who's ever bought a book from me, but I know I won't get round to it.'

'You must. I'll help. Besides, don't forget there's a certain birthday coming up.'

'Don't remind me. The Big Five Oh—that's all I need.'

'I never thought the bookstore would last so long, the number of times you've threatened to sell up,' Mel said. 'I'm really proud of you, Jo, for sticking at it, especially with the divorce and three kids.'

'I'd never have done any of it without you.' Joanne grinned. 'Ten years! Gawd, it's about time I got stuck into something else.'

'You're always saying that.'

'Maybe this time I mean it.' Joanne scooped up a handful of nuts and tossed them into her mouth. 'If I had the money, I'd travel. But since I don't, maybe a health-food store would be good.'

'Health food?' Mel burst out laughing. 'You can't be serious.'

'Why not?'

'What in God's name do you know about eating healthy?'

'More than you imagine,' Joanne said. 'Lucy and Tom are both health freaks.' She pushed her fingers through her wild hair. 'We need to live as many lives as we can.'

'And your new life is *health* food?'

The door burst open and Lucy came in. Her eyes and nose were damply red. There was a backpack slung over one shoulder. 'I'm going down to Hartford to live with Dad,' she announced.

'Does he know?' Joanne asked.

'I'm not staying in this house another moment.'

'That's a shame. I thought we'd call in a pizza, since I burnt the spaghetti sauce. But hey, a girl's gotta do what a girl's gotta do.' Joanne smiled at her daughter. 'I don't think Dad'll let you go to the Prom with Hank Summers, though, any more than I will. Especially after I call him and tell him about what happened to Anna Kirchner.'

'*Mom!*' Tears welled. 'You're so *mean*. You don't give a *rip* about my happiness—oh, hi, Mel,' Lucy said, suddenly turning back into the nicely raised adolescent she usually was. 'How's it going?'

'Just fine,' Mel said.

'I saw an article in the *New York Times* about that girl, Mirja something, you discovered,' Lucy said. 'It even mentioned you.'

'Yeah, I was pretty pleased about that.'

Lucy scowled at her mother. 'If I decided to stick around, how long before this pizza arrives?'

'You can call them yourself. It'll take them thirty, forty minutes to deliver, give me a chance to have a civilised chat with Mel. You can order whatever you like.'

'OK,' Lucy said ungraciously.

When she had gone, Mel whispered, 'What *did* happen to Anna Kirchner?'

'Basically the bastard raped her. And then insisted it was consensual.'

'What a jerk.'

'Precisely.' Joanne raised her glass. 'Talking of the gallery, let's not forget that it's coming up to some kind of an anniversary too.'

'Nearly four years.'

'No thanks to your late husband.'

The two women stared at each other for a moment, then Joanne sniffed loudly. 'Face it, Mel. He wouldn't let you set up the gallery, even after you got the money from your mom. You practically had to wait until he'd died.'

'Let's not go there again.' As so often recently, when Mel thought about her marriage her hands started to tremble. She drank more wine, felt the cool passage of it curl around her brain.

'Time you found someone else, girl.' Joanne gave her hoarse laugh. 'Good-looking broad like you. Three years is a long time to go without.'

'How do you know I have?'

'Because you would have told me.'

'Don't count on it.'

'Mom, does this look like a bomb?' The door from the garage was pushed open and Tom came in, followed by Sam and Lee, two of his friends from school. 'Hi, Mel.' He held up a spherical object.

'Hi, Mrs Sherman,' chorused the other two.

'What do you think, Mom?'

'Honey, my Symbionese Liberation Army days are long gone. I've no idea what a bomb's supposed to look like.'

'What do *you* think, Mel?' asked Tom.

'It does look a bit like something out of a comic strip.'

The sound of an electronic rendering of Beethoven's 'Ode to Joy' came from the pocket of Lee's jeans. 'Oh shit, that'll be my mom wanting to know why I'm not home.'

'I better go too,' said Sam. He looked at Tom. 'See you later, OK?'

'*Not* OK,' said Joanne. 'You've got homework to do.'

Muttering and grumbling, the boys moved back into the garage, slamming the door behind them.

'I wish they wouldn't *do* that,' said Joanne, holding her head.

'It's the mobile phones welded to their ears that I can't get used to.'

'Sign of the times,' Joanne said. 'Talking of signs, how's Lisa doing?'

'I saw her this afternoon. She's a bit depressed at the moment.'

'She came into the shop the other day and bought yet another book on how to be the perfect mother.' Joanne poured more wine into their glasses. 'God, it seems like centuries since I was that dewy-eyed.' She pushed ineffectually at her untidy hair. 'All set for Boston?'

'You bet.'

'The big kids are watching the house while I'm gone—God knows how that'll work out. And Jamie's taking the bus down to Hartford.' Joanne grimaced. 'He really misses his father at the moment.'

'He's such a sweet boy.' Mel leaned back and eyed her friend. 'Ever thought of getting back together with Gordon?'

'Are you kidding? Living with Gordon again would be a fate only marginally better than death.'

'You know that's not true. You two seem to get on really well.'

Joanne gave her a sardonic look. 'I'd rather talk about our trip next week. Are we using your car this time?'

'It's more likely to get us there and back than yours is. By the way, I'm going up to the cabin the day after tomorrow. Want to come along?'

'Gaahd, no. Maybe you're forgetting that the last time you lured me up, there was a spider the size of the Ritz in the shower, and I was nearly chewed to death by a rabid squirrel.' Joanne saw Mel's expression and her voice softened. 'Next time, sweetie. I promise. Just not this time, OK?'

Back home, Mel laid a fire in the big hearth. Even in summer, Vermont evenings could be chilly. She set a bowl of salad on the square coffee table, laid smoked salmon on rounds of fresh multigrain bread, put out a dish of chicken and rice. A plate, a linen napkin, cutlery. Salt and pepper. A crystal vase containing two cream-coloured roses from the garden stood at one corner, the petals slowly opening in the heat.

She looked at the table, checking that everything was exactly where it ought to be. Perfect. It would have been much easier to sit at the kitchen table and read a book while she ate. But self-sufficient though she was, she had not yet grown used to being on her own. Eric had given her a framework within which to operate. Without him, she was often seized with an uneasy sense of displacement. Pattern gave a shape to her life.

She turned to stare up at the portrait above the hearth.

'I hate that thing,' Joanne had said, last time she came round. 'Talk about the Bitch Goddess from Hell. Why don't you take it down?'

'That's Eric's grandmother.'

'I don't care if it's *God's* grandmother.' Joanne had raised her eyebrows. 'I hate to be the one to remind you, sweetie, but Eric is dead, and has been for over three years. Haven't you cottoned on to the fact that you're a free woman? Look at this place. You haven't changed *anything*.'

'I think about it, but whenever I do, I can hear Eric disapproving.'

'Eric had a friggin' PhD in Disapproval.' Joanne made a face. 'I always feel that any minute he's going to come through the door and start plumping up the sofa cushions, the way he used to when he wanted visitors to leave.'

Recalling the conversation, Mel lifted a forkful of chicken and rice to her mouth and thoughtfully chewed it. Joanne was right: the portrait was hideous. But keeping things as they were was a way of holding back the chaos that she felt might otherwise overwhelm her. She glanced at *First Love*, the rosewood statue in its place between the windows. Eric had disliked it, and until his death she had kept it in one of the guest bedrooms. Now, it offered her a kind of solace.

She went to bed early. Over the past few weeks, she had found it increasingly difficult to sleep. In the darkness beyond her windows, she could hear the wind sighing through the branches of the apple tree and the occasional thud as unripe fruit dropped to the ground. The sound reminded her of visits to her grandparents' farm in Maine. She had always appreciated the ceremonious way each season embraced its own rituals, required its own observances: the birthing of lambs, the planting of vegetables, picking fruit to prepare as preserves. Ritual meant order, and in order, she had understood even then, lay safety.

Her life now was ordered too. Neat and tidy. She had a home, good friends, a successful business. Listening to the wind, she wondered why, in that case, she so often felt like breaking down and weeping, why she was consumed by a corrosive sense of waste.

Another sleepless night. In the end, it was easier to get up than to toss and turn. Having dressed quickly, Mel balanced on her hip the box of groceries she had packed the previous night, picked up the black leather backpack waiting by the back door and took them out to the car. It was cold and still dark. Shivering, she set off for the lake, wishing she had been able to persuade Joanne to come along.

It was not until she turned off the highway onto the country roads that the sky began to lighten. By the time she was inching the car down the narrow track towards the cabin, the lake was like a pool of fire, reflecting the rising sun.

Because of her preoccupation with the Koslowski exhibition, this was the first time that she had been up here since the spring, and she wrinkled her nose at the musty, neglected smell of the place. But beyond the high floor-to-ceiling windows, the world looked fresh and clean. The lake shimmered, swallows skimmed the surface of the water and the line of trees on the farther shore was very green.

Mel opened all the windows and doors at the back of the cabin to let in the fresh air. Then she took the rugs outside and hung them over the deck rail, picked up a broom and began to sweep.

It had originally been a poky little guest annexe for the Andersen house next door, but the roof had been heightened so that now the great room soared like the nave of a church towards heavy timber crossbeams thirty feet above the ground. Two large, squashy sofas, covered with cheap Indian-cotton spreads, dominated the floor. Between them and the raised hearth was a low table made from a slab of cherry wood.

Cleaning ashes out of the big fireplace, Mel knocked over a glass bowl full of pine cones that stood on the stone hearth. Before she could grab it, the bowl had fallen and broken, scattering pine cones and dozens of glass fragments across the polished floor. She felt herself flush: Eric would be furious. Eric would be—but Eric was no longer here, could not heap criticism upon her, could not make her suffer the withdrawal of his love before finally offering forgiveness. Picking up the pieces, she remembered how he had bought the bowl in Venice, on their honeymoon. He had looked at dozens before finally settling on one.

'It's for you, darling,' he had said. 'For us, for our house.' He had beamed at her and she did not like to say that she preferred the bowl streaked with blue and red, rather than this muddy brown and green one. Often she had wondered if that honeymoon had set the shape of their marriage. Perhaps because of the age gap between them, almost from the beginning their relationship had resembled that of parent and wayward child. *Do you love me, Daddy? I've been a good girl, Daddy . . .*

Suddenly, she was weeping. She pressed her hands to her face. What had happened to that fine, strong feeling of being in control that had seized her as she signed her cheque for the house on Maple Street? She had felt certain then that, after so much loss, there would finally be gain. And there had been. Yes, there had. Eric, Joanne, Lisa, the gallery . . .

The first time she had come up to the lake after Eric's death, she had been trying to come to terms with his absence. So much of him was here: books, clothes, fishing tackle. During the early days of her widowhood, she could fix on nothing except the fact that Eric was dead. Even the simplest act of brushing her hair or lifting a cup of coffee seemed too much.

Eventually, Joanne, armed with tissues and whisky, had taken the initiative. It was Joanne who drove her to the funeral service and sat beside her in the front pew. Held her hand. Guided her into throwing the first clod of earth onto the descending coffin. It was Joanne, too, who packed up Eric's clothes, removed his shaving things from their bathroom, took away the many pairs of handmade shoes. She put into boxes the albums of childhood photographs, the pipe racks and college-crested humidor, the useless, necessary paraphernalia of a life.

'I wouldn't be able to manage without you,' Mel said weakly.

'Of course you would,' Joanne said.

She had listened patiently as Mel talked about Eric. 'We had a good marriage,' Mel said, over and over. 'How shall I cope on my own?'

'You've got the gallery,' said Joanne, holding her close. 'And me.'

Mel smiled tearfully.

'Why don't you go up to the cabin? Take a break for a few days.'

'I don't want to go up there without Eric,' Mel said.

'Don't be such a wuss,' Joanne had said, finally losing patience, and her sudden irritation had mobilised Mel where sympathy had not.

Ben was down by the shore, cementing in the last of the flat pieces of stone that he was laying to form a little terrace at the water's edge. This place was so full of memories for him that it was impossible not to remember the ghosts. How it had once been. The weekends, the barbecues, the laughter. And how abruptly it had all come to an end.

He straightened up, his back muscles tense from bending over.

Don't think about that.

Think instead about the baby.

Sometimes he was almost overwhelmed by Lisa's pregnancy. He couldn't properly absorb the fact of what lay inside the frail walls of her stomach. A separate person. His child. He was impatient for this new life to begin, yet at the same time he was scared. Lisa seemed instinctively to know what she was doing, what her role was. All he could do was watch. In four months from now, they would never again be just two: they would become three. For always. The demands they made on each other would be different. They would become parents. Not individuals, but part of a family.

He carried over another spadeful of cement and tamped it down. Fitting the stone flags together, smoothing the cement, he envisaged his child—*their* child—leaping into the lake, the way he and Rory used to, Mom and Aunt Evie waving from the porch, holding up a pitcher of homemade lemonade. Such golden days, edged with heat and idleness and the knowledge that school was out and summer would last for ever.

There was movement at the corner of his eye and, turning his head, he saw Mel Sherman wading in the water.

'Hi,' she called.

It was an effort to answer. 'Hi.' If his voice sounded false and unwelcoming, too bad. That was how he felt.

She'd tied her hair into a knot. The first time he'd seen her, he'd thought it was white until he'd seen it in the light, the palest of golds, the colour of corn silk. She waded towards him.

'I didn't realise you were here.'

'Lisa's visiting her father.' He got to his feet. 'Guess I'd better go in, take a shower.'

'Me too. I've been for a hike and thought I'd cool off in the lake, but it's much too cold for swimming.'

'Right.' He lifted a hand and walked up to the house. Later, he decided, he would sit on the porch with a glass of wine and start psyching himself up for Alaska. Lisa was driving up the day after tomorrow—meanwhile, it had become part of his preparation before a big climb to spend a couple of days up here alone.

It was shady in the house, the rooms quiet in the warm hush before evening closed in. Ben smelt the familiar scent of the place: old wood, lake water, garlic, ash, the ghosts of a thousand shared meals.

As he lay in the hammock that was strung between two pine trees beyond the porch, his thoughts drifted between past and present. Denali would be a big climb, and a hard one. Their third attempt. He hoped they would manage to top out this time. He drank from his glass of lemonade, chewed on the sprig of mint he'd added, the way his mother always used to when they were young. The smell of rosemary, mingled with the scent of pine, filled his nostrils with its pungent, almost aggressive odour. 'There's rosemary,' Dad had said, as he had planted the bush, his gaze lingering on Ben. 'That's for remembrance.'

Ben thought of Aunt Evie, hippie, flower child, bangles and beads, a scarf tied round her flowing hair. Half a lifetime away—and yet it still felt as though it had been only yesterday. He supposed that he would never stop missing Rory, his bright, good-at-everything cousin. Always laughing, he was one of those kids that everyone loved.

They'd done everything together. His brother, Neil, was older and had other friends in the neighbourhood, but all summer long Ben and Rory were inseparable. They'd always celebrated their birthdays—just a week apart—midway between the two. The summer they turned twelve, they'd both been given mountain bikes.

He felt the familiar tremor of disaster. Rory in front of him, freewheeling down the hill, hands in the air like a competitor in the Tour de France, yellow top, black cycling shorts, green bike, rounding the bend at the foot of Windrock Hill, his own voice screaming to be careful . . . screech of brakes, tinkle of glass, a horn blaring, knowing already what he would find. Oh God, it had been so awful, blood everywhere, Rory lying at the edge of the road, the driver of the truck bending over him, and the terrible, heart-tearing knowledge that Rory was dead.

It wasn't his fault. Mom and Dad had told him so, over and over. 'It wasn't your fault, Ben. You're not to blame yourself.' They'd sent him to someone, a grief counsellor, who'd said the same thing. But he knew better. He was supposed to look out for Rory. And he hadn't.

When he'd told Lisa about it, she'd asked him if he'd cried, and he had laughed. 'Big boys don't cry,' he'd said wryly. 'That's what my father used to tell us when we were kids.'

You don't cry, not even when your best friend, your cousin, has died. Unless you're alone, in bed, huddled under the covers in the dark. There was nothing he could do to change what had happened. He knew that. He'd gone over it a thousand times. Ten thousand times. It hadn't been his fault. Except that he could not free himself from the conviction that if he looked hard enough, he would find the one essential thing that could—*would*—have made all the difference.

The lake was as flat as a mirror when Mel stepped out onto the deck the following morning. Under her bare feet the wooden boards were cool, pearled with dew; the early sun was still hidden behind light clouds, turning the lake the colour of ashes. She looked to her left across the stretch of stony grass and pine-needled forest floor separating her from the Andersen house. Beyond it, the lake opened out and the mountains thrust into the sky. Shafts of sunlight illuminated the higher slopes.

She dressed in soft jogging pants, a cotton singlet, a fleece, and pulled her hair into a band to keep it off her neck. She laced up her hiking boots, filled her backpack with a waterproof jacket, a plastic water bottle, a couple of apples and a chocolate bar, then set off up the steep track that led away from the lake and up the side of the hill.

Two hours later, she was clear of the trees and had come out at the top of Fitch's Gulley. From here she could see the hills spreading away from her, green blending to hazy blue and topaz before merging with a golden sky. She put her hands on her hips and breathed in the sharp, clear air, then set off along the stony track that led further across the ridge of the hill. By the time she reached the big boulders that marked the summit, the sun was high. Water trickled over rocks somewhere among the trees; a hawk circled overhead, uttering harsh sounds. Otherwise it was silent. She sat down with her back against a boulder and closed her eyes. Up here, alone, there was a chance to look inside oneself. Peace settled on her. And then, when she was almost asleep, she heard someone jogging up the track, feet pounding, breathing harsh. Frowning, she opened her eyes and saw Ben Andersen.

'How did you get here?' he asked, annoyance clear on his face.

'The same way as you did, I imagine.' She too was annoyed.

'I hadn't figured you for—' He stopped.

'For what? The outdoorsy kind?' Mel got to her feet.

'That's not what I was going to say.'

You'd love him if you got to know him, Lisa had said. Yeah, right. Someone who clearly thought that anyone over forty was overdue for a retirement home? She picked up her water bottle, tilted it to her lips. She swallowed, feeling chilly drops roll slowly down her neck onto the exposed skin above her breasts. She stared at Ben, matching his hostile glance with her own. 'Guess I'll start back,' she said.

She was halfway down to lake level when she turned a bend and saw ahead of her a woman and two little kids. As Mel drew nearer, the smaller one suddenly tripped and fell awkwardly onto his arm. For a moment there was silence, then he started to howl.

Mel hurried closer. 'Anything I can do?' she asked.

'I don't know.' The kid was screaming at the top of his voice. 'Sssh, Timmy, let me see what you've done.' The woman took hold of his arm. 'Looks like he's sprained his wrist. Or maybe even broken it.'

'Mommy, fingers *hurt*,' howled Timmy, his small body shaking with sobs that were growing more hysterical by the second.

'It doesn't seem too serious,' Mel said, keeping her voice calm. She looked back up the track, wondering if Ben would be taking the same path down. He might have a better idea of what to do.

'I'm always meaning to take a course in first aid,' said Timmy's mother, 'but I never seem to get round to it.'

To Mel's relief, Ben Andersen suddenly appeared further up the track, then came quickly towards them. Assessing the situation, his eyes flicked from the mother to her sons. Bending down, he smiled at Timmy. 'Looks like someone had a bit of an accident here. What's your name?'

'T-Tim.'

'What'd you do, Tim? Trip over an ant?'

'*No.*' Timmy spoke on a burst of breath, insulted that anyone should think a big boy like him would be so dumb. 'My arm hurts.'

'Mind if I take a look?' As he spoke, Ben gently grasped the little boy's wrist in his big palm. 'Can you feel that?'

Timmy nodded.

'Want to wriggle those fingers for me?'

Gingerly Timmy did so, anticipating pain.

'Know what time it is when your clock strikes thirteen?'

'What?' Despite himself, Timmy was interested.

'Time to get a new clock.'

'I know a better one than that,' said Timmy's brother. 'Why did the kangaroo get arrested?'

'Why?' Ben said, touching each of Timmy's fingers in turn.

'Because it kept jumping the lights.'

'Everyone knows that one,' said Timmy.

'I didn't,' said Ben. He stood up and spoke to the mother. 'We need to splint the wrist—it's almost certainly fractured.'

'Lord,' said the woman. 'All he did was trip over a stone . . .'

Ben looked down at Timmy's brother. 'Want to help me find a couple of straight sticks so we can keep Tim's wrist safe till he gets to hospital?'

'You bet!' The older boy was excited. He joined Ben in searching through the undergrowth at the side of the track.

'That's a big help,' Ben said. 'Tim's lucky to have a brother like you.'

'Am not,' Timmy said, but without conviction.

Ben strapped up the boy's forearm with bandage from his backpack, then hoisted him onto his shoulders. 'You'll be fine,' he said.

Once the little family had been dispatched, Mel had no choice but to walk back to her cabin with Ben.

'You were really great with that kid,' she said. 'You've obviously had some experience.'

'I've got two nephews.'

Where their paths diverged, he nodded at her and walked away to his house without speaking or looking back.

'**B**en?'

He looked up with annoyance. She was standing at the foot of the steps up to the porch, wearing crisp white linen shorts and a rose-coloured blouse.

'Hi,' he said, conscious of the fact that his singlet was torn and faded.

'Um . . .' She raised a hand to smooth her already smooth hair. The sapphire ring she wore was the same colour as her eyes. 'Uh . . . I brought a steak up from town with me, but there's far too much for one person. If you haven't got other plans, I could cook supper for you.'

No, was his first thought. You're not my sort and I'm not yours. But sensing, to his surprise, something needy about her, something unsure, he hesitated for a fraction too long and then it was too late to make an excuse. 'OK,' he said ungraciously. And then, belatedly, 'Thank you.'

'In about an hour?' She put her head on one side, the pale hair falling across her cheek to reveal neat pearl studs in her ears. He remembered the slow slide of the waterdrops down her neck, the way they had lingered on her sunburnt skin.

'I'll bring a bottle,' he said. Dammit. He'd have to change before he went over.

'Just come as you are,' she said, then walked away between the trees.

Putting together a salad, placing baking potatoes in the oven, Mel wondered what on earth had possessed her. The challenge, perhaps? If she was honest, she knew she needed company.

You'd love him if you got to know him . . . I don't think so. She could not imagine anything she wanted to do less, right then, than to eat dinner with dour Ben Andersen. Maybe she could get him talking about mountains, pass the time that way.

What a waste of an evening. He pulled his least crumpled polo shirt over his head, found a pair of reasonably clean jeans. Walking across to the Sherman place, he decided that if he could get her talking about her art gallery, he could sit and look interested and let his mind wander.

He walked along the deck and stepped through the open glass doors into the great room. 'Wow!' he said, his bad mood abruptly forgotten.

She was at the kitchen worktop, holding a glass of wine. 'Like it?'

He stared up at the roof beams. 'This is fantastic. Amazing. When I was a kid, this was just a cramped little overflow guest cabin.'

'My husband called in an architect,' Mel said. She gestured at her glass. 'Wine? Beer? Something stronger?'

'Beer is fine.'

'It's in the fridge.' She pointed. 'How do you like your steak?'

'Medium rare.' Holding the cold bottle in his hand, he walked out onto the deck. The sun was sinking behind the hills in a blaze of vermilion and gold. Near to the shore, a pair of loons were bobbing and diving in and out of water the colour of flamingo feathers. Further out was the black shape of a boat with a hunched figure holding a line. He remembered other summers, him and Rory fishing for eels, Mom and Aunt Evie laughing in the kitchen. Scenes from a life that had abruptly slipped away from him.

'May I look round?' he said, coming back into the kitchen.

'Of course.'

He started up the stairs, scarcely recognising the space above. A sleeping platform was divided from the great room by a railing of finely turned full-bellied balustrades.

'Beautiful, aren't they?' she said. She was standing by the big hearth, watching him. 'I had them specially made. A year or so ago I came across a superb craftsman, an artist, really. He carved them for me.'

He reached out to caress the smoothly polished surfaces.

'I love the way he's brought out the different grains, don't you?' Her voice sounded different now, eager and unguarded.

She walked across the room and stood below him on the bottom step, her pale hair gleaming in the gathering dusk. She had changed into a blue linen shirt and a string of pearls that seemed to be the same colour as her hair. He was embarrassed by her beauty.

'I've been trying to persuade him to do some pieces for my gallery.' She held up a glass of wine and he saw the ruby glow of it in the light from the tall, thin candles she'd put on the table behind her. 'Wine with your steak? Or will you stick with the beer?'

'Wine would be good.'

'OK. Supper's ready when you are.'

Reluctantly he came down to her level. She'd made some kind of peppery sauce to go with the steak, sprinkled chopped chives over the potatoes. He was aware of a grace in her, an absolute need for even the simple things to be right. To be perfect.

He could not think of a single thing to say.

When he had gone, moving through the trees towards the light burning in the living room of his own place, Mel went up to the bedroom platform feeling exhausted. He had insisted on helping with the dishes, he had made coffee, he had been perfectly pleasant. But she hoped she would not have to spend too long alone with him again. He only seemed to lose his inward gaze when he spoke of Lisa and the coming baby. There, at least, they had found common ground.

She sighed. If she had not seen the way he dealt with Timmy's broken wrist, she would have found Lisa's choice of husband almost inexplicable. And yet it occurred to her that, locked away inside him, an entirely different person might be waiting for release.

Chapter Four

HE STOOD AT THE BOTTOM of the back steps and watched Lisa for a moment. Lying in the big old hammock strung between the pine trees, she wore her usual brilliant palette of colours: yellow shorts and a bright blue cotton smock, a green scarf tied round her black hair. Such a contrast to Mel Sherman's pearls and neatly pressed shorts. One bare foot rested on the ground, the toenails a dark silvery blue.

Her eyes were closed: he wondered if she had managed to sleep. She and the baby inside her. Did babies sleep when their mothers did?

He whispered Lisa's name, and she opened her eyes.

'Hi,' he said.

She turned her gaze to him. 'Hi, darling. Had a nice day?'

He nodded. 'But it's good to be back.' He smiled at her.

'God, you're beautiful.' Her voice was still edged with sleep.

'You too.' He reached for her hand and held it against his cheek. The heat hung above them. 'How come your fingers are so cold?'

'Poor circulation.'

'I'm going to get a drink,' he said. 'Want anything?'

'Iced tea, please. There's a pitcher in the fridge.' She smiled at him tiredly. 'A stiff martini would be a lot more fun, but hey, I'm pregnant.'

He pushed a Frank Sinatra CD into the player and stood for a moment listening as the music washed against the wooden walls. He took bottles out of the refrigerator and fixed himself a drink, then poured iced tea into a glass, added a lemon slice and a sprig of mint. Returning to the hammock, he handed the glass to Lisa, then stepped up to the porch and sat down in one of the battered rocking chairs.

The two of them watched the water turn golden, then orange, as the sun sank behind the mountains; in the house, Sinatra sang of love. Ben stared at the softly moving water. 'Isn't it beautiful?' he said.

'Isn't it *dead*?'

It was an old argument between them. 'Would you honestly rather have the big city than this?' he said.

'Where's the excitement? The energy? In New York, we used to be out every night, at the theatre or the movies or meeting friends.'

'We never had time to be still.'

'Honey, I'm twenty-six. I don't *want* to be still. There's time enough for that when I'm *old*. At the moment I want to be out there, living my life, not mouldering in some rural backwater.'

'*This* is life,' he said, bewildered.

'If you're dead from the neck up, I guess it is. I want to be with my friends, with people who can talk, people who do things, people who're in touch with what's happening.' Her voice softened and she reached a hand towards him. 'Sorry, sweetheart. I'm feeling kind of cranky.' She shook her glass so the ice cubes rattled thickly against the side. 'I just wish you could find a job that would use your skills.'

Now was the moment to tell her about Kim Bernhard's offer. Ben opened his mouth to say that it looked like the very job she had in mind had just fallen into his lap. But if he told her, and then decided not to take up the offer, she might find it hard to forgive him.

'I hoped we'd have more time to spend together,' she was saying. 'But you're away climbing as much as you ever were. If not more.'

He took a deep breath. 'I've told you I'd stop climbing if you asked me to.' He wanted to mean what he said, but he knew he didn't.

'It has to be your decision, not mine.'

'I hate it when we argue.'

'Me too.' She sighed. 'I can't wait for the baby to come, but sometimes I wish there had been more time for us to be just the two of us, to *learn* each other.'

It was just what he had thought when she told him she was pregnant, and what, despite the rush of excitement that hit him whenever he visualised the baby, he still thought.

'Thing is,' she continued, 'before I was pregnant, I didn't mind you going away. I mean, I missed you and worried about you, but it didn't matter so much. Now . . .' She laid a hand over her belly. 'Now it does.'

Pinpricks of light were beginning to appear between the trees, their long, bright reflections glinting across the dark water. He went and knelt beside her. 'Lisa, I mean it. If you want me to stop climbing, I will.'

She ruffled his hair. 'What? Give up all that challenge and adventure?'

'I wish I wasn't going to Alaska,' he said, knowing he didn't wish anything of the kind. 'But you mustn't worry. You've met Joe and Ross. They're good guys to climb with. Dependable. And this climb's very important to Joe: he's never summited Denali and he needs to if he's going to establish himself as one of the elite climbers so he can set up his own expedition business.'

'That worries me. It makes him much more likely to take risks. Ben, I've never asked you before but . . . don't go this time. *Please*.'

He spoke soothingly, anxious to calm Lisa. 'Darling, I set this up with Joe and Ross over a year ago. It's only for three weeks.'

'I know.' She lifted her shoulders and let them drop. 'So . . . what time do you leave on Monday?'

'Our flight takes off from Boston first thing in the morning. I have to hook up with the others the day before, which means I'll . . .' He lifted his glass and swallowed the last of his drink. '. . . I'll have to leave here on Sunday morning.'

'The day after *tomorrow*?'

'Yes.'

'But that's a whole day less than I realised.' She wrapped her arms round her chest. 'Suppose you fall? Suppose you're caught in a blizzard and you die, like those people on Everest did?'

'That's not going to happen.'

'You can't be certain, can you?'

'Of course I can't.' He felt a stir of impatience. 'Nobody can. But I've got far too much to live for. You. The baby. Our whole future. You don't think I'm going to risk all that, do you?' He reached for her hand. 'Darling, I'll be thinking about you all the time I'm away, and if I know you're anxious and upset, I'm going to be worrying myself. Nothing's going to happen.'

'Just promise me this is the last climb until the baby comes, OK?' Clumsied by her bulk, Lisa tipped herself out of the hammock. 'Promise me, Ben.'

'I absolutely promise.' He smiled at her. 'Our first baby . . . it's the most exciting thing that'll ever happen to us.' He stopped as he saw the tears start to roll down her face. 'Oh, honey,' he whispered. Overcome with love and remorse, he put his arm lightly around her. 'I adore you,' he murmured into her hair.

She stood stiffly inside his embrace. 'What are we eating tonight?'

'How about the famous Andersen hamburgers?'

'I'd be just as happy with the famous Andersen canned tomato soup. Cold. There's some in the refrigerator.'

'Is soup going to be enough? You're supposed to be eating for two.'

'I'm not sure I can even eat for one.' There was a small frown between her eyebrows. 'I don't think I could keep anything down. It's like there's something . . .' She shook her head. 'Not quite right.'

'But you had a scan a week ago. There was nothing wrong then.'

She shrugged. 'I've got another appointment next week. But I don't think the doctor could care less.'

He hugged her briefly. 'I'm sorry you're going through so much of this on your own.'

She moved away from him. 'I don't have a lot of choice, do I?'

Later, they cuddled up on the sofa, dipping their spoons into a half-gallon of ice cream and watching the news on the TV. Lisa was curled inside Ben's arm, while one of his hands rested on her belly. The baby was dormant this evening; he missed the usual kicks.

'I almost forgot,' he said suddenly.

'Forgot what?'

He disentangled himself from her. 'Just a minute.' He went into the kitchen. 'Look what I bought.' He held up a little box.

Lisa lifted the lid and took out a baby's rattle.

'It's English,' Ben said. 'Coral and silver. A hundred and fifty years old.'

'It's absolutely beautiful.' Lisa reached up and stroked his cheek. 'Oh, darling . . . I'm sorry I've been giving you a hard time.' She shook the silver bells on their coral ring. 'It's lovely, Ben.'

'Our baby . . .'

'I think, if it's a boy, that it'll be tall and rangy, like you, curly-haired and good at sport,' Lisa said.

'If it's a girl, she'll be like you,' said Ben. He touched one of the silver bells. 'Any further thoughts on names?'

'If it's a girl, I still think Rosemary's good, after my mom. We're not doing well on boys, though.'

'What about Rory?' he said suddenly.

'Because of your cousin?'

'Partly. My aunt used to say it was Gaelic for red.'

'Rory,' Lisa said, considering. 'I like it. OK. If we don't come up with something else, we'll go for Rory, if it's a boy, and Rosie if it's a girl.'

On Sunday morning, he hugged her tightly, pushing her against the side of the car, though the bump of her pregnancy kept them apart. Looking at the fragile bones of her arms and the stretch of her slender neck, he was seized with a vague sense of apprehension. Bending down, he kissed her soft mouth, felt the press of her breasts against his shirt. 'I love you so much it hurts,' he murmured.

Lisa nuzzled into the space below his ear, standing on tiptoe to reach it. He could feel tears on her cheek. 'I wish . . . I so much wish you wouldn't go.' Behind them, the bus to Butterfield revved its engine and the driver lightly hooted. Breaking away from him, she stood shivering in the early morning air.

'You'll be all right, won't you? All on your own.'

'I'll be fine.' She held him by the arms. 'Take extra special care, Ben Andersen.' Her face was serious. 'If anything happens to you, it won't be you who suffers, it'll be us. Me and our baby. We'll have to spend the rest of our lives without you.'

Anxious now to be off, he bent and kissed her hair. 'Nothing's going to happen. I left my contact number on your pillow.'

'OK.'

The bus inched forward slightly and the driver stamped on his brakes with a whoosh of squeaky air. 'I love you,' Ben said.

'Love you too, dreamboat.' She leaned forward and kissed his mouth hard so that he felt her teeth under her soft lips. 'Love you too.'

Chapter Five

'WHERE ARE WE GOING to eat tonight?' Joanne asked, halfway to Boston.

'The usual place, I thought.'

'Why don't we try something different for a change?'

'Well, I do know another place,' Mel said hesitantly. 'It's Russian.'

'Great,' said Joanne.

'It might not be there any more, of course. But I remember it as being pretty good.'

Back then, Mel would not have cared whether it was good or bad. It was enough to be up from New York for the weekend with Galen. To be sitting opposite him, candles on the red-embroidered tablecloth, a tureen of soup between them, chunks of black bread in a basket.

He had ladled soup the colour of antique garnets, thick with meat and cabbage, into a bowl, then added a dollop of sour cream from the dish the waiter had brought.

She had picked up her spoon. 'What is it?'

'Borscht. Taste. You will love it.'

And she *had* loved it, had accepted more, dipped the black bread into it, marvelling at the richness of the life he had introduced her to. She watched him eat, her true love, her lover. 'It's wonderful,' she had said, 'Everything's wonderful.'

They spent the afternoon apart, Joanne checking out the bookstores, Mel visiting a couple of the galleries. At six they met up in their shared hotel room and went out to find the Russian restaurant. To Mel's surprise it was still there, scarcely changed since her previous visit, twenty-five years before.

Mel ordered the same dishes she had eaten last time and Joanne added blinis and fish. 'And a couple of glasses of vodka first,' she said. 'I'll have the pepper vodka and my friend will have . . .?'

'Strawberry,' Mel said. 'Just because it sounds nice.'

They drank two glasses each before the borscht arrived. 'God, this stuff goes straight to your head,' Mel said, as the waitress placed a soup dish between them and offered them black bread and curls of butter.

'Not to mention other parts.' Joanne put her glass down noisily on the table and leaned on her elbows. 'OK, so who was he?'

'Sorry?'

'Mel, don't pretend you didn't come here with some really special guy—I recognise the signs.'

Mel played with the glass in front of her. 'We were just good friends.'

Before Joanne could respond, the waitress came back. 'More vodka?'

'What flavours have you got that we haven't tried yet?' Joanne said. Her hair was coming loose from the tortoiseshell combs she had pushed it into and her cheeks shone.

'Peach, raspberry, coffee, orange, mint . . .'

'I'll try the peach,' Joanne said. 'And for my friend, the orange.'

'No,' Mel said. 'I've had enough.'

'Go on. Live a little, darlin'.'

When their fresh drinks had been brought, Joanne spooned soup into her mouth and took a mouthful of bread. 'This is totally delicious,' she said. Then, without pause, added, 'So . . . was this guy Russian?'

The pure alcohol they had drunk was getting to Mel. When she shook her head, tiny flashes sparked at the corners of her eyes. 'Polish.'

'Did you know him before or after you got married to Eric?'

'Before, of course.' Mel took a sip of the orange vodka the waitress had brought. 'But he was just someone I worked with.'

'Shit. And I thought at last I was going to hear something about your mysterious past.' Joanne slathered butter onto black bread. 'Have you ever been really searingly in love?'

For a moment Mel was silent. 'Yes,' she said eventually. But love did not come anywhere near describing the scalding emotions of that lost time. She had walked without feeling the ground under her feet; if she reached out, she could have touched the sky. At the end of each day, she remembered nothing of what had passed since she woke, except for him. Only him. Only his face. His smile. His touch.

'What was he like?'

'He was . . .' What had he been? Warm and strong and angry. Fierce and gentle. A man she had not known how to handle. Which was why she had never again taken on anything she could not control. 'He was what you said, a special guy.'

'What was his name?'

'His name doesn't matter,' she said.

'Hey, come on, Miss Melissa, we're friends, remember?' Joanne swallowed what was left in her glass and signalled the waitress. 'So what happened to him?'

When Mel shook her head, Joanne raised her eyebrows. 'So you went for Eric. Because you loved him, naturally.'

'Yes.'

'Just as a matter of interest, how was he in bed?' Joanne widened her eyes. 'You know something? In all the years we've been friends, we've never talked about sex.'

'*I* haven't talked about sex,' said Mel. '*You* never stop. I'm damned if my love life is any of your business.'

Joanne wiped her mouth on her napkin. 'Go on, honey, tell me. Eric wasn't your first lover, was he? Please, please tell me you and this other man were screwing.'

Mel looked away as the waitress took their soup bowls and brought blinis stuffed with caviar, a platter of smoked fish. When she had gone, Joanne leaned forward. 'It's obvious that you could have gone anywhere, done anything, had anyone. So why Eric, master of the put-down, cushion-shaker extraordinaire, almost old enough to be your father?'

'If you really must know . . .' Mel swallowed the words thick as stones in her throat. 'I was . . . I was trying to get over an . . . an abortion.'

'An *abortion*?' Joanne stared at her disbelievingly. 'I've known you for God knows how many years and you've never hinted at, not a whisper of—of such a thing. Why didn't you ever tell me?'

If the truth be told, Mel thought, I wish I hadn't told you now.

The waitress brought another glass of vodka to the table. Joanne raised the glass and sniffed it. 'Was the . . . was it his?' Joanne said. 'The Russian guy's?'

'Polish.'

'Whatever. Was it his?'

Mel changed the subject. 'Did I tell you I invited Ben Andersen round for supper last time I was up at the lake?'

'Ben Andersen?' Joanne pulled the combs out of her wild hair, letting it fall around her flushed face. 'Hey, now you're *really* cooking with gas!'

'He was there on his own, so I suggested we shared a steak. He's a man completely lacking social graces.'

'But what about other kinds of graces?' Joanne worked her eyebrows suggestively.

'Joanne, that was *not* why I invited him over. Apart from anything else, he's a happily married man and he's young enough to be my son.'

'I was thinking of giving Lisa a baby shower, down at the bookstore. It could be kind of fun to hold it in the kids' section.'

'I should think she'd absolutely love it. She just can't wait to be a mother.' Nor could I, she thought. 'By the way, I'm going up to the lake again—any chance you'd come along, with or without any of the kids?'

'Not for at least another week, hon. We're stock-taking.' Joanne looked at Mel's disappointed face. 'But I promise I'll come up soon.'

Joanne lifted her head and groaned. She dropped back onto the pillow and put an arm across her eyes. 'What happened?'

'Too much vodka.' Showered and dressed, Mel was unsympathetic. 'Want me to call room service, get them to send up a pot of coffee?'

'Make that a cauldron.'

'Here.' Mel handed her a glass of water and two paracetamols.

Joanne swallowed them and closed her eyes. 'I swear that is the very last time I ever touch spirits.'

'I believe you, darlin'.'

When the coffee arrived, Mel poured a cup and placed it beside her friend's bed. 'Best thing I can do is go for a stroll and come back for you in a couple of hours.'

'Fine. Great.' Joanne turned on her side and whimpered.

Mel walked around in the sunshine until she found a restaurant which had outdoor tables separated from the street by box plants in green-painted tubs. With an extra large cappuccino and a chocolate croissant in front of her, she sipped coffee and read the newspapers.

When she returned to their hotel room, Joanne was up and packed. 'I feel much better,' she said. 'What I'd like is some minestrone soup.'

'I saw an Italian restaurant about two blocks away,' Mel said.

As they were passing a terrace of stores, Joanne stopped. Old-fashioned iron railings separated the sidewalk from steps that led down to what must once have been the basements of the buildings. 'Oh look!' she exclaimed. 'It's gorgeous.' She began to step down a stone staircase that ended in a walkway fronting some little shops. 'The hat shop.'

Mel followed her. The shop window, sandwiched between a doll's house shop and a bookstore, contained a single hat, made of pale lilac straw and swathed in lavender chiffon, with a tiny bunch of silk violets lying on the brim. On the other side of the window was a small glass vase containing a bunch of real violets. 'Look,' Joanne breathed. 'It goes perfectly with that scarf you're wearing. Oh, Mel, you have to buy it.'

'It's pretty, but it's not really . . .'

Joanne took her arm. 'Buy it,' she said firmly. 'You can wear it to my funeral.'

'I've never been much for hats.'

'Time you started.' Joanne pushed open the door.

A sad-looking woman was standing at the back of the shop.

'That hat in the window,' Joanne said. 'My friend would like to try it.'

'It's gorgeous, isn't it?' Carefully the woman removed the straw hat from the window. She pulled out a chair and, when Mel had seated herself, settled the lilac hat carefully on her head.

'Beautiful,' she said. 'Especially with your blonde hair.'

'It's wonderful with your eyes,' Joanne said.

'It does bring out their unusual colour,' the hat-shop lady agreed. Darting to the rear of the shop, she came back with two more silk flowers of a deep blue. She pushed them in among the violets. With a threaded needle, she added three or four tiny stitches. 'There . . . that's really perfect.'

'She'll have it,' said Joanne.

'Will she?' Mel said.

'No question.'

'You look lovely in it,' the hat-shop lady said. She brought out a hatbox printed with violets and began to rustle tissue paper into it, but Joanne had seen something else. 'My mother had a hatbox just like this,' she said, holding up a box of lilac silk edged with purple leather.

'It dates back to the twenties,' said the woman. 'As a matter of fact, the box inspired the hat so I guess they should stay together.'

'I can't possibly afford—' Mel began, but Joanne interrupted her.

'I'll pay for the box, darling, if you buy the hat.'

The woman went to the window and brought out the vase of violets. 'Take these too,' she said. 'They have such a wonderful scent.' She tied them up in a purple ribbon, put them in a see-through bag, then wrapped the hat in tissue paper. 'There you are: a souvenir of Boston.'

Mel looked up at Joanne. 'Of friendship,' she said.

Chapter Six

THE CESSNA AIR-TAXI disgorged them onto the rutted-snow landing strip known as Kahiltna International Airport. Stepping out into the cold air, Ben stared up at the vertical granite cliffs and the ice fields far above them, transfixed by the sheer dwarfing splendour of the landscape.

Gearing up, he and Ross and Joe began the tedious slog to the camp at 14,300 feet. They took it slowly; they'd allowed themselves a week to acclimatise to the higher altitudes. Once there, they registered their expedition, as required, then set up their tent. It was cold, with an intermittent wind, but the skies were clear. Despite that, climbers coming into the camp from higher up talked of ferocious winds and worse than Arctic conditions. Joe was developing a chest infection and was anxious to start off before it got any worse.

Despite headshakes from other climbers, they began the climb. The going was tough but not excessively so. They were at 17,000 feet by nightfall and set up their tent. The next day they made two climbs up to 19,000 feet, double-carrying food and fuel, which they stashed in case of emergency, before climbing down again to their tent.

That night the storm hit. Three days later, it was still raging. Dense clouds swirled about the higher peaks and tumbled down the mountain, blotting out the sky. The snow froze as it fell, pounding against the sides of their tent. Stormed in, they stayed inside.

The main thing bothering Ben was the fact that Joe's cough was growing steadily worse. He wasn't about to say so, but, looking at his friend, he began to have doubts about the wisdom of pressing on.

'You don't sound good,' he said, after sitting through a bout of coughing. 'Chest like that, you shouldn't be climbing higher.'

'Turn round, is that what you're saying?' Joe demanded. 'No way. I've been preparing for this climb for a year and I'm damned if I'm giving up.' He coughed again, a gurgling wheeze.

Ben coughed too, felt the premonitory wheeze in his own lungs. He tried to tamp down his fear that it was the onset of altitude sickness. It couldn't be. But up here, at 17,000 feet, the air was thinner, the cold more intense, the dangers more acute. He knew that despite the hard training all three of them had put in over the past twelve months, their physical fitness was deteriorating with every hour they spent incarcerated here. Tomorrow, if things didn't lighten up a little, they'd have to seriously consider trying to battle down through the storm to the camp.

A huge gust of wind buffeted the tent and the sides of the dome were sucked outwards and then in. The poles, designed to withstand hurricane-force winds, bowed inwards, moaning.

'Wow,' said Joe. 'What do you reckon, eighty knots?'

'Eighty-five,' Ross said. 'Minimum. Go out in that and you really will freeze your balls off.'

At least for the moment the satellite telephone was working and Ben had been able to keep in touch with Lisa. He was afraid, however, that as they climbed higher it would become increasingly difficult to get hold of her.

'Guys,' he said. 'It's time to get the stove going.' Speaking was becoming an effort.

'Do we have to?' groaned Joe. 'Damned fumes. Makes me nauseous just to think about it.' He turned his head and retched.

'We have to get something warm inside us.' Ben struggled to sit upright, his body shaking with the cold. 'No way we'll top out if we don't keep our strength up.'

Between them, they managed to light the stove, boil some melted snow water for tea, force down one of the prepacked meals they'd brought with them. Later, Ben unzipped the tent and poked his head out into the raging darkness. To his surprise, he saw that there were a few stars shining up there in the immense cold. Stars. The weather must be clearing. He stumbled back to the others.

'Guess what: looks like it's clearing up,' he said. 'If the weather stays good, we might just make it to the top tomorrow.'

'Think we can do it?' asked Ross.

'We have to,' said Joe. 'If the gale dies down, I vote we go all out, make a dash for the top.'

Revitalised by the change in conditions, they packed their loads and checked their gear. The wind continued to abate. When they looked outside at ten thirty that night, although the temperature was still bitingly cold, the clouds had been swept away and the skies were clear.

Ben put a last phone call through to Lisa, told her he was fine, that, if all went well, he might be back earlier than he had thought.

'Don't worry. I love you, my darling. Both of you.'

'Love you back.'

The other two were ready. 'OK, guys,' Joe said.

The three of them looked at one another, then shook hands.

'I'm not doing any work, apart from wedging clay,' Lisa said, when Mel called her.

'So you might as well be up by the lake, where it's cooler. And I'd enjoy the company.'

'Me too.'

They had driven up earlier in the afternoon. Now, sitting on the deck of the Andersen house, a glass of iced tea in her hand, Lisa said, 'I can understand why you and Ben like it here so much. The lake and everything. It'll be great for kids. Ben's laid a kind of diving ledge.'

'Mmm.' Mel could see them too, those children who would leap into the water, the happy shrieks, barbecues, picnics. She tilted her glass, smelling mint and lemon. 'Ben's in Alaska right now, isn't he?'

'Yeah. I really miss him but he keeps in touch by satellite phone.'

'How's it all going?'

'He called last night. They're stuck in a storm, apparently. Crouched in a tent halfway up a mountain.' She shook her head.

'It sounds horrendous,' said Mel.

'Horrendous is part of the fun,' said Lisa. 'He's up there not in spite of the danger, but *because* of it. It's part of his need to escape.'

'From you?'

Lisa laughed. 'I hope not. If you ask me, it's from the guilt at the death of that cousin of his I told you about.'

'I thought you said he was only eleven when that happened.'

'Eleven, twelve. He still feels it was his fault.'

Not as long as her own guilt had lasted. Mel stood up. 'I'm right next door if you need any help. Just yell.'

The next morning, before setting off for a hike up the mountain, Mel strolled over to the Andersen house. 'Everything all right?'

'Fine. Where are you going?'

'Up to the falls.'

'Wish I had the energy to tag along.' Today Lisa was wearing a green linen top over blue shorts, with a yellow scarf over her hair. 'Instead, I'm gonna veg out in the hammock. I'm still bushed from yesterday.'

'What've you been doing?'

'After you went back to your place, I got a severe attack of the nesting instinct and spent about three hours scrubbing down the kitchen.'

'A lazy morning today, then. And here's something to think about while you enjoy it. I've been mulling over an idea I've had for setting up an exhibition of crafts. Let's talk about it when I get back.'

A scatter of pine needles had drifted up against the door of the cabin by the time Mel returned. She had cut short her hike: the temperature had risen and by midday the heat made conditions unpleasant, even up in the cooler forest. She shucked off her boots, poured water from the refrigerator and carried it out onto the deck.

Clouds were building up behind the hills, purple and black, spreading towards the lower ground. There would be an electric storm later, maybe even some rain. Leaning forward and looking to her left, she could see the Andersen house. Laundry fluttered from a clothes line; beyond it was the hammock. Smudges of green and blue, a patch of yellow. Lisa was enjoying the heat—or perhaps dealing with it the best way she could, by doing nothing.

Mel went upstairs and changed into a swimsuit, found a towel, went outside and walked down to the water's edge. Yearning for the cool water on her overheated skin, she plunged into the lake and began to swim, but the water was cool, then cold, then icy. She turned over on her back and let the sun's rays, dimmed by the thin cloud, warm her until the cold beneath was too much.

Back in the house, she pulled a T-shirt on over her chilled body, poured more water and drank it down. Restless, she walked out onto the deck. Maybe she would go over and see how Lisa was doing. She looked between the trees and saw that Lisa was still in the hammock.

Mel frowned. There was something odd here. Lisa had not moved at all in more than an hour. Stepping down from the porch, she walked slowly through the growth of tree and bush that divided the two cabins. By now, storm clouds were racing across the sky and the wind was rising, ruffling the surface of the lake. It was strange that Lisa did not sense the dropping temperature and wake up.

'Lisa?' Mel called as she approached. Her bare feet winced from sharp-pointed rocks and the roughness of fir cones. Under the trees where Lisa swung, the grass was discoloured, not summer-green but a reddish brown, like autumn leaves.

'Lisa, honey? Are you OK?' Closer to, the immobility of the young woman seemed even more abnormal. Fractions of a second passed while Mel's brain digested what she was seeing. Blood, a crimson glisten on the stained grass, bright drops falling. Then she began to run.

'No,' she said aloud. 'Please, no.'

Her brain absorbed possibilities, spinning through a series of disconnected thoughts. *The baby. Loss. Pain. Ben. The baby. Lisa.*

She bent over the hammock. Lisa's face was as pale as cream, limbs set, body inert. One arm hung stiffly over the edge of the hammock . . . Mel could feel her heart jumping under her breast. 'Lisa!' she screamed, the elongated sound floating up into the blue air. 'Lisa!'

In that hard, still moment, it seemed very clear Lisa was dead. Yet Mel knew that could not possibly be. She pressed her palm hard to her chest, drew in a few deep breaths, then put the back of her hand to Lisa's cheek. It was still warm. So was her bare shoulder. Bracing herself, she leaned down and laid the side of her head against the girl's breast. Deep inside Lisa's body she could hear the slow thud of a heartbeat. The flood of relief was so strong that she felt faint. Was it Lisa's or the baby's?

About to run for the phone, she saw Lisa's eyelids flutter and her eyes open. 'Help me . . .' Lisa's mouth scarcely moved as she formed the words.

'Are you in pain?' Mel seized Lisa's hand and held it tightly.

Lisa moved her head from one side to the other. 'Cramps,' she murmured. One thin hand moved towards her belly. 'My baby . . .'

'I'll call nine-one-one.' Mel looked up at the Andersen house.

'No phone . . .'

'I'll call from my place.'

'I'm bleeding.' Lisa's face creased as though a hand had violently squeezed it. Clots of fresh blood were seeping between the spaces of the hammock, falling in bright red globules onto the grass. Miscarriage, Mel thought. Lisa was having a miscarriage. What am I supposed to do? I ought to know but I don't.

She touched Lisa's arm. 'I'll be right back, honey,' she said. 'I'm going to telephone. Try to keep absolutely still.'

Lisa's pale lips moved but no sound emerged.

Mel ran. Her brain seemed paralysed. Lisa had looked so . . . so dead. The shock made her fingers so clumsy that it took her three tries to dial.

A calm female voice answered. Stumbling over herself, Mel tried to explain what had happened.

'Please verify your phone number and address,' the voice said.

Mel did so.

'How many weeks pregnant is she?'

'I don't . . . five and a half. Months that is.'

'Twenty-two weeks?'

The woman on the other end of the line seemed not to have grasped the urgency of the situation.. 'Send someone quickly, please,' entreated Mel. 'She has to get to the hospital. She's lost a huge amount of blood.'

'Could you bring her in yourself?'

'I don't think I dare move her. There's so much blood,' Mel said, squeezing her eyes shut against the picture of Lisa's body.

'If you'll hold, I'll see what's available.'

'Hurry,' Mel said. 'I don't like leaving her alone.'

After what seemed like a lifetime, the operator came back to her. 'A helicopter will be with you as soon as possible. Where can it touch down?'

Mel tried to think. 'There's a field about half a mile away.'

Ben, Mel thought, replacing the handset. She had to let him know. Running back to Lisa, she tried not to think of the child, Lisa's child, *our* child. For a second, past and present fused.

Lisa was still bleeding heavily. Sensing Mel at her side, she opened her eyes. 'I've lost the baby,' she said clearly.

'You don't know that.' Mel took one of the limp hands in hers.

'It's dead. My baby.' Tears formed in Lisa's eyes and slowly moved down the sides of her face. 'My precious baby.'

'You can't be sure,' Mel said.

'I can. I am.' Lisa's body convulsed and more blood dripped onto the pine needles below the hammock.

'The emergency services are on their way,' said Mel. She listened for the *thock-thock* of the helicopter's rotor blades against the air, but the wind was too strong to hear anything except the tossing branches of the trees.

'It's my fault.'

'Don't be silly,' Mel said sharply.

'I shouldn't have cleaned the house last night.' The words were scarcely audible. 'I should have rested more.'

In the distance, above the roar of the wind, Mel heard a hammering of the stormy air. 'That's the helicopter,' she said.

'Too late.' Lisa closed her eyes and the tears continued to seep from under her lids, each one weighted with loss.

Mel's own throat was constricted as she held the younger woman's cold hand in her own. Above her, the treetops bent and swayed as the Emergency Rescue Service chopper turned looking for somewhere to touch down. She did not look up at it. Instead, she bent her head and squeezed her eyes shut while sobs welled up inside her.

A doctor came into the passage from the recovery room. She pushed herself up from the vinyl sofa, bracing herself for what he had to say.

'We've stabilised her,' he said, glancing down at a clipboard. 'She's lost a lot of blood. They've given her one transfusion already, but she may need another.'

'And the baby? She lost it, didn't she?'

'I'm afraid so. Are you her mother?'

'Her neighbour. Her friend.' Grief burned behind Mel's eyes. 'Her mother died when she was young.'

'Do you know when she had her last ultrasound?'

'I can't remember. It must have been, what, a week or two ago?'

'Mmm.' The doctor stared down at his notes. 'Unfortunately Dr Patterson is out of town this weekend.' He looked at Mel. 'Not that he could have made any difference to what happened.'

'But if I'd called the ERS sooner, it might have . . .'

He shook his head. 'For the record, Lisa's baby, a girl, has been dead for about two weeks. There was nothing you could have done.'

'What? But surely . . .'

'What happened today was a natural process, the body's response to an irregularity. A death in the womb often occurs for a good reason.'

'A *good* reason?'

'The foetus may have been abnormal in some way.'

Lisa had been carrying around a dead child for two weeks? The information was too difficult, too appalling, for Mel to process.

'It happens,' the doctor said. He patted her arm. 'We've cleaned her up, done a D and C. She's young and healthy. She'll be all right.'

'Can I see her?' Mel asked.

'She's still in recovery,' he said. 'An hour or two more should do it. Why don't you find the canteen, have a cup of coffee or something?'

For a moment Mel stood without moving. Then she nodded slowly. 'Thank you for telling me.'

Later, Mel was allowed into the recovery room. Lisa looked so frail, the black lashes lying on her pale cheeks, the blue-veined eyelids seeming almost transparent. The fragility of life, the everyday proximity to extinction, had never struck Mel so forcibly as now. She wanted Lisa to be strong again, to see colour in her white face.

Lisa stirred a little. 'Ben,' she moaned. Her eyes were closed, her voice still fogged with the effects of the anaesthetic.

Mel leaned close to Lisa's ear. 'Lisa, I'm going to go home now to try to track him down,' she said, enunciating clearly, hoping the words would reach her friend's troubled heart. 'I'll come back later.'

Back at the Andersen house by the lake, everything was as it had been just a few hours before. It jolted her to realise that so much had happened in such a short space of time. Outside, the hammock still swung between the trees; even in the early morning light she could make out the discoloured ground beneath it and, without any warning, she found herself shaken again by a grief so severe that she could scarcely draw enough breath into her lungs. 'Oh God,' she moaned.

Upstairs, she finally found what she was looking for. Beside the double bed was a small bottle of Je Reviens scent, and a Post-it note cut into the shape of a heart, scrawled with the words *Je reviens aussi. Until then, you can reach me on this number. Je t'aime.*

Mel read the message several times. This small glimpse into the private side of Lisa's marriage moved her in a way she could not quite define. She had grown used to believing that Ben was an irresponsible husband. Now she envisaged him laying the perfume on the pillow, smiling his fabulous smile as he thought of Lisa finding it. Try as she might, she could not help imagining them together, his big hands on Lisa's small body, her black hair spilling over his chest, the two of them reaching for each other, love enclosing them in a glow of rapture.

She wrenched her mind back to the number in her hand and began the long and tedious business of trying to make contact via satellite radio with a man halfway up a mountain in Alaska.

They had been climbing by the light of their head-torches since eleven o'clock the night before. It was slow going in the corrosive chill, but, as dawn rose, they were making their way up the final headwall. The sky was immense, the colour of rose-tinted honey, changing slowly and magnificently through peach and melon to blue.

Ben stood drinking in the beauty around him, then turned and followed Joe and Ross up the final thousand feet until the three of them stood on the summit. The sun blazed down from a sky of a blue so profound that it was like staring into eternity. The wind was mercifully silent. The moment of purity that he craved when he was earthbound overtook him like an orgasm: tears stood in his eyes and, pushing back his goggles, he brushed them away with the back of his mitten. He knew that if he stretched out his hand, he could have touched the sky.

Joe fell on his knees in the snow and threw his arms wide. 'We made it!' he exulted. His voice was hoarse and he collapsed in an extended bout of coughing.

Ross rolled over and over in the snow, kicking out his legs. 'Oh, thank you,' he shouted gleefully up at the sky. 'Thank you!'

The storm promised by the weathermen held off, and they were able to make good time back to their camp at 17,000 feet. But by the time they reached it the wind was getting up again, and Joe's condition had suddenly begun to deteriorate. When Ben lit the stove, Joe hacked, bent double, clutching at his stomach. 'Oh man,' he gasped and keeled over, bile spewing from his mouth.

'Oh, my God,' said Ross. His face was grey with fatigue. 'Oedema.'

'We have to get him down lower than this.' Ben shook his head, grimacing. 'If we stay up here, he'll die.'

'Hey, I'm whipped out, man.' Eyes closed, Ross gulped hot tea.

'Yeah.' Ben sank back against his backpack. After the efforts of the past eighteen hours, the thought of sleep was irresistible. Outside, the wind howled and shook the tent.

'I gotta have some rest before we go on,' Ross said.

'Two hours, OK? And then we're out of here.'

'I'm fine,' Joe croaked. 'I can go down by myself.'

'Dream on,' Ben said. 'Think I'm going to let you go down alone? But first we've got to get some fluid inside you.'

'My throat's too sore to swallow.'

'Too bad.' Ben crouched over the stove, melting snow, adding cubes of chocolate. Joe needed both fluid and sugar: this was one way to make sure he had both.

An hour later, Joe had ingested most of the warm liquid. Exhausted, Ben swallowed the last dregs from his own mug and wondered whether they should risk staying there overnight. But another look at Joe convinced him that they didn't have that much time to spare.

In the corner of the tent, the sat phone buzzed faintly. Ross picked up. 'Yes,' he said. 'Mrs Who?' His eyes swivelled to Ben. 'For you, man.'

'Who is it? Lisa?'

'Not unless she's calling herself Mrs Sherman these days.'

'Mrs Sher—' Ben's heart felt as if it had stopped beating. The foretaste of disaster struck him with a pain like a skewer being inserted into his brain, so that he cried aloud as Ross handed him the receiver. 'Yeah?'

'Ben? It's Mel Sherman here.'

'What's happened?' A burning rush of anxiety swept over him. He swayed, almost overcome by cold and exhaustion.

'It's Lisa. She's . . . she's had a miscarriage.' Her voice came and went.

'Oh Jesus. Sweet Jesus.' Ben could scarcely breathe. 'What happened?' He looked at the other two men. 'Lisa . . . she's lost the baby.'

'Oh, man, I'm sorry.' Ross reached out to his friend.

Ben's heart was beating so fast he was afraid he would pass out.

'She's still in the hospital.'

'Is she all right?'

'She's . . .' Mel's voice faded again. Phrases emerged through the storm of digital static. '. . . very weak . . . loss of blood . . . no chance . . .'

'*What?*'

'. . . meet you at Boston if you tell me when you'll get here.' The sentence was clear this time, reverberating in the frost-lined tent. Ben was aware of the other two staring at him, their faces gaunt.

'I can't just walk off the mountain at a moment's notice, you know,' he said, anxiety roughening his voice.

'You should be here. Lisa needs you.'

'I know. I know that, for Chrissakes.' He felt as though someone had gripped his heart between a pair of pincers and was squeezing them slowly shut. Tears came into his eyes and froze on his lower eyelashes. 'Oh my God, I can't believe this, Mel.' He pressed his hand against the bridge of his nose in an effort to stem the tears. 'I can't get away I'm snowed in. I can't—'

'Hello? Hello? I can't hear you. Ben? Are you still there?' Her voice faded again, receding away from him into the brutal mountains.

'Lisa,' he screamed. 'Lisa . . . she's OK, isn't she?'

But there was no answer and though he pushed at the keys, he couldn't get the phone working. 'I cart it all the way up here so I can keep in touch with my wife, and it doesn't work worth a shit.' He stared at them with savage eyes. 'My wife . . .'

'Oh man,' Ross said.

'Jeez, I'm sorry.' Joe lifted a hand in Ben's direction, then dropped it.

Ben smeared his face with a half-frozen hand. Pulling down the hood of his parka, pushing his feet into his yellow plastic boots, he tugged down the tent zipper and struggled out into the clamour of the storm. A screaming confusion of barbarous cold and whirling snow greeted him. Each flake slammed into his face with the force of flung pebbles. The sound of the wind had risen to a continuous shriek. Several times its sheer force knocked him to his knees in the snow.

Lisa . . .

An hour later, the new storm had turned into a blizzard. Ben had been unable to rest, though he knew he would need all his strength to help guide Joe safely down the mountain. He couldn't stop thinking about Lisa's small body, torn apart by pain. He groaned aloud. She had wanted the baby so very much. What grief she must be feeling, and he not there to hold her close, kiss her cheeks, tell her it would be OK, it would be all right, they could try again. He should have been there, he knew that.

She'd told him she had a bad feeling about this trip and she'd been right. He looked over at Joe, who seemed semi-comatose. If they couldn't rouse him sufficiently, it was going to be a real problem to get him down to a level at which his oxygen-starved body could start to recover. People died of oedema very easily, very quickly. It was vital that they get him down to the relative safety of the camp 3,000 feet below.

They set off, Ross and Ben assisting Joe as best they could. Roped between them, Joe managed to stagger along under his own steam, but his legs gave from under him from time to time. The first part of the route followed a ridge as sharp as a blade of scissors, with a 2,000-foot drop on one side, a 3,000-foot drop on the other. The slightest inattention could lead to a terminal plunge. They were entirely alone in a landscape where they could barely see each other in the whiteout.

'Oh fuck!' Suddenly, Ross, who was in the lead, stepped onto fresh powder and, in doing so, broke through a thin snow bridge above one of the many narrow crevasses that riddled the terrain. He yelled again as he fell, disappearing into the crevasse.

Joe was yanked after him, his weight pulling Ben down too. Acting on instinct, Ben stamped his feet firmly into the snow and sank the shaft of his ice axe next to his boot before frantically wrapping the remaining rope around the shaft, making it strong enough to hold. He hoped.

'Joe!' he yelled. 'Are you OK?'

Whether it was the adrenaline engendered by the fall, or the lower altitude, Joe seemed suddenly more awake.

'Yeah. I'm anchored,' he called.

'How far down?'

'Maybe twenty feet.'

'And Ross? How far down are you?'

'Another ten feet down from Joe,' Ross said, his voice fainter. 'Except I think I just fucked up my knee.'

Ben secured the rope. 'Can you move at all?'

'Don't know,' Ross said. 'I've got my foot on a kind of ledge here. I'm not gonna fall any further if I keep absolutely still.'

'Joe?'

'If you can pull on the rope, I could try front-pointing up,' Joe said.

'OK, guys,' Ben shouted, thinking furiously. Any moment the two of them could plunge to an icy death. 'One foot at a time. Joe front-pointing, Ross using his axe. You still got the axe, Ross?'

'How do you think I'm hanging on here?' Ross said.

'Lose your pack, for starters.' Getting rid of Ross's gear was a calculated risk: if Ben managed to get the two men up from the crevasse and they then found themselves having to bivouac between here and the camp, it could mean death from hypothermia. But he knew that, weighed down, he wouldn't have the strength to help them both up.

After a moment, Ross shouted, 'Done.'

'Now you, Joe.'

'And make sure it doesn't land on my head,' Ross called.

'I'm going to set up a Z-pulley,' Ben said. Making himself safe, he approached the edge. Snow stung the exposed part of his face and whipped against his goggles, making it difficult to see. Shrugging off his pack, he managed to force one end of it under the rope that led from the embedded ice axe down into the crevasse and constructed a simple pulley system. When it was done, he shouted, 'On the count of three, Ross lifts his axe and sinks it. At the same time, Joe moves up.'

'Can you handle it, Ben?' Joe sounded clearer-headed than he had for many hours. He too must have been calculating the odds.

'No sweat, man,' Ben said. ''Sides, I don't have any choice.'

'Guys . . .' It was Ross's voice, shaky now, frightened. 'Look, I can hang on here for a while. Why don't you cut the rope and leave me here, go and get help?'

'Why don't you shut up?' Ben said roughly.

'That's not an option,' said Joe.

'If I wasn't on the end, you'd find it much easier.'

Ben thought about it. 'He's right. And once you're up, Joe, we can send down a fresh rope.'

'Right. Between us we shouldn't have too much problem hauling the fat bastard up.'

'What do you think, Ross?' Ben asked, though he knew the answer. Ross would be thinking how easy it would be to fall; that once his lifeline was cut, maybe the two of them would leave him to die.

'Makes good sense,' he said.

Even with the rope cut, it took Ben nearly half an hour to pull Joe to the top. Above his head the wind screamed. Snow blew horizontally into his face, obscuring his vision. Finally the top of Joe's helmet emerged and a few seconds later he lay spread-eagled on the snow, gasping.

Ben paid out a rope to where Ross waited further down, precariously anchored by one foot on a tiny ledge, his axe sunk into the ice wall, and only one of his legs operational.

Waiting for Ross to call up that he had secured the fresh rope round his body, Ben thought of Lisa and tears came into his eyes. He'd been a rotten husband to her, he realised. He loved her but he had never come to terms with staying in one place and putting down roots. The baby might have ensured that—*would* have ensured that, he told himself.

Now, in the bleak hostility of the mountainside, fighting nausea from exertion in the altitude, he struggled to maintain control of his senses. He yelled at Joe, but there was no response, which scared him. He would have to do this alone.

'Ross!' he shouted. 'What the hell are you doing down there?'

There was no reply.

'Ross?'

Nothing.

Jesus. Had he passed out? Fallen? If so, had he managed to secure the rope first?

'Ross?' he screamed. 'Where the fuck are you?' He tugged gently at the rope and found that there was weight on the end of it. Ross must have fainted from the pain of his shattered knee.

Bracing himself, Ben gritted his teeth. The muscles round his ribs yelled for mercy as, inch by inch, he used the Z-pulley to get Ross to the surface. His lungs felt as though they were on fire each time he drew breath. How much longer could he keep this up? If he stopped, then all the precious inches he had fought for would go for nothing.

And Ross would die.

Mucus oozed up from his throat, filling his mouth. He spat and saw the snow redden briefly before it was covered again. Joe was half-hidden now under a blanket of snow. If he didn't rouse himself soon . . .

The thought lent Ben new strength. He heaved on the rope again. And again. He was too far from the edge to see what progress he was making. 'One,' he gritted. And tugged. 'Two.' And tugged again. Inch by inch, the rope was coiling at his feet.

Love you too, dreamboat. Out of nowhere, the phrase floated into his head. He thought he could see the letters blazoned on the snow, blue and green and red, like a neon sign flashing through the storm: *Love you too* . . . Lisa, with her shiny black hair. Lisa, Lisa, my darling, the baby, the lost baby, sunlight on the lake, *love you too, dreamboat* . . .

If he couldn't make one last effort, then all three of them were finished. He must not let that happen. Somewhere, in a sane and quiet world far from here, Lisa waited for him.

And then he heard the voice. Ross's voice. Pain-filled. Exhausted. Spurring him onwards. 'Think I lost it there for a while. Way to go, Ben. Almost there. One more try. You can do it.'

The tug on the pulley rope lessened slightly, as Ross used his axe in the ice walls of the crevasse. His bones at cracking point, his muscles torn with fatigue, Ben finally saw one of Ross's mittens scrabbling at the surface, then the other, gave one more body-crunching pull and saw the top of Ross's red hood, his face, his shoulders.

'Jeez, man.' Ross dug his elbows into the snow and pulled himself forward, while Ben, walking backwards, rapidly shortened the rope. 'Oh Jeez.' His voice was full of tears. 'Thought that was it, down there.' He lay with his face pressed into the snow and his shoulders heaved.

Ben, too, sank down and hung his head, fighting nausea. The efforts they'd made weren't going to be enough. There was more to come.

'Your knee—any chance you can walk?'

Ross turned over and sat up. He cradled his knee with both gloved hands and let out a sharp exhalation of pain. 'No way.' He looked at Ben from under frost-caked eyebrows. 'Hey, man . . . thanks.'

'You'd have done the same for me.'

'I might have tried. Don't know if I'd have succeeded.' Ross glanced at Joe. 'What's with him?'

'Hypoxia. Hypothermia. By now, could be anything.'

'What're we gonna do?'

'We're gonna drag you over there.' Ben nodded at a slight mound in the snow, a rock no more than a couple of feet high. 'We're gonna dig you in. Put you inside my sleeping-bag, cover you up as best we can. Then I'm going to get Joe down to the camp and fetch help for you.'

'Can you manage all that, man? On your own?' Ross was worried. 'You'll have to lower him down.'

'No other way.' A huge weariness filled Ben. He turned his back to the wind, hunched over himself, pulled some chocolate from his parka and stuffed it into his mouth. 'Here.' He handed the rest to Ross.

'Are you OK?' Ross said anxiously.

'I'm fine.' He wasn't, but he couldn't give up now. With his axe, he set about cutting a shallow hole at the base of the rock, lined it with his sleeping-mat, then put his hands under Ross's armpits and dragged him over to it. He stuffed his friend's legs into his own sleeping-bag, ignoring Ross's groans, and pulled it up right over his face.

'Don't move,' he said. 'Don't move one inch from here.' He looked down at Ross's face, saw the fear the other man was trying to hide. 'And don't worry. I'll be back. Whatever happens, I'll be back.'

'Yeah, man. I know you will.'

Kneeling beside Joe, Ben lashed his arms to his sides, roped his legs together, round and round until he looked like a mummy in the snow. When he was ready, he began the long clamber down, paying out the rope attached to his belt, lowering Joe little by little, the trussed-up body sliding along the top of the snow like a sledge. He'd told Ross he would be back. He hoped it was true.

He had no idea how long it was before he had dragged himself and his burden down to 14,300 feet. Staggering into the camp, he wasn't even sure if Joe was still alive. But after relinquishing his friend to the staff in the medical tent, pausing only to swallow almost a litre of hot tea and gather a small group of volunteers, he set off again up the mountain. By the time they reached him, with drinks, splints and food, Ross was in bad shape. He rallied a little as he saw Ben looking down at him, and was able to give a tired twitch of the lips. 'Knew you'd make it, Benny boy,' he whispered. 'You fucking hero, you.'

'No,' Ben said, as the hospital aide came towards him, syringe in hand.

The man was brusque. 'I've been told to give you this.'

Ben backed away. 'I've got to get back home.'

'Sorry.' With a swift lunge, the man grabbed Ben's arm, swabbed the vein with alcohol and was plunging in the needle.

'Hey.' Dimly Ben heard Ross's voice. 'He told you he had to get home. His wife's sick.'

'So's he. He's got two broken ribs, severe internal bruising and all the signs of someone suffering from exposure.' But by then Ben was out cold.

Finally, he woke up, disorientated and aching. 'Lisa,' he said, trying to prop himself up on one elbow and falling back with a gasp of pain. Glancing sideways, he could see Ross in the next bed, his leg in traction, bandages covering both hands.

'How long have I been asleep?' Ben asked.

'A day and a half, off and on.'

'Jesus!' Ben smashed a fist down. 'I *have* to get out of here.'

'Joe has telephoned your place a couple of times to explain what happened,' said Ross. 'But there was nobody home.'

Ignoring his body's protests, Ben heaved himself out of bed and made his way to the phone in the lobby. He called the operator to make a collect call, listened to the phone ring and ring, the woman's voice explaining that there was no response.

Fuck it! He slammed down the receiver. Where was Lisa? With her father? With . . . Mel Sherman? Hands unsteady, he called Enquiries, got Mel's number, dialled.

Again he listened to a telephone ringing in a silent house. There was no way he could let Lisa know why he hadn't come home.

Chapter Seven

MEL PICKED LISA UP from the hospital. 'I'm taking you to Maple Street, OK?' she said.

'It's not necessary. I'll be OK on my own,' Lisa said dully.

'You probably will. However, tonight *I'm* in charge.' Mel reached across and squeezed Lisa's hand.

Later, after Lisa had pushed food around her plate, refused a glass of wine, Mel said, 'Let me call someone. Ben's mother? Your father?'

'My dad wouldn't . . .' Lisa's voice trailed away. Then she said, 'Why hasn't Ben called?'

'Maybe he's been trying and can't get through. Or he's called home, and you weren't there.'

'Or maybe he just hasn't tried.' Lisa put her head back and closed her eyes. Tears squeezed between her lids and slid down her face. 'The nurses in the hospital kept telling me it was for the best. For the *best* . . . One of them said, "You'll have some more."' Lisa's voice wavered. 'That doesn't make it any easier to d-deal with the fact that I can't have the one I wanted, that my d-daughter, is dead. Oh, Mel . . .'

'I know.' Mel took her hand. 'I know.'

'I wanted this baby so *much*.'

And so did I, Mel thought.

'I can't believe that somehow I'm supposed to forget about her, just have another baby to replace her.' Harsh sobs shook Lisa's slight body.

'She was . . . oh God, I knew something was wrong . . . They told me she'd been dead for two weeks. Can you imagine the horror of that, Mel?'

All too easily, Mel thought. She could not get the images out of her own mind. 'Oh, Lisa, honey . . .'

'If it's OK, I'll take a shower and go to bed,' Lisa said, abruptly.

'Anything. Anything you want.'

While Lisa was in the bathroom upstairs, the phone rang.

'Ben Andersen here,' a voice said when Mel picked up.

'Thank God!'

'Where's Lisa? I've been phoning and there's never any answer.'

'She's here with me. I've just brought her back from the hospital.'

'How is she? I've been desperately worried about her,' he burst out. 'Stuck here . . . Your phone call . . . I couldn't hear what you were saying.' His voice dropped. 'I've been so afraid . . .'

'Where are you?'

'I'm still stuck in Alaska.'

'You should be *here*,' Mel said angrily.

There was a silence. Then he said, 'I'd like to speak to my wife.'

'She's taking a shower,' Mel said. 'Call back in ten minutes.'

'I'll try,' he said wearily. 'But there are queues to use these phones.'

'Where are you?' Mel asked again.

'In the local hospital.'

'What's wrong with you?'

'Nothing much.'

'I'll tell Lisa you called.' Mel replaced the receiver and went upstairs to the bathroom. 'That was Ben,' she called through the door. 'He'll call back in ten minutes.'

But Ben did not call back.

'**M**y wife is sick,' he said. 'How many times do I have to tell you?'

'It's not advisable,' the doctor said.

'If you won't discharge me, I'll discharge myself,' he shouted. Last night he'd waited hours to use the phone and by the time his turn came again, it was the middle of the night. 'You can't keep me here against my wish.' Remembering that his clothes were gone, he swallowed. 'Please.' He hated the whining note in his voice. Hated himself. 'I feel absolutely fine. There's nothing wrong with me beyond a few bruises.'

It took another hour of argument before they agreed to discharge him. He signed forms, used credit cards, made calls to the airline, to a taxi company, said goodbye to Ross and Joe.

And at last he was on his way back to Lisa.

'Come to the gallery,' Mel urged. 'I don't want to leave you alone.'

'I'm fine,' Lisa said. 'I'm OK.'

'You don't look it. You look . . .' Mel swallowed. Lisa's eyes were deep-shadowed. She was wearing a dark brown skirt, a dull red top.

'It's the sadness that makes me look so awful.' Lisa stared at Mel, her mouth trembling. 'I wish Ben would call.'

'The line was terrible when he phoned last night,' Mel said, finding excuses for Lisa's sake. Surely, somehow, he could have found a way to telephone. 'Maybe it packed up altogether.'

Lisa pressed her fists to her chest. 'Why doesn't he come home?'

The house was filled with the rawness of her pain.

Ben rang from the airport, waiting for a flight out. The weather was atrocious, flights were cancelled, he was on standby.

Lisa wept into the phone while he tried to comfort her. 'I can't believe you said that!' Mel heard her exclaim, as she slammed down the phone, ran upstairs to the guest room and closed the door behind her.

Ben called back. 'What the hell's happening?' he said angrily. 'She just hung up on me.'

'What did you say to her?'

'I was just . . . I said we could try again.'

'Exactly what a woman who's lost a baby wants to hear.'

'I suppose it was tactless.'

'Of course it was bloody tactless,' snapped Mel. 'And cruel.'

He drew a sharp breath. 'Doesn't she realise how much I want to be there with her?'

'I've no idea what she thinks. For the moment, she's all curled in on herself, like a wounded animal.'

'Look . . .' He broke off. Started again. 'Lisa knows that if I could walk from here to there, or swim, or ski, I'd do it, to be with her. But I can't. As soon as there's a flight, I'll be on it.'

'Fine.' She put down the telephone before he did.

When she came home at lunchtime the next day, she found a note on the kitchen table. *Don't worry, I'm OK*, Lisa had written. Knowing how far from the truth that was, Mel wondered if this was her way of asking to be left alone.

But whether she liked it or not, Lisa should not be by herself. Mel spent an uneasy afternoon at the gallery, and, in the end, left Carla to close up while she drove to the old Adams place. Late afternoon sun dazzled on the windowpanes and warmed the mellow tiles on the peaked roof. Herbs—chives, parsley, thyme, mint—flourished beside the barn door and geraniums gushed from the pots Lisa had planted.

Stepping into the hallway, Mel called Lisa's name. There was no answer. She went upstairs. 'Lisa?' she called softly, increasingly apprehensive. Wishing she had not waited so long, she hurried down the landing to the room which had been intended for the baby, and stopped in the doorway. Her throat constricted as she saw Lisa sitting on the floor, rocking back and forth, clutching a tiny T-shirt, sobbing.

'Lisa . . .' Running to kneel beside her, gather her into her arms, Mel recognised a grief that was almost uncontainable. 'Honey, sweetheart, darling . . .' she murmured. Was this what it would have been like, if she had had a daughter? This shared ache, this mutual pain?

She took hold of the younger woman's hands. Lisa had removed the rings she wore: the diamond engagement ring, the thin gold wedding band, the silver love knot from Mexico. 'You're not alone.'

'I am. Without Ben, I am.'

'Sssh . . .' Mel rocked her like a baby.

'She haunts me, Mel. *Haunts* me.' The words were a howl of pain. 'I *want* her. I need to hold her. I . . .' Lisa pressed her knuckles hard against her mouth. 'And I can't reach her, Mel. I can't touch her.'

'Don't . . . don't . . .'

'I miss her, Mel. I never even knew her but I m-miss her s-so . . .' She looked down at the small garment in her hand and began to sob again.

'Darling Lisa . . .'

Mel looked round the room. At the quilt Lisa had sewn for the baby's bed, at the white muslin drapes she had decorated with green leaves to match the ones Ben had stencilled on the sanded pine floor, at the white chest they had found at an auction up in the hills and the mobile of glittery butterflies that danced and sparkled in the sunshine, at the egg-yolk yellow walls. So much anticipation had gone into this room. So much love. And now it held nothing but broken promises.

'The baby was so real to me, and now she's *dead* and I c-can't get my head round it.' Lisa's face contorted, made ugly by grief. 'And I feel so guilty. Maybe it happened because of something I did.'

'It wasn't because of anything you did,' Mel said forcefully. She held Lisa tighter, feeling the thin bones beneath her shirt, the fragile ribs. She took Lisa's hand. 'Let's go back to Maple Street,' she urged gently.

'It's time I took up my own life again. Besides, I have to get ready for Ben coming back.'

'I can't force you to come and stay,' Mel said.

'No.' Lisa hugged her. 'Thank you, Mel. For everything.'

When Ben reached the circular driveway of the house, there were no lights on. He tried the front door and found it locked, as though Lisa wasn't expecting him. Had she gone back to Mel Sherman's house? He felt under the flowerpot for the spare key and let himself in.

He walked through the silent rooms, smelling the familiar fragrances of the old place. In the dining room, he stopped. Oh God . . . he bit his lip. The table had been set for two, with the best glasses, linen napkins. In the middle of the table there were two red roses in a crystal vase. She'd prepared a homecoming dinner and he hadn't shown up for it.

He carried one of the roses upstairs with him. At the far end of the passage, the door of their bedroom was ajar, though the lamps were off. In the moonlight from the window he could see her face on the pillow, looking so frail that he hardly recognised her. In one hand she held the silver rattle he had bought—when? It seemed like years ago. He could see the faint marks of tears on her cheeks. 'Oh, Lisa,' he whispered. He laid the rose on her bedside table.

In the bathroom he showered, brushed his teeth, swallowed some painkillers, then eased himself into bed.

'Ben?' she murmured. 'I thought you weren't going to come.'

In the darkness, he frowned. 'You knew I would.'

He felt her shake her head. 'I wasn't sure. Not any more.'

Wincing at the unspoken reproof, he put his arms carefully around her and felt her cringe away from him as though afraid of being hurt. He thought he could smell her sadness, rising like smoke from her slight body. His own grief stifled him. After a while, he leaned up on his elbow. Looking down at her beloved familiar face in the half-light, at the new sad lines around her mouth, he felt a shiver of misgiving.

She was up in the morning before he awoke. He lay listening for the sounds he had grown used to, but the house was silent. He wanted to talk about the baby, to share their burden of loss.

In the bathroom mirror, he examined himself: the marks across his shoulders, the deep bruises under his ribs and down his legs, the still-raw places on his arms and legs. If he moved too quickly, his entire body protested. On his way downstairs, he paused outside the baby's room. The door was shut. There was something so final about that closed door that he felt cold. He put out his hand and touched the doorknob, then drew back. He wasn't sure he had the courage to walk in. The full force of what had happened hit him like a blow to the stomach.

'Lisa!' he shouted. He went down the stairs two at a time. 'Lisa!'

He found her at the end of the garden, standing motionless among the stunted apple trees. She was wearing black trousers, a grey top, colours he had never seen her in before. The swell of her belly, still in a state of prenatal distension, moved him unbearably.

When she turned her head to look at him, he had the illusion that she had disappeared, not physically, but emotionally, that Lisa herself was no longer there and only an outer casing remained, fragile as eggshell. 'Sweetheart,' he said.

'I should have insisted,' she said. 'On bringing her back here. We could have buried her under the trees.'

'Oh, Lisa . . .' He took her into his arms.

'She'd been dead for two weeks,' Lisa said, in a conversational way.

'The baby?'

'Rosie, yes . . . when I lost her—'

'*We* lost her,' he said.

'She'd been dead for two weeks,' Lisa said again. She turned her head away and her body began to shake.

He stared at her, appalled. She had been carrying a dead child around inside her womb for two weeks. Fourteen days. He tried to imagine it and could not. 'You mean . . .' He put a hand to his mouth. 'Oh God . . .'

'Horrible, isn't it?' she said.

A dead child, inside his wife's body. He pulled Lisa tight against him, heedless of his cracked ribs and screaming muscles.

'Sometimes I wake in the morning,' she said. 'And for a moment, just a split second, I think she's still there inside me.'

'Oh, honey . . .'

Tears gathered again in her eyes. 'I was going to have a baby and now I'm not.'

He looked at her with frustration. 'She wasn't just your baby, Lisa. She was ours.' Sadness had formed a hard lump in his chest.

She stepped out of the circle of his arms. 'I'm sorry.'

'Let me help,' he said, desperate.

'You can't,' she said quietly. 'I wanted Rosie more than anything in the world. She meant everything to me. You can't possibly understand what that's like. Nobody can. All they think is that there's a very simple solution: just have another baby and everything will be fine.'

He'd had the same thought himself. Lying in the hospital bed, drifting on a sea of painkillers, he'd told himself the very same thing.

He breathed a sigh. 'Let me try.'

She shrugged as though it didn't matter, though both of them knew how intensely it did.

'Let's walk by the lake,' he said.

'I don't want to.'

He grabbed her hand. 'Come anyway.'

She followed where he led, putting one foot in front of another, staring down at the ground. The fresh air brought a little colour to her face but no sparkle to her eyes. He walked her down to the shore. 'Look,' he said, wanting to show her that there was still a world out there, beyond her misery. 'Deer tracks.' He pointed at the delicately slotted marks in the sand.

'Yes.'

'Did you know there are bears in these woods?' he said.

She shook her head.

'They come down to the water's edge to fish.'

'Do they?' she said.

'I saw one myself, last time I came down here.'

'Hey, Ben . . .'

'Yes?'

'Like, I really need a nature lesson right now.'

'I just thought you'd be interested,' he said.

'I'm not.' She began to walk away from him. 'I couldn't care less, if you want to know.'

'Lisa . . .' He wanted to ask if she was glad he was back with her, he wanted to say how sad and sorry he was and that from here on in he would be there to love and protect her, but she stared at him with such hostility that he couldn't continue.

'Let me fix you something,' he said, when they got back to the house. 'Anything. Just name it. Anything you like.'

'I'm not hungry.'

'Eat something,' he begged. He took her cold hands in his. 'How about pasta—you know you like pasta.'

'I'm not hungry,' she said again, on a rising note. She pulled her hands away and pressed them to her stomach.

'I could make some pesto sauce,' he said. 'Remember us making it, when I came round to your apartment that first time?'

'I remember.'

'Or we could try a takeout pizza. You know you love pizza.'

'For Christ's sake, Ben, leave me alone. How many times do I have to tell you I don't *want* anything?' She walked out of the room as though she couldn't bear to be in the same place as he was.

God, he was tired. He closed his eyes and wearily rubbed his forehead. He'd expected that she would be depressed. He had been prepared for her sadness. But not for this. Somehow she had disengaged herself from him and from the life they used to share. Even from herself.

He heard a door slam, the sound of her car starting up, the swish of tyres on gravel as she barrelled down the drive. There had to be light at the end of this particular tunnel. He just wished he could see it.

'I don't know what's wrong with me.' Lisa sat on Mel's swing seat, staring at nothing, endlessly swinging back and forth. 'I think I'm going mad. I just felt like I couldn't stand to be in the same room with him.'

'Why?'

'I don't really know.' Lisa fumbled in the pocket of her drab brown skirt. 'And this morning I went to the supermarket and I suddenly had this terrible fear that everything on the shelves was closing in on me.'

Mel remembered the feeling that the world was no longer stable, that any moment it might tip her off, that inanimate objects—chairs or books or buildings—wished her harm. Only much later had she understood that she had probably had a minor breakdown. Lisa was presumably undergoing much the same sort of emotional crisis. 'Don't let the miscarriage change things between you and Ben,' she said.

'Whether we like it or not, things *have* changed.'

'But you still love him.'

'I guess.'

'Of *course* you do.' Mel was surprised at the panic she could feel surging at the base of her stomach.

'It's just that I can't *feel* it any more,' Lisa said.

'Give it a chance. It'll come back.'

Lisa shook her head. 'No. It's gone. I don't mean the love, but the . . . the joy. We can never go back to the way we were, Ben and me.' She drew in a deep shuddering breath. 'Last night, I reckoned he'd be home by eight. I sat at the table I'd set for dinner, and watched the hands on the clock going round, and I realised that I couldn't assume any more that I come first. I was so angry. So hurt.'

Mel took hold of Lisa's hands. 'Listen to me,' she said firmly. 'What's happened has been dreadful for you. You'll never forget it, and you shouldn't even try to. But Ben must be deeply upset about losing the baby too. You should be helping each other to get through this.'

'I don't want his help,' Lisa said painfully. 'He should have come back when he heard about the baby, and he didn't, and I really resent him for it.'

'Aren't you being a bit unreasonable? We all read about the freak storms up there, the airports closing down.'

'I know. I know all that, in my head. But in my heart I feel that if he'd set off as soon as he heard about the baby, he'd have been out of there before the weather changed.'

'Darling Lisa, listen to me. This is the first real crisis you two have had. It's a terrible one, but there'll be others over the years. Love doesn't always turn out the way you expect it to.'

'Whatever I say, he can't possibly understand how it was.' Lisa shuddered. 'It's like a nightmare from which I can't ever wake up.'

As silence fell between them, Jamie Mayfield came cycling up the drive. 'Hi,' he said, dragging his trainers along the cement surface instead of using the brakes, then stopping at the foot of the porch steps, looking up at them. 'I thought I'd stop by because I wanted to ask you something.'

'Go ahead,' Mel said.

Jamie pushed his glasses up his nose. 'It's Mom's birthday soon, and she likes things we make for her, right?'

'Right.'

'But I can't sew or paint or anything, like Tom and Lucy can. And the other day I was thinking about maybe being a chef when I grow up, so I started reading recipes and there was this one for a lemon cake and it didn't look too difficult and Mom likes lemon, so . . .'

'Last week you were going to be a palaeontologist,' Mel said.

He grinned at her. 'I'm keeping my options open.'

'A cake sounds like fun,' Lisa said.

'That's what I thought. Unless . . .' He looked hopefully at Lisa. '. . . I could come by your place and throw a pot for Mom.'

Lisa's pale face flushed. 'No, I . . . I don't think I . . . not at the moment,' she said. 'I'm sorry, Jamie, but no.'

'That's OK,' Jamie said. 'I don't expect you feel like it much. Mom told me you'd lost your baby, so you must be very sad.'

'Yes,' Lisa said. 'I am.'

'"After the first death there is no other,"' Jamie said.

Lisa stared at him, her eyes wide. 'What?'

'It's from a poem by Robert Cormier,' explained Jamie. 'It's kind of an interesting thought. But I don't expect it's much help, is it?'

Lisa bit her lip. 'Not really.'

'Anyway, my teachers keep telling me I lack coordination,' said Jamie, 'so I'd probably've made a mess potting.' His dimple showed. 'And I'd rather make a lemon cake, because Mom's bound to give me a bit.' He turned to Mel. 'One of those with vanilla cream in the middle.'

'Fine.'

'I'd need to practise first, though. And maybe if it turned out good, we could freeze it until Mom's birthday.'

'Good thinking,' said Mel. 'Want me to pick up the ingredients?'

'No, otherwise it wouldn't really be a present from me, would it?' He did a few wheelies in front of them. 'So see you tomorrow, Mel, OK?'

'Don't forget to tell your mom you're going to be home a bit late.'

'I won't.' Jamie raised his hand and sped off down the drive.

'He's a cute kid,' Lisa said, looking after him. 'What does it mean, "After the first death there is no other"?'

'I imagine the idea is that once you've experienced a significant death, gone through all the grief and adjustments and so on, none of the deaths that come after that can have the same impact on you.'

'I wonder if it's true.'

'Hard to say,' said Mel, thinking of Eric, thinking of her baby, and the cold day when her mother had died. Different deaths. Different griefs.

Lisa stood up. 'I guess I better get back.'

'Lisa . . .' Mel touched her hand. 'Don't blame Ben for not coming back. Don't spoil your relationship with him.'

Lisa nodded. 'You're right, Mel. I know you're right. I'll make a real effort.' She walked down the porch steps and Mel heard the sound of her car pulling away from the kerb.

'Where did you go?' Ben said.

'To Mel's.'

'Didn't you think I might be worried about you?'

Lisa stared at him without speaking.

'You're not the only one who hurts, you know,' Ben said loudly. A clot of pain and loss was lodged inside his chest. 'I wanted this baby, too.'

Again Lisa made no reply.

He threw down the book he'd been pretending to read. 'You could at least *answer* me. Why do you have to look at me like I'm some kind of idiot every time I open my mouth?'

'I'm sorry.' She closed her eyes for a moment and took a deep breath. 'I'm sorry, honey.'

'Don't be fucking *sorry*.' Anger crouched between them. 'Answer me. Talk to me.'

'I . . . I haven't got much to say.'

He got up and seized her by the shoulders, hating the way she stiffened at his touch. 'Lisa, Lisa . . . I hurt too.'

He watched her try to relax, try to smile. 'I know, Ben.'

He remembered how she had been earlier in the summer, the brilliant colours of her clothes, her black hair bobbing in a ponytail or pinned up with bright clips, and was aware of a desperate sadness. She'd been slopping around in the same dark top for the last three days. Her hair was dull and lifeless; sometimes she didn't even bother to brush it.

She looked away from him. Inside his chest, the tears he wanted so badly to shed felt as though they were slowly being turned to pebbles.

He grabbed her hand. 'Come with me, Lisa.' He drew her towards the foot of the stairs. 'We're going to talk about this. We *have* to.'

'No,' she said. 'No. I don't want to.' Her voice was suddenly fearful.

'We have to face up to it,' he said. 'Together.'

He pulled her after him up the stairs and along the passage to the door of the baby's room. She hung back, a dead weight on the end of his arm. The muscles of his shoulder and abdomen protested but he took no notice. For a moment he paused outside, thinking of the hours they'd spent sanding down the broad pine planks, the smell of planed wood and wax polish, Lisa looking up and smiling at him, sawdust in her hair. He remembered the soft sweetness of her face as she told him she was pregnant, the delight oozing out of her like syrup. And buying the rattle, ringing the silver bells, imagining it in his baby's hand.

He flung open the door. It was all as it had been when he'd left for Alaska. The quilt she'd made. The chest he'd painted. The willow leaves stencilled on the floor.

Without warning, the tears came, pouring from his eyes, thick and bitter. He let go of her and leaned against the wall, his face on his arm. 'Oh God. Oh, Lisa, what are we going to do?'

There was no response, and when he lifted his head she was standing there, watching him, her own tears streaming down her face, as though there was an invisible wall between them, a sheet of ice through which neither of them could break.

The following afternoon he came back from the supermarket to find her in the barn, staring at the peacock-feather dishes that were supposed to be finished in time for the wedding in Texas. The studio smelt of fresh oil paint and he felt a sudden rush of optimism, until he saw that she had taken the tops off all the metal tubes of paint and squeezed the contents into the bin beneath the sink.

'Lisa,' he said. 'Oh, Lisa. What have you done?'

'I called the Peacockes,' she said tonelessly. She was slumped in a chair and her voice echoed slightly, as though coming from the bottom of an empty vessel. 'Told them I couldn't finish the commission.'

Looking round the studio, he saw that she had removed the damp cloths from the clay, opened the sacking so that the clay would dry out.

She stood up, and he reached out to hold her, but she pushed him away, pressing her lips together to stop them trembling. When she spoke, her voice shook. 'I can't forgive you for being in the mountains instead of with me.'

He hardly recognised her as the girl he had married. 'Don't you understand that I can't forgive *myself*?' he said quietly. 'Would you like me to move out? Would that make it easier for you?'

For a moment she sat still, her mouth quivering. Then she collapsed against him. 'I'm sorry, Ben,' she said into his chest. 'I'm so sorry.'

Both of them were appalled at the cracks, the crevasses, that had suddenly appeared in their marriage.

She was lying on her side, her back to him. The bedroom smelt of her jasmine perfume. A moth fluttered in the circle of light cast by his bedside lamp, drifting away for a moment only to return to the seductive glow. He slid into bed beside her and put an arm round her slight body, wanting to hold her, to protect her from any further harm.

'Don't!' she screamed suddenly, flailing wildly at his arm.

'What?'

She whipped round to face him. 'Don't touch me.'

'For God's sake, Lisa . . .' He moved away from her, alarmed by the hostility in her eyes. Her lips were drawn back from her teeth. 'You're being ridiculous.'

'I know you want to fuck me,' she said.

'Of course I do. You're my wife. But not until you want me to.'

'But it's not because I'm Lisa, is it? It's because I'm a female body lying next to you and you haven't had sex for a while. That's all you want, my body, not my . . . my mind or my heart. You don't give a damn about *me*, do you? You don't begin to understand how I feel.'

'If you'd tell me, I could at least try,' he said steadily.

'You?' she said. In the lamplight, her face was bitter. 'Ben Andersen, Action Man, understand?'

Pain and anger flared in his chest. He grabbed her arms and pulled her closer. Looking down at her, he thought that she resembled some wild animal. 'Is that really what you think of me?'

'That's just the b-beginning.'

He tried to rein in his resentment, remembering what she had been through. He was acutely aware of the silver clock on the bedside table, a box of tissues, the edge of the lampshade, a trinket box carved into the shape of a heart where she put her earrings at night. 'I can't cope with the way you act as if you actually dislike me.'

'Maybe I do.'

'You don't mean that.'

'Don't I?'

He let her go and turned over. The moth fluttered and danced, beating at the sides of the lampshade, its powdery wings growing ever more ragged. He felt as though there was a hole in his chest where his heart used once to fit. He wanted to weep for all that he had lost. He thought how cold and perilous were the mountain ranges of grief.

Time inched by. The two of them seemed locked in some stark and barren place, empty, cold, colourless. He thought of the bright existence they used to have, full of shape and pattern and sound.

'Lisa,' he said, on the tenth evening after his return, as they sat opposite each other, their plates untouched. The effort she made to lift her head and look at him was almost audible.

'Yes?'

'Talk to me, darling.'

'Uh . . .' She drew in a deep breath. 'Tell me about your climb.'

'I already did.'

She seemed surprised. 'Did you?'

'Half a dozen times.'

'Oh.' A pause. 'I'm so sorry.' He watched her reach into her recent memory bank. 'You summited out, didn't you? I'll bet Joe was pleased.'

'That's one way of putting it.'

'And then you had to spend time in the hospital.' She lifted a lettuce leaf to her mouth and chewed it slowly. 'Are you OK? Do your ribs still hurt? You'd think that by now they'd have come up with a way to strap them up while they heal, wouldn't you?' Her face was tight with anxiety as she cast about for something else to say.

Ben got up from the table. 'I'll do the dishes,' he said.

'I'll wash, you dry.' It was an exchange they'd had a hundred times before, but now it sounded like nothing more than a false note in a marriage that was just the skeleton of what it had once been.

As Lisa laid each piece of washed cutlery on the draining board, he dried it and put it away in the drawer.

'Honey,' he said, breaking the heavy silence. 'Don't hate me for saying this, but . . . one of these days we can try again.'

She swung round from the sink and stared at him. '*What* did you say?'

As usual, when he tried to explain things, the words had come out all wrong. He cleared his throat. 'We could . . . think about another baby. When you're up to it, I mean. When you want to.'

'Don't say any more,' she said, through gritted teeth.

'But it's true,' he persisted. He was suddenly frightened.

She leaned on her hands and stared out of the window into the night. 'Stop,' she said loudly.

As she flung a handful of spoons onto the draining board, he picked three of them up and began to dry them. 'I know you need time to get over this,' he soothed.

'What do you mean, *this*? Just what do you think I need to get over?'

'Losing the baby. It'll come right.' He wished he could be sure.

'It will never ever come right,' she said. She looked at him with fierce eyes. 'It *can't*.'

'We can . . . try again,' he repeated. He knew it was dangerous ground but he ploughed on. It needed to be said. It *had* to be, unless she was going to remain forever stuck in a time warp of loss and pain. 'It can't be the same, I know that, it couldn't ever be, but—'

'But what?' She slammed her fists into the water in the sink.

He swallowed. 'Other women have lost their babies and still gone on to . . . to have families.'

The air round her was suddenly raw. 'What do you mean? That I should just get on with it? Pretend it didn't happen? Snap out of it?'

He started to put the dried spoons into the cutlery drawer but suddenly she was screaming at him. 'For Christ's sake, Ben, you know the spoons are supposed to go the other way round.' She snatched the cloth from his hand. 'You *know* that.'

'Does it really matter?' He picked up two more spoons.

'Of course it matters!' She was shrieking at the top of her voice now. 'That's the way we always do it. The bowls are supposed to be *this* end so you can tell as soon as you open the drawer whether they're spoons or whether they're forks. You know that. You fucking *know* it.'

'I don't really give a shit how they're supposed to go,' he said. 'Nothing matters except you.'

She tugged at the drawer, wrenched it out of its casing. As he moved towards her, she flung the contents at him. Forks, spoons, knives cascaded around his head. 'Have you gone raving mad?' he said, trying to shield his face. 'Calm down, will you.' He reached for her but she put her small hands on his chest and, with surprising force, pushed him away. The ends of his broken ribs grated agonisingly against each other. Gasping, he slipped, lost his balance, grabbed at the counter top, landed on his butt among the cutlery, sending a shock of pain up his spine.

'I don't want another baby,' she screamed. 'Are you so insensitive that you can't see I *don't want* another baby? I want the one who's gone.'

He tried to scramble to his feet but she pushed him down again, twisting the muscles in his still unhealed back.

'I want Rosie,' she said. Tears streamed down her cheeks and dripped onto the front of her T-shirt. 'I want Rosie. How can we have another baby when the first one is dead?'

'For God's sake, Lisa.'

She picked up a mug from the counter and flung it at the wall. 'Dead, damn you! Rosie, my baby, is *dead*!' Snatching up a knife from the draining board, she lunged at him, catching him just below the eye.

'Jesus!' He grabbed her ankle, pulling at her so she fell awkwardly as he tried to take the knife from her. 'What the hell do you think you're doing?' He put his hand up to his face, felt blood sticky on his fingers.

Lisa put both her hands over her face and began to sob, her shoulders heaving. 'Oh God, Ben. You do not have the faintest *idea* . . .'

'Lisa,' he whispered. 'Oh, Lisa . . .'

She struggled away from him wiping a palm over her cheeks, smearing flecks of his blood over her wet face. Then she stood with her hands hanging by her sides and sobbed as though her heart was breaking.

Chapter Eight

HE GOT UP EARLY the next morning, while she was still asleep. Jogging along the empty country roads, he wondered if it were possible to run off sadness, sweat away guilt. Above his head the trees whispered. His feet pounded in time to the dull thud of his heart.

When he got back, Lisa was going through her closet. 'I'm sorry. I'm so sorry,' she said as, breathing hard, he leaned against the door of their bedroom. 'I don't know what's happening to me.'

'What're you doing?'

'I thought it was time to clear out some stuff.' She sounded almost like her old self and a huge feeling of relief swept over him. Maybe their fight the evening before had been worth it. She was putting clothes into some boxes lined up against the wall.

He looked at the bright tumble of colours. 'Don't you want those?'

'Maternity clothes,' she said briefly.

It wasn't an issue he was going to push. If they ever . . . they could buy new ones, start over. One day. Some day.

Showered, dressed for work, he said, as he always did, 'I love you,' and, this time, she gave him a smile, nodded at him.

'Love you too, dreamboat.'

Driving back to Butterfield that evening, he crossed his fingers against the steering wheel. Maybe, just maybe, they could start looking forward again, instead of simply marking time.

There were lamps on all over the house when he pulled into the drive, beams of light rolling like rugs across the dark gravel. He pushed open the front door. The hallway was full of cooking smells. 'Honey,' he called. 'It's me.'

He went into the kitchen and saw a casserole sitting on top of the stove. When he lifted the lid, it was cold: she must have made it that morning. 'Lisa?' he shouted. 'Where are you?'

Maybe she was showering. He bounded up the stairs, two at a time. In their bedroom he saw that the boxes had gone. The bed was neatly made, the closets closed, her dressing table tidied up.

'Darling,' he said, opening the bathroom door.

But although the light was on, she wasn't in there. Perhaps she'd gone out to the studio. Perhaps—he clasped his hands together as though praying—she was back at work.

He poured two glasses of wine, then carried them out of the back door and through the apple-scented darkness to the barn. Using a foot, he pushed open the big door. But she wasn't there either. Carefully he set down the wine, trying not to panic. Where could she be?

He ran back to the house and searched the ground floor, peered into the old-fashioned larder and the big utility room. He went upstairs and looked through the three spare bedrooms. Outside the baby's room, he hesitated. 'Lisa,' he called softly.

When he pushed the door open, the room was empty. Stunned, he stared about him. The chest had disappeared, along with the crib. The windows were bare. Only the sunshine-yellow walls and the stencilled leaves on the floor remained.

'You mustn't do that,' he said aloud. 'You can't erase her.' He'd suggested that they might one day have other babies but that didn't mean they had to obliterate the one they did not have. 'Oh God,' he said, and covered his face with his hands while, inside him, something broke.

Coming slowly down the stairs, he saw the mirror that hung in the hall. It had belonged to the Adams sisters, had been in the family for generations. When he and Lisa had moved in they'd said you have it, it belongs with the house. The frame was carved mahogany, all bursting pomegranates and bunches of grapes; the silvering was old and tarnished. Now he saw that there was writing on its surface, red writing. *I can't stay with you*. And, underneath, an *L*.

He stared at the words. *I can't stay with you . . .* He remembered their wedding day, how she had looked up at him when they exchanged rings, the glow in her black eyes, the sense he'd had then that the vows they'd made to each other had a physical existence, like a chain of golden links, binding the two of them together for all their lives.

But this morning she'd said she loved him. *Love you too, dreamboat . . .* She wouldn't leave him if she loved him, would she?

The red words danced on the cloudy mirror. *I can't stay with you . . .*

'Lisa!' he shouted, suddenly desperate, 'Lisa! Where have you gone?'

The echoes of his voice ricocheted around the hall, bouncing up the stairs, beating at the walls. He went back to the barn again. The two glasses of wine were where he'd left them. He drank them both, and felt the cold liquid slide through his body like icy rain.

He punched in the numbers for Mel Sherman's phone. He could feel the rapid beating of his heart as he waited for her to pick up.

'Mel Sherman.' She sounded cool.

'Ben Andersen here.'

'Hi, Ben.'

'Is Lisa with you?'

'No, isn't she—?'

'Any idea where she might be?'

'None. What's happened?' Alarm filled her voice.

'She seems . . .' he said carefully. 'It looks like she's gone.'

He heard her give a kind of moan.

'She wrote on the mirror.'

'Wrote?'

'Said she couldn't stay with me.'

'Oh, Ben. I know she's been in a terrible state but I never dreamed . . .'

He swallowed something thick and bitter at the back of his throat. 'There wasn't even a proper note. Just lipstick on the mirror.' He had a vision of a distracted Lisa racing down the freeways, over the mountains, away from pain, away from *him*.

'She probably just wants some time alone.'

'She's packed up her stuff. Her clothes, make-up, it's all gone.' He made a sound that could have been a sob. 'Oh God.' He drew in a deep breath. 'I'm sorry I called you so late.' Overwhelmed by a sense of emptiness, he replaced the receiver before she could say anything further.

Mel knocked again, louder this time. She had called a couple of times before, but Ben had not come to the door. She banged once more, listening for footsteps. There was no sound. Nothing.

Irresolute, she stepped back and took a couple of paces towards the side of the house. Maybe Ben was out in the studio.

The night was unexpectedly warm and full of scents. Damp leaves. Apples. Something tangy—sage or thyme—from Lisa's herb garden.

A voice suddenly spoke from the darkness behind her. 'Hello, Mel.'

She whirled, clapping a hand to her heart. 'Lord!' she gasped. 'You startled me.' She could see him there, ghostly in the dark. 'I saw the lights on, so I stopped by.'

When he did not reply, she said, 'Any chance of a coffee? Glass of wine? Cup of tea?'

He gave a twisted smile. 'All or any of the above. But if I invite you in, you won't want to stay long enough to drink them.'

As Mel followed him inside, she tried not to show her dismay. The place smelt of decay and neglect. There was a crumpled sleeping-bag on the sofa and a number of mugs on the floor beside it. Dirty clothes lay where he had tossed them. Overloud music filled the room—Mozart, a piano concerto she recognised but couldn't quite identify.

Ben looked around and grimaced. 'Sorry,' he mumbled. 'I haven't . . .' He didn't bother to complete the sentence. Instead he turned down the music and went into the kitchen. Mel followed him. He looked as though he were on the point of collapse. There was several days' growth of beard along his jaw, and his eyes were raw and red from weeping.

'Coffee, you said.' He pulled a mug from one of the cupboards then picked up a jar of instant coffee and stood holding it, as though not sure what to do next.

There was a garbage sack on the floor, half full of empty cans. More stood on the counter. A cereal bowl held baked beans covered with a layer of white fungus, slices of stale bread spilled from a plastic bag. The sink was full of dirty dishes and pans.

'You're not coping very well,' Mel said.

He laughed harshly. 'I'm not coping at all.'

'Would it irritate you if I cleaned up a bit for you?'

He shrugged. 'It won't make any difference.'

'It might make you feel a bit better.'

While she cleaned up, Ben sat at the table, staring at nothing. When the kitchen looked reasonable she started on the living room and the hall, cleaning around him as best she could. Then she located the linen closet and found fresh sheets and pillowcases for his bed.

Finally, she went out to her car, rooted among the groceries she had bought earlier and brought some of them in: fresh milk, honey-roasted ham, a bag of apples and a loaf of wholemeal bread. She fixed a ham sandwich, put it on a plate with an apple, made coffee for them both and put it down on the table. She pushed a mug and the sandwich across to Ben and sat down opposite him.

'I appreciate your kindness in coming round.' Ben gestured helplessly. 'And you're right, it does look better. Nice disinfectant smells in the kitchen. Fresh sheets on my bed that don't smell of my wife, who hated living with me so much that two weeks ago she just upped and left.'

'Lisa loves you.'

'Funny way to show it.'

Mel took a deep breath. 'Ben, losing the baby wasn't your fault.'

He stared at her, his expression bewildered, holding her gaze.

Mel's throat thickened. 'Oh, Ben.' She reached over and took his hand. 'You think it was.'

'If only I'd stayed home . . .' He bent his head. 'I love her so much.'

Not knowing how to offer comfort, Mel stroked the back of his hand. 'Things happen. You can't change them. You can't anticipate them. All you can do is absorb them. And go on.'

'I don't know if I can.'

'When my husband died,' said Mel, 'my friend, Joanne Mayfield, wrote me a letter.' She smiled. 'She only lives a mile from me, but she wrote to me because she wanted me to remember what she had to say. She said that however unfair it might seem, the earth wouldn't stop. She said: "Dust will continue to gather in corners. Moons will wax and wane. Flowers will bloom and fade. Rivers will go on running to the sea. Life goes on." It may seem monstrous to you now, Ben, but she was right.'

He looked at her, his grey eyes bleak. 'And did life go on for you?'

She wanted to say: my life stopped years ago, long before I met Eric. 'Of course,' she said. 'It's the way things are. Though at the time, I didn't want to believe it.' Mel sighed.

Ben squeezed his eyes shut and tightened his fingers around hers.

Another Saturday morning. Lisa had been gone more than three weeks. The lushness of July was giving way to the dusty greens of August. Examining his reflection in the bathroom mirror, Ben scarcely recognised the gaunt face, the bony cheeks and sunken eyes, as his own. It was time he tried to re-establish some kind of order in his daily routine. He couldn't remember when he'd last had a proper meal. If he was going to get his life back again, he'd better start eating properly instead of living off junk food, sandwiches, takeaway pizza.

He drove down to the Farmer's Market. He bought a chicken, new potatoes, lettuce, big slicing tomatoes, red onions, an avocado. There were fresh peaches on the fruit counter and he purchased half a dozen.

Back home, it was still only midafternoon, but he coated the chicken with a mixture of olive oil, salt and pepper, fresh herbs and French mustard, and placed it in the oven. He opened a bottle of Chardonnay. Later, he would start the potatoes boiling and make a tomato salad.

Sipping the cool wine, he flipped idly through a cookbook, and he came across a colour reproduction of a peach tart, the fruit halves set in some kind of custard, the whole thing caramelised. It must have been one of the recipes Lisa had used: there was a smear of butter on the page, two or three grains of sugar trapped in the fold. He licked his finger and collected them up, put them into his mouth, thinking of her standing in the kitchen, stirring, adding, tasting, scattering sugar here and there, dropping a buttery knife onto the cookbook.

The kitchen began to fill with the smell of roasting meat. He poured himself another glass of Chardonnay and walked into the living room. Lying in a drawer was a tablecloth they had been given as a wedding present, made of fine lawn and hand-embroidered with green-leaved yellow daisies. He shook it out and spread it across the table. He laid two places, found a couple of green wineglasses, set out two matching green glass plates. He picked up a photograph of Lisa on their wedding day: an informal portrait of her turning her head, laughing, her black hair, longer then, trailing across her face and fresh white flowers in a crown across her head.

He piled books on the chair and set the photograph on top. Then he saluted it with his glass. 'Lisa,' he said, by now slightly drunk. 'I love you. I will always love you. I miss you. I need you.' He put a pair of candlesticks on the table and lit them.

The tomatoes were warm and plump in his hand. When he lifted them to his face, he could smell the scent of summer heat in the rich, red skin. Slicing them, sprinkling them with olive oil, tearing basil leaves over them, he put them in a dish and set it on the table.

Later, he took the chicken out of the oven and carved it, adding the potatoes tossed in butter and chopped parsley. He stirred some of his white wine into the drippings in the pan and added the mixture to his plate. He carried it to the table, brought over the green salad and dressed it, and then sat down. Lisa laughed at him across the table, insubstantial in the flicker of the candle flames. He missed her. So much. Was it the tears in his eyes or the wine he had drunk that made her image shift and blur? 'Lisa,' he said. 'I love you.'

He picked up his knife and fork, poured more wine. Ate. Carrying on.

Later, the telephone rang and he reached for the receiver.

'Benjamin?'

'Oh, hi, Peter.' Peter Tan, Lisa's father.

'I am telephoning because I had a call from Lisa yesterday evening.'

Ben was surprised at the detachment with which he managed to absorb this piece of news. A short time ago his heart would have begun to vibrate like a tuning fork. 'How is she? Is she well and . . . uh, happy?'

'She's well,' Peter said. 'I'm not sure about happy. She tells me she is moving to California.'

No! he thought. *It's too far*. 'Where in California?'

'She didn't say.'

Silence hung between them. 'If she goes to California, will you be all right?' Ben asked eventually.

'As right as I always am,' the old man said, in his high, precise voice. 'I have many friends and a home with which I am familiar.' He paused. 'Losing one's sight does not have to be a disaster, you know.'

'Of course not.'

'And you, Benjamin . . . how are you coping on your own?'

'Coping is probably a good word to describe it.'

'My daughter has things to work out.' The old man cleared his throat. 'We must hope that it does not take her too long to find her solutions.'

'I love her,' Ben said quietly. 'And I loved our baby. Tell her that, next time she calls you.'

Chapter Nine

BEN PULLED UP beside the little country store at Hallams Cove, turned off the ignition and got out of the car.

Frank Oates, the storeowner, was standing by the pot-bellied stove in the middle of the floor, talking to one of the rangers from the National Park. 'What brings you up here, Ben?' he asked.

'Checking the place out,' Ben said.

'Summer's just 'bout over.'

'So they say.'

'How's things, anyway?' Frank's face was full of sympathy.

'Fine, Frank. You?'

'Gettin' by, thanks.'

Ben picked up a wire basket. 'Need a few stores,' he said. 'Kind of last-minute decision to come up.' He walked round the crowded shelves, taking bread from the bins, bacon and a packet of sausages from the refrigerator, orange juice and apples, eggs and a carton of milk.

The turnoff was two miles further along the highway. A flutter started up in the pit of his stomach. This was the first time he had been back to the lake since Lisa had left. He signalled and turned off onto the dirt track, soft with the accumulation of years of fallen leaves.

Soon, the house came into view and he drove along the gravelled drive and pulled up in front of the door. The stretch of water behind the house glittered in the afternoon sun. Hoisting the groceries from the back of the car, he felt for the keys in his pocket and opened the door.

The house was stifling, heat clinging to the wooden walls and under the ceilings. The shabby living room looked as it always had done, for as long as he could remember. Sand on the windowsills. Dog-eared paperbacks. Full of memories. He dumped the groceries on the kitchen counter and opened the door out onto the deck. Beyond, the hammock swung between the two pine trees. That's where it happened, he thought. That's where she was when she lost the baby. He stepped down and walked slowly across pine needles towards the hammock. Closer, he could see a discoloured patch of grass, a small fir cone dark with blood. Her blood. He forced back the images that threatened to overcome him: Lisa lying here, dozing perhaps, and then suddenly the pain, growing stronger, contractions maybe, as her small body tried to expel the child she was carrying, nobody there to help, the blood streaming from her, not yet knowing that the baby was already dead.

Abruptly, he turned away. At the foot of the steps to the porch, he pulled a twig from the rosemary bush. The scent reminded him of all the lost and golden summers. Of his father's voice: *big boys don't cry*.

But they do.

Joanne stood with one hand on the car door, inspecting the cabin. Sun slanted down through the glowing leaves of birch and maple, lighting the trunks of the pine trees. 'I'd forgotten how terrific it looks, set against the water like that,' she said.

'I know.' Mel began unloading bags from the open hatchback.

Joanne picked up their hiking boots, balanced a box of groceries on her hip and followed Mel to the door. Inside the cabin, Mel set the cool-box on the kitchen counter, then took a bottle of white wine from the fridge and began searching through the drawers for a corkscrew. 'It's not too early to start drinking alcohol, is it?'

'Honey, it's never too early.' Joanne looked appreciatively around. 'You've done a lot since my last visit,' she said. 'Rather . . . um . . . un-Ericy things, if I can put it like that.'

'We always had slightly different ideas about decoration.'

'I like yours better.'

'So do I.' Pulling at the sliding doors, Mel went out onto the terrace and dusted off two chairs. The two women sat back, their bare feet up on the railing of the deck, the wine on a low table between them. The sun blazed down on water that glittered like a spill of diamonds.

'God, it's hot out here.' Joanne wiped her face with her sleeve. 'Must be up in the eighties at least.'

'It'll get cold once the sun goes down.' Mel gazed upwards. 'Funny, isn't it, the sky is actually bluer in the fall than in the summer.'

'That's the difference between you and me,' Joanne said. 'I don't notice things like that.'

'Isn't it glorious?' Mel spread her arms. 'I love to smell the woods. Maybe we'll see a deer—the woods are full of them.'

'And there's not another soul for miles,' Joanne said wryly.

'There are more people around than you think. When it gets dark, you'll see all sorts of lights in the woods and round the lake. You're not really worried, are you? We've been up here before, just the two of us.'

'I know. Hated it then too.'

'You did not.'

'Did so. I only came to keep you company.'

'I'd never realised you were actually frightened,' Mel said. 'You should have brought Jamie with you.'

'He wanted to go see his dad again.' Joanne gave a gusty sigh. 'You know, I never thought I'd ever say this, but looking back, I can see that in his bumbling, insensitive way Gordon was a pretty good guy, even if he did run off with Miss Bubblehead.'

'*What?* That's got to be the first time I ever heard you say anything even halfway positive about him.'

'Could be I'm mellowing.'

'Oh, Joanne, honey, please don't mellow. I couldn't stand it.'

'OK.' Joanne grinned. 'Wanna go swimming?'

'The water'll be freezing.'

'In this heat, can't be too cold for me.'

'No swimsuits.'

'Who cares?' Joanne was already peeling off her shirt.

'OK.' Mel stood up and tore off her T-shirt, undid her bra, pulled at the fastening of her jeans. 'Last one in gets to make dinner.'

Naked, she ran down the steps of the deck towards the edge of the lake. The ground was soft underfoot, slick with pine needles. Flat rocks, crusted with golden circles of lichen, were embedded in the bright green moss. Joanne pounded along behind her as she reached the pale fingernail of almost white sand that formed a tiny beach, and raced across a tangle of twiggy debris into the water.

The chill was sudden and stunning, like an electric shock. Her breath caught momentarily in her throat. She held herself tightly together, unwilling to yield another millimetre of her body to the cold, and then, making up her mind to it, launched herself into the dark water. With a couple of clumsy strokes, she swam out until she was waist deep.

'*Ya* da da *da* dah,' she sang. She winced away as Joanne splashed in, sending a shower of drops of molten cold over her. 'I won!'

'You said *you*'d make dinner,' accused Joanne, panting, laughing. 'Only reason I'm here.' She turned a circle in the water, beating at the surface with flat hands until spray fountained around her. 'Gaaahd, it's *freezing*.' Her heavy, brown-nippled breasts and bountiful hips, her abundant thighs, reminded Mel of some women she'd seen in a hot-spring-fed bathhouse in Budapest she'd once visited with Eric. All were massive of belly and thigh, breast and buttock. This is what real women look like, she had thought then, women who have lived, struggled, borne children and raised them. Now, looking down at her own familiar body—the pale curls of her pubic hair below the surface, the white drift of her thighs down into the sherry-brown water—she felt sad.

On shore, the hammock was still slung between the two pine trees. She tried not to think back to five weeks ago, Lisa's death-pale face, the slow drip of her blood onto the pine needles.

As though following her thoughts, Joanne said, 'Still no word from Lisa?'

'I haven't heard anything.'

'I wonder where she went.'

'Who knows?' Mel spoke lightly. She saw movement at the kitchen windows of the Andersen house. The sun was hot on her back as she cupped water in her hands and hurled it at Joanne, the bright drops golden against the sun.

'Why, you . . .!' Joanne lumbered through the shallows, her generous mouth wide with laughter as she reared out of the water and launched herself at Mel. The two of them clung to each other for a moment, trying for a foothold on the muddy lake bottom, fingers sliding along water-slippery limbs, clutching at dolphin-sleek skin, until, shrieking, they both tumbled, in a tangle of shivering flesh, into the deeper water.

For a moment they clung to each other, faces touching, mouth close to mouth, eyes laughing, breast brushing breast. Then Joanne shrieked, 'I'm outta here.'

'Me too.'

Breath huffing from their mouths, hair plastered against their skulls, they splashed towards the shore, hopping over the stones and across the ground to the warm steps of the deck.

'*Jeez*-us, that water's like ice.'

'You can have first dibs on the shower,' said Mel. 'I'd just hate to have you pass out on me.'

He watched them for a while from the kitchen window. He had never seen women of their age naked before. He was touched by the way they frolicked with the unselfconsciousness of children, faces turned to the sun, light bouncing off their wet bodies, catching the shape of a shoulder, the curve of a breast. He recognised Joanne Mayfield from the bookstore, a big, undisciplined woman twice the size of Lisa—he stopped the thought, since he'd come up here expressly to lay some ghosts. Mel Sherman's hair glinted in the sun. Spun gold, corn silk. Above and below. Her breasts were . . . He felt himself blushing. He tried to look away but found it difficult not to stare.

If she had been up here alone, he might have plucked up the courage to go over later. Apart from Peter Tan, she was his only link with Lisa. Suddenly Mel looked up at the house and he stepped quickly back. He hoped she hadn't seen him; he didn't want her and Joanne coming over, offering sympathy he didn't need, gazing at him with those tolerant, understanding expressions on their faces. He wondered if he was losing the ability to interact with other people.

Outside, the two women laughed and shrieked and he felt a sudden unfocused anger. Part of him envied them, another part wanted to run to the edge of the lake, to yell at them, to ask them how they dared to be so happy when he was in such pain.

Further round the lake, tiny in the distance and darkened by the haze of heat on the water, he could see someone sitting in a rowing boat, a fishing rod extended over the side. A bird circled, close above the water, then suddenly dived, vanished, reappeared with a frantic gleam of silver in its beak. Hugging the shore, two kids came poling a homemade raft, and the sight made him remember the summer that he and Neil and Rory had made their own raft, lashing the planks together, launching it onto the water. The three of them laughing, laughing . . .

For a moment, he squeezed his eyes shut against the memories of the past—and against the future that now would not be.

The kitchen windowsill was dusty. Mel Sherman's voice sounded in his head: *dust will gather in corners* . . . is that what she'd said? *Moons will wax and wane*.

A dead branch stood in a glass jar, along with a black and white feather. He stroked the feather across his arm. Earlier in the summer he and Lisa had found it lying on the fine sand near the water's edge.

'It's an eagle feather,' Lisa said. 'Look, it's black at the end.' Laughing, she had stuck it behind her ear. 'Do I look like a squaw?'

'No,' he said. 'You look like the most beautiful person in the entire world that I'm just about to kiss.'

Was the rest of his life going to consist of memories of her? If Lisa had been there, he would have told her that they could move back to New York if she wanted, go anywhere she chose, anywhere, just so long as she would come back to him.

Nine o'clock. Rain had begun to fall, a gentle patter on the shingles, a tap against the big windows that formed either end of the cabin. Wrapped in rugs, the two women sat close together on the huge sofa opposite the fireplace, staring into the fire.

'If you could travel anywhere in the world,' Joanne asked lazily, 'where would you go?'

'This, right here, wouldn't be a bad place.'

'C'mon, Mel. *Here?*'

'What's wrong with it?'

'It's just up the road from where you've spent the last twenty-five years, that's what's wrong with it. Not exactly adventurous, is it?'

'I leave that to others.'

'But you shouldn't. You should get out there, do stuff, have adventures, *live*.'

'Maybe I like not being venturesome.'

'That is so pathetic.'

'This is the very last time I top up *your* glass.' Mel leaned across and poured more of the Zinfandel she had brought from the cellar at home.

'OK. New question: that abortion thing?'

'I don't want to talk about it.'

'Nor do I. I just wondered what other secrets you haven't told me.'

'They wouldn't be secrets if I had.'

Mel got up and went into the kitchen. When she came back she had a bottle of champagne in her hand and two clean glasses. From behind the cushions of the sofa, she pulled a small, soft package wrapped in fancy paper and trailing long streamers of ribbon.

'What's this?' asked Joanne.

'Your birthday's coming up. Had you forgotten?'

'Forgotten that I'm hitting the Big Five Oh?' said Joanne. 'I wish.'

'Anyway, I thought we'd have a little preliminary celebration.'

'What a sweetheart.' Joanne leaned over and for a moment rested her hand lightly on Mel's sleeve. 'My darling friend.'

'Open this first.' While Joanne ripped the folds of ice-green tissue paper, Mel tore off the foil cover of the champagne bottle and began to untwist the metal guard.

'Oh Jeez,' Joanne said on an indrawn breath. 'Oh, Mel, it's gorgeous.' She let the hand-dyed silk scarf trail over her fingers. 'It's beautiful.'

'I bought it when we went to Boston,' Mel said. 'While you were trying to recover from a hangover. It just screamed "Joanne" at me.'

'Nasturtiums,' said Joanne. She reached across and hugged Mel, kissing her on the cheek. 'My favourite flowers. Yellow and orange.'

'It would look marvellous with your silk jacket. Or with your green shirt.' They knew each other's wardrobes as well as they knew their own.

'Wouldn't it, though?' Joanne tied it round her neck. 'I *love* it.'

Mel eased the cork out of the champagne bottle. 'Here's to birthdays. And to the warmest, wisest, wittiest woman in the world.'

'Me? I'll drink to that.' She wrinkled her nose. 'Does this mean I don't get anything next week?'

'I told you: this is just a warm-up party. I thought it would be good to be just the two of us, so you'd actually listen when I said thank you.' Mel tipped her glass at Joanne. 'For everything.'

Before they went to bed, Mel stepped out onto the deck outside her bedroom. The cold sky was full of stars. There was a new moon hanging over the mountains, a pale lemon curve in the dark blue of the sky, frail as a thread. The lake was silver. She thought of how good she always felt up here. How strong, how secure within herself.

The wooden planking vibrated faintly as Joanne came to stand beside her. 'New moon,' she said. 'What're you wishing?'

'I don't know.'

Joanne slipped an arm round Mel's waist. 'Wish something for me, then. And I'll wish something for you.'

Mel leaned back against Joanne's shoulder. 'I'll wish everything for you,' she said. 'Whatever you want.' Her friend. Her dear friend. She wanted to tell Joanne how much she loved her. 'And neither of us will ever tell, right?'

'Right.'

It was damp underfoot because of overnight rain, and much cooler. Mel and Joanne wore fleeces as they began to hike along the narrow track bordering the creek that fed into the lake. After a while, the sides of the banks began to rise. The angle of the slope gradually increased until Mel and Joanne found themselves walking along the lip of a shallow ravine. Below them, the racing water sparkled and swirled.

An hour in, Joanne began to puff and wheeze. 'I'm not used to this. Why don't I find a nice boulder to sit on and wait here until you come down again?'

'Honestly, Jo, we're almost there.'

'I guess at this stage I've put in so much effort I might as well keep going,' Joanne said resignedly.

'Look up there,' Mel said. 'Isn't it spectacular? Water, rocks, trees.' And floating in the sky above them, an eagle, so close they could see the soft white feathers of its belly ruffle in the wind.

'Terrific.' Joanne stepped close to the edge of the gorge and, holding on to the slim trunk of a birch, leaned out to look at the water far below.

Mel grabbed the back of her mimosa-yellow polar fleece. 'I wouldn't get so close to the edge if I were you. It's quite slippery after the rain. And on top of that, those thin trunks can sometimes just snap in two.'

They walked in silence for a while, one behind the other. 'You never used to be this kind of a fresh-air freak,' Joanne said.

'It wasn't until Eric died that I discovered how much I liked walking.'

That was when she began to hike the mountain trails, enjoying the therapeutic act of putting space between her and the empty places in her life.

'If I come back to earth again,' Joanne broke into her thoughts, 'I'm going to ask to be fifty pounds lighter.'

'Next time round, I'd be happy with non-sloping shoulders, so my bra straps don't keep sliding off.'

As the path took a bend to the right, they heard the subdued drum of tumbling water.

'We're there.' Mel rounded a boulder that protruded across the path and said, as Joanne caught up with her, 'Take a look at that.'

In front of them, across a deep circle carved out of the cliffs, a gush of water rolled over the edge and dropped ninety feet to a dark brown pool before bouncing and skittering along the gorge towards the lake. A rainbow shimmered across the ravine where sunlight caught the spray.

'There's much more water in the spring, of course, when the rains come and the snow melts.' Mel sat down on the boulders above the falls and reached into her backpack. 'Here. Smoked salmon and cream cheese bagels. Grapes. Dried figs.'

'Wonderful.' Joanne eased her back against a rock and unzipped her jacket. 'You were right, Mel, this is great. Just look at that rainbow.'

They ate in silence for a while, then Joanne said lazily, 'The one thing I hope it will say on my gravestone is that I grabbed life by the balls.'

'You do that, all right.' Mel laughed. 'And life's not the only thing.'

'Bet your sweet life, baby.'

'Though, when you come to think of it,' Mel said, 'for all your talk, here you still are in Butterfield when you could have gone anywhere, done anything. Maybe I'm not the only loser round here.'

'Bullshit,' said Joanne.

'OK: if *you* could go anywhere, where would *you* go?'

Joanne was uncharacteristically silent. Then she said slowly, 'When I was a kid, we had an exchange teacher at school, a girl from New Zealand. She used to tell us about this place over there called Rotorua. She said it was amazing, full of hissing geysers and mud pools puking and these boiling hot lakes, and steam coming out of the ground right in front of you. She said it was like hell without the pitchforks—that's always stuck in my head.'

Mel smiled. 'Why didn't you go years ago?'

'The fare out there isn't exactly cheap, plus the cost of hotels, and car hire . . . and once Gordon and I split up, it left me kind of tight. Besides, I still had a living to earn, the kids to raise.'

'A regular little Mother Courage,' Mel said. She looked at her watch and got to her feet. 'Come on. Guess we'd better start back.'

Joanne groaned. 'You're so restless. I was just getting comfortable.'

'We still have to pack the cabin up,' Mel said.

'That won't take long, will it? We can just pile everything into the car and drive off. Back to civilisation, thank God.'

'Don't pretend you haven't had fun.'

'With you, darlin', I always have fun.'

'Me too.' Mel slung her pack across her shoulders and started back down the trail.

Joanne followed. 'Hey, slow down, will you?' she said.

'Sorry.' Mel paused to allow her friend to catch up. The sun had now climbed to the top of the sky and the warm scent of resin was intoxicating. Despite the crash of water from the falls behind them, the forest was tranquil. Something rustled in the undergrowth and she stopped to see what it was.

'Gawd,' Joanne pushed past. 'Nobody ever tells you it's just as hard going down as it is coming up. My knees are killing me.'

'You should come up more often. You'd soon get in shape.' Mel watched Joanne's broad backside move on down the trail, thinking how comfortable they were together. Below them, in the little ravine, the invisible water gushed on its way to the lake.

'Next spring,' Joanne said, over her shoulder, 'I'll be up every weekend, I promise.' She disappeared round the outcrop of granite that jutted out onto the trail. Following her at a leisurely pace, Mel lifted her head to glimpses of sky, drawing the scent of leaf and fern and moss deep into her lungs. She rounded the overhanging boulder. Above the muted boom of the falls, she heard the long-drawn-out shriek of a bird. Ahead of her the trail descended steeply for another 200 feet.

For a moment she walked on, then came to an abrupt stop. Where was Joanne? She should have been ahead. To the right was the sheer edge of the small canyon, to the left an almost vertical slope of boulder and scrub. Mel turned to look back up the trail and her eye was caught by the orange wound of fresh-snapped wood. The lower half of a slender trunk still leaned out over the ravine, the rest of it had broken off.

Not a bird but . . .

'Oh God! Joanne!' Mel threw herself down on the brink of the gorge and edged forward. Damp grasses. Little long-leaved ferns. Her hands clutched, her throat clenched, as she peered down.

Forty feet below, spread across the rocks at the stream's edge, was the yellow of her friend's jacket, like a smudge of mustard powder. Joanne's legs lay half in and half out of the water. Even from here it was obvious that one of them was broken. She was not moving.

'Joanne!' Mel screamed again. Her voice floated out over the sunless spaces of the ravine and the bright golden stain on the rocks, to lose itself in the thunder of the falls.

It was all too easy to follow Joanne's descent by the broken tree stems and the torn bushes at which she must have clutched. Shreds of clothing fluttered from the grey tree skeletons that lined the side of the gorge.

Mel ran further down the trail, boots slipping on the damp soil, feet catching on small rocks, so that several times she tripped and almost fell. As she ran, her thoughts played and replayed what must have happened. She could see it all too clearly: Joanne leaning out to look down at the water, going too close to the edge, grabbing at a tree trunk for support, only to have it break off and send her hurtling downwards.

Remembering that brief glimpse of yellow jacket, denimed legs scattered so carelessly on the rocks, Mel's breath caught in her throat. Her mind clamoured with catastrophe. Joanne with a broken back, with smashed ribs, fractured limbs, head wounds. Maybe dying. Maybe—the possibility was too terrible to contemplate—even dead. But Joanne was not—*could* not be—dying. The height from the trail was less than fifty feet. Surely, surely she could be no more than stunned. Concussed. With a broken leg. But otherwise all right.

When it reached the level of the riverbed, the trail flattened out. Mel turned off and scrambled down onto the slippery black rocks that formed the narrow shore. She started to clamber across them, then paused, irresolute. Instead of trying to make it back upstream to Joanne, would it not be more sensible to leave her lying where she was and find help? But that would mean running back to the cabin, which would take at least twenty minutes, then waiting for the emergency services, then leading them back up the trail, all of which could take hours.

What should she do? Go for help or check on Joanne first, at least move her a little so that she was clear of the river, offer comfort, offer love? It was not a hard choice.

Breath ragged, she began to make her way back upstream. It was cold down here beside the water.

Afterwards, she had no idea how long it took before she finally saw the smudge of Joanne's fleece ahead. 'I'm coming!' she screamed against the sound of the tumbling water. 'Hold on, Joanne, hold on, darling.'

Slipping, stumbling, cursing, she clambered the last few yards and knelt on the stones beside her friend. Joanne was still lying in the same position, but when Mel took her hand she slowly turned her head and smiled. One cheek was gashed and torn.

'What took you so long?' she said weakly. Blood oozed thickly from her wounds. Her eyes looked odd.

Relief rendered Mel speechless.

'Thought I'd snuffed it, didn't you?' Joanne's lips were almost invisible against the clammy greyness of her skin.

'Not for a moment,' Mel lied. Joanne's left hand hung floppily from her wrist. Mel stooped over her. 'I'm going to move your legs out of the water,' Mel said distinctly. 'I think you broke one of them.'

'Can't feel anything,' Joanne said.

Mel's heart went cold. Carefully she moved around Joanne's body and lifted first one leg out of the water onto the rocks and then, hands under thigh and calf, the other. As she moved it, Joanne coughed. Blood-flecked foam appeared at the corner of her mouth, and Mel felt her own face blanch. One of Joanne's lungs must be punctured. Just as she had been with Lisa, she was overwhelmed by her own helplessness.

She pulled off her backpack and then shrugged out of her fleece, which she laid tenderly over Joanne. 'Listen,' she said, trying not to show her fear. 'There's no way I can get you out of here on my own. I'll have to go and call for help.'

Joanne's fingers clamped over hers with surprising force. 'No,' she said. 'Don't leave me alone.'

'It's the only choice we have,' Mel said. She took the end of the silk scarf she had given Joanne last night, in a different, safer world, and gently wiped away the bloody foam.

'Should've brought my cellphone,' Joanne said. Her grin was ghostly.

'It wouldn't have been much use down here.' Mel tried to disengage her fingers. 'Let me go and get help. I'll come right back, I promise.'

Joanne clung more tightly to her. 'I'm going to die, aren't I?'

'Don't be *ridiculous*,' Mel said angrily. 'Of course you're not.'

'Don't let me die, Mel.'

'I've no intention of doing so. But I'll have to leave you for a while.'

'I don't want to die alone.'

'Listen to me.' Mel put her mouth close to Joanne's ear. 'You are not going to die, you hear me? I won't allow it. It's your birthday next week. You've got a party to go to at the bookstore.' Mel forced herself to grin. 'Sorry, but I'm afraid dying's not on the agenda.'

'I'm frightened,' Joanne said. Her face crumpled, a tear oozing from one of her eyes. 'Don't let me die alone.'

'I'm here, darling. I'm here. But just let me go and find help,' Mel's voice was unsteady, her lips trembling. 'Please, Joanne. Because if you don't . . . if you don't . . .' There were hot tears on her own face and she brushed them away with the back of her hand, at the same time pulling the other out of Joanne's grip. She took off her sweatshirt and with infinite care inched it under her friend's head. If Joanne had injured her back, she did not want to risk damaging her spine still further. Reaching for her backpack, she took out the extra pair of socks. Gently she pulled them over Joanne's cold hands.

'I'll be back, sweetheart,' she said, as though Joanne were a child. 'Just as quickly as ever I can. Just wait for me. I'll be back, I swear it.'

Joanne closed her eyes. 'Hurry.'

From the kitchen window, he'd watched them set off. Both in jeans and hiking boots, Mel carrying a small backpack, Joanne in a yellow fleece. Not the kind of gear you'd take for a daylong hike so presumably they only planned to walk for a couple of hours or so. Especially given the meteorological forecast that morning. It was as automatic as breathing for him to check it. To note that despite the fine start to the day, more rain was predicted, followed by a cold front and high winds.

He spent the morning doing nothing very much. Walked down to the store for the newspaper. Swept up the leaves that were beginning to fall. Steeled himself to go out and unhook the hammock, soak it in the lake, hang it to dry from the hooks on the porch.

By early afternoon, the sky was clouding over and the tops of the trees were tossing. Small whitecaps ruffled the surface of the lake, rolling in towards the little beach below the house.

Restless, he stood on the back porch, looking across the lake to the higher hills. He glanced at his watch. None of his business, but he'd spent too many summers as a part-time volunteer for the Emergency Rescue Service for it not to be almost a reflex to watch out for people in the mountains. They should have been back by now.

In the end, he laced on his boots, then he added a couple of sweaters to his pack before setting off along the trail to the falls. The track was still slick after last night's rain. At every bend he expected to meet them coming down, but there was no sign of them.

His attention was suddenly caught by a sapling snapped in half at the side of the gorge. Closer, he saw crushed grass, a scrap of material. Heartrate speeding up, adrenaline beginning to rush, he put down his pack and carefully leaned forward to peer over the edge. Almost directly below where he stood, he saw Joanne Mayfield, arms outflung, her yellow fleece half concealed by Mel's green sweatshirt. No sign of Mel.

He inched himself backwards until he was safely on the trail again and then, snatching up his pack, began to jog back the way he had come. As he ran, he reached into his breast pocket for his mobile phone and tapped out the numbers for the ERS, though he knew the chances were slim that it would work here.

Ahead of him, Mel Sherman suddenly emerged onto the track. Supporting herself against a boulder, she bent double, trying to bring her breathing back to normal. Glancing up the trail, she saw him coming towards her. Her face frantic, she started up towards him, then tripped and almost fell.

He reached her. Took her arm. He could smell her sweat. And something else. The acrid stench of fear. 'Are you OK?' he said.

'I'm fine,' she said, laboured breath rasping from her strained lungs. 'It's Joanne Mayfield. She fell, just up the trail. She's—'

'I saw. What sort of condition is she in? Can you tell?' Again he pressed buttons on the phone. Propelled Mel forward as he spoke. 'Is she conscious?'

'Sort of. Definitely got a broken leg. Something much worse, too. Her back, I think.' Mel's face was full of terror. 'There's a lot of blood. And her head . . .'

'What about her head?' His voice was calm, authoritative.

'Her eyes are strange. And she says she can't feel anything. I think . . . I really think . . . I'm afraid she may . . . she might . . .' Mel pressed her fists to her face, trying to force back the thought. '. . . might die.'

He shook his head, frowning at his cellphone. 'I'm not getting any response. I'd better get to her quickly. She may need stabilising.'

'Oh God.' She was sobbing now, tears streaming down her face. 'Oh God, Ben . . . I'm so. . .' She started to shiver, her teeth chattering.

He put his hand on her arm. 'You're doing fine, Mel.' He swung his pack from his shoulder and took out a sweater. 'Put this on.'

'I-I c-can't.' She seemed to have lost control of her body.

He pulled her forward and with one arm held her against his chest while with the other he slipped the sweater over her head, then pushed her arms into the sleeves. He hugged her briefly and let her go. 'I'll go ahead, and you follow me, at your own pace,' he said. 'Once I've had a look at your friend, and can assess the damage, I'll leave you with her and then find a place where the phone works and I can call the ERS, OK?'

She nodded. 'OK.'

Ahead of her, Ben leapt from rock to rock until he reached the spot where Joanne lay. He knelt down and laid his head against her chest, then reached into his pack and brought out a first-aid kit. As Mel joined him, he began probing Joanne's body: neck, head, chest, legs, his fingers delicately cautious. Rising to his feet, he picked up a sturdy branch and stripped it of twigs and leaves. He looked at Mel. 'Not perfect, but the best we can do.' Carefully he pulled the bloodstained silk scarf from round Joanne's neck and began to tie her twisted leg to the branch.

'How do you think she is?' Mel asked, unconsciously whispering.

'Not too brilliant. But her vital signs are steady, which is good.' He smiled at her. 'Give me your hand towel.' He gestured at the small towel clipped to her waist which she used to wipe sweat from her forehead. 'Luckily, I brought one too.'

Folding the two together to make a thick wad, with infinite care he eased them under Joanne's neck and brought the ends round to overlap under her jaw. He held out his hand. 'Your belt, too.'

She undid the buckle, slid her leather belt out of the loops of her jeans and watched him inch it round and then secure the two towels with it. 'Cervical collar,' he explained. 'I'm not sure how badly she's damaged her spine, but we can't take any chances.'

He took his pack and shovelled some stones into it. 'You do the same,' he said.

Mel filled her own pack and pushed it over to him.

'She mustn't move,' he explained, setting the heavy packs on either side of Joanne's head.

'If I ever find myself in real trouble, I'll know who to take with me,' Mel said, trying to joke, trying to mitigate the sense of disaster that lay like a spreading stain at the edge of her mind.

'You'd be a good person to have along.' He smiled at her, reassuring, encouraging. 'You did a fine job, keeping her warm, moving her legs out of the water. If it wasn't for you she'd be in much worse shape.'

'If it wasn't for me, she wouldn't be here at all,' Mel said. She bit down hard on her lip, determined not to break down in front of him.

He turned cold eyes on her. 'What, you pushed her, did you?'

'No, but—'

'Then don't be ridiculous.' His brusqueness was somehow more comforting than any words of reassurance would have been. 'Stay here and keep Mrs Mayfield company until I get back. Whatever happens, don't let her move.'

He started walking swiftly downstream towards the track, then turned. 'Her neck must stay absolutely still,' he called.

Mel knelt behind Joanne and put a hand on either side of her head. She spoke her friend's name, wondering if she was doing the right thing. Maybe it was best for Joanne to remain unconscious.

'I told you I'd be back,' she said, not sure if Joanne could hear her, hoping to reach into her head, call her back from wherever she was. '*Told* you, and now it'll be all right, because would you believe I found Ben Andersen on the trail, and he's gone for help?'

Joanne's eyelids fluttered.

'He's gone to call the emergency services. They'll airlift you to hospital and put you back together again.'

'Like Humpty Dumpty,' Joanne murmured, the words slurred.

Mel's heart jumped with relief. '*Not* like Humpty Dumpty,' she said, 'because they *couldn't* put him together, could they? But they'll patch you up OK.'

'My leg . . .'

'Yes, you've broken it, but that's nothing, you can hobble around in a cast and everyone will feel terribly sorry for—'

'I can't feel it. Can't feel anything. Can't *move*.' Panic spread across Joanne's bloodied face. She began to struggle feebly.

'Keep still,' Mel said, pressing her hands more firmly against Joanne's head, feeling warm blood on her fingers, the strands of hair slippery under her fingers. 'Ben wants to keep you rigid until they can check out your spine. He's been fantastic.' She remembered the gentle way he had touched Joanne, the care he had taken over her.

'So stupid . . .' Joanne said.

'What is?' The rocks were beginning to dig painfully into Mel's knees.

'You told me not to . . . just wanted to see the river . . . it's not your fault,' Joanne said, her voice suddenly stronger. 'Not your *fault*, you hear?' She coughed, then moaned. Blood glistened on her hair. Fresh blood, darkly crimson. 'Know what I wished last night?'

'You said you'd never tell.'

'Wished you'd fall in love again.' She closed her eyes.

Mel could feel her slipping away again. 'I'll come to New Zealand with you, if you like,' she said. 'To see those mud pools.'

Joanne did not reply.

'And I'll tell you what. After we'd gone to bed yesterday, I thought of somewhere I'd really like to go. When you asked me last night . . . I couldn't think of anywhere I wanted to go but . . . oh, Joanne, wake up, speak to me, Joanne.'

There was no response. Mel shivered. She could feel the thin pulse of Joanne's heart. For the rest of her life she would remember the wet pebbles, the fissured cliff face on the other side of the swirling brown water, the seeping springs that spread across its surface like tears. She would only have to close her eyes to be there again, listening to the rush of the river, with her friend dying in her arms.

'Joanne!' she urged. 'Wake up. Come back.'

Nothing.

The absence grew. Emptiness, total and absolute, filled her. And anger. She wanted to scream, to smash, shatter, destroy.

'Joanne!' she said again, more sharply this time.

There was movement in the body she held so close. 'My legs . . . Can't move . . .'

'I already told you, Ben's got you trussed up like a chicken.'

'Can't feel . . .'

'You're cold, that's why.'

''S bad sign.' Joanne's words were slurring. She tried to turn her head but Mel increased the pressure of her hands. 'Couldn't . . . wheelchair . . . rather die.'

'You're not going to die,' Mel said sharply. 'Don't keep saying that. I told you Ben Andersen's calling the emergency services.'

'Ben?'

'Yeah. I *told* you.' God, had the fall damaged Joanne's brain?

'Poor Ben . . . 'n' Lisa, too.' Joanne sounded as if she were almost asleep.

'I know.'

'Not your fault . . .' murmured Joanne. 'Always was a clumsy bitch.'

'Oh, Joanne.'

'Gotta grab it . . .'

'What?'

'Grab it . . . by the balls.' Joanne opened her eyes. 'Don't . . . forget.'

'I won't be able to, with you around to remind me,' Mel said. Tears filled her eyes.

'Thirsty . . .'

'Hang on.' Carefully, Mel reached for the bottle of water lying beside her. She leaned over awkwardly and held it to her friend's lips.

'Secrets . . .' Joanne said, after a moment, sounding stronger.

'What about them?'

'Kept them.'

'I've kept secrets too,' Mel said. 'Things I should've told you.' Would it have made it more bearable, she thought now, with her friend's grey and bloodied face cradled between her hands, if she had talked about the abortion years before, as she had so much longed to?

'Don Cunningham and me . . .'

'What? Did you have an affair with him? I don't believe it,' cried Mel, pretending outrage.

'How else . . . think . . . could afford . . . bookstore?' A ghost of Joanne's old grin shivered on her mouth.

Mel could not bear to look at her friend's fluttering eyes, at the face from which life seemed almost visibly to be ebbing. 'Not smelly old Don Cunningham. I just do not believe it!'

Trying to keep back her tears, Mel looked down at the wound on Joanne's head. The sweatshirt she had put under there earlier was black with drying blood. Oh, Joanne . . . my friend. My loved one.

She could not stop shivering. The cold she felt was not just of the water and the wet sunless rocks, it was bone-deep, heart-deep. 'Not Don,' she whispered, as if it was that that mattered and not the terrible sense of loss that cut through her, the unstoppable flow of grief.

Chapter Ten

BEN CAME WITH HER to the lounge attached to the intensive care ward.

'You don't have to,' she said, jittery with anxiety.

'I'll stay until the doctor comes out,' he said. 'See what he has to say.'

They sat in the drab little room, together but not together, waiting. A shiny-leafed rubber plant stood in one corner, a bright green fern cascaded from a stand near the door, both of them unwanted reminders of health and vigour. Above their heads the fluorescent lights cast a dead glow that drained the colour from the walls and floor.

Seized by a chill from somewhere deep inside her, which spread until her teeth began to chatter, Mel started shivering.

Ben watched her in silence, then went down the hall to the coffee machine and brought back two plastic cups, one of which he handed to her. She took a sip and grimaced, about to put it down on the scarred table in front of her, but he stopped her. 'Drink it,' he said.

'It's way too sweet,' she complained. 'I don't take sugar in my coffee.'

'Drink it,' he said, and obediently she drained the contents of the cup, and felt the sugar and caffeine work their way through her bloodstream, restoring her depleted energy.

It was another two hours before the surgeon appeared, a grey-faced man in green scrubs. It was nearly two o'clock in the morning, and he looked as if he had not slept for days.

Mel stood up. 'What's the news?' she asked.

'Are you family?' he asked brusquely, too tired for courtesy.

'No—I was—we were with her when the accident happened.'

Ben moved to stand next to Mel. He nodded at the doctor. 'Hi, Jim. You look tired.'

'Oh, Ben. Didn't see you there. Yeah, I'm bushed. It's been a long job.'

'Mel here is Mrs Mayfield's closest friend,' Ben said. 'So tell us what's happening.' He took Mel's hand in his and, comforted by its rough warmth, she was happy to let him handle things.

'We can't say at the moment. Not for at least twenty-four hours. She suffered some fairly extensive damage to both the head and the spine.'

'Will she be able to walk?' Mel said.

'We won't know for a while.' The surgeon shook his head. 'What we're more concerned about is the head injury.' He hesitated, brushed his sleeve, looked at Ben. 'She just might be in a coma.'

'A coma?' Mel was afraid she was going to faint.

He nodded morosely. 'It's too early to say. But we—you—the family should prepare themselves for the possibility.' The doctor pulled at one of his ear lobes. 'Do you live locally?'

'Yes.'

'Then I suggest you go home, come back later.'

'I don't know.' Mel looked at Ben.

'Like me to drive you?' Ben asked.

About to refuse, she realised that he wanted—needed—to do something. 'That would be very kind.'

They walked towards the parking lot, then he took her arm and guided her towards his Jeep. As he opened the passenger door, she caught his eye and for a moment the two of them stared at each other.

'Mel . . .' His fingers tightened round her arm.

'Ben . . .'

The silence lengthened between them again. Finally Mel turned her head away. She climbed into the Jeep and sat staring straight ahead while Ben got into the driver's seat and, without looking at her again, engaged the gears and eased his foot down on the accelerator.

Arriving at her home, she fumbled with the keys and opened the front door. 'Coffee?' she said, walking into the empty house. 'Or something stronger?'

'Do you have any brandy?'

'Over there.' Mel waved a hand. 'Help yourself.'

'Not for me,' he said. 'For you.'

'I have to call Joanne's . . . her ex-husband.' She raised her shoulders and dropped them. She picked up the telephone, then replaced it. She covered her face with her hands. 'How am I going to tell him? And Jamie, too. He's staying with his father.'

'There's no easy way to break bad news.' Ben put a glass of brandy in her hand. 'Drink that first.'

She dialled Gordon Mayfield's number. When he finally answered, clearly roused from sleep, she said, 'It's Mel Sherman.'

'Something's happened to one of the kids,' he said, instantly alert.

'Not the kids.'

'What then? At this time of night it can't be good news.'

She made a tiny strangulated sound. 'I—I . . .'

'Joanne,' he said flatly.

'It's . . . yes . . . she's . . . she's . . .' Mel began to sob.

'She's dead.' He sounded tired; there was a catch in his voice as he added, 'Why do I feel as if I've been dreading this ever since I left?'

'No. It's not that. Oh *God* . . . she's not dead.' Somehow Mel managed to explain what had happened.

There was a long sigh at the other end of the line. 'How am I going to tell Jamie?' Gordon asked. 'And Tom and Lucy?'

'I can't imagine. Do you want me to call any of them?'

'I guess I better do it.' He sighed again. 'You must be devastated yourself,' he said quietly. 'I know how close you and Joanne are.'

'Yes.' Devastated, demolished, destroyed.

'I'll drive up tomorrow,' he said. 'Will you be all right until then?'

'Yes.' What choice did she have? What else could she be but all right?

She put the receiver down and turned round, to find that Ben was standing there, watching her. He held out his arms and silently she stepped into them, laid her head against his shoulder, accepted the support he offered. 'Thank you for being here with me,' she whispered.

Gordon Mayfield and his children arrived the following day and drove straight to the hospital. Exhausted, distressed, Mel waited for them in Joanne's house. When they finally came through the door, all of them looked as though they had been bludgeoned. Tom, who had filled out over the summer vacation, put his arms round her. Mel hugged Lucy, the girl's head burrowed into her neck. When she held out her arms to Jamie, he pushed his spectacles up his nose and frowned, his lower lip quivering, then burst into tears.

'Oh, honey,' Mel crooned, holding him tight against her breast. 'Oh, my little Jamie,' remembering him as a toddler, at four, at seven, solemn, precocious, never without a book. She thought of the lemon cake in her freezer, which might never now be set with candles.

Now, he looked up at her, sniffing. 'Is Mom going to die?' he said.

'She's going to be fine, Jamie,' Tom said, touching his little brother's hair. He seemed finally to have stepped into adulthood. 'You know Mom.'

Was it her imagination, Mel wondered, or did Tom avoid her gaze? She thought she would never lose the images of the water-dark stones, the gushing river, that sulphur-yellow stain at the bottom of the gorge.

Gordon Mayfield put both his hands on Mel's shoulders. He was a big, still-handsome man with a sweep of heavy grey hair, a summer tan. 'This is so terrible,' he said. 'I don't know how we are . . . Lying in that hospital bed, she looks so . . .' His kind eyes were red-rimmed. He sat down heavily on the shabby old sofa and his children gathered around him, Lucy leaning her head on his shoulder, Tom upright, Jamie burrowing into his lap as though he were a baby again.

Superfluous, Mel went out to make coffee. Waiting for the kettle to boil, she was stabbed by the familiarity of Joanne's yellow-walled kitchen. The absence of Joanne's big, ebullient personality was made worse by the memories: the Sabatier knife Mel had bought her, the antique cherry-wood salt box they'd found at a garage sale.

She laid the tray with mugs of coffee, a glass of juice for Jamie, and carried it back to the living room. The others did not appear to have moved. She put the tray down on the battered coffee table then poured coffee, handed it round. Were they blaming her for what had happened? Did they hate her?

Gordon seemed worried. 'What's the best way to handle things like the bookstore?'

'The two assistants, Karen and Wendy, are pretty clued up,' Mel said. 'They'll be able to carry on as usual. It won't matter much until it comes to reordering: they know how to cope with the day-to-day stuff.'

Tom suddenly lost his composure. 'I just can't take it in,' he said. 'Mom, in a wheelchair. That's what they said at the hospital. She might be in a—' He bent his head and his shoulders shook.

Gordon glanced at his elder son. 'Might it be better just to . . . to start trying to sell the store? If she's not going to be able to . . . to get about.'

'Dad, let's not give up on her before we start, OK?' Lucy put a hand on her father's knee.

'Until we know for sure, we shouldn't assume the worst,' said Mel. She was aware that all of them were concentrating on Joanne's possible loss of mobility, in order not to have to think about the much worse options. 'Actually, she *was* thinking of changing direction.'

'Changing?'

'Well, you might not believe this, but she was seriously talking about opening a health-food store.' Mel could not help smiling.

'Joanne was?'

'Mom selling organic vegetables?' Tom said.

'Scrunchy little apples and herbs and stuff like that?' Jamie pushed his glasses up his nose. 'Doesn't sound like Mom.'

'I can't believe it,' Lucy said, mouth curving in a smile.

'I can,' said Gordon, 'for about three minutes!'

And then suddenly all of them were laughing, falling about in their seats, the images bright and clear: Joanne surrounded by sacks of pulses, buckets of basmati rice, organic wholefoods.

'Can you imagine?' gasped Lucy, trying to catch her breath. 'Mom selling herbal tea! She hated—*hates*—the stuff.'

Laughter turned quickly to tears.

Mel's head was way too heavy for her neck. It kept falling forward onto her chest. She blinked awake again. Her eyelids felt like sandpaper and her mouth was dry and foul. How long had she been sitting beside Joanne's bed? Hours? Days? Waiting, talking, hoping for some sign.

A couple of times Joanne had sneezed, little snickerings that shook the sheet covering her chest. Occasionally she turned her head on the pillow, muttered something.

Seeing her for the first time since surgery, Mel had felt as though she had been punched in the stomach. One side of her face was encrusted with thick red scabs and her eyes were swollen shut, the skin around them startlingly purple against the waxy grey of her cheeks. Most of the hair had been shaved from her head, leaving her skull—where it was visible—as vulnerable as a baby's. Bandages. Plaster. And those tubes. Dozens of tubes. Up the nose, in the mouth, attached to the arm, snaking under the covers to feed and monitor. How could anyone expect to recover from such injuries? What hope was there that Joanne could ever take up the life she had lost?

Yet, over the following days, the nursing staff remained positive. They came and went, checking Joanne out, feeding her, washing her. 'The vital signs are stable. Her response to external stimuli is the same as it was,' they said. 'We're not seeing any change for the worse.'

'But she's not waking up. She's . . . not *there*,' Mel said wildly, after a long night of sitting beside her friend's bed, holding the limp hand, watching the expressionless face.

The nurse, Beverly, glanced across at Joanne and laid a finger on her lips. 'Hearing sensitivity is very acute in coma cases,' she said softly. 'Let's try and be positive. Just accept that she's there, somewhere. Gotta have faith, Mel!'

Faith: Mel was not sure if she had enough faith to restore Joanne to health again, or if any single person could possess that much faith. She had worked out a visiting rota with Gordon, but in between her own sessions at Joanne's bedside, she was unable to sleep. Now, she cranked up her eyelids again. Exhaustion coated her.

Desperately she wished to get back to normal, then wondered if there still existed a normal to get back to. This room, this chair, this figure in this bed, Joanne and yet not Joanne, was her normality now. She had offered to move into the Mayfield home, to take over the role of carer of the family, to make dinner for them at night, pack Jamie's lunch box, but Gordon had shaken his head, squeezed her arm.

'Concentrate on Joanne,' he said. 'I'll cope with the kids.' And, though she knew that had not been his intention, she had felt excluded. All the years shared with her friend meaningless now.

Going home to eat, shower, change clothes, she scarcely slept in her own bed, slumping down, instead, on the couch, falling instantly into a deep and consuming sleep, only to start up after a couple of hours, fretting that Joanne had woken, was calling for her.

She found time to drop in at the gallery, sign a few letters, agree with whatever Carla suggested, but the Koslowski show seemed remote and inconsequential, something that no longer had any relevance.

Now, she took her friend's hand and lifted it to her mouth, kissed it. 'I wish you'd wake up,' she said. 'I want to hear you laugh, not that you've got much to laugh at, I know that, God, don't I know.' Mel pressed her friend's fingers. There was no reaction from the still figure on the bed. Mel took a sip of water from the glass on the bedside cabinet. Her throat was raw and scratchy, and she felt as though she had been talking for days. She paused, drew a deep breath, started once more. 'Tom cut the grass in your back yard yesterday. And I personally raked up the leaves under that big old maple. And if you don't believe me, I've got the blisters to prove it, and as I've said to you before, that tree definitely needs to be trimmed down before a branch falls onto someone's head. Oh, I wish you would wake up, Joanne, I really wish you would come back to me and be my friend again.'

Tears filled Mel's eyes. It was the sort of thing a kindergarten kid might say. *Will you be my friend?* She reached for the glass of water again; her throat was beginning to seize up and her chest felt tight.

She had not known she could keep up a verbal barrage like this for so long. At first her brain used to run ahead of her mouth, desperately searching for something to say, trying to shape sentences, to make sense. Sometimes she had read aloud from *Great Expectations*, always top of Joanne's list of books if she was marooned on a desert island. But latterly she had simply let the thoughts emerge in whatever order they wanted, talking to Joanne in the easy freewheeling way that had developed between them. She had no idea whether it was doing any good.

'Do you remember,' she began once more, then suddenly tears were splashing down her cheeks and grief rose inside her, a huge heavy ball of it, swelling, stifling her.

So many *do-you-remembers*. So many things shared.

'Oh, Joanne, wake up,' she whispered. 'Squeeze my hand, blink, smile, *anything*, so I know you can hear me. Please wake up so I can stop feeling so terribly *guilty*, because it's tearing me apart. *Please*, Joanne.'

But there was no response. No squeeze. No flicker. No twitch. Nothing to show for all the words. Nothing to ease Mel's misery.

He had bought flowers for Joanne. Roses, orangey-brown ones, with a sprig or two of some green stuff to set it off. She wouldn't know, of course, wouldn't give a damn whether he brought her anything or not, but he'd decided, passing the florist shop, that it might comfort the family to know that people cared enough to bring flowers.

It was late as he drove into the hospital parking lot. He turned off the ignition, stepped out of the car and gazed up at the sky. It was sprinkled with the hard clear stars that announced the coming autumn. Fall used to be his favourite time of year. He'd liked the crisp days, the bite of frost in the air. And the colours, so many reds—wine, crimson, scarlet, cranberry—and yellows, everything from palest lemon to amber to mustard, and oranges like fire or copper . . .

His mouth twisted. Who gave a rat's ass what season it was? What the hell did it matter, without Lisa there to share it?

He walked in through the entrance, then down long passages and past darkened rooms. He knew that Joanne was still in a coma. The intensive-care ward was quiet, most people either asleep or out of it on medication. When he reached Joanne's room, the lights were on and he could see Mel sitting by the bed, her back to the door. She was holding her friend's hand and had her head down on the covers.

He wondered what to do. Then he tiptoed in and laid the flowers on the high hospital table that had been pushed to the end of the bed.

As he turned to leave, Mel lifted her head.

'Hi.' He was shocked at the change in her. She seemed ten years older than she had only a few days earlier.

'You've brought flowers,' she said, and he wasn't sure if she thought they were for her or not.

'How is she?' he asked.

She stared at him as though she hadn't heard, then gave herself a small shake. 'They don't know. There might be brain damage. There might be . . . they don't really know.'

'When she wakes up,' he said awkwardly, picking them up again and laying them down on the end of the bed, 'she might like to see some roses.'

'She loves roses,' Mel said. 'They're her favourite flower.'

'Good.' There were dozens of vases in the room, full of flowers, and for a moment he felt ridiculous, standing there. 'I guess the last thing she wants is more of them.'

'Can anyone ever have enough roses?' She smiled tiredly. He could see the exhaustion in her eyes.

'Right. Well . . .' Lifting his hand in farewell, he walked away. Mel was obviously exhausted. Even her hair looked tired, not so much blonde as colourless. She probably hadn't even noticed he'd left.

Chapter Eleven

ANOTHER WEEK WENT BY.

The first delivery of Koslowski's work arrived at the Vernon Gallery. The United Parcel Service man carried the three big crates into the gallery and set them carefully down on the polished maple floor. Handing over a sheaf of papers to be signed, he reached into the pouch he was carrying and pulled out an envelope. 'There's this too,' he said. 'Special Delivery, supposed to go with the other forms. Mr Koslowski was real insistent about it. Follows me all the way down the stairs. Yells at me. "You gotta hand it over personal," he says. "I'll hold you directly responsible if anything goes wrong." I'm like, "Look, mister, I'm just the messenger boy here," but he's not listening. "Hand it over personal," he's going, real loud, with people stopping to see what's goin' on.'

'He's quite a character,' agreed Mel.

'I'll say. No shoes on his feet, hair all mussed. Anyhow, here's the letter and I'm handing it over personal, like he said.'

Mel took the white envelope and looked down at the ungainly black script: **TO WHOM IT MAY CONCERN ! ! !** She was surprised by the complicated sensations that swept over her. She remembered notes stuck to the door of Galen's studio, sudden postcards from Rome or Calcutta when she had believed him to be in Oregon, angry letters fired off to critics who had failed to understand his work.

In the office at the back of the gallery a phone rang and Carla hurried to answer it. Mel dealt with the paperwork and signed the delivery note.

When the UPS man had gone, Carla fixed coffee for them both and Mel sat down at the table in her office and opened the envelope. Inside was a sheet of A4, torn from a pad, with strong black letters and a mass of exclamation marks. The sculptor had jabbed at the paper so hard that in places he had gone right through.

TO WHOM IT MAY CONCERN ! ! !

All the pieces have been labelled very clearly. Do NOT mix them up ! ! Contour IV is to be displayed in a corner! Harbinger should stand in water. These conditions MUST be met!

Galen Koslowski

'What do you think of this?' Mel said, handing it to her assistant.

Carla scanned it. 'Well, that's telling you.' She laughed. 'He sounds like he's kind of off the wall.'

'He's eccentric, but not nuts. He's . . . he's actually one of the kindest people you could ever meet. He just gets very frustrated.'

'What about?'

'Like a lot of creative people, he feels that nobody really understands his work.'

Carla dropped a heavy hand onto Mel's shoulder, made a severe face. 'Mind you don't go making a mistake, now, Ms Sherman. Stick *Contour IV* in a bowl of water, instead of *Harbinger*, for instance. What does he mean, anyway, displayed in water?'

'It's something he does. He's probably packed in a marble or granite basin which we'll have to fill.'

'Will plain tap water be acceptable?' said Carla. 'Or does it have to be designer water? And—oh my!—should it be still or sparkling?'

'I'm amazed he hasn't specified it,' Mel chuckled.

'I had another call from that couple up in South Burlington,' said Carla. 'They got the invitation to the preview and are going to bring some art-dealer friends who're over from Paris. And the *Boston Globe*'s confirmed that they're coming and want to do an interview.'

'Terrific. But I'm so sorry you've been landed with everything while I deal with my . . . my crises. First Lisa Andersen, now poor Joanne.'

'Don't give it a thought.' Carla patted Mel's shoulder. 'Much better you should be with Mrs Mayfield. Anyway, I love it, you know that.'

'When this is over, we'll have a talk, get things on a better footing, yes?'

'Fine by me.'

'OK. Let's get the new stuff unpacked.'

It was gone eight o'clock at night, but Mel was still prowling through the gallery, inspecting the exhibits. Now that so much of his recent work was assembled in one place, it was easy to see how Koslowski's style had evolved over the years. The early Koslowskis had spoken to the dark places of the human soul. There had followed a period of exuberance, when his pieces had flowered like roses, before he began to get fussy, less pure in form. Now, he had turned to a sparer kind of work.

She stopped in front of a heavy piece of black basalt. *Woman*. A female body, squat and heavy, cut off at the thighs and the shoulders. The stone was undressed, except for the heavy breasts and distended belly, which had been polished to a high sheen.

Another recent piece caught her eye. Called *Birth*, it was simply a face, reaching out of the stone, contorted by an expression that could have been anything: agony or grief or ecstasy. Or perhaps all three.

She wondered whether to add *First Love*, her own sculpture, to the show. A tender, personal piece, he had made it specifically for her; she was not entirely sure whether it would fit in with the other work. She would have to think about it some more before she decided.

Butterfield continued its usual routines: the Craft Fair, the historical pageant, civic council meetings, events in which Mel would normally have taken part. But since Joanne remained comatose, Mel divided her time between home, the hospital and, when she could, the gallery. She was home now. A fire burned in the hearth of her living room; outside, a strong wind was tugging at the turning leaves and smacking them against the windows.

Jamie was curled up on the sofa beside her, looking at a picture book. 'Mom told me I'd enjoy something called *Orlando*,' he said, looking up at her. 'By this English writer called Veronica Woolf or something. No, not Veronica . . . Virginia.'

'You're on O's now, are you?'

'Yes, but I couldn't . . .' He looked at the fire and bit his lip. 'I know she didn't mean *Orlando the Marmalade Cat*, which anyway I've read hundreds of times, but . . . at the moment it just seems sort of less complicated to read something I already know.'

'No demands,' said Mel.

'Right. And also, I really like the pictures. They're kind of . . . comforting, aren't they?'

Oh, my poor little Jamie, she thought. At least, when your world turns upside-down, you can always bury yourself in a book. 'When I was little, I loved the way Orlando wears his watch on his tail,' she said.

Jamie's eyes rounded. 'Wow! He's been around since *you* were a kid?'

'You ageist swine, you.' Mel snuggled him closer to her. 'How's Gargery doing?'

'He's pretty sad,' Jamie said. 'I took him for a walk this morning and he just walked. Normally he . . . he . . .' Jamie pressed his lips together, holding back. '. . . he runs about all over the place.'

'Want something to eat?'

'I had a hamburger at the hospital.' He closed the book on his knee. 'Mel. Is Mom going to get better?'

So many things she could say. So many lies she could tell. 'Honey, I just don't know.'

'What will happen to us if she . . . if she dies?'

'You've got a loving dad. You and Tom and Lucy would probably go and live with him.' She knew this because she and Gordon had discussed it as a worst-case scenario. 'So you'd still be together.'

Jamie gave a deep sigh, started to say something but choked instead. Suddenly he was sobbing against her, shaking his head from side to side. 'I don't want her to . . .'

'Jamie, Jamie.'

'I dream about her all the time. Sometimes she's there, but not really. Sometimes she's falling, falling . . . . Sometimes I'm falling with her. And when I wake up I can hear Lucy crying or Tom. Or me.' Blindly he burrowed against her, questing for comfort.

Mel held him against her breasts, rocking back and forth. She cupped her hand over his skull as though he were newborn, soft against her palm, and her tears fell onto his hair. He was too young to have to bear this burden, but who else could bear it for him?

They were sitting like that when Lucy and Gordon arrived. 'How is she?' Mel asked, already knowing the answer.

'The same,' Gordon said. 'Just the same.'

Lucy dropped her bag. She looked at her little brother and her forehead creased as she tried not to break down in front of him. Distractedly, she ran her fingers through her long loose hair.

It was a gesture Mel had seen a hundred times. Joanne had always shared her children, as she had shared so much else, leaving Mel a legacy of memories associated with them: Lucy in her first long dress, going to the Prom, Tom taking first place for his clarinet-playing in the State musical competitions, the tears and histrionics when Carter Longstrom dumped fourteen-year-old Lucy, Tom falling out of a tree, mealtimes and picnics and trips to the ocean.

Gordon leaned over the back of the sofa and put his hand on Mel's shoulder. 'We're so lucky to have you,' he said. Gently he touched his son's head.

Mel wiped her eyes with her free hand. 'I'm the one who's lucky.'

'We've always thought of you as family, you know that,' Lucy said suddenly. 'Christmas, Thanksgiving, birthdays. All those summer picnics.' Her shoulders lifted in a sob and she turned away. 'I better get down to the hospital and take over from Tom. You coming with me, Jamie?'

Jamie hesitated. Then he stood up and squared his shoulders. 'OK.'

Lucy took his hand. At the door, she turned back and stood staring at the floor. 'I hate this, Dad.'

'We all do, sweetheart.' Gordon went over and put his arms round her and Jamie.

'Oh, Dad . . .' Lucy leaned into his shoulder. 'Oh God, this is so terrible. Mom lying there, like she doesn't exist any more. I can't bear it.'

'It's OK, hon.' He smoothed her hair. 'It'll all come right in the end.' The ritual words of childhood, a magic incantation left over from the days when children believe their parents to be omnipotent.

'Dad . . .'

'Women like your mom don't give up easily. She'll be back with us before we know it and then we'll all miss the peace and quiet.'

'Da-ad . . .' But Lucy was half smiling now, wanting to believe him, longing to be convinced. Jamie said nothing. His face was set. He knows, Mel thought. He's prepared for the worst.

'She may not be the mom we're used to,' Gordon said. 'But she'll be back, one way or the other.' He held his daughter at arm's length, his hands on her shoulders. 'Apart from anything else, we're coming up to party season, and you know how much your mom loves a party.'

'I so much want to believe you.' Lucy planted a kiss on her father's cheek and pulled open the front door, letting in a swirl of cold air.

'You better.' It was the voice dads used to ward off the demons and Mel could see that even Lucy was half convinced.

'See you,' she said, then she and Jamie were gone, slamming the door behind them.

Gordon sat down again. 'My kids are everything to me,' he said simply. 'They're my whole life.'

'You're lucky to have such a good relationship with them.' Mel could see little resemblance in this tired, sad man to the demon that Joanne had so often painted.

'Joanne is a generous woman. That's why she moved here after the divorce, so that they wouldn't be too far away from me. I doubt if she's ever said a bad word about me to them.' He turned and looked directly at Mel. 'She probably saved it all for you.'

'Well . . .'

'It's OK, Mel. I can imagine. I know what she's like in full flight.'

They sat in silence for a while. 'Joanne always wanted to go to New Zealand,' Mel said as another unconnected thought rose to the surface. 'I was thinking that maybe I could go with her when . . . if . . .'

'There's no reason why she shouldn't have gone long ago.'

'Except money.'

'Money?' He raised his eyebrows.

'The bookstore doesn't exactly lose money, but there's not a lot left over by the time she's covered the overheads. She can't afford the flight.'

'Baloney.'

'What do you mean?'

'I've lost count of the number of times I've offered to buy her a ticket to Auckland.'

'Perhaps she didn't want to be beholden.'

He lowered his head and glanced at her from under his eyebrows. 'Truth is, she's afraid to travel on her own, afraid of a lot of things.'

'*Joanne* is? I don't believe it. She's always telling me to grab life by the balls, get out and live.'

He smiled tiredly. 'Joanne always thinks there's a more perfect life somewhere over the rainbow. Nothing's ever quite good enough but she never wants to go for the dreams, in case they turn sour on her.'

'The bookstore was a dream she went for.'

'Buying the bookstore was the biggest decision she ever took, but she was terrified it would fall apart in her hands. In the end, she only went ahead because I said I would underwrite it for her.' He gave her a quizzical look. 'I bet you didn't know that either.'

Mel made a movement of the head which could have been a nod. But in fact, no, she had not known.

He leaned back against the arm of the sofa. 'Oh God, Mel, when I think of the way I've wasted my life. All these years with my kids lost because of a single moment of madness, chasing off with some bimbo from the office. God knows what possessed me. I knew the day I left that it was a terrible mistake, that the one I really loved was Joanne.'

'She was coming round to realising that,' Mel said. 'Maybe she even felt the same way, though she'd never admit it.'

Gordon wiped his hands over his face. 'Guess I'd better get along to Joanne's place and make sure there's something for Tom to eat when he gets back from the hospital.'

At the front door, he patted her shoulder. 'She'll be back with us soon,' he said. 'The same old feisty Joanne, bossing us about, telling us how to run our lives.' He suddenly looked uncertain. 'She *will* be back, won't she?'

Mel nodded at him. 'Of course she will.'

The telephone bleeped and she ran to answer it, while Gordon still hovered in the open doorway. 'Hello?'

'Mel! It's Lucy! Oh, Mel, guess *what!*'

'What?'

'It's Mom . . . she woke up!'

'That's . . . oh heavens, that's *wonderful*! That's just so . . .'

Jamie pulled the phone from his sister. 'Mom woke up. Just like that. She said hello, Jamie.' His voice swooped like a swallow, bubbly with joy. 'She asked me what I was reading.'

'Hang on, honey. You can tell your dad all about it.' Mel handed the receiver to Gordon, who was now standing beside her. Joanne awake, alive? It was almost too much to take in.

'Oh my . . .' Gordon said, his eyes shining as he listened to his children. A tear rolled down his cheek and he brushed at it. 'Did she really? Isn't that typical of . . . Yes, I'm absolutely . . . I'll come right over . . .'

He put down the telephone and drew a deep breath. 'Oh God, Mel,' he said. 'I've been putting a brave face on things for the sake of the kids, but all this time, I didn't really . . . I honestly feared the worst.'

'I did too.' Mel seized his hand. 'I can't believe it.'

The two of them looked at each other, smiles splitting their faces. 'I'm off to the hospital—come with me,' Gordon said.

'No. It's a time for family.'

'You *are* family, you know that.'

'I'll go in later.' She pressed her hands to her mouth. 'Oh, Gordon, I'm so happy.'

'Me too.'

When he had gone, Mel walked through the house, picking things up, setting them down again. She looked at the phone, needing to share her joy with someone. She called Ben's number, but there was no answer. As she replaced the handset, she heard a car pull up in front of the house and someone running up the path, leaping the wooden steps onto the porch, rapping at the door using the heavy brass knocker, over and over until she opened the door.

'Joanne's OK!' It was Ben.

'I know, I know!'

'I dropped in at the hospital to check up how things were going,' Ben said, coming inside and shutting the door behind him. 'They told me she'd just, like fifteen minutes ago, come out of the coma.'

'It's marvellous!' Mel hugged him. 'Miraculous!' She sobered suddenly. 'Is it going to last?'

'Who can say, Mel. But it has to be a good sign, doesn't it? Which is why I brought some champagne.' He brandished a bottle at her.

'It'll be all fizzed up if you shake it around like that.'

'Who cares!'

Mel laughed, whirled around the room, wanting to jump, to leap, to fly, feeling as though she had been given back the world.

In the kitchen, Ben opened the bottle over the sink while Mel held two flutes under the neck, managing to catch about half the contents.

'To Joanne,' Ben said, taking one of the glasses from her. 'To . . . I don't know . . . life and love and . . . happiness.'

'I'll drink to that.' Mel raised her glass to her mouth. 'Oh, Ben, I can't really believe she's woken up at last.'

'It's only a first step,' he said, suddenly cautious.

'I know. There's all sorts of stuff still to go through. I know we're not out of the woods yet. But all the same . . .' She held out her glass. 'It's worth celebrating.'

Ben pressed the switch on the player Mel kept on one of the counters. Something jazzy filled the kitchen and he pranced round the table, snapping his fingers, his hips undulating. 'Yeah, *man*!' he growled, guttural as Mick Jagger. 'Go, baby, go!' while Mel leaned against the counter top, laughing. She had never seen this side of him.

The music changed to something slow and sweet and he strummed a few bars on an air guitar, then came over to Mel. He took her champagne out of her hand, set it down on the table and put his arms round her. Together they swayed in time to the music. 'I feel so darn good,' he said. 'So . . . what's the word I want?'

'Unreal?'

'That'll do.'

His hand was on the small of her back, pressing her against him. She laid her head on his shoulder, smelling his sweat, and closed her eyes. 'Mmmm,' she said.

He held her away from him. 'Sometimes, in this sorry life, things do actually come good, don't they?'

'Sometimes. Maybe.' Mel still could not entirely believe it.

Lightly he kissed the tip of her nose. 'Hold the thought.'

Mel read aloud two more chapters of *Great Expectations*. In the gritty grey hours at the heart of the night, Pip and Miss Havisham and Estella appeared to have more reality than she herself did. Sometimes it seemed as if there had never been anywhere else but the four walls of this hospital room, filled with flowers Joanne could not see, books and magazines she had not read. There was a magnum of champagne standing on a table under the slatted blinds of the window, an act of faith, now that the hopelessness had fallen upon them once more.

Mel came back from one of the occasional breaks she allowed herself during the harsh span of time between midnight and dawn, to find Beverly frowning as she marked something down on Joanne's notes. 'She's not doing so good,' the nurse said. 'Pulse rate's way down.'

Mel pressed her fingers against her temples. 'But you told us she was holding her own.'

'She was, honey. Just took a bit of a downturn this morning.'

'Is she going to be all right?' Joanne lay quiet on the bed, her face smooth and expressionless, all emotion wiped away.

'Gotta have faith, Mel,' Beverly said, her voice gentle.

It seemed unbelievable that only two days ago Joanne had roused herself, spoken to her children, made a feeble joke. By the time Mel and Ben, merry with champagne, had arrived at the hospital, she had relapsed. She had remained in a coma ever since.

Mel pulled the chair up to the bed, sat down, took hold of her friend's hand. 'Joanne!' she said urgently, squeezing the fingers so tightly that they cracked. 'Joanne, wake up! Come back!' But, as usual, there was no response from the still figure on the bed.

Wearily Mel reached for the book she had left on the bedside table. '*Great Expectations*,' she said. 'Remember we'd got to the bit where Mr Jaggers arrives to inform lovely Joe Gargery that Pip has great expectations and tries to compensate Joe for the loss of his apprentice.' She smoothed the pages down with one hand and began to read.

'"Pip is that hearty welcome," said Joe, "to go free with his services, to honour and fortun', as no words can tell him. But if you think as Money can make compensation to me for the loss of the little child . . ."' For a moment Mel could not speak. '"—the little child what come to the forge—and ever the best of friends!"' she said with difficulty. She laid the book on the bed. 'Ever the best of friends, eh, Jo?' she said softly.

'Bes' of frens . . .' The voice was hoarse and weak, but the words were unmistakable.

'Joanne!' Mel was instantly alert.

The woman in the bed cleared her throat with a visible effort. Her head was turned on the pillow and her eyes were open, staring at Mel.

'You . . . you *spoke*.' Mel was trembling, on the verge of tears that had nothing to do with sorrow, flooded with an upsurge of emotion so profound that she could scarcely contain it. 'You're back again . . .'

Gently she took hold of the hand that lay palm upwards on the cover.

Squeezing the fingers, she felt pressure in response.

Joanne's pale face crinkled in what was recognisably an attempt at a smile. Her tongue moved slowly over her cracked lips and Mel reached for the lanolin on the cabinet and smoothed it round her friend's mouth.

'Wha's go'n' on?'

'You're in the hospital, darling.'

Lines of incomprehension gathered between Joanne's brows. 'Kids?'

'They're OK, Jo. Missing you like crazy. Lucy's looking gorgeous, Jamie's grown at least an inch, Tom's got a new girlfriend. But it's no fun without you there—for any of us.'

Joanne's hand moved faintly on the bed cover. 'Hos . . . pit'l?' Her forehead creased again.

'Yes.'

'Why?'

'Do you remember coming up to the lake with me?' Mel asked.

A faint nod.

'You had a fall,' Mel said. She glanced at the dark square of the window. It was lighter now; dawn was approaching. Already she could see the palest flush of rose above the town, and the outline of the white spire of the Episcopalian church. First light. The hour when the body's defences are at their lowest ebb. The hour at which people die.

As though she were recounting the plot of a film, she went through the sequence of events that had led from the falls, from blue sky and birdsong and the deep murmur of the leaves, to the slippery grass at the edge of the cliff and a stain of yellow on the black stones below, Ben Andersen's ministrations, the helicopter swinging up into the sky.

'Ever the best of friends,' Joanne said, very clearly.

Mel smiled at the pale face on the pillow. 'Oh, Joanne, I can't tell you how . . . I just can't begin to . . .' She sniffed. 'Wot larks, eh?'

'Wot larks,' echoed Joanne faintly.

Her hand tightened on Mel's fingers and relaxed. Then, while Mel continued to smile at her, unaware, she went away. Gently, like a swimmer striking out from the shore, heading for deeper waters, pushing further and further towards a greater silence, she moved away until finally she was out of sight.

Ben sat nursing a mug of coffee. Last night, as most nights, he had fallen asleep on the sofa and woken to a chilly room, grey ashes, dawn light seeping through the drapes.

He heard a car turn in off the road and crunch up the short drive, circle the apple tree, pull up at the door. He frowned. Kind of early for visitors. Getting up, he drew back the drapes and saw Mel standing on the porch, holding the collar of her coat close under her chin.

He ran to the door, tugged it open. 'Has she woken up again?'

'Ben.' She bent her head but not before he had seen the way her mouth was distorted by grief. 'I wanted to tell you first because you . . . without you . . . you were there when . . .'

'Come in,' he said quietly.

Mel covered her face with her hand and squeezed her eyes shut. 'Oh, Ben . . .' It was a moan of pain. 'She died. She *died*.'

'When?'

'Two hours ago . . .'

'I'm so sorry, Mel.'

'She . . .' Mel pressed the backs of her hands against her eyes, looking utterly lost. 'She wasn't supposed to die.' She shook her head. 'My best friend,' she said, in a high childlike voice. 'And she's dead.'

'Come inside,' he said again. When she stayed where she was, he put an arm round her. 'Come on, Mel.' He guided her into the house.

'I just wanted to come and tell you.' Vaguely she looked about her. 'It's too early. I hope you don't mind.'

'Of course not, I was up, anyway.' He took her hand and led her into the sitting room. 'What happened? I thought she was doing OK.'

Mel sat down and began to pick at the material of her coat. 'One moment she was there in the room with me,' she said, sounding bewildered. 'The next she was . . . she was so *not* there.' She gave a small sob, and then was silent. 'I was sitting by her bed, and suddenly she spoke to me.' Mel's shoulders shook. 'And then she looked at me, and . . . and she went. I watched her, Ben, I thought she was going to talk some more and instead she . . . she died right there in front of me.'

He put his hands on her arms and gathered her against his chest. 'Mel, Mel . . .'

'I sat there,' she said, leaning back so she could look at him. 'I sat there, Ben, smiling at her, and all the time she was dying.'

'That could be a good way to go,' he said. 'Remember that the last thing she saw was her best friend's face. Someone she loved.'

Mel stared at him. The fatigue of the past few days was imprinted on her face. 'I hadn't thought of that.'

'Smiling,' he said. 'That's good.'

They sat quietly for a while, not speaking, nursing their separate griefs. She said simply, 'I loved her.' She gave a sad little smile. 'Far more than I ever loved my husband. She was . . . she was all the family I had.'

He made an inarticulate soothing sound.

Her hand plucked restlessly at the navy-blue wool of her coat. 'At the beginning, you think it's all going to be straightforward. You think you can see the milestones ahead, and all you have to do is reach them, go past, on to the next one.' She shook her head. 'It's not a bit like that. When you're young, you don't make allowances for the . . . the losses.'

'If you're lucky, you don't have to.'

'I'll never be able to go up to the lake again,' she said. 'Not after what's happened. First Lisa. Now Joanne.'

He wanted to hug her, to comfort her, but she sat stiffly against his arm. Last time he had touched her, he'd been able—or so he hoped—to offer her some solace. The warmth of her body pressed into the sleeve of his sweatshirt. She smelt of vanilla and salt and ironed cotton.

She sniffed back tears, tried to wipe her face but he leaned in close, gently stubbed his thumb into the tears pooling below her dark blue eyes. 'Cry, Mel. Sometimes that's all there is.'

'I'm not just crying for myself,' she said, her voice unsteady. 'I'm crying for all of us. For Joanne. For her children. Lisa. Your baby.' She closed her eyes. 'For all the lost babies.'

She looked so defenceless. He felt a profound need to console and comfort her. When he pulled her closer, she shifted against him. He lifted her hand to his mouth. 'Mel,' he said. Her fingers were cold against his lips. 'Mel.'

He looked down at her, tucked into the curve of his shoulder. Her mouth was slightly open. He could feel the heat from her body, sense the beat of her heart. Her hands were long and slender, the nails short and unpainted. She wore no wedding band, only the sapphire.

When she lifted her face and looked at him, a collage of images rolled through his mind: Mel leaning against a sunlit rock, her gleaming body as she played in the lake with Joanne, her mouth by candlelight, her smile, the vanilla smell of her.

Unsurprised, he recognised that this moment had been building for a long time. She needed comfort and he sensed that he was the only one who could offer it. Putting his hand beneath her chin, he tilted her head. For a fraction of time, her lips parted, her body moved against him. The space between them was frantic with possibility. 'Mel,' he said.

'I want . . .' Moaning, she twisted her head away. 'I need . . .'

He turned her face up to his and gently kissed her wet eyelids.

Mel was stunned by the strength of feeling that had so suddenly swept over her. She wanted—needed—to feel his mouth on hers, to touch his gold-tipped curls. She longed to press onwards, to touch him, taste him, bury her grief in the wonder of their two bodies, drown her sorrow in desire. A dark warmth lingered in her belly. Her face burned. His mouth was on her mouth, his hands on her breasts. She closed her eyes, felt his strength reach out to her, his cheek against hers, his searching mouth. Whatever it was he offered her, however temporary it might be, she wanted it.

He raised her hand to his mouth, kissed each knuckle, then turned it over and pressed his lips to her palm. He put his big hands on either side of her face and brought her closer to him. He kissed her, tiny kisses, on her forehead, her eyebrows, her ear, the hollow of her neck. The stubble of his chin rasped against her cheek. One of them moaned as he pulled her coat from her shoulders, but she could not have said which. It was enough to be there with him, insulated for a while from the world and its numbing griefs.

Holding her face with his right hand, he slid his left hand under her shirt. His fingers were cold and she shivered slightly. His hand touched her breast, stroking the nipple through the lace of her bra, and she turned to look into his eyes, hardening under his touch.

'Ben,' she said. 'I need you.' And then again: 'I *need* you.'

He lifted the shirt over her head. Reaching behind her back, he undid her bra and slid the straps down her arms. Gravely, he looked at her breasts, then put out his hands and held them as though they were something infinitely precious. He bent his head to caress them with his lips.

His tongue moved lightly across her body as she undid the buttons of his shirt. She was clumsy; it was years since she had undressed a man. Yet how easily the actions of love returned. As she pushed the shirt from his shoulders, he pulled his arms through the sleeves so that his torso was naked. She embraced him, let her breasts graze his chest.

Undoing the zip on her skirt, he gently tugged it down over her hips while she lifted her body towards him. She helped him out of his jeans, her hand brushing across his back and his hips and his buttocks. His belly was hard and flat, with a line of golden hairs running towards his groin. He pushed her down until she was lying on her back then stretched alongside her, the two of them lying naked, skin touching skin. He put a hand under her back and held her against him. She spread her hand across his heart and felt the beat of it under her fingers.

She knew she ought to say, 'We shouldn't be doing this: you are married to another woman, this is wrong.' Instead, as he kissed her, his mouth moving over her body, she was filled with a hunger to possess and be possessed. I need him now, she thought. I need him to show me there can be something other than grief.

Joanne was dead, but she herself was alive. Celebrate that fact, she told herself. Just for once, do not feel guilty. He put a hand between her thighs and touched the wetness there. Slowly he slid a finger inside her and she felt she would explode. When he entered her, she knew a thankfulness so enormous that when she came, rising to meet him, convulsing suddenly, then clasping him, holding him motionless inside her while she twisted around him, she sobbed aloud. Slowly he increased his tempo until he was soaring towards his climax and she felt the heat of him gushing into her body.

Silently she began to weep, tears falling down either side of her face. Yes, she was alive—but Joanne was gone. Joanne would never kiss her children again, or touch a man with love, with desire. Joanne lay still and cold, alone now, for ever.

'Don't cry,' Ben said.

'I can't help it. I'm here with you and she's . . . Only the blink of an eye separates life and death.'

She pulled his head down to her breasts. For years she had not dared to unzip her heart and permit herself to feel an emotion such as love. Her marriage had offered her a niggardly sense of warmth, but in the generosity of Ben's lovemaking, the rich scents of his body, she was aware of an overpowering sense of fulfilment.

Chapter Twelve

WHAT DO YOU WEAR to your best friend's funeral? Your beloved fifty-year-old friend, who you would miss for the rest of your life. And another question: was it seemly to go to your best friend's funeral with a lover's caresses still warm on your body? Smiling slightly, Mel rather thought that, given this particular friend, it was.

Rummaging through the clothes hanging in her closet, Mel found a silk scarf in shades of mauve and purple. She let it slip through her fingers: she had last worn it when she and Joanne had gone to Boston.

'We had fun, didn't we?' she whispered, crushing the silk in her hand.

From her closet she took out a skirt of lavender wool and a matching linen shirt. On the shelf above it sat the hatbox of lilac silk, edged with purple leather. She pulled it forward, took off the lid, lifted out the hat.

Outside, clouds full of rain hung low on the hills, heavy as concrete. The trees shook in the wind. Last week, before Joanne died, it had seemed as though they were still at the end of the summer. Now, a cold autumn was upon them, with winter already hovering. Definitely not the weather for a straw hat. Mel dabbed her make-up on her face, found a lipstick and outlined her pale mouth, scrabbled in her drawers for a pair of sunglasses to hide her eyes.

She got into the car, switched it on and set the heater working. She laid her coat on the passenger seat. About to back out of the drive, she hesitated, pulled on the handbrake, shook her head.

'*You can wear it to my funeral . . .*' Joanne's voice came back to her, and her smile. Mel got out of the car, went back into the house and ran upstairs to her bedroom. Tears stung her eyes as she picked up the beautiful lilac and purple hatbox and took it out to the car.

As she parked beside the neat stone walls that bounded the graveyard, freezing rain blew into her face, stung her eyes, drenched the black slate headstones. Leaves whirled in the sudden gusts of cold air blowing beneath the trees. Black coats, black cars, grim under wet black branches, black umbrellas, a biting wind. Mel shivered. Joanne had hated the cold. She should have been laid to rest on a day of sunshine.

Mel pulled on her coat, wrapping it round her body, wrapping the pain inside herself. As she walked between the graves to join Joanne's family, she felt empty of all emotion but grief. That a simple hike through the woods should have ended in this bleak moment still seemed incomprehensible. Lucy's hand touched hers, and she held it tightly as the girl began to sob. She still had not found an opportunity to spill out the corroding guilt she felt. On her other side, Gordon Mayfield took her arm while Tom stood with his arm round his sister, his hand on Mel's shoulder. Diminished by his loss, Jamie leaned against her, forlorn.

A fierce gust of rain battered Mel's face as they began to lower the coffin into the ground, and she blinked, stepping back a little. Gordon's hand tightened on her arm, as though he was afraid she might collapse. On the other side of the grave, she saw Ben watching her from the back of the crowd. She remembered him making love to her that morning, learning her with his mouth as she lay in the cradle of his arms, kissing his smooth skin. Could people tell that they were lovers? That they were consumed by each other?

We are two hurt people, she thought, who have been fortunate enough to find and help one another. We are blessed. She smiled briefly at him. Love had come so unexpectedly that she scarcely recognised it.

Now, she thought, I love you for so many reasons. Because you listen to what I'm saying. Because when your eyes rest on my face, they are no longer remote. But mostly because when you touch me, I am not me, but someone made of fire and air, a creature of the elements. Because you give me back the Mel I once was.

What kind of a woman was she, to be thinking such thoughts as they lowered the coffin of her dearest friend into the earth? Joanne would have loved it. 'You heartless bitch!' she would have said, her eyes crinkled with laughter. 'Your best friend's dead and you're *happy*?'

As the final words were spoken, people began to drift away to their cars. Mel stood at the graveside for a moment, looking down at the earth-spattered wood, then turned and walked blindly away.

The room was crowded. It seemed as though half the town had come to say goodbye to the Bookstore Lady. Chairs had been set in a semicircle in front of Joanne's family, who sat together, holding hands.

'Joanne would have been delighted to know that she was held in such affection,' Gordon told them. His face was grey, rutted with care and weariness. 'She often said to me that there was nothing she wanted more than a full turnout at her funeral.' He gave a crooked grin, and then spoke for a few minutes, shaping for them a younger Joanne whom none of them had known but could easily imagine. Afterwards, Lucy recited a poem, then Tom read a piece he had written about his mother when he was in high school. Finally, Jamie stood. Unaccustomedly neat in a tie, a too-big jacket that had once been Tom's, he pushed his glasses back up his nose. 'She's still my mom,' he said. His voice broke. 'And I love her. That's all I want to say.' He sat down again and stared at his lap.

Mel held the hatbox on her knee. When Gordon indicated that it was her turn to speak, she stood up and reached into the box. 'Joanne and I bought this together in Boston, earlier this year,' she said steadily. 'The minute she saw it in the window, Joanne told me I had to buy it, so I did, because, as you all know, she had the most phenomenal powers of persuasion—or do I mean coercion?' Laughter rippled warmly round the room. 'It's not a funeral hat. But that doesn't matter.'

She put the hat on her head, settled it there. Tears filled her eyes. 'I'm wearing this for her,' she said. 'And I just hope *you* all like it because *I* was never sure that it suited me, and . . .' She looked up at the ceiling. 'And whatever you say, Joanne, I'm still not.'

After Mel sat down, others took their turn to reminisce about Joanne, and then, later, wine was poured, food served. Mel wandered around, spoke to friends, murmured. There is nothing you can say, she thought, not at a time like this, and yet we all try so hard, as though words can bring someone back, or soften the blow.

As she passed the entrance, someone slipped into the room. It took Mel a moment to realise who it was, then the blood rushed to her face.

'Lisa!' she said.

'I had to come.' Lisa put her arms round Mel. 'I only heard about Joanne yesterday. I'm so so sorry. I . . . what is there to say when something like this happens?'

'Nothing,' said Mel, shaking her head. 'There's nothing.'

'Poor Joanne. Poor Mel. You must be totally devastated.'

'I am.'

'I'm so sorry. I should never have taken off like that without getting in touch with you.' Lisa's small face looked strained and tired. 'It all suddenly seemed more than I could handle.'

Mel tried to smile. 'And how is it now?'

'I'm managing.'

'Where are you living?' Mel found it hard to meet Lisa's black eyes. 'What plans do you have?'

'Plans?' Lisa gave a tight smile. 'I've given up on making plans. They always seem to go wrong.'

'And what are you doing at the moment?' Over Lisa's head, Mel saw Ben staring at them, his face grim.

'Teaching art and ceramics. In Montpelier,' Lisa said. 'At a little private school.' She clutched Mel's arm. 'Please don't tell Ben where I am.'

Ben was pushing between the chairs, moving towards them. Before Mel could say anything more, he was beside them.

Lisa's face paled. 'Hello, Ben.'

'I can't believe you're here.' His eyes flicked to Mel's and for a second the corner of his mouth lifted.

'I'm not here for us,' Lisa said. 'I'm here for Mel—and Joanne.'

'Lisa . . .' He put out a hand towards her and she stepped back. 'Can we talk?' He looked at Mel and she saw apology in his eyes.

'I'm not ready to discuss anything,' Lisa said, averting her eyes.

'All right. OK.' He pulled back. 'Any idea when you will be?'

'Maybe never.' She looked up at him.

'I see.' Ben clenched his fists and his expression grew distant, hostile. Then he swung away from them and out of the room.

'Oh God.' Lisa bit her lip.

Mel was furious on Ben's behalf. 'You had no reason to be so . . . so mean, so spiteful,' she said.

'It didn't occur to me that he'd be here.'

'Of *course* he would. If it hadn't been for him, Joanne would have died right where she fell.'

'Mrs Sherman?'

Mel swung round. Two men were standing beside her.

The smaller of the two shook her hand. 'Jim Trotter and this is Bill Faraday. We were part of the ER team who rescued Mrs Mayfield.'

'I'm sorry she didn't make it,' Faraday continued. 'She looked pretty bad at the time, but you have to keep hoping. Ben Andersen did a terrific job.'

'Thank you for coming,' Mel said. 'I know Mrs Mayfield would have appreciated everything you did for her.'

'We just wanted to tell you . . .' They moved off together.

'I wasn't exactly pleasant to Ben, was I?' Lisa said.

Mel merely raised cold eyebrows.

'I hardly recognise myself any more.' Lisa's eyes filled with tears. 'Ben looked at me as though he hated me.'

'Are you surprised?' Mel turned away from her. Across the room, Jamie was standing alone, tears rolling down his face.

'I better go,' she said. She started to move away, then turned back. Thinking how miserable Lisa looked, how wounded, she touched her arm. 'Good luck.'

The last mourner had left and the room was empty now except for the remains of the wake. 'I'll go now,' Mel said. Since Lisa's appearance and Ben's abrupt departure, she had felt restless and unsettled.

'Thanks, Mel.' Gordon put his arms round her. 'For everything. Not just for today.'

'Mom would have been pleased, don't you think?' Tom said. 'She always liked a party.'

'We gave her a fine send-off,' Mel agreed.

'Remember the good things, Mel,' Gordon said.

'I will. I do.' Mel lifted her hand in farewell.

When she reached the parking lot, Ben was waiting for her, leaning against her car, his expression bleak. 'Let's go,' he said.

'Where to?'

'Does it matter?'

But, after a while, when she realised where he was headed, she put a hand on his arm. 'No, Ben,' she protested. 'There are too many bad memories up there.'

'You'll have to face them some time.'

'We only buried her today.'

This is not what I am about, she thought. I do not do this sort of thing. But as the skies darkened over the mountains, she heard Joanne's emphatic voice ringing in her head: *then it's high time you started.*

They stopped for supplies at the store in Hallams Cove, then drove on to Mel's cabin. Stepping out of the car, Mel looked up at the star-studded sky. A sliver of new moon hung above the green-black forest. It had been warm when she was last here. Now the cold, pure air struck her lungs like a spear.

Ben lit a fire while she sliced onions, grilled a steak, halved tomatoes, cut bread, poured wine into green glasses. He had lighted candles, too, which gave the dark room a soft and intimate glow.

They pushed one of the sofas close to the hearth, and ate in front of the fire. It seemed like only a few short days since Mel was last here. She recalled the dolphin-feel of Joanne's naked body against hers in the lake, the strength of her arms as they stood on the deck in the moonlight; silk nasturtiums, champagne and laughter. Friendship. Things that would never come again.

Suddenly she broke into sobs.

Ben took her hand. 'What is it, my sweet Mel?'

'I wish . . . *so* much . . . that I could have said something to Joanne's family. I couldn't, I couldn't, when they were suffering so much—but I so much wanted to apologise. To have their—their forgiveness.'

'What for?'

'It was all my fault, all my fault. If I hadn't made her come with me, she would never have been up here in the first place.'

'She was a grown woman,' Ben said. 'Nobody made her do anything she didn't want to. It was her own choice to come up here with you.' He tilted her face up to his. 'You weren't at fault.'

'I am in my heart.'

'No.' He kissed the side of her neck, just below her ear. 'Remember what she wrote to you, when your husband died?'

'"Dust will continue to gather in corners. Moons will wax and wane. Flowers will bloom and fade. Rivers will go on running to the sea,"' Mel quoted softly.

'That's right,' said Ben. 'And over the past weeks I've realised how true that is. For both of us. I've blamed myself for everything that ever went wrong, for as far back as I can remember. But we have to learn to take the people we've lost with us into the future.'

He shifted so that he was sitting right up close to her, then slipped off his shoes and socks and lay back against the cushions. Mel curled her fingers round his thumb, like a baby. She started laughing. 'Remember when you came out above Fitch's Gulley and found me sitting there?'

'Sure do.'

'You looked so mad.'

'Not mad, more astonished.'

'That a little old lady like me could have made it all the way up there?'

'No, nothing like that.' He smiled to himself. 'I hadn't realised until then how beautiful you were. Your hair in the sunshine . . .' His big hand covered the top of her head. 'In fairy tales, the princess always has hair like spun gold. Until I saw you that day, I never knew what it meant.'

Her stomach tightened. Little pulses, sharp as electricity, sparked across her skin. 'Oh, Ben . . .'

'I saw you,' he said. 'That afternoon, you and Joanne in the water.'

'I guessed there was someone in the house.' With an ache in her heart she recalled that carefree, rainbow-glittering moment.

He put a hand over her breast. 'When I saw you then, I thought how beautiful you were.'

'Do you still?'

'Now, I think you are more than beautiful.'

He kissed her and she tasted the wine on his tongue. Her throat contracted. This moment will stay with me for the rest of my life, she thought. The warmth of his hand, the shadows on his face, candlelight, moonlight, firelight, like sips of champagne from someone else's glass.

Except that this time, the glass was her own, even though the champagne was not. She turned her mouth into his, desire clawing at her, insistent. She put her hands on his back, felt the knobs of his spine under his shirt, the shape of his shoulder blades. She unbuttoned his shirt, watched the play of light and shadow on his torso, touched his ribs one by one, felt the solid beat of his heart. 'Ben . . . Ben,' she said. Under her hand his skin was cool, satiny. She pressed her lips to his belly, closed her eyes, drew the good scent of him into herself.

His hand burrowed into her hair. She could feel the heat between his thighs, feel the movement of his body. The years of desire repressed, of feelings denied, could never be regained or relived. She had thrown them away, accepted second best, knowingly exchanged the fires of her long-lost lover for the cold kisses of her husband. She had squandered her life.

'Make love to me,' she said fiercely, gripped by passion, scarcely recognising her own voice. 'Love me.'

'I do.' He undid the buttons on her lavender jacket, lifted the blouse over her head. Firelight warmed her naked breasts as he knelt between her legs. He moved his hands up her body, lingered on her hips, her breasts, her shoulders. 'Beautiful, beautiful Mel,' he murmured.

She grabbed his hair, pressed him closer to her body. Even as she lifted her hips to him, felt the urgent rush as he came into her, tears squeezed between her eyelids. 'Yes,' she gasped, arching as he held her, looked down at her, his mouth swollen. 'Oh yes.'

They got up late the next morning, having lingered for hours over each other's bodies, having strolled, sprinted, galloped, through each other's physical territories with as much certainty as if they had created them.

'We're going for a hike this morning,' Ben said, cutting bread, making toast for Mel, while she poured orange juice from a carton.

'Are you telling, or asking?'

'Let me rephrase that.' He paused, looked across the lake at the far mountains. 'I'm going for a hike this morning. Do you want to come?'

'Yes. But I told you: I'll never be able to walk here again.'

'Mel.' He put his arms round her and held her close.

She shook her head. 'I can't. Not after what happened.'

'It happened here to both of us.' His face was suddenly sad. 'You must. *We* must.'

'More therapy?'

'Yes.' He kissed her fiercely. 'But this isn't.'

'What is this, then?' She was saturated with desire.

'This is love.'

The word spun into her consciousness. Light as a bubble, heavier than concrete. It *felt* like love. She put her fingers over his mouth.

'It is,' he insisted. 'You know it is.'

She smiled at him, briefly moved her head from side to side.

'Say you love me,' he demanded.

She could imagine him as a child, eager, impetuous, demanding what he wanted and getting it. A child, sixteen years younger than she was. Child. Mother. Young. Old. She thought wearily: with all the love in the world, the years between us cannot be expunged. I have lived too much longer, I started too much earlier, this relationship cannot last.

'I love you,' she said.

Her body was so different from Lisa's. Softer, more used. And yet so obviously unused. Overlaid with her past. She reacted to him in ways that were new to him. Looking out at the lake, he felt he had been granted an immense privilege. Mel. Melissa. He was younger than she was. So what? All that mattered was that she was Mel and he loved her.

They climbed towards the cold sunshine that splashed gold on the tips of the higher trees. Though the sun shone out of a cloudless sky, frost-edged leaves lay under the trees. At the turn where the path led upwards, away from the river, he squeezed her hand. 'I'm here,' he said.

When they came to the point where Joanne had fallen, he stopped. The broken sapling was still there, though the scar where it had snapped had weathered. 'I told her,' Mel said, her face crumpling. 'On the way up, she got much too close to the edge, and I told her it was dangerous. There'd been rain the night before and the ground was wet.'

'I remember.'

'I pulled her back,' said Mel. 'Grabbed her jacket and pulled her away from the edge.'

'But she did it again on the way down?' He smiled at her for a moment, with his head tilted. 'Your fault? I don't think so.'

Mel bit her lip for a moment. 'No,' she said, decisively. 'No.'

At the top of the trail, where the slope flattened out along the stream that came down from the higher hills to become the falls, they stood panting in the clear crisp air.

'It's so beautiful,' she exclaimed, easing off her pack.

Ben took off his own pack and put his arm round her shoulders. 'One of the things I love about you is that you're happy up here.' He nuzzled into her neck. His hands moved inside her clothes and caressed the bones of her back. He tugged at her shirt, freed a shoulder, kissed it.

'Oh,' she groaned. 'I can't *not* do this.'

When he opened her clothes and closed his hand over her breast, she shivered with delight. He could feel her melting. Feel her sadness loosening, washing away on a stream of love. Always, before, he had stood outside, seen himself feeling. With Mel, he was part of a whole.

Before they set off again, she raised both arms to the sun. There was something pagan, something primitive, about the gesture. Seeing him watching her, she laughed aloud, then put her arms round his neck. 'You've given me so much,' she said.

It was two o'clock in the morning. They lay in bed in a tangle of bedclothes. Ben had brought up chilled champagne and two glasses.

'Why didn't you have any children?' he said.

'My husband didn't want any,' she said lightly, as she had always done when the question was asked.

'And you let him decide?'

She opened her mouth to say yes, to let Eric bear the responsibility. But she found that here, with Ben, she had no desire for deceit.

'No,' she said. 'It was my decision.'

He sensed something important here. 'Why?'

'Because . . . years ago I had an abortion.'

He was astonished. '*You* did?'

She touched the side of his jaw. 'You must have realised by now that nobody is ever what they seem.'

'But why should an abortion stop you having a family?'

'It was simply . . . simply that if I couldn't have children with . . . with the man I loved, then I didn't want them with anyone. Particularly Eric.'

He poured more champagne for them and turned towards her.

'Tell me about your cousin,' she said.

He sipped slowly from his glass. Beads of condensation rolled down the sides and onto his chest. 'He was such fun, always planning something new: swimming by moonlight, picnics out on the lake in the middle of the night.' He blinked away the tears that suddenly stung his eyes. 'He lived by his own rules, and I loved that. And then . . .'

Mel reached for his hand.

'Then he was killed.'

'How?'

'It was a stupid accident. We were on our new bikes, riding down the hill to the main road. He was ahead of me, and instead of slowing down at the corner, he picked up speed and went straight under the wheels of a truck coming the other way. I didn't see it, but I heard it.' He gritted his teeth. 'I'll never forget the sound. And then the silence.'

'Not your fault, Ben.'

'And after Rory died,' Ben said, as though he had not heard her, 'my Aunt Evie went to pieces. In the end, she took an overdose.'

'You can't blame yourself for that.'

A complicated expression crossed his face. 'I knew that Rory's death wasn't down to me. I really knew that. But Aunt Evie . . .'

'Where do consequences begin?' Mel asked. 'Think about it, Ben. It's like you said about Joanne. It was your cousin's choice to go down that hill too fast, not yours. None of it had to do with you.'

He took a deep breath. 'I'm trying to believe that, I really am.'

'Is that why you climb, why you spent time working with the mountain rescue people? Because you couldn't save Rory, you try to save the rest of the world instead?' She cupped her hand round his cheek, so tenderly, so full of love. 'Ben,' she said. 'My Benjamin.'

He turned his head so he could kiss the vulnerable veins on the inside of her wrist, lick the soft places between her fingers. 'Why do you look so sad?'

She half smiled, but didn't answer.

'You do love me, don't you?' he demanded.

'Yes.' Her voice was so low he had to bend his head to hear it. 'Always.'

'Me too.'

'But I have to go back tomorrow,' she said. 'I have a show to organise.'

'Another day,' he begged. He didn't want to return to the real world, to take up the frayed edges of his life again. 'Call your assistant. Don't go back just yet. Please, Mel. Please.'

In the end, she telephoned Carla and said she was still too depressed to think about work and would come in the following day.

She had forgotten that such uncomplicated happiness was possible. Somewhere down in the valley lay Butterfield, lay duty and expectation. For the moment, she was happy to stay here in the hills and let the world flow by. Lisa, Joanne, the past and the future, did not for the present exist. For a few precious hours she was able—she had the *right*—to lose herself in Ben. She watched him sleep. He is part of me, she thought, reaching out to touch the tip of a curl, and always will be.

And yet, lying beside him the next morning—their last morning—she was seized once more with the thought that this joy was not hers to take.

Ben leaned up on his elbow to look down at her, kissed her breasts, lifted one of her hands. 'I love you.'

I love you too, she wanted to say. So much more than you can imagine.

'The stone in your ring is the same colour as your eyes,' he told her.

'That's what the person who gave it to me said.'

'Who was he?' When she did not answer, he said, 'Not Eric?'

'Eric didn't believe in giving me jewellery.'

'Did he love you?'

'I don't know.'

'Why did you marry him?'

'He was lonely,' she said. 'Like me. And . . . and completely different from the man I'd been with before him.'

'The man who gave you the ring?'

'Yes. Eric was very ordinary, very average and conventional.'

'Why would someone like you marry a man like that?'

'I thought that there might be a kind of sanctuary in ordinariness. That being conventional could be more appealing than passion. And . . .' She hesitated. 'My father hadn't wanted a child. He didn't . . . he really didn't love me. I think I saw Eric as a father figure. One who'd love me, this time round. My second chance.'

'You're *my* second chance.'

'Oh, if only . . .' She felt like weeping.

'It's true, Mel.' He turned her face to his and kissed her, his mouth pressing into her, his hands gently holding her breasts. He danced his fingers down a scar below one of them. 'Where did you get this?'

'An accident, when I was seven or so,' she said. 'I fell off a slide.'

'You'd have thought it would have disappeared by now.'

'Wounds heal,' she said. 'Scars don't.'

The white light from the window glittered on the honey-coloured hairs springing from his skin. She lifted his hand and began to stroke it, smoothing the skin over the knuckles, outlining the shape of his nails.

'The man who gave you the ring,' said Ben. 'Did he know you were pregnant?'

Her answer was oblique. 'From the moment we met, he was everything to me. He lit up my life. But he didn't want children. So I never told him about the pregnancy. I could *not* let a child be born to a father who wouldn't love it.' There were tears in her eyes. 'So I . . . *murdered* it.'

She had often thought the words but never, until now, spoken them aloud. Here, with the sounds of the lake on the shore, the noise of rain on the roof, the swish of wind in the trees, they seemed melodramatic.

'And you've never told the father?'

'It wouldn't have changed anything.'

But what would have happened if she had stayed in New York, instead of running away? If she had made a different choice, that awful afternoon, when the path her life was to take still hung in the balance. She had wanted to tell Galen, but the remembrance of her chilly father had passed through her head and she had kept silent. She had packed her bag and taken off, already knowing, as she took the empty roads north, that she had made an irretrievable mistake.

'Do you know where the baby's father is?'

Mel nodded.

'Maybe you'd feel better about all this if you told him about it now.'

'He's not the kind of person . . .' She broke off.

'How do you know? You've changed—why shouldn't he have done, too?' Ben caught her wrist and kissed the inside. 'I love you,' he said.

She touched his mouth with her finger. 'Me too,' she said.

Later, over breakfast, she said, 'Have you heard anything from Lisa?'

'Nothing.'

'She's still trying to come to terms with what happened.'

'How long does it take?' He poured coffee, sipped his, shook his head. 'I've had a lot of time to think about her leaving. I know it would have been better if I'd been there when she lost the baby. But I wasn't. I came back the minute I could. I wanted to help, to share it with her, and somehow we couldn't seem to communicate.' He remembered Lisa's face, mouth open in a howl of rage and grief, and felt a tightness around his heart. 'I always thought we had such a strong . . . such an idyllic marriage. And when the first real test came, we failed.'

'Pain takes people in different ways.'

'Running away wasn't going to make things better.' The way Lisa had spoken to him at Joanne's funeral still hurt him. Whatever there'd once been between them had come to an end. 'Let's not talk about it.'

Chapter Thirteen

AFTER SOME THOUGHT, Mel had decided to include *First Love*, her own carving, in the show. She carried it into the office and set it down carefully on her desk. The light on the answering machine was blinking so she picked up the handset and jammed it into her shoulder, turning over papers on her desk as she listened to the messages. They were routine, except for the final one. Koslowski's agent. 'Something's come up. Call me. Doesn't matter what time.'

Almost certainly Koslowski was playing up again, wanting to impose more conditions. Angrily she pushed the numbers for the agent's cellphone, heard him pick up, told him who she was.

'You better brace yourself, Mrs Sherman.'

'Consider me braced.'

'Putting it bluntly, Galen wants to cancel the show.'

'You are joking, aren't you?'

'I wish I were,' the agent said heavily. 'I've told him he can't do that, but I might as well be talking to a wall.'

Furious, Mel held the receiver so tightly she was afraid it would crack. 'Just let him try.'

'I know that. I told him. I'm with you. I just thought I'd warn you.'

'Thanks.'

The agent's voice changed. 'You sound tired.'

'I *am* tired, dammit. I've put a lot of work into this show, and on top of that my . . . my closest friend just died and I really, *really* don't need this kind of crap.'

'I'm sorry to hear that.' He sounded genuinely concerned.

'An agent with a heart?' Mel said wryly. She paused for a moment, options racing through her mind. 'Might you be prepared to compromise your deepest principles for a woman you've never met?'

'Depends what you want.'

'Galen's phone number.'

'I can't do that. Client confidentiality—you know how it is.'

'Maybe, just for once, you could forget yourself.'

'You mean, like, get all confused, reel off some numbers at random?'

'That sort of thing.'

'It wouldn't be my fault if they turned out to be his phone number, would it?'

'Could happen to anyone.'

Impatiently she pushed buttons on her handset. Allowed the phone to ring, on and on. *Come on, damn you* . . . The answering machine kicked in. She did not wait for the message, just rang off, redialled, rang off when the machine came on. She did this for five minutes, imagining him lying in bed, cursing. *Answer the darn phone, for Pete's sake* . . . Mel dialled for the twenty-sixth time and, at last, someone picked up.

'What?' a voice barked. Koslowski's voice. 'Are you mad?'

'Extremely mad,' she said. A catch of the breath at the sound of his voice, a clutch at her heart.

'I am asleep,' he said loudly. 'Who is this?'

'Mrs Sherman. From the Vernon Art Gallery in Vermont.'

'What are you doing, calling me so early?'

'Your agent has just told me you want to cancel the show I've spent eighteen months or more setting up, and I want to tell *you* that if you lay so much as a finger on a single one of the sculptures that I'm exhibiting at my gallery for the next three weeks, then I will sue your ass off.'

'Those pieces are my children,' he said.

'They *are* for sale, right? I mean, if someone wants to pay you good money for them, you'd take it, wouldn't you?'

'Of course.'

'Mr Koslowski, I don't know how it is in Poland, which is where I believe you come from, but in this country, people don't usually sell their children every time they need money.'

Sounding sulky, Koslowski said, 'I have to make a living.'

'So do I. And I've spent a lot of time and even more money on getting this show together and there is no *way* you are going to cancel it now.'

'But I have to.'

She could hear police sirens wailing in the background, the sound surging through his windows. 'You do not.' She pressed the receiver closer to her ear.

'There is something odd about you, Mrs Sherman,' he said. 'I am wondering how safe my works will be in your care.'

'Whether they'll be safe or not, you don't have a lot of choice, Mr Koslowski. We signed an agreement, remember?'

There was another silence.

'What did you say your first name was?' he asked eventually.

'I didn't.'

'And you are from Vermont?'

'That is correct.'

'Have we met before? Your voice is—'

'No.'

'Well, Mrs Schumann from Vermont, I'm warning you that—'

She ran out of patience. 'And I, Mr Koslowski from New York, am warning *you*, don't start fucking me about of I'll fuck you about much *much* worse.' Mel slammed down the phone.

By half past seven that night, she was exhausted. Carla had gone home an hour ago, but Mel wanted a period of time to herself to relish the stillness, to walk round her gallery, check that everything was in place.

She paused in front of *Harbinger*, a block of granite that had been highly polished on one side, left unfinished on the other. It was a powerful piece, but its full significance was only made clear when it was placed, as intended, in water in the carved granite bowl that the sculptor had provided. She had trained a spot on the piece to emphasise the fluidity of the carving.

'Beautiful,' she said aloud. She reached forward, slid her fingers along the polished planes, felt them snag on the rough ones.

The telephone bleeped in her office and she hurried to answer it.

'Vernon Gallery.'

'I did not think you would be there so late,' a voice said.

Mel was suddenly breathless. 'Then why did you call, Mr Koslowski?'

He waited a heartbeat, then said gruffly, 'I apologise for my discourtesy this morning. And naturally I will not spoil your show.' He coughed. 'I hope very much that it will go well.'

'We have followed your instructions to the letter,' Mel said. 'Of course it will.'

She would have liked to prolong the conversation but she replaced the handset and went out to her car. The temperature was falling. She was always disconcerted by the sudden change from crisp fall to icy cold as each day dragged them nearer to the chilly beauty of a New England winter.

Back in the kitchen at Maple Street, she opened a bottle of wine, filled a glass and grabbed something to eat. Then she picked up the telephone and called Ben's number, but the line was engaged. My lovely Ben, she thought. His scent, his smile, his gentle fingers on her skin, the passion in his eyes.

In the living room she sank down on one of the sofas, pulled the woollen throw from its back, then wrapped it round her body. On the wall above the hearth, Grandmother Sherman stared down as she always did, eyes full of cold disdain.

So like Eric . . . selfish, controlling, cold Eric. Defiantly, Mel got to her feet, jerked the picture off the wall and carried it out into the hall, then she opened the front door and threw it out into the wet and chilly darkness. Now she ran up to her bedroom and lifted the calmly glowing icon off its hook between the windows. Downstairs again, she hung it in Grandmother Sherman's place and stepped back to look up at it. Perfect. She should have changed things years ago, as Joanne had always urged her to.

The doorbell sounded, followed by the knocker. Ben? Smiling, she went out into the passage and opened the door.

Lisa was standing outside, a bag slung over her shoulder. She wore a red woollen hat pulled down over her ears, and a matching scarf. Despite the sharpness of the bones in her face, she looked like a child. 'I know it's late . . .' she said. Behind her, rain fell heavily onto the grass.

'Come in.' Guilt flushed through Mel. Could Lisa smell the scent of love that rose from her like a precious balm? Could she see Ben's kisses on her body, the sweet, glittering marks of his passion?

Closing the door, Lisa pushed Mel gently ahead of her into the hall, where she took off her coat and hat. Then the two women walked towards the kitchen. 'You look tired. Let's have coffee,' Lisa said, easy and familiar with Mel and Mel's home. Like she used to be. Like a friend.

Or a daughter.

'I'll heat some,' Mel said. 'What are you doing here?'

'I came to talk to Ben.'

Mel felt the beat of her culpable blood. 'I see.'

'I thought about what you said. I wanted to apologise to him for the way I behaved at Joanne's funeral,' Lisa said.

Mel filled two mugs with coffee. I also have rights, she wanted to say. I deserve a measure of happiness. 'What . . . uh . . . what did he say?'

Lisa took a mug and raised it to her lips. She shrugged. 'He didn't want to know. He was really angry, Mel. You know Ben . . .'

'Yes.'

'. . . he's not angry very often. But I guess in one way, I can't blame him. He wanted to help me over the miscarriage but he didn't know how, and instead of realising that, I did my best to hurt him.'

'Did you tell him that?'

'I tried.' Lisa's mouth trembled a little. 'After I lost the baby, I felt so . . . *wounded*. I think I must have had a kind of breakdown. I did such silly things, cruel things. And now he's fallen out of love with me. If you'd seen the way he looked at me—so cold and remote . . .'

'So . . . uh . . . what are you going to do?'

'What can I do? I just have to admit that we should never have got married in the first place.'

'Do you really believe that?'

For a moment the younger woman stared at nothing. Then she said softly, 'No. Of course I don't.'

'Do you still love him?'

'Yes. I do.'

Mel cleared her throat. Somewhere at the very core of her she could feel a grief so monstrous that she was afraid it might split her apart. 'Then . . .' I can't do this. I cannot.

'Then what?'

'T-tell him.'

'He wouldn't hear me if I did.' Lisa raised her hands to her face. 'Once he's taken a stand on something, it's impossible to shift him.'

'Can you take a stand on love?' Mel reached for a chair and sat down. 'I did once,' she said slowly. 'I've regretted it ever since. It was the most stupid, the most destructive thing I've ever done. It ruined my life.'

Lisa stared at her, a frown between her dark brows.

'Don't make the wrong decision.' Mel pressed her hands to her heart. 'If . . . if you still love Ben . . . don't walk away from him.' Each word felt like a tombstone planted in the graveyard of her love.

'He said he'd found someone else. He had that look, Mel.' Lisa's face crumpled as though a cold wind had blown across it. 'You know, that kind of shiny look that people in love have?'

'Yes.' I know, I know. His hands on my face, the smell of his skin, his beautiful face above mine . . . Oh, can I give that up, can I lose that?

Lisa lifted her thin shoulders and dropped them again. 'I shan't come back to Butterfield. At least, not for a while. But I couldn't go without saying goodbye this time. I didn't get in touch after I left because I was afraid you'd disapprove. On top of everything else, I couldn't have coped with that. So I just . . .' She spread her hands, began rooting in the bag she had been carrying and took out something wrapped in tissue paper. 'I brought you one of my new pieces.'

Mel unwrapped it carefully. In her hands she held an oval-shaped bowl thickly glazed in a smooth honey colour. The sides curved outwards and in again, like a boat, then doubled back onto themselves so that the bowl almost seemed to be self-lined. Simple, strong, beautiful. 'Oh,' she said, turning the piece in her hands. 'This is simply stunning. How do you get this marvellous glow from the glaze?'

'I've been experimenting. Recently I've been firing the pots as many as three times, to make them come to life. I've made one for Ben too. But I didn't want to give it to him when I was there earlier, in case he threw it at the wall or something. I wondered if you could—would you, Mel?—take it round some time and give it to him.'

The telephone began to trill and both women stared at it, startled, before Mel picked up.

'Mel? It's me.' Ben's voice, urgent.

'Hi,' Mel said, overbrightly.

'What's wrong?'

'I can't talk. I've got company.'

'Anyone I know?'

'No. I'll call you later.' Mel put down the telephone.

'Everything OK?' Lisa said. She smiled.

'Just fine.'

'The show's opening any time now, isn't it?'

'Next week.'

'Will the sculptor—Koslowski—come up from the city for it?'

'I hope not.'

'Didn't you tell me you knew him once?'

'It was years ago.'

'I'll bet that was exciting.'

'It was.' Mel remembered that constant sense of life enhanced, of choices, dreams, magical possibilities. 'I had it,' she said suddenly. 'I had it and I threw it all away.' Impulsively, she grabbed Lisa's hands, squeezed them hard. 'Lisa, don't do what I did. Don't let it go.'

'There's nothing left to let go.' Lisa gathered her things together, walked out to the hall and began to pull on her coat. She tugged the hat down over her hair. 'Thank you for . . . for being my mom. I'll be in touch.' Lisa flung her arms round Mel. 'I love you,' she murmured. 'I miss you.' She opened the door, stepped out onto the porch and went down the steps to the path. She waved once and disappeared.

Mel went back to the kitchen and picked up the telephone.

There was a light on over the porch, and more lights in the living room behind the drapes. Ben parked on the road and ran through the rain up the stone path. When Mel opened the door to him, he smiled happily and followed her into the living room.

'I was afraid I wasn't going to see you today,' he said. He stared at the icon on the wall above the hearth. 'You've changed this room around.'

'Minimally,' she said. 'But crucially.' Her voice sounded strange.

'I see.' He sensed that there was much he did not, *could* not see. She stood on the other side of the room, looking severe, her pale hair pulled back from her face, an unreadable expression in her eyes.

'I can't do this any more,' Mel said, without preamble. Grey shadows lay above her cheekbones. 'You and me . . .'

'What do you mean?'

She leaned her head against the wall behind her. 'You and Lisa . . .'

'What about us?' he said gently.

'You . . . the two of you have to start over.'

He could see the effort the words cost her. 'I don't think so.'

Mel's eyes were full of pain. 'I've thought about it, I can't think of anything else, and this . . . what we have between us . . . can't be.'

Ignoring the hand she raised to stop him, he went over and put his arms round her. 'I love you.'

'It's not *right*.'

'If I think it is, and you do, then it is.' Her body was as tense as a statue. 'Are you ashamed of loving me?'

'Never.' She closed her eyes. '*Never*. But you . . . don't you see, this is the second chance for you both?'

'Lisa and I are through.'

'We m-mustn't s-see each other again.' Her chin trembled.

'You don't mean it,' he whispered into her hair.

'I do.' She gave a kind of gasp.

'You will break my heart.'

'And mine,' she said. 'But hearts can be mended.' She stared at him, his lovely, clear-eyed Mel. 'We don't belong together. You should be with Lisa. And I—' She shook her head slightly. 'I'm not quite sure where I belong. But it can't be with you, Ben. Beautiful Ben. I'm too old for you.'

'Your husband was much older than you. What's the difference?'

Tears came into her eyes. 'That's one of the mean tricks that nature plays on women.'

'I don't give a shit about your age,' he said angrily.

'Maybe not now. Maybe not in a month, a year, even two years. But sooner or later, you will. You'll look at me and you'll wonder why you are in bed with someone old enough to be your mother. Why there are no children in the house. You'll want children, Ben.'

'Not if you don't.'

'That's not true.' Mel put a hand on the back of the armchair. 'I lied to you when you called me earlier this evening. I told you I had company. I said it was nobody you knew. It was Lisa. She told me she wouldn't be coming back to Butterfield. She left that for you.' Mel nodded at something on the table beside him. 'It's a piece of her recent work.'

'I don't need this,' he said.

'Open it, Ben.'

The bowl inside the wrapping was oval-shaped, with the round fullness of an egg. Like an egg, it contained a yolk, a softly fertile second layer in a different glaze, the two together combining to produce something powerful and solid, yet infinitely vulnerable. He held it carefully between his hands. He pictured her at the turning wheel, her shining hair falling over her face. Lisa the potter. The artist. His wife. 'Oh God,' he said softly, feeling the future change. 'Her other stuff was beautiful, but this is so much more . . .' The right word eluded him.

'Mature,' Mel said. 'She told me you two had quarrelled earlier.'

He grimaced. 'The truth is, *I* quarrelled. She didn't.'

'She wants to come back to you. She wants to come home.'

Home . . . him and Lisa again, fitting together again. Home. 'You don't know what you're talking about,' he said harshly. There was an ache under his ribs, a hollowness.

'She loves you,' Mel said. The words were like acid in her throat.

'Did she tell you that?'

'Yes.'

'Love wasn't enough, last time round.'

'Give it another try,' Mel said. She had gone very pale. 'And another after that, if necessary. You had so much going for you.'

'Lisa isn't the person I married any more.'

'Of course she's not. After what happened, how could she be?' Mel looked down at the ring on her hand. 'How could any of us?'

'I want *you*,' he cried. 'I love *you*.'

'Oh, Ben.'

'Our marriage didn't work.'

'It worked fine until she lost the baby.'

He spread his arms wide. 'It's too late.'

'It's never too late.'

He walked over to her hearth and kicked at the logs, sending up a plume of grey ash. He buried his face in his hands.

'Find her, Ben. Tell her you want her to come home.'

'Mel, I love you.'

'And I you. But . . .' She had to force the words out. 'But we weren't meant to be together.'

'How many times do I have to say it? It's over between Lisa and me. I even told her I was in love with somebody else.'

She brushed angrily at her wet cheeks. 'Ben,' she said sharply. 'Promise me something.'

'Anything.'

'Swear that you will never, ever, whatever the provocation, whatever quarrels you have, you will not ever tell her, Ben, that it was me. *Never*.'

He was taken aback by her vehemence. He tried to take her hand. 'The question doesn't arise, since she and I aren't together any more.'

'I know where she is,' Mel said abruptly.

'Oh?'

'She asked me not to tell you . . .'

His expression hardened. Blood drummed behind his ears. 'Doesn't that exactly prove what I'm saying?'

'. . . but I think you need to know,' she said.

'Much better not to break her confidence,' he said, angry now.

Picking up Lisa's bowl, he walked rapidly out of the room. He pulled open the front door and walked down the steps. As he climbed into his car and pulled away from the kerb, did he really hear her say 'I love you,' or was it just the blood pounding in his ears, the hammering of his heart, the need for her that he would never be allowed to assuage? Because he knew she spoke the truth; there was no hope for the two of them.

She heard his car start up, saw the wheel of his headlights across the trees, and the redescending darkness. She thought of his hands on the wheel, the way he raised one finger and tapped it up and down as he drove. She thought of his body, strong and scarred, the line of blond hairs on his belly. His face in repose, the sun-whitened eyebrows, the full mouth, the way his eyes lit up when he was happy.

These memories were to be her punishment. As she had once arranged to have her unborn child torn from her body, so now she had wrenched her lover from her heart. Then, she had acted without recognising the value of what she was losing, without fully realising the consequences; now she knew the value of what she had given away.

I am waiting for my true love . . . she had written, thirty years ago. She had fled from one true love; she had just sent the other away.

Closing the front door, she leaned against it. You will break my heart, he had said. She could feel the sound of her own as it chipped, cracked, fractured, fell into shards.

That night she lay open-eyed, hungry for Ben. Moonlight drifted through the half-open windows. The drapes billowed gently in the chilly breeze, in, out, in, out, like lungs pumping to keep a life going, a heart beating. But her heart was in hibernation: she was alive, but not living.

With the Koslowski exhibition opening in a few days' time, she was able to immerse herself in her final preparations, keep her head empty of him. But when the telephone rang two days later, and she heard his voice, the thump of her heart was almost painful.

'Mel, I love you.'

She stared out at the rain falling in heavy sheets over the outdoor sculptures in the meadow at the front of the gallery.

'Don't do this, Mel.'

'Go and bring Lisa home.'

There was a long pause. Then he said slowly, 'I'd need to find her first. And since I haven't the least idea where she is, how can I?'

Rain outside, rain in my heart, Mel thought. With that question, he has given himself the answer. 'She's teaching,' she said. 'At a private school in Montpelier.' Gently she put down the receiver.

Chapter Fourteen

AT FIRST, HE COULD SCARCELY BELIEVE she had been serious when she sent him away. He assumed that she would eventually change her mind. But he hadn't seen her now for more than a week. He'd gone to her house, but she wouldn't open the door to him.

But gradually, with each slowly passing day, he had begun to see the value of the sacrifice she had made for him and Lisa. She had insisted that Lisa loved him. Had urged him to go and find her. Despairingly, he saw, too, that she was right. Especially since, somewhere deep inside himself, he'd always known that his relationship with Mel couldn't last.

Montpelier. That's where Lisa was. Just an hour or so's drive away.

If you wanted to find someone in Montpelier, how would you begin? You would have to get hold of a list of the private schools in the area—there couldn't be that many—and then you'd call them up one by one and ask if they had a teacher called Lisa Tan on the payroll. If you really wanted to find someone.

Mel and he had offered each other something immensely valuable. It would remain a secret that was not to be shared, one that only he and she would ever know about. He thought of her full breasts resting like fruit in his hands, the endearing curve of her belly.

And yet . . .

Memories came back to him: New York in the rain, Lisa's sleeping face on the pillow, an eagle feather on the lake shore, the brush of skin against skin, the sweet scents of lovemaking. The precise and particular textures of happiness. He would want her to know how she had made him feel. How . . . his mind hesitated over the thought. How they might make each other feel again.

If he was lucky.

He parked across the wide street from the Hanson School. Behind a wall broken by tall iron gates sat an imposing building in the style of an eighteenth-century French country house. Girls spilled out of the grounds onto the sidewalk, standing in groups as they waited to be picked up by their parents. Ben rolled down the window into cold, brisk air and heard female voices rising through the overhanging branches like the chattering of birds.

After a while, the girls thinned out until there were only a few older ones, heads bent together as they discussed something. A man came out onto the top step and paused, holding the door open for a woman behind him. The woman was Lisa. She looked up at the man, laid a hand on his arm.

Without thinking, Ben scrambled out of the Jeep and ran across to her, dodging traffic, ignoring the angry toots of horns. 'Lisa!' he called.

She turned. She murmured something to her companion, who looked at Ben with interest, before nodding vigorously and moving away. She came slowly towards her husband, frowning.

'How did you know where I was?' she asked.

'Mel told me you were teaching in Montpelier.'

'I asked her not to.'

'Mel is . . . a very wise woman,' he said. 'She thought it was better for both of us if I knew. Is there somewhere we can go for a coffee or something? I need to talk to you.'

'Do we have anything to discuss?'

'Yes,' he said firmly, suddenly sure. 'We most certainly do.'

'There's a place on the edge of town,' she said.

He took her elbow and guided her towards the Jeep. It was the first time he had touched her for months. Two or three silver earrings arched along the curve of her right ear. He hadn't noticed them when she'd come to the house.

She directed him to a small shopping mall. He found a parking place behind a bank, and took a plastic bag out of the Jeep before they walked together, not speaking, to a place with its window full of hand-blocked patchwork quilts and cushions. They found a table and sat down opposite each other. A waitress came and took their order for coffee.

'Well,' Lisa said. 'What do you want to talk about?'

'I wanted to say . . .' He hesitated. Mel hovered at the back of his mind. 'I wanted to apologise. When you came by the other night, I didn't give you much of a chance. I should have listened to what you had to say.'

'It doesn't matter any more.'

'Why not?' Her indifference stabbed him.

Her black eyes were opaque. 'You told me you'd fallen in love with someone else.'

He recognised this as a defining moment. His future lay within his answer. Whatever he said, he would be betraying a woman he loved.

'I . . .' He lifted his coffee to his mouth, staving off the necessity for an answer, thinking of Mel. *You belong with Lisa* . . . how hard had it been for her to say that? 'I just said that because I was angry.'

A kind of tremor moved across her face, leaving the skin smooth and unwrinkled. 'You mean it's not true?'

'No, I . . .' He swallowed. 'I said it to hurt you.'

'Oh, Ben.'

'What happened this summer,' he said. 'The baby. We can never make it not have happened.' He reached across the table and took her hand. 'Let's try again,' he said, not even knowing if he meant it.

At first she didn't respond. Then she smiled briefly at him. 'Do you think that's possible?'

Regret and longing clogged his throat, desire for the innocence they had once possessed, regret for what he was losing. For a moment he was afraid his eyes would fill with tears.

'Do I think it's possible,' he repeated slowly. Yes. The word sounded inside his head. Mel was right. 'Yes. I do. And there's something I'd really like to do. It means you'd have to come back to Butterfield with me. Right now. This very minute.'

'Why?'

He lifted the bag he'd been carrying and put it on the table between them. 'Because of this.'

'What is it?'

'A last reminder,' he said. A crushing sorrow waited somewhere in his chest. Something he would have to deal with later. He wondered how it could all have come to this when there had been—still was—so much love. 'I want us to plant it together.' He pulled open the top of the bag and a sweetly pungent scent of herbs hung in the air between them. 'It's a rosemary bush. I thought . . .' His voice cracked. 'I thought it would be a way of remembering her. Remembering Rosie.'

'Listen, Ben. I really—'

'Whatever you say or do, please, Lisa, remember that I also miss her. She was my child too. And whatever happens in the future, she will always be my first child, our first baby. Always.'

She stared at him for a moment, then she shut her eyes. 'I know. And I never took that into consideration.' Tears squeezed between the lids and moved slowly down her cheeks.

'I didn't mean to hurt you,' he said, reaching across the table for her hand again. 'I never *ever* meant to hurt you.'

She opened her eyes, bit down on her lip. 'Nor I you.'

The waitress came over to their table.

'May we have the bill?' said Lisa. 'We're just leaving.'

The two of them walked down to the till and Ben paid.

'So, will you come with me?' he asked her as they walked to the Jeep.

Lisa stood in the middle of the parking lot. A few cold raindrops drifted down. 'Is it really a good idea?'

'Yes,' he said.

'I guess I could spent the night at . . . the house.'

'I'll drive you back here tomorrow.' He looked up at the already darkening sky. 'We could plant the bush in the morning.'

'Yes.'

They looked at each other without smiling, then he opened the door of the Jeep, helped her up into the passenger seat. They drove down to Butterfield without exchanging more than a dozen meaningless words. Lisa sat quietly with her hands neatly folded in her lap. Ben was too full of heartache and regret to want to talk. If he kept silent, he could kid himself that everything was all right and they were a couple again.

As they neared the house, Lisa spoke. 'Is there anything to eat?'

'Not much. We could stop at the store, if you like.' He was hesitant to do this, in case they ran into someone they knew. He didn't want to have to explain that no, they weren't back together.

'Let's not stop.'

The light was beginning to fade as he turned into the drive and parked under the apple tree. A faint sliver of new moon already hung over the fields across the lane, colourless and bleak except for the thick green of the pines.

Once inside, he set a match to wood in the fireplace, added scrumpled newspaper and a half-burnt log left in the ashes from the last time. Lisa sat on the old blue sofa, like a guest, watching him.

'Want something to drink?' he said. He felt absurdly shy.

'A glass of white wine, please,' she said. She didn't make any kind of move to follow him into the kitchen, or find glasses. His heart dropped. The messages she was sending were loud and clear. *This is not my house any more. This is no longer my marriage.* He wondered how they were going to get through the rest of the evening. He gripped his hands together and pressed them against his chest. 'Please,' he said, under his breath. '*Please . . .*'

Please what? He had no idea.

He took two glasses and a chilled bottle from the refrigerator into the living room. The fire was burning comfortably and Lisa sat on the raised hearth, feeding it with pieces of kindling.

'No one can resist fiddling with a fire, can they?' she said.

'Two reasons for that,' he said, painfully aware that they were manufacturing conversation. 'One because fire is so elemental. The other because everyone in the entire world knows that no one can make a fire work better than they can.'

She laughed. 'You're probably right.'

He removed the cork, poured for them both, handed her a glass. He sat down and tipped his glass at her in a kind of toast. 'So tell me about the new job, how things are going.'

'Just about OK.' She made a face. 'I only took it because they promised me unlimited use of the kilns and the wheels in the art studio. Turned out their idea of unlimited wasn't exactly the same as mine.'

'But you're managing to get some work done.' He picked up the bowl she had left with Mel. 'Some great work. This is the most striking piece of yours that I've seen.' He thought of Mel handing it to him, the pain that had shadowed her face. Thank you, he wanted to say. For loving me, for healing me. Thank you, my generous Mel.

Lisa inspected the bowl. 'Yes, I'm pleased with it.'

'Are you hungry?' he asked.

'Very.' Carefully she put down her glass. 'Tell you what,' she said. 'We could make pesto sauce, if you like. That first time, when you came to my apartment, you said anything could happen. I don't know about you, but it sure worked for me.'

There was a dimple in her cheek: it seemed like years since he had last seen it. *That first time* . . . It had been so easy then. He put his arms round her and smiled into her upturned face. 'Sign me on,' he said.

'**B**oy, that pesto sauce.' Lisa pushed her chair back from the table, pressed a hand to her belly. 'I feel so full.' Her mouth shone as she stared at him through the candle flames.

'Me too.' He poured more wine into their glasses.

'Funny thing is,' she said, putting her elbows on the table and cupping her face in her hands. 'I have this weird feeling that, like you said, anything could happen.'

'Any idea what form this "anything" might take?'

'Oh, yes.' She laughed. 'Absolutely.'

She came round the table and bent to kiss his lips, her mouth slippery on his, fragrant and exciting. But when he reached for her, she slipped away.

When she went up to bed, he blew out the candles, hearing water rushing in the ancient plumbing system, the clank of radiators, the wheeze of the pump. In the living room, the fire was no more than a red glow, the logs crumbled in on each other. He turned off lights, locked the front door, slowly went upstairs. He wasn't dreaming. Lisa was back. The evening really had happened. And the rest, please God, would follow. Mel's image, her moonlight-coloured hair, her night-blue eyes, hovered briefly behind his eyelids. He felt no guilt, just a secret kind of loving. What had happened between them had been necessary, for both of them. The brief time they'd shared had enriched and strengthened them, given them the fortitude to go on with their real lives.

He lay in bed, alone, listening to the sound of Lisa in the other bedroom. Once he thought he heard soft footsteps in the passage, her bare feet on the polished floor, and hoped she was coming to him. Then he heard the door of the nursery open, and—after a while—softly close.

I shall never take this . . . this privilege for granted again, he thought. I shall never ever assume anything again. In the distance of his mind hung the mountains he had loved: mysterious, eternal, unconquerable.

He realised suddenly that however many times he reached the top, standing as close to heaven as any man was able to, they would always remain unconquerable.

In Lisa's studio they chose one of the glazed earthenware pots and filled it with potting compost. Together they planted the little rosemary bush, tamped down the compost round its roots, watered it with rainwater from the barrel behind the house. They would transplant it in the spring. 'Ben,' Lisa said, holding his hand. 'This is a beautiful idea of yours.'

'It was the name,' he said. 'Rosemary for remembrance. Whenever we see it, we'll be able to think of Rosie.'

'All the things she might have done, might have been.'

'That's what I thought.'

She looked at him with shining eyes. 'We can move on, Ben. Do you realise that?'

'Yes, I do.' He took a deep breath. And another. 'Lisa.'

'What?'

'I promise I'll never go climbing again.'

She put a finger across his lips. 'Best not to make promises you may not be able to keep.'

'But I mean it.'

'Ssh,' she said.

Chapter Fifteen

ACROSS THE FIELDS, trees stood against the clear sky, fiery, brilliant, and beyond them the encircling mountains. White birds rose and wheeled through the air, the sun catching the underside of their wings. A fox parted the long grass on the opposite verge and peered carefully out before trotting across the road, its brush momentarily vivid in a slice of sunlight. Mel could see its ruthless yellow eye, the shine of its wet nose.

Overhead, a gust of wind shook down a shower of flaming leaves then lifted them along the lane in front of her, scarlet, apricot, saffron and plum, like a flight of exotic butterflies. Her life in this place had been made up of countless small moments such as these, images laid down like paint on the canvas of her mind. These fields, those hills, that sky, were as familiar to her as her own reflection in the mirror.

Last time she had taken the road south from Butterfield, Joanne had been with her. This time she was going down to visit Joanne's children. When she had called Gordon to suggest it, he had been delighted, told her that they had missed her, hoped she would stay.

'Just one night,' she had replied. 'My exhibition is in three days' time.' She did not add that along with her desire to see how Tom, Lucy and, above all, Jamie were doing, was the need to be doing something, anything that would prevent her from thinking about Ben.

'Jamie,' she said, sweeping him into her arms. 'Oh, Jamie, sweetheart, how are you?'

'I'm doing OK.' He led her into Gordon's designer kitchen, and, lifting an elegant chrome kettle, asked if she would like a cup of tea.

'Tea would be good.' She pulled out a chair and sat down. The immaculate counters and polished floor were a far cry from the warm and homely kitchen he had grown up in. 'Do you like your new school?'

'It's OK.'

'What are you reading?' She delved into her bag and brought out a package. 'Here's a book for you. Save it until you reach the Cs again.'

He picked it up. 'Maybe I won't wait. I already broke the pattern.'

'Is that good or bad?'

'Good, don't you think?' There was a new maturity in his voice. 'I was getting kind of set in my ways. Dad says that's OK when you're older but not so cool when you're twelve.'

'I think Dad's probably right,' she said gravely. 'So open it.'

He tore off the paper and his face lit up. '*Catcher in the Rye*: perfect. It's on my reading list.' He bent and kissed her cheek. 'Thanks, Mel.'

'How's Gargery liking it down here?'

'Sure doesn't like the traffic, but otherwise he's fine. Lucy's just taken him for a walk with her new boyfriend. Boy, what a geek *he* is.' He poured hot water into a pot, and took down two mugs.

'And how is your dad?'

'He's . . . I guess happy isn't the right word 'cause of losing Mom, but he's real glad to have us staying with him.'

'I'm sure he is. And you, Jamie . . . are you all right?'

'I guess,' he said slowly.

'It'll take time,' she said. 'Maybe the rest of your life.'

'That's what I thought.'

'Do you know what your mom's very favourite book of all was?'

'What?'

'*Great Expectations* by Charles Dickens. It's where she found Gargery's name.'

'Is it?' He assimilated the information. 'Maybe I'll read that next. If you don't mind. Save *Catcher in the Rye* for the book after that.'

Gordon and Tom arrived at the same time as Lucy. 'Oh, Mel, we've missed you so much,' Lucy said, flinging her arms round Mel. She looked well; she even looked happy. Tom too: like his little brother, he seemed to have gained a veneer of confidence in the past weeks.

Lucy and the boyfriend, a handsome sophomore at Brown, and not in the least geeky as far as Mel could see, had volunteered to cook supper.

'This is called *spana kopitta*,' Lucy said, putting an oven dish on the table in the dining room, 'and it's really, really good.' The boyfriend produced a sophisticated lemony salad that contained, among other things, snap peas, artichoke hearts, mangoes and rice. They brought in garlic bread and baked potatoes topped with melted cheese, and sliced tomatoes with a pesto sauce. 'Vegetarian, as you can see,' said Lucy.

'Sometimes we get to eat steak,' said Tom.

'Especially when it's my turn to cook,' Gordon said. 'Steak's about all I can handle.'

'I make roast chicken when it's my turn,' said Jamie. 'With roast potatoes. Wicked.'

'Do you have plans, Mel?' Gordon said, taking the cork out of a bottle of wine.

'I can only think as far as my exhibition,' she said. 'After that . . . who knows.' She felt like a kite, free but tethered.

'You know what you ought to do, Mel?' Jamie said.

'What's that, honey?'

'You should go to that place Mom talked about. In New Zealand.'

She smiled at him. 'I don't think so.'

'Why not?' Gordon asked mildly. 'What's to stop you?'

She remembered him telling her Joanne had always been too scared to travel on her own. I'm scared too, she thought.

'No, really,' insisted Jamie. 'I've been reading all about New Zealand. That place, Rotorua, sounds totally wicked. I wish I could go.'

'I'll take you one day,' she said.

'Will you really?'

'A graduation present.'

'That's cool.'

'You might not want an old lady along by then, of course,' she said, smiling at him. At his father and siblings.

'I'll always want you, Mel,' he said.

'Creep,' said Lucy, but she was smiling. 'You're part of the family,' she said, reaching out a hand to Mel.

'Thank you, sweetheart.'

Driving back the following day, she felt content. I need no longer worry about Joanne's children, she thought. Gordon was taking over where Joanne left off. The three of them were travelling onwards, as they needed to.

Moving on, Mel thought. And I must move on too.

On the morning of the exhibition preview, Mel arrived at the gallery to find a UPS truck waiting outside. The delivery man—a different one this time—walked in behind her, carrying a small wooden crate.

'I thought we had all the exhibits,' Mel said.

He shrugged. 'I was asked to deliver this, is all I know.' While she signed the necessary documentation, he put an envelope in front of her. 'Plus this.'

When he had driven away, she sat down at the table in her office and opened the commercial envelope he had left. Inside was another envelope, which contained another note from Koslowski. Like the first, it was scrawled on a sheet of A4, thick black writing enlivened by capital letters and exclamation marks.

Mrs Sherman,

This is Lost Love, my most recent work. I must emphasise that it is MY OWN PERSONAL POSSESSION and is not, repeat, NOT FOR SALE ! ! ! ! !

Galen Koslowski

His most recent work! With extreme care, she broke open the crate and lifted the piece inside clear of its wrappings.

Lost Love. The breath caught in her throat, blood pounded in her ears. She looked at her own piece on the table, and then back at the new one. Despite the more than twenty-five years that separated them, the two were almost identical. But the first figure was that of a girl, slight, barely pubescent, while the second had been modelled by a woman of riper years, rounder of breast, curved of belly.

She picked it up and ran her hands over the wood. Below the left breast, running towards the inward crook of the waist, was a narrow, almost imperceptible slash. It was clear it had been added deliberately.

'Oh, Galen,' she said softly. She tilted the sapphire ring on her finger so that the stones caught the light and blazed with blue fire.

'Did that go well, or what!' Carla eased her feet out of her pumps and propped them up on the table in the gallery office. The last invitees had left the gallery ten minutes ago, and finally they could relax.

'It was terrific. Absolutely terrific.' Mel poured the remains of a bottle of Chardonnay into a glass and handed it to her assistant. 'Here's to us.'

'And our future success.' Carla lifted her glass to her mouth. 'The piece that arrived this morning looked marvellous, right in the middle of the floor like that, especially with the other one. I never knew you already owned something by Koslowski.'

'That's partly where I got the idea of setting this show up.'

'If they'd been for sale, you could have sold them both five times.'

'I know.'

Carla looked at her watch. 'Well, I better get on home.'

Mel reached up and clasped the other woman's hand. 'Thanks, Carla, for everything. You're an absolute star.'

She listened as Carla's footsteps receded down the wooden floor of the gallery. There was the creak and clank of the heavy ring-handle, the bang as the door closed behind her. It was time she went home herself. But she stayed where she was, picked up another bottle of wine and poured some into her glass.

God, she was tired. And, despite the success of the evening, forlorn. Loss weighed her down. If only Joanne were here. Over the years there had been so many gatherings, so many parties, when the two of them had kicked off their shoes and sat down with the remains of a bottle of wine to pick over the details, relive the evening, post-mortem it. Although she was exhausted, she was wired, elated, she wanted to talk, to exclaim, to describe. But there was no one to share her excitement with.

Except . . . Slowly she reached towards the telephone and as she did so, it bleeped, the sound echoing through the silent gallery, bouncing off the stone pieces, rippling the surface of the water sculpture. She snatched it up.

'Vernon Gallery.'

'Mrs Sherman?'

Her low mood dissipated, her weariness vanished. 'Mr Koslowski. I was just about to call you.'

'How did it go this evening?'

'Brilliant! Fantastic!'

'That's wonderful.'

'Three pieces were sold in the first half-hour,' she said. 'Isn't that marvellous? And at least four other people will almost certainly buy later.'

'It sounds like the hard work paid off.'

'I'll say. Three sales in the first *half-hour*? How good is *that*? And the show doesn't even officially open until tomorrow.'

'That's really something.' He sounded impressed. 'Did many people come?'

'Nearly two hundred.'

'Mrs Sherman, you are obviously a genius.'

She laughed. 'Thank goodness they didn't all show up at the same time. My gallery is quite small.'

'As a matter of fact, I intended to come tonight. As a surprise. But I'm afraid I left it too late.'

'You missed a terrific evening,' she said.

'The extra piece I sent you yesterday, it arrived safely?'

'*Lost Love*,' Mel said. 'That was surprise enough.' She hesitated. 'I wanted to ask . . . who was the model?'

'There was no model.'

'I thought perhaps . . . someone you know.'

'Someone I *used* to know. I made it from . . . from the heart. From my memories. She was young then, we both were. I wondered how she might be now, changed by the years. This piece is the result. Describe for me how you displayed it.'

'Well'—Mel tipped more wine into her glass and leaned back—'in the end, I grouped it with the companion piece.'

'The companion piece?'

'Yes, they seemed to fit together so well, to illustrate the damage that time causes and how, despite that, even in middle age, a woman's body can still be beautiful.'

There was a long silence. She heard the clink of glass against glass, a deep-drawn breath, almost a sigh. Silence.

'Mr Koslowski?'

'The companion piece,' he repeated. 'Mrs Sherman, there is no companion piece.'

'There is. It's a carving you did a long time ago.'

'Called?'

'Uh . . . *First Love*.'

There was another lengthy pause. 'Ah,' he said finally, drawing the syllable out. 'I have often wondered where that piece was.'

The two of them sat without speaking, companionable. The polished floor of the gallery stretched away to dimness, lit by the occasional spotlights Mel had not yet switched off.

'She left me,' Koslowski said into the silence. 'The beautiful woman who was the model for that. It almost killed me. It was only then, in that moment of separation, that I realised just how much she meant to me. Without her, I couldn't work. I needed her. She was my inspiration.'

'Why didn't you go after her?'

'Where? Where would I start looking? America is a big place. She would have married, changed her name. And then, I realised that I could not waste the rest of my life waiting for her to return, or I would never produce anything worthwhile again.'

'So you're over her now.'

'What do you think, Mrs Sherman? Am I over her? You have seen my newest work.'

From her office, Mel could see the whole exhibition stretching in front of her. 'The piece called *Birth* is absolutely magnificent.'

'Was it one of the pieces that sold?'

'I bought it myself, before the show started.' She refilled her glass and laughed, for no particular reason.

'You sound happy,' he said.

'I do believe that I am.'

'Do you have children, Mrs Sherman?'

'No.'

'Why not?'

'I . . .' What am I doing? she asked herself. For a moment she hesitated. 'I had an abortion when I was young.'

'Oh no . . .' He drew a sharp breath. 'I see.'

'I've never forgiven myself. After that, I never considered that I deserved to have children.'

'I have none either,' he said abruptly.

'Why not?'

'At first because I thought I must not bring children into a world like this one. By the time I changed my mind, the only person I wanted children with was gone. This woman whom I loved wanted to have children with me and I refused.'

'That's probably why she went.'

'I regret it now. I bitterly regret it.'

'Maybe one of these days you'll see her again.'

He gave a deep sigh. 'If I do, I shall certainly ask her to give me back the icon that she took from our apartment.'

Mel's mouth curved upwards. 'Are you sure you didn't offer it to her as a gift?'

'Only on the assumption that we would be staying together.' He sighed, and she heard wine being poured into a glass.

Do you still have nightmares? she wanted to ask. Do you still wake shuddering in the night to reach out for someone, to weep into her hair? Do you miss me, as I have always missed you, as I missed you still even as I lay in the arms of my young lover?

'You sound about as tired as I feel,' she said.

'Not tired. Just . . . old. And I don't always sleep so well. Also—why do I tell you this?—I am lonely. What about you, Mrs Sherman? Are you also lonely? Or do you lead a life of social gaiety? I imagine you up there, surrounded by cows and buttercups, the queen of Butterfield, the hostess with the mostest.'

'A social butterfly? Hardly.'

'Perhaps Mr Sherman drags you to functions and business dinners, where you sparkle and shine.'

'Mr Sherman has been dead for some time.'

'I see. And, of course, you miss him.'

'The one I miss is Joanne, my dearest, closest friend, who died a few weeks ago. She was the nearest thing I have to family.'

'So you are lonely, too.'

'Yes.'

'And I must have added to your worries at a bad time for you.'

'That's the way it goes. Highs and lows. Ups and downs. The best you can do is enjoy the ups and endure the downs. Trouble is . . .' Mel pressed her lips together.

'Are you crying, Mrs Sherman?'

'Since you ask, Mr Koslowski, I guess I am.'

'If I was with you,' he said, 'I would hold your hand. It's not much, but it would show you that you still have a friend, even if it's only a crabby old shabby old sculptor like me.'

She found herself smiling again, despite herself. 'Are you crabby?'

'A little bit. There are so many things here in New York that drive me mad. Cellphones, for instance. Why must people walk down the street talking on the phone? Why can't they wait until they get home?'

'Isn't that just the most irritating thing?'

'Something else I hate is the way, in restaurants, the waiter tells you his name and then gabbles off the specials so fast you cannot remember a single one when he's finished. I do not wish to hear a three-act play, I tell him, give me the menu and I will read for myself what you have.'

Mel laughed aloud.

'You have a lovely laugh,' he said. 'What kind of cuisine do you like, Mrs Sherman?'

'Most sorts. The last time I went to Boston with Joanne,' said Mel, 'we ate in a Russian restaurant.'

'I used to know a Russian restaurant in Boston—I wonder if it was the same one. Let me guess what you ate: borscht, and pirozhki, no?'

'Pretty standard choices, Mr Koslowski. We had blinis, too. And some fish.' Mel giggled, wondered if she had drunk too much wine. 'And a truly wicked amount of vodka.'

'Mrs Sherman!' he said. 'I don't want to call you Mrs Sherman. It's ridiculous to be so formal. By now we have become friends. I feel I have known you for years. The formidable Mrs Sherman. The sometimes sad Mrs Sherman.'

'People of our age are bound to be sad from time to time,' she said. 'We've lived long enough to have experienced loss and grief.'

'Of course. What keeps me going is the certainty that happiness is waiting for me around the next corner. Or the one after that.'

'Do you believe in second chances, Mr Koslowski?'

'Without any question.' His chair creaked. 'One moment.'

She heard hollow noises and then the sound of Mahler's Symphony No. 2. When he picked up the receiver again, she said softly, 'The "Resurrection Symphony"—one of my favourites.'

'I thought it might be.'

Mel smiled secretly. They had been on the telephone for over forty-five minutes; she felt as though she could go on talking for the rest of the night. 'What are you working on at the moment?'

'Nothing. But I'm thinking about something.' There was a familiar rise in his voice. 'I have this piece of marble, from South America. Green marble, with the most wonderful streaks of gold. I've had it for years, waiting for the right moment to use it.'

'And now it's come,' she said.

'Is coming,' he corrected her. 'For the moment, I'm just considering it, trying to see what is hiding inside, waiting to appear.'

'Like Michelangelo.'

'I wouldn't put myself anywhere near him, but yes. Now tell me, Mrs Sherman, what plans do *you* have? Other exhibitions, maybe?'

'I have at least two I'm considering, rather like you and your piece of marble.'

'Anything more? A visit to New York, perhaps?'

It suddenly came to her. Excited, she sat up straight. Jamie's suggestion was exactly the right one. 'No. Not New York. New Zealand.'

'But why?'

Mel wrinkled her forehead. 'Sounds crazy, I know. But Joanne—'

'Your friend who died?'

'Yes. She always dreamed of going there, some place called Rotorua, and she never did, even though she had the chance.'

'Why not?'

'Her former husband told me she was too scared of travelling on her own.' And there's that other worry, Mel thought. The fear that the reality will prove to be less than the dream. 'I'm scared too,' she said. 'Travelling to strange places on my own. But I'm going to go.'

Carla would jump at the chance to look after the gallery, to use her own judgment. The journey would mean a fresh start. More than that, it would be a journey that might lead anywhere.

'I could come with you,' he said quietly. 'If you're scared.'

'Oh . . .' she said. 'Mr Koslowski.' She remembered how once she had been so in love that, if she had wanted to, she could have reached up and touched the sky. There were tears in her eyes.

'Are you crying again, Mrs Sherman?'

'Yes, Mr Koslowski, I do believe I am.'

Before she left, she drove to the dam and stood looking down at the frozen water, hands jammed deep into the pockets of her coat. Her breath hung in the air like smoke, like melancholy. The wind hurled snow spray into her face, tiny stinging dots of cold. Dark birds flapped slowly above the water and disappeared among the black-spired pines. Cold had bleached the colour from the trees, from the sky, the wintry hills. She used to walk here with Joanne and the children, on winter holidays. Now she saw her friend lifting away from her, propelled like a time-warping spaceship into the distance, further and further, until she was no more than a prick of light in a sky full of stars.

And Ben, too, was charting new territory. Sometimes she caught glimpses of him, crossing the common, buying flowers. Lisa was often with him, enough for Mel to be aware that the two of them had moved into a resumption of their lives together.

The air was sharp as glass. She imagined that she could smell the scents of summers past: roses, jasmine, lilacs. Deep down, like a silver fish on the bottom of a fathomless pond, she knew that if she had the courage to go out and find them, choices, dreams, magical possibilities still existed. I've lived safely for too long, she thought. I shall be better at living in the future than I have been in the past.

From the airport, she took a cab into the city. At the hotel, she hung up her clothes, took the icon from her bag and laid it on the bed. She stared at her reflection in the mirror, saw her mother's face behind her own and—for the first time—her father's. Lifting her pale, heavy hair from her neck, she felt the weight of it in her hands. The sapphire ring shone on her finger. She smiled at herself.

The familiar street had scarcely changed since she last walked away from it, twenty-five years before. At the deli on the corner she stopped to buy rye bread, the big Polish pickles Galen used to love, unsalted butter, curls of smoked ham, pastrami. She carried the brown paper sack to the familiar steps, took out the key she had kept all these years, let herself in. Two floors up she could hear the chip of hammer on stone. She started to hurry. Faster and faster. The stone stairs sped away from her feet. Running down the passage, she turned the handle of the door—*their* door—and found, as always, that it was unlocked. Pushing it open, she saw him against the window, head on one side, staring intently at the stone before him, green streaked with gold.

He looked up. Opened his mouth to say something, shut it again. He began to smile, lighting up the room. Lighting up the world.

'Mr Koslowski,' she said.

'Mrs Sherman.' He opened his arms to her. 'Melissa. My honeybee.'

SUSAN MADISON

The restaurant where I had arranged to meet Susan Madison was an oasis of calm after the bustle of Oxford. Filled with plants and white, linen-clad tables, the pretty Victorian conservatory where we lunched could have been a candidate for one of her mouth-watering descriptions of meals and restaurants. 'I first knew this place when it was a greengrocer's shop with flowers at the front and I was passing it on my way to school,' she laughs.

The author still has a house in the city, but now lives for part of the year in Australia, where her husband, John Donaldson, is a university professor. In fact, when we met they had just arrived in England and were about to leave for a month in Minneapolis. How, I marvelled, does she find the time to write, given her busy lifestyle? 'It's difficult,' she admits. 'Until my recent marriage, I'd lived on my own for a long time and I could write at any time I liked. It's hard to get into a routine with a husband around.' Her expressive brown eyes sparkle. 'The whole story of our meeting is very romantic.' Which is also the perfect way to describe *Touching the Sky*, with its searing passions. 'It is a hugely complicated novel, with lots of threads and ideas, and I think the apprenticeship, if you like, that I had as a crime writer helped. It taught me the discipline of tying up all the ends. That is, after all, what the reader expects.'

Susan went on to explain that she wanted to explore the tearing grief

that people feel upon losing someone close to them. 'The loss of a child is terrible, nothing could be as bad. But I also wanted to write about other forms of loss. There are an awful lot of people walking around with unresolved grief, not being allowed to mourn. Those feelings were pivotal to the story.'

Also pivotal are the glowing descriptions of Vermont, where much of the book is set, and I wondered if she had ever lived there. 'No, but I just love New England. If I could live there I'd be ecstatically happy—I live an ecstatically happy life anyway, but . . .' So would she tell me a little about the man who makes her so happy? I ventured. 'He's gorgeous,' she says, hugging herself. 'I mean, a really beautiful man.' She rushes on to tell me how they had met at a dinner party in Australia just three weeks before she was to return to England at the end of her time as a visiting fellow at the University of Tasmania. The attraction was mutual and instant, but their time together was brief. When he flew into Heathrow, and they saw one another again after months of courtship by emails and phone calls, they both knew absolutely that they had to be together. 'Every morning we wake up and say, "We are just so lucky." We have seven grown-up children between us and now all this as well.'

Anne Jenkins

Claire Calman
I like it like that

The effect of a mother's death on a young family is always devastating—and no less so for the Abrams family. Luckily they have Georgia who, from the age of ten became 'mother' to her younger brother, sister and disorganised father. Now grown up, the family have gone their separate ways, but they still meet for brunch every Sunday, to talk and argue. The main topic is usually Stephen, Georgia's rather boring fiancé. If only they liked him a little more. And her delightful friend Leo a little less.

ONE

A nice, normal family

SO I'M STANDING IN LINE at the orphanage and these prospective parents have turned up to choose a child. We're all stretching up straight and tall and we've pulled up our socks and had our noses wiped so that we look like nice, clean children who'll be no trouble. Inside, we're all thinking the same thing and you can practically hear the words rushing out of us like the wind: 'Pick me! Me! Me! Pick *me*!' The couple are coming down this way, stopping kindly to talk to each child, smiling and fussing over everyone, and making it worse—because now we all really, really want to be picked more than ever. Now it's my turn. I think I should do something adorable, something that would make me irresistible—perform a pirouette or an on-the-spot tap dance? Or just give them a dimply-cheeked smile instead of my usual serious face. But here they are now, right in front of me, and I can't even seem to manage my own half-smile never mind a pirouette, so I just hold out my hand to shake theirs and say, 'Hello, I'm Georgia, how do you do?' And this is the best bit, because this is when the mumsy-looking woman turns to her husband and whispers into his ear and he smiles and nods and they each take one of my hands and draw me out of the parade and that's it, they've chosen me. *Me*.

Then they sign a piece of paper and my new *Daddy* picks up my small suitcase and we all get into their big, shiny car. The house is not especially grand or big, but completely perfect with a green front gate and a thatched roof. There's a straight path leading up to the front door, flanked by flowerbeds full of candy-pink roses and purple lavender. We go in and *Mummy*—she asks me if I'd like to call her that and I loop my arms round her neck and give her a big hug and she wipes a tear from her eye—says she must just pop in the kitchen and find me a nice treat, and I feel as if I'm the happiest, luckiest girl in the whole wide world.

And then the picture fades and that's the end.

That's it. That was my all-time favourite fantasy when I was growing up—that I was an orphan. I used to play it in my head like a videotape, exactly the same every single time, and sometimes, even now when I can't get to sleep or if I'm bored, I let the fantasy return.

Now that I'm thirty-four, I presume that I've blown it on the being-adopted front. I don't suppose there'd be many broody prospective parents queuing up to have me unless I offered myself on the Net and posted a photo of me when I was about two and a half. I was moderately cute back then. But it's hard not to be cute when you're two and a half because you're all soft and dimpled and even when you fall over you look adorable whereas if you fall over when you're thirty-four, people think you're drunk and you have to walk round with holey tights and a bleeding knee until you get home.

Also, I don't have angelic blonde hair or appealing blue eyes or a cherubic smile. My hair is dark brown and what you could call curly if you were feeling generous, but not gorgeous film-star tumbling curls, like my sister Ellen has—it resembles a nest of burnt noodles. If a man dared to run his hands through it, you'd have to call in the fire brigade to cut him free. My eyes are brown, not blue, and I'm not sure what my smile is like because I tend to scowl when I look in the mirror, but my habitual expression is serious. When I'm walking down the street, total strangers call out to me, 'Cheer up, love! It might never happen!' A couple of times, I've said, 'Actually, my mother just died . . .' and done my ultra-sad face, then they look guilty and feel compelled to apologise.

It sounds kind of horrible, the orphan fantasy, because I'm already half an orphan. My mother really is dead, she died when I was ten and no, I'm not playing for sympathy, I'm just telling you. My father's alive though and now I feel even worse about the orphan thing because it's not as if I don't love my dad. And I'm not an only child either. I've got a little sister, Ellen, she of the proper curls. She's twenty-seven now but she'll always be my little sister. And there's Matthew, my brother, who's thirty-one. That's my family, not counting Quinn, who's my stepmother so she's not real family, and Unc, who's Dad's brother, and a whole bunch of cousins too many to list here, then there's Quinn's daughter from her first marriage to this poxy artist, but we don't really count her.

It's not that I don't love my family exactly—it's just that you've never met a bunch of people more guaranteed to drive you crazy. Other people's families always seem so nice and so, well, normal.

I wasn't always the sensible one in our family. When I was two and a quarter, I clambered up onto the lavatory seat in the upstairs bathroom, then onto the cistern, and hurled Mumu, my toy monkey, out of the window 'to be a birdy'. Not being tall enough to see where—or even if—he'd landed, I was on the verge of following him when my mother rushed in and grabbed me, startling me so much that I burst into tears, she later told me, and could only be consoled by a jam tart and a ride on Daddy's back round and round the kitchen table until he lay flat on the floor and said horsey had to have a rest now.

Then Matt was born and I wasn't the baby any more. I was 'a big girl who must be ever so gentle with little Matthew'. I was always being told to shush and not to run up and down the landing for fear of waking him because he hardly ever slept and to 'please behave, because Mummy's far too tired to run round after you'. As far as I was concerned, he should have been taken right back to the hospital because all he did was cry and eat and poo and be sick and take up Mummy and Daddy's time, so what was the point of him? It wasn't as if you could ride him round the garden like a tricycle or bounce him across the floor like a ball.

At the age of five, only two weeks into my first term at school, I dabbed green paint onto the nose of Martin, a boy I had a crush on. He retaliated with a blob of blue on my cheek and a riot of impressionistic brushwork soon covered our faces, arms and hair, until the teacher stormed over to separate us. I was ordered to say I was very sorry, which I did, but the very next day, I refused to come in from the climbing frame at the end of break. I sat right at the very top, perched on the bar and swinging my legs and they had to send for Mum to come and talk me down, like a police negotiator with a person on a window ledge.

And then, when I was seven and three-quarters, things went from bad to worse—because that's when Ellen was born. It was bad enough having to share everything with Matthew, but at least I was used to him by then. When my mother told me, 'Soon there'll be another baby brother or sister for you,' apparently I uttered a single word: 'Why?'

'We thought it would be nice,' my father had said lamely, though, as I later discovered, they were both as surprised by the prospect of another baby as I was.

Ellen was bound to make an enormous difference to my life, no matter what kind of a baby she was. But the fact that she was Ellen from Day One—irresistible, irrepressible, impossible—made it much, much worse. Ellen had blue eyes and soft curls and she smiled on cue. She refused to sleep when out in her pram, preferring instead to bask in the admiration and sickening goo-goo talk—'Who's a *boo-ful* baby? Yes, *you* are'—of neighbours, shopkeepers, strangers.

It was also then that things started to change in the family. Anyway, no point droning on about it now, it's years ago. The key thing is that Mum died when Ellen was only three so she doesn't even remember her. Nothing—not her face, her voice or anything. She looks at the photos though and sometimes she says she thinks she can sort of remember her, but we both know that she can't really. She still gets me to tell her stories about when she was little. 'Tell me the bit about when you cut off all my hair,' 'Tell me the time when I peed in Matt's wellie,' 'Tell me how Mum used to sing when you were out in the street with her,' and, endlessly, 'Tell me what Mummy was like.' Matt never does that. Never. It's as if she never existed.

Anyway, Mum died. End of story. It happens to lots of people all the time. I can't remember exactly how it happened, not Mum dying, I mean, I'll never forget that—but my becoming the sensible one in the family. All I know is that now it's been that way for so long that I can't even remember how not to be any more. Was it really me who was on the verge of hurling myself out of the bathroom window to fly like the birds? Could I have dared to smear paint on a boy I didn't know? It may not sound much to you, but no one who knows me now would believe that I'd ever been naughty or even silly when I was growing up. I wasn't even wild as a teenager—a couple of token blonde streaks in my hair for a few months, letting myself be groped by some creep in his car after a date, getting drunk when I drank quite a lot of lager and, weirdly, given that I can't remember ever having liked it, Southern Comfort and lemonade. Anyway, I managed to get home only to find my father sitting at the kitchen table in his dressing gown. I was sixteen. It was nearly two in the morning. To say that he was not happy would be an understatement. And remember, this is my dad we're talking about, the mildest, gentlest man you could ever hope to meet. First of all he shouted at me because it was 2.00am and I hadn't phoned and that was the absolute Number One rule. Then he noticed that I wasn't entirely steady on my feet and he went even more crazy. How could I? What was the one thing that I knew he minded about more than any other thing in the world? Did I want to flush my entire life down the drain, is that what I wanted? Then he grabbed a black Magic Marker from the dresser and drew a straight line all the way across the cork-tiled floor. Well, I got the giggles then and the more he stood there stony-faced, the worse it got until I thought I was going to wet myself. I walked the line with exaggerated care as if it were a tightrope, and he said I was drunk and I was incredibly bloody stupid and I absolutely wasn't to drink again, he was dead serious about that, and did I understand? And, even though I was drunk, I could see that he was serious as hell and I never was much of a rebel anyway. The black pen couldn't be washed off and it remained there for another three years—a one-line testament to my shame—until the floor was finally too scuffed and grotty even for us and was replaced.

These days, I don't even touch lager. A single glass of wine with dinner sometimes. When we're out, I order a glass of white and Stephen has a glass of red. He's my boyfriend, fiancé really, and he's not a great one for overdoing it either. We're very compatible. Stephen's very sensible, too, and reliable. That's one of the things I love most about him. And, unlike everyone in my family, he doesn't expect me to come to the rescue all the time. When Matt and Ellen used to squabble or fight, it was always me who intervened and stood between them telling them they must make it up again. When Dad thundered upstairs and slammed his study door because some stupid client had changed her stupid mind for the forty-fifth time, it was me who waited ten minutes then tapped on his door to ask if he wanted a cup of tea. Even now, I guess it's me they all turn to in a crisis, real or imaginary—nearly always imaginary. Still, all that early training—being the family peacekeeper (Matt calls me 'our one-woman UN')—has stood me in good stead. I'm a counsellor, so I listen to people talking about their problems all day long. Looking on the bright side, at least now I get paid for it.

TWO

Twenty-four years and one day . . .

YESTERDAY WAS THE ANNIVERSARY of Mum's death—and the first time in my memory that I haven't spent the day with Ellen. It's not a sacred ritual or anything; it's just a day when we do Mum-ish things like going to an exhibition then having tea and cream meringues afterwards while we argue about which pictures we liked and, much more fun, which ones we didn't. We don't go to the grave any more because that's not how we want to think of her, lying cold and alone beneath a slab of stone. 'Oh, you don't want to visit me—I'm just a bundle of old bones now!' That's what Mum would say if she was still alive—except then she wouldn't be bones, of course, would she? Mum had no time for sentiment or floaty notions that your soul lives on after you die, or you go to heaven. She said when you die you become food for the worms and then part of the earth. It's a good thing, she said, because it means that, in a way, you're still part of the world even though you're dead, still around the people you loved, the people who loved you. You become the ground and the grass beneath their feet, the trees that shade them, the water that trickles through the soil, the chalk, the rock, the water they drink, the sky, the clouds, the rain, even the air that they breathe.

Now, I realise that it *does* sound mystical, but that was the thing about Mum—I suppose she could be quite fey at times, but it never sounded affected, it was just the way she was.

When I went through my brief pious phase, kneeling by my bed each night, praying for things to be different, and begging to be confirmed, Mum just smiled and didn't say anything even though there was no question of my being confirmed because a) Dad's Jewish so I'm not baptised and b) she knew I only wanted to do it so I could have a white dress and little white gloves.

And then Mum died and that pretty much put paid to my brief flirtation with God.

I don't know what went wrong with Mum's Day this year. Well, I do. Ellen forgot and went tootling off with a friend to some wholesale place miles away in quest of a particular type of crystal bead. Ellen makes jewellery. She doesn't earn a living at it because, well, because she's Ellen, so, despite the fact that she's bursting at the seams with talent she manages to undercharge for her pieces or she leaves her best things behind at home when she rents a stall, so that there's not the slightest danger of her accidentally turning her talent and skill into a real career. 'In the meantime'—one of her favourite phrases—she works part-time in a wine bar called The Warm South.

Ellen forgets things all the time, so that's nothing unusual, but she's never forgotten Mum's Day before. It's not fair to blame it all on her though because, in fact, it was really *my* fault. I forgot last week, which is when I'd normally call Ellen to remind her and to fix up what we were doing. We see each other all the time in any case, but we always make a proper arrangement for Mum's Day and plan what we're going to see so the time doesn't just drift away from us. Yesterday was the Day and I woke up and looked at my diary and I had three clients all in the morning, then one at 7.00pm and I saw the date and suddenly it clicked, August 8, and I rang Ellen so that we could meet up in the afternoon and she wasn't there.

I sat through all my morning sessions, then ran upstairs to check the answering machine, but there was nothing.

I thought about what we would have done if Ellen had been there, and I went to the Tate Modern. By myself. Mum would have got such a kick out of it—there's a vast open space when you go in and it's very unstuffy and unpompous, and everyone was talking at a normal level instead of in those special hushed, reverent whispers that people seem to reserve for when they're in the presence of Art. There was a huge stone abstract sculpture, a bit like a squashed circle with strange wooden spheres suspended in the central gap—the sort of thing I normally dislike because it makes me feel as if I'm missing something, that it *means* something only I don't know what it is and everyone else is looking at it and making little ah-I-see nods to themselves because they get it and I just stand there feeling like an idiot. Still, despite the fact that I didn't know what it was or what it meant, I liked the way the stone was all smooth and curved, and, without thinking, I ran my hand down the cool inner slope of it until one of the guards scooted up to me and told me not to touch. At the time I felt incredibly embarrassed, but afterwards I thought how proud of me Mum would have been because it was exactly the kind of thing she was always doing only she wouldn't have gone bright red or apologised—she'd have got into a discussion about the accessibility of art and why we should all be allowed to touch sculpture rather than just look at it.

Eventually, Ellen rang me back.

'Oh, George, I'm so sorry! I can't believe I forgot. I feel so bad!'

'It's all right. Don't worry, babes. It doesn't matter.'

'It does! It does!'

'Ellie, come on. It doesn't mean we've forgotten her. Let's meet up tomorrow instead. At the café?'

'OK. And you don't hate me?'

'Don't be silly.' Ellen loves to dramatise everything.

***J**oy died on a Tuesday and was buried on Friday. David believed that Ellen was too little to attend the funeral, but he sat down with Georgia and Matt and asked them solemnly what they would like to do, it was up to them to decide. Matt, not quite eight, leapt up and kicked his father hard in the shin* *and said he wasn't going, no one could make him, then he ran out to the garden and rode his bike round and round and into the flowerbed. Georgia sat very still for a moment, then she said, yes, she thought it best if she went. David pulled her onto his lap and said into her hair, 'You don't have to go, little chick, if you don't want to. Mummy wouldn't mind.'*

Georgia slid off his lap and nodded and said it was fine and she would go.

Georgia has never seen a real coffin before, only ones on the news and in the newspaper. She knows that her mother is in that box, and she knows that she is dead. Daddy says it is just like being asleep, only for ever and ever. So that was what being dead was and then you got put in the ground and then the worms got you and after ages and ages you became like earth. That was what Mummy said when their kitten died, and the goldfish, and even Daddy said that it was natural and not really a bad thing because, in a way, you were carrying on and, most of all, he said, you lived on in people's heads, their memories and thoughts, the way Mummy would, for ever and ever.

Georgia holds Daddy's hand tight and her face is white as a shroud, but she does not shed a single tear. Her father, by contrast, cries continuously from the moment the coffin appears. The tears just keep falling down his face, like the leaky tap in the kitchen. Every few minutes he blows his nose loudly and wipes his face, and then the tears leak out again, rolling down his face and inside his shirt collar.

Afterwards, people come back home and Georgia helps make cups of tea. Auntie Audrey puts sugar in Daddy's tea, 'to keep your strength up, it's good for shock,' and he drinks it even though he doesn't take sugar.

In the middle of the lawn there is a table, and in the middle of the table is a big glass jug of sweet peas. Pink and mauve, purple and white, and one nearly the colour of red wine. The jug looks as if it has been besieged by butterflies, the sweet-pea petals in the wind fluttering and fragile like wings.

Georgia tips her head back to look at the sky; it is hot blue, the blue she has painted as a strip at the top of the paper a hundred times. Around her, the grown-ups are talking and drinking and making lip-smacking noises when they kiss each other. It is rude to smack your lips when you are eating, but maybe it is allowed when you are kissing.

Matt and Ellen are brought back by the neighbour and Matt stands by the buffet table, cramming crisps into his face and throwing peanuts into the air and trying to catch them in his mouth, until Uncle Howard gives him fifty pence to stop and he goes upstairs to look at his comics. Ellen works the room, tugging at trouser legs and skirt hems and smiling until she receives attention and Amaretti biscuits, stuck out of her reach on the table.

Unc pats Georgia's head and pulls out a coin from behind her ear. She stands next to Daddy, leaning against him. He looks down at her, rests his hand on her head, draws her closer. He is nodding, saying yes, yes, he knows it will get better in time, of course it will.

All is going as swimmingly as could possibly be expected given the nature of the event, until Ellen, catching sight of the jug of colourful sweet peas, runs towards the garden and takes a tumble on the back step. She is quickly scooped up, but she is crying now, really sobbing. 'M-u-u-m-m-ee-e-eee! I want Mu-u-u-mm-eee-ee!' A cluster of women coo and fuss around her, soothing her and offering her cocktail cherries, toys, anything to make her stop.

And now the guests are starting to leave, and they are kissing each other all over again. Mummy's best friend Briony and Auntie Audrey stay behind to clear up while Uncle Howard and Daddy walk to the bottom of the garden. Georgia can see Unc light a cigarette, then, after a moment, he holds out the packet to Daddy. He must be pretty silly because Daddy doesn't smoke. Unc can't have forgotten, but maybe Daddy has because he takes a cigarette and dips his head towards the flame.

Georgia goes to the kitchen to ask Auntie why Daddy is smoking, but she stops at the door when she hears them talking.

'. . . manage with them all, I don't know,' Auntie is saying. 'How's he going to get any work done? He'll have to get much more help.'

Daddy used to work in a proper office like everyone else's dads, but now he says he is going to work at home. He is called a designer and he does things like books and posters for exhibitions and he tells people what sort of lettering is best to have and how it's supposed to look.

'Of course it'll be tough.' Briony is slotting plates into the dishwasher. 'But I'm most worried for Georgia. She seems so grown-up, so calm. I've not even seen her cry. It can't be healthy to bottle it all up.'

Georgia slides back into the hall.

Back in the garden, Briony comes out onto the lawn and takes away the jug of butterflies to put in the kitchen.

'I must have a big hug with my favourite girl before I go,' she says. 'You be sure to come see me with your dad, OK?'

Georgia nods and buries her face in Briony's neck. 'You smell like Mummy.'

Briony blinks hard, then smiles.

'Oh—what? Yes! You're right. Your mummy gave me this perfume. It's the same as hers. You clever thing. Fancy you noticing that.' She turns away then and runs back into the house. Probably she is going to the loo, it's best to go before you get in the car or when you're on the motorway everyone gets cross and says you should have gone before you left.

When she comes out, her face is all pink and she stands by her car talking to Daddy, saying she could stay, it's no trouble—and Daddy saying no, no, he won't hear of it, it's all right, he wants to be alone. Really he does. Honestly. Auntie Audrey is looking at her watch about fifty times a minute and saying they ought to be making a move too. Unc gives her a funny look and says for God's sake, there's no rush, of course there isn't. And Daddy says, never mind now, they should go. Please go. Will they all just go now?

THREE

Queen of Communication

I NODDED AND CLASPED my hands loosely in my lap in my attentive-and-supportive-listening pose.

'Hmm-mm. And how did that make you *feel*?'

And hurry *up*, I thought, flicking my gaze to the carefully positioned clock on the side table. Three minutes and counting, I mentally intoned, like the villain's henchman in a Bond film.

'We-e-e-e-ll . . .' My client paused, as if unsure whether this might be a trick question and she might give the wrong answer. 'A bit hurt reelly. And a teenthy bit—' her voice dropped as if she were about to blaspheme in front of a priest—'croth?'

Ah-hah! Now we were getting somewhere.

'I *see*. And did you tell him how you felt?'

'We-e-e-e-ll—not reelly, I thuppothe, but . . .'

Oh, hurry up, will you? I'm meeting Ellen.

'. . . I did throw thomething at him . . .'

'*Mmm?*' One minute and thirty seconds. 'Which *was*?' I prompted.

'Theodore.'

Theodore? Who the hell was Theodore? Her son? Her ex-husband? Oh, bollocks. Bollockth. I should have checked my thodding notes.

'*Teddy*,' she added. Oh dear. Not a good sign in a woman of forty-one.

'Well, we need to come back to this next session . . .' the well-timed pause before sending the traumatised client out with all their emotions freshly unleashed, '. . . but I'm afraid we do have to end now . . .'

She gathered up her bag and jacket. 'Bye-bye.'

I nodded. 'See you next week.'

I stayed in my chair, a figure of perfect repose and calm wisdom, a bit like Buddha only with slightly less of a tummy. As soon as the door clicked behind her, I sprang to my feet, straightened the items on my desk, tucking a stray paperclip back into the correct compartment of the drawer-divider, aligning the notepad so it was square to the edge. Then I pulled open the door a crack and peered out. Coast was clear. Locked up, then tiptoed along the corridor. That's the trouble with a block like this—if you're not careful, the neighbours buttonhole you at every opportunity wanting to chat and tell you about their knee operations or ask you in for cups of tea.

Thirty-two seconds later, I unlocked the front door of my flat on the floor above. Ah, home. An identical studio flat to the one I use as a consulting room on the fourth floor. Or rather, the layout's the same—a studio room that includes the world's smallest kitchen. But, whereas downstairs all I need is a kettle and a sink, and the rest of the room holds only a sofa bed, my armchair and a desk, my living accommodation has to be bedroom, sitting room and kitchen all rolled into one.

I had the bed specially designed for the room and it folds up each morning into a discreet cupboard. Aside from that, I've kept the furniture to a minimum—a boxy sofa like the one downstairs, a rectangular beech table and six pale chairs. Roman blinds in textured fabric the colour of caffè latte, cushions covered in velvet, bouclé and mohair in soft smoky greys, creams and milky chocolate colours. A beautiful parlour palm in a square ivory pot. On the whole, I manage pretty well. This I achieve partly by being naturally tidy—or 'an anally-retentive control freak' as Ellen puts it with her usual charm—partly by storing half my clothes in the hall cupboard of my consulting flat downstairs. The only major problem is the kitchen, which consists of a cupboard—literally—in which lives a sink, draining board, a worktop the size of a table mat and storage space. To one side, I've added a diminutive fridge which doubles as a plinth for a mini-cooker with two rings and a small oven. It's an ideal set-up for a student or someone with a wild party-going lifestyle who never eats in. No, really it is. It's just that I *love* to cook. I'd have people round for dinner every night if I could, but cooking for six is a struggle when you have to kneel on the floor every time you want to chop a mushroom.

I slowed my steps, trying not to be so predictably punctual—not that Ellen would know if I were punctual or not. Ellen is always late. It's a law of Nature, like gravity or the tides being governed by the moon.

And it's never only by five minutes either. If she's only twenty minutes late you feel honoured because sometimes it's forty. Needless to say, it is never her fault; it's always the traffic, the tube, the bus, she had stopped to direct a lost tourist, got talking to a mime artist in Covent Garden.

It is almost as rare for me to be late as it is for Ellen to be on time. Sometimes, I deliberately try to be a little late—to prove to myself that I'm not some obsessively punctual, uptight control freak. But, for some reason, the ticket machines will be working and I'll reach the platform just as a train's pulling in and for once there won't be a points failure or a signalling fault or a body on the line and I'm the first one there. Again.

So yet again guess who arrived at our café first? It had become 'our' café, mine and Ellen's, although it was my discovery, and barely a day goes by when I don't pop in to read or make notes over a cup of tea away from the all-too-close confines of home.

I was deep in my book by the time Ellen finally put in an appearance, her first word, as it so often was, not 'hello' but 'sorry'.

'Sorry, sorry, sorry!' She kissed me and gave me a hug. 'I had to run half the way here—the tube—'

'Yeah, yeah. I know. You had to listen to the driver tell you all about his prostate problem before the train would move off . . . Never mind, you're here now.' She was wearing an orange tie-dye T-shirt and red velvet hipster trousers, a combination that only she could possibly carry off. Ellen's one of those people who can throw on a disgusting pair of jeans tugged from the bottom of her laundry basket and some manky old top that you wouldn't pay 20p for in a charity shop and she'll look gorgeous and stylish but in a blasé, couldn't-care-less kind of way.

The waitress came over, deposited my tea on the table, and kissed Ellen on both cheeks.

'*Ciao*, Elena!'

'*Ciao*, Paola!'

'Caffè latte? Almond croissant?'

'*Sì*, Paola. *Grazie*.' Ellen sank into her chair and started divesting herself of her usual array of baggage: hat, Filofax, magazine, two bags, mobile phone, sunglasses, cigarettes . . .

'I don't get it. You go somewhere all of three times and already the waitress knows what you want and treats you like her long-lost sister.'

'Oh, George. It's only because I got into a chat with her about her little boy and the problems he's been having at school.'

'How do you get into these conversations?'

'You do it too.'

'I don't.'

'You *do*—only you're clever enough to have made it into a career.'

'It's *so* not the same thing.'

Ellen tucked her hair behind her ears and sipped at her latte.

'Touchy toots. Why isn't it? You're good at listening, finding out what makes people tick.' She lit a cigarette. 'And don't sigh at me, George. I need a fag after the journey I've had.'

'You said you were giving up.'

'I *am*.' She took an exaggeratedly long drag. 'But probably not today.'

I waved away the smoke and she gave me a look, the two of us slotting into our regular performance we have acted out a thousand times before, the way sisters do.

'Anyway . . .' I stirred my tea to make a questioning pause, 'so who are you in love with this week?'

'Bitch.' Ellen pretended to be aggrieved.

'Trollop.'

'That's so unfair!' But she laughed, scattering almonds from her croissant as she waved it around. 'Promise not to do your teacher-face? He's called José. He's one hundred per cent drop-dead gorgeous and—'

'Never mind his blazing brown eyes and cute bum—what's he *like*?'

'Well, he writes poetry . . .'

'Oh. *Poetry*. So he's got a steady job then? I *am* glad. I thought for one second you might have gone for someone who had less career sense than a battery chicken.'

'Oh, shut up. He's got a real job, too.'

'No—let me guess. He's a corporate lawyer? A TV producer?'

'Ha-ha. No, he's not some dull suit type . . .'

The words '*like Stephen*' hovered, unspoken, in the air between us.

'. . . He's a motorbike courier actually, but it's only temporary.'

I slid my teacup to one side and laid my head on the table.

'Call me when it's all over, will you?'

Ellen is clearly making some sort of world-record attempt in the 'Longest Succession of Unsuitable Boyfriends for One Woman' challenge. Mostly, they fall into one of two distinct categories: the earnest, intellectual ones who wear fleeces and talk about fractals, and the dumb, gorgeous ones who barely know what a fleece is, never mind a fractal, but they stroke bits of Ellen's anatomy in public and as long as they're good in bed she doesn't care that they don't attempt to make conversation. Neither type tend to be especially well endowed in the job department. Ellen claims she just doesn't fancy 'career types', insisting that they are boring, arrogant workaholics who 'don't have a real life'.

'Not everyone is lucky enough to have Mr Perfect, you know.' Ellen exhaled sharply. 'Anyway, how is Stephen-with-a-p-h?'

'Oh, behave.' When I first met Stephen, he tended to introduce himself as 'Stephen—with a "p-h" ', as if the other person was about to write his name down. Ellen witnessed this a couple of times and now calls him Stephen-with-a-p-h or Mr P-h or even *the* P-h—often right to his face. Stephen, being Stephen, is never quite sure whether Ellen means it as an affectionate joke or whether she's just taking the piss.

'He's fine. We were thinking of looking at this hotel near Oxford next weekend.' I shrugged. Going to Look at Prospective Wedding Venues is an activity we revive from time to time; I love it really, it's just I get depressed because they're never *exactly* what I had in mind.

'Ah, the blushing bride-to-be, all aflutter with nerves and excitement as the Big Day draws near . . . only another three and a half years to go.'

'Oh, fuck off.'

'Why don't you break it off, George? If you really wanted to marry him, you wouldn't keep pissing about looking for the perfect venue and the perfect car and the perfect dress, would you? You could wear tartan pyjamas and hitch a ride on a rubbish lorry and it'd still be perfect.'

'I'm *so* glad I didn't ask you to organise the wedding. You know I *am* going to marry Stephen. At some point. I just want everything to be exactly right, that's all. Why do I have to be in such a rush?'

'Er—because you're thirty-four and your eggs will soon be wanting little walking frames?'

'Thank you for that, sister dear. I told you. I'm not having children.'

'Yes, I *know* you say you don't want sproglets because you might die and leave them motherless . . .'

'Like us, yes. That seems perfectly reasonable.'

Ellen rolled her eyes. 'And what does the love of your life think?'

I sighed. 'We don't discuss it all that much . . .'

'But you have told him, right?'

'I'm pretty sure he knows how I feel, yes.'

'Eh, hello? Queen of Communication?—i.e. you haven't told him?'

'Well . . . I've made it crystal clear in my own way.'

'You're being mean. If you really loved the P-h, you'd tell him that little peeps are off the agenda and give him the chance to find someone else if he wanted to.'

'He knows. I told you.'

Ellen licked her finger and dabbed at the scattered flaked almonds on and around her plate, not saying a word.

'He *does*.'

FOUR
The Abrams Sunday Brunch

EVERY SUNDAY, WHOEVER'S AROUND heads home to gather for brunch, which is something of a mixed blessing. On the plus side, there's seeing Dad and Quinn and Ellen and Matt and Izzy and the kids. And, on the minus side, there's seeing Dad and Quinn and Ellen and Matt and Izzy and the kids. I love the moment of anticipation when the doorbell rings and you don't know who it might be: Unc, with or without Audrey and the cousins in tow, or a neighbour or one of Quinn's friends or an entirely new face; but then comes the moment after that moment, when you see who it actually is. And if it's Unc, well then that's sort of nice because I love Unc to bits but, on the other hand, he does insist on asking me every single time when Stephen and I are going to name the day. Or if it's one of Quinn's floaty friends, then you find your shoulders sinking because they're barely in the door before they're requesting soya milk for their coffee and wittering on about their auras or their chakras.

Years ago, when my parents were first married, Mum used to cook Sunday lunch, with a roast and crispy potatoes and carrots and cabbage and gravy. But when I was five or so, Dad went to New York to see his sister Rachel and when he came back he was singing the praises of *brunch*. Once he explained that, with brunch, a) everyone helped themselves and b) you didn't need to make lunch as well, my mother became an instant convert.

Over the years, we've tinkered with the details, but the fundamentals of the original winning formula have remained unchanged. Any time from 10.00am onwards—well, up until one-ish—you can turn up, eat, talk, squabble or just read the Sunday papers. You can bring anyone you like, an old friend or even someone you've only just met, so long as you phone before Dad has left to fetch the bagels. Everything is set out on platters on the big kitchen table and there's tea and coffee and orange juice and a massive bowl of fruit.

So the point of Sunday brunch is that it's supposed to be a family thing—but that it's always better if you have at least one non-family person there. Having a non-Abrams, Mum said, stopped squabbles getting out of hand because you had to behave in front of other people.

The alleged 'proper' grown-up in my family is my dad, David, who's sixty-two. He's quite wise, I think, but no one, least of all Dad, would call him a Real Grown-Up. He still lives in the same house he bought with Mum over thirty-five years ago, only now he lives in it with Quinn, my stepmother, who shares his deep, abiding love of never throwing anything away. Dad believes that it's simply not possible to be a truly creative person if you have a tidy desk. But he is brilliant; my dad has a way of looking at the world that's completely original—just when you feel you know exactly what you think about something, then he'll say something that makes you question it all over again.

Quinn answered the door. Quinn isn't her real name, but I presume you worked that out already because it's ridiculous. Her real name is Margaret, which she hates, and most of the people in her life have called her Maggie, which she hates too. Then she met Dad about ten years ago, no, it was twelve, because someone brought her along to his surprise fiftieth birthday party and introduced her, saying 'This is Maggie Quinn,' and what with the music and everyone talking and my dad being a bit deaf, he only heard the Quinn bit, so he called her that and then they did awful, embarrassing, jiving round the sitting room and the next thing we knew they were snogging in the kitchen and generally making us all want to vomit.

Quinn's not so bad, aside from her name and the fact that her hair is about fifteen shades too red for a woman of fifty-three and her cooking . . . and her clothes. Don't get me started on the clothes.

'Georgia! How nice.' She leaned forward to kiss me on both cheeks and I turned my face so as not to be impaled on her lightning-bolt earrings. The outsize earrings are quite at odds with her clothes, which have that faded, comfy, worn-and-washed-a-thousand-times look. They're all slightly shapeless: skirts with no proper waistbands, jackets with no lapels, flat shoes that look like larger versions of the sort that children have so that their toes won't be squashed. This morning, she was wearing a green crushed velvet skirt—not a skirt made of crushed velvet but a velvet skirt that had obviously been scrunched up in the bottom of the wardrobe—a sludgy-green T-shirt that had seen better days and, inevitably, her famous patchwork jacket. Quinn calls it her 'Joseph's coat' and claims that 'it goes with everything' because it contains so many colours whereas, in fact, it goes with absolutely nothing except possibly the contents of a skip.

'Is Stephen coming today?' Quinn really likes Stephen, a fact which makes me feel slightly beholden to her because she's the only one of our lot who is actively nice to him.

'Yes, he is for once. Later though.' I came into the hallway.

My father was sitting on the stairs, peering at the spines of the books next to him. Bookshelves line the stairs all the way up—a sensible use of space in theory but in practice means my father spends endless hours trundling up and down the stairs, shouting to anyone who happens to be within earshot, 'Have you seen that Kowalski book? Paperback, brown jacket, white lettering.' He can never remember the title of anything, but he always recalls what a book looks like. My family mock me because my books are arranged in a logical way—fiction separated from non-fiction, non-fiction divided by subject, fiction ordered alphabetically by author name. That way you can find the book you want in less than a minute. But Dad *likes* having everything mixed in together, he *likes* to be sidetracked. That's why you find him sitting on the stairs reading a dictionary or completely absorbed in one of our cherished childhood Tintin books. In fact, if by chance you catch sight of him and he's not clutching some form of reading matter, he doesn't look quite like himself, slightly unfamiliar.

'Hi, Dad. Have you done the bagel run yet?' I bent to kiss him. Needless to say, as it's Dad who fetches the bagels, it does not involve any kind of a 'run'. He usually drives and then he doesn't even need to put on shoes. He wears his slippers.

'Yes, I have, bossy-boots. It's all in the kitchen.'

'Good.' I squeezed by Quinn to go to the kitchen. I was bracing myself to expect the worst, but it only registered about a five on the Abrams Chaos Scale. There were the inevitable papers on the table, the worktop was crowded with last night's dirty dishes, there were bowls of soaking pulses on the window ledge and the dishwasher door was open, waiting to trip someone up, but it can be a lot, lot worse.

Underneath the mess, there's quite an attractive kitchen, with wooden worktops and a quarry-tiled floor. There's an old dresser at one end packed with a plethora of odd crockery, each piece with its own story: there on the top shelf is the rosebud plate, sole survivor of a set of six, one of our parents' wedding presents; two misshapen pottery cats with pocked glaze I made when I was eleven; four 1930s cocktail glasses that shine with rainbow colours when they catch the light—those had been Grandma's, Mum's mother; a peculiar earthenware cow Matt brought back from Morocco; and, tucked out of harm's way near the top, the three egg cups from when we were little, with our names painted on by Mum: Georgia, Matthew, Ellen. Mine has a hen painted on it, Matthew's a cockerel, and Ellen's a little yellow chick. I remember Mum painting them and me saying they were lovely, but really just feeling horribly envious; I wanted to have an egg cup with a little fluffy chick on it—especially as that was Dad's name for me—not a boring old stupid hen, but I couldn't say anything.

'Georgia, any chance you could do the scramblies?'

The only cooked element of our brunch is scrambled eggs—or 'scramblies' as they're known in our family, which sounds horribly self-conscious and cute, but it's just because that's what I called them when I was little and the name stuck. There's nothing worse than other people's family expressions, is there? I hate it when Quinn uses our family words for things, it sets my teeth on edge. Also, I always do the scramblies, the scrambled eggs, I mean, whenever I come to brunch, so why does she always ask me as if it's only just occurred to her to mention it?

'Of course. Perhaps we should clear the table first?' I said pointedly.

Dad was surrounded by his usual nest of papers. He looked up vaguely, like a tortoise waking from hibernation. 'Mm?'

'Dad! Table! *Please* can you clear your papers off the table?'

He started slowly shuffling the bits together into a pile, then looked round and balanced them right on the edge of the dresser, the only surface close enough for him not to have to get up again.

'Or they could go in your study maybe?' The study's even worse than the rest of the house. God knows how Dad manages to work in there, because it's more of a room-sized in-tray than a study.

'Do I surmise correctly that Stephen will be turning up later?'

'I'm not asking you to roll out the red carpet, am I? Just make the place look passably civilised.'

Quinn, wiping the table and swooshing the crumbs straight onto the floor, looked up for a moment, but she didn't say anything.

'Oh—*civilised*? Well, of course, that's the most important thing.' My father leaned back in his chair and laughed softly to himself.

'Don't be annoying.' I took out the eggs from the fridge and ventured into a cupboard for a large bowl.

Out of the corner of my eye I noticed Quinn piling the bagels into some awful dark brown palm-leaf basket. Quinn favours tableware made out of old bits of twig wherever possible, although they've got a perfectly good set of matching plain white china which I prefer to use.

'Or we could use one of the white platters?' I said, cracking the eggs into the bowl, and not looking at her.

'*Georgia* . . .' Dad's voice came from behind his newspaper.

'Oh,' said Quinn. 'Yes. A plate. If you like.'

I caught Dad looking at me.

'No. Sorry. The basket's fine.' I delved under the sink for a new cloth and surreptitiously shoved the old one into the bin while Quinn had her back turned, then I gave the worktop a proper wipe-down.

'I brought some flowers if you want to stick them in a vase.' I gestured to Quinn. She drew out the bunch of white lilies from their paper and buried her face in them, emerging again with a streak of orange pollen on her nose.

'Oh, how lovely! Thank you, Georgia.'

'That's OK.' I don't know why she was thanking me; they weren't for her really, just for the house.

I was dishing out the eggs when my brother Matt arrived with his wife Isobel and their kids, Bonnie and Daniel, who came running up to me and clutched me round my legs. 'Auntie Gee! Auntie Gee!'

I squatted down to hug them. Being an auntie seems to me the best of both worlds: you get to spend a small amount of time with children, children you love enormously and who seem to be quite fond of you, then after an hour or two—just when you're thinking that's enough hilarity and riot for one day—you get to give them back. Bonnie is four and destined to be a major captain of industry, I suspect. Daniel is two and his main ambition in life so far is to be Bonnie.

Isobel came and gave me a hug. 'Hi. D'you want a hand?' she said.

'No, you need a break. Sit down. Matt—pour Izzy a coffee, will you?' Matt rarely helps unless he's prodded.

'Yes, ma'am!'

Matt is two and a half years younger than me and a lot less hopeless than Ellen, but that's not saying much. He does at least have a normal job—he edits reference books and his office floor has even more piles of paper on it than Dad's does, so it must be a family trait.

At about eleven thirty Stephen appeared and, as there was no safe haven next to Quinn or Isobel, he was forced to sit next to Matt, who immediately started to quiz him.

'So, how's tricks? What's the latest news from the fascinating world of management consultancy?'

'Matt, bugger off! Stephen, just ignore him if he gets too annoying.' Matt's always winding people up about their jobs.

Stephen sat perched on the edge of his chair, as if he might make a run for it at any moment. 'Actually, you may mock but it really is rather interesting at the moment—' I saw Matt doing his pretending-to-find-it-all-fascinating face and shot him a warning look. I wish Stephen would just give as good as he gets, but he's far too nice.

Then Ellen turned up.

'Hiya, everyone!' She breezed in, then came to kiss each of us in turn. 'Have I missed the scramblies? I'm *starved.*'

'They've all gone, babes . . . but I can do you some more.'

'Oh, will you? Thanks, George. Budge up, P-h.' She squashed in next to Stephen. 'So . . . what's occurring? What's the news? Is there any coffee?' Ellen's always asking questions then not waiting for the answers because she's incredibly impatient and doesn't listen properly. 'God, I feel completely wrecked. We went on *such* a bender last night.'

'Weren't you at work?' I caught Dad's eye. Ellen normally works at the wine bar on Saturday nights.

'Nah. I swapped shifts with Tony—but I forgot to tell Brian. He went totally apeshit, left about a thousand messages on my mobile.' Brian is Ellen's boss and we all think he's in love with her, but Ellen says he's 'too old' (he's thirty-six), 'too short' (he's about five foot eight) and 'called Brian' (which he is, but I don't see why that has to disqualify him).

'Aren't you a bit *old* to be going on benders?' Matt said.

'You're just envious because you've traded in your social life for a sofa, a video and a pair of comfy slippers.'

'*You're* the one who should be envious.' Matt squeezed Isobel's hand. 'At least I'm not still pretending to be a teenager at nearly thirty.'

'I'm not even twenty-eight yet!'

Stephen was looking from one to the other of them, then over at me, as if wanting to be rescued. He never knows quite how to take our family squabbles. His family don't believe in disagreements, all that raising your voice and getting heated, so even the most minor altercation he regards as the beginnings of World War Three.

I handed Ellen a cup of coffee and she stood up.

'Just going to check on the garden.' Dad hates the fact that Ellen smokes but he doesn't stop her smoking in the house because that would go against his belief in the importance of personal freedom. Matt hasn't got time for such high-flown idealism but just insists that she's not to smoke in the same room as the children.

'Don't be long—your eggs are nearly ready.'

Matt gave me a look. 'You shouldn't run round after her the whole time. Let her cook her own eggs if she's missed them.'

'I cooked yours too. I didn't notice you begging to make your own.'

'I was here before they ran out. Crucial difference.'

I noticed Isobel squeezing his arm. 'C'mon, Matty, don't give her a hard time,' she said. 'The eggs were delicious, Georgia. Thank you.'

I smiled at Izzy. 'Thanks.'

Matt came over and kissed the top of my head. 'I didn't mean to upset you, Gee. Just—you know—Ellen's old enough to take care of herself.'

'Yeah,' I sighed. 'I know.' Then I tipped the scrambled eggs out onto a plate, laid two neat triangles of buttered toast alongside. 'Give her a shout, will you? Before it gets cold.'

It was seven o'clock the following Saturday and I was upstairs, helping Matt give the kids their bath. Ellen had volunteered to baby-sit so that Matt and Izzy could go out to dinner on his birthday, but Izzy had refused to leave the house unless there was a 'proper grown-up there too'. So Matt had asked me to go round so that Ellie's feelings wouldn't be hurt.

'You be the shark!' Bonnie bossed me. 'I'm the diver and Daniel is all eaten up.'

'I'm not eaten!' Daniel stood up in alarm. 'I'm a diver too!'

'Sit down or you'll slip.' Matt squeezed out the flannel and attempted to wash Daniel, who squirmed out of his grasp like a slithery fish.

'All divers have to have their wet suits wiped with special anti-shark deterrent before diving,' I said to Bonnie. 'Chief Diver—present yourself for inspection.' Bonnie stood to attention and I seized my chance to wash her down with a soapy flannel. 'Chief Diver—Passed and Ready!'

'Me now! Me pass and ready!' Daniel pulled at my arm. I started to wash him, then caught Matt watching me.

'What?'

He smiled. 'You're so good with them. You should have your own.'

'No. This is easy. I'd go crazy doing it full-time. Come on, Daniel—out you get! Here's your special cloak.' I lifted him out and enfolded him in a towel.

'Why? You're good-tempered and very patient. You're miles better than I am and even I manage.' He got Bonnie out and started to dry her.

I shook my head.

'It doesn't have to be with Stephen, you know.'

'It's nothing to do with him. Why do you say that?'

Matt laughed. 'Well, it should be to do with Stephen as you're engaged to him, wouldn't you say?'

'I didn't mean that—don't be annoying.' I lowered my voice. 'I meant I don't want kids of my own, full stop. Stephen isn't the issue.'

'Listen, Gee, all I'm saying is that I never thought I'd have kids either before I met Iz. If you're with the right person, suddenly it all slots into place and you start thinking, "God, I might actually be able to do this." '

'Well, Izzy's great, she'd be the right person for anyone—but I don't think it's practical for me to have kids with her too, is it?' I stood up, then scooped Daniel into my arms. 'Anyway, Stephen is exactly right for me,' I added. 'He really is.'

Stephen arrived just before eight, but Matt and Izzy had already left for the restaurant by then, of course. I was quite glad they'd gone—after my conversation with Matt, I knew he wouldn't be able to resist trying to winkle out Stephen's views on having children.

'Hello, darling. Are they in bed yet?'

'Only just. I'm about to read them a story.'

He came into the sitting room and switched on the TV.

'Just want to catch a bit of the cricket.'

'You're not tempted by the joys of *Babar* or the *The Cat in the Hat* then?'

'Who could resist? Tell you what—you make a start, sweetie, and I'll come up in a minute.'

Daniel was happily settled into his cot with a final bottle, so I went through to Bonnie's room. I asked her to pick a story but she claimed to have read them all.

'OK, let's make one up then, shall we? How shall we begin?'

'Don't know. *You* make it up.'

'Well, I'll start it off. Once upon a time, there was a clever and beautiful princess . . . and what do you suppose her name was?'

'Her name was Bonnie and then what happened was she had all magic powers and there was a bad witch and then this prince—'

The doorbell rang. I hoped Stephen would answer it but it's hard to lever him away from a cricket match once he's engrossed, so I stood up. 'Lie still now and I'll be back in two minutes. No getting up.'

Stephen was opening the door as I came down the stairs. It was Ellen.

'Well, well—it's the P-h! This is a most unexpected treat. Am I babysitting you too?' Ellen swept in, kissing Stephen on her way past.

A nervous laugh from Stephen as he said hello.

'Hi, babes.'

'Where are Matzo and Izzy? Have they gone?'

'Yes, of course. It's ten past eight.'

'God, I'm only a couple of minutes late—he said to come at eight.'

'Really?' Stephen dug his hands down into his pockets. 'I believe their dinner reservation was for eight. Georgia's been here since before seven.'

'It doesn't matter—you're here now,' I said.

Ellen thundered up the stairs to see the kids.

'Sssh, Ellen! Don't get them all hyper—please.'

Stephen rolled his eyes at me, then returned to the joys of the cricket.

I followed Ellen up. She went into Bonnie's room. 'Auntie Ell! Auntie Ell!' Bonnie leapt out of bed and started jumping up and down.

'*Ellen*. She was nearly settled.'

Ellen made a face at Bonnie, as if I were the big bad wolf. Thanks, Ellen, that's really helpful.

'Let's play dressing up,' said Bonnie, marching over to the dressing-up box and fishing out a battered crown I'd made for her from a gold cardboard cake box. 'I'm the king and—' she pointed at Ellen, 'you're the queen—'

'What about Daniel?'

'Daniel's the servant and he goes in the dungeon for being bad.'

'It's the servant's day off,' I told her. 'We're not to disturb Daniel, so this is to be a nice, quiet game.'

'And what about Auntie Georgia?' Ellen asked. 'Is she the guard?'

'Hilarious.'

'Auntie Gee,' Bonnie corrected her. She thought for a moment. 'Auntie Gee's the queen.'

'But you said *I* could be Queen.' Ellen sounded aggrieved, as if she really were playing the game with the same seriousness as Bonnie.

'No.' Bonnie pointed at Ellen again, as if ordering a courtier. 'You're the little princess.'

'Five minutes and no more,' I said. 'You start—I'm just checking on Daniel.' I shut the door and went through to Daniel's room.

Daniel was deeply asleep, his arms flung back in total abandonment, his bottle lying beside him. I pulled up his cotton blanket then kissed my fingertips and gently touched his forehead.

I stood there, watching him for a minute, seeing the slight rise and fall of the blanket as he breathed, then I went back into Bonnie's room. She was already drooping with tiredness.

'Hail, Majesty—it is dark and we must retire to our bedchambers.'

'But I was about to get my coronet,' Ellen said.

'The coronation has been adjourned until tomorrow,' I said firmly, bending down to pick up Bonnie. She reached her arms up round me. I squeezed her tight then tucked her under the covers.

'Night, night, King—sleep tight.'

'Ni-nigh.' Her voice was sleepy.

I motioned to Ellen with my head to go, then stayed to stroke Bonnie's hair for a few moments, until she was asleep. I love her when she's awake but she does zap your energy in no time. Now, when she was like this, her eyelids fluttering as she drifted into sleep, I felt almost overwhelmed with love for her.

Sometimes, when Georgia comes home from school, she gets herself a glass of lemonade with a slice of lemon and ice cubes going clink, just like a grown-up drink. Matt still prefers milk, like a baby, like Ellen. Georgia spreads two slices of bread with butter and thick honey, then folds each one over to make a sandwich. Passes one to Matt with instructions not to drip honey everywhere.

Then Matt plays with his Bat Cave, a papier-mâché one which Mummy made before Ellen was born. If Mummy is not having a little lie-down before supper, she plays with Georgia for a while: they raid the dressing-up box or her own wardrobe, for Joy doesn't mind a jot about Georgia trying on her things; Georgia goes clack-clacking along the tiled hall floor in strappy gold sandals or black suede high heels, an antique fringed shawl cascading over her small frame. They are princesses in the palace, sporting cardboard crowns and ordering people's heads to be chopped off. Or they shed their shoes and dance barefoot round the kitchen table and into the sitting room, leaping from the sofa in grands jetés, *pointing their toes, prima ballerinas at Covent Garden, pirouetting from one side of the stage to the other then falling, dizzy and delirious with giggles, onto the rug. They lie there, letting their limbs be used as ramps for Matt and his collection of vehicles.* 'Ner-ner, ner-ner, ner-ner,' *he imitates a siren,* 'here's the fire engine.' *Georgia and Joy, softened by play and dancing, humour him. 'Help! Help!' Joy calls. 'Fire! Fire!'*

Ellen sits on the rug, watching the circus in full swing around her, and laughs and claps her hands.

As we were halfway through our Chinese takeaway, my bribe to Stephen for spending Saturday night baby-sitting, we heard crying coming from upstairs.

'Probably stop in a minute,' said Stephen.

'Izzy always says it's best to leave them sometimes,' said Ellen.

'I'll just have a quick look,' I said.

It was Daniel. And it was my fault. I hadn't secured his nappy tightly enough when I dressed him and he'd leaked onto the sheet so he was all wet and cross and uncomfortable. I lifted him out and carried him through to the bathroom.

Stephen popped his head round the door. 'All right, darling?'

'Me? I'm fine. Daniel's a bit wet, that's all.'

'Oh. Right.' He shifted from foot to foot. 'Erm, do you want a hand?'

I bundled up the soggy nappy. 'Actually, I need to change his bottom sheet—can you have a look in that chest there?'

Stephen tentatively opened the top drawer.

'Oh. It's got—women's things in it.' He recoiled as if he'd discovered the contents crawling with maggots.

'Stephen, come on—you've seen tampons before. They won't bite you.'

He looked in the other drawers and eventually extracted a white cotton sheet, while I finished Daniel's nappy.

'There we go, all clean and dry again.' I handed Daniel to Stephen. 'Here. Hold him a sec, will you? I'll remake the cot.'

Stephen held Daniel slightly away from him, as if Daniel might possibly explode or, worse, expel noxious fluids.

'Er, hello, baby. Baby Daniel. Er. *Hush-a-bye, baby*. Um, how's it go? On the tree top? *La-la-la-lah!* The cradle will rock?'

I took Daniel back again.

'Here we go, little one. Nighty-night. Sleep tight.' I kissed him and tucked him under the blanket once more.

'You're good at this baby stuff, aren't you? Where did you learn it?'

'I didn't learn it. You just do it.'

Stephen put his arm round me as we stood by the cot. 'I suppose I'll pick it up.' He turned to kiss me. 'You can teach me.'

FIVE

Mr P-h

STEPHEN AND I have been together for three and a half years, and engaged for two and a half years. In fact, we became engaged on the first anniversary of our very first date—'so we'll only have one date to remember,' Stephen said. He was joking, of course, but actually it is kind of handy.

The night we became engaged, we'd gone out to dinner, to what had quickly become 'our' restaurant, an old-fashioned Italian place five minutes' walk from his flat.

'Is everything OK? You seem a little on edge,' I remember pointing out, as Stephen tweaked at his cuffs yet again.

'I'm fine,' he said, stretching across the gingham tablecloth to squeeze my hand. 'Shall I order a bottle of bubbly?'

'Why? Oh! You got that big client?'

He gave me a considered half-smile, a cautious nod. 'It's not one hundred per cent as yet. But I think it's in the bag.'

'Wonderful! And well deserved. I know how hard you've worked.'

'Thank you. Shall we have that champagne?'

'I hate to be a wet blanket, but I really can't drink all that much . . .'

'A half-bottle then? It is our anniversary after all.'

'Lovely.'

After dinner, we'd walked back to his flat and I made us some coffee, and I went and sat by him on the sofa. He was looking at me and smiling in a very un-Stephenish way.

'What?'

'Well.' He took my hands in his. 'We've been together a year now.'

I smiled.

'And I think it's time to move on to the next square . . .'

At the time I had thought he meant he was going to dump me. And I thought everything had been going so well.

'Oh.'

'Hang on—no point doing these things if one doesn't do them properly, eh?' He slid off the sofa and balanced on one knee, wobbling slightly. 'Georgia, you know how I feel about you. I think it's time I asked you to marry me.'

I was so relieved that I wasn't being dumped that I gave him the most enormous smile. 'Oh, Stephen! I can't believe it! Are you sure?'

'Of course I'm sure.'

Then he took out this little box from his pocket and opened it at me. It was a diamond solitaire.

Call me a horrible person, but my first thought was, 'Eek—I never wear gold.' I mean, I know engagement rings are almost always gold, but what if you prefer silver? Anyway, I took out the ring and put it on my finger. It went on easily. Too easily.

'Does it fit? It's too big, isn't it?' Stephen slid the ring up and down my finger. 'Oh, sweetheart, I'm sorry.' He patted my arm.

'Don't be silly. It's not your fault. Still, I'd hate to lose it . . .' I tucked it snugly back into its box.

The following weekend, Stephen took me back to the jewellers.

'I wonder if we could change this ring?' Stephen unfolded the receipt from his wallet.

'Different size or different style?' The assistant looked at me with one of those unpleasant smug faces, like he felt he knew what you were going to say before you said it.

'Well, we could look at some others maybe . . .'

'I thought you *liked* it,' Stephen said.

'I *do*. Of course I do. I just thought, you know, now that we're here anyway . . .' my voice tailed off.

The assistant gestured to a display case. 'Aside from our extensive range in the window, these are the diamond solitaires,' he pronounced.

'Do you have anything in silver?'

'Silver?' He said it as if the word was 'Shit?' He gave Stephen one of those 'Women! What are they like?' expressions and said, 'Silver is rarely used for those truly special items, betrothal rings and suchlike, because it's so *common*, you see.'

'Oh.'

'We do carry a limited selection of white gold pieces, of course. And platinum in our "Once in a Lifetime" range, though obviously they aren't in the same price range . . .' This last remark directed at Stephen.

'That's no problem—' Stephen began.

'May I see the white gold ones then?' Stephen's sweet, but the rings were a ridiculous amount of money as it was.

The assistant unlocked a case and brought out a tray. They were pretty enough, but there was something soulless about them, like they'd been churned out on an assembly line, given a final polish, then—plonk, now they were going to end up on someone's finger. Mine.

'You haven't got anything a bit more . . .'

'Look at the platinum ones if you like, sweetie.'

'No, I mean, have you something more, sort of, battered? Er, old, I mean.' Another smirk from the assistant.

'We do have a small selection of antique rings, miss.' He locked the first tray away, then went to the back and returned with another.

'But, don't you mind having a secondhand ring?' Stephen rubbed the back of my hand.

'No. Quite the opposite. An old one has a history, like an heirloom.'

I wished I hadn't said that, because it set me off thinking of Mum's wedding ring, which Dad had kept for me. Dad hoards absolutely everything, as you know. He never has a clue where anything is—except for the ring. Every now and then he gets it out for me to try on and then he tells me all about the day they got married and about how I would have the ring whenever I marry because I'm the eldest and Mum always said I should have it. It's a plain gold band, and it's inscribed on the inside 'Jumping for Joy' with the date of their wedding. I bit my lip, told myself *I* should be jumping for joy at being engaged, not being morbid and thinking about Mum. Then I started thinking about how one day I'd get married and Mum wouldn't be there to cry or kiss me or do her awful, embarrassing dancing at the reception.

I fumbled in the tray and picked out one with tiny pearls and diamonds in it. 'Silver?' I asked, already knowing the answer.

The assistant nodded..

It was much cheaper than the other one and they weren't exactly falling over themselves to refund the difference, so we bought Stephen a new watch, and I felt much better then because it seemed a bit fairer somehow even though it was still his money.

After that, we went for coffee and I kissed Stephen and thanked him.

'I want you to have whatever you want,' he said.

'Thank you for being so nice about it.'

Still, it's moments like that that make you sad when you should be being happy. On key occasions, like when I graduated from college, I wished so strongly that Mum could be there—even if only for a minute, just so I could hug her and hear her tell me how proud she was.

Stephen is sympathetic about all this stuff because he's a nice person, but he doesn't really *know*. It's like being a virgin and trying to imagine what sex is like—you sort of understand the mechanics of it, but you can't know deep down until it's happened to you, can you?

'**O**h, yeah. Cooling. Mr and Mrs Cooling. You're in 206. Harry—take these bags up to 206.' The youthful hotel clerk called this last bit over my shoulder to another boy in a too-large uniform.

'*Mr* Cooling and *Miss* Abrams,' I pointed out, icily. 'We've arranged to look at your banqueting rooms for our *wedding*—it *should* say.' I peered over the ridiculously high counter to see if he had any notes. 'So, not Mr and Mrs Cooling—*yet*.'

'Wooden hangers, not wire,' Stephen pronounced approvingly once we were installed in our room. 'And a decanter of sherry.'

'Bottles, not sachets,' I added, checking out the shampoo and bath foam. 'And cotton wool in a little china dish.'

He lay down on the bed and plumped up a couple of the numerous rose-spattered cushions behind him. 'Bed's not bad,' he said, and patted the space on the mattress beside him. 'Care to join me, Miss Abrams?'

I lay down next to him and he shifted onto his side and kissed me.

'Don't suppose you fancy a little . . . predinner . . . appetiser?'

I smiled and put my arms round him.

'Aren't they expecting us downstairs to show us the Gainsborough Suite?' Why do these places always have these stupid names? I bet they don't have an actual Gainsborough painting gracing the wall.

He sighed and looked at his watch.

'OK . . . Now, darling, promise me you'll give this one a fair chance. We can't keep ruling places out because the wallpaper's not a hundred per cent to your satisfaction.' He smiled at me.

I nodded. 'I promise not be too picky.'

'That's my girl.' He swung his legs round and stood up. 'Ready?'

We looked at the rooms and murmured appreciative noises, then the child-manager person asked us about our proposed dates.

'Late spring maybe?' Stephen said.

'Perhaps we should check our diaries and get back to you,' I said.

'Well, if you like, but we're getting well booked up for next year,' the youth said. 'You don't wanna leave it too late.' When he'd gone, we walked out to the garden. 'This is really very nice,' Stephen said. 'And it's a good location, isn't it? Not too far for people to get to.'

'Yes. It really is pretty. Shame we can't do it here.'

'What? Georgia, why ever not? If it's about the cost—'

I shook my head. 'Well, aside from the reception staff who are all clearly incompetent and barely out of school, the room's too small.'

'But he said it holds up to seventy.'

'Exactly. Darling—work it out—that's only thirty-five guests each—and by the time I count in my family, including the American contingent and everyone's children and my friends . . .'

'OK.' Stephen sighed heavily. 'Well. *I* don't need thirty-five—if I only ask, say twenty-five, you can have forty-five. Is that enough?'

'You're so unselfish. Still . . . I'm not sure. We'll have to work it out.'

Stephen wanted us to draw up a list before dinner, so we could book a date while we were still at the hotel, but I was longing for a lovely deep bath. I was lying back in the bubbles, letting thoughts waft through my mind, picturing myself in the perfect dress, trying out different fabrics—heavy satin or sheer chiffon, silk dupion or layered organza. I was just adding Stephen into the picture, when he tapped lightly on the door and came in. 'Fancy some company?'

'Sure.'

He handed me a small glass of sherry. 'Nice bath?'

'Gorgeous.'

He undid his cuff and rolled up his shirtsleeve, dangled his hand in the water, brushing along the side of my arm. 'Shall I do your back?'

'Would you? Thank you.'

I sat up and leaned forward while he slowly soaped my back, then rinsed it down with a thick white flannel. 'Mmm-mm.'

'You like that?'

'Mmmm. Lovely.'

He leaned in closer and I turned towards him. He kissed me softly then pulled away slightly, a question in his gaze. He held out a towel for me and I stepped onto the bathmat. 'Shall I dry you?'

'Uh-huh. Do we have enough time before dinner? We don't want to have to rush.'

He checked his watch. 'Nearly an hour.'

'Fine. You go through. I won't be a minute.'

When I went through to the bedroom, he was already undressed and under the covers. He drew back the sheet for me to climb in.

We lay side by side, then we started kissing. The good thing about having been with Stephen all this time is that we're completely familiar with each other's bodies and preferences. There's none of that awkwardness you get at the beginning of a relationship when you're having to find out what he likes and doesn't like, all that stuff.

Having devoted a couple of minutes to my breasts, he slid his hand down between my legs. After a couple of minutes more, he said, 'Shall I get something?'

OK, I admit it, that's the one thing that drives me crazy about Stephen. He always pauses when I'm just beginning to get excited and says exactly the same thing: 'Shall I get something?' And it's usually several minutes before I'm ready. I don't know—am I especially slow to warm up? Anyway, why doesn't he just get a condom or say what he means, 'Shall I put on a condom now?' Sometimes I say, 'Can't we carry on just touching each other for a bit longer?' but then, after a while, he looks kind of impatient, so you think, 'Oh go on, might as well, even if I'm not quite ready.'

Anyway, given that we didn't have loads of time because I'd still need to dress and do my face, I thought we'd better cut to the chase. He rolled on the condom, then slowly eased into me with a sigh of relief.

His eyes were closed, as usual. Do other men do this? It's so long since I've slept with anyone else that I can't really remember. It's not as if I think he's fantasising about doing it with someone else—it's only that sometimes I'd like him to look into my eyes, to linger on my face, just enjoying the fact that he's with *me*, making love to *me*, rather than concentrating so intently on the actual act.

'Darling?' I said.

'Hmm?' He opened his eyes. 'What? Is this OK? Am I going too fast?'

'No. It's fine. Just—hello—that's all.'

He smiled. 'Hello, beautiful.' Then his eyes closed again.

Do you ever have that thing when, suddenly, you just *know* you're not going to come no matter what? Well, I had that feeling.

I want to make it clear that I have never, ever faked an orgasm, but I do occasionally slightly *emphasise* my enjoyment a tiny bit more than is actually the case. Don't get me wrong—if we've got plenty of time and I'm in the mood, I usually come. But don't you ever have times when you really can't be bothered? So you lie there, saying 'Mmm, mmm' in an encouraging sort of way, thinking, If he comes in the next minute or so, I won't miss the start of the late-night film.

It was a shame because, when you're spending all that money on a nice hotel room, you feel as if you deserve a seriously decent orgasm—to sort of *go* with the room. Anyway, so I didn't fake it, not at all, but I did make one or two extra mmm-mmm noises that were somewhat surplus to requirements. After a minute or two more he came, in any case, then he carefully pulled out and lay back next to me.

'That was wonderful.' He tilted his head to kiss me. 'I love you.'

'I love you too.'

'Was it nice for you?'

'Yes. It was lovely.'

When Stephen says, 'Was it nice for you?' what he really means is, 'Did you come?' which he can't bring himself to say for some reason. But it's not as if I was really lying to him—after all, it *was* perfectly nice. And I don't mean it sneeringly at all—it was lovely being held and kissed and I was pleased that it was so good for him, I really was, I hardly minded about not coming myself, and besides, we still had a delicious dinner to look forward to, so, all in all, I felt almost perfectly content.

SIX

An end to life as we know it . . .

'. . . AND THEN I WAS BEING chased by a courgette . . .'

One of my new clients is prone to having peculiar dreams, which she likes to recount in some detail.

I imagined a giant courgette bouncing along the road—or perhaps it had legs?

'I think maybe it symbolised my mother.'

'Uh-um . . . and why do you think that?'

'Well, she was always making us eat ratatouille when I was a child . . .'

Why wasn't it accompanied by its old buddies Messrs Aubergine,

Tomato & Capsicum, I was tempted to ask. A rampant courgette seemed to me to indicate classic sexual anxiety.

'Had you considered—' I began.

There was a sudden, violent crash against the outer door and both Dream Woman and I let out a simultaneous cry. For one moment, I imagined it might be the courgette on the rampage.

'I'm sure it's nothing' I reassured her, 'but if you'll excuse me for a second I think I'd better just check.' I smiled with considerably more confidence than I felt, opened first the inner door, then the outer one.

'Holy fuck!' A man was sprawled on the floor in the hallway, surrounded by enormous bags and metal cases.

'Sssh!' I said automatically, thinking of my client, then more softly, 'Are you all right?'

'Yes, I'm fine. I always like to lie down in the corridor with half a ton of equipment on top of me. God, that hurt!' He rubbed his left knee.

I pulled the door to behind me, noticing a dent and a deep, long gouge in the wood. 'Have you broken anything?'

He leaned up on one arm and looked around him.

'I can't tell yet—I'll have to unpack and check it all.'

'No, I meant *you*. Bones, I mean.'

He sat up a bit more. 'I guess I'll live.' Suddenly, he smiled, a crazy, warm smile, displaying a chipped front tooth. 'Hello, by the way.'

'Right. Yes. Hello. Sorry—I really can't help you now. I've got someone here. Sorry. But I must—' I started to open the door, catching sight of the damage again. 'Um, perhaps you could just leave your details with the porter?' I gestured at the scarred door, thinking he'll probably do a runner and I'll have to get it off the insurance.

'Oh God—I'm so sorry. Let me—' He started to struggle to his feet.

'No, really. *Not now*. Leave your address. It's fine.'

I closed both doors behind me and nodded at Dream Woman.

'Nothing serious,' I said authoritatively. I sat down again. 'I do think there might be a sexual element to your dream.'

'No, I don't think so. I'm not all that keen on sex, to be honest, so I don't think it could be sexual, could it?'

Later on that day I was in another session when there was a knocking at my door. When I moved in, I had the doorbell removed to minimise unexpected interruptions. You can't have people interrupting every three minutes when a client is sitting there sobbing her eyes out, can you? At first, neighbours knocked on my door, but I ignored it, then I put up a discreet notice where the bell had been: 'Please knock only if you have an appointment; for any other purpose, please contact Flat 511.' Still, people can be quite slow to take the hint. Sometimes, one of the neighbours waylays me in the lobby or the corridor and it's hard to get away. Mrs Patterson is the worst. She's very sweet but very lonely. She must have some high-tech sensor laser beam by her front door, because a mouse couldn't tiptoe across the corridor carpet without her opening a crack to see who it is.

Anyway, there was a knock at my door, and not the tentative tap-tapping of an elderly neighbour, but a more assertive kind of a knock.

'Just ignore it,' I told my client. 'Please, do go on.'

He glanced nervously at the door.

'. . . erm, OK, so then she said, "Well, *I* didn't come—were you in a rush or something?" and I wasn't sure if she was expecting me to—'

Another knock, louder this time.

'I'm terribly sorry—please excuse me a moment while I just check the building's not on fire or anything.' I smiled brightly.

I pulled the inner door closed behind me and opened the outer one.

'Yes?' It was that man who'd taken a gouge out of my door.

'Ah, hello—you *are* there. Look—I just wanted to say—'

'Hang on a second.' I raised my hand, like Canute trying to hold back the waves. 'Let me put you on pause for one moment. I have a *client* here. We *cannot* be interrupted. It may have escaped your notice but many people actually work for a living and cannot spend hours idly gossiping at the front door. You've already interrupted my work once today and, bizarrely, you seem to feel the need to do it again.'

He flushed. 'I was only trying—'

'I'm sure you were, but if it's about my door, please speak to the porter or leave your card there for me . . . if you have one. Georgia Abrams, Flat 411, as you can see.' I gestured to the number and the sign saying only to knock if you have an actual appointment.

'All right, Miss Abrams,' he said tightly. 'But it wouldn't take—'

'*Ms*. Sorry—was there some part of that sentence you didn't understand? Do I need a DO NOT DISTURB sign swinging from my doorknob?'

'Sorry, Ms Abrams, there's no need to be so snotty. I was only trying to apologise, but forget it. For God's sake, who rattled your cage?'

I closed the door. Well, I half slammed it. I stood in my tiny hall for a moment, trying to regain my composure. I'd have to give my client another few minutes at the end of the session, it wasn't his fault.

'I'm *so* sorry for the interruption.' I sat and nodded for him to continue, thinking about the interruption. Could you believe the gall of that man? Some people just have no idea how to behave, do they?

'Hey, Georgy, love!' Barry, one of the porters, called out to me as I strode across the lobby. I've given up trying to explain to him that it's Georgia not Georgy, but I do hate to be called 'love'. I've told him before.

He was waving an envelope at me.

'It's from that new bloke, the photographer what just moved in. Said he took a tumble with some gear against your door.'

'Yes, he did.' Well, at least he hadn't disappeared without trace.

'I could come and take a look if you like, love. P'raps I can fix it?'

'Thanks. But I don't think so—there's a deep gouge out of the wood.' The idea of Barry seeing to anything more challenging than a defunct light bulb is ridiculous. 'No, really, Barry. Thank you, but I can manage. Really. And, er . . . I don't mean to be rude but do you mind not calling me "love"? Georgia is fine—but not love. OK?'

He looked down at the desk.

'Oh. Sorry, love. Oh—sorry. I mean . . . yeah, sorry.' His voice dropped to a mumble. 'Didn't mean to cause offence like.'

'No, of course not. Good.' Looked at my watch. 'Well, I must dash.'

I ran down the front steps, started opening the envelope, thinking about my door. It was most annoying, and it looked so bad—as if one of my clients had gone bonkers and tried to attack me.

The note just plunged straight in, no hello or Dear Ms Abrams or anything:

Sorry, but somewhat baffled that my attempts to apologise for accidentally scraping your door have proved so offensive to you, for some reason. Had no idea that you were in the middle of defusing a nuclear bomb or otherwise caught up in some matter of global importance. Perhaps, if it won't interrupt your pressing schedule too much, you could find out whether the damage to the door is covered by your buildings insurance. If not, I will, of course, be happy—no, ecstatic, over the moon, delirious with delight—to pay for it and, as you're too busy to speak to anyone for three seconds, I will also arrange for the work to be done. Let me know.
Leo Kane

It was a compliments slip, with *Leo Kane, Photographer* at the top and an address in Glasgow, which had been scored through and Flat 418, Weedon Court written in. Oh, marvellous, the rudest man on the planet has just moved in onto my floor.

I read the note again. No phone number. Well, I would have to drop a note back through his letterbox, I suppose.

Stephen was already waiting at the bar when I arrived at Vats 'n' Vintages, a wine bar halfway between his office and my flat.

'Hi, sweetie! Good day?' He bent to kiss me.

'No, actually. Fucking awful.' Stephen raised his brows—he's kind of old-fashioned about women swearing. 'It's been one thing after another and then some stupid prat busted my office door.'

'No! Not a burglar? While you were there?'

'No, no, just some idiot. It was an accident.' I felt silly for being so melodramatic about it now. Stephen tends to take everything you say a bit literally. 'Never mind anyway, I'll get it fixed. Tell me about *your* day.'

'First-rate.' He turned to the barman to order. 'Sparkling mineral water with a twist of lime, and a glass of the Beaujolais.'

'Actually, hang on a sec—' I said, 'I think I'll have a glass of wine too.'

Stephen looked surprised. 'Sorry, darling, I just assumed.' Normally, I only have wine when we're out for dinner.

'It's fine.'

'Two glasses of the Beaujolais?' said the barman.

'Fine. Thank you.' He was rather attractive actually. I smiled at him a second longer than was strictly necessary and he smiled back.

What are you doing? I said to myself. Here you are with lovely Stephen who's handsome and six foot two and you're very, very lucky.

'So, can I tell you what happened?' Stephen loosened his tie and put his briefcase down on the floor.

I could hardly blame him for not being eager to hear about my day of disasters. 'Of course,' I smiled. 'Tell me all about it.'

On the way into my block the next morning, I stopped to talk to Vernon, another porter, to explain about my damaged door.

'Yeah, I know all about it. Leo had a word with us. First you got to notify the managing agents, then you have to get three quotes—'

Leo? Vernon made him sound like an old friend. The man's hardly been in the building two minutes.

'And how long will that take?'

'Shouldn't be more than three, four weeks, I reckon.'

'I can't possibly wait that long. Can't we just get it done *now*, then claim the money back?'

Vernon rubbed his chin. 'Well, no, see, you have to get three quotes . . .' Vernon is fond of repeating himself so even the simplest exchange takes three times longer than it should.

'Yes, I appreciate that,' I said firmly. 'But if I can find a handyman . . .'

'Hi there!'

I swung round. Oh, marvellous—the Door Destroyer.

'Ah, it's you. The man who doesn't know his own strength. A gentle knock should more than suffice in future.'

'I'll bear it in mind next time you invite me round for tea and scones. Now, about your door—'

'Vernon told me. It's far too slow. I can't let my clients see it like that. It looks *appalling*.'

'Hmm. You wouldn't say you were exaggerating just a tad? But . . . OK.' He checked his watch. 'What say you if I sort something out for later on today—four? Five? What suits you?'

'Really? Well. Four then. Thank you.'

I must have looked as if I didn't believe him, because then he said, 'I *will* be there.'

He smiled suddenly and it was so unexpected that I found myself grinning back at him even though so far he'd done nothing but be rude and damage my property. Still, at least now he was trying to make amends.

'So. Um—were you all right then?' I asked. 'You weren't hurt?'

'Nope. All in one piece.'

'Good. That's good. I'm—' I was on the verge of apologising; I felt embarrassed that I'd been so brusque.

'So, see you at four?' he said.

I nodded and headed for the stairs, hearing Vernon taking up his thread once more. 'We're really supposed to get three quotes, you see . . .'

'**B**ut how do I know if Donald really is *right* for me?' my client said.

'We've talked before about your difficulties in committing to a relationship in the past . . .'

'Yes. That's exactly the problem. How do I *know* whether it's just me getting cold feet again as soon as things start to get remotely serious or if he's simply the wrong person for me? I do like him . . .'

I nodded. Well, it's a start.

'And I sometimes think that I really love him . . .'

I flicked my gaze over to the clock. It was coming up to ten to four. The number of people who wait until near the end of a session to discuss their most pressing issues, you wouldn't believe. It's because that way it feels safe, of course, it's all right to delve into risky territory because they'll be saved by the bell before they get in too deep.

'But then we'll be having a meal out and I'll look across and see another couple and they'll be laughing or leaning in close, like they're desperate to hear what each other has to say, and then I find myself looking at Donald and thinking, I should be feeling more . . .'

'More . . .?'

'Yes. *More*. More—more *everything*. More excited to see him, more interested in what he has to say, more pleased at the prospect of spending my entire life with him.'

'Relationships do go through a series of stages,' I pointed out.

'Yes. Of course. But if it was right, wouldn't I just *know*?' She put her hands up to her face. 'But I so don't want to be on my own again. I've done all that. Staying in with a video every bloody Saturday night or going out with a girlfriend who you don't like all that much but she's the only other woman you know who's free on a Saturday night, and the waiter gives you the worst table by the loos. It's so awful. I can't face it.'

'But do you believe that's a good reason to stay with Donald—out of fear? Do you think that's fair on him?'

'No. It isn't. But he says I make him happy, so why not? I may as well be with him and at least let him be happy rather than ditching him so we'll both end up miserable.'

She looked directly at me, for the first time beginning to acknowledge just how unhappy she was.

'I think you know that's not really the answer—you'd end up resenting him,' I said gently. 'We need to look at this further next time, but . . .'

She twisted to look at the clock, then stood up and said goodbye.

Four o'clock came and went. Five past. I might have known. The kind of person who damages your door then sends you a rude note is hardly likely to be punctual. I was on the verge of phoning the front desk to ask Vernon if he'd seen any sign of a handyman, when there was a firm knock at the door.

'Hi!' It was Mr Rude. No handyman in sight.

I peered past him into the corridor. 'I assumed you were bringing a handyman.'

'I am. That's me.'

'I thought you were a photographer. I don't want someone to take a nice snapshot of my door—I want someone to mend it.'

'Look!' he said suddenly, slapping the door. 'Your door isn't actually cracked or broken, so I can probably hide the scrape with wood-filler.'

'But won't that show?'

'Not if I sand it then paint it.'

Currently, aside from the scrape, the door is a rather nasty, institutional dark brown—a sort of shit-brown, to be honest. Originally, every door in the block was identical, but gradually the rules have been relaxed and now some doors have been painted other colours.

I stood there, thinking about it.

'Or wait for the insurance and have a new door. It's your call.'

'And you think you can really make it look perfect?'

'It'll look fine. Better than fine. But *perfect*? Who knows?'

'I'm not sure . . .'

He smiled and covered his mouth with his hand for a moment. 'Tell you what—I'll fill it and rub it down and paint it . . . Then, when you discover it's not quite *perfect*, call me and I'll come and smash it down—and then you call the insurers and get yourself a new door, OK?'

I looked at him and he stared back, unblinking.

'Well. What's it to be? Time's cracking on.'

'Filler then. Please. When can—'

He checked his watch. 'Bugger—I'm running late now. Tell you what—I'll do the filler tonight, then paint it at the weekend. No—not tonight—it might be after twelve—I don't want to keep you up . . .'

'It won't. I don't actually live here.'

'Are you house-sitting or something?'

'No. I do live *here* . . .' I waved an arm expansively to indicate the building as a whole. 'But I don't live *here*.' I slapped the door, as he had done.

'So—where do you live then?'

'Upstairs. On the fifth. The flat directly above this one, in fact.'

He made a face. 'That's a bit weird, isn't it? *Two* flats on different floors.'

'Not so different from having a house—besides I like to keep my work and home life separate. It's neater that way.'

'They're not that separate if you only live upstairs.' He was smiling.

'Psychologically separate,' I explained. 'More than geographically.'

'Ah-ha!'

Don't you hate it when people act as if they've got you sussed? I gave him a withering glance. 'Anyway. So—the *door*. It would be great if you could do it tonight. As long as you won't disturb my neighbours?'

'I'll wear slippers and muffle my spatula.'

I suppressed a smile.

'Oh—and get some paint, will you?' he called back down the corridor. 'We need undercoat and gloss. And for God's sake pick something jollier than this disgusting Hint of Turd!'

On Saturday night, if we're not away for the weekend, we sometimes meet up with Stephen's friends Mike and Liz. I usually see my own friends during the week; Stephen's not mad keen on most of them, to be honest. Liz and Mike are tremendously nice and it's great that we both get on so well with both of them. And they're very easy company, too—

you can just chat away about nothing at all and then you look at your watch and realise that the whole evening's gone by.

We were having supper at their place, a small terraced house in Dalston or, as Liz and Mike call it, 'Islington Borders'.

'Of course, this area's really, *really* coming up now,' said Liz.

'Yes—you can get a proper cappuccino down the road,' Mike added.

'Gosh. How are the schools?' Stephen asked, although Mike and Liz don't have any children.

'We-e-e-ll. We're planning to go private.' Mike topped up our glasses.

'Are you—thinking of starting a family then?'

'Of course.' Liz smiled. 'We thought we should have our first, say, end of next year, then the second about two and a half years after that.'

'Right. Great.'

She probably had it all scheduled in their joint diary: *Conceive Baby No. 1 for delivery in November*.

'And how about you two? C'mon, Stephen, I have mega-mega plans for the ultimate stag night!' Mike gave him a manly slap on the back.

'We're thinking of next spring or summer, aren't we, sweetie?'

I took a sip of wine. 'Mmm. But we still need to find the perfect place. We found somewhere nice recently but the room was too small.'

'*Oh!*' Liz let out a squeal and clapped her hands together.

Then she launched into an account of the most perfect, perfect wedding venue. She wished she'd seen it before they got married and she knew for sure that I would just love it. A friend of hers had taken her there last week and they'd been able to look round while the staff were preparing for a wedding and everything—the flowers—the room—the setting—it was all perfect. *Completely perfect.*

'We must make an appointment. Why don't you note down the details, darling?'

'Yes, of course.' I fetched my handbag and fished out my notebook.

'It sounds ideal.' Stephen raised his glass. 'Here's to the *perfect* wedding.'

I raised my glass and smiled. 'I hope it's not too expensive,' I said.

Stephen winked at me. 'Let's not worry about that now.'

'Ooh—leave the finances to Stephen!' Liz nudged me. 'You're so lucky, Georgia. You wouldn't believe the fuss Mike makes every time I buy so much as a pair of shoes!'

'Why?' I was puzzled because Liz works and earns quite good money, certainly enough to buy the occasional pair of shoes if she wants them. 'You don't expect him to pay for them, do you?' I laughed.

She looked at me as if I were being stupid. 'It's a joint account.'

'Yes, but surely you each have your own too—for personal stuff?'

'No. Whatever for? It's so much easier this way.'

I tried not to look too horrified. I would hate to have to explain myself because I've dared to take Ellen out for a meal, or something.

'Just you wait and see,' Liz attempted to reassure me. 'Once you're married, you'll be the same.'

Mike waved the wine bottle over my glass once more. Normally, I refuse after the first glass, but I was feeling quite thirsty for some reason. 'Thank you.'

SEVEN
The open door

I TRIED TO COAX Stephen to brunch on Sunday morning, but he said he wasn't in the mood. 'You go, darling,' he said, 'and give everyone my best. I've got loads of work to do.'

'OK. Sure you don't mind if I go?'

'No. Really. See you later.'

I stayed at brunch until nearly one, but Ellen didn't show up. Unc came with Auntie Audrey, and a neighbour popped in, a rather interesting man with one of those shaggy, untrimmed beards that look as if they've been dug up from the bottom of an amateur dramatics props box. But brunch is never the same without Ellen. I love Unc and Auntie, but Auntie frowns at you if you put your elbows on the table, and she wears an unbelievable amount of make-up. Even at ten o'clock on a Sunday morning, she looks as if she's just heading off to the opera. And her eyebrows have been overplucked, and they're too arched so she always looks rather surprised, as if she's just sat on something nasty. I kept looking round for Ellen, wanting to see her doing her Auntie Audrey face.

When I got back to the flat, I found a note had been pushed under my door.

'Filler all done. Need to have door open to paint it and while it's drying. When's good for you? Or let me have the keys (if you can trust me not to demolish the rest of your flat). Leo the Barbarian
PS—Did you get the paint?

At least he'd thought to put his phone number this time.

'Hello, Mr Kane? Er . . . Leo?'

'Yup.'

'It's Georgia Abrams, about the—'

'Yup—now please don't tell me you're not happy with the door. It'll look fine when it's painted. Did you buy the paint?'

I explained I hadn't even seen it yet, because I was in my upstairs flat, but that I'd bought the paint. He said he could do it tonight or I'd have to wait another week because he was going to Dublin at the crack of dawn the next day.

'But, don't worry—I wouldn't dream of emigrating until I've completed the door to your satisfaction.'

'Do you always take the piss out of people you barely know?'

'No. Only the ones I like.'

'You're very direct, aren't you?'

'I find it saves time. Why—does it bother you?'

'Not at all. No. Why should it?'

'Well, we could go on like this all night, I'm sure, but I'd better get on with it. So do you want to lend me the keys or what?'

'Oh, no—I'll let you in. I need to do some work down there anyway.'

'OK. Bang on my door when you're ready—number 418.'

'It's really good of you to fix my door yourself,' I said, when he came to the door of his flat. 'I do appreciate it.'

'No problem. I broke it—I'll fix it.' He picked up a set of keys. 'Right, let me at it then.'

I unlocked the door of my flat and gestured to the bag of paint and brushes I'd bought yesterday.

'It's all in there. What about your clothes?'

'You're kidding?' He gestured to his, admittedly rather faded, shirt and well-washed jeans. 'I don't think I own a single item of clothing that wouldn't be improved by a fresh lick of paint. But—do you have a dust sheet or anything to protect your floor?'

'No, I don't think so. But we can use newspapers, can't we?' I retrieved some from the cupboard in my hall and started spreading them out.

'Here, I can do that. You get on with your work or whatever.'

I sat at my desk and took out my notebook so that I could write up my notes from yesterday's sessions properly. Fired up my laptop and switched on my printer.

'Hey—glad you resisted the dubious delights of Dried Turd!' he called through. 'Perhaps you'll start a trend.'

'Perhaps.' I wasn't really listening, to be honest. I was hoping he'd just shut up and get on with it, but he was obviously one of those people who have to keep talking the entire time.

'Do you want a coffee or anything?' I asked him.

'Er, yes, please. Black, no sugar.'

A couple of minutes later, he stuck his head round the door.

'Er, hi?' venturing a step into my inner sanctum.

'Yes? I'm just bringing the coffee.' I stood up, crossed to the kettle.

'Hey, isn't this great!' He came in uninvited. 'How do you keep it so—empty? It's like something out of a magazine.'

'Well, you have to be tidy in such a small space or it'd drive you crazy. Besides, I see my clients here.'

'Why—what do you do?'

'I'm a counsellor—as in couns*el* not coun*cil*, as in trying to help people with their emotional and psychological problems, not trying to push through dodgy planning applications.'

He raised his eyebrows but said nothing.

'You think counselling's not a *real* job, I suppose? That people should just pull their socks up and get on with their lives rather than seeking help. That's so English—the ridiculous belief that if you're unhappy you should just soldier on regardless. It really annoys me.'

'So I see. Have you finished?' He looked like he was about to laugh.

'Yes. I suppose so.' I handed him his coffee. 'Biscuit?'

'Please. I can't imagine how you got it into your head that I'm anti-counselling. Quite the contrary. But of course, now, I'm rather curious to know why you're so defensive about your chosen profession.'

'Are you trying to analyse me? A lot of people seem to find it amusing to try to prove that a counsellor has problems too.'

'Well, it wouldn't be how I'd get my kicks, but if you say so. I can't imagine that being a counsellor means you never have a single problem—but I guess you're maybe a bit more mature than the rest of us in the way you deal with them.'

How annoying. Just when I thought I had him figured, he turns out to be quite thoughtful and intelligent after all.

'Well, I don't know about that . . .' I said modestly. Then I looked up to see two of my neighbours blatantly peering in at us through the open door. I gave them a chilly look, which would have sent them scurrying on their way, had not this stupid Leo character *waved* at them and called out, 'Hi there!' Then he went out to talk to them, and showed them the door, patting it, chatting away as if nothing could be more enjoyable than to stand there discussing door decoration with two old ladies.

'So, you come and bang on my door anytime, OK? It's 418, just along the corridor there! Bye-bye, girls—behave yourselves now! Don't talk to any strange men!' There were shrieks of laughter then they moved on. I so wanted to close the inner door but I felt I ought to leave it open, partly so I could keep an eye on him. He continued to enter into conversation with every single person who went past him along the corridor, so that each time I attempted to settle back into my work, I'd be interrupted by the sound of people chattering away.

'Do you feel compelled to speak to every person you see?' I called out.

'Why—don't you?'

'No. Of course not. Why should I?'

'Because people are interesting? Because you might hear something you've never heard before? Because someone who starts out a total stranger might become a friend for life?'

'Oh, come on.'

'Why? Have you known all your friends for your entire lifetime? Of course not. So they were all strangers at some point.'

'Yes. *Obviously*. But—'

He smiled. 'But?'

'It's hardly the same thing.' I turned back to my work.

'This undercoat's done now.' He came further into the room. 'Shouldn't take long to dry, but I'm desperate for a bite to eat, so I'll slope off now and get a pizza, then come back and do the gloss, OK?'

'Fine.' God, I could just murder a pizza. I wondered if I could possibly ask him to pick one up for me, seeing as he was going anyway. Maybe I should have been a bit more polite to him.

He paused by the door. 'Can I get you one? I'd say come with me, but it's better for the door to dry while it's open.'

'Um, no, of course. Actually, yes, could you get me one?' I reached for my handbag and took out my purse. 'Where are you going?'

He told me.

'There's a Pizza Express just a bit further, if you don't mind . . . the pizzas are miles better.' I described how to get there. 'Can I have a Giardiniera, only with artichokes instead of leeks and no black pepper, please? Should I write that down or will you remember?'

He sucked in his breath through his teeth. 'God, I'm really not sure—what was it? Baked bean and pineapple pizza with extra garlic?'

I peeled off a yellow stickie and quickly wrote it down.

'I really don't need that. Artichokes, not leeks—see?'

'Yes. And no black pepper. Please will you be sure to get it exactly right? I like it like that.' I started to hand over the money.

'It's OK. I think I can stump up for a pizza.'

'It's not necessary. I can buy my own.'

'I'm sure you can but I would *like* to pay for it. Call it compensation for the door if you like.'

I passed him a plate, cutlery and cloth napkin, which were met with another of those lopsided smiles and the raised eyebrows.

'Pepperoni pizza with many, many extra anchovies,' he said, passing me a box. I opened the lid. Giardiniera. Artichokes, not leeks. I searched for telltale dark specks of black pepper, but by some miracle he seemed to have managed to order it correctly.

'Does it pass muster?'

'It does. Thank you.' I passed him a tumbler and a corkscrew for the wine he'd bought. 'Sorry, I haven't got any proper wineglasses down here.'

'But cloth napkins?'

'I prefer them. Even if I'm just having a bowl of soup on my own.'

He laughed, then started to open the wine.

'I suppose you think that's very prissy?'

He shook his head. 'It's not that. Don't get cross, but it reminds me of my mum, that's all. She always has proper napkins. Even if we're just having takeaway fish and chips.'

I asked him about his family and he explained that his parents had moved from London to the outskirts of Glasgow over fifteen years ago, when his father had taken early retirement.

'But he's dead now, alas. He died a couple of years ago.'

'I'm sorry—was it sudden?'

'Yeah. Stroke. He'd had two before so I guess it was on the cards.'

'That doesn't make it any easier. We imagine we can somehow protect ourselves by saying we expect the worst—'

'Then when it actually happens, you're still knocked for six. True.' He held out the wine to offer me some. 'And you—what about your parents?'

'My dad lives up in—'

My mobile started to ring.

'Sorry, please excuse me—hello?'

'George, hi, it's me.' Ellen. 'Where are you? You're not at home.'

'No. I am allowed out occasionally. Actually, I'm in my office.'

Leo stood up and made a walking movement with his fingers, jerked his thumb towards the door—a question.

'No, it's fine. It's only my sister.'

'*Only* your sister?' said Ellen, loud in my ear. 'I'm not an *only*.'

'Behave. What do you want?'

'Can I borrow your car tomorrow? Who've you got there? Not the P-h?'

'No, it isn't. What do you want it for?'

'Why are you being mysterious? It's a man, isn't it?'

'Yes, it is, but—' I turned away from Leo. 'Anyway, yes, you can borrow my car, but I want it returned with at least the same amount of petrol in it as there is now.'

'OK, OK, I promise. I'll come by at six or so tomorrow evening to get the keys, yeah?'

'Fine. See you then. Take care. Bye.'

Leo had stood up. 'I'd better get on with that gloss.'

'I think we may have a small problem,' Leo said, knocking at the inner door just as I was backing up my files.

'What kind of a small problem?'

'A should-have-read-the-paint-tin-first kind of problem. The first coat won't be properly dry till tomorrow morning so you shouldn't really shut the door.'

'I can't leave it open all night.' I stood up and went into the hall, then stopped dead in disbelief. 'Why is it *red*?'

'What do you mean—"why is it red?"? It's red because that's what you bought, see?' He held up the tin. 'Pillar-box Red', proclaimed the label.

'But that's not what I chose! I *know* I picked up the black.' Ebony Black. Professional. Authoritative. That's what I chose, I'm sure of it.

He shrugged. 'Well, it's way better than the brown you had before.'

'But it's not what I was planning to have.'

'Maybe not, but it's what you've got. Look—why not live with it for a week, then, when I come back from Dublin, I can either do a second coat of this or go over it in black?'

'I suppose so . . .'

'Now, the bigger problem is the drying time.'

'Well, I can't sleep here with the door open—anyone could stroll in.'

'OK—so, either both of us stay up all night here, talking, reading, arguing, playing cards, trading insults or whatever—'

'I can't—I've got a session first thing. I'll be shattered.'

'Or I could sleep here.'

I thought about it. 'Well, if you really don't mind . . .'

'Course not. It's my fault—I should have checked the tin first.'

'No, I should have.'

'You're right. It is your fault.' He laughed. 'But I must pack for Dublin.'

'Do you want a hand?' I said it without thinking, partly because I often help Stephen pack when he has to travel for work, I suppose.

'What—really? I loathe packing.'

It seemed mean to withdraw the offer, even though I'd sort of said it by accident. 'Sure,' I said.

We pulled my door to slightly, and wrote a 'Wet Paint' sign to put on the floor outside, then went to his flat. There was a long table against one wall and a couple of plain wooden chairs, an unexpectedly smart dark red sofa and a lot of equipment.

'Leave my door open too,' he said. 'Then we'll hear anyone coming along and you can stick your head out to check it's not burglars.'

'How will I know? What if they're not wearing stockings on their heads and carrying a jemmy?'

'You'll have to ask them. Now, what do I need?'

'What are you doing there? Work or pleasure?'

'Work *is* pleasure—well, on a good day. It's work. Pretty much non-stop—I'm doing some stuff for a travel guide to Dublin. You ever been?'

I nodded.

'So, tell me what to see. I've got a list from them, but it never does any harm to shoot extra stuff.'

I made a number of suggestions, while he pulled bits of clothing out of the cupboard.

'Right,' I said, sitting on the floor by the holdall. 'You're going for, what, a week?'

'Four or five days.'

'Right. Jeans? Trainers?'

He passed them down to me.

'Pants. Socks. Shaving things. Toilet bag plus razor, toothbrush et cetera. What else? Aftershave?'

I balled the pairs of socks and stuffed them into the trainers, then suddenly felt embarrassed as he dropped five pairs of underpants into the bag in front of me. I looked up and we both laughed.

'Sorry. I don't normally throw my underwear at women I hardly know.'

'That's OK. I don't normally pack for strange men either.'

He smiled. 'Now what?'

'Do you need something smart? For meetings?'

'Dunno. I might go and see a couple of magazine bods while I'm there.'

'What've you got?'

He held up an awful old grey suit and a crushed linen jacket with too-narrow lapels.

I shook my head. 'What else?'

'Not a lot.'

'You ought to have a few decent things for when you see clients.'

'I know. I'm hopeless. I hate clothes shopping.'

'Now. Shirts . . . um, I could come with you sometime if you like. Shopping, I mean.'

'God, that'd be great.' He rummaged in the cupboard once more then emerged with an armful of shirts. 'Don't suppose you want to come to Dublin too, by any wild chance?'

I wasn't sure if he meant it flirtatiously—or if he just needed someone to help him run his life. 'As your personal valet?' I said.

Tell him, I thought, why haven't you told him about Stephen yet?

'I don't suppose my boyfriend would be too happy about it.'

'Oh. I guess not.'

'Fiancé, I should say.'

'Oh. Right. Congratulations. When's the happy day?'

God, I do wish people would stop asking me that.

'Whenever.' I waved my hand airily. 'There's no rush.'

'Why no rush? Life's all too short.'

'It is. But that's no reason not to plan, is it?' I tucked the last things into the holdall and zipped it up. 'It's just like packing—plan properly and everything will be fine. No getting caught out. No surprises.'

He raised his brows and did his peculiar lopsided smile once more.

'No surprises? Now, where's the fun in that?'

It's 3.22am and there is a strange man sleeping in my consulting room. He could be prowling around, looking through my things or—dear God—my cupboard. He could have broken open the locked filing drawer and be reading my clients' confidential case notes. I must be bonkers. Perhaps I'll just nip down and check that the contents of my office are still there at least. That can't do any harm, can it?

I put on my dressing gown and tiptoe down the stairs.

The front door is open, of course, and there's a dim light from within. Perhaps he's reading? I hover outside by the Wet Paint sign for a minute, trying to hear the turning of pages, but there's no sound. I push open the door a bit further—the paint's only very slightly tacky.

The inner door is shut. Of course. But I can see the light beneath it. He could have simply fallen asleep with the light on. Or he could be reading. Or he could be going through my stuff. I quietly get down on my knees and crouch right down to the floor to listen at the gap. Maybe he snores? Wait—what was that? There was definitely—a noise. A small but distinct noise. Oh, for God's sake. This was such a stupid idea. Now what do I do? Throw open the door and demand an explanation? Or perhaps I should just creep back upstairs. Another noise—a creak.

Suddenly, the door flies open and he's standing over me brandishing the wine bottle.

I scream and he lets out a yell.

'Shit—it's you! What the hell are you doing, creeping around? You nearly gave me a heart attack!' He lowers the bottle. 'Why are you scuttling about on the floor? What *are* you doing?'

He puts out a hand to help me up.

'I—I was just—checking,' I said feebly. 'I was, you know . . .'

'Hang on a tick.' He steps out into the corridor, standing there in just his jeans with no shirt on. Not surprisingly, the noise has roused a couple of the neighbours, who are peering out of their front doors. 'Everything's fine,' he tells them, with solemn authority, as if he is used to handling this sort of thing all the time. 'No need to worry. Georgia saw a huge spider and had a bit of a panic. Sorry, folks. Very sorry.'

He comes back inside and stands aside to let me in. 'Come in—come and see that I haven't damaged anything or bundled all your belongings out the window.'

'I feel incredibly embarrassed.'

He laughs. 'It's fine—you should have just banged on the door and said, "Oi, *you*! You're not messing with my stuff, are you?" You can't go creeping around a respectable block like this in your dressing gown, sneaking into strange men's bedrooms—whatever will your neighbours think?'

'I didn't think anyone was going to see me.'

'There, I told you. You can't plan for everything. Life's full of surprises.'

'Your life—maybe. Not mine.'

'That's fine as long as you live in a cocoon and never have any contact with anyone else—'

'Especially not peculiar photographers with a tendency towards clumsiness and a complete lack of regard for all social conventions—'

'Especially not anyone like that. Bound to cause no end of trouble. Do you want a coffee now that you've dropped in unexpectedly? Says he, blithely offering you your own coffee in your own flat.'

'I'd better not.' I clutch my dressing gown round me more tightly. I'm beginning to feel extremely self-conscious. 'Good night then. I'm very sorry. See you in the morning.'

'Yes. Sleep well. And don't worry. I only booked the van to remove all your stuff for half seven—you can get plenty of rest before then.'

EIGHT
A suitable mate?

'ELLIE, I MUST TELL YOU—I've met *such* a lovely man,' I said, when she finally arrived at our café.

'Ooh, who's this then?' She started shedding her various belongings, creating a nest of jacket, scarf, and numerous bags around her.

'He's called Leo and he's a freelance photographer. He's just moved in, on the same floor as my office.'

'Hang on, wasn't he the guy who bashed your door down? The one you said was abominably rude?'

'He didn't bash it down. It was just a scrape. And, he's not *that* rude, just direct. Do you want to hear about him or not?'

'Go on then. What's his shag potential?'

'Well, he's not exactly what you'd call handsome—'

'Is he what you'd call pig-ugly?'

'No!' I banged down my teacup. 'Absolutely not! He's really attractive, just a bit crumpled-looking, you know? His hair is slightly receding—well, retreating at a gallop might be more accurate, but—'

'Wow—sounds gorgeous . . .'

'Oh, shut up! OK, so he's not good-looking in a boring, bland, film-starry way, so what? But you wouldn't push him out of bed. There's something really . . . moreish about him. And he's warm and bright and funny—and he's always in a whirl—I think he's a bit chaotic—'

'Just as well he's met you then. You'll soon sort him out.' She waved at the waitress, who mouthed, 'Latte?' at her, then turned back to me. 'What about Mr P-h? Have you told him?'

'No. What's it got to do with Stephen?'

'I can't believe you're being so casual about this!'

'*I'm* being casual? *You* don't even seem all that excited. I thought you'd be really pleased.'

Ellen leaned forward and took my hands. 'Oh, I *am*, George. I am. It's just it's so not like you to go sneaking around. Or are you trying to keep Stephen on standby just in case things don't work out with Baldy?'

I clunked down my cup with a bang. 'What on earth makes you think that *I'm* interested in Baldy? In Leo I mean? I'm *immensely* happy with

Stephen as you know. I was telling you all about Leo because I thought *you* might like him—though God knows why I bother.'

'But why the hell are you trying to pair him off with me when you're the one who's obviously bonkers about him?'

'I'm NOT!'

Faces turned towards us and I ducked my head and glared at Ellen.

'Well, you were doing a bloody good impression of it. You looked all lit up and were going on and on about his lovely shiny bald head—'

'He's not bald for the forty-fifth time, all right?'

Ellen sat back and lit a cigarette.

'Right. You're not in love with him even the tiniest bit. You were only playing matchmaker for me, but you leap to defend him and his acres of naked scalp. Try taking all that bloody wisdom you're so proud of and direct it at yourself, why don't you? You're gagging for him.'

The thing was to remain calm. 'I can see now how you might have got the wrong impression,' I said. 'I shouldn't have gone on so long trying to sell him to you. My mistake. But—look—you'll see. Meet him. He's not remotely my type. He'd drive me up the wall.'

'OK then.' Ellen took a dramatically deep drag on her cigarette, even though she knows I think it's disgusting. 'Have us both round to dinner or bring him to Sunday brunch and let's see if I like the look of him.'

'No problem.' I opened my bag to find my diary.

'And I take it Stephen will be coming too, of course?'

I paused, eyes down, toying with the ribbon marker of the diary.

'Mmm? Well, he's pretty busy right now. Probably easier with just us in any case.'

Leo was lying on the floor of my office, something he seemed to be doing quite a bit in the last few days because his studio was too full of equipment and there was nowhere to get comfortable. I was stretched out on the sofa, where my clients normally sit.

'Any more coffee going?' He looked up at me.

'I'm not here just to wait on your every need, you know. Can you not navigate your way through the vast echoing recesses of my kitchen? The kettle's due north once you come out of the east wing, OK?'

He heaved himself up to his feet, suppressing a smile.

'D'you want another one?'

'Oh, all right then. God, I've done practically nothing this afternoon. Look, it's after five already. I'm supposed to be going out at seven.'

'Then it's miles too late to start messing about with your face now. You'll have to cancel.'

'No one asked for your opinion, did they?' I got up and peered at my reflection in the mirror in the hall. 'It's not that bad, is it?'

'Grotesque. I'm not playing this game. Why do women always do this? Anyway, are you up to anything this Sunday?'

Stephen is off at a conference on Monday, so he was planning to stay in on Sunday to pack and practise his speech. I had been intending to go home for brunch, then see Stephen in the afternoon, help him pack.

'Sort of. We always have a kind of informal family brunch thing at my dad's on Sundays. We just talk and read the papers and eat bagels. Why don't you come too? You can meet my sister, she's really gorgeous, and my dad would like you. He can't bear people who are too polite.'

'Thanks.'

'You know what I mean. And, if you get bored, you can always take a turn teasing my stepmother.'

He looked surprised. 'Don't you like her?'

I'd never really thought much about liking Quinn or not liking her—once she'd become ensconced in the household, I mean. She's just Quinn, who happens to have been married to Dad for over ten years.

'Well—do you?' He stayed looking at me.

'I—I don't really know. She's just Quinn, you see? We've always teased her a bit because—well, she's such fair game. God, that sounds so mean. It's just that she wears these awful earrings and her clothes are peculiar—I don't know, strange, smocky dresses that nobody wears any more and patchwork jackets, like she's trying so desperately hard to be arty and bohemian when really she's quite ordinary and normal. And there's the cooking—her casseroles have always got things in them that you don't want—raisins or chickpeas or great big stalks of sage.'

'Ah, but do you *like* her?'

'You're very persistent, aren't you? Actually, I suppose I *do*. Quinn's fantastically fair. Same as Dad, come to think of it, though he's much ruder than she is. Also, she's not bitchy. Not like the rest of us. She's kind. Decent. Only a bit comical.' I felt ashamed. Am I really so low as to take the piss out of Quinn just because of her earrings and the fact that she puts chickpeas in everything? 'Anyway, you can see for yourself on Sunday. Unless you've got other plans of course.'

'No, that'd be great. It's just—' he thrust his hands down into his pockets, suddenly looking embarrassed. 'Thing is—I dunno—it's kind of a bit—see, there's someone I have to see on Sunday. I think you'd get on, but—um—could I bring her too? No, sorry.'

'Um. No. Yes. Of course. That's fine! Brilliant! Another new face. Dad's always telling us to bring new people along.'

I had a horrible feeling in my insides, a heavy, churning feeling as if someone was tumble-drying a whole load of rocks in there. Why had I just said my father was always begging us to bring more guests? Why? Now I'd look rude if I tried to backtrack. Bugger. No. Why should it make any difference to me whether he brought anyone or not?

I grabbed the notepad by the phone and scribbled down the address. 'There you go. Any time from ten on is fine.'

'Probably be about half past then, because I have to go—'

'Yes! Great!' I felt I was sounding peculiar and falsely jolly, babbling on and getting carried away like a merry-go-round at speed, but I couldn't seem to stop myself. 'Half past! Excellent! God, I hate to throw you out, but I must get on—all that make-up to layer on with a trowel . . .'

'Yes, of course. Sorry—do always feel free to chuck me out.'

'I will, don't you worry.'

Leo smiled, as if on the verge of laughing to himself.

I closed the door behind him and collected the mugs to wash up. Why do I feel like this? Please tell me it's not that I'm at all jealous. I'm not. Absolutely not. Just a bit disappointed on Ellen's behalf.

The annoying thing about all my training and experience as a counsellor is that I can only kid myself up to a point. You are such a pathetic liar, I told myself. OK, so I like him a little bit. So what? It's a very minor crush. This happens to people all the time. The important thing is to recognise it for what it is and not let it get out of hand. By next week, I thought, I'd be laughing about this with Ellen, saying, 'You know, I think you were right—I did have a little bit of a soft spot for Leo, but it was nothing and it wore off after a day or two.'

Clearly, Leo already sees me as some trusty old friend whom he can rely on for a sensible opinion on choice of shirt, choice of car, choice of girlfriend. Next, he'd be asking my advice on the best way to propose. What on earth makes him think I'm interested in meeting some bimbo he's managed to chat up? Honestly. Well, I'm not going to lie just to flatter his ego. If he insists on asking for my opinion about this woman, then fine, I will give it. 'I'm glad you asked me, Leo. Yes, suppose she is attractive in a humdrum, banal, supermodelish sort of a way, but I really can't see it lasting. Not exactly overburdened with brain, is she?'

I don't want to be his sodding pal. Now I really am being ridiculous. What do I want then if not to be friends? Well, I do want him as a friend, of course I do. He's sparky and provocative and he makes me laugh and he's quick, too: I don't have to keep explaining what I mean the whole time. And he's never boring. But it would be nice to think that he at least finds me vaguely attractive, attractive enough that he wouldn't dream of asking my advice about his stupid love life. God, just because I'm a counsellor doesn't mean I don't have feelings like normal people, you know. I still feel hurt, jealous, anxious, ashamed, guilty, resentful, just like everyone else. The only difference is that I'm supposed to keep recognising my feelings, acknowledging them in a responsible, grown-up manner—'Ah, I notice that I am feeling a little jealous. Hmm, what can I learn from this?' Perhaps I'd give myself a day off from being so bloody grown-up. Maybe I'd just be unreasonable and jealous and pathetic and wallow in it all weekend.

NINE

And then it was Sunday . . .

SUNDAY, 7.55AM. In five minutes, I will get up and make some coffee, then have a lovely long bath and annoy myself by reading the style supplement of the Sunday paper. It's the best thing to read in the bath because it's small and glossy and I don't care if it gets wet because it's entirely dreadful from front to back, but I enjoy being cross with it and its pretentiousness, its injunctions for you to shell out £200 for some stupid stone bowl that would mark if you put anything in it or £90 for a suede cushion that—again—you clearly weren't supposed to touch. Stephen was at a friend's stag night last night, so I had my bed all to myself. Stephen and I will live together one day. I could be living with him now if I chose to. I want to, naturally, but not right this minute. Of course, we'll have to if we're going to get married. *When* we get married.

Anyway. Brunch. Good, I could murder a bagel. Fresh and chewy and still warm. Weirdly, this brought Leo's face to mind. Why did eating a bagel make me think of him? It didn't. It was just that he would be there. With some awful, giggling girlie, skinny enough to wear one of those little strappy dresses and an itsy-bitsy cardigan perched on her shoulders. She'd laugh at his every utterance and he'd smirk and be insufferable. Well, thank God I don't care, I reminded myself. My crush was fading already, I knew it would. It was a shame for Ellen, of course, but mind you, once he sees her he'll realise how stupid he is to be fooling about with this other woman, because Ellen is warm and bright and gorgeous. Yes, he'll see Ellen and he'll be completely captivated.

Funny how this wasn't making me feel any better.

Maybe I was coming down with something. My stomach definitely felt a bit—strange. But I couldn't kid myself. There's nothing wrong with you, you just don't want to see him with another woman. It's truly pathetic. You're jealous and you have absolutely no right to be. You've got a wonderful, kind, sweet, loving boyfriend and here you are getting yourself in a state over some ridiculous man who'll probably troll off to New York tomorrow for work. How could I have thought for even a moment that I was interested in him? And, worse, I'd even tried to palm him off onto my own precious sister!

I got to Dad's just as he was shuffling down the front path in his slippers to get in the car for the bagel run.

'Georgia!' He hugged me. 'Looking well and beautiful. You look like a woman in love—are you?'

'Oh, Dad! Of course not! Don't be ridiculous.'

Then I realised what I'd said. 'I mean, yes, of course. With *Stephen*. Of course. But not *like that*. Oh, you know what I mean.'

'Any special requests while I'm there?'

'Oh, I've invited my neighbour—you don't mind?'

'Course not. Long as she's not boring. Who is she?'

'*He's* not boring. And he's bringing someone, his girlfriend I presume. She probably won't eat a thing though. I bet she's one of those "Ooh—none for me, thanks! I ate last Tuesday!" types.'

Dad smiled and shuffled off to the car. 'See you in a minute.'

I waved him goodbye and rang the bell. It was answered by Quinn, still wearing the black and white kimono she uses as a dressing gown.

'Ah, Georgia, thank God it's only you. I mean, it's lovely that it's you, but I'm glad it's only family because I haven't had a moment—I was just about to tidy—you know.' She led the way through to the kitchen. 'Now, let me make you some coffee . . .'

The supper dishes were still on the worktop from last night. There were numerous mugs containing varying levels of coffee of varying vintages. The sink was full of pots and pans. The kitchen table had stacks of papers at one end and a tray full of dirty crockery at the other.

Quinn stood still, like a rabbit caught in the glare of headlights, unsure which way to jump.

She took a tentative step towards the dishwasher.

'Why don't you go upstairs and finish getting dressed?' I said, tactfully, 'and I'll load the dishwasher.'

Quinn's face brightened.

'Would you really?' She probably had some vague idea that she would get round to doing it all, but then got flustered about where to start and so gave up. God knows what it's like when I'm not there.

I switched on the radio, emptied the murky contents of the coffee-maker, cleaned the jug and scooped in fresh coffee, then I found a vase for the roses I'd brought and began to empty the clean things from the dishwasher so I could reload it.

By the time Quinn re-emerged, wearing a maroon needlecord dress, bright yellow tights and flat black shoes, Dad had returned with the bagels and was sitting at the table surrounded by newspapers.

The counter was as clear as it was ever going to be and the dish-washer was thrumming away. A stack of plates and a basket of cutlery and napkins were on the worktop and the bagels were piled on a platter. Dad had brought cream cheese and smoked salmon from the deli. I added pots of honey, jam and Marmite from the cupboard.

I started cracking eggs into a large bowl. 'Do people want salmon in the eggs, chopped up into little bits, or just on the side? Dad?' I sloshed in some milk and ground in some sea salt.

'Mmm, lovely,' said Dad, not looking up from the paper. 'Did you hear about this exhibition of plastinated corpses?'

'What—real ones? People, you mean?' I said, whisking.

'Oh, no, David! Surely not?'

'Mmm—the so-called artist says it has enabled him to "democratise anatomy". What's that supposed to mean?' He looked up from the paper. 'Salmon's in the bag there. Huh—plastinated—I'm not sure that's even a real word. Is it the same as plasticised, do you think?'

'Actually, maybe I'll leave the salmon on the side, so people have the choice. Why would anyone want to look at dead bodies in an exhibition anyway? It doesn't make it art just because this bloke comes up with a whole load of bollocks about democratising anatomy. You can't democ-ratise anatomy. It just *is* what it *is*. Where's the butter?'

Quinn brought it over from the dresser.

'Still—no need to talk about dead people, over breakfast, is there?' Quinn, for all her coloured tights and soaking pulses, frequently forgets how to pull off her bohemian eccentric act and betrays her upbringing.

'It seems that any old scam merchant now thinks that he can shove his grubby sheets or his toenail clippings onto a plinth and—dah-*dah*, suddenly it's art and it's got a message,' I said, ignoring Quinn.

'Well . . .' Dad leaned back in his chair and pushed his spectacles up onto his head. 'He could be saying something about the nature of the body, dehumanised and viewed purely as an object—at core, we're all equal, a collection of bones, muscles, tissues and so on . . .'

'No, he isn't, Dad. He's just yet another would-be rebel who thinks that shocking people is the quick route to becoming rich and famous.'

'Does anyone want any of my homemade hummous with their scramblies?' said Quinn.

'No,' I said quickly. 'I mean, no, thanks. Maybe after the eggs.' I felt mean. 'Quinn—sorry—can you pass a plate for the salmon?'

'Did you say you had a friend coming?' Dad looked up from the paper. 'Who is he again?'

'Leo. He's a neighbour. And his girlfriend I think. Eggs coming up in *one minute*! Have your plate ready!'

'And Stephen? Is he coming?'

'No, he's going away yet again for work tomorrow—he has to pack.' I scooped out scrambled eggs onto three plates and left the remainder to keep warm over a large pan of hot water.

'Uh-huh,' said Dad.

Matt arrived next with Bonnie and Daniel, who came running in, shouting, 'Auntie Gee! Auntie Gee!'

'Hey, everyone, how's it going? Iz sends her love.' He dropped a bag of croissants onto the table. 'She's having a much-needed lie-in and a bit of quiet time without the monsters.'

'I'm NOT a monster, Daddy!' Bonnie shouted. '*You're* a monster!'

'*I'm* a monster!' said Daniel.

'Yes, you *are*!' Matt picked him up and turned him upside-down until Daniel was shrieking with laughter. 'Who wants scramblies?'

'I don't like eggs!' said Bonnie.

'I don' like eggs!' repeated Daniel.

'Yes, you do, Daniel. Don't be a pain. Scramblies aren't eggs in any case, they're scramblies. Bonnie is a bit off eggs just now, Gee, but she can have a croissant.' He took one out of the bag and put it on a plate. 'Who else is coming?' he said. 'Mr Interesting?'

'Ho-hum, Matt, that's original.' It isn't that Matt dislikes Stephen exactly, it's just that he can't resist winding me up about him. 'Anyway, no he isn't. He has something important to do.'

'Whoo-oo!' Matt let out a whoop. 'Something *important*. Well, we can't possibly compete with that, can we? Lucky old Stephen.'

The doorbell rang again. Oh God, this might be Leo. Please don't let her be beautiful. Or bright.

It wasn't Leo. It was Unc.

'Greetings, all!' He handed a bag of satsumas and a pineapple to Quinn. 'Any eggs?' He came over and kissed me.

'Just making some more, Unc. Sit yourself down.'

'No Stephen today, Georgia? When are you two going to name the day?'

'I gave him time off for good behaviour.'

'In fact, Georgia's got a *special guest* coming . . .' Dad said, as if announcing news of great significance.

'He's NOT a *special guest*. He's just a neighbour. No big deal.'

'Goodness!' Quinn's the only person I know who still uses the word. 'Are you not seeing Stephen any more, Georgia?' She looked concerned.

'Have you really ditched the P-h? Wow! And just when I was warming to the guy . . .' Matt spoke through a mouthful of croissant. 'So, who's this new man? That was fast—or was there an overlap?'

'Oh, just *stop*, will you?'

The doorbell rang again.

Unc went to the door, with Bonnie tailing him. I heard him opening it, his booming 'Hello!' followed by Leo's, considerably quieter, then Bonnie saying, 'Who are *you*?'

I feel sick. Why did I even ask him in the first place? Stupid, stupid woman. I'd go in a minute. Say I had to be off, had to meet Stephen.

'No.' Unc's resonant tones again. 'I'm Georgia's uncle, Howard—but you can call me Unc if you're Georgia's new man. All the family does.'

Oh, ground, please swallow me now. *Please*. How could Unc be such a blundering fool? Couldn't he see Leo was with someone? This is mortifying. I might actually die from embarrassment. Leo will think that I've been going round claiming he's my boyfriend, that I'm totally barking. Hang on a sec. I haven't heard a woman's voice. All I could hear was Unc, then Leo—surprisingly quiet—and Bonnie jumping and squealing. Maybe he has come on his own after all. I start to whisk the eggs, keeping my back to the door where he would come in.

'So this is Leo, Georgia's *friend*,' Unc bellows.

'Hey, everyone. Hi.'

'. . . And this is his beautiful companion, Cora,' Unc concludes.

No, no, *no*. Oh shit—I can't bear it. Tears prick my eyes. Pull yourself together, for God's sake! Now, just turn and smile and stretch out your hand. Be friendly, charming, the perfect hostess.

'Well, hello there!' Dad's voice, unexpectedly warm and interested. She must be devastating.

'Hey, Georgia!' Leo's voice, like a hand, warm and strong against my back. I can feel the beginning of a blush creeping over my face.

'Sorry—just at the crucial whisking stage. Give me a couple more secs!' Trying to crank a smile into place before I turn round.

Everyone round the table has fallen silent, a virtually unknown occurrence in Abrams land. Dad clears his throat and rustles the paper.

'So, has anyone seen this new Brazilian film . . .?'

'Hi there!' I twirl round, still holding the whisk and sending a trail of egg spinning out into the air in front of me.

His smile nearly knocks me over. The sight of his chipped tooth induces an inexplicable surge of tenderness. I desperately want to touch his hair.

'And this is Cora . . .' She is indeed quite beautiful, with huge, dark eyes and shiny hair, and she's holding a big bunch of glorious sunflowers.

And she is no more than five years old.

'Cora, this is Georgia, the nice lady I told you about. Georgia—meet Cora, my daughter.'

TEN
Sardines

NEEDLESS TO SAY, NO ONE BELIEVED my claim that I had burst into tears because I'd dropped the egg whisk onto my nice suede shoes. But even Matt knows that there's a time for taking the piss and a time for shutting up and leaving things well alone. I can't even explain it myself—I'm probably just tired, I didn't sleep too well last night.

'I didn't realise you had a daughter,' I said quietly to Leo, as Bonnie took Cora's hand and towed her away: 'We're playing ships and *I'm* the captain. Watch out for sharks.'

'Join the club. Neither did I until very recently.'

'What? How? Surely even you must have noticed a small person tailing around after you and calling you Daddy?'

He cocked his head on one side.

'Finished? I didn't *know*,' he lowered his voice, 'because Hazel, her mother, neglected to inform me of this minor development in my life until—look, can we talk about it later? I don't want to discuss it while Cora's around.'

'Of course.' I laid my hand on his arm, then caught Matt looking at me, reading too much into everything as usual.

Leo sat down and I gave him a plate so he could help himself.

'So . . . Georgia has told me little about you other than that you're a neighbour.' Dad put down the newspaper and even folded it.

'You should feel honoured,' I said. 'It's rare for Dad to relinquish his paper. It may mean that he's even going to listen.'

The doorbell rang. It was Ellen, with yet another new man in tow.

'Hiya! This is Jürgen. Ooh, croissants! Jürgy, grab a plate and help yourself while I fill you in on who's who.' She seized a croissant and dunked it in Dad's coffee mug. 'OK—now this is my dad, David, that's his brother Howard but you can call him Unc. Quinn, my stepmother. Great tights, Quinny! Then that tall guy at the far end is Matt, my annoying brother, the person holding a tea towel and doing all the work is my lovely sister, Georgia. Those are Matt's kids playing through there in the sitting room—Bonnie and Daniel—and I don't know who that other gorgeous little girl is, friend of Bonnie's, presumably?'

'No, that's—'

'And who are *you*?' She turned to Leo. 'Are we related? I thought I'd met all the cousins by now.'

'No. Well, not as far as I know. I'm Leo. I'm—'

'Oh, *you're* Leo. But you're not *bald* at all. Well, not really. You've got loads more hair than Jürgy—hasn't he?' She addressed the entire room.

'Er, thank you.'

'Ellen, please feel free to shut up at any point, won't you?' I started collecting the used plates to give me something to do.

Leo shoved me playfully. 'I see—so you said I was bald, did you? Remind me not to hire you as my PR manager.'

'I *didn't* say that—I said—'

'Anyway,' my father interrupted. 'Leo—do carry on with what you were saying. You're in Georgia's block?'

'Yes, I'm renting a flat on the same floor as her office. I'm a photographer so it's ideal being so central. The only trouble is that it seemed quite big before I filled it with all my equipment—I'm thinking of annexing a section of the corridor to sleep in.'

'You should get a fold-down wallbed, like I've got.'

'Don't let Gee start organising your life, whatever you do,' Matt chipped in. 'You'll be tidied up to within an inch of your life.'

'Sorry, was anyone asking for Matt's opinion?'

'I must apologise for my children, Leo,' Dad said. 'I used to think that they would grow up eventually, but it was just a foolish dream.'

'That's so unfair!' Ellen spoke through a mouthful of croissant.

'Mouth!' I cautioned. She's always eating and talking at the same time.

'Shut up! I was just going to be nice about you. I was going to say that at least Georgia's a proper grown-up, but I shan't bother now.'

'Gee isn't anyway.' Matt turned to Leo. 'She's just as bad as Ellen. Worse in some ways, because Georgia seems so sensible on the outside—'

'But underneath she's passionate and deeply silly, thank God,' Leo added, turning to smile at me. 'I know. It's a well-kept secret, but bits of it do have a way of leaking out when she lets her guard down.'

'He's interrupting already. He's definitely one of us.' Ellen laughed.

'Apologies again, Leo.' Dad shook his head. 'I think Ellen meant that as a compliment.'

'I take it as one. You lot remind me of my own family. What's left of it.'

'Oh?' Quinn, getting a word in edgeways at last.

'Yeah, my father died a couple of years ago and my mum lives in Glasgow near my two sisters. I was living up there too, so I saw them all a lot, but I couldn't get enough work so I moved to London.'

'You must miss them.' Dad passed him a dish of pickled sweet-sour cucumbers, as if to compensate.

'Yeah, I really do.' Leo took one and crunched into it. 'I didn't realise how much. It seems a bit pathetic to be homesick at my age. And little things remind you—' he held up his cucumber—'my dad loved these.'

There was a moment's silence, then my father nodded.

'Well, you're very welcome here—come and see us any time you fancy a bit of family life red in tooth and claw.'

'Quite. It will probably make you miss your own family even more,' I added. 'We're not exactly your classic happy family, are we?'

'Oh, that's a bit harsh.' Quinn, taking things too seriously as usual.

'Dissent is very healthy,' Dad pronounced. 'I've always been deeply suspicious of families where no one ever argues—in my experience it usually means that they never talk much either.'

'But we *are* a happy family, aren't we?' Ellen's voice sounded very young, as if she were a child again.

'Of course we are.' Quinn, smoothing things over. 'Now, Leo, would you like some more coffee?' She came forward with the coffeepot.

He held up his cup for a refill.

'That's lovely, thanks. Georgia says you have a daughter, too?'

'Yes.' Quinn flushed. 'Simone. She's in marketing, she's doing very well, but she works too hard. You young people all do. It's very stressful.'

'Oh, Quinn—you make it sound as if you're ninety-four,' I protested.

'You work hard too.' Quinn's involved in arts administration.

'And does she live close by? Is she a regular at your Sunday brunches?'

Quinn shook her head. 'Not really. She's in Holland Park.' Simone's got a gorgeous flat with high ceilings and three bedrooms, she must be loaded. 'But she's very busy,' Quinn added defensively.

'Can't be arsed more like,' Ellen said, not quite quietly enough. Ellen's always louder than she thinks she is. I gave her a kick under the table.

'Anyway,' I tried to turn the conversation round, 'Simone's very—um, lively, isn't she? You'd like her a lot, I'm sure.'

Quinn looked placated.

Cora came up and tugged shyly at Leo. He ducked his head so she could whisper to him.

'Well, perhaps we can play something else then, hmm?'

'Is Bonnie bossing her around?' asked Matt.

'Er . . .'

'Bonnie!' Matt got up and went through to the sitting room.

'Let's all play something!' Ellen said, jumping up from her chair.

I rolled my eyes at Leo.

'I'm sorry. You don't have to join in. You probably want to sit and have a civilised conversation and enjoy your coffee in peace.'

He smiled, showing his chipped tooth. 'I can't remember the last time I had a *civilised* conversation, thank God. So what are we playing?'

'Charades!' said Ellen, who relishes the chance to show off.

'No!' Matt and I chorused, remembering the last time we had played it.

'What about Sardines?' I suggested.

'God, *Sardines*—' Leo began. 'I haven't played that since I was—'

'A child?' I finished. 'Wow—aeons and aeons ago.'

'Thank you.' He reached out and squeezed my waist, making me yelp. 'Actually, no. I haven't played it since I was about twenty-five.'

'A late developer then?'

'Yup. Going to hit my prime any day now.'

'Call me when you do, won't you? I'd hate to miss it.'

'Don't worry—you'll be there.'

Dad and Quinn excused themselves, claiming that they were too old to fold themselves into cupboards, and Ellen explained the rules to Jürgen.

'So one person hides and then all the others look for him separately and one by one you all pile into the same tiny space and then the first person who found him hides . . .'

'My study's off limits, people,' Dad said, returning to his newspaper.

'OK. Georgia hides first,' Ellen said. 'Two-minute head start. Everyone else stays in here. Talk loudly, everyone, so you can't hear her! Go!'

'As if you lot need to be told to talk loudly . . .' I said, slipping out of the kitchen.

My heart was pounding. We haven't played Sardines for ages but, when we do, Ellen usually finds me first because she knows the kind of place I'd choose, just the same way that I always find her before anyone else. Thoughts raced through my head as I rejected one potential hiding space after another. In the shower? Too obvious. Stretched out behind the sofa cushions in the den? Beneath the desk in Matt's room? Could I fit into the chest on the top-floor landing? Hurry, hurry.

It wasn't ideal, but it would have to do.

Footsteps on the stairs, the sound of the door opening. I am trying not to breathe, keeping as still as I can, but my heart is thumping and it seems as if I can actually feel the blood racing round my body.

'No, Daniel—she won't be in here. It's too grubby. There's dust everywhere.' Ellen's voice. 'Come on—quick!—let's look in the shower.'

Footsteps thundering downstairs to Dad and Quinn's bedroom.

The door opens again.

'Do you think she's in here?' Leo. He must be hunting with Cora. Of course. I feel myself sag a little with disappointment.

Cora's reply is so quiet that I can't hear it.

'What about behind that curtain? No? What about under that cushion? You think it's too small? Yes, she's *much too big* to hide there . . .'

He knows I'm in here, the rude sod.

'That's a strange lump, isn't it? What about under . . . here?' A glimpse of legs close by, then he ducks down and I am looking straight into his eyes. 'Cora, you've found her!'

'We found you!'

'Sssh! We have to be quiet as mice until everyone else finds us.' Leo pulls aside the roll of carpet and the cardboard boxes that I had dragged across to conceal my hiding place. 'Shove up a bit.' He leans over Cora to pull the boxes back in place. 'Cora—are you in properly?'

'Sssh, Daddy!'

I have never been so close to him before. That is his shirtsleeve against the flesh of my bare arm, his leg pressing against mine. He is lying next to me, the way he would if . . . No, I must stop this. But now he is looking at me, here in the half-dark, his eyes shining.

He isn't smiling, yet still I notice his mouth. It's so close to mine, you see, our faces barely more than a hand's width apart. I can't believe I picked such a ridiculously small place to hide. Well, it is Sardines.

'Are you OK?' he whispers.

I nod, although I'm not remotely OK. I try to move then but there isn't a speck of space to move to. I slide my hand down, by my side. The edge of my hand brushes his. It's an accident, of course. It just—happened. Then, in the half-light, his little finger hooks itself round mine. It doesn't really count or anything—it's only because we're playing Sardines and squashed close together. You can't avoid touching, it's part of the game, a little playful, totally harmless flirtation.

Downstairs, on another floor, in another world, the doorbell rings once more. Dad would have to get it.

Footsteps running up the stairs now and Bonnie comes hurtling in with Matt. 'Gee, are you in here?' Matt's voice.

'Let me find her! Granddad says we've all got to come down now.'

'Gee?' Matt's voice again. 'It's not a trick. Game's over.'

We crawl out.

Matt looks at me, then down at my clothes. My black trousers look as though they've been used as a duster.

'We'd better go down,' he says. 'Guess who's just shown up?'

ELEVEN

A wonderful surprise

'HELLO, DARLING.'

By the time I had extricated myself from under the bed and brushed off the worst of the dust, Stephen was sitting in the kitchen, perched on the edge of a chair, and still wearing his jacket.

'Hi!' I said brightly. 'What a nice surprise!' I bent to kiss him although I found myself feeling decidedly cross about his impromptu appearance. It was nothing to do with Leo. It's just that the whole thing about Stephen is that he is predictable. In a good way. A way I like. 'We weren't expecting you.'

He gave me a sharp look, I thought, that said, 'Apparently not . . .' but I ignored it.

'I did try calling you on your mobile. You look like you've been spring-cleaning.' He swept some dust off my trousers.

'We were playing Sardines. You know, for the children.'

'What fun,' said Stephen, as if he couldn't imagine any activity on the planet that could be less fun. 'I'm sorry I missed it.'

'Hi,' Leo took a step forward. 'I'm Leo, by the way.'

'Stephen. With a—' Stephen cut himself short, with a nervous glance at Ellen. 'Georgia's *fiancé*,' he added.

'Oh, yes, sorry, haven't you two met yet?' I tucked my hair behind my ears. 'I was sure you had. Leo's recently moved into my block—you remember, Stephen, I did mention it?'

'And this is my daughter, Cora.' Leo rested his hands on her shoulders.

'Hello, Cora,' said Stephen, visibly relaxing. 'Well, I packed in no time, so decided to come and whisk you away for lunch.' He turned to the rest of the company. 'With my folks,' he explained.

'Oh, but I'm stuffed!' I waved a hand at the table.

'That's all right. Mum won't mind.' He rebuttoned his jacket. 'You *are* coming, aren't you?'

A glance at Ellen, at Matt, at Dad. A final one at Leo.

'Great,' I said, feeling like a kid who's been dragged away from the party before they've served up the birthday cake. 'Of course I'll come.'

The front door opened as we were getting out of the car. I'm sure Stephen's mother, Trish, must hover by the glazed panels in the porch whenever she's expecting someone so she can open the door before they've even reached the front gate.

'Stephen!' She tilted her face up as he bent to kiss her, looking up at him as if he were a Greek god. 'And Georgia! 'Scuse me still in my apron!'

I laughed automatically, knowing that I was expected to. Trish has a way of talking, her voice rising as if she's telling you a joke even when—which is always—she's telling you something completely prosaic. But then she laughs in this rather girlish way and you feel mean if you don't join in.

'I hope it's not putting you out, having me to lunch as well.'

'Putting me out! You're one of the family! And I popped in a couple of extra potatoes as soon as Stephen phoned me, so we won't be sending you away hungry, will we!' She laughed again.

'I won't eat all that much actually, because I just had brunch at—'

'Oh, I know. Your family! Breakfast all the day long! I don't know how your, how your father's wife manages. She must be run off her feet!'

She's never met Quinn, so she doesn't realise just how ludicrous the idea is of Quinn's being 'run off her feet'. Quinn never runs.

'Now. Nice cup of tea, Georgia? Or will you be naughty and take a sherry?' What I really fancied was a glass of wine, but I've long since given up saying yes to any wine offered in the Cooling household after a couple of how-can-I-tip-this-into-the-aspidistra experiences.

'Well . . . a sherry would be nice. Yes, let's live dangerously.' God, I'd started talking like her; it was rubbing off on me.

'Ooh, shall I join you?' She looked as if she might just explode from the excitement of it all. 'Ted, dear!' she screeched at him in the other room. He came shuffling through, smiled warmly, then waited passively for me to kiss him hello as usual.

'We girls are having a sherry!'

'I'll do the honours then, will I?'

I used to love coming here. I remember my very first visit. Trish was so kind, so solicitous, topping up my teacup and pressing de luxe selection chocolate biscuits on me rather than leaving me to fend for myself the way Stephen has to with my family. Everything was so clean and tidy and polished. It wasn't that it was my taste—it wasn't at all, but I loved it that their window ledges weren't piled high with stacks of books or old newspapers. I loved the fact that I could sit down without checking my chair for pens or keys or mouldering fruit. I loved it that Stephen came from such a family, such a house, I really did.

But, suddenly, I desperately wanted to be away from this well-ordered, brightly lit room. I wanted to be at home again—so much so that I almost cried out. Not my flat, I mean, but *home* home. I wanted to be sitting at the big old kitchen table with Dad reading out bits of the paper. I wanted to be listening to Ellen bitching about her customers at the wine bar and making me laugh. I even wanted to see Quinn with her patchwork jacket and her earrings swinging wildly as she talks. Suddenly, I craved the sheer, chaotic, ridiculous excess of it all.

'. . . top up?'

'Mmm? Sorry?'

'You were miles away! I was thinking I'd have to wave a flag and ring a bell at you!'

'Sorry.'

'Not at all. Don't you think of it. Get Ted to top your glass up. Ted! Georgia's glass is empty! It must be going all the way down to your ankles, Georgia, I can't keep up with you!'

'I'll be under the table by teatime,' I said flatly.

Trish exploded into great gales of laughter.

I leaned back in my chair and shut my eyes. I could feel a headache gathering behind my eyebrows, brewing like a storm.

TWELVE
About Cora

I RANG LEO THE NEXT DAY, desperate to find out more about his mystery daughter. He suggested we hook up in the evening because he had a real live job to do that day, photographing some author in a club in Soho.

'I can't, I've got my supervision then and I'm not usually home till ten. What about then—or is that too late?'

'Not for me, but if you still need supervision in the early evening, can you be trusted out on your own after ten?'

'I won't be on my own though, will I?' As Leo well knows, it's not that kind of supervision. No matter how long you've been counselling, you still discuss your cases with a supervisor if you've any sense.

'Just bang on my door when you're back.'

In my supervision session, I talked about various issues that had come up with clients, and how I had handled them. Supervision isn't therapy, and there was no reason to mention the events of the weekend, but I couldn't stop thinking about it all and, frankly, I don't know anyone who has more sense than Marian does in these matters.

'Why do *you* think you burst into tears when you saw Cora?' asked Marian.

'I just don't know! But maybe it was because I did have a bit of a tiny, insignificant crush on Leo and . . . oh, I don't know—his having a child puts him off limits because I don't want to be a stepmother. Hell, I don't even want to have kids of my own, as you know.'

Marian smiled, but remained infuriatingly silent.

'You don't think that's it?'

'Do you?'

I cupped my face in my hands and looked at her. 'I guess if that was really all it was, then I might have been disappointed, frustrated—even angry . . . but I don't think I'd have cried.' A small nod from Marian. 'I suppose that I was upset because my emotions were in conflict. Which means that I was ambivalent in some way. At some level, I was also—excited—maybe even happy. It doesn't make sense.' I shook my head. 'Can't you just tell me and put me out of my misery?'

Marian laughed. 'Now, Georgia, you know it's not like giving you a solution to a crossword puzzle. There's nothing I could possibly tell you that you don't know already.'

'But I *don't* know . . . you're saying I should go away and think about it?'

'No.' She shook her head. 'You do more than enough thinking. I'm saying you should go away and let yourself *feel* about it.'

I felt buzzing with energy, even after the brisk walk back to the flat, when I drummed a rat-a-tat-tat tattoo on Leo's door.

'Hey, you—come in. Has your supervisor let you off the leash?'

'No, I did a bunk while she was looking the other way.'

He smiled. 'I'm starving—have you eaten?'

'Pizza?'

He nodded and reached for his jacket. 'Let's get a takeaway.'

When we got to Pizza Express, he opened the door and waved for me to go ahead of him to the counter. 'Let's see . . .' He looked down the menu. 'You want a Giardinièra, but with artichokes instead of leeks, right? And no black pepper.'

I always have the same thing, but I hate feeling that I'm quite so predictable. 'No, I'll have the—' I scanned the menu, but nothing else seemed half as nice, then looked back at him. Leo was smiling knowingly. 'OK, I give in. I'm a boring old fart. I accept it. Same as usual.'

He ordered.

'. . . and a Four Seasons with extra cheese and extra garlic, please.'

'Now tell me all about Cora. Fill me in,' I said, as we walked back. 'Who is Cora's mother? Hazel, you said?'

'Yes—we had a brief thing over five years ago. It was never serious. We were so different—Hazel was quite . . . floaty . . . I think is how you'd put it. She drifted from one creative phase to another—making candles, batik wall-hangings. Also, she never got up till about noon and she used to smoke dope during the day and speak really slowly, like she had to think about everything for half an hour before she said it, drove me up the wall. I wanted to get up and get on and *do* things.'

'Was this in Glasgow?'

'No. She lived in Edinburgh, so I used to drive there at weekends to see her.' He turned to look at me as we walked. 'Don't go putting on your counsellor face at me—I know it wasn't a proper relationship, but it was fine at the time. Hazel was a nice person. Kind. Decent.'

'And where is she now? Presumably Cora lives with her?'

'No. Cora lives with Hazel's sister in Cricklewood. Look, maybe I should show you her letter—that explains it better than I can.'

Back at Leo's flat, he went and looked for the letter while I cut the pizza. We sat side by side on his sofa, eating straight from the boxes, and he handed me the letter.

Dear Leo,

I hope this letter reaches you. I wrote before to the last address I had for you but there was no response—so I don't know whether you received it or not. If you did—and chose to ignore it—please, please reply to this one because it is now urgent.

I hope you don't think me weird for writing to you out of the blue like this—I know what we had, our relationship or whatever you like to call it, lasted only a few months and wasn't even what you'd call serious. I don't remember even saying 'I love you' though I feel as if I did in my own way.

Leo—you got me pregnant. Remember that time—just a week or two before we split up? It was the middle of the night and my room was hot and stuffy and neither of us could sleep. I turned to you then, pulled you towards me and, half in a dream it seemed, we made love. Did I know I would get pregnant? No. Of course not. Did I hope for it? I was scared, but yes, I have to say I did. My fortieth birthday was round the corner and who could blame me for thinking it might be my last chance?

I know we'd never have lasted as a couple—less so with a child, I truly believe that. As soon as I knew, I moved back south, to Devon where I grew up. I rented a tiny cottage by the sea. I used to think of you sometimes, when I walked by the water's edge with my—our—baby in a sling, thinking of how you would have loved to photograph it there—the views across the water to the other side of the bay, the light changing hour by hour.

Forgive me for not telling you sooner, for waiting until it was too late. Leo, I—we—had a beautiful baby girl. Her name is Cora Anne—I hope you like it. She is nearly five now. She's a daily delight—sweet-natured though rather shy, with bright, sparkling eyes like your own. She has been my joy, Leo, so thank you for that. I didn't tell you before because I was sure you'd show up, determined to 'do the decent thing' and I didn't want that.

But now I'm so angry with myself. Ashamed too for not letting you know because—remember what you used to say? 'Life doesn't go according to plan'? How right you were.

I'll be blunt. I'm dying, Leo, and there's not a bloody thing I can do about it. I've got ovarian cancer and they tell me that if they'd caught it earlier, perhaps they'd have been able to save me. You'll no doubt be pleased to know that I didn't waste time with my crystals but went straight for the chemo. We've moved back to London, and we're staying with my sister in Cricklewood.

I've given Cora a photo of us together and told her that you live a long, long way away—in case you don't want to see her. But it would be good for her to know she still has one parent to turn to. Please, please get in touch as soon as you get this—if you get this—for Cora's sake, for yours—if not for mine. This is my sister's phone number and address . . .

I'm so sorry.

With love and many regrets,

Hazel

I swallowed hard and looked up at him as I finished the letter. His eyes met mine.

'Quite a letter, hmm?' He clicked his tongue, the way he does sometimes when he's feeling stressed or doesn't know what to do next. 'It didn't reach me for over three months. By the time I phoned her sister, Hazel had been dead for a month.'

'Oh—how awful. I'm so sorry. Poor Cora.'

'Yup. Poor little mite. I felt pretty gutted.' He sank back into the cushions. 'And now all Cora's got is me—and her aunt's family, of course. At least they're pretty steady.'

'Hey—you're not so bad yourself. She's lucky to have you.'

That lopsided smile again. 'Thank you, but I haven't got a clue how to be a dad. I've barely got my own life together, for God's sake.' He waved an arm at the semi-unpacked boxes, the tripods and equipment.

'You can learn. That's only what every parent has to do anyway. At least you've managed to skip the crappy nappies and sleepless nights . . .' Watching his face, his eyes. 'I'm sorry, now is not the time to be flippant.'

'That's OK. Sometimes flippancy is more useful than sympathy.'

I leaned back on the sofa. 'So what happens now?'

'Now I'm a weekend dad—I get to take Cora out for the day on Saturday or Sunday. But, boy, do I know I'm on probation. Hazel's sister is one tough cookie—pick her up on time, bring her back on time, don't buy her sweets, don't fill her up with fizzy drinks, hold her hand when you're crossing the road.'

'Most of that's pretty sensible, surely?'

'Oh, sensible, schmensible. I want Cora to have fun—I want her to know that the world's wonderful and exciting and weird.'

'She *will* have fun. She can discover how wonderful the world is—but you have to be sensible for her, don't you see that? Just think—she's had this huge loss and a massive upheaval—she's lost her mother, her home, everything. It'll be all she can do just to keep her head above water—but you can help her by being the rock in her life.'

He looked at me, assessing. 'You're not just a pretty face, are you?'

'Oh, hush—or I'll start taking myself seriously.'

He cleared away the pizza boxes then and offered me a coffee.

I looked at my watch. 'No, thanks. I can't believe how late it is. I must go. I've got a client at eight o'clock tomorrow morning.'

Leo made a face. 'OK.' He showed me out. 'Hey—and thank you. For what you said.' He leaned forward suddenly and kissed me on the cheek.

'Any time.'

'Maybe you could come with us some time?' He dug his hands deep into his pockets. 'Cora and me, I mean.' I looked into his eyes and saw that it wasn't just a casual invitation. 'She liked you,' he said.

THIRTEEN

Close to the edge

'I MEANT TO SAY—I had a good chat with your dad on Sunday, after you left,' Leo told me.

'He's great, isn't he? Well, great if he's someone else's dad, I imagine.'

Leo frowned. 'I thought you got on well with him? You seem so close.'

'We do OK—I just get a bit exasperated by him at times. When he doesn't listen properly because he's reading the paper at the same time as ostensibly having a conversation, or when he plays devil's advocate just to keep an argument going. And you should see his study—it looks like a paper-recycling depot. He never, ever files anything.'

'Well, he's the one who has to live with it. Why don't you just not go in his study if it annoys you so much?'

I made a face. 'Will you please not be so rational and sensible? That's my job. And I suppose you and your family never exchange a cross word? You never find them annoying?'

'Of course I do. We talk, we argue—we're a family. It drives me bonkers the way my mother insists on keeping every single leftover item of food, even one lone boiled potato.'

'She sounds wonderful.' And I meant it. I loathe waste.

'So, is your mum still on the scene or what?' Leo settled back into my sofa. 'I didn't like to ask your dad, or—'

'She's dead.'

'I'm sorry, I didn't mean to sound flip about it—was it recently?' He sat forward again, his face serious.

'God, no. Years and years ago. I was ten.'

'That must have been awful.' He shook his head, as if remembering it himself. 'So, do you mind my asking—what did she die of? Was it cancer?'

I shook my head. 'Funny how people tend to assume it was cancer.' I stood up, walked over to my rubber plant and dipped to feel how dry the compost was. 'Must give this a water.' Crossed back to the sink, started filling a jug. 'She—well, she fell down the stairs at home, the ones down to her studio and—' I shrugged. 'Well, that was it. She slipped. Her neck was broken. At least it was quick.'

He stood up and came nearer, but I avoided his eye and started watering the rubber plant.

'I'm sorry.'

I moved away to put the jug back by the sink.

'No need to be. Really. I'm not saying I never miss her or that I don't care. I've just . . . moved on, that's all.' I nodded. Subject closed.

'OK. If you say so.' He stood up and started fingering the edge of one of the plant's glossy leaves. 'I'm surprised your dad didn't want to sell the house afterwards—it must be a painful reminder for you all.'

'He did want to, but I—we—asked him not to. It has lots of good memories, too. And we don't have much else that's connected to her.'

'Oh?'

'Well, there are photos, of course, and a handful of her paintings but most of those were—but home is still home—that's the house she first bought and decorated with Dad. And very little's changed really. That big dresser in the kitchen—Mum found it in a junk shop and stripped off all the paint to get back to the wood. Things like that—they hold your memories, don't they?'

He nodded, considering. 'And don't you find—' he began, his voice serious. 'I notice—in myself, I mean—traits I've got from my dad, like the fact that I can whistle really well but can't sing to save my life and I love sweet-sour cucumbers but don't like olives—'

'But surely most of that's just because you grew up around him?'

'You'd think so, wouldn't you? But what's weird is that I didn't used to be like that. I couldn't whistle before and I didn't like sweet-sour—'

'You think it's mystical? What?'

He shook his head. 'No. You know me—arch-sceptic most of the time. I don't know what I think really—maybe some of the things were already there in me, but I just didn't recognise them until after he died.'

'But I'm not like my mother at all, so bang goes your theory.'

'You must be. There must be some qualities . . .'

'No. Not at all. I take after Dad's side more. My mother was very sparkly, you know? Full of life. She was not exactly beautiful, but charismatic, bubbly. Ellen looks quite like her.'

'So Ellen got all the breaks? What a shame . . .'

'Hilarious. I'm just *saying* you can't assume that children always take after their parents. I'm completely different. You've seen what the others are like—I'm the inexplicable white sheep in the family.'

'But—I'm not sure you are that different . . . granted, I can see you're fiendishly organised and they're not—but you're all—how can I put it? You're all—cut from the same bale of cloth. And I bet, if you think about it, there'll be some way in which you take after your mum—like your cooking maybe or your amazing eyes or—or the way you half poke your tongue out when you're really concentrating on something—'

'I don't do that!'

'Yes, you do. You did it the other day when you were chopping something very finely with that big scary kitchen knife of yours.'

I paused, remembering. 'She used to do that when she was painting.'

'There then. You see?'

'Mmm.' I cleared my throat. 'Still, that's only one tiny thing. I'm not like her in anything significant.'

He looked into my eyes for a moment, seemed about to say something, then he simply smiled and reached for his jacket.

'See you tomorrow then?'

'Yes. Tomorrow.'

Half-term. Thursday. Georgia, now nine and a half, and Ellen, nearly three, are hungry. Matt, as usual, has sloped off to a friend's house. It is well past lunchtime.

Georgia knocks timidly at the door of their mother's studio and, when there is no answer, puts her head round.

'Mummy? What's for lunch?'

Joy is painting. Tongue poised between her lips in concentration, she scrunches her eyes half-closed at the canvas in front of her. Every inch of the table next to her is crowded with jars jammed with old brushes, dirty cups, tubes of paint.

'Hmmm?'

'Lunch. We're hungry. Ellen's hungry.'

Joy peers at Georgia as if about to transfer her dimensions to the canvas. 'You can find something, can't you? There's plenty of food.'

'No.' Georgia, patiently. 'There isn't.'

'Oh, well, there must be something. Make yourselves cheese on toast, you're good at that. Mummy's painting just now.'

'There isn't any cheese.'

Joy turns away again, back to the fragments of light and dark, the play of shadows demanding her attention once more.

'Well—just toast for now then, hmm? Mummy will take you both out later somewhere nice. Special treat.'

Georgia doesn't bother to ask where or at what time because she knows there is no point. Joy stabs her brush into an extrusion of burnt umber on the dinner plate she is using as a palette. Georgia goes back up to the kitchen and heads for the breadbin. There are three slices of bread left and two of them are ends. Georgia fishes down into the wrapper, then recoils as if she has been stung. The bread is spotted with blue mould circles. She pushes the lot into the rubbish bin.

In the larder, Georgia finds a packet of breadsticks and, on the table, the butter from breakfast is still out, as are jars of jam and honey. Georgia shows Ellen what to do, dipping the end of a breadstick first in the butter then directly in the jam jar. Ellen is delighted.

'You're very lucky,' Georgia informs her. 'Breadsticks are what people have for lunch in posh restaurants.'

'**S**o what would you do if you were my counsellor and I was your patient?' Leo digs his spoon deep into a tub of Belgian chocolate ice cream and offers it to me.

We sit side by side on his jacket, looking out at the lights of the city from the roof of our apartment block. I had no idea you could get up here, but Leo had discovered that the door marked 'Fire Exit' on the top floor led out onto the roof. The view is amazing, breathtaking.

'Client, not patient. And you wouldn't be.'

'Why? Am I beyond help?'

'Undoubtedly, but that's not why. I couldn't take you on because I'm—' I stop myself short. It's weird—whenever I'm around Leo, I find myself thinking out loud, saying things I would never say normally. 'Because I see you socially already, it wouldn't be—appropriate,' I say.

'Why?' He's like a child sometimes. Why, why, why, all the time. 'That could be seen as a good thing, because I'm already relaxed with you.'

'I don't make the rules. But you can see it makes sense. If you already have some kind of relationship with the prospective client—'

'That would be me.'

'Yes, you or whoever—some sort of relationship, no matter how *slight or superficial*, there's a risk that the client may already have some feelings regarding the counsellor that are not part of the process and—'

'What about the counsellor? Is he or she immune to all this or . . . '

'No, that's right. The counsellor is also human, of course, so he or she may not be able to be one hundred per cent impartial either.'

He swings round to look at me. 'I see. And is she?'

'Is she what? Who?'

'She, the counsellor—you, then. Impartial, I mean.'

'Impartial as regards . . .?'

'The potential client. Um—me.'

I get up and take a few steps towards the edge of the roof, stand there with my back to him—but whether it's so I can't see his face or he can't see mine, I'm not sure. 'Not one hundred per cent impartial. No.'

'And why are you announcing this vital fact to the dome of St Paul's?'

'It's important to keep significant landmarks well informed, I always feel, don't you? Most people neglect to.'

'When you've finished chatting to the rooftops, do you think you might turn round and look at me?' I hear him stand up.

'I've still got Big Ben and the Houses of Parliament to talk to.'

'What say you talk to me about this not quite hundred per cent impartiality and we notify the architectural highlights of Central London a bit later?'

I nod slowly, then turn to face him.

'So—if you're not a hundred per cent impartial, just how impartial are you?' He comes one step closer. 'Ninety-seven per cent? Eighty-nine per cent?'

'Bit less than that.' I step towards him.

'Seventy-two per cent? Sixty-three?'

'Mm—lower.'

'Thirty-one per cent?' He seems to be standing right in front of me.

'I think it might be more of a fraction of a percentage.' I look up into his eyes. 'More like, say, two-fifths.'

'Didn't your teacher tell you never to mix fractions and percentages?'

'Yes. They're too different. You mustn't mix them. It doesn't work.'

'Except . . .' He puts his hand on my waist and pulls me gently towards him.

'Except?' I echo, tilting my face up to his.

'Except when it does.'

A minute later—or perhaps it's an hour?—I pull away.

'This isn't right.' I shake my head. 'I can't do this.'

'Well—why *are* you doing it then?' He is smiling that funny lopsided half-smile of his, but the question is serious.

'I don't know.'

'Cheers—flattery will get you nowhere.'

'I'm sorry.' I rest my head against his chest for a moment.

'Is it because of Stephen? Or because of Cora?'

'Stephen, of course. What on earth has Cora got to do with it?'

'I don't know—just a feeling. I mean, you seemed really good with her, but you told me that you can't see yourself ever having kids and—you know—I come as a package deal now.'

'I can't see how having one kiss with you has got anything to do with—'

'Of *course* it has. Come on, we're not fifteen any more. It *matters*.'

'Don't have a go at me.' I pull away from him.

'Hey, hey.' He takes my hand. 'Look, I'm not the kind of person who goes round busting up other people's relationships, but you and Stephen—I mean—you've been engaged all this time yet—'

'So?' I pull my hand away. 'What's wrong with that? If more people took their time and didn't rush into marriage, there'd be a much lower divorce rate. There are so many things to go wrong.'

'True.' He nods. 'Such as who you choose to marry.'

'That's a really nasty thing to say. You don't know Stephen, you don't know anything about him. He's a wonderful person.'

'So why are you kissing another man on a rooftop?'

'I'm not.' I take another step back. 'It was a mistake. I'm sorry.'

'And you see no reason why you shouldn't carry on with Stephen as if nothing's happened between us?'

'Nothing *has* happened—just *one* kiss. What on earth makes you imagine I'd even want someone like you?'

'Thanks. So what am I then? Did you just think you could have one last fling before you get that ring on your finger? Thanks a million.'

'Don't be ridiculous—you know I'm not like that!'

'Well, what are you up to then? You want Stephen? Fine—you've got him. If you only wanted to be friends with me, Georgia, that would've been OK, you know. But if you're not interested, then don't bloody keep looking at me like that with those great big eyes of yours, don't melt into my arms as if you were meant to be there and don't go kissing me as if you—' He clamps his lips shut, then opens them again only to make that soft clucking noise he does with his tongue. 'I'm sorry. As you say, it's only a kiss.' He nods towards the door. 'Coming?'

'Mmm.' I check my watch. 'Oh, I'm late. I'm never late!' I cannot meet his eye. 'I *am* sorry. I wasn't thinking—'

'Hey, no big deal, OK?' He laughs it off. 'Forget it—it's just a kiss. Kids of ten get up to more mischief than that these days.'

I nod. He's right, of course. No big deal, no big deal at all.

'**A**nd don't forget Ellen's birthday party on the 10th,' I said to Stephen as we went through our diaries. 'Brian's letting her have the upstairs room at the wine bar. And giving her the wine at cost. And throwing in free bruschettas and stuff.'

'Which he's doing purely out of the goodness of his heart?' Stephen smiled knowingly.

'Quite. It's strange, actually, because Ellen's not usually slow to notice men being besotted with her. Anyway, you know what she's like—if a man's halfway decent and suitable, then she's not interested.'

'I'm glad you're not like that.' He patted my leg and smiled again. 'We don't have to stay long, do we?'

'Don't force yourself if it's that much of a penance. I'll go on my own.'

'Silly. Course I'll go. I just don't want some *barman* having a go at me because I do a job that involves wearing a suit. Her friends all act as if working in an office means you've sold out to the capitalist oppressors.'

'Don't exaggerate. What's wrong with being a barman anyway?'

'That's rich. You're the one who's always saying that Ellen's "wasting herself" working at the wine bar.'

'Well, she *is*.'

'So, what's good enough for some people isn't good enough for your family?' He laughed.

'Well, if you had a child, wouldn't you want it to grow up to be—an MP, say, rather than a barman?'

He laughed again. I hate it when he laughs during an argument. It makes me feel he's waiting for me to stop being a stroppy little woman.

'Can I just point out that MPs don't earn particularly good money, so that wouldn't be my first choice—going into the law or, if he were creative, perhaps advertising, would be preferable. Of course I'm ambitious—why shouldn't I be? Unlike Ellen, I don't think having a proper job makes me a boring person and, by the way, Ellen isn't actually your child, so it's not really a valid comparison, is it?'

God, he can be infuriating.

'You know that's not what I meant. Don't deliberately misunderstand.'

'I'm not. It's sweet that you want to protect her, very sweet—you're a lovely, kind person—and I do understand, but—'

'No.' I shook my head. 'I don't think you do.'

'Well, all I'm saying is if you stopped bailing her out every time she has some trumped-up crisis, she might start growing up a bit.'

I dug my fingers into my thigh in an effort to combat a strong urge to punch him.

'Come on, darling.' He put his arm round me, but I shook it off. 'I'm only saying what you've more or less said yourself enough times.'

'Stephen—everybody occasionally gets irritated by their own family. It's normal.'

Stephen, of course, though certainly the most 'normal' person I know, never, ever criticises his family. 'The point is,' I continued, 'that it doesn't give outsiders a licence to join in. I never criticise Trish or Ted, never.'

Stephen sighed. Sometimes I feel like a naughty child in his company. 'Sweetie, you don't *occasionally* get *irritated* by your family. You're always moaning about them. Of course it's not the same with my family.'

He was exaggerating ridiculously. Everybody whinges a little about their family, don't they? 'Why isn't it? Because they're perfect, I suppose?'

Don't get started on this, I told myself.

He smiled. 'Come on then—let's have it.' He sat back. 'I won't be offended. I can listen to criticism without getting worked up, you know.'

'It's not a criticism of *you*.'

'I know that. That's exactly my point. So my family. Their less positive traits. Carry on.'

'Well . . .' I hesitated and I could see him thinking I was having trouble coming up with anything. 'You know I'm fond of your parents . . . but sometimes . . . I mean, not all the time—don't you ever find them just the tiniest bit . . . boring?'

He looked at me for a moment, and then he laughed. A great big, hearty laugh. 'Is that all? So what? It's hardly a big deal. I thought you were going to come up with something serious for a moment.'

Hardly a big deal? Not serious? If you'd accused anyone in my family of being boring—Bonnie, Daniel even—they'd have been distraught.

Stephen patted me as if I were an errant puppy and stood up. 'Come on, let's hit the hay.'

It really gives me the creeps when he says that. It's like he's *trying* to be old before his time.

Ellen's birthday falls on a Thursday this year, but the party is on the Saturday after. She always asks Dad and Quinn to her parties, but this time we'd just found out that Quinn's daughter Simone would be around too. Simone's been off working in New York, so she's let her flat, which means she sometimes descends on Dad's house when she's over.

'George, save me from the dragon!' Ellen said on the phone. Scary though Simone is, the dragon tag in fact relates to her habit of exhaling through her nostrils when she's smoking—i.e. all the time.

'Look—Simone won't want to hang out anywhere that doesn't serve nonstop champagne. She's not going to drag over to some celeb-free wine bar for two glasses of Rioja and a tomato bruschetta, is she?'

'Yes, she is. She's not busy—Quinn said so.'

'Well, you're having how many people? Thirty? Forty?'

'Fifty-eight and rising. Brian's going to throw a major wobbly. I swore I'd keep it to no more than forty-five.'

'He's so in love with you, you could invite everyone you know to doss down in the bar for a week and he'd probably end up tucking them in.'

'So untrue!' But she laughed. 'He gave me a total bollocking last week because he said I'd been late three nights in a row.'

'And had you?'

'No. I was only late Tuesday, Thursday and Friday—that's not in a row.'

I sighed. I can't believe he puts up with her.

'Anyway, with any luck Simone will spend the whole evening standing outside bellowing into her mobile and you won't even see her.'

'Perhaps. By the way, I asked Leo too—you don't mind?'

'No. No. Why should I?'

There was no reason to mind. So far, I'd managed to fight the urge to confide in her about the kiss. Knowing her, she'd make a huge deal out of it then casually let it slip in front of Stephen. I can't think why I let Leo kiss me. It was just being on the rooftop, the lights all around us, like being in a different world. It's easy to get caught up in some ridiculous romantic fantasy, but, sooner or later, you've got to come back down to earth and accept what you *know* is best for you.

'Good. He's nice, isn't he? Quite sexy, too, despite the lack of hair.'

'Mmm. Suppose so. I haven't really thought about it.'

Ellen laughed. 'You are the world's most crap liar. Don't worry, I won't tell Stephen about your secret lust for your next-door neighbour—'

'He's not next door—and I don't have—'

'Yeah, yeah, we know. Never mind—see you on Saturday and please come early,' Ellen begged. 'I need you to be rent-a-crowd at the start, otherwise it looks all sad and empty.'

'Then we can piss off when your real friends arrive, you mean?'

'No way—you've got to stick it out till the bitter end. Till the last guest is lying in the gutter.'

'How lovely.'

'Hi, Georgia. On your own?' Brian, Ellen's boss, waved me over.

'Yes. Stephen's not coming till later.'

'Oh. I meant Ellen.'

'She's not here yet? I knew I was stupid to get here so early.'

'It's fine. Come on up and have a glass of wine.'

The room looked great, with two huge vases of flowers, chairs and tables pulled back round the edges so there would be a small area of floor for dancing later, and a long table for the food.

'Red or white?'

'Perhaps I'd better start with water. I don't want to get carried away.'

'Very sensible. Some of my customers think they've entered some kind of drinkathon the second they walk in the door.'

I laughed. 'It's really kind of you to do all this for Ellen.'

'Ah, get away,' he said in his soft Irish accent. 'She's a good worker.'

God, he must be seriously in love.

I laughed again, then he laughed too.

'OK, no she's not, but she is good with customers and that counts for a lot. Quite a few of the guys fancy her, so they keep coming back.' He looked away from me, concentrating on opening a bottle of wine. 'She's very attractive, isn't she? You can't blame them. I mean, I think she is.'

'She *is* very fond of you.'

He snorted. 'Great. I'll crack open the Dom Pérignon, will I?' He poured me a glass of mineral water.

'So, how's your love life, Georgia? Cheer me up. Tell me it can be done.'

'Oh, well—you remember Stephen?'

'Tall, handsome bastard, right?'

'That's him. Well, we're engaged. We have been for a while.'

'Good on you—when's the Big Day?'

'We haven't finalised the actual date yet.'

'Oh, rightio. And are you wanting the big family do, or are you planning to run off to Las Vegas just the two of you?'

'I couldn't get married without my family. Well, they're more important than the groom, aren't they?'

He laughed and I did too, though a moment later I realised how weird it sounded.

'I'll tell him that when he turns up, will I?'

'Brian!' One of the bar staff called over to him. 'Phone! It's Ellen!'

'You'd think she'd manage to get here on time if she wasn't having to work, wouldn't you?'

A few moments later he came back and said, 'She's having a crisis, she says. She wants me to drive you over to her flat.'

Two minutes later, we were on our way to Ellen's flat.

'Shall I come up too?' Brian asked.

'Better not in case it's a girlie-type crisis.'

'Give her a boot up the arse and tell her to get cracking. Tell her I'll wait ten minutes, no more.'

When I got up to the flat, Ellen was running around like a headless chicken, struggling to put up a dilapidated ironing board.

'It won't go up! What can I do?' Her voice was starting to take on the note of hysteria Ellen reserves for completely minor setbacks.

'Phone the fire brigade? I'm sure they won't mind coming to sort out your domestic accoutrements. Oh, give it here—I'll have a go while you get the rest of your clothes on.'

'What rest of clothes?' She held up an extremely crumpled dress.

I battled with the ironing board, but it was like trying to set up a deck chair in a Force 10 gale.

'Anyway, I thought ironing was against your religion? You never buy anything that needs ironing.'

'I know. This is Siobhan's.'

Ah-ha, the flatmate's. 'And does she know you're borrowing it?' The catch suddenly loosened and I managed to release the legs—but only to get the board up at knee-height.

'She's not fussed. Unlike *some* people, she doesn't go into a total strop if I borrow something of hers for a couple of hours.' She knelt down at the semi-prostrate ironing board and spread out the dress. 'This is *really* hard, you know.' She said it the way she used to when she was about seven or eight and struggling to wrap a present neatly or wipe the table, wanting someone else to do it for her.

'It's not exactly scaling Everest in stilettos, is it? It's *ironing*.'

'It's all right for you . . .' she said, somehow managing to iron a crease into the shoulder strap. 'You're so neat. You don't even have to try.'

'Of course I try. What makes you think I don't?'

'Because Georgia equals tidy plus neat plus . . . whatever.'

'Plus uptight plus controlling plus bossy plus . . .?' Is that really the sum of me? How other people see me? 'What a wonderful equation.'

'Don't be daft.' Ellen stood up and put the dress on. 'You could say plus warm-hearted plus clever plus funny plus unselfish plus longing to do her little sister's hair in a French plait.'

'Go on then. Sit down. Where's your brush?'

'It was in the kitchen, but someone moved it. Siobhan's is on the table there—you can use that. She won't mind.'

I reached for the brush and started taming Ellen's hair.

'Tell me about the time you cut my hair,' she said.

'What—again? You know it better than I do by now.'

She nodded.

'Good grief. Well, it was a few months after Mum died and we were playing hairdressers, and you said, "Cut my hair! Cut it!" So I *did* but . . .'

'. . . it was all crooked . . .'

'. . . and it looked really silly. And I thought you'd start crying, but when you looked in the mirror you thought it was funny.'

'Yes, and you thought it was hysterical too, didn't you? And we both laughed and laughed. And then Dad came down and—'

'Your plait's done. We'd better get going.' I held the end tight in my fingers. 'Have you got an elastic thingy?'

FOURTEEN

Fun, fun, fun

'DO YOU REALISE,' SAID STEPHEN, 'that there are well over a hundred piercings in this room? That girl over there has got five in her left ear and one in her tongue!'

'And that's only the ones you can see.'

Stephen winced. 'Can we go yet?' It wasn't even half past ten.

'I really can't. You go if you like. I don't mind.'

Just then, Leo appeared. I watched him saying hello to Dad, Quinn and Simone, then he got scooped up by Ellen.

'Leo! Leo!' She threw her arms round him and started introducing him to her coterie, clutching him as if he were one of her oldest friends. I saw him half craning his neck round, trying to catch my eye, as three of Ellen's giggly friends clustered close round him.

'Well, if I'm not going I might as well have another drink,' Stephen said, as if I'd insisted he stay. 'Sweetie?'

'I'd better switch to water now. Thanks.'

While Stephen was at the bar, Leo appeared by my side. I peered to either side of him, pretending to be surprised. 'No groupies?'

'I chucked them some jelly babies then ran the other way. Do I get a kiss hello or what?'

I smiled and turned my face slightly so he'd kiss my cheek.

'You smell gorgeous.'

'Thank you. Stephen's here by the way.'

'So? Does he smell gorgeous too?'

I punched his arm lightly, as Stephen came back with the drinks.

'Stephen! Good to see you again!' Leo held out his hand.

'Wasn't expecting to see you here.' Stephen shook his hand. 'Glad you could make it.' It was hard to imagine anyone sounding less glad.

There was an awkward silence.

'I was just saying to Georgia how incredibly young everyone here seems,' Leo said, swigging his beer from the bottle.

'Yes. Very true. We feel like that too, don't we, darling?'

Just at that moment Ellen came over and dragged me away. 'Just borrowing George. You two can manage without her, can't you? Good.'

'What are you doing? You can't leave those two alone together. You could cut the atmosphere with a knife.'

'Good. Let them fight it out between them, then you can swoop in and claim the victor.'

'I don't want the victor. I want—I don't want all this tension. There's no reason for them not to get on. No reason at all. It's not rational.'

Ellen rolled her eyes. 'This isn't about being rational. It's about biology—whose sperms will be successful?'

'I don't want anybody's sperm—successful or otherwise. Where are you dragging me?'

'Simone's having a go at Quinn, as usual. Come and make them play nicely. I've got to get Brian to whap the music up. I want to dance.'

'**Y**ou're looking very nice,' I said to Quinn, hoping to cheer her up a bit. 'Um, interesting earrings—are they new?'

Simone sat there silently, taking deep drags on her cigarette, alternating with large gulps of wine. She stood up to go to the bar for a refill, vaguely gesturing at the rest of us. We all three shook our heads.

'You OK, Dad?'

He smiled as the music suddenly got a lot louder and Ellen bellowed: 'Come on, everyone! Dance!' She started dancing at once, pulling people away from their small groups to make them join in.

'Feeling a bit old for all this,' Dad shouted in my ear.

'Same here.'

'Not at your age. Come and have one dance before we head off.'

As Dad spun me round, doing the strange, slow, all-purpose jazz-jive-type dancing he performs to every sort of music, I spotted Stephen, talking to the pierced-tongue woman, apparently deep in conversation. Leo was behind me, dancing with Quinn. Ellen was gyrating madly and thrusting as if she were on show in some seedy lap joint.

'Why don't you dance with Quinn, Dad?'

'Good idea.' He sashayed over to her in an embarrassing, Dad-ish way, did a silly mock bow, then took her hand.

Leo took a step towards me, brows raised.

Stephen joined us.

'Hi! Saw you'd been abandoned—so I've come to your rescue!' He held my elbow, then started to dance.

Leo backed off and I saw him go to the bar. A slow number came on and Ellen swooped in on Stephen, like a hawk to a dormouse.

'Mr P-h! Come on! Dance with me!' She looped her arms round his neck and he put his arms round her waist.

Leo is still standing by the bar, next to Brian. They are both looking at me, smiling. Suddenly, I feel as if I'm fifteen again, waiting to be asked to dance. This is silly. I could dance with either of them. It would be perfectly natural. Rude not to really.

Now Leo is standing next to me. He doesn't say a word, just takes my hand, pulls me closer, his hand on my waist. And we are dancing. He is holding me the old-fashioned way; it's perfectly respectable. We are barely touching—just the occasional accidental bump of hip against hip, my breasts almost brushing his chest as we turn. I can feel him looking at me, then I feel his breath in my hair and I look up at him. He gives me the smallest of smiles and squeezes my hand, but so slightly that I am not sure whether he really has or if I have imagined it.

The track ended, then glided seamlessly into another. Dad tapped me on the shoulder. 'We're just off,' he said.

Ellen broke away from Stephen to hug Dad. She was unsteady on her feet, hanging on his arm. Dad looked at me, frowning, for reassurance. I nodded and mouthed, 'It's OK,' and shooed him away.

I was talking to Brian, when Ellen came up to me.

'George—tell Brian he should serve some frozen vodka. It's fantastic.'

'I'm not doing it, Ellen, so save your breath.' Brian wiped down the bar. 'Half of them are well pissed as it is. And it's not in your budget.'

'Who cares? Take it out of my wages.' Ellen put on her sulky face.

'Ellen! Stop it!' I was mortified, knowing Brian had already provided all the drink at cost price. 'There's plenty to drink. No one needs vodka as well. And you certainly shouldn't be having any vodka—you're drunk.'

'I'm s'posed to be drunk! It's my birthday! You should be drunk too.'

I turned to Brian. 'I'm so sorry—she's just awful when she's like this.'

'But George doesn't get drunk, does she?' Ellen was practically shouting now. 'Does you? Do you? No. No—George *doesn't* drink. George *doesn'* have fun. George *doesn'* get good sex with the P-h, do you? No wonder she's so uptight.'

'Ellen! For God's sake.'

'Ellen—' Brian laid a hand on her arm. 'Enough now. C'mon—have a coffee with me.' She shook him away and returned to the dance floor, joining three or four friends who had also had way too much.

A couple of people cast sympathetic glances at me.

'Did Ellen just say what I thought she said?' Stephen said, furious.

'Yes. I can't believe it. Can we go now?'

'Why did she say that?'

'Why are you sounding cross with *me*? It's not because of anything *I've* ever said to her—if that's what you're worried about.'

'Where's your jacket?'

I pointed to the back of a chair beside the bar.

Leo came over. 'You OK?'

I nodded dumbly.

'Take care of yourself,' he said quietly. He bent to kiss my cheek, his hand briefly holding the flesh of my bare arm. 'I'll call you.'

Stephen came back and held out my jacket for me, I waved goodbye to Brian, and we left.

FIFTEEN

The morning after

I RANG DAD AND TOLD HIM I couldn't make brunch because I'd be going to Stephen's parents. I know Ellen—she'll have conveniently forgotten all about last night and won't even apologise, then I'll look like I'm mean and pathetic for still being cross about it.

Then I took Stephen breakfast in bed, poached eggs on toast.

'Thank you for spoiling me. Aren't you having any?'

'I've had some toast. I'm saving myself for lunch.'

'Good.' He nodded. 'Mum's really pleased you're coming.'

'I'm very sorry about what Ellen said—last night—I hadn't said anything—I'm completely content with our sex life, you know that . . .'

'Georgia, I know you share everything with Ellen. Almost everything,' he amended, seeing I was about to protest. 'But if you swear that you never tell her . . . personal things . . . what happens between us in the bedroom, then I'm content. I take your word for it, of course I do.'

'Good. But I'm sorry she said it. She can be so embarrassing.'

'But, darling—are you going to spend your whole life apologising for Ellen all the time?' He shook his head. 'She carries on as if she's still seventeen or something. If she was a member of my family, there's no way I'd let her get drunk and carry on like that.'

'Hang on a sec—one minute you're saying I shouldn't be apologising for her, then the next you seem to be implying that it's somehow my problem and I ought to be able to control her.'

'Not at all. But surely your father could have a word with her?'

'If Dad started laying down the law she'd laugh in his face.'

'Well, he should have instituted a bit more respect earlier on. We're not going to let our kids be like Ellen, are we, darling?' Stephen frowned. 'Children need a bit of discipline, you know.'

'Stephen . . . um—you know when you talk about having kids . . .?'

'Yes.' He smiled.

'How much do you want them? I mean, do you think having them would be the most important, amazing thing you could ever do?'

He laughed.

'Hardly that, darling. No, of course not.' He wiped the last crumbs from his mouth neatly then scrunched up his paper napkin. 'They're just part of normal life, aren't they? Meet someone you like, fall in love, settle down, get married, have two or three kids, then watch your life savings get eaten away by school fees!' He laughed again.

'It's just—you know—I thought you knew—that I'm really not—I'm not sure, you see—if I want to have any . . .'

'Don't be silly!' Stephen waggled my knee to and fro. 'We can hire lots of help—a live-in nanny, au pair, whatever you like.'

'No, it's not that. It's just—' I shrugged. 'I don't think I want them.'

'Oh.'

'I'm sorry. I should have spelled it out more clearly before.'

'Of course, we don't *have* to have children.'

'What?'

He took my hand and rubbed his thumb across the knuckles.

'I'm not one hundred per cent dead set on it, darling, if that's what you're worried about. You sweet thing—you've been giving yourself a hard time over it, I can tell. I don't see kids as being the be-all and end-all of my purpose in life. We can make a great life for ourselves, just the two of us. To be honest . . .' he rubbed his thumb back and forth over my hand, 'if anything, I'd say I'm quite relieved. Just think,' his voice brightened, 'no school fees, so we can have topnotch holidays—the Caribbean, the Seychelles, wherever we fancy.'

'You're just trying to be nice. I can't possibly deprive you of children.'

'You're *not* depriving me, I swear. The more I think about it, the more it makes sense.' He pulled back the covers and leapt out of bed. 'Right, then. Let me at that shower.'

I have an unwritten rule not to venture into certain subjects when I'm in the confines of Stephen's family: religion, politics and sex are just for starters. We don't exactly see eye to eye on these things, and normally it's easy to avoid the taboo subjects because Trish would rather talk about less contentious topics in any case, such as what she cooked for Ted each night this week, what the chiropodist said to her about her bunions, how much Jif she gets through in a single week.

However, we were drinking tea after lunch when Trish made some slightly unpleasant remark about refugees. Part of me was thinking, Leave it, don't cause trouble, it's not worth it. Unfortunately, the other part of me wasn't listening. I pointed out that my father's parents had come to England not long before the Second World War and that I wouldn't be sitting there drinking tea right now if they hadn't been allowed in.

'I didn't realise your family were—that they came from abroad.'

'Oh? Surely I mentioned it before? This is my dad's side, of course, the Jewish side. My mother's family come from Wiltshire.'

'We had a lovely holiday in that part of the world, didn't we, Ted? Remember? Ever such a good cream tea, we had. Ted?'

Ted turned to me. 'So, where were your father's parents from then?'

It's so rare to hear Ted actually utter an entire sentence that I practically splurted my tea all over the nest of tables.

'Lithuania. Of course, it's just as well they left when they did or they'd almost certainly have been killed.'

Trish reached for the teapot and started topping up everyone's cup.

'Bit more for you, Georgia? Still, it's nice to be good with money, isn't it? Ted and I, we've always been careful, haven't we, Ted?'

'I'm sorry?'

Trish stopped pouring.

'Well, it's just what they say, isn't it? About Jews. No offence.'

Have you noticed how people always say 'no offence' just after they've said something unspeakably offensive?

'Oh, what's that?' I feigned ignorance. 'What do *they* say?'

'You know, that Jews are mean. I'm not saying *I* think that—*I* think it's good to be careful with your money.'

Stephen patted my leg gently, trying to pacify me. 'Leave it, darling,' he said under his breath. 'You know she doesn't mean it—'

I shook his hand away.

'Really? And why do you suppose they say that then?'

'Well, I wouldn't know. It's just one of those things, isn't it? Like a saying or what have you, that Jews are mean, it's like the French being—' she dropped her voice, 'dirty, or the Irish being stupid.'

I sat there open-mouthed and aghast. 'I'm sorry, but I can't *believe* you think that. Every time you meet someone who's Jewish—or French or Irish—I mean, you must *notice* the huge gulf between the stereotype and the reality?' I realised there was no point even attempting to go into an historical account of the origins of Jews becoming bankers and money-lenders. Trish would never grasp it anyway. 'You do see that it's simply racist and wrong, don't you?'

Stephen's hand pressed firmly into my leg. 'Now, steady on—'

Trish's cheeks flushed red.

'But I'm not racist, am I, Ted? What about that coloured nurse I had when I was in hospital having my—you know? I always said good morning to her. She was a nice lady.' She started towards the kitchen, avoiding meeting my eyes. 'I'll just put the kettle on for a fresh pot of tea.'

Stephen and I walked in silence to the car. Trish was waving chirpily to us from the front door. I waited until we'd been driving for a few minutes before I spoke.

'Well,' I said, 'that was fun.'

He sighed.

'I'm sorry if Mum upset you, sweetheart, but you must make allowances. That generation haven't got the hang of the whole PC thing.'

'What the fuck's being PC got to do with it? I'm talking about being a decent human being. And, excuse me, but her generation should be more understanding, not less—it's not history for them, it's in living memory. I know she was only a small child in the war, but Quinn wasn't born till after the war and she's the least racist person I've ever met.'

'Steady on, now. My mother's not a racist.'

'Well, what would you call it then?'

He sighed again and paused while he concentrated on checking his rearview mirror. 'It's just the kind of thing people say without thinking about it. You shouldn't let every little thing bug you.'

'Stephen! This is exactly why these things get out of hand—it starts with *harmless* little jokes and stereotypes and people who should know better saying it doesn't matter, then pretty soon you've got people turning their neighbours in or burning crosses on their front lawn.'

Stephen was silent. I could tell he'd decided to end the conversation. He does that when he thinks the other person is being irrational.

'I really don't think I'm overreacting about this, Stephen,' I said.

'Mmm-mm.'

'Can you stop the car, please. I want to get out.'

'What? Now, let's not be silly. Let's all calm down and talk—'

'Oh—which *all* is this? You sound reasonably calm to me. I'm fucking angry and upset, so perhaps you meant me? Stop the car now.' I started to open the door.

'Hey! Hey! That's dangerous! Don't be stupid. Let me at least drop you at the station—then you can hop on a train and not endure my repulsive, fascist company, OK?'

'Stephen, don't be like that—I'm not cross with you, really I'm not, but I just want to be in my own place.' He pulled over by the station and I opened the car door.

'All right, sweetie. Call me later then?'

'Yes. Take care. Bye.'

There was a train drawing in as I was buying my ticket, so I had to run for it. I hurtled down the stairs, but slipped near the bottom and fell headlong onto the platform.

'Hold the train!' I shouted to the guard. 'Please!'

A man came over to help me up. 'Thank you, but I *must* catch that train.' He helped me to the open doors.

'Mind the doors!' the guard called.

During the interminable journey back to town, I had time to inspect the damage: my hands were badly grazed and stinging like crazy, my trousers were filthy, with the fabric ripped at one knee, and my ankle hurt from where I'd twisted my foot as I fell.

A woman sitting opposite gave me a sympathetic smile, then everyone returned to their newspapers, their books, and ignored me. I rubbed at my ankle and thought about Trish—how on earth was I going to get out of seeing her in future? It's not practical. Obviously. If you're going to marry someone, you can't avoid their family for ever, can you? Of course, Stephen would gladly not see my family for . . . ever. If he could. It's not that he dislikes them exactly, it's just that his family are cut from a different bale of cloth, in fact they're in a whole different warehouse, aren't they?

SIXTEEN

The 2.00am test

THE PHONE'S RINGING. Dear God—it must be the middle of the night. I fumble for the phone in the dark. 'Hello?'

There is someone crying at the other end. Not just someone. Ellie. I sit bolt upright, wide awake.

'Ge-g-George?' She's hiccupping with sobs. 'Can you come? I need you to come.'

'Yes, of course. But what's happened? Tell me what's happened.'

'I—I—there was a— I *can't*—please come. I'm at the flat.'

'I'm on my way, Ellie. Sit tight.'

I leap out of bed—straight onto my dodgy ankle, and crumple to the floor as it gives way beneath me. The pain is so bad I cry out. I can't possibly drive like this. Stephen? No. I can't phone him, not after yesterday.

I haul myself back onto the bed and call the taxi firm I always use. Sure, I can have a car, they say. In an hour. Very busy tonight. Shit, shit, shit.

I'll *have* to ask Stephen. I hate asking people for favours.

His voice is sleepy. And cross.

'Stephen! Darling. I'm so sorry to wake you—'

'What's the matter? Are you ill?'

'No, no. *I'm* fine. It's Ellen—'

'Oh, *Georgia*! Not *again*? It's two o'clock. What is it this time?'

'She sounds seriously upset. I wouldn't ask if—'

'Sweetheart.' He's got his being-patient voice on. 'If you keep running to her rescue every five minutes, she's never going to grow up.'

'I'm not arguing about this now. I'm sorry I phoned you—I shouldn't try and drag you into my family's messes, but . . .'

A heavy sigh down the line. 'Why don't you find out what this is about? She's probably forgotten she even phoned you by now.'

'I have to go. I'll call you tomorrow.'

'Night, sweetie. Just ring her. I'm sure she's perfectly all right.'

But there is someone else. Someone who won't give me a hard time, someone who might even still be up. Leo.

'Urgh?' Oops. Not still up then.

'Leo. I'm sorry—'

'Georgia? What is it? Are you OK?'

'Yes. No. It's Ellen. I need to get to her now and I can't drive because I've hurt my ankle—and I can't get a taxi—and I phoned—'

'Give me two minutes.'

I crawl round the room, dragging on yesterday's clothes. A knock at the door. I hop to answer it.

'Sheesh—what the hell happened to your ankle?' He sees how unsteady I am and puts his arm round me. I tell him.

'Shoes?'

I sit down while he kneels in front of me to ease them onto my feet.

'My van's right outside. Lean on me.'

I take a tentative step, clutching his shoulder, but even that sends shooting pains up my leg.

'I take it we're in a hurry?'

I nod, feeling too faint and sick even to speak.

'Okey-doke. Hold on to your bag, lady. Prepare for liftoff.'

'Wha—'

With that, he crouches quickly and bends me over his shoulder in a fireman's lift. 'Sorry. I know it's undignified, but I'll do my back in if I try to carry you bridegroom-style . . .' He half jogs to the lift.

When we reach the lobby, he carries me out through the front door to his van. 'So—tell me—where are we headed?'

'Ellen's flat. It's near Swiss Cottage, off Finchley Road.'

'What's going on? What's happened?'

'I don't know. Of course, I know she can be a bit of a drama queen, but she sounded so upset. She was really, really sobbing and—and—' I start to cry myself then, 'she's m-my little sister . . .'

'Hey—it's all right.' He pats me on the knee, but in a comforting way. 'We'll get you there faster than you can say snotty handkerchief.'

At Ellen's flat Leo comes round to my side and gets ready to haul me over his shoulder again.

'You can't. She's on the third floor and there's no lift. It'll kill you.'

'Well, you can't hop all the way up there, can you? I'll survive.'

'What if I'm too heavy?'

'Then I'll drop you and you'll bounce all the way down to the bottom.' He hefts me onto his back again. 'Top bell is it?'

'Yup.' He turns me round so I can speak into the entryphone.

Ellen buzzes us in and we begin the slow climb to the top.

'Ohmygod!' Ellen said. 'What happened to you?'

'It's nothing—I sprained my ankle, that's all—fortunately, I never travel without Sherpa Leo . . .'

He unloaded me, rather hastily, onto the sofa and Ellen came and sat down for a long hug while Leo went into the kitchen to make some tea.

'Do you want to tell me?' I asked her.

'This, this man—f-followed me . . .' she began, crying again as I cuddled her close. She and her flatmate Siobhan both work at the wine bar, so they usually walk home together. But tonight Siobhan had swapped her shift so Ellen was walking on her own.

'There was a bunch of blokes shouting and walking in front of cars in the road so I ducked down a side street to steer clear of them—but then I heard footsteps behind me. I turned round to look—but there was only a man some way back down the street, who'd stopped to light a fag, so I thought it was OK. I carried on but then I heard him again—faster this time—I speeded up and dug down into my bag for my mobile—but it wasn't there—I must have left it at the bar. And then he started to run.'

'Oh, babes.' My hands felt clammy, as if I was reliving it all myself.

'So I ran too—as fast as I could—I could hear him panting and I tried to scream but I couldn't—I was running so hard I couldn't make a sound—I cut left into another street, trying to head back to the main road—but then—then he caught up with me, and grabbed me and pushed me against this wall. He was—just *horrible*. So horrible. I *can't*—' I stroked her hair back from her face and then she sat up straight. 'He started kissing me—and he *reeked* of beer and sweat—I kept trying to push him off, but he was stronger—and then he jammed his knee between my legs—and I was so *scared*. I managed to scream then but he pressed his hand over my mouth so I could hardly breathe.'

'And then what happened? Did he—?'

'No—I—you know that pencil you gave me?'

'What?'

'The purple glittery one? It was in my coat pocket and I managed to reach in and grab it and then—I stabbed him with it as hard as I could.'

'My God—well done! Where did you get him?'

'Only in the cheek—but he jumped back and it gave me a couple of seconds to run for it. He shouted, "You fucking bitch!" after me, but I ran and ran until I made it to the petrol station. And they rang the police. The police drove me home and took my statement and a description. When they'd gone I went to the loo 'cause I had the runs, and I threw up as well. And then I rang you.' She snuggled up closer to me.

Leo brought the tea and we ate all of Siobhan's chocolate digestives.

'I wish I'd got him in the eye. I bet he tries to attack someone else.'

'Maybe he'll die of graphite poisoning.'

'George?'

'Yes.'

'I feel a bit weird about being on my own now. It's just I keep thinking he's going to find me somehow and climb in through the window or break down the door. Is that silly?'

'Not at all. Of course I wouldn't leave you on your own. You're staying with me. It'll be fun. We can have midnight feasts and talk in the dark until we fall asleep the way we used to.'

'Can we have popcorn?'

'Of course. And cheesy Wotsits and Toblerone and Iced Gems.'

I turned to look at Leo. 'Can I come?' he said.

Ellen smiled and hugged him.'Thank you. For being our white knight.'

'No sweat. Anyone would have done the same. Let me take you home.'

Stephen phoned the flat a little after nine the next morning, while Ellen was in the shower.

'Oh, hi.'

'You sound a bit off. Sorry—did I wake you?'

'No. We haven't slept much though.'

'We?' He cleared his throat.

'Ellen came back here.'

I could sense rather than hear his slight sigh at the other end of the line. 'Why? What happened? Is she all right?'

'No. She was nearly raped on her way home last night.'

'How awful! I'm really sorry. I would have come if I'd known.'

'Yes. Anyway, she's physically OK, but pretty shaken up, I think.'

'How did it happen?'

I told him.

'What was she doing walking on her own at that hour?'

'Er, excuse me? She was going home from work.'

'Well, come on—it's a bit silly to go wandering about the streets at midnight in this day and age with all these muggers and nutters about.'

'Are you saying it's her fault? I suppose *you* think all women should have a curfew after eight o'clock at night?'

'Now don't go jumping on the feminist bandwagon.'

I managed to suppress the urge to scream and keep my voice low.

'It's not a matter of being a *feminist*. It's a matter of being a decent human being. Everyone should have the right to—'

'Darling, *darling*. Calm down. This isn't about rights. It's about acting with due caution. You must admit, Ellen's not exactly the most sensible person in the world.'

'How dare you try and turn her into the guilty party! And don't fucking tell me to calm down!'

'Give me a call a bit later when you're feeling more like yourself.'

'I *am* feeling like myself! I've never felt more like myself.'

'We'll talk a bit later then,' he said calmly and hung up. I slammed the phone down with a crash.

SEVENTEEN

Sisters

'DO YOU WANT TO TALK about it any more?' I asked Ellen in bed the next night.

'Not really. I can't stop thinking about it as it is.'

'It might help.'

'The trouble is,' she turned towards me, 'I feel like a sitting duck and that he's out there, lurking in the bushes waiting to pounce on me.'

'I won't let him get you,' I said.

'Oh, George, how can you protect me? Twenty-four hours a day? You *can't*. At least he doesn't know where I live.'

'And he wasn't out to get you personally, was he? I mean, he wasn't a customer at the wine bar, someone you knew?'

'No. Definitely not. I was just in the wrong place at the wrong time.'

'Maybe you could do a self-defence course? Judo, or something.'

'What—me? God—do you remember that strange guy I went out with a couple of years ago?'

'Couldn't narrow it down a bit, could you?'

'Tee-hee. The *strange* one—who was totally fascinated when he discovered that I was half-Jewish? He kept wanting to talk about my roots and calling it *Judo*-ism, instead of Jud*a*ism—remember?'

'Yes! Judo-ism!—the ancient art of self-defence using only a bagel and a small accountant from Hendon.'

'Learn to survive armed only with your wits and a side order of latkes!'

'Subdue your foe by urging him to eat fifteen portions of lokshen pudding so he can't move . . .'

Ellen laughed and flumped back against the pillows.

'Aaah—I never have half this much fun when I'm with a bloke.'

'No. Me neither. Except—'

'You mean the P-h doesn't keep you up giggling half the night?' Ellen affected a look of astonishment.

'Oh yes, we roll around night after night, weeping with laughter.'

'I'm supposed to be the bitchy one.'

'I'm just cross with him. I'll get over it. Giggling isn't everything. Stephen's very . . . he's very *good* for me. Very stable. Trustworthy.'

'But what are you going to do once you're married? About the giggling. You can't keep having me over to stay then desert the marital bed because you want to sit up talking all night, can you?'

'But you'll come often, won't you?'

'Oh yeah—like Stephen's really going to want me turning up on your doorstep every week.' She wrinkled her nose. 'Can't you marry Leo instead?'

'What—would that suit you better?'

'Yeah.'

'No problem. Whatever you say. Stick it down on my "To do" list.'

A couple of days later, I was in the bathroom pinning up my hair, getting ready to go out with my friends Emma and Susie, when there was a knock at the door—rat-a-tat-tat—Leo's signature knock.

'Get that will you, babes?' I called through.

Through the closed bathroom door, I could hear them saying hello to each other, an exchange of kisses.

'Hi! Leo? I'm going out,' I called through. 'Just finishing my face.'

'Shall I come back in three hours then?'

'Gosh, that's original! You must tell me who writes your jokes . . .'

As I came into the main room, Ellen emerged from where she'd been half-hidden by the screen.

'Coffee, George?' She was wearing a pair of black jeans and a bra. No top. My face must have fallen because then she said, 'What? What is it?'

I went right up to her and mouthed, 'Why aren't you *dressed*?' pulling her back behind the screen. 'I can't believe you're *parading* around in front of Leo with no top on. What do you think you're doing?'

'Oh, for God's sake!' Ellen stepped out from behind the screen defiantly, as if striding out onto a stage.

'George is giving me a hard time about the fact that I'm *improperly dressed*, apparently—but a bra's no worse than a bikini, is it?'

'Er, no. I guess not.' Leo said, looking decidedly uncomfortable.

'Ellen! Of course he feels he *has* to agree with you—to be polite.'

'No, he *doesn't*. He's not polite.'

'Don't mind me, will you? I *am* still here, in case you—'

'Leo—tell me,' Ellen demanded. 'Do you honestly care about seeing me in my bra?'

'Why can't you just put a top on?' I asked. 'All this time you're arguing—how long does it take to put on a top? Two seconds?'

'I couldn't decide what to wear—I haven't got anything I like here.'

'Well—*ask* then. You can borrow something of mine.'

Ellen slid open the wardrobe door and started to rifle through the contents. She plucked out a black stretchy top. 'So, Leo—you didn't answer my question—does it bother you seeing me in my bra?

'Actually, no it doesn't.' He was perched on the edge of the sofa. 'But I only dropped by to say hi. I'm off out myself.' He stood up and headed for the door. I walked with him.

We stood for a moment in the corridor. I felt I should say something.

'It's OK,' he said. 'She's bound to be acting a bit oddly—she's had a hell of a shock and maybe this is her way of dealing with it. Don't worry about me. Just look after yourself, hmm? You look tired.'

'I *am* tired. I've barely slept for three nights. I'd sooner be sinking into a deep bath with a good book, not heading out for pasta and the latest instalment of Decent Men, Are They All Hiding In a Cave Somewhere?'

He smiled. 'Not as bad as going to some awful magazine bash.'

'Why are you going then?'

He curled his lip. 'Might be useful. I've got to get some new clients if I'm ever going to be able to afford somewhere bigger.'

'Oh.' I looked up at him. 'You're going to get rich then swan off to a swanky loft with twenty-foot-high ceilings, aren't you?'

'Yup. Soon as I make my first couple of million.'

'You won't be in too big a rush, will you?'

He smiled and bent to kiss my cheek. 'What do you think?'

Georgia and her friend Ruth are outside in the garden. They are playing Spells, standing either side of a large stone urn as their cauldron. Ellen is in the sandpit, flicking sand onto the grass with her spade.

Georgia has dug deep into the dressing-up box to find her magic silver wand, which she waves to and fro over the ivy and periwinkle that spill down the sides of the urn like a potion boiling over.

'Abracadabra—fabracadabra . . .' *she intones.* 'Put a pebble in the pot—' *Georgia nods sternly at Ruth, who throws in the stone she has been clutching hotly in her right fist*—'then you get to wish—*a* lot.'

Ruth shuts her eyes to make her wish.

'I wish,' says Georgia, 'that Mark Evans kisses Ruth in the playground.'

'No! Take it back. It's not your wish!' Ruth's cheeks are flushed.

'Too late now. You can't undo the spell.'

'You can, Georgia. Please *undo the spell.' Ruth's face is full of trust and absolute belief that Georgia has the power to grant or undo wishes.*

Georgia relents and chants once more to reverse the spell.

'Have you got any lemonade?'

'Don't know,' says Georgia, knowing they haven't.

They hear the doorbell as they go inside, a long, insistent ring.

'It must be my dad, come to fetch me.'

Georgia runs through the kitchen to answer the door, but she is too late. Her mother is thundering down the stairs. 'I've got it!'

Before Georgia can speak, the door is open. Ruth's father stands on the doorstep.

'Oh—I'm so sorry. I didn't—I wasn't sure if the bell was working—Sorry, perhaps I have the wrong house . . .'

'Perhaps you have.' Joy, laughing. 'The bell does work, but I was just upstairs—' She is standing by the front door in her tights, waist slip and bra. No blouse, no skirt, no shoes.

'Er, yes. Sorry. I'm Max, Ruth's father. Is she here?'

'Who knows? We may have to hunt for her, you know what children are like! Do please come in.' She turns then and sees Georgia. 'Georgia, darling, who's the friend you're playing with? Ruth, is it?'

Georgia nods.

'Hello, Georgia,' says Ruth's father. 'How are you?'

'Hello. I'm very well, thank you.'

'You must come in and have a little something,' Joy urges, tugging at Max's jacket sleeve.

Georgia is praying silently inside her head, Dear God, please, please, PLEASE make her go back upstairs.

'Well, that's very nice of you, but we'd best be making a move, hadn't we, poppet?' Ruth is looking at Joy's lacy bra, wide-eyed.

'Ruth has such a pretty face,' Joy smiled at Max.

Max smiles while Ruth presses her face into her daddy's jacket.

'Bye then,' says Georgia.

'Bye,' says Ruth. 'Thank you for having me.'

Georgia waves at Ruth and then the front door is closed once more.

'Well then—did you girls help yourselves to lemonade?'

'There isn't any.'

'Oh. Isn't there?' Frowning, then thoughtful. 'We could go and get some now.'

'It's too late now. And besides I don't want any lemonade.'

'Don't be silly.' Joy checks the kitchen clock. 'The off-licence doesn't shut for ages.'

Georgia winds a strand of her hair round and round her finger.

Joy looks down at herself.

'Oh! Look at me—about to go out half-dressed! Give me a minute and I'll be right down.'

As Joy disappears Georgia goes back out to the garden. Closing her eyes, she puts her pebble in the magic urn and makes a wish.

EIGHTEEN
Being together

I CAN'T LIVE LIKE THIS. Ellie's driving me crazy. If this is what being married is like, then I may just stay engaged for the rest of my life. At least Stephen manages to cross from one side of a room to the other without leaving a trail of devastation in his wake. Why can't she put anything away. How have her flatmates put up with her all this time? Clearly, they must be just as bad as she is.

While Ellen was having a bath, I rang Leo.

'Hey, you! How's it going?' he says.

'Not great. I'm in danger of doing serious damage to my house guest.'

'Come down. I could do with a second opinion on some pictures.'

I banged on the bathroom door, called through to Ellen.

'Just nipping downstairs. Won't be long!'

'How's Ellen doing?' Leo asks, as I stand at his table, looking at contact sheets of photographs through a magnifying lens.

'She's OK, I think, but still pretty jumpy understandably. I know this sounds mean, but I just find it so hard having her in my flat. I wish I could be more relaxed and not keep whizzing round after her with a damp cloth.'

'It's tricky to have someone else suddenly in your space when you're used to living alone. But it's OK to be annoyed—it doesn't mean you don't love her. I couldn't live with either of my sisters, either, yet I love them to pieces.'

'Why? They can't be worse than Ellen.'

'Because when it's family, every single thing you say has got thirty-odd years of subtext to it. If a friend asked me about the state of my love life, I'd say, "Crap, thanks, how's yours?" but if my sister Linda asked me, I'd think, Here she goes again, getting at me about not being married yet, and I'd probably say, "Get off my back—I'm happy being single!" '

I laugh. 'And are you?'

'What do you think?'

'Do you always answer a question with another question? You're like a bloody politician.' I look away from him and back at the images.

'In answer to your question, Ms Abrams, that would have to be a straight no.'

'So why *are* you still single then?' I point to some of the frames in the contact sheets. 'I like these two here, and that one, this, this and this.' He follows my finger and hunches over them with the lens.

'It's one of life's little mysteries.' He bends over the contacts once more. 'These two are fine, that one's not so hot, this is OK, and I agree—that one, and that one. Good.'

I like the way he looks when he is concentrating. When I first met him, my impression of him was that he was disorganised, always running to catch up with himself, but when he's working—taking pictures, or selecting which frames to print up, or even just looking at something—he suddenly acquires this wonderful sort of stillness.

He straightens up again, marks the images we've picked out.

'I'm single because I'm too old to pick women up in bars, don't want to face the fact that my days of messing about in a series of cul-de-sac affairs are over, and too irresponsible to feel ready to settle down—only now I've got a child so I'm not exactly number one on every single woman's wish list when they're looking for the man of their dreams.'

'Oh, come on! Cora's lovely. If anything, she's one of your chief selling points. Possibly your only one.'

'Oh, ha-ha.'

'Anyway—I'm sure you won't be single for long. There are always tons and tons of gorgeous, bright, single women and hardly any decent single men—it's a known fact.'

'I don't want tons of women.' He looks at me directly. 'I just want one.'

'Well, there you are then. If you're not looking for an entire collection, just the one—I mean—well—that's not difficult, is it?' I am babbling, I know, but cannot seem to stop. 'God, I've got some great women friends, Emma's lovely and Susie, she's very attractive and amusing.'

'I'm not interested in your women friends.'

'Right.'

'The other reason I'm single . . .'

I want to hear this and I don't want to hear this.

'. . . is that I've become rather attached to someone already and I'm trying not to think about her, but it's proving rather difficult.'

'Oh. Is she—OK-looking?'

'Well . . . so-so if you like that kind of thing.' He sighs. 'No. She's rather beautiful, I think—but I'm not sure she even knows it. And she's bright but without shoving her intellect in your face—opinionated and passionate—strong and fierce but also sensitive, warm—'

'Huh. She doesn't sound real to me.'

He laughs. 'She's very real. And she's tough too. She knows what she likes and she doesn't want it any other way. She can be inflexible, judgmental, hard to please, even shrewish, pedantic.'

'Now she sounds like a bitch.'

'Not at all. But she's not perfect—and thank God for that, say I.'

'So—this all-too-imperfect individual . . .?'

'Yes. I'm trying to get her out of my system because, if I can't, then I'm in danger of gathering her into my arms and peeling off all her clothes and getting the pair of us extremely hot and sweaty and, given that she's engaged to marry another man, it just wouldn't be right.'

I nod. 'No. It wouldn't be.' I could barely speak.

I move towards the door, as if to make a run for it.

'Georgia?'

'Yes.' I cannot look at him.

'I—I'm sorry if I—I shouldn't have said—but. Oh, shit. Still—it's not exactly as if it were much of a secret anyway.' He waves me away. 'Go on, get out of here before my principles run out on me.'

NINETEEN

Under a green sky

ON SATURDAY, STEPHEN AND I spent most of the day peering in estate agents' windows at houses we can't afford. We weren't seriously *looking* looking of course, because we haven't put our flats on the market yet—but Stephen says it's vital to recce in advance so we won't waste our energies looking at houses in streets that are a no-no.

On Sunday, Stephen went off to his parents and I went to brunch on my own. Then Leo and Cora turned up too—Dad's issued a standing invitation to them. Leo settled in as naturally as if he'd been coming every week for years, while Cora was as quiet as before, watching everything going on around her with saucer eyes.

Leo was trying to coax her to eat something, but she refused scrambled eggs, smoked salmon, even a plain bagel with a polite 'No, thank you'. Quinn then said, 'How about a banana sandwich? Anyone?'

How revolting, I thought, but I noticed that Cora didn't immediately shake her head as she had done before.

'Will you help me make it, Cora?' Quinn smiled. 'I'm hopeless at doing sandwiches.'

Cora nodded and stood by the worktop.

'Sit up here.' Quinn patted the worktop.

Cora, I noticed, was watching Leo's face, checking it was all right with him. 'There you go,' he said, picking her up. 'A front-row seat.'

'Now some people have just butter on the bread . . . And some people have a little bit of honey . . .'

Cora smiled and nodded. 'Can I have honey?' She swung her legs. 'Please,' she added quickly. She really is almost spookily polite. Doesn't get that from her dad, that's for sure.

Leo sidled over to me. 'Quinn's great, isn't she?' he said quietly. 'I can never get Cora to eat anything other than apples and crisps.'

'Yes, Quinn's very patient.'

'So are you.'

'No, I'm not—look how Ellen drove me up the wall when she was staying? How on earth would I manage with a child?'

'I bet you'd find you could deal with it when it came to it.'

'Fortunately, we'll never know, because I won't *have* to deal with it. It's not part of my master plan. So chuck me a bagel, fat-face.'

'Still,' he said, peering at me through the hole of the bagel as if it were a monocle, 'for someone who claims not to be keen on kids, you seem to do all right with them. No chance of your coming to the park with us later, is there? Just to have a go on the swings and stuff.'

'Aren't you too old for swings?' I took the bagel, tore it in two and handed him half back again.

'Nope. Never too old for swings.'

Cora had a go on the slide and the swings. Then I tried to show her some clapping games, from when I was a child, but I couldn't remember the words properly. It was funny, though, I hadn't done them for—

what?—twenty-five years or so—but, as soon as I started, all the hand movements came back to me perfectly.

Inevitably, it started to rain, so we ran back to the block and they both came up to my flat for tea and orange juice. It was getting on for half five by then and Leo had to take Cora back by seven.

'Are you hungry?' Leo asked her. 'I could go and get a takeaway pizza? Would you like that?'

She nodded.

'So,' I said, once Leo had left to fetch the pizzas. 'What would you like to do?' I suddenly felt ridiculously nervous, as if I'd been left alone in charge of a grizzly bear rather than a small, shy, five-year-old girl.

'Don't mind.'

'Well, we could . . . I've got paper if you want to draw?'

'OK.'

I couldn't find any felt-tip pens, so she had to make do with some old crayons that Bonnie and Daniel had left behind. She sat at the table, hunched over her drawing.

'Is he coming back?' she asked after a little while, without looking up.

'Who? Your daddy? Yes—of *course* he is.'

'OK.' She sorted through the crayons. 'There's no blue,' she said. 'For the sky.'

'Oh, I'm sorry.' I sat down at the table. 'I think that one must have got lost. Maybe you could pick another colour?'

'Sky's supposed to be blue.'

'Well—ye-e-e-s. But it isn't always—look, now, when it's rainy, it's more a sort of grey really. And, you know when the sun sets, then it goes all sorts of colours, doesn't it? Pink and red and orange, even purple.'

'Can it be green?'

'It can be any colour you want it to be—it's *your* picture.'

'When is he coming back?'

I checked my watch and showed her.

'See—your daddy left twenty minutes ago, when the big hand was here. See—that's five, ten, fifteen, twenty minutes,' I pointed it out with my fingertip. 'So he'll be back any minute now.'

I got her another glass of juice. How long does it take to fetch a couple of pizzas?

Five minutes ticked by. Another five. Cora finished her picture.

'Sometimes when people go away they don't come back,' she said.

'That's true. But mostly they do.' I sat with her at the table. 'Your mummy went into the hospital and didn't come home—is that right?'

She nodded. 'But I knew she wasn't coming back because she told me she was going to die. I had a kitten and it died and we put it in the ground in a shoebox.' She drew a girl on the ground beneath the green sky. Picked out a pink crayon to draw flowers around her.

'Even when we *know* that someone isn't coming back, we can still be sad.'

'I'm not sad. I'm drawing. Was that your mummy, who made the banana sandwich? The red-hair lady.'

'No. That's Quinn—she's my—she's married to my daddy, but . . . I haven't got a mummy. My mummy died—like yours—a long time ago.'

'Did she die in the hospital?'

'No. She was at home.'

'Is the red-hair lady like a mummy?'

'Well. Sort of. Um. A bit.'

'She looks like a mummy. Only older.' She added a cat in the garden, next to the girl. 'Are you a mummy?'

'No. I—no, I'm not.' I stood up again. 'Not yet anyway.'

School finishes at three forty-five. Most of the mothers are already there before the children come spilling out, swarming like ants to honeycomb, clutching at their mothers' offerings—a tube of Smarties, a two-fingered Kit Kat, a packet of cheese-and-onion crisps. Joy, when she remembers, brings a handful of raisins; she refuses to give them sweets other than as a rare treat.

Two minutes to four and Matt and Georgia stand alone. Mr Dawson comes out and asks if they want to wait inside.

Matt sits on a chair, swinging his legs. 'When is Mummy coming?'

'In a minute.' Georgia gets up and walks to and fro on her heels.

'Why isn't she here now?' Matt is near tears, Georgia can tell.

'Because she got held up. Maybe she'll bring us some chocolate.'

'Everyone else has gone.' Matt's voice takes on a tragic note. He has a knack for pointing out the obvious. 'And I need to do a wee.'

Georgia takes his hand and walks with him to the door marked 'Boys'.

'Go on then. Hurry up.'

When they come back, their mother is there, standing talking to Mr Dawson. They are laughing, Joy's laugh echoing round the hallway.

'You're late,' says Georgia.

'I know. I'm sorry. I had a really bad headache and then I fell asleep.'

Georgia looks up at her mother, unsmiling.

'Can we have some chocolate?' says Matt.

'Maybe.' Joy takes Matt's hand and reaches for Georgia's on her other side,

but Georgia keeps her arms folded. 'Well, OK then.' She turns to smile at Mr Dawson. 'Thanks so much for looking after the little horrors!'

'Not at all, not at all!' Mr Dawson adjusts his tie and shifts from foot to foot. 'And I hope you're feeling better, Mrs Abrams.'

'I am. And it's Joy!' She calls over her shoulder. 'Joy!'

Rat-a-tat-tat—Leo's knock. At last.

'Where have you *been*?' I pull the inner door to behind me.

'I couldn't find anywhere to park. Cora's all right, isn't she?'

'Yes—but you don't understand! You can't just swan about taking as long as you like—she was getting anxious, worrying whether you were coming back.'

He comes into the main room and starts admiring her drawing.

'I'm sorry I was longer than I said I would be.' He puts his arm round her. 'Let's put your drawing here so it doesn't get pizza on it, OK?'

She nods and I show her the bathroom so she can wash her hands.

Leo comes over to me as I'm getting out the plates and cutlery.

'I think she's OK. Maybe *you're* the one who was worrying?'

'Me! Why should *I* worry? I'm just saying you need to be rock-solid reliable—for *her*. It's no good being late all the time.'

'I am not late all the time. I never let people down. I'm *reliable*.'

'Well—start acting like it then!' I thrust the plates at him, then begin to set the table.

'**H**ey,' says Leo, turning up again after he'd taken Cora back. 'Sorry about earlier. I know you were only thinking of Cora—you're great with her.'

I shake my head.

'Not at all. I wish I was more relaxed with her—with Bonnie and Daniel, it's more about containment and crowd control than anything else. But Cora's so different—like a little adult in some ways—she reminds me . . . anyway, thanks for the pizza.'

'No sweat. Can I make you a coffee?'

'Would you? I'm shattered. Can I have peppermint tea instead, please?'

'You can have whatever you like.' He starts filling the kettle.

'Good. In that case, can I also have a Georgian house with huge windows and proper fireplaces and an enormous garden?'

He pats his pockets. 'Nothing like that on me, I'm afraid.'

'I was looking at estate agents yesterday—everything's so expensive.'

'*I*?'

I shrug. '*We*. Of course.'

His back is to me as he delves into the box of tea bags.

'When *are* you planning to move?'

'Oh—whenever. No rush really. Still—don't suppose I can put it off for ever.' I laugh feebly, as if I have made some kind of joke.

He doesn't reply, just passes me a mug of tea in silence.

'**W**ould you mind watching telly?' I ask him. 'I quite fancy a spot of rubbish—I feel wiped out today, don't know why.'

'Me too. Shall I turn the TV round a bit?'

'Actually, I normally pull down the bed and watch from there . . .'

'Do you now?' He tilts his head and gives me that look.

'Oh, behave—it's just more comfortable. It wasn't a subtle attempt to seduce you.'

'Thank God for that.' He grabs the knob and pulls down the bed. 'If you do ever decide to seduce me, by the way . . .' he sits down and starts taking off his shoes, '. . . don't be too subtle—I might not get it.'

'Fine.' I hurl over some extra cushions from the sofa at him. 'I'll hold up a huge placard.'

A few minutes later we are sitting side by side, propped up against the pillows, channel-hopping. 'This is nice,' he says. 'Do you think we'll still be doing this in forty years' time?'

Forty years. I attempt to gauge his expression without turning round to face him. He's teasing, of course he is. He must be.

'Surely I'll have found somewhere else to move to before that?'

'This really *is* rubbish, isn't it?' Leo changes channels for the fortieth time. 'And not in a good way. Can't we play a game instead?'

'Such as . . .?' I fold my hands neatly in my lap. 'I've only got cards and Scrabble, I think.'

He slides further down the bed, and turns to face me. 'Too tired for Scrabble—you'd wipe the floor with me.' He yawns. 'Sorry.'

'That's OK. We really ought to go to bed soon,' I point out. 'School day tomorrow—I've got a client at nine.'

'We're *in* bed already. Well—on it.'

'To sleep,' I add.

'Of course to sleep.' He looks into my eyes, then slowly traces a fingertip across the back of my hand, making me shiver. 'What else?'

In my dream a phone is ringing. It's all right, I say in my dream and in my head, it's only the telephone, someone else will get it. I snuggle up closer to the nice, warm body next to me, curl my arm over it, mmm, lovely soft material. Phone still ringing then, close by, a clunking as a hand—mine? No—scrabbles to pick it up, then a deep, sleepy voice

says, 'Urgh? *Wha—?* Oh, *shit.*' Suddenly, said body is sitting bolt upright.
'Ssh-ssshh . . .' I say. 'Lie down.'
'Georgia!' A hand shaking me. 'Er, yes—she's right here, but—'
'It's Stephen.' He covers the mouthpiece for a moment to whisper, 'I'm sorry—I forgot where I was—I just grabbed it.'

Oh fuck. Fuck, fuck, fuck.
I swallow and sit up, suddenly one hundred per cent wide awake.
'Oh, hi, Stephen—I—' Click.
Stephen has never hung up on me before. 'Oh, shit.' I look at Leo.
'I'm sorry,' Leo says again. 'I didn't realise where I was. I'm an idiot.'
'Yes, you are, but it's done now. Still, at least nothing actually—We just fell asleep—it couldn't have been more innocent, really—'
'True—there was no getting naked, I'd remember that—and no snogging . . .' He is smiling. 'What a terrible, terrible waste.'
'Don't you dare smile! This is very, very serious. Poor Stephen!'
'But he trusts you, surely? As you say, nothing *happened*.'
I cover my face with my hands. 'What can I possibly tell him?'
He gets off the bed. 'The truth?'
'Don't be ridiculous.'
'Well, why don't you tell him that I'd just popped round this morning?'
'But you sounded all groggy and sleepy and, anyway, why would you be answering my phone?'
'Because you were in the shower?'
'Oh, marvellous idea—Stephen, Leo was only answering my phone because I was lathering my naked body just a few feet away.'
'Perish the thought. No, you'll have to tell him the truth—that you wanted to make mad, passionate love with me but that you didn't because you're a decent person and you wouldn't be unfaithful to him so we spent an entirely chaste night together—unfortunately.'
'There's a time and a place for complete honesty, Leo, and frankly I don't think this is it.' I slump back down onto the bed.
'Ah-ha!'
'Ah-ha what? Have you thought of a sensible excuse?'
'No, but look at what you said, Dr Freud—complete honesty—so you *do* want to have sex with me?'
I hit him with a pillow. 'No, I don't. Not remotely. You're insufferable, irritating and arrogant—but I don't have time to argue with you when I need to come up with something credible for Stephen.'
I look at the clock—8.57am.
'Oh God! I've got a client at nine! I have to go!'

I ran downstairs, raking my fingers through my hair, then licking a finger to rub away any mascara smudges under my eyes. With any luck she'd be late. I turned into the corridor. She was there, outside my door. Bugger it. I slowed my steps to a dignified pace, calmly said hello and let her in. Her gaze flicked over my face—perhaps I hadn't quite erased all the mascara, so what? I took my seat sedately and she sat down. I was desperate for a pee, but I crossed my legs—only fifty minutes to get through—and attempted to concentrate.

As soon as she left, I dashed to the loo. Checked my face in the mirror. Oh. I see. That explains the look. Mascara and eyeliner smudged not just under my eyes but also at the sides. Worst of all, right in the middle of my forehead, there was a small G in blue pen where Leo had attempted to write my name until I grabbed his arm and stopped him and—ah, I remembered, I'd only managed to divert him to my arms. Yes—my upper arms: three games of noughts and crosses on the left one, some silly anagram on the right—VOLE AGREES IGLOO—I must get all this stuff *off*.

I had to scrub at the blue G to get rid of it and, even then, the pale ghost of it remained. I was desperate for a shower but, no, better ring Stephen first. I tried his direct line but it went straight through to his voicemail.

'Stephen. It's me. It really isn't what you think. Honestly. Please, please call me as soon as you get this.'

Then I rang the switchboard and spoke to the receptionist, who told me Stephen wouldn't be in all day. He was going straight to a meeting. So I rang to leave a message on his machine at home.

'Hi, Stephen. I'm really, really sorry about this morning. It *so* isn't what you imagine.' An inspired thought suddenly popped into my head. 'Leo was just messing about—he happened to drop by this morning early to borrow a book I'd mentioned and I was looking for it when the phone rang and he grabbed it as a joke and pretended to sound groggy as if—well—he said he thought it would be Ellen and it would be a laugh—he was just being silly. Look, call him yourself if you want to check, here's his number . . .'

OK, I realise now that it did sound just a tad far-fetched but it was exactly the kind of thing Leo *would* do. Stephen had already made it all too blindingly obvious that he considered Leo to be an utter twat, so he shouldn't be too astonished, ha-ha, just silly old Leo being daft.

I must warn Leo that Stephen might phone him. I was pretty sure he wouldn't, but just in case, better get our stories consistent, right? Pulled on a cardigan in case my arms got any funny looks in the corridor and ran downstairs. Banged on Leo's door. 'Corridor patrol! Anybody up?'

Leo opened the door.

'Hi!' His voice sounded strained, as if he had a pistol dug into his back and was 'acting normal'.

'Great, you're here. Stephen's here,' he said.

'Hi!' I tried to smile and look relaxed.

'Hi.' Stephen smiled back. 'Oh, darling.' He came across and hugged me. 'Leo's explained what happened. I'm sorry I hung up on you, but I—' A glance at Leo. 'Well, let's go for a coffee, eh?' He took my hand and led me to the door.

'Er, yes! Fine! Lovely, let's do that.' I looked back at Leo, trying to communicate a thousand questions with a single glance. He made a discreet thumbs-up sign at me. Not helpful.

'Two cappuccinos, please,' Stephen ordered. I was in dire need of a cup of tea actually, but I didn't think now was the time to be highlighting our differences.

'Lovely,' I murmured.

What had Leo said? Presumably not the truth, oh no, that wouldn't be interesting enough for him.

Stephen reached across the table and took my hand. 'Why didn't you just *say*, you silly-billy?'

He waggled my hand about as if it were a floppy toy.

I shrugged. I'd just have to be vague until I'd worked out what Leo had said. 'Oh, well, you know . . . Anyway, you hung up before I—'

'I know. Not like me. I thought for a minute—crazy, I know—you wouldn't do that.'

'No,' I shook my head. 'I wouldn't.'

Just thinking about it doesn't count, right?

' . . yes, quite an upheaval, with a kid and everything.'

Upheaval? With a *kid*? Something to do with Cora? How the hell could Leo have roped Cora into it? Oh, shit!—the message! I left that message on Stephen's answering machine about it all being a joke with not a mention of an upheaval or Cora. OK, just keep calm. It's fine, completely fine. I know the remote code for Stephen's machine—I can delete it as soon as I get home.

'So, do you know when he's off exactly?' Stephen was still stirring his coffee, round and round. 'He just said imminently.'

'What? Um, I'm not sure. Quite soon, I think.' I took a sip of my coffee. Shit. Is Leo really leaving? He could hardly have lied about that—or he'd have to hide in his flat every time Stephen came over.

He nodded. 'And he'll have to sort out his plumbing problem before he goes.'

Plumbing problem? One minute he's talking about Leo dashing off somewhere with Cora, now he's talking about plumbing. What does he *mean* plumbing problem? With Stephen's tendency to be euphemistic, he might mean Leo's having trouble peeing or something.

'Oh, I'm sure he will.'

I wish I had at least some idea of what was going on.

Stephen started doing up his jacket, he ought to be getting on, he said, had a client to see, but wasn't it naughty skiving off like this? Quite fun really. He stood up.

I must, must, must talk to Leo.

'**O**K,' I say, 'what the hell did you tell him?'

'Keep calm—you'll like this. I take it you managed not to blow it by saying the wrong thing?'

'I hardly said a word. Unfortunately, I left a message on his machine saying you'd just been messing around, pretending to sound sleepy as you thought it would be Ellen on the phone—you know, that you'd done it as a wind-up?'

'Why did you say that?'

'Because I couldn't see Stephen going for the "we lay side by side all night like little lambs and didn't get up to anything" story.'

'But he *did*.' Leo throws himself onto his sofa, then budges up to make room for me. 'I told him that I'd stayed the night at your place—'

'Because you'd missed the last train—to the floor below?'

'No, I don't think he'd have bought that.' Leo grins. 'I said my boiler was leaching noxious carbon monoxide and it was too dangerous to sleep there in case I was asphyxiated during the night . . .'

'Chance'd be a fine thing. Hang on a second, you don't have a boiler, do you? Isn't your heating on the communal system, like mine?'

'Yes, of course it is. But Stephen doesn't know that.'

'But he must have thought it odd that you have one when I don't? That must have made him suspicious?'

'Georgia, I don't know. Maybe Stephen lies awake at night contemplating other people's plumbing systems or maybe, like most men, he spends his idle moments thinking about sex, worrying about work, or wondering whether God is balding too . . .' He runs his fingers through what's left of his hair. '*Anyway*, I thought he'd be a lot less uptight if I said I'd had Cora staying too—so, if he asks, you gave Cora and me the bed and you took the couch.'

'But what was all this stuff about an upheaval and your going off somewhere?'

'Ah, yes—well, after I'd told Stephen the stuff about the boiler, he was still acting kind of twitchy. He started looking my prints up and down as if he didn't think much of them, then he said, "So, do you manage to earn a reasonable living by taking snapshots?" Pretty rude really. But I clicked—he needed to believe that I'm just some hopeless failure who's no threat to your domestic bliss. So I said I was short of work but going to Canada for a few months with Cora to do a job. I mean, you're hardly going to trail halfway round the world with an unsuccessful photographer who barely earns a crust, are you?'

'Why wouldn't I? Is that how you see me? That I'd only love a man if he were rich and successful?'

'No—not at all. I thought *Stephen* might see it that way. Sure—from the outside you look all neat and tidy and sort of aloof—but if you could just *relax* for more than five minutes—long enough to accidentally enjoy yourself—you'd realise how amazing and extraordinary life can be when you don't keep trying to pin everything down the whole time. If you'd only tell your brain to shut the fuck up for two seconds and pay attention to your guts and your heart and—'

I leap to my feet in anger. 'Who the *fuck* do you think you are? How *dare* you decide what sort of person I am. I suppose you think I'm like some librarian in an old movie—that if I only let my hair down, you can say, "Gosh, you're beautiful after all" and I'll fall at your feet in gratitude? Well, dream on. I'm extremely happy with the way I am, thank you.'

'Hey, hey! Calm down.' He stands up and lays a hand on my arm, but I jerk away from him. 'I'm sorry—I didn't mean to patronise you. Shit. Please don't go off in a huff. You might not see me for ages.'

'What's that supposed to mean?'

'What I said before—I'm thinking of going to Canada. I've been offered this major job, taking shots for a travel guide, covering the whole of Canada. It'll take three, four months at least, maybe more.'

'Three or four *months*?'

'Yup.'

'Congratulations,' I said flatly. 'It sounds great. But what about Cora? You can't take her out of school all that time, can you?'

He frowns. 'I couldn't *possibly* take Cora with me. I'll be working.'

I stand there, mouth half-open but silent, like a photograph. Who is this stranger? How could I have thought I even *knew* him? 'You can't abandon her *now*! Not now you're a part of her life!'

'I'm not *abandoning* her. Don't try to pull a guilt trip on me.'

'Children need a rock-solid grown-up in their lives, someone who won't keep letting them down.'

'I *don't* let *anyone* down. And *you* don't even want children, so excuse me if I don't come rushing to you for advice on how to be the *perfect* bloody parent, OK?'

'Fine—go on then—fuck off to Canada with your cameras! I hope you're very happy together. You're right—Cora will be a lot better off without you waltzing in and out of her life as the mood takes you—' I fling open the flat door so it bangs back against the wall. 'You can be her daddy by postcard. That should suit you down to the ground.'

TWENTY

The truth is out there

By the time I unlocked the door to my own flat my whole body was shaking. I yanked off my cardigan and hurled it across the room onto the sofa. Looked at my arms again. Bloody Leo. He's happy to be all flirty-flirty and amusing and isn't-this-fun-drawing-on-Georgia, but come the next day, look who's stuck with arms covered in pen. Canada's welcome to him. I shut my eyes, recalling the feel of his fingers as he held my arm, drawing the grid for noughts and crosses . . .

'Love and kisses,' he said. 'That's what we call it in my family. Let's play love and kisses.'

'I can see the crosses could be kisses, but why do noughts represent love? Isn't that a bit sad?'

'Nope. It's from tennis—thirty—love. Love is nothing, see?'

I'd nodded. 'I suppose so, yes, love is nothing to most men.'

'That's so untrue. Come closer and say that.' His mouth, smiling, close to my face. The feel of the pen on my arm, nerve endings tingling.

'I know you want to seduce me, but in all honesty I think I'm too knackered.' He flopped back on the pillow.

'You shouldn't say things like that. What about Stephen?'

'What *about* Stephen? Does he want to seduce me too?'

I shoved him. '*No one* wants to seduce you, bighead.'

And then we'd had three rounds of love and kisses—noughts and crosses—all draws, inevitably, and had fallen asleep.

Right. Please, no more distractions for the next two minutes, then I could wipe the message from Stephen's phone and dive into the shower.

I dialled Stephen's home number. It was engaged. Oh-oh. Someone else must be calling him. Hopefully they'd hang up without leaving a message. Or it could be something completely insignificant, something I could erase without a second thought.

I redial. Dring-dring. At last.

Stephen's outgoing message, then that annoying singsong tune. I pressed the code number and the creepy electronic or digitised voice or whatever it is came on: 'You have *three* messages.'

The first one was mine. It sounded ridiculous. I am such a bad liar. Then—surprise, surprise—a message from his mother, telling him the astonishing news that she was planning a shepherd's pie for this evening and that her hairdresser had had a very nice holiday in Portugal.

Then a third voice came on.

'Hi, Steve—it's me . . . um, Denise—obviously—' This surprisingly familiar introduction was followed by a girlish giggle. 'I didn't want to leave a message on your voicemail at work for obvious reasons. Last night was . . . aah, really super! It really was. Super. Thank you. I'm feeling really, really excited about it. I know there are some obstacles, so I won't hassle you, but call me, OK? Byeee!'

I pressed the delete code, stabbing at the button with rather more force than was strictly required.

Steve? No one, but no one, calls Stephen anything other than Stephen. And—*me*? Who the hell is *me*? I'm the only *me* in his life. Denise? Who do we know called Denise? And just what are these obstacles, I'd like to know? Me again, I suppose.

Here I am trying to cover my tracks as if I'm some kind of desperate criminal when all I've done is spend a completely innocent few hours *asleep* in the company of another man, while Stephen's getting sneaky, secret messages from a giggly 'me' who has no right to call herself 'me'. I wish I had bloody gone ahead and slept with Leo—not that I wanted to—just to even things up a bit. But no, why relax and enjoy myself like a normal person when I could mess things up completely instead?

'Stephen—I've got a bit of a confession to make,' I said at supper the following night.

'Nothing serious, I hope?'

I shook my head. 'Of course not. It's silly really, but I left this message on your machine, then I—I—rang up and used your code to delete it. Only you had a couple of other messages, too.'

'And you erased those, did you? I see. What were the messages you decided I didn't need to hear?'

'One was only from your mum.' I poked at my pasta with my fork, pointlessly moving it around the dish. 'And the other was from some woman—Denise? Thanking you for dinner. Perhaps *you* have a confession to make too?' I sat back and looked him in the eye.

'Fortunately, I called Mum in any case so the one *only* from her was taken care of. As for Denise, she's a PA in another department, but I want her to come and work for me. I took her out so we could talk away from the office—otherwise I could be accused of poaching her. I gave her my home number, so she could call me and let me know if she's going to apply via the official channels.'

'Oh.'

'Quite. Is that the sum total of your confession? Why were you so desperate to wipe your own message in any case?' he asked as if I were about five years old, being told off by teacher.

'I wasn't *desperate*, I just . . . Look, you know when Leo stayed in my flat the night before last?'

'Oh, *Leo*. What a surprise that he's mixed up in all this.'

'He's not "mixed up" in anything. It was only—my message—Leo ended up staying because we were talking and we were tired and we both fell asleep. That's it. End of story. We were both fully dressed and absolutely nothing happened, I promise.'

He remained silent.

'But I didn't think you'd believe me. I thought you'd be suspicious even though there was no reason to be because you don't like him.'

'And why shouldn't I believe you if you were telling the truth? Why concoct that ridiculous lie? Yes, I did hear it. I checked my messages after I'd left you at the café, on the way to my meeting. And as for that absurd story about his boiler . . . After I'd heard your message, I should have gone straight back and—and sorted him out. Now—just what exactly is going on with you and this—this clown?'

'Nothing. Absolutely nothing.'

'You swear you've never—nothing's ever happened between you?'

'He—I—we had one kiss. Once. Ages ago.'

'And that was it?'

I nodded.

He sighed heavily. 'And are you planning a repeat performance?'

'*No*. Of course not. It was nothing—a stupid mistake.' I looked into his eyes. 'I *am* sorry, Stephen. I—I—he doesn't *mean* anything to me.'

'Well . . . if that's really true . . .'

'It *is*.'

'Good. Promise me you'll never see him again then.'

'*What*! That's ridiculous! You're treating me like a child! Anyway he's flitting off to Canada soon, we won't be—it won't be a problem.'

'Well, I can't say I'll be weeping at the airport.'

'Oh, don't go *on*, Stephen—I don't care about bloody Leo, I told you. Left to myself, I'd happily never see him again anyway.'

'Good—that's all sorted then. If you're happy not to see him anyway, I can't see what the problem is. We both want the same thing.'

'But I—' What was the point? It didn't matter any more. Stephen was right, it would be better this way. 'Fine. Whatever. Can we just . . .'

'Move on to the next square? Certainly. We've had our plans on the back burner for far too long. Let's crack on with selling our flats. You can move in with me in the meantime. Rent a consulting suite.'

'I—'

'Or not? If you don't want to be with me, Georgia, just say so. I'll get along perfectly well without you, you know. Otherwise, let's for Christ's sake just get married and get on with our lives.'

'Of *course* I want to be with you. It's just—my flat—my office—everything—all at once.'

'Well, it's not as if it's a surprise, is it, darling?' His voice softened. 'We have been planning this for a long time. Just move your bits and bobs in for now, then we can organise a van early in the New Year to bring the rest of your things.'

'Yes, of course.'

He raised his glass and motioned for me to do the same. 'To us then?'

I smiled and our glasses clinked. 'To us.'

This morning there was a brief ring on my doorbell.

'Excuse me, dear?'

'Oh, Mrs Patterson? Hello. How are you?' I asked. I felt something more was called for, felt suddenly embarrassed, ashamed of the way I'd been so distant with her since I moved in. 'I hope you're well?'

'Oh, you know, fraying at the seams!' She laughed, a frail, papery laugh. She's a small, slight woman who always wears a mackintosh even on a gloriously sunny day. 'Now, you're Leo's friend, aren't you?'

I wondered if she'd forgotten me altogether. I felt slightly annoyed—I've lived in the building for nearly five years, so how come I'm 'Leo's friend'? How has everybody come to know him in such a short time?

'Well, yes, I suppose so.' Not something I could swear to with confidence, given that a) I haven't seen him for days, b) he's obviously not talking to me and who could blame him? and c) I have just promised Stephen not to see him? He must have left for Canada already.

'You see—he asked me to feed Cora's cat while he's away.'

So he *has* gone then.

'Cat? But cats aren't allowed here,' I said.

'You won't tell?' she shrank back a little.

I reassured her I wouldn't report it to the pet police.

'The thing is, dear,' she continued, 'he gave me his keys but I've looked high and low for them and they're not where I thought I'd put them . . . and then I said to myself, well, Leo's . . . friend may have a set, so I . . .'

'I did have once, but not any more, I'm afraid.'

'Oh.' She clenched her tiny hands into fists. 'But it'll starve to death if it doesn't eat for a week!'

'A week?' I frowned, puzzled. 'He's gone to Canada for a week?'

'Canada? No, dear. He's gone back to Scotland, to sort out his house.'

'Of course,' I said confidently, aiming to reassure her so I could find out what the hell was going on. 'The house. I'd forgotten. Well, have you checked with the porters?'

She shook her head and I suggested she return to her flat while I nipped down to the lobby.

I walked down the stairs, thoughts racing through my head. What on earth was going on? What had happened to Canada? Was he still planning to go? And why had he gone back to Glasgow? Was he sorting out his house because he was moving back there?

Down in the lobby, Barry, the porter, nodded at me.

'All right, lo—' he cut himself off short. 'Miss Abrams.'

I flushed, remembering that I'd once asked him not to call me 'love'—'Georgia is fine, but not love, thank you.' How pompous, how uptight it sounded in my head. I knew what Leo would have done if I'd told him about it—he'd have called me 'love' every second word, would have said that it built up my immunity to it or something.

'Georgia, please. I'm fine, thanks, Barry.' I smiled warmly. 'And you?'

'Back's playing me up again. Still, mustn't grumble, eh?'

I explained the problem, modifying the forbidden hungry cat for a collection of thirsty houseplants. 'Mr Kane. Flat 418,' I said.

'Should have a set for him.' He went into the back room to check. 'Can't have our Leo's plants turnin' up their toes now, can we?'

Our Leo? Does everyone know him as well as I do? Did. Suddenly I felt keenly, irrationally jealous.

Barry returned, jangling the keys. He handed them over, with strict instructions to return them afterwards. 'And while you're there?'

'Yes?'

'Better feed his cat too, eh?' He grinned and gave me a wink.

'I'll come in with you, shall I? See if the cat's all right?'

Mrs Patterson looked relieved.

As soon as I opened the door, the cat came running through, circled herself round Mrs Patterson's ankles, and mewed plaintively. On the table were several tins of cat food, a box of chocolates, and a note:

Dear Joan—

THANK YOU for being Blossom's personal chef for the week. Please can you top up her water too? You're a doll.

Love, Lx

PS Chocs are for you, not Bloss. Save me the nutty ones!

She smiled. 'A doll? At my age? That Leo!' She tutted, though she was grinning fit to burst. 'He always has the ones with nuts in, you see, when we have a few choccies. I can't manage them, not with my teeth. Now then . . .' She looked around vaguely, not quite sure what to do next. I went and found a tin-opener and Blossom immediately transferred her attentions to me as the potential purveyor of food.

With Blossom happily stationed at her bowl, I turned my attention to Leo's two wilting houseplants and gave them some water. I looked at the sofa we'd sat on together. I wanted to stretch out on it, be on the cushions where he had sat so many times before. Then I caught sight of the latest photos on his pinboard. Leo says he needs to live with his pictures a while before he knows if he really likes them. There was a new one of Cora, looking sweet but desperately serious, a characteristic Cora expression, I thought. Then one of Cora and me together in the park, when I was trying to remember the clapping rhyme. I hadn't even realised he was taking shots—he always has a camera with him and I'd got so used to his taking pictures that I'd stopped noticing. It's a good photograph. We're both in profile, facing each other, and because we're both concentrating and gazing intently straight ahead, at each other and our rhythmically moving hands, we look oddly similar. The effect is rather striking.

And there was another one I'd never seen before—a woman laughing—I mean really, really laughing. Her eyes were all creased up so they looked almost closed, and her mouth was open, showing her teeth. It was so unfamiliar that it took me a moment to realise that it was me.

I sensed Mrs Patterson hovering at my shoulder. 'Is that you, dear?' Her head tilted, assessing. 'That's a lovely picture, isn't it? Unusual.'

'Mmm.' I nodded, unable to speak for some reason. 'Mmm.'

Blossom started mewing like crazy when we made motions to leave.

'I'd have her in with me, I like a bit of comp'ny, but it's the smell, you know . . .' Her voice tailed off as she looked down at the cat-litter tray.

I was surprised she could smell it. Her own flat has the same kind of smell that pervades the whole block, an odd intertwining of aromas: a whiff of overcooked cabbage, the slightly sick-like smell of floor polish, and some strange, other scent that's hard to put your finger on—the smell of old clothes and musky wardrobes, mothballs and faded lavender sachets—it is the smell of loneliness, of people who live alone by necessity rather than choice, each of us in our own box, battery chickens—clucking gossip and eating by the clock and waiting for night-time with its hope of sleep and the long, sweet hours of forgetfulness.

A hand on my arm.

'Oh, I'm sorry—I'm miles away.' Blossom smooched up against me, looked up at me with beseeching eyes. How can you resist me?

'I could take her up to my flat, I suppose. She must be lonely.'

'Would you? I could still feed her if you're too busy—with your work—or perhaps you'd rather not . . .' Mrs Patterson looked awkward, remembering no doubt my former chilliness to her.

'That would be lovely. I'll feed her first thing, then why don't you pop upstairs at four tomorrow? We can have a cup of tea together, too—if you want—if you can spare the time, I mean.'

She smiled warmly. 'I'd love to, dear.'

I picked up Blossom. 'Come and sniff your new territory, Bloss.'

I ran, naked and dripping wet from the shower, to grab the phone before the machine cut in. 'Yes! Hello! I am here! Don't hang up!'

'George—it's me.'

I felt my whole body sag. I can always tell when something's gone awry in Ellie's universe from the tone of her voice. 'Hi. What's up?'

'It's Brian—he's refusing to sleep with me.'

'Er, sorry, have I missed an episode in the nonstop soap of your love life? I thought *you* didn't want to sleep with *him*?'

'I know, I know. Will you just *listen*.'

'Sorry. Let me grab a towel.' I zipped into the bathroom and back.

'You know, since I was attacked, I haven't wanted anyone to touch me—I mean, not at all, not to kiss me or anything.'

'That's only natural, babes. Don't rush it.'

'It's not natural for me and it feels weird. So—' She paused, a rarity in itself. 'So I thought, who do I really, really trust? Who could I sleep with and it would make it OK for me again?'

'Ah . . . Brian?'

'Of course. Brian. I trust him completely. But when I explained about it and I told him I'd picked him, he said no!'

'Oh, Ellie—can't you see why?'

'No. You always told me he really liked me. Now I feel such a prat.'

'He *does* like you. What did he say exactly when you asked him.'

'OK, I think he said, "I couldn't do that, Ellen," and I said why not and he said, "Because I'm half crazy over you as it is and making love to you will only make it worse,"'

'Oh Ellie, you can be so thick sometimes. Why don't you just stop for a minute and consider his feelings as well as your own. Did you tell him also that you wanted it to be him because you *trust* him—not just because he happens to be around?'

'Don't know. Can't remember.'

'Why are you so anti trying to see how things would work out with him? Not just sex. A relationship.'

'That's the thing where you have less and less sex as it goes on, right?'

I laughed. 'Not necessarily. Besides, in theory the quality usually improves even if the quantity's not what it was. It's the thing where you talk and go out to dinner and phone to say sorry if you're running late rather than just assuming the other person will sit and wait—the thing when you find yourself looking at the person's face and thinking you'd still like to be looking at that face in ten, twenty, fifty years' time—when you know that if he were suddenly gone from your life you'd drift about like an empty shell, as if part of you were missing. And, God knows, it's also the thing when you say, "No, it's *your* turn to change the sodding bed linen," and you argue about who should phone the plumber or pick up the dry-cleaning. You know—a real relationship. Real life.'

There was another pause.

'Ellie?'

'I didn't want to interrupt you—you sounded as if you were just getting into your stride.'

'Sorry—I didn't mean to lecture you.'

'It's OK. Do you really have all that with Stephen?' she said.

Silence.

'So, George—why have you stayed with him so long if you don't want to argue about the plumber with him? Or whatever.'

I sighed and it felt as if I were letting out a long, long breath.

'Because . . . Stephen seems such a perfect match, you see? I *need* someone like Stephen in my life. Someone who's a hundred per cent steady and reliable.'

'And predictable. And boring.'

'Oh, shut up. That's unfair. See—after Mum—I can't be around people who might just disappear at any moment.'

'But you've got us, too. You can rely on us—you know we'd be there if you needed us. Matt would, Dad would, I would. Quinn too.'

'I know.'

'You mean I'm right? That's a first.'

'No, it isn't.'

'It is, but what about my problem? Brian? Solutions, please.'

'Give him a chance—bring him to brunch one Sunday, then it won't be like a date and there won't be any unrealistic expectations—on either side. And we can all get another chance to stick our noses in.'

'OK. Thanks, George.'

'Any time.'

'Are you going on Sunday? Dad wants to sort out Christmas.'

'Yeah, I suppose so.'

'And George?'

'Mmm?'

'You're OK, aren't you?'

'Yeah. I'm fine.'

For a man who supposedly doesn't celebrate Christmas, my father certainly frets a disproportionate amount about December 25. It's not that he fusses about the presents or the food or any of that stuff. Quite the contrary. All he really cares about is having the whole family gathered together. For us, it's always been a strange mishmash sort of festival. When I was small, we used to celebrate Chanukkah, the Festival of Lights. Unc and Auntie used to come round with the cousins and we were given a small present on each of the eight days of the festival. Sometimes Chanukkah falls so it overlaps with Christmas and sometimes it doesn't, but it didn't matter because, either way, we still had roast turkey on December 25 and stockings to open in the morning. But then Mum died and we didn't do Chanukkah any more. Dad said it was because Chanukkah is for children and we were getting too big, but Ellen was only four. I think—before—that Mum wanted to celebrate it for Dad's sake—and that he wanted to mark Christmas Day for hers. Nowadays Quinn usually has some weird women friends round on December 21 for a Solstice get-together.

As early as September, Dad starts raising the subject of Christmas. He likes to plan it like a military operation, trying to arrange who is going to be where at what time and who is bringing what: the satsumas, the bubbly, the nuts, the proper Cheddar from the posh cheese shop.

'And is Stephen coming?' he asked the following Sunday at brunch.

'No,' I sighed, trying to keep the impatience out of my voice. 'Not until after lunch anyway.' We eat Christmas lunch at about four o'clock. 'He's turning up around six, after he's spent the day with his parents.'

'But who will we tease if there's no Mr P-h?' Ellen said.

'That's not actually his sole purpose in life, you know, to be a comic punchbag for you and Matt,' I replied, grabbing a bagel.

'Isn't it? But he does it so well.' She leaned across me for the butter.

'And the other thing . . .' Dad lowered his voice and I instinctively leaned towards him. 'Simone will be joining us.' Quinn was upstairs in the bathroom, and I knew he'd picked a moment when she was out of the room to tell us, just in case Ellen complained without thinking.

'Oh, no! *Why* is she?' Ellen sounds like such a spoilt brat sometimes. 'Last year she was nonstop hideous from the second she walked in the door. And she was foul to Quinn,' she added.

'Ha! And like *you're* not!' I shook my head. Unbelievable.

'Ellen. Any guest in this house is to be made welcome. She's Quinn's daughter and I expect you to be polite to her at the very least.'

Ellen pouted.

'Ellen, Quinn is endlessly hospitable to you, and puts up with all your teasing and your sulking. It's not much to ask in return that you behave half decently towards her daughter for a few hours, is it?'

'Huh.' Ellen sat sideways on her chair and gnawed at a piece of her bagel. 'Well, it won't be the same, that's all I'm saying. At least tell me you'll be doing the cooking, George.'

'Of course I will.'

Dad peered at me over his newspaper battlements, brows raised.

'I mean, if that suits everyone? If Quinn doesn't mind,' I added.

'If Quinn doesn't mind what?' Quinn came back into the kitchen.

'Um—about Christmas dinner, would you like me to do—to help you with it or . . .?'

'Goodness, I was hoping you'd do the whole lot, Georgia. I did it last year, you know, and the turkey was very dry. I don't know how you always get it to be so delicious.'

'Your roasties were good. Really crunchy,' Ellen offered, attempting to redeem herself.

Quinn positively beamed.

'Let's share the cooking then. Quinn can do her legendary potatoes—'

'And George can do all the rest.' Ellen's terrific at volunteering other people to do things.

'And what's *your* contribution going to be?' Dad asked her.

Ellen looked shocked, as if he'd asked her when she was planning to retile the roof, before or after lunch? 'Um—I'll—I could—well—I—'

Dad was still looking at her, went so far as to lower his paper.

'Maybe I could chop the carrots or something?'

'I tell you what—why don't you do the table? Sort out candles and napkins and all that. But you've got to do it *properly*.'

She nodded, happy again. 'I *will*. Don't boss. What about Matt?' Ellen can't bear the idea that anyone else will get off with doing less than her.

'Matt will have the kids to look after.'

'But Iz can do that! It's not fair!'

'Ellen,' Dad sighed. 'Until you have children of your own, you don't realise how much work it involves.'

'Quite,' I said.

'What would *you* know?' Ellen turned on me. 'You're no expert!'

'Ellen!' Quinn rebuked her, which she never does. We were all so surprised that we turned to look at her. 'That's not very diplomatic,' her voice softened. 'A childless woman in her mid-thirties is bound to feel a little bit . . . *sensitive* on this subject.' She smiled sympathetically at me.

I was outraged.

'What? Quinn—thank you for your intervention, but it's quite unnecessary—if you're referring to my ageing ovaries and my cobwebbed womb, let me assure you that I'm more than happy for them to atrophy with disuse. I have no intentions of having children. Absolutely none.'

Quinn cocked her head on one side and directed a small, infuriating smile at Dad who, annoyingly, smiled back.

'Meaning *what* exactly?' I addressed both of them.

Quinn and Dad stayed silent.

'Why does everyone think they know me better than I do myself? If I say I don't want children, you have to accept that a) I might be telling the truth and b) it's none of your business in any case. OK?'

I pulled one of the colour supplements towards me and started to leaf through it.

'But we all know that you *do* want them really . . .' Ellen reached across me again to grab the apricot jam. 'And if you're going to end up with Leo, you'll have a child whether you want one or not.'

'It may have escaped your notice, but I am NOT with Leo, nor am I likely to be EVER—is that clear? And it's nothing to do with Cora—she's a really sweet child—but I have absolutely no interest in Leo in any case and, even if I had, there's no way I'd ever want to be a stepmother—what could be worse than being some awful, unwanted substitute and knowing that you're always going to be second-best and never—'

I'd been going to say about knowing that the children are only putting up with you and don't really want you there, when I realised what I'd just said out loud. The room was absolutely silent. I swallowed and stole a quick glance at Dad. He looked angry, very angry. Even Ellen was completely quiet.

Finally, I looked up at Quinn.

'Quinn, I'm really sorry—I didn't mean—' I was floundering.'

'It's all right, Georgia. We all say things we don't mean sometimes.' Her hand flew instinctively to Dad and he reached out and squeezed it.

'Well, I'd best be getting on.' She looked up at the kitchen clock. 'I've got—some—some—things—to do.' She smiled, a valiant smile, then left the room and I heard her running lightly up the stairs.

'**H**oly fuck,' said Ellen. 'And *you* call *me* Queen of Tact!'

'Dad—I'm so sorry—'

'Don't apologise to *me*.'

'I—I—wasn't thinking—you know I don't think of Quinn as a substitute mother—'

'As you made all too clear. Georgia. Honestly. How must she be feeling?'

'But Quinn's never tried to mother us—she wasn't even around when we were growing up . . .'

'Quinn's never tried to mother you lot because she's got more sense than that, but she's always hoped you might let her into your lives a bit more that you have. Half the time you treat her as if she's some comical cameo, getting in little clever asides about her cooking and her clothes. I have never interfered because I hoped you were grown-up enough to moderate your own behaviour and see that it upsets her. But I was wrong.' He looked down, away from me. 'I was wrong and I was stupid. Sitting on the sidelines as usual, hoping things would fix themselves.' He shook his head, but more at himself than at me it seemed. 'No one's saying she's a replacement for Joy. And no one is saying you've got to think of her as a mother. But I will not have you talk to her like that. Quinn is my wife and this is her house too—don't look like that—*it is her house too*, and while you're in it, I expect you to treat her with the same respect you'd accord anyone else.'

'**U**m, Quinn?' I tapped on her bedroom door.

A pause. A long pause.

'Oh. Georgia? No. I'm—just—I'm—changing just now.'

'I wanted to say I'm sorry—really sorry—I—'

'Thank you, dear.' Her voice sounded artificially bright.

'Can I come in for a minute?'

'Not just now. I'm having a lie-down. I've got a bit of a—a migraine.'

'Oh. I'm sorry. Really I am. I—well. I'll be off then I guess.' There was no response. 'Hope you feel better soon. Bye then.'

Still no answer.

I went downstairs and back into the kitchen.

'She can't talk to me now,' I said flatly. 'She says she has a migraine.'

'I'll go up.' Dad shook his head. 'It's not like you to be so thoughtless, Georgia. I expect better from *you*, you know I do.'

'I know.' I couldn't even meet his eye, I felt so ashamed. 'I'd better go.'

'I'll come with you, George.' Ellen sprang up.

Dad gave each of us a cursory kiss. 'Let yourselves out,' he said, then he turned away from us and headed up the stairs.

TWENTY ONE

Homecoming

LEO'S BACK. He's been away for eleven days. It was supposed to be a week, but he phoned Joan to ask her if she could carry on feeding the cat a bit longer. Naturally, she told him I'd taken Blossom into my flat, to save messing about with the keys each time. I thought that then he'd have to talk to me, even if only to ask for his cat back. And that would give me a chance to apologise properly. I've moved a lot of my stuff into Stephen's flat, stay there most nights now, but when I went home yesterday to feed Blossom, I found this note on my doormat:

G—

I gather that you are in possession of something that belongs to me—i.e. one cat (black, white flash at throat, name of—but not necessarily answering to—Blossom). Kindly return same a.s.a.p.

L

That was it.

I phoned him, but got the machine, so I left a message, but I was so nervous that I started babbling about Blossom and how she'd been and how sorry I was for what I'd said. I probably would have carried on until I'd used up the whole tape, but then he picked up the phone and said, 'Hey!'

'Hi. I—I was just leaving a message.'

'Sorry—I didn't hear the phone—I've just come in.'

'I've got Blossom. Shall I—'

'You're not holding her hostage, are you?'

'No, of course not.'

'Hello? Joke.'

'Oh, of course. Yes. Right. I'll bring her back now, shall I?'

I walk down the stairs with Blossom in my arms. The corridor is full of people talking and clinking glasses. Music—Ella Fitzgerald?—emanating from someone's flat.

'Hey, you!' Leo appears in front of me.

'Hi. Here she is then.' I want to look into his eyes, but I cannot.

'Thanks for looking after her.'

'That's OK. She's lovely. Well, bye then.' I put her into his arms, then turn to leave.

'Where are you going?' he says.

'Going back upstairs—for the litter tray and stuff.'

'Are you mad? We're having a party—in case you hadn't noticed. Don't you want to be at it?'

'I didn't think I was invited.'

'No one was invited. It just—happened. I got back an hour ago—saw Joan and she said let's celebrate you being back, so I got the wine and crisps and here we all are. Of course, there's no reason why you might want to stay, ask how I am, how my trip went, any of that stuff—'

'But you're not talking to me.'

'No. That's true. To the naked eye, it might look as if I'm standing here talking to you, but that is merely a sophisticated illusion.'

'I'm so, so sorry about what I said about you—and Cora—I felt terrible about it—wretched—it was mean and horrible and I don't blame you a bit for not talking to me—I wouldn't talk to me either if I was you—anyway—your note—I knew you were still angry.'

'Hello—are you awake yet? The note was a joke. Can't I leave you alone for a few days without your losing your sense of humour? Look—yes, of course I was upset. Very. And angry too—but do you really think I'd hold a grudge all this time, you dope?'

'I didn't think. I just felt angry then guilty then completely and utterly crap. It's been horrible.'

'Now, stop all that and come here and give me a hug and tell me how much you've missed me.' He puts down Blossom who coils round and between us, mewing for attention.

'**O**ne good thing did come out of what you said.' He lets me go and picks up Blossom again. 'It made me realise something. You were right about that Canadian job.' He lowers his voice. 'I mean, there I was—with this extraordinary, miraculous gift of a *child*—and I was about to chuck it all out the window and not see her for months, making out this *job* was some amazing once-in-a-lifetime opportunity when the real opportunity was right here under my nose—only I couldn't handle it. I was scared, Georgia. Shit-scared.'

'It *is* difficult. And scary. And I'm glad you're staying. Not just for Cora's sake.'

'Did I mention how much I missed—Blossom?'

'No. Did you?'

'Yes. I missed—her—very—very—much indeed.'

'You could have phoned her.'

'Nope. I decided not to. The problem is I'm never sure how she feels about me. One minute she's purring, the next she's sinking her claws into me. I figured if I didn't have any contact with her for a week or two, I might stop thinking about her. I thought it might help.'

'And did it?'

'Nope.'

I step slightly closer to stroke Blossom as she purrs there, cradled in his arms. 'She missed you a lot too. She used to curl up close to me just for comfort—because I reminded her of you.'

He smiles.

'And how's everyone else doing? Ellen? Your dad left me a nice message inviting Cora and me for Christmas—really kind of them. Come on, give me all the news. And, dare I ask, how's things with Stephen?'

Stephen. Oh shit. What am I doing? I promised I'd never see Leo again. But I had to return his cat, obviously. I couldn't help it.

'What is it? You've gone white as a sheet.'

'Stephen—he—I—we. I said I wouldn't see you.'

'You *what*?' He puts the cat down.

'I felt so awful and I *thought* you weren't speaking to me.'

'So you offered to drop me faster than a week-old haddock? Cheers.'

'It wasn't like that. He wanted me to move in with him and—'

'I see. And you're going along with that as well, are you?'

I drop my head.

'Great. Well, that's wonderful, wonderful news. Boy, do I feel stupid.'

'No—it's—I didn't think—'

'No, you certainly didn't, did you? Fine—you just stay stuck in your good old trusty rut, it suits you. Thanks for bringing Bloss back.' He looks down to find her, but she's scampered off along the corridor.

'No, Leo. *Please*.'

He holds his hand out as if to keep me at a distance.

'*Enough*. I've *had* it with all this. Just forget it. Forget *everything*.' Then he strides away, calling for Blossom.

I think my car's been stolen. At first I thought I'd just forgotten where I'd parked the bloody thing. But after I'd spent two hours wandering up and down the streets, the awful truth dawned on me.

How am I going to get home on Christmas Day? I could walk if I have to—except I'll have loads to carry and . . . I ring Quinn.

'Oh, Georgia! How are you? I'll just call David.'

'Actually, I was calling to speak to *you*.'

'Oh. If it's about the other day, I'd virtually forgotten all about it . . .'

'I am very sorry. It all came out wrong.'

'Well, not to worry now. Anyway . . .?'

I told her that my car seemed to have gone AWOL and asked if it might be possible to stay.

'Of course! No need to ask, this is your home too.'

Then I went round to the police station to report the theft of my car. They said it's unlikely I'll ever see it again—unless it's been nicked by joyriders, in which case it might turn up totally trashed. Terrific. It's shaping up to be a wonderful Christmas.

TWENTY TWO

Pieces past and present

I SHUT THE ALARM OFF QUICKLY at 8.00am so as not to wake the others, then came downstairs, put on a pot of coffee and brought the turkey out from the cool larder to start preparing it.

For once, downstairs really did look nice. Quinn had made swags of greenery—laurel and bay with trailing strands of creamy-margined ivy—to go above the fireplace in the sitting room, along the shelves of the dresser, and over the big mirror in the hall. I nipped out to the garden to pick the herbs for the turkey. Grated zest from a lemon and an orange. Peeled a couple of onions. It was nice being here, in the calm before the storm, with no one else making a noise or getting in my way.

So I was standing in the kitchen with my hand halfway up the turkey, shoving in bits of onion and lemon and sprigs of thyme, and singing a sort of bluesy version of 'We Three Kings' when a voice right behind me said, 'Is there any coffee?'

Simone. Oh, hello, good morning and happy Christmas to you too. I'd forgotten she was even in the house.

'Oh!' I said, making a bit of a thing of it. 'Hi. You *startled* me.' She didn't bother to apologise, just slumped into Dad's big carver chair at the end of the table. 'Happy Christmas,' I added, with not much feeling. 'Or do you go for Winter Solstice?'

She shrugged. 'My mother only pretends to be into all that Solstice shit because she's still desperately trying to rebel against the nuns.'

'The nuns?' I took a mug from a hook and filled it with coffee for her.

'Yuh.' She arched a single eyebrow. 'Didn't Ma tell you? She went to convent school. Her parents weren't especially religious—they just wanted her to speak nicely and not mix with the nasty rough children at the state school.' She delved into the pocket of her silk dressing gown and came out with a packet of cigarettes. 'Ashtray?'

Honestly. I wish Quinn had sent *her* to convent school—at least then she might say please and thank you occasionally.

I handed her a saucer. 'No. Quinn never talks about her schooldays.' And I don't think I've ever even asked her, I thought.

'No surprises there. A couple of the nuns were frightful, frustrated old bitches, if you ask me. They used to smack the girls over the backs of their hands with rulers. And they were always telling them to keep their hands on their desks so they would know that the girls weren't touching themselves—*down there*, as they used to say.'

'No!'

'Exactly. Who'd want a wank in a roomful of schoolgirls and decrepit nuns? Not my idea of a turn-on.'

'How bizarre.' I suddenly felt sorry for Quinn, picturing her as a girl, holding out her hands to be struck, her eyes welling up with tears.

'Better not say anything to Ma. She's quite ashamed of her convent-school past—I think it's 'cause she's tried to reinvent herself as this right-on arty-farty earth-mother type, and it doesn't fit with her being a repressed Catholic girl from a semi in the suburbs.'

'Well, we all react against our pasts, I suppose, don't we?'

She looked straight at me, unblinking. 'You mean me, right?' She took a deep drag of her cigarette. 'Fair enough. Still—better to be a stressed-out yuppie shrew than an ageing wannabe hippy.'

'I wasn't thinking of you at all. I meant just generally.'

'Really?' She mashed out her cigarette firmly.

'Well.' I shrugged. 'And me, I suppose.'

'I hadn't figured you for a rebel. You and your family—' She cocked her head on one side while she thought. 'You *fit* together—like a jigsaw.'

'Us?' I laughed. 'But we're always squabbling and interrupting and getting up each other's noses. Not exactly a pretty-picture jigsaw, is it?'

'So? At least you're all part of the same puzzle. You know . . .' She looked down. 'Many people would be kind of . . . envious of you lot.'

I stared at her incredulously. I couldn't imagine Simone's being envious of anyone. She's so successful and clever and immaculately groomed. Besides, she's normally so dismissive of other people.

'Yuh,' she continued. 'Even when you're arguing you all mesh—like a real family. You're all different, sure, but you're at least all on the same wavelength. Shit, when I'm talking to Ma, half the time I feel as if we're not even on the same planet. And take your dad, he's like a real designer, right? He earns a living and everything, he's not wafting around banging on about expressing himself.'

'Mmm. I suppose you're right. I always think of Dad as being hopelessly befuddled and incompetent—but he *does* earn a decent living and he managed to bring up the three of us virtually single-handed.'

'Ma said your mother painted, too. Have you any of her work?' She picked up a piece of toast and started eating it.

'Very little. She didn't just paint though—she did etchings, sculpted in clay and wax, made tapestries, ceramics, she loved to experiment.'

'Why haven't you got much of her stuff left? Did you flog it or what?'

'No.' I almost wished I hadn't started on this, except that it was still so calm here in the kitchen and it suddenly seemed easy to be talking about it to someone I didn't know so well. 'A lot of it was . . . destroyed.'

That arched eyebrow again, but no comment.

'My brother, Matt—he went a bit ballistic after our mother died. He—he smashed up a lot of her stuff.'

'Christ. He doesn't look the type. But wasn't he just a kid at the time?'

'Yes, not quite eight. One morning Dad went downstairs and found him in the studio—surrounded by broken glass, smashed ceramic heads, busted canvases. With poor Matt in the middle of it all, curled up into a ball.' I felt at once relieved to have said it but also guilty for having told someone outside the family. 'Please don't say anything.'

'Whatever.' She shrugged. 'All families have their skeletons.'

'Of course. But he's so happy and settled now, he doesn't need to be reminded of that time. And also . . .'

I looked down into my empty mug.

'Ellen doesn't know.'

After a typically raucous brunch, and buck's fizz provided by Simone, Ellen barricaded herself in the kitchen, pulling the dividing doors closed so that nobody could see in.

'I shall now prepare . . . the table,' she intoned. 'Do not enter under any circumstances—on pain of being pelted with squashy satsumas.'

As I was unwrapping my present from Matt and Izzy—a beautiful, soft cream jumper—the phone rang. Quinn answered it.

'Hello? . . . Ah, hello, how are you? . . . Happy Christmas to you too. Are we seeing you later? . . . Ah, I see. OK. I'll just get Georgia for you.'

Stephen, presumably, though I had already rung him earlier to say happy Christmas. I laid the jumper carefully on my chair and stood up.

'It's Leo,' she said.

I stood with my back to the others. 'Hello?'

'Hey, you. It's me. If you're really not speaking to me, just nod, OK?'

'And for those of you listening in black and white, the red cracker is the one to the left of the green.'

He laughed.

'Tell me you're having a good Jewish Christmas over there—good food, good jokes and good arguing, with not a sausage roll in sight.'

'Well—more or less.' I dropped my voice. 'I'm glad you've rung. I—I really am. I wanted to say sorry. I never meant—God, I'm hopeless. Are you having a good time? How's Cora?'

'No, I'm not. I've eaten six mince pies out of boredom. Cora's fine though. Look, Georgia—you *can't* not talk to me. This is the season of goodwill. And if Stephen's not happy with that, well he'll just have to see me about it—he's not as fit as he looks, is he?'

I laughed.

'Tell him we've saved two places at the table,' Dad called out.

'Did you hear that? . . . Of course he's being serious . . . yes, I'd love you to, too, that's OK . . . it doesn't matter a bit . . . no, of course not, don't be silly . . . yes, whenever. Good. See you then. Take care.'

I turned round and they were all looking at me except Bonnie and Daniel who were 'helping' Dad open his presents.

'Leo's coming too, then, is he?' Matt said. 'Excellent.'

'Ellie?' I knocked on the dividing doors. 'Ellie—I have to get in there to baste the turkey and turn the potatoes. Can you *please* hurry up?'

'Can't you do it blindfolded?' she called.

'Of course—nothing I'd like more than to wrestle a fifteen-pound lava-hot turkey out of the oven and spoon hot fat over it blindfold.'

'OK—you can come in—but no one else.'

She led me in from the hall, covering my eyes with her hand.

'OK—ready?' She removed her hand. 'Open your eyes!'

Along the centre of the table was a line of six ivory candles, each one in a most unusual-looking holder, half sprayed gold and half left unsprayed—'Oh my God—they're *bagels*!'

'Right. You like?'

'I *like*. This is brilliant!'

Around the bagel candleholders, trails of ivy entwined, with subtle touches of gold here and there on the leaves. The place mats were beautiful, some sort of wonderful dark green slate and the napkins were plain calico, secured in spiral coils of more ivy.

'It's beautiful, Ellie. It really is.'

'I kept thinking, all the time I was doing it, would Georgia like this or would she think it was naff? But you haven't seen the best bit. Look up!'

Suspended above the centre of the table was a mobile, with small pipe-cleaner figures dressed in coloured tissue, dangling from invisible threads. 'What are—oh God—Ellie!'

There was a male figure, hands clutching a miniature newspaper.

'Is that *Dad*?'

'Of course.'

One had wild curls and pink jeans and was holding three bags—Ellie. One had yellow-painted legs and ridiculous outsize earrings made of wire and tinfoil—Quinn. Another was tiny and hanging upside-down as if from a trapeze—Daniel. Bonnie. Matt. Izzy. Even Simone. And there—right in the middle—was a Christmas fairy or angel. Except that it wasn't. It didn't have wings, just a tiny wand, with a silver star at the end. Aside from this one festive touch, the figure was plainly dressed, wearing black trousers and a white top.

'But why—?'

'Because you *should* have a magic wand—you're always the one who tries to make everything all right again—whether it's your clients or us.'

'God, I wish that were true. All I've done recently is make a total hash of things left, right and centre.'

'You haven't. You've just—' She shrugged. 'Become a bit less Georgia-ish and a bit more like a normal person. It's *good*.'

'Hi, everyone! Happy Christmas, Happy Solstice et cetera, et cetera.'

A burst of hellos as Leo goes round the table, kissing cheeks and shaking hands. He sets two bottles, port and champagne, on the worktop.

'Now, have I missed anyone?' Leo says, as he's about to sit down.

'Only the chef. No one of any importance.'

'Auntie Gee!' shouts Bonnie.

'The chef? You mean I have to kiss the *staff*?'

He comes up next to me.

'Best not to get too witty while I'm wielding a large knife.'

He puts his arm round me then kisses my cheek in a chaste manner.

'Ohh,' says Ellen, 'call that a kiss?' She tips the last of a bottle into her glass. 'Pass that other bottle along, will you, Matzo?'

We eventually wind to a halt, weighed down with turkey and too many potatoes, and slump onto the sofas and cushions in the sitting room. After a while, Bonnie and Daniel start to get tired and fractious, so Izzy suggests taking them home. Dad, who hardly drinks at all, volunteers to take Matt back later. Cora's eyelids, I notice, are drooping.

'And I see my little one is fading fast too . . .'

'Oh, don't go!' says Ellen.

'She can go to sleep in our room.' Quinn stands up. 'Then you can wrap her in a quilt to take her home.' She leads the way upstairs.

Ellen reaches across me for what must be the fifteenth time, knocking over my water glass to get to the wine.

'Ellen!'

'Oops! Sorry. Sorry, sorry, *sorry*! Relax—it's only water.' She dabs vaguely at me with a stray napkin, pours yet more wine into her glass.

'Don't you think you've had *enough* now?' I say, keeping my voice low.

'Come on, George, light'n up,' she says, voice slightly slurred. 'If you don't want to enjoy yourself, fine, but don't spoil it for everyone else.'

I stand up to start clearing away the coffee cups to the kitchen.

'So . . . Leo . . .' Ellen says, loudly. 'Tell me, before the P-h arrives to spoil the fun—are you madly in love with my sister or aren't you?'

'Ellen! For God's sake!'

'Personally, I think you *are* . . .' she continues, ignoring me.

'Ellen. Just shut up. Right now.' I turn to face her. 'Leo.' I cannot look at him. 'I'm terribly sorry. Ellen's just being stupid and ridiculous—'

'It's OK. Really. Don't worry about it,' he says calmly.

'Because she's had way too much to drink and—'

The doorbell rings.

'Saved by the bell!' Ellen calls out, rolling her eyes.

'That'll be Stephen. Ellen—don't you dare carry on like this in front of him.'

'**H**appy Christmas, darling!' Stephen puts his arms round me and kisses me on the lips. 'Are you all having fun?'

'We were, but Ellen's had too much to drink. She's behaving appallingly—promise me you'll ignore her if she gets too awful.'

'I'll do my best. But never mind, eh? She'll have a lousy head in the morning and say she's sorry, I'm sure.'

It's not like Stephen to be so laid-back.

'And also—now don't go mad, but Cora and Leo are here. Dad invited them ages ago, and they only decided to come at the last minute—so I didn't know, I swear. But can we please not get stressed out about it? It's Christmas—let's not spoil it.'

He nods, though he looks decidedly unhappy about it.

'All right. But we're not staying long.'

'**H**ello, everyone. Happy Christmas!' Stephen nods at Leo.

'Mr P-h—you don't know how much we've missed your sparkling company,' Ellen says. 'Sit here and entertain me!'

Oh God. Why won't she just stop?

Stephen takes a seat and Dad attempts to hold a normal conversation with him, but with Ellen sitting between them, it's impossible.

'Isn't there any more wine?' she demands.

'I stuck another bottle of bubbly in to chill,' says Simone.

Oh, thank you. That was helpful.

'Will you have some, Stephen?' Quinn stands up and goes to fetch another glass while Matt opens the champagne.

'Thank you. I will. Just the one though as I'm driving.'

'Don't forget me, Matzo,' says Ellen. Her eyes have that out-of-focus expression, as if she is looking at someone over Matt's shoulder.

'Why—not exactly dying of thirst, are you, Ell?'

'God—you're getting like George. Nag, nag, nag.'

'Come on, Ellie. Have some coffee instead.'

'Oh—STOP getting at me!' Ellen stands up suddenly, knocking over her glass. 'I'm perfec-ly fine. Mr P-h? You don' want to marry George—she won't let you have more than one drink at the wedding—'

'Ellen! Cut it out!' I grab her arm but she jerks away from me.

'Don' boss me! You're just cross 'cause I asked Leo if he was in love with you and he never answered!'

Stephen's face is as if carved of stone.

'*Ellen*.' Dad's voice is serious and deadly calm. 'You have clearly had more than enough to drink and you're now embarrassing our guests as well as yourself. Go upstairs right now and have a lie-down.'

'Why's everyone havin' a go at *me*?' she wails. 'What've *I* done?'

'Oh, Ell. Give it a rest.' Matt sounds angry. 'You know something? You're turning into a real lush. Wake up for God's sake! Just because Dad and Gee try to pretend it's not happening—'

'Matt—no—*don't*—'

'*Matthew*,' Dad says, making it sound like a warning.

'No. It's ridiculous. Everyone treats Ellen like a child and that's why she still acts like one. Ell—face it, you're nearly thirty—time to grow up! You can't go round getting pissed the whole time like some teenager. It's becoming a real problem and you should take it seriously—'

'No, Matt—please!' But I can see that nothing will stop him now.

'Take it *seriously* . . . Because Mum—Mum—she . . .' His voice fades and he slumps into a chair.

Silence. Then Stephen looks at me, suddenly comprehending, utterly shocked. Leo, unsurprised, sends me a look of sympathy.

'What do you mean?' Ellen's voice is like a child's.

'Do you need everything spelt out for you? She was an alcoholic.'

'But—she *can't* have been.' Ellen looks round at Matt, at Dad, at me. 'I'd *know*. George would have told me. Dad would have.'

She turns to me once more, but I look away. She faces Dad. He sighs. 'We thought it would be easier for you not to know. That's all.'

Ellen looks round the room, assessing the expressions of the others.

'*You* knew.' She accuses Quinn, who nods. 'And Matt—is that why you never talk about her?' He drops his gaze and I can see that the enormity of what he's said is starting to hit home.

All these years and I have never been sure whether Matt really knew or not. I knew he remembered smashing up her studio because he was so angry with her, but I thought he was just angry about her dying, not about . . . everything else. I was never sure if he *knew*.

'I don't remember all of it, just bits and pieces.' Matt's shoulders are hunched. 'Her mood swings—her little naps to sleep it off—never being on time—lying—letting us down again and again—embarrassing the shit out of us.' Dad hangs his head, Quinn's hand on his shoulder, a silent support. 'But Georgia bore the brunt of it, trying to hide the bottles when she found them, getting Mum up and bullying her to get dressed—she was running this household well before Mum died. Gee's been a way better mother to you than Mum ever was.'

Georgia and Joy are preparing the lunch. Joy is rummaging through the contents of the vegetable basket, saying she can't find the carrots.

'No, Mummy. We have to start the turkey or it'll be ever so late.'

The bird is sitting in a roasting tin, looking large and pink and naked.

'It's no great shakes whether we serve it at one o'clock or three o'clock, is it? Besides, grown-ups are more than happy to relax with a little something while they wait for lunch.'

'But it won't be lunch. It'll be supper. We have to put it in the oven.'

'Oh, darling, don't look so cross. It's Christmas! Come on—come here and give Mummy a kiss.'

Georgia slowly comes forward to comply. Her mother hugs her tight.

'Let's dance! We should be enjoying ourselves, not doing boring old cooking!' She whirls Georgia round the kitchen, singing, 'Deck the halls with boughs of holly! Fa-la-la-la-lah-la-la-la-laaah! 'Tis the season—' Stops as she catches sight of Georgia's face.

'Well.' She draws back a pace. 'Perhaps we'd better get that bird in.'

At half past twelve, Unc turns up with Auntie Audrey and the cousins. As well as presents, they bring chocolates and two bottles of wine to join the single bottle David has put out.

Unc is driving, so has just one glass. Auntie Audrey claims to get tipsy if she even so much as looks at a bottle of sherry, but she lets David pour her a glass all the same.

There are presents to be unwrapped, family stories to recount as they have been recounted for years. There is laughing, drinking, nibbling of crisps. The smoked salmon starter is devoured, then everyone leaves the table again for the turkey is still not cooked through.

At four o'clock, the immense turkey is finally brought to the table and David begins to carve.

'Won't you open some more wine for our guests, David dear?'

'Mmm . . .' he looks round, then sees the empty bottles on the worktop. 'Oh. Well—does anyone want any more?'

'Not for me,' says Unc. 'I'm driving.'

'Go on,' Joy urges Audrey, 'live a little. Come on. God, you're all such bloody stick-in-the-muds, you lot!'

Unc laughs, his eyes avoiding his brother's. Audrey smiles awkwardly. 'Just a sip then. Only if you're opening it, mind.'

'Of course we are! Aren't we?' Joy gets to her feet, disappears into the hallway, can be heard clanking about in the depths of the clutter under the stairs. 'Found one!'

'That was lucky.' David's voice, sounding bright and jovial.

Mummy's voice gets louder and louder when she is being like this. She laughs when people say things that are not funny and when you look at her, her eyes are strange, all shiny like polished stones, or as if she is looking at something just beyond your shoulder and not really at you at all.

When Mummy is being like this, Daddy hides behind the newspaper, but now, today, all the family is here and the papers have been stuffed out of sight in the dresser. Daddy smiles and fills Audrey's glass almost to the very top when she is looking the other way. After the meal, when Georgia comes to sit by him, he pulls her close and kisses the top of her head, then smiles at her.

Unc starts singing, quietly at first, then his voice growing stronger, deeper, hamming it up a bit, signalling for David to join him—an old Hebrew song, the words at once strange and familiar to Georgia. 'Our Chanukkah carol' Unc calls it, the song he and David and their sister Rachel had to sing as children for Chanukkah, the Festival of Lights. Then Joy joins in, for after all these years she knows the words almost as well as David does. A smile passes between her and her husband, a real smile, like the silver, heart-shaped locket that Georgia got as her most special present this very morning, small and precious and rare, something to treasure and keep.

And then the song ends and David and Unc give each other a big hug and Georgia and Matt and the cousins roll their eyes, already old enough to be embarrassed by their parents' singing and hugging.

Now, when it is like this, sitting on the sofa, her father's arm stretched round her shoulder, Georgia can make believe that everything is all right. Her mother is sitting on the floor, with Ellen sprawled across her knees—thumb in mouth, eyelids drooping. Unc is telling a long story but Georgia does not hear the words, just lets the deep waves of his voice roll over her, wrapping round her like Granny's old eiderdown, safe and familiar and comforting.

Suddenly, there is a loud snorting noise in the middle of Unc's story. Joy is snoring, her head fallen askew against the arm of the sofa, mouth gaping. The cousins laugh at their Auntie Joy snoring like a pig.

'So much for my skills as a raconteur!' Unc says, laughing. He casts around for Audrey, brows raised. 'We should be heading off soon . . .'

'Of course.' Audrey gets to her feet. 'It's a lot of work catering for the troops. Let's not disturb her, she looks . . . worn out.'

'Yes.' David nods. 'She's worn out.'

Georgia stands by her father's side on the doorstep, smiling, stretching up on tiptoe to kiss Unc and Auntie, thanking them for their gifts. Matt leans against her, not saying goodbye properly. Normally she'd push him off, stupid Batzo-Matzo, but not now, not today.

In the sitting room, sprawled on the floor, Joy and Ellen sleep on.

TWENTY THREE
A lifetime of lies

'ELLIE?' I KNOCK ON THE BATHROOM DOOR.

'Go away.'

'Can I just talk to you for a minute?'

Silence.

'At least let me explain.' I rest my forehead against the door.

The door suddenly swings open and she stands there, red-eyed and smudgy-cheeked. 'Well, this should be interesting. Just how do you plan to explain away twenty-four years of lying?'

I step inside and she plonks herself on the bathroom floor.

'We—I—wanted to protect you . . .' Even to my own ears it sounds pathetic, one of the classic feeble excuses: we did it for your own good.

Ellen snorts with derision.

'Why? I'm not three years old any more, am I? Just when exactly were you planning on letting me in on this minor family secret—when they're wheeling me away to the twilight home?'

'I'm sorry. Of course, it's only natural for you to be angry—'

'Don't you *dare*!' She leaps to her feet. 'Don't you dare try and load any of that calm-and-reasonable counsellor shit onto me! Everyone else is some sort of emotional fuck-up according to you—you're the only one who's perfect. Well—you're not perfect, not even close, are you? Look what you said to Quinn—and you've been stringing Stephen along all this time when I don't think you even *like* the guy all that much, never mind *love* him. And you'd have to be dead, blind or wilfully self-deluding not to see how you really feel about Leo. And Cora. I suppose it's been easy to lie to little Ellie, hasn't it? Ellen's clueless—everybody knows that. Ellen can't even manage to get from A to B without being an hour late. Ellen can't keep a boyfriend for longer than it takes him to get dressed again afterwards. Ellen—titter, titter—is still waiting to find out what she's going to be when she *grows up*. This wasn't some silly little lie to protect my feelings. You kept the truth from me about my own mother—year in and year out. I can understand Dad doing it, in a way—he'd rather hide behind the Review section than have to deal with anything real and messy—but *you*? You're supposed to be dealing with this kind of crap all the time—you're always on about the importance of open, honest communication! How *dare* you?'

Her words whip against my face like sharp sand in the wind. I flatten the palms of my hands against the solid door behind me.

I wish I could be angry too—angry like she is—throw something, anything, back at her. But how can I when I know that she is right?

I shake my head, unable to speak at first.

'You don't know what it was like—'

'No.' She folds her arms and stands steady, straight and tall. 'Well, how could I as you've never told me? And—what about all our stories—' She bites her lip, her eyes welling with tears. 'Were *any* of them true?'

'All true. I swear. But—I edited out the—the difficult bits—bits I thought you didn't need to know. I wanted you to have the perf—the mother you *should* have had—the way she was before she—'

'Who are *you* to judge what *I* need to know? You've fed me a fucking fantasy my whole life—and now I don't have a clue about anything any more.' She slumps to the floor again, huddling close to the bath.

'I'm sorry.'

She shakes her head then and hugs her knees up to her chest.

'Leave me alone.'

'Maybe I could—?'

'No.' She will not look at me. 'Just fuck off.'

Stephen unwrapped the food parcels his mother had given him: cold turkey, ham, mince pies, swathed in layers of foil and plastic bags.

'What I don't understand, Georgia,' he said, avoiding my eyes, 'is how come you couldn't tell me?' He wanted to ask why Leo knew and not him, but he was afraid to. And I could not give him an answer, not an answer he could take. *Because I knew he wouldn't judge me. Or Mum. Because I knew he wouldn't give that little smug look on finding out about yet another of the Abramses' numerous flaws. Because I knew I could trust him.*

'I don't know. I was always scared you might—judge me somehow. I know you think my family are all hopeless. And you're right—we *are*.'

'Silly—you're not. Not at all. No one's perfect.'

He came closer and put his arms round me.

'Come on, sweetie. Let's not dwell on this. Forget about it for now. Let's have a bath and go to bed, eh?'

On Boxing Day, Stephen and I went to stay with some friends in Sussex for a couple of days. It was good to get away from everybody and everything. I did almost nothing but read and sleep. When I returned to my flat afterwards, to pick up some more clothes to take to Stephen's, there was a message on my machine from Leo, so I rang him back and he came up for some tea.

'Hey—how are you doing? Have you managed to talk to Ellen?'

I shake my head and he puts his arms round me and just holds me.

'Listen—you're not to beat yourself up about all this. You and your dad did what you thought was right.' He puts one finger gently under my chin and tilts my face up so that I'm looking into his eyes.

'But we were *wrong*.'

'You don't know that. Just because Ellen's angry about it—you can't possibly know how things would have been if you *had* told her. And even if you were wrong, it wasn't out of malice.'

'I can't let myself off the hook so easily.'

'OK. You're a vile, nasty, evil person—happy now?'

'Oh, *don't*.'

'Now, if you've finished with the sackcloth and ashes for the moment, can I demonstrate my usual chutzpah and ask if it's OK to stop by at brunch with Cora on Sunday?'

'Of course you can, silly. How is she doing?'

'So-so, I guess.' A shrug. 'But she's so quiet. I told her I'm going to find a bigger place so she can come and stay with me every weekend, have her own room, and she just smiled her funny, polite little smile and said "thank you"—as if I were a stranger.'

'You need to be patient. She *will* come to love you and to *know* you as her daddy, I'm sure of it. But she just needs to feel . . . completely safe.'

He frowns. 'But she *is* safe. I'd do anything to protect her. Anything.'

'I know you would but that's not what I meant. She needs to *feel* safe. My guess is she can't risk getting close to you because she fears losing you as well as her mother. How's she to know that you won't run off to—to Canada or wherever?' I laugh at myself then. 'Sorry—doing my counsellor schtick, you don't need that.'

'No. I do.' His eyes light up and he nods as if considering something. 'That makes sense.'

Sunday. A quiet brunch. No Matt and family. No Ellen. Brunch without Ellen. It's like smoked salmon without lemon juice. Dad phoned her but she said she didn't fancy it and wouldn't say any more than that.

As I chewed halfheartedly at a bagel the doorbell rang. I went to answer it.

'Hello, Cora.'

She smiles shyly back at me, half-hidden behind Leo's leg.

'C'mon, Cora—say hello, hmm?'

I explain that Bonnie and Daniel won't be coming today as Matt and Izzy have taken them away for the weekend.

'It might be better,' I tell Leo. 'Bonnie can be so dominating.'

Dad fetches some paper and coloured pencils for Cora and she sits there, quiet as a statue, drawing. Once more, she draws a girl standing alone in a garden, surrounded by grass and flowers.

After the meal Simone goes out into the garden to have a cigarette. At least she's stopped smoking in the house.

She leaves the back door open, creating a huge draught. I roll my eyes at Leo. 'No one in this family *ever* shuts the door.'

I leap up to close it, but then there is a sudden clanging noise, at once metallic and musical. Cora's head snaps up. Her eyes are open wide, like a startled fawn. 'Do you know what that noise is?' I ask.

A silent nod.

'Do you want to come and see?'

Another nod.

I motion for Leo to follow us. Cora slips her hand into mine and I give it a small squeeze as we walk out into the garden.

'Oh, hi. Come to join me?' Simone says, puffing away.

Another sudden gust of wind. That sound again. Quinn's much-maligned wind chimes, hanging from the old apple tree.

Cora points, then runs towards them, laughing. She stops under the bough, her face tilted upwards, transfixed.

'Did you used to have these?'

She nods. 'Yes, but not the same. In Mummy's room. By the window. They're called wind chimes you know. They're very lucky.'

It is more in one go than she's said all day.

'Shall we get you some more then?' Leo says. 'Would you like that?'

Quinn comes out to the garden, to see where everyone has gone.

'Quinn—can we take down your chimes for a sec? Just to show them to Cora?'

'Certainly. Here we go—' Quinn unwinds the wire from the branch and hands the chimes down to Cora.

'Thank you.' Cora holds the chimes high up in front of her as she goes back inside, like a flag borne aloft in victory.

'Quinn?' I touch her arm, as Leo and Simone go on ahead.

'Yes?'

It is hard to meet her gaze. 'I—what I said—that time—'

'Oh, that's OK. It's all in the past.'

'No. No, it isn't. I just want to say that I am really and truly sorry—I know I've never treated you—properly—like a—a—but I—'

'I've never tried to replace your mother, Georgia.'

'No. I know. But that doesn't mean I—' I look down at the rough lawn, then force myself to meet her eyes again. 'I do know that I've teased you—and been kind of—well, mean, really—and I'm sorry. I do—I really do appreciate how—how much Dad loves you and how good you are for him. And I do—I do actually like you. And I'm really fond of you. I just—don't know how to show it.' My hands fall to my sides and I look down once more. Why don't I know how to do this properly?

'Well, here's a secret—I like you too. I must confess I've always been a little scared of you—but I do like you.'

'*Scared?* Of me? Why?'

'Oh, Georgia—do you have any idea how you come across sometimes? You're so efficient and capable. You're so good at everything—and I've always been so clumsy—I feel like an awkward girl of twelve again when I'm around you and I feel as if you're judging me and waiting for me to make a mistake . . .'

I try to swallow.

'I *am* very judgmental. I know.' I shrug my shoulders, defeated. 'I've been like this for so long I don't know how to be any other way.'

'Be patient with yourself. Everything takes time.'

I exhale a long breath, nod slowly.

'Friends then at least?'

'Yes, please.' I suddenly want to hug her. All these years and we've only ever exchanged polite cheek kisses. I stand there awkwardly. Perhaps it is too late, it would be too strange after all this time.

But she opens her arms wide suddenly, like a bird about to soar, unafraid to take the risk. I half crumple against her.

'I don't know what's wrong with me,' I mumble into her shoulder. 'I seem to keep driving away everyone who matters most to me.'

'Sometimes it's easier that way. Safer.'

'Why is it?' I ask, although of course I already know the answer.

'Because then we don't have to worry so much about losing them.'

'But it doesn't work that way, does it? You miss them anyway.'

'That's right. Because you can't really stop yourself from loving people—not if you're someone like you, you can't.'

She fishes out a crumpled tissue from her pocket. Her pockets are always full of old tissues. Pens that don't work, and crumpled tissues.

I laugh and wipe my eyes. 'That is such a *Quinn* tissue.'

She laughs too then, and we go back inside for a pot of tea and some of her raisin bread. Even Cora has a piece and Simone, who seems to have come to some sort of cease-fire with Quinn, admits that it's 'not bad for one of Mother's culinary endeavours'—high praise indeed.

When Leo and Cora had left, with a plan to see the dinosaurs at the Natural History Museum, I asked Dad if Ellen had phoned. He shook his head.

'But it'll be OK,' he said. 'Ellen can never stay angry for long.'

'Yes—but, Dad?'

'Hmm-mm?' he said, still keeping one eye on the newspaper.

'Do you think we were right not to tell her?'

He put down the paper and sat back. 'No. I think I was wrong—*I* was wrong, Georgia, not *we*. It wasn't up to you at all. *You* shouldn't have had to worry about—anything else. I—*failed* you. I know I did. Very badly. I *wish*—it's too late to go back—but I wish so much . . .'

I reached forward to pat his hand.

'No, Daddy, *no*. You didn't fail me. Or us. Never, never. You were always the best dad in the world for me. *Always*.'

Ellen hasn't spoken to me since Christmas Day and now it is New Year's Eve. Six days. Just six days and I am living in a different world. A world without Ellen. Again and again I reach for the phone, forgetting that I can no longer reach so casually for one of our endless, aimless chats, talking and giggling, flitting from subject to subject in apparent non sequiturs, the links unguessable to anyone other than us.

New Year's Eve. For the last three years, Stephen and I have had a dinner party for a few friends on New Year's Eve. Just eight or ten of us for a quiet meal and a civilised champagne toast at midnight. Nothing wild. Sometimes we all declare our resolutions out loud, unless they're too embarrassing. I still have last year's list in a notebook, a purple sparkly one that Ellen gave me last Christmas. Looking at it now, it seems pathetic: the most ambitious resolution there is to tidy out my hall cupboard—and I haven't even managed to do that.

I open the notebook at a fresh page. This year, my resolutions should be ambitious, adventurous, challenging. I sit there for maybe half an hour, chewing the end of my pen. The best I can come up with is this:

1. Get new life.

Yup. That just about covers it.

This evening, the dinner party is at Stephen's flat—just us and three other couples, a neat number. The menu is virtually identical to last year's; I couldn't seem to set my mind to thinking of anything else, so here we are again, a whole year on, looking forward to hot vichyssoise followed by poached salmon, then lemon tart and flambéd fruits. A toast at midnight, champagne in chilled glasses. Here's to next year, here's to us.

Alongside the two bottles of bubbly in the door of the fridge there are another two bottles of white wine. A rather expensive Chablis, the one Stephen always buys when we want something 'classy' to drink. Stephen prefers red wine, but he never buys it when we have guests in case they knock over a glass and it spills onto his beautiful pale carpet.

Tonight I am poaching the salmon the way my mother used to do it. You wrap it loosely in foil and put it in the oven in a roasting tin with a little water and wine in it. Once you open the wine, you can have a glass of it too, of course. Chef's perk—that's what Mum called it, only in her case it was a perk even if she was only making two slices of toast. I tuck a couple of bay leaves around it, a sprig of fresh tarragon, chuck a few peppercorns over it, rub some sea salt into the slit along its length.

A little more Chablis for the chef is in order, I think. Chablis-dabbly. Plenty of time before anyone arrives. I'll put the salmon on now, anyway, then I can skin it while it's still hot and serve it warm or cold. Last year, Ellen dropped in and she helped me cut 'fish scales' from slices of cucumber. They're supposed to be so thin that they're translucent, but the ones Ellen cut were much too thick, so she and I stood in the kitchen, eating them while I sliced some more. We got the giggles and started being silly, doing impressions of everyone we know and suddenly saying 'penis' loudly every now and then to annoy Stephen.

I take the cucumber out of the fridge and cut a slice but the knife slips, leaving just a misshapen sliver. 'Penis,' I say loudly, but it is not the same.

It's really not at all bad, this wine, though I hadn't realised I'd used so much of it in the fish. There's barely a glass left in this bottle. Anyway, there's still the second one and we won't run short because everyone brings a bottle or two, don't they?

Now, look, here's the salmon still sitting in its tin on top of the hob. That's not going to get us very far, is it? Put it in the oven and turn on the cooker hood thing so no fishy smells. That's that sorted.

Ah-ha. Stephen's back.

'Hi, sweetie. How's it all coming along?'

I nod and smile. 'Fine. Fine. It's all very lovely.'

'I'd love a glass of wine. Shall we open a bottle now, do you think?'

He comes into the kitchen, sees the empty bottle on the counter. 'Good God—did you use all that Chablis for the salmon?'

I nod again. 'I'm really sorry. I couldn't find anything else.'

He sighs, and puts another two bottles to chill. Takes out the second bottle of wine from the fridge.

'Fancy a glass, darling?' He is looking at me in a slightly odd way. 'Are you all right?'

'Fine. Yup. Fine. Bit of a headache, that's all. I've taken a tablet.'

He pours himself a full glass, and a third of a glass for me, then goes through to the sitting room. I hear him settling himself on the sofa, putting his feet up on the coffee table.

'Mum and Dad say Happy New Year,' he calls through to me, as I take out the salad stuff from the fridge. 'But I'll phone them later anyway, so you can wish them a Happy New Year properly then.'

'Great.'

'God, it's nearly eight!' Stephen goes through to the bedroom. 'I'll just change my shirt and shave.'

The doorbell goes. Jason and Sandra. Stephen's friends. They are terribly, terribly nice. I know they are nice because Stephen told me so. They thrust bottles and chocolates into my arms and kiss me somewhere near my cheek. As they come in, Stephen emerges from the bedroom, and there is more kissing and patting of backs and 'great to be here's'. Then, in quick succession, Liz and Mike and Tim and Jools arrive. More kissing. Stephen opens bottles and fetches glasses and gives me cross looks.

'Darling? Where are the nibbles?'

Stephen comes into the kitchen, spots the bowl of olives on the counter, the nuts and rice crackers bafflingly still in their packets.

'I thought you were doing these,' he says.

'I *am*.'

'Darling?'

He is standing in front of me, looking at me with the face he uses when members of my family phone after eleven o'clock at night. 'You haven't been . . . drinking, have you?'

I suppress a sudden snort. Ridiculous. Everyone knows that Georgia doesn' drink. Georgia doesn' have fun. Georgia doesn' have a life.

He comes nearer. 'Breathe on me.'

I shake my head.

'Come on, I think you've been drinking.'

I shake my head again, then get a fit of the giggles.

'It's not funny, Georgia.' He clicks the kettle on. 'I think you'd better have some coffee, don't you, if you're not to ruin the evening completely.'

I nod. Prob'ly best to have some coffee.

From the sitting room, I can hear him explaining to our guests. His guests.

'I'm afraid the chef's started seeing in the New Year a bit ahead of time . . . Georgia's had a drop too much . . .' Laughter, a single whoop from Jason. Someone calls out, 'We'd better catch up with her then.'

Stephen comes back in. 'Where's the soup? For God's sake, Georgia, haven't you done anything?'

I point to the fridge and he opens it and takes out the big pot of soup.

'I thought we were having it hot? How do we heat it?'

'Vich-soise,' I say. 'Serve chilled.' I point to the big white bowl on the counter, slopping it onto the worktop, the floor, his good black shoes. Stephen tips the soup into the bowl and I follow him through to the sitting room, where the guests are already seated at the dining table.

'Georgy!' shouts Jason. 'Stevie says the chef's been at the sherry! You naughty girl!'

'Sack the chef!' someone calls.

Stephen nods for me to sit at the other end while he ladles soup from the big bowl into the small ones. I reach for my wine.

'It's very tasty,' Liz says quietly.

'What are your resolutions then, Georgia?' asks Jason. 'Go on the wagon for a bit, eh?' Everyone laughs, except Stephen.

'Mine is to have more sex,' shouts Tim. 'Some of it even with Jools!' Jools simpers by his side.

'My resolution . . .' I begin.

Suddenly, everyone stops talking and looks at me. I look at Stephen. He is frowning, worrying that I'm going to embarrass him.

'My resolution for next year—' I take another gulp of my wine '—is very simple, actu'ly in fact. My resolution is to *live*.'

'What?' says someone.

'Georgia's not ill, is she?' someone half whispers to Stephen.

'To live?'

'Yup.' I nod. 'To *live*. Really *live*. Not just exist. I'm going to eat ice cream on rooftops—I shall cry in the cinema and eat spaghetti bolognese without a napkin—and I'll laugh loudly in restaurants and get drunk every now and then and let myself fall in love . . .'

There is a silence, then Jason says, 'Sounds like an excellent plan!'

Stephen has got up from his seat and is now at my side. He bends to speak in my ear. 'Go and drink your coffee.'

Slowly, I get up and go back through to the kitchen. Stephen comes in, carrying the empty soup bowls.

'I hope you're happy. You've made me look like a complete fool.'

'Mmm?' I am definitely not going to laugh. Clamping my lips shut and doing my sensible face.

'For Christ's sake, Georgia, this *isn't* funny. I would think that you of all people would take this seriously—given your *background*.' He strides back to the sitting room.

The timer buzzes—that's right! Come along now!

I open the oven door, reach in to pull out the salmon. Jump back as I touch the tin, realising I should have used the oven glove.

But I'm not burned. It's not even warm. The oven's not on.

Oh-oh.

It's important, when you're doing the cooking, to put the oven on. Otherwise, the things will not be as hot as you want them. Or cooked.

I can hear Stephen clattering the dishes, his friends telling jokes.

'No, I've got one—listen to this. There's this Englishman, an Irishman and a Scotsman, right . . .'

I tiptoe out to the hallway and take my coat from the rack, pick up my handbag. Then, quietly, I ease open the door and let myself out, and then I'm tottering down the street, pulling on my coat, the night air fierce and cold on my face, stumbling in my high heels.

On the main road, I get a portion of chips from the greasy takeaway that Stephen says is guaranteed to give you food poisoning. The chips look clean enough to me. I smother them in salt and vinegar. As I come out, I see a bus and I run to the stop to flag it down, leap on.

'Finchley Road, please, near Fortune Green.' Finchley Road. Where Ellen works. The Warm South. Brian's wine bar. Ellen.

I hold out a handful of change. He pokes through my palm for the right money.

'Happy New Year, love. Sit down before you fall down.' He smiles and winks at me then. 'Any chance of a chip?'

The Warm South. The windows are lit up, and as I press my face to the glass, I can see it's packed with people.

There is a bouncer at the door. 'Got your ticket?'

'No. I—I left it at home. But I'm a friend of Brian's.'

'Yeah—isn't everyone? Wait here.'

He opens the door a fraction then squeezes his bulk through the gap.

Then Brian appears.

'Georgia! Brilliant! Sorry—didn't know you were coming or I'd have put your name on the door. Ellie didn't say. Come in, come in.'

I blow the bouncer a kiss as I waltz inside.

At the top of the stairs, I cross the landing and enter the main room. It is very crowded and I can't see Ellen. There is nowhere to sit down so I lean against the wall for a minute and close my eyes. Just a little rest.

'Georgia!'

I open my eyes. There is a man standing in front of me. He looks like Leo, very like Leo. This is a dream. I think I have drunk a little bit too much and now I am dreaming what I want to see.

'Georgia! Are you all right?' He has such a nice face, I bet you've never noticed that about him, but he has a lovely face.

'You've got a lovely face,' I say, as I start to cry.

'Thank you. So have you. Why are you crying?' Gently, he smooths away my tears. 'Come and sit down. We're over here.'

He takes my hand and leads me to a table in a corner.

'George!' says Ellen.

'Hi,' says Simone.

'Gee-gee!' says Matt, getting up to come and hug me.

'Hello,' says Isobel. 'What's the matter?'

'You're all here,' I say, which is true. 'You're here without me.'

'You're here now,' says Leo.

'We thought you were at Stephen's,' says Izzy.

'I was. I ran away.'

'What did he say?'

'I don't know. I didn't tell him I was going.'

'Holy shit,' says Ellen, handing me a glass of wine. 'Wish I'd been there.'

'No, you don't,' I say, drinking my wine. 'It was horrible.'

'Oh, George—don't cry.' Ellen comes round the table and puts her arms round me. 'Please don't cry. I can't bear it if you cry.'

'I ca-can't help it. You won't talk to me an' I messed everything up.'

'I am talking to you, George. I *am*.' She laughs. 'I've never, ever seen you this pissed—I think we've swapped places.'

I shake my head.

''m not pissed. Just had a little tiny bit wine for cooking. Chef's perk.'

'Yes, I think we've gathered that.' Leo puts his arm round me. 'Did anyone ever tell you that you're dead cute when you're tipsy?'

We are talking and drinking. Matt says, 'I'm sorry about what happened at Christmas. I shouldn't have said it. You know I love you, Gee?'

'I love you too, Batzo-Matzo.'

I lean across to Ellen and say, 'I'm sorry, I'm so so sorry,' and she says, 'Sh-sssh, Georgia. It's OK now. Don't worry about it now.' She pulls me close for a hug.

'Am I still your favourite sister?' she asks.

I nod. 'Am I yours?'

'Always,' she says. 'You'll always be my favourite sister.'

Brian weaves between the tables but always comes back to us, resting his hand lightly on Ellie's shoulder for a moment. 'Two minutes to go, folks!' he says.

Leo is looking at me and I am looking at him. It is all right to kiss someone on New Year's Eve at midnight. Even a total stranger. It's practically compulsory. It doesn't have to mean that you love this person, does it? Love him so much that you're getting tears in your eyes just thinking about it. Love this face, this face you could look at for a lifetime. This is the person you want to talk with, make love with, laugh with. This is the person you even want to argue with. Whose go is it to empty the dishwasher? Did you call the estate agent today? Shall we paint the baby's room sky blue or primrose yellow? With this person, you could be the person you never dared dream you could be, the person you really are.

And it *is* terrifying. Of course it is. But it is also too late to turn back now, to inhabit a life that no longer fits me, a life I no longer want.

'**G**et ready!' shouts Brian to the room.

'Ten!' Leo's eyes lock on mine.

'Nine!' Everyone shouts, sort of together.

'Eight!' Brian steps nearer to our table.

'Seven!' My brother puts his arm round his wife.

'Six!' Brian lays his hand on Ellen's shoulder.

'Five!' I look down at my hands, resting in my lap.

'Four!' I look back at Leo.

'Three!' My heart is thudding.

'Two!' Leo takes one of my hands between his own and cradles it as if it is something infinitely precious.

'One!' He gathers me to him and I tilt my face up to his.

In some part of me, I can hear the shouts and the cheers and the 'Happy New Year!'s. But that is there, outside of us. Here, there is no noise except the beating of my heart. I can hear the roar of my blood as it rushes round my body, quick and hot and full of life. And it seems to me that I have been waiting my whole life to notice the simple fact that I am alive.

One minute past midnight. A new day. A new year. A very good time to begin to *live*.

EPILOGUE
L'chaim

I WORE RED IN THE END. We organised the whole thing in one hell of a rush so there wasn't time to mess about having something made. Ellen came with me and banned me from even looking in the same three shops I normally use. Used to use. We found this dress made of deep red velvet—off-the-shoulder and quite low-cut.

'That is so *you*!' she said as I stood there, tentatively stroking the fabric. 'What are you waiting for? Try it on, try it on.'

When Leo sees me in it, he just stands there with his mouth open for a few seconds. 'Now *that*—' he says, moving closer, 'is what I *call* a *dress* . . .'

'That's because it *is* a dress.'

'What would I do without you to point out these things?' He steps towards me. 'Aren't brides supposed to look demure and virginal?'

'A little late for that, don't you think?'

We decided to forgo the formal sit-down affair and just have everyone free to roam and mingle and sit wherever they damn well please. The buffet tables are laden with food, an eclectic mix of cultural treats. There are bite-sized potato latkes and deep-fried fish balls, four sorts of bruschetta, garlicky chicken tapas, huge piles of crudités with felafel and tsatziki—we even had trays of mini-pizzas (no leeks, no black pepper).

I look round the room then, catching my dad's eye. He smiles and raises his glass and mouths: '*L'chaim*'—to Life. His arm rests along the back of Quinn's chair. Her earrings sway madly as she bobs her head, deep in conversation with Unc. There is Anne, Leo's mother, bright and animated in her emerald silk dress, nattering away to Simone. And Leo's sisters, Rebecca and Linda, helping to push back the chairs to make more space for dancing. Beyond the open French windows on the lawn, there is Matt, whirling Daniel round and round, screaming with delight. Izzy is watching Bonnie, who has tucked her long bridesmaid's dress into her knickers and is being a ballerina. And there is Cora now, running at full pelt to join her, then twirling round and round in pirouettes, her bridesmaid's dress swirling round her, shrieking with joy. And there is Ellen, stationed by the buffet, picking out the biggest, plumpest strawberry she can find, turning now and feeding it to Brian.

And here, by my side, is my husband, with his lovely, much-loved face and his thinning hair. He smiles then and the sight of his chipped tooth stabs me with such love and tenderness that my eyes fill with tears.

'You look *so* beautiful,' he says, laying his hand on the swell of my tummy, already starting to show. 'My bride with a bump.'

He takes my hand and nips it softly with his lips. 'We've some family between us, hmm?' he says.

We look round together at them all—talking and arguing, eating and drinking, the children shouting and laughing and pushing each other, the adults—well, doing pretty much the same.

Leo shakes his head. '*What* a bunch . . .' But he is smiling.

'Mmm. But, you know what?' I cuddle up close to him.

'No. What?'

'I'm beginning to think I like it like that.'

CLAIRE CALMAN

When I first met Claire Calman after the publication of her debut novel, *Love is a Four Letter Word*, she was very much a single woman enjoying her first publishing success. Now, just two years later, her life has changed beyond measure. Not only is she a well-established author but she has also recently married and bought a house in north London with her husband. 'Well, when I say we've moved in, I mean me, my husband, sixty-three boxes of books and the builders!' says Claire. 'There is dust and debris everywhere.' Something which Claire admits is not helping her to get ahead with her fourth novel. 'When I'm writing I have to confess that I use any excuse to put it off,' she laughs. 'I find I'm suddenly overcome by the urge to wash the kitchen floor or start dusting the bookshelves, which is particularly pointless just now because the house is one big dust cloud!' And Claire insists that mundane chores are still easier than staring at a blank page and writing. 'Unfortunately, I suppose, I do make it harder for myself because I don't write in sequence. I have a sort of patchwork approach then put it all together.' When I asked Claire just why she doesn't write from first page to last, as most authors do, she grinned. 'It's just the way I work. The way I've always worked. It's like do you always put your right sock on before your left? Try doing it the other

way round and if feels odd. There is absolutely no difference in the end result, but it feels strange because you've meddled with your own ritual.'

Meeting and being welcomed into her husband's extended family was very much the starting point for *I Like it Like That*. 'We were in America and having a meal on the beach with some of his fourth cousins. We were all talking and laughing at once and it felt so good to be part of a big family for the first time in my life. It made me think about all the little things that go into making a real, warm close family—the history, the personalities and, especially in a Jewish family, the meals! Like the Abrams in the novel, my own family has always enjoyed "scramblies" with their bagels, but with a slight difference. My mother once accidentally burnt the scrambled eggs and, as money was tight, we ate them anyway and found we loved them. Now my sister and I still prefer to cook our eggs that way—much to my husband's horror!'

In *I Like it Like That* there is a relaxed family wedding and I asked Claire if that was how her own wedding had been. 'Absolutely,' she beams. 'The best day of my life. And everyone expected me to wear red, as that's the colour Georgia wears in the novel, but in fact I wore purple. I can't be dictated to by my characters, now can I?'

Jane Eastgate

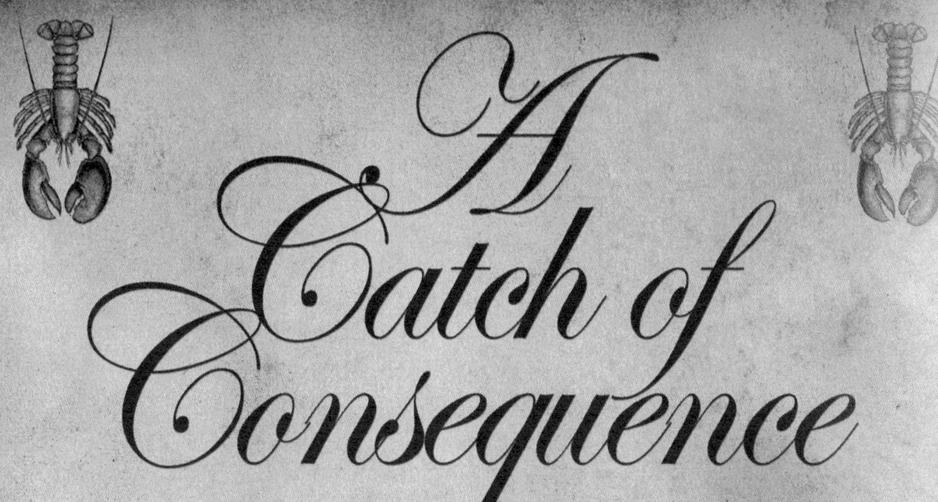

A Catch of Consequence

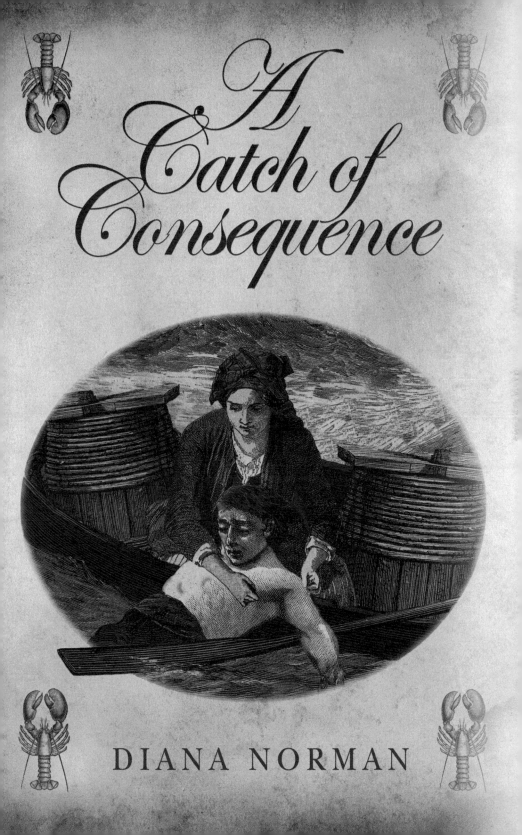

DIANA NORMAN

The year is 1765, and in the American port of Boston rebellion is stirring against oppressive British rule. These are dangerous times for those with divided loyalties, as tavern-keeper Makepeace Burke is about to discover. For one fateful morning, as she rows out to check her lobster pots, she sees a man drowning and rescues him. Unfortunately for Makepeace, her catch that day is Sir Philip Dapifer, one of the hated British aristocracy, and the consequences of her compassionate action will change her life for ever.

Chapter One

THE WOMAN FEATHERING her boat round the bend of the Charles River into Massachusetts Bay that early morning on August 15, 1765 was about to save someone's life and change her own.

Later on, in rare retrospective moments, she would ask herself, 'What if I hadn't?' A useless question; Makepeace Burke could no more watch a fellow creature drown without trying to help it than she could stop the wind blowing. That's not to imply that Makepeace was a gentle woman. She wasn't; she just hated waste, and unnecessary death was wasteful.

If her boat was dirty, she was clean in a scrubbed sort of way, or as clean as you can be when you've been hauling in lobster pots. A gangly figure in faded brown cotton, a leather cap tied under her chin to hide her hair, she propelled her boat with the professionalism of a sea dog.

About to have her life changed.

To Makepeace Burke, emerging into the great harbour's North End, the damage that she saw had been done to her waterfront overnight was change enough. Some of the damage was old and caused by the English: empty warehouses, wharves sprouting weed. Boats that had once been respected smugglers delivering cheap sugar lay demasted on the hards, killed by the newly efficient British Customs and Excise. Only sugar from the English West Indies, the *expensive* English West Indies, could be imported now—and that was unloaded further down.

But last night, in protest against the English and their Stamp Tax and Navigations Acts, Boston had gone on the rampage and done damage in return. *Hadn't* they, by hokey! Even from this distance, she could see the depredations to the Custom House. And the new warehouse Stamp Master Oliver was having built was now no more than a pile of broken timbers. Serve the old bugger right.

Makepeace Burke disapproved of rioting—not good for trade—but she disapproved of the Stamp Tax a mighty sight more. The tax fell heavily on taverns and she was a tavern-keeper.

The August heat had been near suffocating for a month, like a volcano grumbling under the town in sympathy with the discontent of its inhabitants. Last night the cone blew off. Customs officials, known English-loving Tories, lawmen: all had been hunted through the streets by Sons of Liberty smeared with war paint and howling like Mohawks, bless 'em. The town had been streaked with flame and pounded with the beat of drums until it seemed that light was noise and noise was light. If that was riot, Lord knew what revolution'd be. Well, maybe it *was* revolution. Sam Adams was preaching something suspiciously along the lines of it being time Americans threw off the English yoke.

Customers had run into the Roaring Meg to pass on the latest news, down a glass of celebratory flip and rush off again to join in. 'Don't you go outside, now, 'Peace,' Zeobab Fairlee'd said. 'The Sons is lickered up. Got at a few cellars. No place for a respectable female in them streets.'

So she'd stayed with her tavern in case they tried to get at her liquor stock—Sons of Liberty or no Sons of Liberty, she wasn't in the business of free drinks—but, come the revolution, she'd march against the British with the best of 'em.

She liked these lovely mornings, collecting lobster pots. Peaceful. More peaceful than ever this morning. Usually, down at the business end of the harbour, cranes emptied incoming merchantmen and filled the holds of those getting ready to set out. Greetings, commands, farewells—sounds of human busyness floated across the water. But not today. Captains, worried for their cargo, had stood their ships further off where the Sons of Liberty couldn't board them.

She had to feather so that, by standing in the prow, she could negotiate between the detritus that had been thrown in the water during the night. All of it a hazard to little boats like hers as it was carried out to sea on the current. Lord, it was quiet. There was Tantaquidgeon waiting for her as he always did, standing on the Roaring Meg's gimcrack jetty and staring out to sea like the statue of a befeathered Roman emperor.

She was heading towards him when a prickle of movement a hundred yards further on caught her eye. A knot of men on Fish Quay. One was standing still, keeping watch, while the others threw objects into the harbour. Something heavy had just splashed in.

With her free hand she shaded her eyes to see who the men were. The one acting lookout was Sugar Bart, recognisable at once by the crutch that did duty for his missing leg. *Mackintosh?* What was he doing this far north of town? No mistaking his swagbelly. She'd seen it too often parading at the head of the South End mob. Couldn't make out the others.

Sugar Bart had seen her; she saw him stiffen and point.

Now what? She looked behind her. From her vantage point, Makepeace saw what Sugar Bart couldn't: a patrol of armed redcoats from North End fort marching down the wharves towards Fish Quay.

Makepeace put two fingers in her mouth and whistled a warning. Bart looked. She nodded towards the redcoats. One of the soldiers advanced to the edge of the wharf. 'You. Seen anybody?'

She cupped her ear, wasting time. The Mohawks had legged it; Bart was hobbling off.

'Seen. Any. Body, you deaf bitch.'

She held up one of her pots. 'Lobster. Lob. Ster.' And may you boil in the saucepan with him, thee red-backed bastard.

The soldier gave up, the patrol resumed its advance down the waterfront and there was no time for reaction because, while dealing with the problem, she *had* seen a body. Wreckage from last night twirled on the current; from the corner of her eye she'd noticed a piece slipping off from the rest. And the new bit of flotsam was a man.

She feathered the boat to where the current would bring the fellow near it. He was alive; a hand moved before he was carried under. Je*hos*ophat, wouldn't you know it? The fool couldn't swim. He was being sucked under again.

Makepeace kept standing, waggling her oar through the water with a friction that took the skin off even her toughened hands. Passing her jetty, where Tantaquidgeon still contemplated the horizon, she shouted: 'Git, will you?' angling her head towards Fish Quay, and saw him start off in the right direction in his infuriatingly unhurried stride.

The current was taking the drownder further and further away from the quay. As he rolled, she saw a face white as cod, eyes closed in acceptance of death. Frantically, she feathered harder and closed the gap between them. She yelled, 'Hold up,' unshipped her oar and ran it forward under his left arm. The blade was caught between waistcoat and sleeve, held by the pressure of water, and, with all her weight, Makepeace pressed down on her end of the oar so that the man's upper body came up, nose and mouth blessedly free. There was never anything so heavy but if she let go she'd lose him. The boat tilted wickedly. She cricked her neck, looking for help. Tantaquidgeon was on the quay.

'Boathook. Fast.' He strolled off to find one. She couldn't control the boat and keep the man out of the water at the same time; he wasn't helping, just hung there, dipping under, coming up, eyes half closed.

'Wake up,' she screamed. 'D'ye want to die?'

The shout jagged through nothingness to the last cognitive area of the drowning man's brain and found a flicker of response.

Not actively die, he thought, and then: But life's not worthy of effort either. The water swam with the image of two naked bodies writhing on a floor, neither of them his own. Wounded long before the sea decided to kill him, he was slowing to languor. Not worth effort, not worth it.

As always when frightened, Makepeace became angry. Fury helped her haul in the oar until the body was against the boat starboard. Holding the blade with one hand—buggered if she'd lose a good oar—she grabbed at the man and hooked his jacket over the rowlock so that he hung from it, head lolling. 'An' you *stay* there.'

Somehow, keeping her weight to port, she feathered back to where Tantaquidgeon was kneeling, boathook in hand. She caught the hook's business end and shoved it under the man's coat. The Red Indian pulled. A long, wet body slithered onto her lobster pots and flopped among waving, reaching claws. She nudged his face to one side then pressed her boot on his breadbasket, released it, pressed again, until water began dribbling from the man's mouth and he coughed.

Makepeace Burke and her catch looked at each other.

Through a wavering veil of nausea, the man saw bone and freckles, a pair of concerned and ferocious blue eyes, all framed by hair the colour of flames that had escaped from its cap and which, with the sun shining through it, made an aureole. It was the head of a saint remembered from a Flemish altarpiece.

Makepeace saw a bloody nuisance.

Here was not, as she'd thought, a lickered Son of Liberty; the Sons didn't sport clothes that, even when soaked and seaweeded, shouted wealth. Here was gentry. 'Who are you? What happened to you?'

He really couldn't be bothered to remember, let alone answer. He managed, 'Does it matter?'

'Matters to *me*.' She'd expended a lot of effort.

Long time since I mattered to a woman, thought Sir Philip Dapifer. He drifted off, oddly consoled, into unconsciousness.

Makepeace sat and considered. If the bugger hadn't fallen, he'd been pushed *and she'd seen it done*. Mackintosh had thrown the poor bastard in like he was rotten fish. *And* worked on him first from the look of him—his face was livid and bruised. So he was enemy. Customs, excise, taxman, Tory, British bootlicker: whatever he was she'd rescued him.

What to do? If she handed him over to the authorities right now he could identify his attackers; and say what you like about Mouse Mackintosh and Sugar Bart, they were at least patriots and she'd be damned if she helped some Tory taxman get 'em hanged.

But, from the look of the drownder, he was on his last gasp. And that, thought Makepeace Burke, was pure foolishness, a waste of the trouble she'd taken in the first place.

She looked up at the quay and jerked her head at Tantaquidgeon to get into the boat. 'The Meg. You row.'

Behind him, appearing to stand on an island, though actually on a promontory, was their destination, the Roaring Meg, two storeys of weather-beaten boarding. Ramshackle maybe, but an integral piece of the great ribbon of function which provided incoming ships with their first view of the town. Here was Boston proper, not in its wide, tree-lined streets and pillared houses, but in a salt-stained, invigorating seaboard generating the wealth that sustained all the rest.

Makepeace was proud that her tavern was part of it. But it was a matter of shame to her, as it was to all right-thinking citizens, that there was yet another Boston. In the maze of lanes behind the waterfront, out of sight like a segment of rot in an otherwise healthy-looking apple, lay gin houses and whoreshops where the crab-like click of dice and a tide-line of painted women waited for sinners.

A voyager disembarking at Boston's North End had a choice. If he were heedless of his purse, his health and his hope of salvation, he would disappear into those sinning, acrid alleys. If he were wise, he would make for the Roaring Meg, with its smell of good cooking and hum of decent conversation. Named after the noisy stream that ran alongside it before entering the sea, Makepeace kept it free of the devil's flotsam by perpetual moral sweeping, brushing harlots and their touts from her doorstep, plumping up idlers like pillows, ejecting bullies, vomiters, debtors and those who took the Lord's name in vain.

A little stone bridge led over the stream to its street door above which was displayed the information that John L. Burke was licensed to dispense ales and spirituous liquors. John L. Burke was in the grave these three years, having energetically drunk himself into it, but a man's name above the door inspired more confidence in strangers than would a woman's, so Makepeace kept it there. North End magistrates conspired in the fiction, for Makepeace was acknowledged 'a crisp woman'. An accolade, 'crisp': American recognition of efficiency and good Puritan hard-headedness. Makepeace took pride in it but knew how hard it had been to win and how easily it could be taken away. One word of scandal or complaint to the magistrates, one impatient creditor, and she would lose her vaunted crispness *and* her tavern.

And now that she had a calm moment, suspicion grew that she might be jeopardising both by harbouring the drownder under her roof.

The Cut, the lane at the sea end of which the Meg stood, was as respectable as the tavern itself, a narrow row of houses that passed through the surrounding wickedness like a file of soldiers in hostile Indian forest. Eyes at its windows watched for any falter in its rigid morality and one pair in particular was trained on herself. 'Makepeace Burke's picked up a man.' She could hear the voice now. And, because the Cut was as patriotic as it was respectable, she could also hear the addendum: 'A *Tory* man.'

It hadn't been easy, a woman running a tavern. One of the proudest moments of her life—and the most profitable—had been when, with the imposition of the Stamp Tax, the local lodge of the Sons of Liberty had chosen the Roaring Meg for their secret meetings. Good men most of 'em, driven to desperation by an unemployment that was the direct result of British government policy. And among those very Sons was at least one of the group that had thrown the drownder into the harbour. Mighty pleased *they'd* be to find Makepeace Burke succouring the enemy. No decent patriot—and all her clientele were patriots—would set foot in the Roaring Meg again.

'Lord, Lord,' she prayed out loud, 'I did my Christian duty and saved this soul; ain't there to be *no* reward?'

And the Lord answered her plea by skimming the last word of it across the surface of His waters until it hit a wharf wall and bounced it back at her in an echo: *Reward, reward.*

Receiving it, Makepeace became momentarily beautiful because she smiled, a rare thing with her, showing exquisitely white teeth. The drownder was in her debt. In return, he could reward her with a promise of silence. Least he could do. She looked down fondly at the richly clad bundle by her feet. 'And maybe some cash with it,' she said.

She was intrigued—more than that, *involved*—by the man. As someone who'd fought for survival all her life, this drownder's 'Does it matter?' had excited her contempt but also her curiosity and pity. Look at him: fine boots—well, he'd lost one but the other was excellent leather; gold lacing on his cuffs. A man possessed of money and, therefore, every happiness. So why was he uncaring about his fate?

The boat bumped gently against the Meg's tottering jetty. Makepeace looked around. Nobody there. Boston kept the sleep of the hung over.

She threaded her lobster pots together and dragged them up and through the sea entrance to her tavern with Tantaquidgeon behind her, the now tarpaulined Englishman draped over his forearms like laundry.

The Roaring Meg's kitchen doubled as its surgery, and the cook as its doctor, both skills acquired in the house of a Virginian tobacco planter who, when Betty escaped from it, had posted such a reward for her capture that it was met only by her determination not to be caught.

She might have been—most runaway slaves were—if she hadn't encountered John L. Burke leaving Virginia with wife, children, Indian and wagon for the north after another of his unsuccessful attempts at farming. John and Temperance Burke weren't prepared to hand Betty back to her owner, however big the reward. She'd stayed with the family ever after, even during her late, brief marriage.

She examined the body on the kitchen table deftly. 'Collarbone broke. Lucky he keep faintin'.' She squeezed her eyes shut and ran her fingers along the patient's shoulder. 'Ready?'

Makepeace put a rolled cloth between his teeth and then bore down on his arms. 'Ready.'

There was a jerk and a muffled, 'Aaagh'.

'Oh, hush up,' Makepeace told him.

Betty felt the joint. 'Sweet,' she said. 'I'm one sweet sawbones.'

'Will he do?'

'Runnin' a fever. Them Sons give him a mighty larrupin'.'

'I thought maybe Tantaquidgeon could row him to Castle William after dark,' Makepeace said hopefully. 'Dump him outside, like.'

Betty pointed to a meat cleaver hanging on the wall. 'You've a mind to kill him, use that,' she said. 'Quicker.'

'Oh . . . oh, *piss*. He's got to stay, I guess.' Makepeace sighed. It had been inevitable. 'Which room?'

Betty grinned. The Meg was a tavern, not an inn, and took no overnight guests. The bedroom she shared with her son Josh was directly across the lane from the window of the house opposite. Makepeace's brother Aaron's, too, faced the Cut. The only one overlooking the sea and therefore impregnable to spying eyes was Makepeace's.

'Dam*nation*.' The problem wasn't just the loss of her room but the fact that its door was directly across the corridor from the one serving the meeting room used by the Sons of Liberty.

'Oh well,' as her Irish father used to say, 'let's burn that bridge when we get to it.'

They put the bad arm in a sling of cheesecloth and Tantaquidgeon carried the semi-naked body up the tiny, winding back stairs, followed by Betty with a basket of salves.

Left alone, Makepeace looked round the kitchen for telltale signs of the catch's presence in it. Nothing, apart from a bloodstain on the table that had seeped from a wound on his head. She was still scrubbing when Aaron came in, having rowed back from Cambridge after a night out. 'All hail, weird sister, I expect my breakfast, the Thaneship of Cawdor and a scolding. Why all the smoke? Did Boston catch fire?'

'It surely did.' He looked dark-eyed with what she suspected was a night of dissipation, but she was so relieved he'd missed the rioting that he got an explanation, a heavy breakfast and a light scolding.

He was horrified. 'Imbeciles. I blame Sam Adams. What's he thinking of to let scum like that loose on respectable people?'

'They ain't scum,' she said. 'And Sam's a good man. Respectable people? Respectable lickspittles, respectable yes-King-Georgers, no-King-Georgers. I wished I'd been with 'em.'

'It's a reasonable tax, 'Peace.'

'You don't pay it.' Immediately, she was sorry. She didn't want him indebted; she'd gone without shoes and, sometimes, food to raise and educate him and done it gladly. What she hadn't reckoned on was that he'd become an English-loving Tory.

She broke the silence. 'Aaron, there's a man up in my room—'

He grinned. 'About time.'

'You wash your mouth out.' She told him the story of her dawn catch. He thought it amusing and went upstairs to see.

'Reckon he's English,' was Aaron's verdict on his return. 'A lord to judge from his coat.'

An Englishman, by hokey, worse and worse. Aaron could be trusted on fashion; he made a study of it. 'That important, somebody'll be missing him, so keep your ears open today. Maybe we'll find out who he is.'

The Cut was awake now, shutters opening, brushes busy on doorsteps, its men coming up it towards the waterfront. Only Aaron went against the flow, heading with an easy swagger towards the business quarter, where he worked in marine insurance.

Few wished him good morning and she suspected he didn't notice those who did. Already he'd be lost in the role of Romeo or Henry V; he was mad for Shakespeare. The Cut, however, didn't see youthful play-acting, it saw arrogance. From a doorway further down came a sniff. 'You want to tell that brother of yours to walk more seemly.'

'Morning, Mistress Busgutt. And why would I do that?'

'He may think he's Duke Muck-a-muck but the Lord don't 'steem him any higher'n the rest of us mortals. A sight lower than many.'

Makepeace returned to her empty kitchen. '*I'll* 'steem you . . .' In place of Mistress Busgutt, two lobsters died in the boiler, screaming. ' . . . you shite-mongering, vicious old hell-hag.'

Cursing was Makepeace's vice, virtually her only one. Today, she reckoned, having sent her both a dangerous, unwanted guest and Goody Busgutt all in one morning, the Lord would forgive her.

It was a busy day, as all days were. With Tantaquidgeon stalking in her wake, she took her basket to Faneuil Market for meat and for mention of a missing Englishman. She doubted if she could have heard it if there had been; Faneuil's was always noisy but today's clamour threatened to rock its elegant pillars.

Boston patriotism, simmering for years, had boiled out of its clubs and secret societies into the open. 'We showed 'em. We got 'em running.' She heard it again and again, from street-sellers to wealthy merchants to lawyers fresh from the courthouse, as exhilarated as any Son of Liberty at last night's mayhem. All litigious documents were subject to Stamp Duty; the tax had hit the legal profession hard. Even newspapers—another taxed item—had increased in price.

'Mistress Burke.'

'Mistress Godwit.' Wife to the landlord of the Green Dragon in Union Street. They curtsied to each other.

'Reckon we'll see that old Stamp Tax repealed yet,' shrieked Mrs Godwit. 'Don't approve of riotin' but something's got to be done.'

'Long as it don't affect trade,' shouted Makepeace. 'Hooray to that.'

'Sam Adams'll be speechifyin' at the Green Dragon tonight, I expect,' announced Mistress Godwit, loftily.

'Always ends up at the Roaring Meg.'

Honours even, the ladies separated.

Men on upturned boxes harangued crowds gathered under the shade of trees to listen. Barefoot urchins ran along the streets, sticking fliers on anything that stood still, or even didn't. Makepeace caught one of them by the shirt and cuffed him. 'You come on home.' She took a flier from his hand. 'What's that say?'

Joshua sulked. 'Says we're goin' to cut Master Oliver's head off.'

'It says "No importation" and if you kept to your books like I told you, you'd maybe know what it means.'

She was teaching Betty's son to read; she worried for his literacy, though he'd gone beyond her in the art of drawing.

He trotted along beside her. 'Don't tell Mammy.'

'I surely will.' But as they approached the Roaring Meg she let him slip away from her to get to his room without passing through the kitchen.

'Going to be a long, hot night, Bet. I don't know what about the lobsters. Can the Sons eat *and* riot?'

'Chowder,' said Betty. 'Quicker.'

'How's upstairs?'

'Sleepin'.'

'Ain't you found out who he belongs to?'

'Nope. Ain't you?'

Maybe she could smuggle him to Government House—she had an image of Tantaquidgeon trundling a covered handcart through the streets by night—but information had Governor Bernard holed up, shaking, at Castle William along the coast.

When she went up to her room, the drownder was still asleep. Tying on a clean cap, she crossed to the bed to study his face. Wouldn't set the world on fire, that was certain sure. Nose too long, skin too sallow, mouth turned down in a parody of melancholia. '*Why* did thee never learn to swim?' she complained.

As she reached the door, a voice said, 'Not a public school requirement, ma'am.'

She whirled round. He hadn't moved, eyes still closed. She went back and prised up one of his eyelids. 'You awake?'

'I'm trying not to be. Where am I?'

'The Roaring Meg. Tavern. Boston.'

'And you are?'

'Tavern-keeper. You foundered in the harbour and I pulled you out. What's your name?'

'Oh God. Philip Dapifer. I don't wish to seem ungrateful, madam, but might you postpone your questions? It's like being trepanned.' He added querulously, 'I am in considerable pain.'

'You're in considerable trouble,' she told him. 'And you get found here, so am I. See, what I'm going to do, I'm a-going to put my'—she paused; she never knew how to describe Tantaquidgeon's position in the household—'my footman here so as nobody comes in and you don't get out. You hear me?'

He groaned.

'Hush up,' she hissed. She'd heard the scrape of the front door. 'No moaning. Not a squeak or my man'll scalp you. Hear me?'

'Oh God. *Yes*.'

'And quit your blaspheming.'

Chapter Two

THE ROARING MEG was a good tavern, popular with its regulars. 'Going rioting again?' Makepeace asked, serving the early-comers.

'Ain't riotin', Makepeace,' Zeobab Fairlee said severely. 'It's protestin' agin bein' miserably burdened an' oppressed with taxes.'

'Ain't nobody more miserably burdened and oppressed'n me,' Makepeace said. 'A pound a year, a *pound a year* I pay King George in Stamp Tax for the privilege of serving you gents good ale, but I ain't out there killing people for it.'

'Who's killin' people?' Sugar Bart stood in the doorway.

'I heard as how George Piggott got tarred and feathered down South End last night,' Makepeace said quickly.

'Tarring and feathering ain't killin', Makepeace,' Zeobab said. 'Just a gentle tap on the shoulder, tarrin' is.'

'I'd not've tarred that Tory-lover, I'd've strung the bastard from his eyelids 'n' flayed him,' Sugar Bart said as he tip-tapped his way awkwardly across the floor to his chair by the grate.

Immediately the injured man upstairs became a presence. Act normal, Makepeace told herself. She said evenly, 'No cussing here, Mr Stubbs, I thank you.' She heated some flip and took it to him.

'*Was* you whistlin' this morning, weren't it?' he asked.

There was no point denying it. 'Saw the redcoats coming.'

'See anything else?'

'Lobster pots. What else was there?' She was an uncomfortable liar so she carried the fight to him. 'And what was *you* doing there so early, Master Stubbs?'

His eyes hooded. 'Sweepin' up, Makepeace, just sweepin' up.'

'They got Mouse Mackintosh today,' Zeobab said, 'so you be careful, Bart Stubbs. Noon it was. I was near the courthouse an' redcoats was takin' him into the magistrates.'

'What they get him for?' asked Makepeace. 'Custom House?'

'Don't know, but he was the one broke into Oliver's house,' Zeobab said. 'They say as Oliver's resigned from Stamp Masterin' already.'

'Still got to pay the tax, though, ain't I?'

'You have.' Sugar Bart's voice grated the air. 'That's a-why we'll be on the streets again tonight.'

Conversation ended for her after that; the taproom was filling up with men whose thirst for the coming rampage was only equalled by that for liquor. Hungry, too. She wished she'd caught more lobsters.

When Aaron came back from work they managed a brief moment together in the kitchen. 'Do you know who he is?' Aaron was excited.

'Philip Dapifer,' she said.

'*Sir* Philip Dapifer. They reckon he's a cousin of the Prime Minister. Staying at the lieutenant-governor's house. There's a search on; if he ain't found soon the British'll send in troops.'

'Holy, *holy* hokey.'

There was no time to pursue the matter; voices were calling from the taproom for service. With Aaron, she entered a wheeling dance between kitchen, casks and customers. Sugar Bart caught at her skirt as she went by. 'Where's Tantaquidgeon tonight?'

'Poorly,' she said. There it was again, that instinct he had.

Conversation was reaching thunder level, pierced by the hiss of flip irons plunging into tankards.

And stopped. Sam Adams was in the doorway. He stood to one side, smiling, threw out a conjuring hand and there, shambling, was the self-conscious figure of Andrew 'Mouse' Mackintosh.

Little as North Enders had reason to love the South End and its violent gang, Mackintosh had become an instant hero. The taproom erupted. Even Makepeace was pleased; it was a bad precedent for Sons of Liberty to be in jail, and anyway, she *loved* Sam Adams.

Everyone loved Sam Adams, Whig Boston's favourite son, who could spout Greek and Latin but preferred the conversation of common Bostonians and who frequented their taverns talking of Liberty as if she were sitting on his knee. He marched to the carver Makepeace always kept for him by the grate, his arm round Mackintosh's shoulders, shouting for 'a platter of my Betty's lobscouse'.

'How'd ye do it, Sam? How'd ye get Mouse out?'

Aaron took his hat, Betty came tilting from the kitchen with food, Makepeace tied a napkin tenderly round his neck and, less willingly, offered the same service to Mackintosh. As she did it, she saw one of his hands had a grubby bandage that disappeared up his sleeve and seeped blood. 'You hurt, Mr Mackintosh?'

'Rat bit me.'

An English rat, she thought. Her drownder hadn't gone down without a fight.

The room was silent, waiting for Adams's answer. 'Told the sheriff,' he said, spraying lobscouse, 'if Andrew wasn't released there'd be general pillage and I wouldn't be able to stop it.'

'That'll do it, Sam,' somebody called out.

'It did, didn't it, *General* Mackintosh?' He looked around. 'Yes, we're an army now, my Liberty boys, a *disciplined* army. By displaying ourselves on the streets like regular troops.'

''Scuse me, Sam.' It was Sugar Bart, struggling up on his crutch. 'Seems to me you're talkin' strategics. I reckon as how you should do it upstairs so's we shan't be overheard.' The man was looking straight at Aaron.

Sam got the implication. He crossed to Aaron and put his arm round the young man's shoulders. 'I've known this lad since he was in small clothes. We're *all* good patriots here, ain't we, boys?'

The room was silent.

It was Aaron, with a grace even his sister hadn't suspected, who resolved the situation. 'We're all patriots right enough, Sam, but this one's going to bed early.' He bowed to Sam, to Sugar Bart, to the company, and went upstairs.

'That's as may be,' Bart said, 'but how d'we know he ain't listenin' through the floorboards?'

Makepeace was in front of him. 'You take that back, Bart Stubbs, or you heave your carcass out of this tavern.'

Sam Adams stepped between them. 'We mustn't quarrel among ourselves and spoil this happy day when Liberty arose . . .'

While he calmed the room down, Makepeace went angrily back to her barrels and resumed serving, listening carefully to what Bart had called the 'strategics'. Sam and Andrew Mackintosh were playing the company between them.

Sam's rhetoric was careful, reiterating the need for caution in case the British government reacted by sending an army.

'No,' agreed Mackintosh, 'we ain't ready for war agin' the redcoats.' And then, 'Not yet.'

Sam: 'On the other hand, we can achieve the Act's repeal peacefully through the embargo on British goods.'

Mackintosh: 'Peacefully break the windows of them as disobeys.'

In other words, thought Makepeace, Sam was advocating reason yet allowing Mackintosh to inflame his audience for another night of rioting. He'd got a tiger by the tail; if the tiger learned she'd sheltered a representative of British tyranny, broken windows and lost custom'd be the least of it. Did they tar and feather women?

Having lit the fuse, Sam Adams and Mackintosh left. Makepeace turned back to a taproom that, without the restraint of Sam's presence, was exploding. Was that old Zeobab climbing up on a table? 'Let's drub 'em, boys,' he was shouting. 'Let's scrag them sugar-suckers.' An exhortation causing stool legs to be broken off for weapons and pipes to be smashed against the grate like Russian toast glasses.

Makepeace yelled for Betty and, with her cook, managed to snatch back two stool-legs with which to belabour heads and generally restore order. She went to the door, holding it wide. 'Git to your rampage, gents,' she called, 'but not here.'

She saw them out as they rushed past her to begin another night of liberty-wreaking.

Sugar Bart was in front of her. 'That redskin were healthy enough earlier,' he said. 'Saw him with you in town. Where's he gone?'

Sure as eggs, he knew she'd seen what he and the others had done to the man on Fish Quay this morning and found Tantaquidgeon's unusual absence from her side suspicious. She loathed the man; he frightened her. 'You ain't welcome at the Meg any more, Mr Stubbs,' she told him stiffly, 'not after what you said about Aaron.'

He stared straight into her eyes. 'The Sons is at war now,' he said. 'Know what they do to informers in war, Makepeace Burke?'

'Yes,' she said. 'And you still ain't welcome.'

Tantaquidgeon opened the door at her rap; the room was an oven that, from the smell of it, had been cooking Tantaquidgeon and vomit. 'Dammit, what'd you let him do that for?' The Englishman had been sick on his pillow.

She pushed Tantaquidgeon from the room, fetched a basin of water and a cloth, sponged the Englishman's hair and face clean, and found a fresh pillow. He slept all through, with no care for the extra washing he was giving her, let alone that someone—she—must now sit up with him all night in case he be sick again and choke on it. Her eyes pricked with tears of fatigue.

She lit a lamp, snatched up her Bible and sat on a stool beside the bed, opening the book at Matthew 25 for some encouragement.

'For I was hungry, and ye gave me food, I was thirsty and ye gave me drink, I was a stranger and ye welcomed me, I was naked and ye clothed me, I was sick'—all over your pillow—'and ye visited me, I was in prison and ye came unto me.'

As always, it calmed her. She fell asleep.

She woke up in darkness to find her head resting sideways on something hard. She had been asleep across the drownder's body, her cheek against his knee. Knee? *Christ have mercy.* She jumped up.

'Pity,' a voice said sadly. 'I was enjoying that.'

Shocked, disgusted, Makepeace walked to the window. Her cheeks were hot with embarrassment, so was her ear where it had lain on his . . . A view of the jetty's mooring post down below, sheeny in the moonlight, did little to restore her composure.

'Still in Boston, am I?' the voice asked.

'Yes.'

'And to whom am I indebted for my delivery from the waters?'

'Name's Makepeace Burke.'

'Thank you again, Miss Burke.'

His voice was a pleasing tenor. Her answers came like a crow's caw in contrast.

'It's been a curious day, Miss Burke . . . Did I at some point gather that my presence in your hostelry is a cause for concern?'

She said, 'English ain't welcome here.' Ready for him now, she turned round and went back to the bed. 'How'd you fall in the harbour?'

'I was set on, belaboured and, presumably, thrown in whilst I was unconscious.' He squinted so that he could read her frown. 'Or did I imagine it?'

He was no fool. 'You imagined it,' she said. There was no point in pit-patting around. 'That's my price for pulling you out.'

'Ah.' He thought about it. 'Do the imaginary ruffians who hypothetically threw me in know that you pulled me out?'

'Not ruffians,' she said, 'patriots. Like me. No, they don't.'

'And would not rejoice that you did?'

'No,' she said, 'they wouldn't.'

'Presumably they are not aware that I am at this moment, ah, in residence in . . . what's the name of your tavern?'

'The Roaring Meg,' she said. 'No, they ain't. And mustn't.'

'Why *did* you pull me out, Miss Burke?'

She frowned again, surprised. 'You was drowning.'

'I see.'

Awake, his eyes, which were brown, took away from the plainness of his face. She saw they were studying both her room and her person. A rectangular attic of lumpy whitewashed plaster. A sparse woman of twenty-four years. Makepeace saw no reason to be ashamed of either, both were homely, clean, serviceable and free of fleas.

He was silent for a minute, then said plaintively, 'I've got a hellish imaginary headache.'

Makepeace went downstairs to the kitchen. She poured a dose of physick into a beaker, ladled still-warm chowder into a bowl and pumped up a jug of water. Before she went back upstairs, she made sure no tendril of hair escaped her cap. Respectable women kept their hair hidden—especially when it was a non-Puritan red.

She slipped an arm under the Englishman's neck to lift his head for his dosing. 'Betty's Specific against pain and bruises,' she told him when he made a face. 'Also kills worms.'

He swallowed. 'I don't wonder.'

She gave him some water, then the chowder, spooning it into his mouth for him.

'You've got children?' he asked.

'Ain't married yet,' she said. 'You got childer?'

'No.'

'Used to feed my brother like this when he was little,' she said. 'Our ma died when he was born.'

'Who set my collarbone? A large black lady?'

She nodded. 'Betty.'

'And did I dream an even larger, red gentleman?'

'Tantaquidgeon.'

'His pomade is . . . unusual.'

She grinned. 'Bear's grease.'

The lamp guttered and went out and Dapifer was left with the memory of an astonishing smile. Her arm was instantly withdrawn from his neck and he saw her go to the window, her head in its dreadful cap outlined against the moonlight, like a carapace. He recalled from the kaleidoscope of the day's feverish images that she had equally astonishing hair, a halo round her head like an autumn bonfire.

He said gravely, 'It appears, Makepeace Burke, that I over-indulged last night. With great carelessness I stumbled into a ditch, thereby breaking my collarbone.' Well, he owed her.

'That's what you'll tell 'em?'

'Lieutenant Governor Hutchinson, who is my host in this town, will be so informed. The matter will proceed no further.'

'Swear on the Book?' She picked up her Bible and placed it on the counterpane; he took it and swore.

She was holding out her hand. Moonlight showed wet on the palm. God, she'd spat on it. He held out his good hand and they shook on it, making him wince.

She went to the door, carrying the dirty plate and spoons. 'Go to sleep now,' she said.

He heard the stairs creak as she went down.

Resisting the pain in his head, his shoulder, everywhere, he tried to take stock. A waterfront? At night? In a town already in turmoil? What had he been thinking of, walking it, exposing himself to such risk? What he always thought of, he supposed: two entwined naked bodies, one of them his wife's, the other—its arse bobbing up and down like a ball bounced by an invisible hand—his friend's.

Ludicrous image, all the more ludicrous that it was set against his own drawing-room carpet. But it had hooked itself into his brain like some flesh-burrowing insect and festered, debilitating him, making him careless of life in general, his own in particular . . .

Gritting his teeth, Dapifer concentrated. What had he done *before* venturing along the waterfront? That's right, he'd been saying goodbye to Ffoulkes. Dear, good Ffoulkes. They'd gone aboard the *Aurora* as she readied herself to sail and Ffoulkes had tried to persuade him to make the voyage. 'For God's sake, Pip, come back home with me. Don't let her infect all England for you, old fellow. Nor him.'

In all the weeks the two of them had spent in Massachusetts, that had been the first time either had broached with emotion the matter that had brought them there. Even then, Dapifer remembered, it had been difficult for him to respond to overt concern. He'd said lightly, 'Odd, isn't it? One almost regrets his defection above hers, friends being more difficult to acquire than wives.'

Bare feet had pattered overhead like heavy raindrops; they could hear the bosun rousting out the crew's women from their rats' nests below. 'All ashore as is going ashore.'

But in Ffoulkes's cabin a silence had been enjoined by the ghost of Sidney Conyers demanding recognition of a past that went back to schooldays. Not quite of their birth nor wealth but qualifying as a friend by his eagerness to be one and by the orphaned state they all shared, he'd joined them like a frisking, abandoned puppy. At university they'd drunk, gambled and whored together as befitted young gentlemen, cementing a friendship that had survived Conyers's entry into the army.

It was a ghost, a past, due some sort of salute and Dapifer had found himself honouring it. 'Despite it all, I believe he loved us.'

'He loved what we were,' Ffoulkes had said, less forgiving. 'He always wanted what we had—and you were the first to marry.'

'Well, he had her. On my own bloody carpet.'

Ffoulkes hadn't smiled. 'Come back with me, Pip.'

'Shall, old fellow,' he'd said. 'Back in a year or less. But if you'd be good enough to lodge the papers and see she's out of the place by the time I return. Embrace that boy of yours for me.'

'He's the only reason I'm leaving you now.'

'Of course he is, you've got to go. Just thought I might as well squint at what lies beyond the Alleghenies.'

'Scalping knives probably.'

'More likely to be scalped in Boston. When they hear my accent nearly every Puritan looks at me as if I'd raped his mother.'

'Exactly. A sullen and uncouth continent. Listen to it.'

What had begun as confused and discordant noise in the centre of town, whistles, horns, war-whoops, was now rising into an orchestration of pandemonium with a relentless, underlying beat.

'Will you be safe on the streets?'

'Hutchinson's sent an escort.'

They'd said goodbye at the taffrail. He'd tried to thank this best of friends. 'All you've done, Ffoulkes . . . over and above the call of.' They embraced stiffly, like true Englishmen, and he'd stood on the quay, watching water widen between them. A slightest lightening of the sky beyond the ship had suggested the beginning of dawn.

By that time the town had developed a patchy flush as if it had become feverish, which it had. Boston was burning to the beat of drums. And yet, knowing the danger, he'd dismissed the lieutenant governor's escort, meandering away from the bonfires along a waterfront that grew ever meaner and quieter. The depression at this end of the harbour equalled his own.

Good God, he thought now, it was suicide. Had she brought him to this? That he *wanted* to die? How hideously . . . commonplace.

Yet he remembered fighting the bastards who'd set on him. Illogical, that. Remembered clinging to the wreckage in the water and wondering if survival was worth it and deciding it wasn't.

And then the God he didn't believe in had sent an interfering tavern harpy to whom, it seemed, his life had mattered. Couldn't argue with God . . . Sir Philip Dapifer fell asleep.

Downstairs, Makepeace did the same on one of the taproom settles.

Makepeace heard a thump and sat up, rigid. Movement again; her room, not Aaron's. She raced upstairs.

The Englishman was on the floor, trying to get up. 'Shaky on the pins,' he said. 'Where's the bloody receptacle?'

She got the chamber pot from under the bed and steadied him while he pissed into it; he clambered back, querulously. 'Who constructed this bed, Procrustes? And where are my damn clothes?'

She fetched his clothes, dry now but wrinkled, and his one surviving boot, then sat down on the stool. Get 'em to talk about themselves: first rule of tavern-keeping. 'And why was you on Fish Quay, Philip Dapifer?'

'I'd been bidding farewell to a good friend, Makepeace Burke. He was sailing back to England on the *Aurora*.'

'Why'd you come to Massachusetts Bay in the first place?'

Gloomily, he said, 'To divorce my wife.'

There was an appalled silence.

He wondered why he'd told her. Apart from Hutchinson, who'd expedited the matter for him, the judges—granters of the decree—were the only Americans who knew. In England, just Catty and, presumably, Conyers. Why blurt it out to a tavern wench?

'What do you want to do that for?' Makepeace was horrified. She said, 'Is she American then?'

'No, she's English. In England.' He wished he hadn't started this. 'I wanted to save her the publicity.'

Makepeace thought, You been saved, Makepeace Burke. He's nothing but a heathen. In disapproving silence, she picked up the Bible and began reading.

Dapifer thought, Whom was I actually sparing? Her or myself?

Was it that he couldn't have borne the public vindication of those who'd warned him not to marry her? A swathe through your fortune, they'd said, a scandal to your house, viciousness and charm handed down through the blood of dissolute generations.

And they'd been right. If she'd ever stopped menstruating, which she hadn't, he'd have had to count to be sure the child was his.

His passion for her had cooled into guilt; her father had forced the match on her, though she'd seemed willing. But indulgence had infuriated her. 'Why do you let me? Why don't you beat me?'

A spaniel, a woman and a walnut tree,
The harder you beat them the better they be.

He wasn't the beating sort; she could only cure herself. Tormented, she'd cast about for more exquisite ways to hurt him: his friends. Ffoulkes had refused her, Conyers had not. She'd smiled up at him from the carpet when he and Ffoulkes had walked in on them, bringing down the tree of his remembered past, his schooldays, Cambridge, with an ease that proved one of its roots had been rotten all along.

She'd engineered it; he saw that now. Even then, amidst disgust, he'd experienced pity at her craze for self-destruction.

No, he'd had to spare her; the world shouldn't know what she was. And in doing so he'd had to spare Conyers; a duel would have been the delight of the gossip rags. Very gentlemanly, Dapifer. You should have shot the bastard. Christ, it rankled. He hadn't realised how much. *My own bloody carpet.* Was that, in essence, what had taken him along the waterfront last night? Throwing out a challenge to the low life of Boston that he hadn't issued to the adulterer?

Introspection brought him full circle. And the silence from his companion was becoming too pointed to ignore. He was aware he'd lost ground with her and must make it up; whatever else, he was dependent on the female to get him out of this place. He said, 'And what of you, Miss Burke? Is there a lover on the horizon?'

She wanted to maintain her silence in order to show her disapproval. Then she thought, He'll think nobody's asked. So she said, 'I'm handfasted. To Captain Busgutt.' The name blasted the trumpet of the Lord into the quietness. 'Sailed for England six months gone. Should've been back in three.'

'I'm sorry.'

'No need,' she said. Captain Busgutt was alive, she was assured; there were a thousand things other than disaster to account for the delay. Both she and Goody Busgutt expected that one of the ships from England, now anchored out in the bay until it was safe to come in, might have news of his ship the *Gideon*.

She said viciously, 'It's your fault I'm still waiting.'

He blinked. 'Never met the gentleman.'

'Your government, then.' She was wagging her finger now. 'Captain Busgutt must go back and forth to London 'stead of trading where he'd wish—and the Atlantic passage is dangerous.'

'Ah,' Dapifer said. 'What age is Captain Busgutt?' he asked.

She picked up the Bible again. None of his business.

There was a mutter from the bed. 'I'll lay he's an old man.'

'Captain Busgutt,' said Makepeace clearly, 'is fifty years old and a man of vigour, a lay preacher famed throughout the bay for his zeal. Let me tell you, *Mister* Dapifer, Captain Busgutt's sermon on the Lord's scourging of the Amorites caused some in the congregation to cry out and others to fall down in a fit.'

'Pity I missed it.'

When she'd told Aaron that Captain Busgutt had asked for her, he'd said with the coarseness he'd picked up from his Tory friends, 'That old pulpit-beater? What d'you want to marry him for?'

The answer was that Captain Busgutt's was the best offer. She wasn't getting any younger and keeping the Roaring Meg's shaky roof over all their heads was becoming a losing battle. Captain Busgutt was that unique phenomenon, a rich man—or what passed for rich in Makepeace's world—who was also a good man. She thought now, Captain Busgutt didn't divorce his first wife, though she was sickly and gave him no children.

True, he was twice her age and didn't set the mermaids singing but he was admired in the community. The drunken reputation of Makepeace's father, her trade, the colour of her hair, the dislike accorded her brother: all these had kept her on the edge of social acceptance. Captain Busgutt would cloak all of them in his own respectability.

'Captain Busgutt seems to believe in long engagements,' said the voice from the bed. 'Why are you still waiting, Miss Burke?'

'None of your business.' Then, because, despite everything, conversation with this man was curiously luxurious, she said, 'Goody Busgutt.'

'Another of the captain's wives?'

'His mother.'

Goody Busgutt had strongly objected to the marriage, and, like the good son he was, Captain Busgutt had agreed to delay the wedding until his return from England—the hiatus to be a term of trial during which his mother could assess Makepeace's fitness for the position of Mrs Busgutt. At first the thought of being tested by Goody Busgutt had very nearly led Makepeace to break off the engagement. Then she'd thought, Why let that lip-sucking old sepulchre ruin your future, Makepeace Burke? She can't last for ever.

Suddenly, Makepeace was angry. 'And if she hears of it . . . if Goody Busgutt knew you was here . . .'

'She wouldn't look kindly on the wedding?'

'She would not.'

'What *would* she think we'd got up to?' he said mournfully.

Unsettled, she got up and went to the window. Dapifer, watching her, thought how unusual she was; like this damn continent, new and disrespectful. Too good for Captain Busgutt, he knew that.

He saw her stiffen. Dapifer struggled out of bed and limped across to her. 'What is it?' He kept his voice low.

She shook her head and pointed. An unaccountable shadow had moved in Thompson's boatyard. He caught hold of her shoulder to steady himself and felt the tension in there, the skin of it only separated from his hand by a thin layer of material.

After a while they both heard the tip-tap of movement receding down an alley. She let out a breath and the muscle under his hand relaxed as tension went out of her—to be replaced by the awareness of how close he was. She stood still for another second and then turned. He didn't move. 'Are they watching us?' he asked.

She nodded.

He was taller than she was, her nose was level with his chin. Makepeace could smell his skin. She knew he'd said something, but there was another conversation in progress between their bodies and she found difficulty in attending to anything else.

'What you say?'

'Is it trouble?'

Trouble. She pushed past him. 'We got to get you away,' she said. Away from me. But the damage was done, something had been established.

'It's the Sabbath today,' she said. 'The Sons won't be on the streets tonight. We'll smuggle you away then. Now get your sleep and let me get mine.' Determinedly, she plumped herself on her stool. She should leave, she knew, go down to the taproom, but the weird enchantment of the night insisted she stay out its last moments.

Dapifer closed his eyes obediently, wondering at a rioting mob that left off rioting on Sundays—and at a shared moment in a window with a tavern-keeper that had proved as erotic as any in his life.

Two hours went by.

Downstairs there was a rap on the door. A squall of camphor and propriety swept up the stairs to Makepeace's bedroom, awakening the two sleepers in it with a voice that could have clipped hedges. 'And what is this?' asked Goody Busgutt.

Chapter Three

CHURCH. OH GOD, God, I should've been in church.

Behind Goody Busgutt was Goody Saltonstall; they hunted as a pair. Saltonstall being exceptionally fat and Busgutt thin, they resembled an egg and its timer in petticoats. In fact, they were the area's moral police.

As Goody Busgutt was saying, still from the doorway, 'I knew, I *knew*. Moment you wasn't in church, Makepeace Burke, I smelled licentiousness. 'Twas my duty to sniff it out.'

And it was. Though innocent, Makepeace did not question Goody Busgutt's right, either as a future mother-in-law or as Puritan Boston's licentiousness-sniffer, to invade her house. She was ruined. She'd been caught alone in a bedroom with a man—*in flagrante delicto* as far as the Goodies were concerned. No marriage to Captain Busgutt now. She would be condemned as a trull; the Roaring Meg closed by official seal as a house of ill repute . . .

Dapifer saw her face age with defeat and became angry.

'Thank the Lord for you, mistress,' he said. 'Rescue, rescue.'

Goody Busgutt's mouth paused in a quirk. 'Eh? Who are you?'

'Madam, my name is Philip Dapifer. I was thrown into the harbour yesterday by rioters. This woman and her Indian dragged me out and, since there was nowhere else, brought me here. Most unwillingly, I may add. You look a kindly soul, will you get me food?'

'Eh?'

'Mistress,' said Sir Philip Dapifer, 'I have been here all night and this female has done nothing but lecture me on my politics and my soul. She has read to me from the Good Book without ceasing . . .' He pointed to the Bible lying open on the little table. 'Did not our Lord minister to the sick as well as preach? Not a morsel has she given me, not a sip.'

'Not a sip?' Goody Saltonstall's wattle quivered sympathetically.

'And my head aches most damnably. I'm ill.'

Saltonstall was already won; Goody Busgutt was holding out. 'Thee talks fast enough for a sick 'un, Englishman.'

'There you have it,' Dapifer said. 'She holds it against me that I am from England. For some reason, she blames me that her fiancé has not yet married her. Since she learned that I have connections at the Admiralty, she has been on at me to find out what happened to his ship. I suspect he has sailed to the Tortugas to get away from her. I tell you, mistress, were I her fiancé, I wouldn't marry her either.' He fell back on his pillow and closed his eyes.

Goody Busgutt walked round the bed like a woman searching corners for cockroaches. In the morning light, Dapifer's pallor looked deathly, a man without enough energy to raise his eyelids, let alone any other part of his anatomy.

'Thee *could* have fed him some broth, miss,' she said.

Makepeace's wits came back. ''Tis the Sabbath,' she sulked.

'When did the Sabbath stop the Lord's work? What were thee thinking of? Now fetch this poor soul some broth.'

Makepeace got up, still astounded. He'd rescued her as surely as she'd rescued him. He'd worked the oracle on the two flintiest women in Boston. Downstairs she fell into Betty's arms, babbling.

'Never believed you was jus' talkin', did they?' asked Betty.

'They believed *him*. And it was true,' Makepeace said. She ran her fingers round her neck, still feeling the noose. 'In a way.'

'Oh-ah.'

'Don't you start. And get that fire going. Pop in a couple of lobster and I'll run up some pastry for patties.' She was exhilarated by escape.

When the trays were ready, Betty stopped Makepeace from carrying them up. '*I'll* take 'em, gal.'

She was right, of course, she usually was. Makepeace sobered. If he'd rescued her from one danger, another loomed for them both. The Sons of Liberty and everybody else in the Cut would be aware of the Englishman's presence in the Meg as soon as the Goodies left it; her marriage was saved but her custom was ruined.

Makepeace went upstairs and woke Aaron. He was to take Tantaquidgeon with him and go to Hutchinson's house and tell the lieutenant governor to send a sedan chair for Dapifer with an escort.

'A chair *and* escort? Why not trumpeters while they're about it?'

Makepeace shrugged. 'Might as well, there'll be a crowd whatever we do. I want him safe through it.'

Aaron winked, as had Betty. 'Ooh-er.'

She said wearily, 'There wasn't no ooh-er.' She suspected that her exchanges in the dark with the magical fish she'd caught would be all she had to sustain her from now on.

For the rest of the day, he was the Goodies' catch. Every so often one of them would come down to berate her for her neglect of him and command some recipe for his improvement.

The lobsters and patties had gone down well. Betty came down with trays on which no scrap was left. She frightened Makepeace with a high keening as she flopped onto the settle with her apron over her head.

'What is it? What is it? What did they say to you?'

The apron moved slowly from side to side. 'They're snorin'. But he ain't. He . . .' Betty's voice failed. Makepeace waited a full minute before Betty was able to continue. 'Ladder.'

'He wanted a ladder?'

'A ladder . . . for him and Goody Saltonstall is plannin' to elope.'

Makepeace sat down beside her friend and wailed with her.

Aaron came back while they were both sweating over the next collation, lobscouse and flummery. His news lacked amusement; what he'd found in town had shaken him.

It was Sunday. Boston, as ever, was a ghost town, only a murmur of prayers breaking the silence. Today, to Aaron who had missed both riots, it was shocking. Because no work should be done on the Lord's

Day, avenues were still littered with the black scatterings of bonfires. Fences and flowerbeds lay trampled; broken glass winked in the gutters. In Hanover Square the huge, hundred-year-old oak tree that stood in its middle had sprouted new fruit. A figure was hanging from one of its branches. Close to, it turned out to be an effigy of Andrew Oliver, the Stamp Master. Last night the old man had been made to stand before it and apologise for his offence of administering the Stamp Act.

Where Lieutenant Governor Hutchinson's white, pillared mansion had stood among trees there was an empty shell surrounded by wreckage, as if it had vomited semi-digested furniture onto the lawns.

'Well, where is he now?'

Aaron shrugged. 'Maybe he's taken refuge with Governor Bernard out at Castle William.'

Betty asked, 'What we goin' to do with him upstairs?'

'Get him away by boat,' said Aaron. 'I'll row to Castle William and get them to send an escort for him tonight.'

'Take him with you,' Betty said. 'Save time.'

'Too risky. The Sons ain't observing the Sabbath that religiously. If they're patrolling the water like they're patrolling the streets, he'll get tipped back in the harbour—and me with him.'

Makepeace groaned. Her brother, usually incautious, was showing common sense. Nobody would question him alone in a boat—but if Sugar Bart saw him with Dapifer . . .

What Aaron didn't realise was how disastrous it was going to be for the Roaring Meg's local reputation when a bunch of redcoats turned up to rescue an Englishman from its midst. As well run up the Union Jack and be done with it. The Sons would never drink here again. Probably nobody else either, she thought. But what else to do? Nothing.

'Go up and tell the Goodies we got lobscouse and brandy for their supper in the taproom,' she said to Aaron. 'You can tell the English your plan while they're down.'

While the Goodies gorged in the taproom, Zeobab Fairlee came to the kitchen door asking for them. 'There's news, 'Peace,' he said. 'I come to tell Goody Busgutt. It's the *Gideon*.'

Betty paused over the fire. Makepeace sat down, gripping the knife with which she'd been cutting bread until her knuckles showed white. Her face was impassive. Don't let him be drowned, Lord, she prayed. Batting your eyelashes at Englishmen and your fiancé drowns—it's the Lord's punishment. 'Dead?'

Zeobab shook his head. 'Press-ganged.' The words tolled through the kitchen like a passing bell. It was almost as dreadful.

The knife in Makepeace's hand stabbed into the loaf and stabbed it again. She was so angry. How *dare* they? King George and his shite Admiralty. Kidnap your own men but you leave ours alone. Here it was again: British tyranny. Stab. Silence closed in on the kitchen with another question. Eventually Betty asked it. 'Who's goin' to tell her?'

'I ain't,' Makepeace said. But in the end she accompanied Zeobab into the taproom and held Goody Busgutt's hand while he told her. The old woman diminished before her eyes; she kept pleading 'I'll not see my boy again, will I?'—a question to which, terribly, she knew the answer.

They helped her back to her house.

The news had spread—most of *Gideon*'s crew consisted of local men, and further down the Cut was a large cluster of women that hurried towards Zeobab. 'Was my man pressed along of the others?' 'Did the press take Matthew?' 'Pressed.' 'Pressed.'

'Ask *her*.' Saltonstall's voice rose above the clamour. 'She'll know. She's took in a English lord as is a friend to them as steals our poor lads. Ask her what she's a-doin' with him in her bedroom.'

Unbelieving faces in unison turned towards Makepeace, the women's go-to-meeting caps like the frill of spume on an advancing wave. She began gabbling: *Drowning. What else to do? Where else to take 'un?* Every hurried word an apology and admission of guilt—and unheard.

Mary Bell from Number 25 shifted her baby more firmly onto her hip. She came up so that she stood on one side of the little bridge that led to the tavern, Makepeace, with her back to the door, faced her on the other. They were friends. Mary's young husband was second mate on *Gideon* and had sailed before his child was born. 'What's she sayin', Makepeace?' Her face crumpled. 'Where's my Matthew?'

Wordless, Makepeace stared at her. Useless, useless to say she'd saved a man from drowning not knowing who he was; her actions had no relevance to this woman.

Had *Gideon* gone down with all hands, Mary could have grieved and recovered. But there was no formula for putting to rest the victim who disappeared into the jaws of His Majesty's authorised monster. Though he didn't come back, he remained the man who might or might not be dead, the husband of a wife who couldn't remarry; he was a disembodied scream that went on and on.

Somebody would have to pay. Pain must be subsumed in revenge, a shriek of protest go up against the distant, arrogant, little island that inflicted such suffering. And this time, there was a scapegoat on their doorstep, trailing blood. Not a governor, not a stamp master—hirelings who took their orders from 3,000 miles away—but a real, live

Englishman who, on his own admission, had connections with the same Admiralty that commanded the stealing of men.

Helplessly, Makepeace went into the Roaring Meg, shut the door, bolted it and began preparations for a siege.

Would Aaron be safe going to Castle William? Yes, she decided, he would, as long as he set out immediately.

When Aaron came down from upstairs she apprised him of the situation. 'You tell them soldiers to lie out from the jetty an' keep quiet,' she said. 'We'll row him to their boat.'

She accompanied her brother to the jetty and watched him go. She put Tantaquidgeon on guard at the jetty, then went upstairs to take out her anger and discomfort on the English gentleman.

'Well,' she said, storming in, 'you cost me my marriage. You gone and got Captain Busgutt pressed. Ain't I lucky?'

He had the sense to listen, giving a nod from time to time. When she finally ran out of breath, he said, 'I can get him out, you know.'

The sheer omnipotence of the statement made her angrier. 'And what about Matthew Bell and the rest of the crew?'

'I'll get them out as well.'

'Oh.' She paused. 'Do it then.'

Then he said, 'I thought I heard the voice of Mrs Saltonstall. She was using the words "English lord" in tones that suggested a blight on our former intimacy. She's blaming me.' He looked at her. '*And* you.'

He's quick, Makepeace thought. She hadn't meant him to know how much trouble she was in. 'They got to blame somebody. It'll pass.'

'Will it?' He shook his head at her. 'You really should have let me drown, shouldn't you, Makepeace Burke?'

'You wanted to, di'n't you? I saw.'

He shrugged and turned back to the window. 'As I remember, my situation appeared unpropitious.'

'There's *always* propitions—whatever they are. You struggle 'til the Lord sounds the last trump. See him?' She pointed out of the window to where Tantaquidgeon stood on the jetty below them. 'He'd be dead now if he'd thought like you.'

She told him the story. At the time John L. Burke had been playing at frontiersman along the fur-rich edges of the Great Lakes. Makepeace, then four and a half years old, had found Tantaquidgeon lapping from the stream to which she'd gone for water. The wound in his skull was horrific. The Burkes discovered later, from other sources, that an Iroquois war party had raided his settlement—he was a Huron. 'His brains was coming out, Pa said he was a-dying. But Ma said he di'n't need to less'n he had a mind to it.' Temperance Burke had prayed over him as she nursed him and become heartened by his repetition of 'Jesus', his only word. 'He was a praying Indian, see,' Makepeace told Dapifer triumphantly. 'The Lord hadn't sounded the trump for him yet and he knew it and he fought to stay living. He wouldn't be beat.'

'And you've kept him ever since?'

Makepeace was as surprised at the question as she had been when Dapifer had asked her why she'd saved him from drowning. 'Couldn't manage on his own, could he?' The Indian's devotion to her mother had been absolute; after Temperance's death it had been transferred to herself. 'He's family.'

'Can he say anything at all?'

'He says "Jesus". Ma said that was enough. Tantaquidgeon's a remarkable man. You want to be more like him.'

She means it, thought Dapifer. That overgrown doorstop down there is being held up as an example to me. He said meekly, 'I'll try.'

There was that ravishing grin again; she was extraordinary. He said, 'They're going to punish you, aren't they, Procrustes?'

The smile went. 'It'll pass.'

'I'd better stay.'

'That'd rile 'em more.'

'What then?'

With hideous honesty, she said, 'I was minded there'd be a reward.'

'Good God.' Fooled by the relationship that had grown between them, he'd forgotten she was a member of a class that grubbed everywhere for money. 'And what are you *minded* my life's worth?' He added, with assumed calculation, 'Don't forget I saved you from the Goodies.'

'Not for long, you didn't.' She pushed an errant red ringlet back into her cap as she reckoned the cost of him. There was the expenditure on the Goodies' food and drink, the loss of her custom, the loss of Captain Busgutt. *And*—here she doubled the figure she'd first thought of—there was the cost of falling in love with an Englishman who was about to leave her, the memory of whom would keep her incapable of loving another man for the rest of her days. That was worth something.

She took a deep breath. 'Forty pounds?'

Sir Philip Dapifer, born to an income of £15,000 per annum, appeared to consider. 'Cheaper to marry you,' he said. 'Will a draft on my Boston bank be acceptable?'

'Cash,' she said.

'Cash.'

She spat and they shook on it. She went abruptly out of the room and he returned to the view. The pain inflicted by his drubbing was beginning to recede, though his shoulder still ached and he could hear the wheezing in his ears which tormented him when his heart skipped and then redoubled its beat as it often did nowadays.

The moon was rising like a transparent disc, giving a sheen to the little islands in the bay so that they looked like a school of curved dolphins arrested and pewtered in the act of diving. The view almost gave the lie to the violence enacted against it. It was hard to believe the rioters meant it.

And in London, Dapifer thought, they don't believe it.

Before setting out for America he'd gone to Prime Minister Grenville, suggesting he take soundings of the situation in New England. George Grenville had been courteous—the two were friends—but dismissive. 'Mere grousing,' he'd said. 'Your Boston Whig may grumble against the Stamp Tax, yet be assured, *au fond* he'll do nothing to jeopardise his God, his King and his business.'

But he will, George. He is.

The whole colony, perhaps the entire continent, was angry. From here he was vouchsafed a view of the government as the Americans saw it: complacent, arrogant, demanding obedience, snatching Captain Busgutts from their rightful employment as if they were of no account.

And here, again as he could witness, was a nation that wouldn't stand for it. These, its lesser people, had an energy, a newness he hadn't encountered before. The fat, black cook, the two grotesque old women, had addressed him as if they were his equal.

Most extraordinary of all was Makepeace Burke, provincial, unpolished, brave, smelling of fresh air, and with a validity that made the painted scenery of London society appear stale in contrast.

You struggle 'til the Lord sounds the last trump.

What was amazing was that she'd invested him with the will to do it. Even more surprisingly, God knew how, that gawky body of hers had revived the old Adam in his. Just as he'd begun to think he'd lost the lust for women, a tavern-keeper in appalling clothes was concentrating his mind on what lay underneath.

Dapifer gritted his teeth. The best return for what she'd done for him was to leave her alone. The lemans introduced to society by some of his fellow bucks embarrassed everybody. What *could* he do for her? More a matter, he supposed, of what she would allow him to do . . .

Two boatloads of soldiers arrived at the jetty just before midnight, with a clatter of disembarkation that could have been heard at Cape Cod. Makepeace moaned; there went secrecy. She met them on the jetty, looking for Aaron. A graceful civilian in a feathered hat was being bowed up the steps; the lieutenant governor himself. She tried to waylay him: 'Excuse me, sir . . .' but was pushed aside by a soldier's musket. She stood back until the last man had tramped past her. There was no sign of Aaron. She went inside, pushing her way through a taproom now ablaze with red and blue. Sir Thomas Hutchinson was embracing Dapifer like a returned prodigal son.

'Excuse *me*. Where's my brother?'

The lieutenant governor looked down. 'Ale for these men, my good woman.'

'Sir Thomas,' Dapifer said, 'I should like to present my saviour and our hostess, Miss Burke.'

Instantly a bow. 'Miss Burke, we owe you a debt of—'

'Yes,' said Makepeace. 'Where's my brother?'

Sir Thomas declared himself at a loss; so did the officer in charge. A sergeant eventually said, 'The lad as fetched us? Still rowing, I reckon. Came back in his own boat. We passed him.'

Makepeace was comforted; it would take Aaron longer to cover the stretch of water from Castle William than for the swift launches of the army.

'*May* the company be provided with the wherewithal to drink your health, Miss Burke?' Sir Thomas was all charm.

'Who's paying?'

He blinked. 'I suppose I am.'

While she, she supposed, ran a public house and was obliged to serve paying customers. Grumbling, she called Betty and the two of them went to the barrels.

A sinuous little man clutching a hamper of clothes saw his chance to greet Dapifer himself. '*Now* then, Sir Pip, we managed to rescue some of our habiliments from the *ruin* those *savages* made of poor Sir Thomas's house. What a night, I thought our last hour . . .'

Sir Thomas was explaining the size of the armed contingent he'd brought with him. 'I'm deploying men round the town but if trouble breaks out again tonight, I shall have to ask London for troops. The *Lord Percy* is standing by to take my dispatches to England tomorrow. The first I sent went down with the *Aurora*, of course, but—'

'*What did you say?*'

Makepeace, glimpsing Dapifer's face from the other side of the room, elbowed her way towards him.

' . . . tactless and unthinking,' Sir Thomas was saying. 'My dear fellow, I'm so sorry. Yes, I fear she went down almost as soon as she got out of the bay—an unexpected squall. They've found no survivors.'

'Leave him alone,' Makepeace said, moving in, but the man—Robert, Dapifer had called him—was before her.

'This way, Sir Pip.' He looked round for an escape route, nodded as Makepeace pointed to the kitchen and guided his master to it.

Sir Thomas, elegantly sad, watched them go. 'Such a loss, Lord Ffoulkes. They were great friends, great friends.'

'Broke it to him gentle, though, di'n't you?' snapped Makepeace and returned to the task of drawing and handing out ale pots, suffering for the man who'd just been stricken as if they were twinned.

As soon as she could she made for the kitchen. He'd managed to get himself in hand. 'I'm taking ship for England right away,' Dapifer said, briskly. 'Robert, give us a moment and then fetch Sir Thomas in here.'

Robert minced back to the taproom, eyebrows working.

They faced each other in the firelight. 'There you have it,' Dapifer said, 'I have to go back. Ffoulkes's wife is dead and he has . . . had a young son. I'm the boy's guardian, I'm responsible.' There was a cleaver on the table and he lifted it and drove it deep into the pine. 'I'm responsible for everything—Ffoulkes's death. You. All this.'

'Not me,' she said. 'I'm responsible for me.'

He pointed to a purse on the mantel. 'The reward,' he said.

'Thank you.'

'Thank *you*. Would you do me a favour before I go?'

'What?'

'Take that bloody cap off your head.'

She thought about it for a moment, then pulled the strings at her chin and took the cap off, knowing it was the most sensual and abandoned thing she had ever done or would ever do.

The curls came warm onto her neck. His arm reached for her and the Meg's kitchen twirled into a vortex that centred on the two of them, bodies absorbing into each other in its centrifugal force.

Somebody from another dimension was coughing. Robert and the lieutenant governor were in the doorway. Dapifer was unconcerned. He kept his arm round her. 'I want this woman protected, Tom. An armed guard, if you please. And I shall need a passage on the *Lord Percy*. I have urgent business in England.'

'Certainly. My dear fellow, I trust . . .'

Makepeace wrenched herself free and Dapifer strolled away from her to the taproom, chatting. The man Robert was still in the doorway. She was suddenly very tired. '*What?*'

He quirked a hand towards the mantelshelf, his little face twisted.

'There's a hundred guineas in gold in that purse, did you know? What *did* you do to earn it?'

The taproom was emptying as soldiers left to take up guard duty at points around town. Two men were being detailed to stay at the Meg. She went up to the sergeant. 'I don't want redcoats here.'

He shrugged. 'Orders, miss.'

'But . . .' No doubt they thought they were protecting her, but a guard on her door put her on the same footing as Stamp Master Oliver and the lieutenant governor—and look what happened to them.

She and Betty stood hand in hand on the jetty to watch the embarkation. As Dapifer went down the steps with Hutchinson a drum began to beat somewhere on Beacon Hill. The beat was answered by another in the east, then west, then others joined in, until Boston palpitated as if infested by a thousand giant crickets. The Sabbath was over.

Makepeace didn't look at Dapifer as he was rowed away, nor he at her; she kept watching for Aaron. Behind her the glow of bonfires matched the tangerine of an extraordinary moon.

'Boat out there,' Betty said.

Makepeace could see a light floating on the sea directly opposite the jetty; somebody appeared to be fishing. 'Ain't Aaron,' she said.

The projectile came at them almost lazily, not seeming so much to get nearer as to grow in size, a bit of comet with fire at its centre, getting bigger and bigger. There was a splatter against the end of the jetty and little trills of flame began running along the grooves of planking. Another point of light from the darkness widened into a ball, a plate, then into a cartwheel of fire spinning towards them. Another splatter, this time from above them and sparks came down in a shower.

Batting at her head and shoulders, Makepeace looked up. There was a pale glow and a movement of shadows in the bedroom where none had been before. 'Fire,' she said gently to herself and then shrieked. 'JOSH!'

Betty was already lumbering into the inn; Makepeace passed her. 'I'll get him. You get them bloody redcoats.'

It'll go up, the Meg'll go up. In this heat . . .

The boy was asleep on his small bed. She could hear crackling through the partition between his room and hers. As she snatched the child up and took him downstairs and then out into the garden she tried to think. What to do? What to do?

For a moment she stood, rocking with indecision, but the sight of Tantaquidgeon, stalking past her from the jetty to fetch the ladder and bucket by the privy wall, brought back her senses. One of the soldiers was trying to stamp out the flames on the jetty, looking for buckets. She showed him where they were and fell on the pump. He disappeared upstairs with one bucketful, she followed him with another.

Flames licked the furniture and ran along the ceiling beams. Her bedroom was a copse of fire with new trees springing up every minute. She and the soldier ran down for more water, ran up, down, up, getting in each other's way. In the midst of her panic, she remembered to pluck the purse off the kitchen mantelshelf as she passed it.

They had to surrender the bedroom; the corridor began to burn. There were people around now, through smoke and panic she saw faces, some of them dear to her, one very dear, but couldn't have put a name to any of them. Down to the kitchen again, crowded now. The bottom of her petticoat was smouldering, somebody picked her up and carried her out to the slipway to dump her in the shallows. 'Thank you,' she said.

'Not at all,' said Dapifer and went back to the battle.

The sea was cool on her blistered feet and an odd remoteness allowed her to stand in it for a few seconds longer. There were figures on the roof, a rope had been slung round a chimney to take up buckets provided for it by a chain of people that led down to the slipway beside her. Half the Cut was here: Zeobab, Mr and Goody Saltonstall . . . Very organised. And hopeless as hell. But she joined the chain. Praying Bostonians passed buckets to goddamning English soldiers who passed them up to swearing, scorching British sailors who threw their contents onto the common enemy howling back at them. The Roaring Meg itself was on their side: its oak beams had weathered to virtual iron over the years; although fire ran along them, it couldn't gain purchase.

A Cockney voice shrieked from a perch on the kitchen chimney: 'She's going out, we're winnin', she's going out.'

Makepeace stared at her misshapen tavern with its smoking upper ribcage and was washed by a terrible gratitude for the miracle of its deliverance. She joined the other Puritans on their knees while Mr Saltonstall trumpeted a prayer of thanksgiving before she hobbled to the barrels to dole out ale and rum to her various saviours.

At which point the miracle faded. The people from the Cut melted away. Makepeace called, pleading, to Zeobab, 'It's on the house.'

Old Zeobab looked sadly at the rum glass in Makepeace's hand. 'Cain't drink here no more, 'Peace,' he said. 'You let us down.'

She poured bumpers for the servicemen of the British army and navy who sat slumped among the detritus of her taproom.

'Didn't need to light a fire to welcome us, miss,' one of the men said. 'We was warm enough.'

She peered at him. 'Was that you up on the chimney? Could have killed your fool self.'

He raised scorched eyebrows. 'Was that a chimbley? Gor damn, thought I was back up the crow's nest.'

They ain't so different from us, Makepeace thought as she kissed him. She led them into the kitchen to give them some food and treat their burns. Dapifer was already there. Betty was resetting the collarbone which had been dislocated once more by, he said, 'carrying lumps of women around'.

'Back again, then,' Makepeace said to him.

'I was passing. Thought I'd drop in.' He'd seen the flames and made the rowers turn the boat round.

Betty heaped the table with what food she could find and Makepeace added her largest jug filled with best Jamaican.

Dapifer took her into the taproom. 'Don't get them drunk. When they've rested I want those sailors searching the bay in case the boat that did this is still out there. We saw it as we turned back. It had some sort of catapult rigged up in it, like a siege engine.'

'God have mercy,' she said dully. 'I thought they were meteors.' Only five years before Boston had been devastated by one of the worst town fires in colonial history but Sugar Bart—she *knew* it was Bart—had risked starting another in his haste to injure one small tavern.

She realised something else. 'Aaron,' she said. '*Aaron*.'

'We'll look for him,' said Dapifer gently, 'but there's no reason yet to believe he's come to harm. Isn't he a Harvard man? He could have gone to see friends in Cambridge.'

Yes, he'd gone to Harvard—she'd slaved to send him there. No, he wouldn't have gone tonight without letting her know.

There was no comfort he could give her so he left her and went to organise the boat party. As the men were clambering down into the boat, one of the oarsmen said, 'Best leave it to the navy, me lord. We'll find the lad.'

When the boat had gone, Betty came to inspect Makepeace; the soles of her feet were blistered where the slippers had burned through. She fetched a chair for Makepeace to sit in while she did some salving and bandaging. 'Best talk to her,' she said to Dapifer. 'Keep her mind off it.'

'What will you do about the Roaring Meg? Rebuild?'

She tried to concentrate. 'Sell,' she said. 'We'll move on.'

'You'll get your customers back,' he reassured her. 'One insane arsonist can't stand for a community. And people forget.'

'Not round here.'

It was as Zeobab Fairlee had said. *You let us down.*

So she had. While they'd been discussing protest, thinking they were in a safe house, she'd concealed a representative of the very rule against which they were to take action. They wouldn't drink here again.

Ain't that punishment enough, Lord? Don't take Aaron as well.

Dapifer was thinking of his wife and wondering how she would have borne the afflictions being visited on the woman by his side.

'A spaniel, a woman and a walnut tree . . .' Makepeace Burke was being beaten, and with every buffet showed more quality.

Perhaps, he thought, it was Catty's affliction that she had never loved anybody or anything sufficiently to be wounded by its loss. Had he loved *her*? He supposed so—until she'd run through his affection as carelessly as she wasted everything else.

'I should have divorced her in England,' he said, 'but the process is akin to a public hanging. I couldn't inflict that on her, though, God knows, Ffoulkes urged me to. Better for everybody, I thought, if it were done discreetly three thousand miles away. She signed her consent readily enough; she's set her sights on Conyers to be her next husband, poor devil. So Ffoulkes came with me to give the necessary evidence—because I decided it was easier. *Easier*, by Christ.'

Makepeace was aware he was stripping his soul for her sake; such a marriage was beyond her social experience, but when it came to his friend, she could imagine what he imagined and hear, as he must be hearing, the voices of men calling on God to save them from an empty sea. She could hear Aaron's.

'A squall's quick,' she said. 'Chaos, they say. No time to think, everything blotted out. It would've been all over for him in seconds.'

It wasn't much, all she could offer, but he was grateful for it; he'd been haunted by the image of Ffoulkes clinging to a wreck for hours, praying for help until his strength failed. There'd been no Makepeace Burke to lift Ffoulkes from the sea. He mustn't lose her as well.

'I think you should come to England with me,' he said.

'What for?'

'You know what for.' Her own appalling honesty deserved better than the taffeta phrases he used on other women. After all, when he'd scrupled at making her his mistress he hadn't known how important she'd become to him, nor what disaster his presence would bring to her.

'A kept woman?'

'It's about time somebody kept you,' he said, 'and I don't think marriage to Captain Busgutt is going to come off.'

'Holy hokey,' she said, 'a kept woman.' It took her breath away. If one of her customers had made the suggestion, she'd have slapped his face. That this man, who set her blood fizzing, had made it was, in his terms, the greatest compliment he could pay her. He wanted her. That he could marry her didn't occur to Makepeace any more than it occurred to Dapifer. As it was, she understood this offer from a scion of the ruling class to be Olympian; she'd cherish it for the rest of her life.

But she'd be damned if she accepted it. Not from prudery; the Puritan corseting of years had been shaken loose during the last two days. If, earlier, when they'd kissed, they'd been alone in the house, she would have let him take her. That was one thing; to be *kept* was another. It was prostitution. She thought better of herself—and him—than that.

'I know you mean well—' she began.

'No, I don't,' he said.

She almost smiled. 'Got to keep my independence.'

'Oh Jesus. Very well, I'll set you up in the biggest inn in England, Betty, the boy, Aaron, the Indian, all of you. You can work until you drop. Just come with me.' England would be a lonely place for him now.

She'd felt England's contempt for its colonials from 3,000 miles away; she could imagine with what derision it would treat the ignorant Yankee mistress of a favoured son.

'Wouldn't they just love me.' she said. Here, she was confident on her own territory; there, he'd be as hamed of her within the week.

'I've got to go, Procrustes. Ffoulkes would expect me to.'

'Then go,' she said.

He was sitting on the doorway sill, elbows on knees, chin in hands, morose. *Lord*, she loved him. 'I know,' she said. The noise of riot from the town had become part of the night, now and then pierced by a scream—always Aaron's. She clutched at her head. 'Where is he?'

He put his arm round her. The moon was seeping colour now and hung like a huge Chinese lantern over an empty sea. There was a grunt from Tantaquidgeon and they heard a call outside.

'Makepeace Burke.'

High, fluting, strange, not human. So frightening that, when Makepeace opened her mouth to answer, she couldn't make any sound.

It came again.

'Makepeace Burke. Here's your brother, Makepeace Burke.'

Somehow her legs walked her outside, Tantaquidgeon behind her with a knife in his hand, and then Betty. Makepeace looked to the right; difficult to see but, yes, figures passing and repassing against the glow of a bonfire in the square beyond, carrying something on a rail, an effigy. As she squinted, trying to make them out, they tipped the rail so that the scarecrow they'd made slid off onto the ground.

Dapifer was telling her to get back inside.

Makepeace kept her eyes on the effigy. They'd made it of hay, untidily; black hay that gleamed when it caught the light. She watched it rise to its feet and start stumbling up the Cut. She didn't move.

The tarred and feathered thing was bowed so that the prickles along its back curved, like a hedgehog's, and it zigzagged as it came, lumbering from one side of the lane to the other, mewing when it bumped into a wall. I must go to it, she thought, it's blind. And stood there.

In the end it was Tantaquidgeon who strode down the lane and carried Aaron home.

Chapter Four

THE LANDLADY of the Roaring Meg, her brother and staff sailed for England aboard the *Lord Percy* on the evening tide.

Dapifer, finding himself in charge, had reasoned that a surgeon on a ship, where tar was used extensively, would be used to treating its burns and therefore well qualified to help Aaron. Makepeace had to be taken out of danger and the *Percy*'s captain, charged with speeding Sir Thomas Hutchinson's dispatches to London, would not delay sailing. His own imperative was still to support Ffoulkes's son; neither could he desert Makepeace in her trouble. Ergo: they must sail with *Lord Percy* together—and today.

This was explained to Makepeace who merely nodded; anything, anything. Dapifer had turned to Betty. 'She can return later if she wants to but I'm not leaving her in Boston,' he said. 'The thing is, are you prepared to come with us?' To separate the two women was unthinkable.

'Ain't leavin' me behind in this place. Nor my boy neither.' Betty's face was drawn, though she was taking the horror of what had happened to Aaron better than his sister.

Tantaquidgeon was not consulted but strode up the *Percy*'s gangplank with his usual impregnable serenity.

The ship's doctor was youngish, Scottish and irritable, and blamed his patient's condition on those who'd brought him aboard. 'Will ye see this? Have ye revairted to savagery on this continent?'

Aaron lay face down on the cot in the surgeon's own cabin, semi-conscious and moaning. He'd been naked and in a foetal position when the hot tar had been poured on him so that most of it had been retained by his upper back, head and arms. Makepeace hung over him, trying to smear him with butter and coming between the doctor and the lantern.

Dr Baines glanced up. 'Will ye remove this female?'

Dapifer, who'd already tried, shook his head. 'Can you help him?'

'How can I tell? It's depaindent on the depth of the burns and that I'll not know until they're uncovered. And on how many useless questions I'm paistered by in the meantime.'

The man's rudeness was oddly reassuring and some measure of his competence penetrated Makepeace's brain enough for them to get her outside to the companionway, though she refused to go further.

Dapifer went up on deck to make arrangements for the passage with the captain. The *Percy* was one of the navy's new frigates, small but fast. Most of her time was spent shuttling between London and Boston, carrying dispatches and, occasionally, a passenger or two on official business. This trip her captain was stretching the point and obliging the governor of Massachusetts Bay by giving passage to England to one of his female relatives and her maid.

Captain Strang was happy to stretch the point even further and oblige Dapifer and his connections in the Admiralty, despite that gentleman's curious entourage. 'We should make England in six weeks, perhaps less.'

Satisfied, Dapifer left the captain to his preparations and waited on deck for the doctor to report.

'Wail,' said a voice at his side, 'we can thank the Almighty it's not as extensive as might be.'

'A full recovery?'

The Scotsman shook his head. 'The scarring will torment him the days of his life, nor will he aiver grow hair on the back of his haid. I ask ye, what sort of people? Medieval, so it is.' The doctor drew in a breath. 'Is there a reason they punished the boy?'

'His sister saved me from attack by so-called Boston patriots the day before yesterday. She and her brother paid the price.'

'A spirited young lady,' Dr Baines said thoughtfully.

As the ship drew out into the bay, the sun glistened on the prim, white-painted steeples of Boston's churches, accentuating the messy, blackened tideline of its waterfront. It shone through the bared beams of the Roaring Meg's roof and the open door of its taproom. Betty sobbed then. Makepeace remained below with her brother and didn't see it.

Since Makepeace refused to leave Aaron, her food was taken to the surgeon's cabin. Betty stayed with her. Dapifer was invited to dine with the officers in the wardroom. Dinner was cheered by the presence of Susan Brewer, the niece of Elizabeth Murray, owner of Boston's smartest ladies' outfitters, who was on her way to study metropolitan shopkeeping and send back the latest London fashions. A lively young thing, Miss Brewer, of bouncing laugh and bosom, excited by this, her first voyage, and the presence of so many eligible men—though, for propriety's sake, she had asked that her black maid, Jubilee, join her for meals.

After the meal there was a rush to invite the young woman to promenade with the officers on the quarterdeck. Dapifer, tired, excused himself. Miss Brewer was disappointed and whispered, 'Sir Philip, I hope you ain't offended that Jubilee is eating with us? I saw the other two maids on board are having to eat below and—'

'Two maids?'

'White one and another black one, and I wondered—'

Gently, Dapifer explained Makepeace's situation and Miss Brewer was momentarily silenced with embarrassment.

New England heat extended far into the Atlantic and tarpaulins were slung for the passengers to sit under and watch porpoises frisking in a sapphire sea, but Makepeace still sat by Aaron's side.

Dapifer called every morning to enquire after the patient but Makepeace kept her eyes averted from his and did not talk to him.

Aaron's pain was kept at bay for the first two weeks by laudanum but it came snarling in as the doses were gradually reduced.

'Give him more,' Makepeace demanded.

'Now, now, ye'll not want the lad depaindent on it?'

There was an argument, not their first. Aaron's agony lacerated Makepeace as if it were her flesh that lay in open strips; Baines soothed her as he would a defensive dog until she saw sense. That she made trouble seemed to increase his admiration. 'A strong-willed lassie,' he reported to Dapifer, 'but from true concairn for her brother.'

He was her only concern. She was vaguely aware that all the things that had anchored her life were being left behind. And it didn't matter.

Even if the choice hadn't been made for her, she would have left Boston anyway. Overnight every memory it held for her had become smirched with tar. People she knew had disfigured a seventeen-year-old boy, people she knew. *Because of me.*

Betty sat down beside her. 'It weren't your fault.'

'Yes it was.'

'Held him down while they poured the pitch, did you?'

'I brought the Englishman to the Meg.'

That was the one needless action. She should have landed him along the quays and sent for the magistrates. Had she been attracted to Dapifer from the first? Had her sin of lusting after him fallen on Aaron?

Shock had left Aaron's memory of events fragmentary. Rowing back alone from Castle William, he had decided to tie up for a while at White's Wharf. Then a sack over his head, the smell of cordage as if he were in a rope-walk, a glimpse of whooping, painted men as they stripped him, searing pain. He hadn't recognised any of the men's voices—an omission that seemed to comfort him slightly. Random assault was less terrible than if it had been inflicted by people he knew.

He had his own guilt.

'What did you stop off at White's for?' Makepeace asked him.

He turned his head away. 'There was a girl.'

At first she didn't understand and then she did and she was angry. 'All those nights you said you was at Cambridge . . . ?'

'I'm sorry, 'Peace, I'm sorry. Wages of sin.'

She sat back, suddenly appalled that she'd been cross with him. He'd only done with a girl what she so nearly had with a man.

'Wages of *what*?' she said. 'Wages of being young? Being human?' By absolving Aaron, she was able to absolve herself. 'I tell you this, Aaron Burke, there's only one man owed the wages of sin and that's Sugar Bart and one day I'm a-going to see he's paid 'em.'

She felt cleaner after that; they both did. It was not enough, though, to help Aaron through the next stage of his hurt. Her brother had displayed considerable courage but as the pain lessened and he absorbed the extent of the permanent damage done to him, he declined into grief. It was mainly for his hair. 'I'm piebald.' It was a howl of despair.

'Och, b-barley-cakes,' shouted the doctor, exasperated, 'for why do ye think the Lord invented wigs?'

The wig was a success. Robert, who had been almost tearfully attentive throughout, produced it from Dapifer's wardrobe. Once Makepeace had lined its hessian interior with a silk handkerchief so that it would not rub the still raw flesh, Aaron put it on and was transformed. Robert clasped his hands: 'Oh, *yes*. Pale and interesting, *just* like Hamlet.'

A shirt of softest linen, a cor de soie coat and breeches were selected for the patient's first sortie to the quarterdeck. Aaron was helped up the companionway but he shrugged off assistance when he reached the deck, walking stiffly to the chair set for him under the tarpaulin next to Miss Susan Brewer. Dapifer set another for Makepeace on her opposite side, then strolled away unthanked.

Susan Brewer began a pleasant but determined questioning.

Aaron's replies were revealing. 'An Indian attack, best left unmentioned . . . and you, Miss Brewer, why do you go to England? . . . Oh, a mere actor off to seek my fortune in London's theatres.'

Makepeace's horror at the tarring and feathering had overlooked its humiliation, yet, obviously, Aaron felt it deeply. Oh, bless him. But an *actor*? In *London*? Makepeace's Puritan upbringing had trained her to regard the theatre as a form of whoring.

For a second, his glance met hers with a challenge.

She nodded back. If that particular ambition returned the spark to her brother's eye, then amen to it. Boston prejudices must remain in Boston. But she was overcome by a wave of depression; she was being sailed to a country she didn't know, didn't like and had little idea what to do when she got to it. Furthermore, she had fallen out of love with the man taking her there. It was as if the cataclysm that had overwhelmed her household had swept away with it such feeling as she'd once had for him. Mainly, she wasn't used to powerlessness; she had become his dependant and resented it.

He needn't think I'll be his doxy just because there ain't any other living for me.

Being Makepeace, she had to tell him so right away. She found him in the stern, gloomily watching the ship's wake.

'Thank you for what you've done for Aaron, Sir Philip,' she said, 'but matters ain't changed. I still won't be your mistress.'

She had his hundred guineas. Maybe she'd buy an English tavern with it, get her own boat, trade with the natives, *something*.

He seemed reluctant to leave his contemplation of the water, but eventually looked at her. 'Mistress Burke, I am your servant in everything. That particular offer, however, has been withdrawn.'

'Oh,' she said. 'That's all right then.'

He turned to watch her walk away. She'd bound her hair in a piece of sailcloth and topped it with a ragged straw hat more suitable for keeping flies out of a horse's eyes. Small wonder Susan Brewer had taken her for one of the lower orders. Well, so she was.

Dapifer shook his head. He'd suffered his own revulsion. Her hostility to him since coming aboard had been unreasonable. Here he was, burdened with sole responsibility for a bad-tempered American scarecrow and her entire entourage. He'd set her up, of course, and the family, but it was a relief to find she was holding him to nothing more.

Betty, who was plucking a chicken while sitting on the hen coop—she'd formed an alliance with the ship's cook—saw them part, two people leeched by life's unkindness. Give 'em time, she thought.

Aaron, tired from his first outing, had been taken back to his cabin by Robert. Makepeace sat herself down in his chair. Miss Brewer turned to her. 'I hope you will forgive that I mistook you, Miss Burke. I didn't know 'til Sir Pip told me you'd lost all your clothes in the riots but I said to your brother, "Sakes, she can borrow some of mine."'

Susan Brewer was dressed in glossy white lace-edged lute-string over which rampaged pink and green flowers. She could have attracted butterflies. Makepeace glanced down. Her clothes had been laundered; the hat she had borrowed from Boocock, Dr Baines's assistant, to keep the sun off. In Puritan eyes she fulfilled the requirement of cleanliness and decency. In Miss Brewer's she was a fright.

Abruptly she excused herself and went off in search of a looking-glass. A pocket mirror was supplied eventually by the invaluable Robert. She took it to her cabin and held the thing up.

After a while she put it down again. Of *course* he'd been relieved by her rejection. The way she looked now would stop clocks.

Before dinner there was a tap on Miss Brewer's cabin door . . .

'**A***gh*. Are you sure?'

'Certain,' puffed Susan, her foot on Makepeace's backside. 'I can't think how you went without one.'

'Wore my, ow, mother's. Can't breathe.'

'You're not supposed to.'

Miss Susan had accepted the challenge with enthusiasm. Makepeace had been scrubbed with soap and unguents and her head held out of the porthole to dry her hair. Now, with a nineteen-inch waist and her arms crossed in embarrassment over her breasts, she was hooped into a contraption like a fruit cage while Susan Brewer considered the next stage. 'This blue or this blue?'

'Anything.'

'That, if I may say so, is your error; you should *care*. Look at you: Aphrodite up from the waves of wherever. Such hair . . .'

The dress decided on was of deep blue and its décolletage even deeper. 'You sure?' Makepeace asked again, hoisting the front so that her feet nearly left the ground.

'Trust me.' Susan yanked it down. 'Are we or are we not out to catch the eye of a certain gentleman?'

'We ain't.'

But Miss Brewer wasn't listening. 'Only a *little* set of the cap should do it, I think, the good doctor already—'

'Dr *Baines*?'

'Certainly Dr Baines. Sir Pip apart, he's the most eligible creature on board, and he was telling me only last night he intends to find a wife and settle on land as soon as may be . . .'

Makepeace was distressed; Alexander Baines was an angel of healing but, for her, he had the sexual appeal of a bottle of physick.

She noticed that Susan did not suggest she set her cap at Dapifer. Presumably he was excluded as too aristocratic for her or because Miss Brewer was setting her own pretty headgear at him. Makepeace felt a constriction round her ribs that wasn't caused by the corset.

They had a difference of opinion over the matter of rouge. 'I ain't trying for a husband,' Makepeace insisted, appalled.

'*Every* woman's trying for a husband,' Miss Brewer said, dabbing anyway. 'There.' She handed over a fan. 'Ye-es, if only we could walk a *little* less like we were bringing the cows home.'

Arm in arm they stepped out of the cabin onto the deck and Captain Strang, emerging from his, rushed to open the door of the wardroom for them, just beating his lieutenant to it.

Makepeace found the meal unnerving. Her opinion on his ship was sought by Captain Strang, on the weather by Lieutenant Horrocks. Her plate was piled higher with pickled beef than anyone else's by the steward. Dr Baines directed the conversation so that it could display his familiarity with her. This, then, was what curls and a dab of rouge could do; men responded to the wrapping, not the content.

Only Dapifer remained aloof, though Dr Baines's tenderness did not escape his attention. He thought, Wants her, does he? And an excellent match for them both. *Dammit.*

The warm, indigo current of the Gulf Stream pushed the *Lord Percy* lazily eastwards towards the coast of Europe and the heat followed it. At night the sea was illuminated by phosphorescence, a phenomenon of such beauty that the inclination was to stay late on deck to watch it, but Makepeace would sense Dr Baines, moved by its romance, edging towards her with a proposal on his lips and was forced back to her cabin before he could make it.

'But he's so worthy, poor man,' protested Susan Brewer.

'You have him then.'

Susan shook her head in apparent sadness. 'In Dr Baines's opinion and therefore, of course, that of the Lord, I am too giddy.'

Makepeace grinned. Her life until now had lacked the friendship of a congenial young woman. They were by no means like-minded: Susan was high Tory and had been brought up without the angular Puritanism that Temperance Burke had instilled into her daughter. What they shared was not only an appreciation of female independence but a rare knowledge—Susan's from her enterprising aunt, Makepeace's from her own experience—that it was achievable. It was extraordinarily pleasant and did a good deal to recover Makepeace's equilibrium to exchange life stories, to discuss men and manners. Of the latter, Susan knew a good deal more than' Makepeace, being an avid reader of novels imported from England, especially those of Mr Richardson.

'You saved him from *drowning*? Sakes, he's *bound* to marry you.'

'Oh, very likely.'

'But he *is*. King Cophetua and the beggar-maid. He's practically a peer you know. Captain Strang said he turned down the King's offer of a dukedom as too vulgar but is mightily well connected with half the Cabinet.' Susan gave a sacrificial sigh. 'I suppose I must yield him to you now, you having saved his life and all, and creep off to fade away of unrequited passion.'

'Have him,' said Makepeace generously, 'I don't want him.'

But, after all, she found that she did. Her health was returning with rest and sea air and, with it, the realisation that the two days during which he'd been closeted at the Roaring Meg had been the most terrible yet the most wonderful of her life.

But she saw quite clearly that their relationship was now alienated beyond repair. There was nothing to be done except keep her pride intact by being as remote towards him as he was to her.

Makepeace allowed Susan's rants against the Sons of Liberty to go unrefuted. The very words echoed with Aaron's screams. But when talk in the wardroom turned to what the English government should do when it received the *Percy*'s news, that was a different matter.

'"No taxation without representation", the saucy rogues,' said Captain Strang. 'Why, your common Englishman is not represented in Parliament yet submits to being taxed and do you hear him complain?'

'I rather think I do,' Dapifer pointed out.

'That's beside the point, Sir Pip, if I may say so. The point is that the plantations must obey the will of their King and his government. Concede the vote to any agitating colonist with straw in his hair and your ploughman and cowherd at home will be demanding it too.'

'Reform, certainly,' Dapifer said.

Dr Baines said, 'Captain, ye're surely not advocating sending an army to enforce the Stamp Tax?'

'Why not?'

'Ye'd have war on your hands.'

'Why not just repeal it?' said Makepeace.

The interjection of a soprano voice into an opus for basso profundo brought only a deliberate silence in which it was supposed to consider its temerity and withdraw.

She didn't care. 'Colonist with straw in his hair . . .', she'd give him straw in his hair. 'We don't *want* it,' she said.

Even Dr Baines changed his position in order to repel female boarders. 'Aye, well, Miss Burke, we can't always have what we want.'

Only Dapifer met her as an equal. 'It was wrongly applied, I grant you, but it wasn't an unfair tax.'

'You didn't have to pay it.'

'The war with France had to be paid for.'

'It wasn't our war.'

'I thought it was a war for all Protestants. Had the French won it, their Roman Catholic compatriots in Canada would even now be swarming over the New England border. Imagine yourself under a Canadian pope—racoon mitre and bear claws. Doesn't bear thinking of.'

She imagined it and grinned—and the men at the table forgave her on the instant. Two of them made up their minds.

Dr Baines said, 'We'll not bore the young ladies with our politics. Miss Burke, will ye give me the privilege of your company on deck?'

He proffered his arm but Dapifer had beaten him to it and already proffered his. 'Tonight, sir, that privilege is mine.'

Makepeace found herself hustled through the captain's—now Dapifer's—cabin and out onto the open stern gallery. 'What are you doing?'

'Saving our good doctor from a fate worse than death. He was about to propose.'

The Boston moon she'd shared with Dapifer had been replaced by another, which, in its turn, was waning, a frail thing like the curve on a capital D. She felt an anguish for the time they had stood together in another place looking out on this sea. Why doesn't he leave me alone? She said dully, 'None of your business.'

'I rather think it is. I want you to marry me.'

Her jaw dropped and then she was so angry that she attacked him. He had to hold onto the rail to avoid falling. 'Don't you dare. You . . . you shite-poke, you—'

'Ow! A simple "No thank you" would be—'

'I don't need your pity and your marriages,' she hissed at him.

She was appalled that he should offer her charity. He'd made it clear that he no longer desired her. Now, out of some dreary sense of obligation, he was suggesting a marriage that he didn't want. Did he think she'd be grateful? *Thank you for your patronage, kind sir, I'm beholden to you?* Beholden be buggered. She was Makepeace Burke, American. She had one hundred guineas. She could stand on her own feet.

She turned to go.

'I can't help feeling,' he said, holding her back, 'I can't help feeling—stay still, woman—that we are at cross-purposes.'

'No, we ain't. You think you're beholden. Well, you ain't. I can manage. Marry you? I'd sooner marry Boocock.'

'Boocock? Is he the one with the squint?' He had hold of her fists now. 'Calm *down*.'

'Leave me alone.'

'Take a deep breath.'

She took one, and another.

'Now then,' he said. 'Do I understand that you believe my offer to be made out of gratitude and condescension? You are an extraordinary female. Most women would at least have pondered the proposal. I admit my looks may not measure up to Able Seaman Boocock's but I'm certainly richer than he is.'

'I don't want your stinking money.'

'So I gather.' He let go of her hands. 'I came to America in disgust at women, society and, most of all, at myself. There I was plucked from the briny deep by a female who was . . . well, I can only describe it as *healthy* in both mind and body. So much so that she managed to imbue me with a vigour I haven't felt for years.'

'Makes me sound like a patent medicine.' But she was coming round.

'More a tonic,' he said. 'In fact, Mistress Burke, if I may say so without offence, you give new meaning to the term "rude health". Of course, had I understood your passion for Mr Boocock I would not have offered, but I thought your inclination might lie in the direction of poor Dr Baines.'

'And what's wrong with Dr Baines?' Blast it, he always managed to amuse her.

'Nothing, nothing. An admirable consort for you—could dress his own wounds and everything. It's just that I thought you might accept him and I wanted to get in first.'

'Oh, hell,' she said, defeated. 'What d'you want to marry me for?'

'Not out of gratitude or pity, I can tell you that. The man who pities you, Makepeace Burke, will have to wear chain mail.'

'What then?' She was beginning to fill up with an unbidden, rapturous happiness. It was true she was good for him; despite his sorrow for the death of his friend, he'd clearly lost the pervading despair that had led him to want to drown. She'd done that.

'Because I was wrong in asking you to be my mistress, I see that now. There's little point in making a dishonest woman out of one of the most honest females I've ever met. I don't know how you'd go down with London society and I don't care, you go down with me. I need you, as a permanent fixture. To forgo that privilege merely because of the outworn shibboleths of prejudice would be the act of a fool.'

She said nothing, thinking of the consequences for him and for her, the launch into unchartered difficulties and whether they could survive them.

Her silence unnerved him. '*Please*, Procrustes.'

Until then he'd been assured, amusing, but there was that in his voice now which echoed with the loneliness he was going back to. Holy Hokey . . . 'Oh well,' she said, 'if it's a matter of doing you a favour.'

'I'd be obliged,' he assured her, catching her tone. 'Since making you my mistress is out of the question, marriage is the only way I can think of to get your clothes off.'

'Oh,' she said, and took in a deep, glorious breath. 'I see. Why didn't you say so? In that case, I accept.'

Captain Strang, who was authorised to perform weddings, married them the next day.

Chapter Five

IMMEDIATELY THEY'D ANCHORED in the Thames, Robert was sent ahead to prepare the staff of the London house for its master's arrival. He was rowed ashore with Captain Strang and the dispatches.

After Makepeace had thanked the crew and while her husband distributed largesse, she and Aaron stood at the taffrail with Susan Brewer to be introduced to the landmarks by Lieutenant Horrocks.

Ahead, the great span of London Bridge was outlined against a dusty, lowering sun. Opposite, a modern Custom House gleamed and the mouth of Traitors' Gate yawned at the water's edge of William the Conqueror's Tower. All around loomed a bespired, cupolaed, multiroofed skyline of such history, complexity and loftiness that it demanded obeisance from those looking on it for the first time.

'Shakespeare,' Aaron said, 'Dryden.'

'Gloriana,' Susan breathed.

'They ought to do something about these docks,' said Makepeace.

The hurry of wharfingers; squawking, scavenging seagulls; a smell of weed and sewage; the bluster of sails; boats ferrying back and forth: these were Boston again. But in a comparison of the two ports, the Pool of London, main artery of the trading world, came off worse.

Where Boston's forty or more quays provided ease of access to shipping, London itself had twenty and these were crowded side by side together between the Bridge and the Tower. All the way up from Woolwich, merchantmen had congested the river, waiting three or four abreast for lighters to unload them.

'Wait for weeks, some of 'em,' Lieutenant Horrocks said, 'by which time they can lose a quarter of their cargo from pilfering. Oh yes, you've got to keep your goods and your purse battened down in London.' He offered the information as if both his capital's beauty and its criminality were a matter of national pride. 'But don't be afraid, ladies.'

Susan, who wasn't, rewarded him with a tremulous, 'Oh my.'

Makepeace wasn't either, although she knew she should be. She was entering this ancient city as Lady Dapifer and had no idea how to fill the space encompassed by those two words. Already some of the difficulty she would encounter had been exemplified by, of all people, Dapifer's manservant. Robert had shown much kindness to her and Aaron during the bad weeks of the voyage, but the marriage brought a change. His 'And what does Lady Dapifer require?' and 'Certainly, Lady Dapifer, of course, Lady Dapifer', were issued, out of his master's hearing, with a deliberate grotesquerie of subservience which made it clear that, in his eyes, she couldn't fulfil the role and never would.

She'd actually heard him say with apparent sadness to Susan, 'Of course, the first Lady Dapifer was *such* an exquisite dresser.'

She recognised jealousy, pure and simple, but it was, she knew, a mere foretaste of the hostility and mockery awaiting her.

They had consummated the marriage ahead of time. One consensual, unstoppable, liquid move had taken them from his proposal in the stern gallery to his bed and what was officially, deliciously, still a sin. No preparation, no bridal rites, no waiting, nothing to make her tense, just an unthinking swoop into passion.

When, later, he'd asked her what her experience of losing her virginity had been, she said, 'I enjoyed myself.'

He groaned. 'You sound as if you'd been out to tea.'

But she *had* enjoyed herself and continued to do so, more and more. She'd nudged her husband-to-be in his ribs. 'And so did you.'

If there'd been a lingering suspicion that he'd married her from a sense of obligation, that night and all the subsequent nights swept it away. He loved her; she made him laugh, she made him happy; there'd been a great need in him and she fulfilled it.

They were becoming very close, not just sexually. She was discovering that he was an extremely kind man. Already, for Aaron's sake, he'd offered to set Dr Baines up in a London practice and, for Makepeace's, had invited Susan Brewer to stay with them, suggesting he buy her a year's pupillage with Madame Angloss who, he said, was the most influential adviser on fashion in England. This easy disposal of people, however, brought home to Makepeace how powerful a position Sir Philip Dapifer held and how unfitted she was as his consort. In bed in their cabin, she'd said, 'What are you going to do with me?'

'This.'

All very pleasant but later she returned to the problem. 'But what do you want me to be? What do you want me to *do*?'

'That.'

'In public?'

In the end she'd got out of bed, put on a wrap, and pursued the matter out of his physical reach. 'What I mean is, you'll be entertaining royalty and—'

'We won't be entertaining royalty.'

'Because of me?'

'Because I'm divorced. The King and Queen are strait-laced about these things.'

'Oh.' That was a relief. 'But you got society friends . . .'

'And we'll be able to tell whether they're friends or not, won't we?'

'But there's fish knives and how to address a duke . . .'

'Fish knives are definitely a problem.'

'I mean it, Pip.' For the first time she approached the nub of the business. 'Your first wife knew all this taradiddle and I don't.'

He shook his head at her. 'Procrustes, I don't care. I don't *care*.'

She crawled across the bed to hold him.

Afterwards, he said, 'Ffoulkes's opinion was the only one worth a damn and, if it's any consolation, he'd have proposed to you quicker.'

So that was all right. By the time she viewed London from the deck of the *Lord Percy* that morning, she was armoured by love.

Dapifer came up to say it was time to go. A coach was hired, luggage and Tantaquidgeon were placed on top, the rest of the party squashed inside. It was a measure of London's extraordinariness that the sight of a large Red Indian, complete with feather, sitting atop a vehicle did not attract more attention than it did.

There was no comparison with Boston here: Makepeace, peering over the head of Josh, saw pigtailed Chinese, gaberdined Jews, astrakhan-hatted Russians, an Indian robed like a maharajah and another in a loin-cloth. Negroes with slave collars, dressed like princes; free negroes in patches; beadles in tricorns; aldermen in scarlet; running footmen in wigs; two dancing bears; a snake-charmer; lawyers clutching briefs: all of them bustling about their business.

Trades came in blocks, with their stench and noises: Smithfield mooed and baaed and ran with blood; Poultry held them up to let by a flock of turkeys with their feet tarred into boots. One street seemed entirely given over to the melting of metal, another ticked with clocks.

Aaron spoke for them all. '"Behold, the half was not told me."'

Once out of the twists of the Middle Ages, the going became straighter and more genteel but just as congested, with shoppers, play-goers and carriages delivering well-dressed men to their clubs.

The coach turned north into gridlike squares of restrained elegance. 'Grosvenor Square,' Dapifer said, 'and this is Dapifer House.'

The mansion they had stopped at dominated the row on this side of the great square with a pediment and six-columned façade.

Robert came down the steps at a flurried run. He and Dapifer held a whispered conversation at the coach door; the rest of the party kept their seats. A woman appeared in the doorway, smiling, holding out her arms. 'Husband,' she called. 'Welcome home.'

It was a pretty sound and it carried. For Grosvenor Square it promised interest; heads appeared in some of the windows.

She came down the steps and stood on tiptoe in an effort to kiss Dapifer's cheek. He moved back out of the way so she continued forward to the coach and stood on its step to look in.

'I wasn't expecting so many Americans,' she said, 'but how delightful that you've brought your own totem pole with you.' To Makepeace: 'Robert's told me about *you*, my dear. *What* an interesting style of dress—and a little piccaninny on your lap, how free-*thinking*.'

'Exquisite' was the *mot juste*, pinning her delicacy and petiteness; cloudy dark hair was set off by a primrose gown, and her scent had the fleeting sweetness of bluebells. She had animal quickness with a smile of tiny, white, backward-sloping teeth.

Makepeace knew she'd been born to hate her.

'Oops. Sorry.' Makepeace had opened the carriage door so that her enemy was forced to cling on and be swung ridiculously outwards. Robert ran forward to lift his former mistress down.

'My letter with the divorce decree told you to leave this house. Leave now,' Dapifer said quietly.

'Very well, my darling. Where to?'

'Great Russell Street. I've given you Great Russell Street.'

'Thank you, dearest. Robert, run and tell Maria that Lady Dapifer wants her things. I'll sit here and wait.'

She returned to the steps and sat on them, arranging her skirt.

Dapifer addressed the coach. 'I apologise. I'm afraid I must ask you to wait here.' He didn't look at Makepeace.

A weeping maid with hatboxes put them on the steps, followed by a train of footmen with luggage. She was already packed, Makepeace thought.

Every window in the row now had heads peering out of it. Residents came out of the houses. The square had spawned people, chimney sweeps, footmen, maids. A female neighbour hurried solicitously round to the figure on the steps—'My dear, my dear'—and was waved away. The first Lady Dapifer needed no help; she was managing nicely. It was the man standing and watching, arms folded, by the hired coach and those inside it, who appeared boorish.

Makepeace felt larger and lumpier than at any time in her life. I look stupid. Tantaquidgeon looks stupid, we all look stupid. The *bitch*. It was an exercise in humiliating that touched genius.

After nearly half an hour a coach drew up. As it left the square, the two Lady Dapifers were level with each other for a moment. The first smiled.

When they were all going into the house, somebody in the crowd threw a lump of horse manure which hit Dapifer on the back of his coat.

The entrance hall was chillingly beautiful and as high as the house itself. It was lit through a glass dome roof from which hung a great glass and filigree lantern. An oval staircase, cantilevered and in marble with a wrought-iron balustrade, rose to a gallery of rooms.

Susan Brewer opened her mouth to express wonder but after the first 'Oh my', shut it again. This was not the moment.

An incredibly old, powdered footman, looking as if he'd collapse under the weight, relieved them of their wraps. A large and severe woman came forward. 'Welcome home, Sir Philip.'

'Makepeace, may I introduce Mrs Peplow, my housekeeper. Peplow, this is Lady Dapifer.'

'How de do, Mrs Peplow. Hope we ain't a bother to you.'

The housekeeper addressed Dapifer. 'With such little notice, I fear there is nothing in for dinner, Sir Philip. *Madame* was going out.'

He didn't notice the snub to Makepeace, he was struggling out of his manured coat. 'Serve whatever you're having.'

'Yes, Sir Philip. Do I assume that the darker persons in your party will be eating in the basement?'

'Tonight they will dine with us.'

'The feathered gentleman too?'

'For God's sake, Peplow. *Yes.*'

It was a gruesome meal. Dapifer barely spoke. Susan was the only one to rise to the occasion with chatter that became more maniacal as nobody joined in. The array of cutlery was bewildering. Makepeace took the bit between her teeth, a fork in her hand and followed Betty's example of using it for everything.

The only person at the table enjoying himself was young Joshua. He kept squeaking and drawing attention to details of the room: the superb coffered plaster ceiling, painted panels on the walls, the gilt-backed chairs, the statuary in their niches at the far end.

There was nothing wrong with the food. Smoked fish, pâtés, oysters, buttered shrimp, roast beef, capons, broiled mutton, pastries, flummeries . . . Makepeace caught Betty's eye: if this was what the servants ordered for themselves they were living high off the hog's haunch. If I was running this here establishment . . . It occurred to her that, as the new Lady Dapifer, she was.

Since everybody was tired, the housekeeper was ordered to show them to their rooms. Makepeace went with them, leaving Dapifer still at the table. Portraits of past Dapifers lining the staircase wall looked down their noses as they followed Mrs Peplow to the gallery. Makepeace took against them. Her own pilgrim ancestors had defied bullying by men and women of this species and, by God, so would she. Any sauce from you lot and I'll spit in your eye, she thought.

She glowered at the housekeeper's ample backside ahead of her. Yours an' all.

Actually, Peplow had done well by them. Betty and Josh had an attic room considerably better furnished than the Roaring Meg's, and so did Tantaquidgeon. Joshua, hopping from foot to foot, tugged at Makepeace's sleeve. 'Where can I piss?'

She'd been wondering the same herself. Was there a privy in the yard? If so, where was the yard? During the meal she'd been shocked when a footman opened one of the dining-room cupboards to see a chamber pot in it—a most insanitary arrangement.

Mrs Peplow pointed grimly to the underside of the bed. 'Unless, madam, you wish your people to share your water closet.'

What's a water closet? 'Oh, piss in the pot, Josh.'

They left him to it and went down to the next floor where Susan had been allocated a guest bedroom panelled in powder-blue flock matching the coroneted tester and coverlet of the bed. Miss Brewer winked at Makepeace and gave a die-away sigh. 'I guess this will have to do,' she said. Makepeace winked back. *Good girl*.

Aaron was being accommodated in equal luxury. He bade his sister good night, went into his room and then reopened the door to utter an Indian war-whoop that stiffened the housekeeper in her corsets. Makepeace grinned; her brother was back to form.

A corridor ran off the gallery. 'The family apartments, madam,' said Mrs Peplow. She opened a door. 'The Yellow Room.'

Makepeace looked in. Yellow was too crude a word for the first suggestion of dawn that some Chinese dyer had transformed into wallpaper. It smelled elusively of bluebells; it was exquisite.

'No,' Makepeace said.

'It's your room now, madam.' The woman was smirking.

'No.'

'Then I don't know where, madam. There's only the master's room further along.'

Hadn't they slept together? Or did this class keep separate beds?

'Show me.'

Dapifer's apartment had a Roman motif and could have housed the Praetorian Guard. Makepeace settled herself in its antechamber, which served as a dressing room and contained a divan. 'This'll do.'

'Very well, madam. Should you need anything more, there is a bell pull in the corner. And a bagnio through that door.' Mrs Peplow twitched her nose. 'Perhaps madam would wish to take a bath?'

The inference was she needed one. Which she did, but damned if she'd take it at this woman's instigation. 'No, I thank you.'

'As you please, madam. Shall I send your maid to assist you in undressing?'

'What maid? Oh, Betty. She ain't my maid.' Makepeace smiled at the woman—a last attempt at rapport. 'I take my own clothes off.'

'I'm sure you do, madam,' said Mrs Peplow with meaning, and went.

You sailed into that one, Makepeace Burke.

To cheer herself up, she explored, stroking materials, sniffing, opening cupboards and doors. This, then, was a water closet, a little room where you sat on a mahogany seat over a marble bowl with a hinged metal pan in its base. Makepeace studied it, then tentatively pulled at a handle which stuck out from the contraption's top. Immediately the pan tilted downwards; she glimpsed a water-filled tank below before it tilted back into its place. So that's how it worked. She saw no advantage to it—some poor soul still had to clean the pan and empty the tank.

And this door . . . here, oh Lord, here was the bagnio. A tiny double staircase led to a plinth on which stood the statue of a naked youth and from which another flight led down to a plunge bath big enough to swim in. It was a long way from a tin tub on the occasional Sunday morning in the Roaring Meg's kitchen.

As in a trance, Makepeace retreated to the dressing room and tugged the bell pull. 'I *will* bathe, Mrs Peplow, iffen you'd fetch the water.' It would be some gain to see the woman carrying buckets.

Instead there was a smile, like the Sphinx. Mrs Peplow crossed to the bagnio, bent over and did something that resulted in a rush of water and steam. 'We call it *plumbing*, madam.'

Makepeace called it the eighth wonder of the world. She was awestruck and couldn't pretend she wasn't. When the housekeeper had gone she rushed to spreadeagle herself over the side of the bath to see how it was done. Underneath each of two cunning caps shaped like dolphins was a cock, one permitting a flow of blisteringly hot water, the other cold. They'd raised water to first-floor level and heated it.

Once she'd closed off the magical water, Makepeace covered the statue's eyes with her petticoat and leaned back in soapsuds and steam to consider her position.

A sour place, England. 'Better is a dinner of herbs where love is, than a stalled ox and hatred therewith.' For all the marble and gold herewith, hatred was what she'd encountered so far. She'd expected to be looked down on by the society Dapifer moved in but she hadn't reckoned on the servants' attitude. She was suddenly racked with longing for the Roaring Meg. Hatred there, hatred here. Lord, why d'you allow so much hatred?

The water was growing cold. Makepeace wiped the tears from her eyes, found one of Dapifer's robes, and went downstairs to find him.

He was still sitting in the dining room, a decanter of port in front of him, a document in his hand. 'Where have you been?'

'Bathing. There's this bagnio upstairs, it's a wonder.'

'Yes,' he said. 'The first Lady Dapifer had it installed. Very far-sighted, the first Lady Dapifer.'

'You're drunk. 'What's her name?' she asked. 'First Lady Dapifer. What's she called?'

'Her name,' he said, 'is Catherine. Everybody calls her Catty.'

Not surprising, Makepeace thought. 'Servants and all?'

'They addressed her as Lady Dapifer.'

'Not madam?'

'Lady Dapifer.'

So that was cleared up. 'What's the matter?'

He held out the letter. 'This is from her. She's had it sent round by messenger. Quick work. She says she will be petitioning for divorce on the grounds of my bigamy.'

She tried to take it in. *'Bigamy?'*

'With you. Maintaining that she's still married to me.'

'But you divorced her.'

'Always a gamble. Legal opinion's divided on whether an American divorce pertains in this country. Fact is, my solicitor wasn't happy about it.' He was speaking with careful and remote judiciousness. 'Took the risk. More a nominal gesture—had no intention of marrying again.'

'She agreed to it, though.'

'Oh yes. Signed her permission, would comply with the decree.' His fist crashed down on the table, making its epergne and Makepeace jump. 'Never kept her word. Should've known.'

'Can she do this?'

'Ah yes. That'll be interesting. Whether an English court upholds a New England decision, whether *Parliament* upholds it. Got to be done through Parliament. Private Bill. House of Commons'll be full that day. Spectator sport, that'll be. Better than bear-baiting.'

He wasn't looking at her; he didn't want her to look at him. She thought, He's ashamed because he's been a fool. Well, he has. She said, 'She wants money, doesn't she?'

'For dropping the case? I imagine so. Given her a bloody great settlement already but she's profligate with money. In effect, this bit of paper's a demand for what I imagine will be a ruinous sum. Good case she's got now. Even if I counter petition it's only my word against hers. Ffoulkes is dead, the only other witness is dead.' Dapifer's mouth twisted. 'Robert commiserated with her on Ffoulkes's death. She laughed.'

Makepeace leaned across the table, took the letter away from him and put it out of his reach.

'"A spaniel, a woman and a walnut tree . . ." Should have beaten her but tried to spare her, y'see. Ffoulkes warned me. "She wouldn't spare you, old man. Don't turn your back on her fangs, Pip." Wouldn't listen. Made him go with me to give evidence. Killed him.'

She put her hands round his face and turned it to her. His eyes were appalled and appalling. He said, 'Drowning again, Procrustes. And this time dragging you under with me.'

'Oh no, you ain't. We're going to fight her. Pay her off and she'll only ask more. I'm your legal wife and we're going to prove it.'

'Didn't want this for you.'

She said what he'd once said to her: 'I don't care. Pip, I don't *care*. We got each other, we're going to fight her and we're going to win.'

Somehow she got him to his feet and up to bed. She sat beside him after he'd gone to sleep, as she'd done in her room at the Roaring Meg.

Ain't fair, it ain't *fair*. He's a good man. She got cross. Adultery was adultery. Why *should* Dapifer pay that corrupt little besom for sleeping with another man? All the impotent fury of her countrymen returned to Makepeace as the contempt in which they were held came to be personified in the beautifully dressed figure of one woman.

By *God*, I'll show her I'm her equal.

Not just her, either.

Carefully, so as not to wake him, she went out. In the dressing room, she rang the bell pull. Rang it again, and went on ringing it.

After a while, she heard angry feet.

'Yes, madam?' Mrs Peplow was in a flannel nightgown and curlpapers.

'Yes, Lady Dapifer,' Makepeace said.

'Eh?'

'Say it.'

Mumble.

'Bit louder.'

'Yes, Lady Dapifer.'

'You remember it. That's all, Mrs Peplow. Good night.'

The second Lady Dapifer had gone to war.

Chapter Six

ON ENTERING THE SALON, Madame Angloss gave a dramatic stagger. '*Mon dieu, quelle rousse. Qu'est-ce qu'on peut faire?*'

Left to herself, Makepeace would have given the job of choosing her wardrobe to Susan Brewer but Dapifer had said no. 'Too provincial yet. Give her a year with Madame Angloss and then we'll see.'

Susan's pupillage had already begun and her obsequiousness to Madame Angloss suggested she was happy. 'Sakes, she's the tsarina of *haute couture*,' Susan said when Makepeace had wondered whether she did not object to being ordered about like a dog.

Susan and a depressed-looking seamstress were now running back and forth to the entrance hall where hatboxes, dress boxes, shoe boxes, wicker hoop cages, materials, ribbons, lace, were being delivered. The matter was urgent. Makepeace could not appear in public until she was suitably dressed. It had been a bone of contention between her and her husband that she should appear at all. 'I ain't a public person.'

'What are you going to do? Rattle in a closet like a skeleton? I'm not ashamed of you.' He'd recovered his self-possession.

'But ain't we *persona non* whatsit?'

'That's at court. But the court is not society, in fact the two are inimical, Their Majesties being undoubtedly worthy but undoubtedly dull. I think you'll discover that there are still some among the powerful eager to make your acquaintance.'

'Glad to hear it.' But privately she thought, They ain't falling over themselves. (So far not one invitation had been delivered to Dapifer House.) Even next door don't talk to me.

Accustomed to a community that chatted over the yard fence, the silence of her neighbours was thunderous in Makepeace's ears. At least, it was silence only as it extended to her; actually, the Judds on her left were a noisy family with an apparently inexhaustible supply of leather-lunged children. To hear their play over the wall accentuated her own exclusion and it broke her heart to watch Josh listening to it as he wandered alone in the Dapifer back garden.

Dapifer said that Sir Benjamin Judd, a Birmingham manufacturer made rich by the Seven Years' War, was too unsure of his own social position to risk bolstering Makepeace's. So, nothing for it but to be ready for invitations when they arrived from elsewhere—if they ever did. Hence Madame Angloss.

'Yes, I apologise for my wife's hair, madame,' Dapifer said, leaving the room. 'A sore trial. No point in hiding it, though; you know my opinion on heads. Excuse me.' He went out.

What *were* heads? And how did this female know his opinion on them?

Blast him, Makepeace thought, Madame Angloss dressed his wife.

He'd already been amazingly casual on this matter. 'What's wrong with the Yellow Room?'

'It was hers.'

'We'll have it changed then.'

Immediately there was Signor D'Amelia, tall, sinuous and, it appeared, to rooms what Madame Angloss was to fashion.

'What is your inclination, dear lady?' Not, his expression added, that it mattered; he was the artist.

She was lost. 'Clean, I guess, and no fleas.'

She could have said nothing better, it seemed. Signor D'Amelia spread the word that the second Lady Dapifer was a wit.

D'Amelia's sketches were lovely: a restrained freshness of pearl-grey plaster panels picked out in white, and white pieces by Sheraton. 'I see purity, *purity*, lady, only the colour of your hair to blaze it.'

Madame Angloss was seeing purity as well. 'Line,' she said, pointing at Makepeace but addressing Susan, 'line is everysing. We follow client, not fashion—I spit me of fashion. *La mode* is what I say it is. What is it we 'ave here?'

'Hair?' ventured Susan.

Madame Angloss made a 'taa' with her teeth; hair was obvious. 'Skin,' she said, dragging Makepeace's bodice down, '*boules de neige*.' She patted Makepeace's head: 'Height.' Then Makepeace's cheek: '*Voici la dame posée, bien sérieusement*. Not a furbelow will I have, no *falbalas*. Nothing *jolie* for zis one. Pretty? I spit on it.'

'Absolutely right, madame,' said Susan. Makepeace sighed.

The preliminary sketches were of breathtaking, simple, sweeping elegance. Low, uncluttered necklines, tight sleeves over a plain cuff instead of the usual shower of lace, less emphasis on pannier hips and more on the bustle. 'I create a new 'oop for the world.'

Oatmeals, greys, donkey, olives and fawns highlighted the cream-white chalk with which Madame Angloss represented Makepeace's skin. Caps—the 'heads'—were almost an insult to the word, tiny strips or mere filets on a simple chignon.

'For ze daytime. For ze evenings . . .' Grape-dark purples, leonine tawny, bronzes—a stand-up-and-fight challenge to an era of pastels.

'You . . . I'll be *noticed*,' protested Makepeace.

For the first time, Madame Angloss addressed her directly. 'Madame, you are in a situation zat is noticeable all ways. Be ze mouse and zey laugh, ha-ha. Show panache and zey are angry, ooh-hoo, but I tell you, wiz zees creations in two months all ladies scream to wear what you wear.'

Makepeace looked at her carefully. '*All* ladies?'

Madame Angloss's lips curved very slightly. 'All.'

'Go ahead.'

They had a scuffle over the riding habit.

'I cain't ride.'

'And what has that to do wiz it? Brewer, fetch ze 'abit we take to

Marchioness Londonderry.' Madame Angloss's point was that a riding habit enabled Makepeace to wear black, a colour otherwise reserved for funerals. 'An' zat hair was made for black.'

So much was apparent when Makepeace, still protesting, was put in the Marchioness's habit and looked at herself in the pier-glass.

A silence, then Susan said, 'Guess you better take up riding.'

Makepeace released her breath. 'Guess I had.'

The sound of wheels stopping at the house took her and Susan to the window. A man was being bowed out of a carriage.

'D'you know him?'

Madame Angloss from behind them said, 'It is Lord Rockingham.'

'He . . . but he . . .' The man who had replaced Grenville as Prime Minister was calling on—not summoning, but *calling on*—her husband.

'Now, madame, may I recommend . . .' The consultation continued until a footman appeared to say her husband required her presence.

Dapifer wet his lips on seeing his wife. 'Where's the horse?'

'Left it in the parlour.'

'Your lordship, may I present my wife? Makepeace, the Marquis of Rockingham.'

'The pleasure is mine, Lady Dapifer.' He was surprisingly young, mid-thirtyish, and with all the attraction of power, riches and a good tailor. Dapifer had said he was on the side of the angels, which meant that he was a Whig and a liberal Whig.

'You want something to drink, your lordship?' Makepeace asked, trying hard. 'Tea? Brandy?' She explained kindly, 'The footman gets it.'

'Thank you, no. This is a flying and very surreptitious visit. Lady Dapifer, as an American your views on the situation in our esteemed colony would be valuable. Your husband tells me you believe the Stamp Act should be repealed?'

'It surely should.'

'So do I. There are . . . *elements*, however, who will oppose a repeal tooth and nail, thinking it would be regarded as weakness.'

'Ain't weakness to admit a mistake, that's strength.' She leaned forward to tap his knee. 'Your lordship, we got "elements" too and you gave 'em their chance to turn nasty, with all your Acts taking away our work, taxing us, telling us what to do in our own land. We'd trade with you happy enough iffen you just stop telling us how.'

The marquis said, 'And Sam Adams?'

She was enchanted that he knew the name, and smiled. 'You listen to Sam Adams more and a darn sight less to Lieutenant Governor Hutchinson and we'll all do just fine.'

Dazzled, Rockingham asked, 'And *iffen* we don't?'

Her smile faded. 'You got a revolution on your hands. It's war. And I don't see how you can win—not against a whole continent.'

'I don't either.' He got up, his face suddenly older. 'Thank you, Lady Dapifer.' He turned to Dapifer. 'And how is young Ffoulkes?'

'Stoical.' The day after their arrival in England, Dapifer had travelled to Eton to see his ward.

On the way out the marquis kissed her hand. To Dapifer, he said, 'Well, Pip, your sibyl is not only beautiful, she is honest and wise.'

'Thank you, Charles. I know.'

They stood together on the steps to watch the carriage pull away. '*Sybil?*' Makepeace said. 'Ain't good on names, is he?'

The purpose of the call had been to ask Dapifer to go secretly to Bath, there to persuade Mr William Pitt to attend the House of Commons and speak for the repeal of the Stamp Act.

'But why you? You ain't in Parliament.'

'I am what Aaron's friends in the theatre would call a behind-the-scenes man. Rockingham knows that Mr Pitt, though gouty and sulking in his tent at the moment, trusts me. And I am a persuasive fellow.'

'Don't I know it.' She was proud of him.

Dapifer was to be away at least a week. Since Robert was accompanying his master, Susan would be following the peripatetic Madame Angloss about her business and Aaron, to his joy, was about to join a London acting company, it meant that Makepeace must be left in authority at Dapifer House without allies other than Betty, Josh and Tantaquidgeon.

Word that she'd taught Mrs Peplow a lesson had spread and the servants now treated her civilly, if with a coldness that stopped just short of insolence. Their resentment, she saw, was because she was an interloper of no higher class than their own.

Given a free hand, she would have dismissed the lot, but the Dapifers were an old and traditionalist family, their servants nearly all men and women who'd inherited their posts from a mother or father who had inherited theirs. Makepeace considered it a system that had led to laziness and corruption, but Dapifer refused to let her change it.

The household accounts were alarming. Jack, the decrepit senior footman, had already retired on a Dapifer pension but, returning to work, now received pension *and* wages plus two new uniforms a year. 'But why's he need a powder allowance? His hair's white already.'

'Procrustes, if you wish to make economies, do. But we've trouble enough with America without you stirring up revolution at home.'

When Dapifer had gone, she began to do it, poring over the accounts with Betty. Makepeace had hoped her old nurse could assume her former occupation in the Dapifer kitchens but Betty had taken one look at the enormous charcoal range, the wet and dry larders, copper fountains, ice moulds, dripper, hastener, mills, had studied the menus of previous banquets—'A man-of-war made of pasteboard to float on a great charger in a sea of salt to have trains of gunpowder to fire at eggshell boats filled with confection and rosewater'—and confessed herself beaten. 'That ain't cookin', that's archi'ture and I cain't do it.'

What Betty didn't say anything about—it was Joshua who told Makepeace—was the hostility of the cook and her staff. 'She said she di'n't want Ma's dirty black carcass in her kitchen.'

Raging, Makepeace had set off but Betty pulled her back. 'Leave it, gal. Sir Pip's got troubles enough. Let's bide our time.'

'All right, but they ain't swilling like hogs while we're biding. Look here, three dozen larks. You eaten a lark since we been here? I ain't.'

At least she could put Betty in charge of victualling the household—and did. Butchers, grocers and wine merchants who had supplied the Dapifers for generations suddenly found their bills questioned. If the answers were not satisfactory, Betty found new tradesmen who were eager to supply Dapifer House at more competitive rates.

The new stringency led to a formidable deputation of protest consisting of Mrs Peplow and the cook, Mrs Francanelli.

'When His late Majesty visited unexpected in '59,' Mrs Francanelli declared, 'I had the wherewithal to serve dinner as'd suit a emperor . . . twenty dishes a course, finishin' with my special fantasy, Transparent Puddin' with Silver Webb—'

'Famous, Mrs Francanelli's fantasies are,' Mrs Peplow interjected.

'Ain't they just,' Makepeace said. The woman had been over-ordering and selling off the surplus. 'Well, the new King ain't calling, ladies, so get used to it.' Household frigidity increased but the bills went down.

With Betty busily employed, Makepeace took on a personal maid; Catty Dapifer had taken hers with her. She promoted young Fanny Cobb from the scullery because she didn't sneer. Dapifer had discovered the child begging on the streets and broken with tradition by giving her a place in the household where, though she suffered as an outsider, she did it on a full belly.

Fanny's two years in the scullery had given her no reason to feel loyalty for the rest of the staff, but she had a great deal for her master and new mistress. Her knowledge of toiletry was negligible but, by using her Cockney acumen and poring over illustrations in *The Ladies' Pocket*

Book, she began to hook her mistress into her clothes more or less correctly—it couldn't be done by the wearer alone—and make a passable job of dressing her hair.

Strangely, the only American who fitted a niche in Dapifer House was Tantaquidgeon. He'd taken a liking to a wall-hanging embroidered with dragons and wore it in place of his blanket. In this, a pair of breeches, and smeared with a pomade Dapifer had given him to replace the bear's grease, he'd begun to stand on the back of the carriage when Dapifer went out. Dapifer said he discouraged footpads.

Soon there was to be an excursion to collect Lord Ffoulkes's young son from school and take him to the Dapifers' ancestral manor in Hertfordshire for the Christmas holidays. 'I think you'll like Hertfordshire,' Dapifer said. Makepeace was prepared to, and she was looking forward to mothering the orphaned little baron. With no work other than to check the accounts and make herself pretty, Makepeace found herself idle for the first time in her life, and her hands twitched for gainful occupation.

She and Betty took to going for walks in Hyde Park with Josh or Tantaquidgeon. There was always something new to discover: a little wooden lodge of a Cake House where they bought cheesecake or a mince pie and washed it down with a mug of milk warm from the cow. There were skiffs on the Serpentine and an engine house where horses turned the mill that pumped water to Chelsea.

Once, in early morning, they were stopped from approaching too close to a clearing in an oak grove by a gentleman who told them there was a duel in progress. On another occasion they had to run out of the way of a four-in-hand, driven by a hatless man with a pretty female passenger, which came careering towards them across the grass. The woman's shout floated back to them: 'Faster, faster, Sidney. Make 'em jump.' They'd heard the voice before.

'That was her, wa'n't it?' asked Betty, brushing herself down. 'She tryin' to kill you?'

'She didn't know it was me; she don't care who she kills.'

There was an elderly woman who set up an apple stall every morning and who was ejected every afternoon, swearing loudly, when the park's beadles made their rounds. Another thorn in the side of the beadles was the sellers of pamphlets and scandal sheets. Makepeace was acquainted with political pamphlets—they'd been a powerful weapon in the hands of Sam Adams—but scandal sheets were new to her. She bought one, the *North Briton*, which seemed both political and scandalous, and carried it home to Dapifer. 'Are they allowed to write this about Lord Bute and the Princess Dowager? 'Tis very rude. Do they . . . ?'

'Probably not. Wilkes is an irreverent rake who enjoys stinging his opponents any way he can. Oh, come on, Procrustes—even you must have heard of John Wilkes.'

'"Wilkes and Liberty"? That trouble the other day?' There had been riots over the import of foreign silks that was ruining London weavers.

'That's the one. Actually Wilkes is in France, saying that the establishment is trying to kill him, but his name has become synonymous with protest against the government.'

'Is he against the Stamp Tax?'

'He is.'

She left the room a Wilkes supporter.

When they set out for Hyde Park the next morning, it was the first occasion she wore one of Madame Angloss's designs outdoors. It was a walking dress, almost a coat, of dark blue velvet with white linen peeping from deep, masculine revers and cuffs. The brim of her matching hat swept up daringly over one ear. Fashions in the park were still fussy, the only change of the season belonging to the head, where hair was rising like dough in an adornment of feathers and lace. The severity of her own ensemble, by comparison, would command attention. And deserves to, she thought, looking in the pier-glass.

However, even Tantaquidgeon attracted a few stares as they went into Hyde Park today because their entrance coincided with the exit from it of the man with the umbrella. He was one of the sights of the West End, invariably accompanied by a fascinated crowd which, deciding he must be a foreigner and therefore probably homosexual, minced along behind him. He had the moral courage not to abandon what Makepeace, who hadn't seen an umbrella before either, thought a strange but sensible precaution against English weather.

Passing the stall where she'd bought the *North Briton* the previous day, Makepeace awarded the young pamphlet-seller a we-Wilkesites-must-stick-together smile without receiving one in return. He was not a prepossessing object, being pasty-faced, badly dressed and scowling.

They had reached the duelling grove when a grunt from Tantaquidgeon made them look behind. A figure was running towards them, hampered by a board under one arm and a sack in the other hand. 'That paper fella, ain't it?' Betty said.

It was—and frightened. As they watched, he dropped his table and ran on. They could hear the pursuit: ' . . . in the name of the Law.'

It was Boston again, excise men after innocent smuggler. Makepeace signalled the man to come in her direction. The young man doubled back, crouching, and hurled himself and his sack among the tree roots behind Makepeace like a rabbit into its burrow. Makepeace felt the back of her skirt lift; the man had crawled underneath it. 'Keep still, blast you.' She pushed back her cloak so that the excise-men could see the quality of her dress and hat.

There were two of them. 'Where'd he go, ma'am?'

She pointed deeper into the grove. 'That way. What'd he do?'

'Libel.'

Court bailiffs, then, not excise. But all against liberty. Satisfied with her blow for freedom, she waited until the sound of running feet had diminished to nothing, then moved forward and round in order to receive the young man's tearful thanks.

He wasn't offering any. Horrified, she saw that instead of crouching beneath her skirt he had crawled in face up. He still lay on his back, blinking. 'Never saw a red quim before,' he said.

For a moment, she couldn't think that she'd heard what she'd heard. He'd . . . 'You dirty little shite-hawk.' She kicked him in the side and he rolled over, whimpering. 'You worm, you peeper.'

Tantaquidgeon, seeing her anger, placed his moccasined foot on the young man's none-too-clean neck.

'Ow! Get that heaving great Huron off me.'

Makepeace teetered in the act of kicking. 'How'd you know he's a Huron?'

'Bigwigs ain't got a monopoly on education. He's got the haircut. Right feather, too. You American?'

'And a good job for you I am, you sneaking little turd. I saved your fat from frying, hokey knows why. What's your name?'

'John Beasley. What's yours?'

'Cut off, Beasley. I ever see you again, I'll have you charged.'

Betty had been picking up the sack and some of the papers that had spilled out of it. 'Better see this first, girl.'

Makepeace took the printed sheet. It was a cartoon in which two women were battling next to a street sign bearing the legend 'Grosvenor Square'. One of the figures held a raised tomahawk with a banner streaming from her mouth reading: 'He's MY husband, Lady Dapifer.' The other was saying: 'Help! Help! MY husband, Lady Dapifer.'

'Oh God. That's *me*.' This filth was being circulated, people would see it, laugh at it. 'Who printed this?'

'Me.' He was proud of it. 'My new paper, I'm calling it *The Passenger*. To be read on coaches and such. What d'you think?'

'Who told you about this?'

'Sorry. I can't reveal my sources. It's in the public domain anyway. If that's *you*'—he put a long-nailed and grubby finger on the female with the tomahawk—'*she's* just started an action in the church courts against *him* for aggravated adultery. That's bigamy if you didn't know.'

For the first time Makepeace saw the full extent of what was to come. This nightmare beside her had not only looked up her skirt, he was lifting it for the public's amusement.

Beasley said, 'You want to publish your version of it?'

She shook her head. 'Go away.'

'Ought to. Important, the printed word. I'll call, shall I?'

'Young fella,' Betty said, 'you come near us again an' this here Indian's goin' to take your scalp off an' wear it.'

Beasley nodded and took the sack from her. As he slouched away he thrust his card into Makepeace's hand. Had Makepeace known it, a gun as big as Lord Rockingham had just been added to her future armoury. At that moment, however, she'd have shot him with it.

Another outcome of that day was that she ordered Madame Angloss to design something which neither she nor, as far as she knew, any woman had worn before: a pair of short pantaloons to encase the thighs and the part between.

Just before they left for Hertfordshire, Dapifer took her down to Wapping to await the arrival of a ship bringing a secret gift he had ordered for her. 'I trust you'll approve.'

They sat on the rickety balcony of the Anchor, where an easterly wind brought the smell of sea from the estuary. Boats circumvented the tangle of hulls to land sailors and goods ashore.

'Miss it?' Dapifer asked.

'A bit.' She daren't tell him how much. 'Pip, there's the *Lord Percy*.'

'She's returning to the West Indies. Calling in at Boston first. May I present Captain Dobbs? He brought you your present.'

She thanked a middle-aged naval captain, though he appeared empty-handed. 'Mighty kind of you, sir.'

'A pleasure, ma'am. If you look down there, Lady Dapifer, my jolly is about to unload it.'

A boatload of sailors, wearing the divided calico petticoat of ratings, was clambering up a ladder to the dockside. 'They don't look happy,' Makepeace said.

'They'll be happier in a minute,' Captain Dobbs said, 'when I tell 'em they're discharged and going home.'

And then she knew what the present was.

Matthew Bell—he was the least changed—Laurie Crumpacker . . . all the *Gideon*'s crew. And there he was, the fluttering ribbons on his hat unsuitable to the granite dignity his face always kept.

Captain Dobbs was saying to Dapifer: ' . . . a fine seaman, Busgutt, but always admonishing me as if I were a heathen.'

'Do you want go down, Makepeace?'

She managed to shake her head. What could she say to him?

The tears plopping onto her face dried cold in the wind as she watched them scramble up the nets over the *Percy*'s side. She felt for her husband's hand. 'Thank you,' she said.

'Wish you were going with them?'

'No,' she said, 'I'm already home.'

Chapter Seven

IT WAS A LANDSCAPE out of Bruegel, brown figures following a plough, white earth livid against a bleak, grey sky. The horses' hoofs made muffled squeaks on the snow as the coach turned to go through an ancient archway and ploughed along a village street.

They turned in through open ironwork gates to begin the drag uphill between two lines of sweet chestnut trees, past a small church and cemetery, to the top and the manor called Dapifers.

The modest keep Eudo Dapifer, steward to Henry I, had built on this Hertfordshire hilltop had been patched and recrenellated for the War of the Roses and again when Roundheads and Royalists battled across the surrounding countryside. A fifteenth-century Dapifer had attached a hall to which an Elizabethan descendant had added a turret with a cupola. His Jacobean heir had waded in with an Italian garden and a stable block. The house spread along the crest of its hill as artless and untidy as the River Drift meandering through the valley below it.

Catty Dapifer had disliked the place; too bucolic.

That day, with its firelit windows and the snow rounding its roofs, it blinked down at Makepeace like a line of huddled, wide-eyed owls on a branch, and she loved it; this was deep, deep countryside, biting air tinged with earth and manure, the Middle Ages of her ancestors. But she looked doubtfully across at the child on the seat opposite her. 'I hope it won't be too quiet here for you, my lord.'

Lord Ffoulkes said with some energy, 'I hope not, ma'am.' He was a round-faced, sturdy little boy with lamentably ginger hair.

'Don't worry, Andrew,' Dapifer said. 'At Dapifers we celebrate Yuletide until it surrenders. We shall *not* be quiet.'

Makepeace suppressed an 'Oh dear'. Popish practices.

As it turned out, Christmas at Dapifers was not popish, it was pagan, as much to do with ancient invocations for the return of the sun as it was with Christ made flesh. And Makepeace was too busy with the preparations to worry about it. A list of her duties compiled by Mrs Bygrave, Dapifers's housekeeper, was mountainous.

Makepeace went to challenge her husband with it. 'Thirty-eight silver spoons? Why?'

'Each adult on the demesne gets one every Christmas. Tradition. Gratitude for saving their Dapifer lord in the Stephen and Matilda war.'

'When was that?'

'During the 1140s. And don't forget the bean in the plum cake for the Lord of Misrule. Oh, and the wassail bowl is kept in the church vestry, tell Simmonds to get it out. The orchard needs to be thoroughly wassailed or the apples won't grow next year.'

She groaned. 'Goody Busgutt would report us to the magistrates.'

'She should see us burying the Corn Dolly. Have the dinner invitations gone out?'

'Yes.' She looked at her list. '*Two* cows? Who're we feeding? The whole damn county? Suppose they won't come because of me?'

'They'll come. Around here you don't offend a Dapifer, however many wives he's got. Sir Toby, for instance, is the local Member of Parliament, a Whig, his seat's in my pocket and he does what I tell him. He likes Forc'd Cabbage Surprise with his meat.'

Sir Toby and Lady Tyler. Top table. 'I know. Mrs Bygrave said. The surprise is how long it takes to bloody make.' She leaned across the escritoire. 'You're doing this deliberately, ain't you?'

'You said you lacked employment,' he said sadly. 'I'm giving you employment. Lock the door.'

'I ain't got time.'

'Lock the damn door.'

They made love on the threadbare Persian carpet in front of the fire. 'I understand they refer to you as "missus". A compliment.'

'What did they call *her*?'

'"My lady".'

The hall echoed with calls from ladders as greenery was hung, the back yard with the bellows of animals unappreciative of having their throats cut in a good cause.

One morning she found Sam the pigman having the blood from his nose stanched by Fanny Cobb and the blacksmith, Edgar Croft.

'Only lifted Betty's petticoats, didn't he,' Fanny told her.

'Wanted to see if she were liquorice all a way down, tha's all,' Sam said.

Betty was grinning. 'Felt my liquorice fist instead.'

There was a general air of relaxation. The village faces had a stoniness which, Makepeace was learning, in Hertfordshire passed for laughing. She took in a breath of relief. They'd melded. She nudged Betty. 'Told you to wear drawers.'

Two days later, Makepeace, furious because she'd been frightened, faced two small, shivering, blanketed boys. 'You varmints. I *told* you the ice wasn't thick enough, didn't I tell you? You stay off that damn lake till I say it's safe—I know about water.'

'Yes, Miss 'Peace.' That was Josh.

Lord Ffoulkes stared her out. 'Josh says you can sail a boat.'

'And you're sailing to bed this minute.'

But there was something there and when she'd stopped shaking she went up to his room. She lay down next to him, carefully staring up at the ceiling. 'What's this about sailing?' At least his father's death hadn't given him a horror of the sea.

'I want to learn. I want to sail to America.'

'Surely. I'll teach you. But why?'

'My father's there.'

She said quietly, 'You know he drowned, Andrew. You went to his memorial service.' Dapifer said the child had stood it like a guardsman.

She watched his grubby little hand tighten. ' . . . goodbye.'

'What?' She leaned over him.

'I didn't say goodbye.'

Perhaps a goodbye couldn't be said in Westminster Abbey among pomp and dignitaries and bloody incense.

She clenched her teeth against an old, childhood agony; they hadn't let her say goodbye to her mother, either. Lord, let me help him. All she could do was tell him what she'd once told Dapifer, how quick it must have been . . . She ended, 'But that's one good thing, it was the same sea the Thames goes into. Souls don't have any difficulty navigating the Atlantic. How about when we get back to London you and me sail down the Thames to the estuary and give it some flowers for your pa?'

She'd done the same thing when her father died, to help float his soul back to Ireland. Goody Busgutt had called her a heathen.

'Will he see them?'

'He surely will.' She added with difficulty, 'No need to say goodbye, neither. You and him ain't finished just because he drowned.'

The boy turned to her and she put her arms round him.

Aaron and Susan arrived from London on the day before the dinner at Dapifers for the local dignitaries. They brought with them a copy of the latest scandal sheet, *Picknicks*.

'Susan didn't want you to see it,' Aaron said, 'but I reckoned you'd better. The item's short but it's dirty.'

> The woman Sir Philip Dapifer now parades as his wife is reported lately to have been serving ale in New England. A tavern wench, Sir Pip? The original Lady Dapifer has entered a suit in the Court of Arches against him, alleging his criminal conversation with this person.

Catty Dapifer was finding her range.

Dapifer pulled the paper from her hand. 'Not worth bothering with.'

'Excuse me, but I think it is.' Aaron, usually in agreement with his brother-in-law's every word, was standing up to him. 'This needs action, Pip. People are ingesting this poison. You've *got* to counter it.'

Susan said, 'And forgive me, Sir Pip, but we all know who's doing the poisoning. It's the talk of the drawing rooms.'

'I appreciate your concern, my dears,' Dapifer said, 'but a libel suit would merely compound the frenzy. And now excuse me. Lord Ffoulkes, Josh and I have an appointment to build a snowman.'

The three of them watched him go. 'Too good for this wicked world,' Aaron said.

'Well, I ain't,' Makepeace said. 'I'll give that Jezebel "tavern wench". Me and my friend John Beasley, we'll splatter her over the sidewalk.' A sudden alarm made her grimace. 'Was it on sale in Hertford?'

Aaron nodded. 'We picked it up at the stage inn.'

It was apparent the next night that copies of *Picknicks* had circulated with speed among the manors and farms of Hertfordshire. Makepeace, standing with her husband in the great hall, could see snow-bespattered cloaks being flung without regard onto the poor footmen as their owners' eyes hunted for the first glimpse of Sir Philip's tavern wench.

Some, hoping for a harlot in full garish fig, showed disappointment as they lighted on her. Others, equally expectant, rejected her as improbable and hunted elsewhere. Still others looked relieved—and these she marked down as people bearing goodwill to the House of Dapifer.

Susan had dressed her carefully for the occasion: they went for simplicity, a closed, olive-green velvet gown, its bodice trimmed round the wide neck with gold-embroidered white linen that ran to a point over the stomacher, matching her cap. Guests with an eye for cloth and cut were not fooled but Sir Toby Tyler MP, guest of honour, was deceived into thinking her ensemble unsophisticated and, from the kindness of his heart, reassured her.

'See, my dear'—this was to his wife during their introduction—'Lady Dapifer has no need to run after the vogue to look pretty, nor to cost her husband a fortune in pursuit of it.'

'I'm going to kill him,' muttered Makepeace.

'You'll have to stand behind Lady Tyler,' Dapifer muttered back.

She had splurged on candles in an effort to warm the hall, with little effect; outside the direct radius of heat from the great fireplace it was arctic. But at dinner the tables sparkled with reflecting crystal and silver as brightly as the guests' eyes at the food.

The footmen—Edgar and Sam had also been co-opted into livery and floured wigs—trotted like horses on a training rein between kitchen and hall with covered chargers of dishes: turkey, capon, roast beef, mutton, pork, stews. Makepeace had thought a hundred stomachs could not accommodate so much meat. She was wrong. Vegetable dishes had to be served individually, there being no room for them on the board. Wine sank in the glasses like water into sand.

When the tables were cleared, the small orchestra hired for the occasion took up its position on the dais for the dancing. And here was Sir Toby again, wonderful man, bowing, puffing and indefatigable, asking her to lead the first set with him. It had been anticipated that he would and the orchestra had instructions to begin with a gavotte, which was as far as Makepeace's dancing lessons had yet taken her.

She managed to prance through the quadruple metres before escaping to devote herself to those sitting out. There were still icicles to be thawed, especially among the elderly.

Assisting the relict of a cloth merchant to a glass of mulled punch, she was told acidly, 'I suppose you're used to serving drink, young woman.' Mrs Higgs, who now ran her husband's company, had once met Queen Anne and therefore considered herself entitled to speak her mind.

'I surely am. Being a tavern-owner, I didn't expect my staff to do what I couldn't. As a businesswoman, Mrs Higgs, you'll understand that.'

'Oh, you *owned* the tavern.' That was better. It wouldn't have done for the nobility but it warmed the representatives of a society interlinked with trade. Mrs Higgs was later heard to remark that Makepeace Dapifer might not have breeding 'like t'other one, but she's more our style, a good, plain girl with a head on her shoulders'.

She was invited to dance again, this time by Dapifer's agent, Peter Little. 'Is this a gavotte?' Makepeace had a tin ear for music.

'A minuet, I believe.'

'Ain't learned that one yet.' She looked around; the festivities had achieved their own impetus, she wouldn't be missed for a minute or two. 'Let's get acquainted.' They went up to the minstrels' gallery and leaned on the fretted balcony to watch the swirl below. 'See,' she said, 'I need to go round the place, learn about it.'

'Really . . . well, do you hunt, Lady Dapifer?'

'No.'

'Then perhaps . . . There's a meet after Christmas. While everyone else is chasing the fox, perhaps you would accompany me in the trap and we could do the rounds.'

They stayed on a while; the scene in the hall was worth lingering over: a blazing tableau of light and colour. Aldermanic stomachs bounced, breasts bobbed, sweat ran, coiffures uncurled.

Heat created by energetic bodies rose up to the gallery and Makepeace found herself oddly moved, as if she had opened an interior door of an unwelcoming house and been confronted by the glow of a good fire. How irritating these people were and how unexpected. The men and women below had a rough humanity their ruling class did not; here, in its greed and good humour, was the England that built empires.

She and Dapifer stood in the doorway for the farewells, invitations to cards, to suppers, to balls, falling on them like the snowflakes that blurred the light spilling out into the speckled darkness.

As the lanterns of the last carriages disappeared among the ghostly trees of the drive, Dapifer said, 'Well done, Procrustes.'

They hailed the Yule Log. They obeyed the Lord of Misrule. They buried the Corn Dolly. They went through night-time orchards carrying flares, a fiddle struck up and they sang:

'Old apple tree, old apple tree,
We wassail thee, hoping thou wilt bear,
For the Lord doth know where we shall be
When apples come another year.'

They discharged a volley from their flintlocks to waken the god of the apple tree from winter slumber and went back to the house and drank lamb's-wool from the wassail bowl.

Popish, pagan, polytheist, whatever it was, as she knelt in the freezing little church Makepeace knew she was as close to the stable in Bethlehem as she ever had been or probably would be. Her periods were as regular as the moon; now, for the first time since puberty, she had missed one.

The shire turned out again for the meet, splendid in hunting pink and black, the horses jostling on the manor's front apron and so big she had to stand on tiptoe to present the stirrup cup to their riders.

They tantivied away and the air was left to the cawing of rooks. Peter Little drew up in his trap. He and Makepeace set off down the valley. Makepeace was shown the village's strip fields, pigsties, cow byres, sheepfolds, most of them emptied by the annual winter slaughter.

Peter Little shook his head over them. 'It's inefficient, that's what it is,' he said. 'We should be keeping the beasts alive during the winter with root crops. I could double our production of wheat as well.'

'How?'

He swung his hand in a generous arc. 'Enclosure. Those woods should be cleared and the common should be fenced for arable land.'

The subject of enclosure was the talk of the day. Some of the neighbouring landowners had already applied to Parliament for the passing of an Act that would allow them to fence in their common land. To them it meant better production that would benefit the country by cheaper corn, fresh meat all the year round and general stability of the food market. And themselves, of course. But to the villagers, who pastured their cow on the common, fished its streams, used its firewood, enclosure meant dispossession. Already processions of displaced families were leaving homes they had occupied for centuries to seek work in the towns. It was the passing of an age.

'And Dapifers will pass as well,' Little said. 'I tell you, Lady Dapifer, we either advance out of the Middle Ages or go under.'

She was alive to that now. 'What does Sir Pip say?' she asked.

'He says the villagers have the same rights to the land that he has, they've been on it as long.'

'He would.' It was typical, lovable, of her husband that he should hold fast to his people and the ancient, ramshackle economy that kept their lives turning. It was also irritating. Her business instinct recoiled at inefficiency. She broached the subject a few days later as she and Dapifer took a walk down the avenue through trees as still and as white as statuary. 'Peter Little said the big estates either enclose or go under.'

'I know.' He surprised her. '*Fugit inreparabile tempus*. Irretrievable time is flying. But we'd be taking the land my people, *those* people'—he looked towards the village—'have occupied for six hundred years. We'd have to compensate them hugely, then there's the investment necessary for the new cultivation.'

'I thought you was rich,' Makepeace said. 'It's why I married you.'

'I wondered what the reason was. But the wealth arises from income, not capital. I shall need such capital as I've got.' He hesitated and then said, 'I meant to tell you. I've decided to pay off the first Lady Dapifer. She's agreed to drop the case if I pay her another hundred thousand.'

Makepeace stopped, appalled. 'There ain't that much money in the world.'

'If I'm any judge it will barely cover her gambling debts. So you see, enclosure is out of the question, even if I were inclined to it.'

She clutched at him. 'Pip, don't do it. We'll fight her, Pip, you agreed. She hurt you enough in the past without mortgaging our future as well.'

From a branch overhanging the stream, a kingfisher dived into the twirling, icy water and came up with a wriggling arc of silver in its beak.

'Can you face it?' he asked.

'I can if you can.'

He sighed. 'Very well.'

As a reward, she told him he was to become a father and watched the future unroll before him as if a curtain had been raised. It was almost painful; she'd never seen his face as naked.

The phrase 'halcyon days' had always brought an image of summer to Makepeace's mind but from that day, and in all the years that followed, it was replaced by the image of a blue-tan kingfisher flickering into a winter stream and out again, in the last hour of a dream.

Chapter Eight

ON HER RETURN from Hertfordshire in March, Makepeace went immediately to see the family solicitor in Lincoln's Inn. Gentry usually insisted that their lawyers come to them but she enjoyed walking in London, unsafe though its streets had become. The poor harvest of the previous year had put up the price of bread, which had led to greater numbers of beggars and cutpurses.

Makepeace, an inveterate early riser, held to the belief that beggars and cutpurses were in the sinful habit of sleeping late, and that therefore even London streets were safe of a morning. However, like a respectable woman, she took Fanny Cobb with her. Betty had stayed behind in Hertfordshire with Josh. Tom, the most reliable of the footmen, accompanied her in the place of Tantaquidgeon who, Dapifer said, was too noticeable and likely to attract brickbats.

They passed Brooke Street where Dr Baines was now successfully installed, and the house where Handel had lived. Eastwards, the elegant houses of music and medicine gave way to dingy courts. London was extraordinary. Having negotiated a narrow, urine-scented passage, they were confronted by the hidden, breathtaking surprise of space, trees and Inigo Jones frontages that was Lincoln's Inn Fields.

The chambers of James and Hackbutt, Solicitors, when they eventually found them, were like the Law itself: dark, fusty and forbidding. Mr Hackbutt, on the other hand, was another surprise, with the appearance of a middle-aged country squire come in from a shoot. He hailed Makepeace as if he'd sighted her fifty yards off in a greenwood.

But he was still a lawyer. 'You do realise, Lady Dapifer, that I can reveal nothing of Sir Pip's affairs without his permission.'

'He's very busy just now, Mr Hackbutt.' Makepeace held out the letter Dapifer had written to say that she was in his confidence. 'The Stamp Tax debate's coming up.' Dapifer had gone to Bath to remind Mr Pitt of his promise to speak for the repeal in the House of Commons.

'These colonials,' Mr Hackbutt said resignedly, then remembered. 'But of course, Lady Dapifer, you yourself are from the colonies.' He bowed to one of Madame Angloss's most attractive walking dresses. 'One would never guess, if I may say so. How may I help you?'

She hoped he was a better lawyer than he was a diplomat. 'This case my husband's first wife's bringing. We're going to fight.'

'Sir Pip's not settling then? Splendid, splendid.'

'How much damage can she do?'

'She will be a difficult bird to bring down.'

Divorce by Act of Parliament was a long process, Mr Hackbutt said. It had to begin with a successful civil action for 'criminal conversation' against the accomplice in adultery. 'But that, Lady Dapifer, can only be brought by the husband, not the wife. The husband can sue his wife's lover because, as you know, in legal terms a wife is the property of her husband. A wife has no property in her husband and therefore she has no grounds for suing any woman with whom he has sexual intercourse.'

'But she's suing us.'

'Ah.' Mr Hackbutt rubbed his hands, as if presented with a particularly good pork pie. 'She is suing not simply for adultery but *aggravated* adultery, a course open to you ladies. That is, adultery aggravated by some circumstance such as bigamy, incest or, forgive the word, Lady Dapifer, sodomy.'

'It ain't bigamy,' said Makepeace wearily. 'Sir Pip divorced her.'

'Therein lies our defence to her action. But we are on untrodden ground, Lady Dapifer. Will an English court recognise a divorce decreed in Massachusetts and therefore a subsequent marriage? We'll be making legal history, Lady Dapifer.'

'Expensive legal history?'

'It won't be cheap. However, we hope, not as costly as the settlement the first Lady Dapifer is demanding as her price in order not to proceed with the matter. It is of considerable importance to you because in the event of Sir Philip's death . . .' He saw her flinch and went on more gently, 'In the *unlikely* event of Sir Philip's early death, his estates pass to his wife or, of course, a subsequent legitimate child. They are not entailed, he has no near male relatives and on his first marriage he made the first Lady Dapifer his heir. He has since changed his will, leaving everything to you and any children you may have instead.'

Makepeace shook her head; she couldn't cope with that. 'I don't want to think about it.'

'Let us hope you don't have to.' Mr Hackbutt stopped and became shifty. 'There's another cost, of course.'

'The scandal rags,' said Makepeace flatly.

'Are you prepared? In human terms the price may be high.'

Suddenly she liked him. 'Not as high as paying blackmail.'

'You're sure?'

She grinned and stood up. 'I'm an American, Mr Hackbutt, I ain't prepared to be taxed.'

Wandering back home through Clare Market, Fanny pointed to a newspaper on a stationer's stall. 'Bloody *Picknicks*'s at it again.'

Makepeace snatched up a copy. There she was, front page, tomahawk aloft, chasing caricatures of Rockingham and Dapifer, both of them with rabbit's ears, into the House of Commons. The balloon issuing from her mouth read: 'Repeal the Stamp Tax!' She grabbed the stall-holder by the throat. 'Who prints this shite? Who *prints* it?'

'Don't think he'll say, missus,' Fanny said happily, 'you're throttlin' him.'

Makepeace turned to leave, sweeping all his papers to instant ruin on the mud-splattered, well-manured market cobbles. 'Here,' the boy shouted after her, 'what'm I going to do with this lot?'

'Wipe your arse with 'em,' was Fanny's Parthian shot. She caught up and proffered a handkerchief for the tears of fury spurting from Makepeace's eyes. 'That's where they'll be tomorrow,' she said consolingly, 'hangin' from a hook in everyone's shite-house.'

In the meantime, half the House of Commons would have read them. Catty was ensuring she'd get her price from Dapifer by making Rockingham pay it too. 'Where's Great Russell Street?'

'Bloomsbury.' Fanny looked startled. 'Here, you're never goin' to—'

'Oh yes, I am. Tell Tom to find me a cab.'

Face-to-face confrontation was what Makepeace understood.

It was a short journey. The village of Bloomsbury lay to the north of town, separated from Holborn by farms and open land. Great Russell Street came up suddenly, a wide road bounded by tall, handsome houses with steps up to a portico. A maid pointed out Lady Dapifer's house. Makepeace told Fanny and Tom to wait in the cab.

The footman who opened the door to her was puzzled. 'Did you say Lady *Dapifer*, madam?'

'Lady Dapifer,' said Makepeace firmly.

She was shown into a hallway. The footman opened the double doors of a room leading off it, exposing candlelight and letting out stale air. She heard her title announced. There was silence, an outbreak of incredulous questioning, then a loud shout of laughter.

Oh Lord, she's got company. What's she got company for this hour of the morning? Then it struck her: Catty hadn't gone to bed. Some gathering had extended through the night and was still in progress. If Makepeace had needed confirmation of her enemy's depravity, she had it now. Decent people did not carouse into the next day.

'This way, please, madam.'

She stood in the doorway while twenty or so beautifully dressed people looked at her with amused hostility. Shaded candles cast downward light on a large table in the centre of the room and smaller ones round its sides; cards lay everywhere alongside piled coins.

'But how nice.' Catty Dapifer came forward. 'Ladies, gentlemen, may I present my husband's Red Indian, Makepeace?'

She belonged on her own mantelshelf, a Meissen figurine, rigid hoops at her hips exaggerating the little waist. She was wide awake, with a febrility that belonged to audiences in places where animals were killed for entertainment.

'Can we talk alone?' Makepeace said. 'I've come to make peace.' The phrase sounded dull; Catty had pre-empted it.

'Oh, she *has*.' Even the shout was pretty, it rang out in arpeggios. 'My dears, there's actually to be a pow-wow. Christopher darling, your pipe. We do need a peace pipe, don't we?' She sat down on the floor, and one of the men gave her his pipe.

Outside this heavy, candlelit room there was fresh air; Makepeace wanted to run back to it. *I don't know what to do.* The animosity around her was almost physical, like being stoned with jeers.

Another man moved forward, put his arms under the first Lady Dapifer's armpits and lifted her up. 'Now, now, Catty.'

She struggled. 'Put me down, Sidney. I want to play.'

'I know, me dear. But it's got to be *fair* play.' Still in a sitting position, Catty Dapifer was carried to a sofa and set on it. Then the man led Makepeace gently to the other end of the sofa and bowed to her. 'Major Sidney Conyers, ma'am. First Regiment of Foot Guards.'

Makepeace was surprised at how unvillainous this still boyish pleasant-faced man appeared. But she knew, with absolute assurance, that even while he could estimate Catty Dapifer's faults to the uttermost farthing, he was helpless, enslaved to her body and soul.

He shooed the other people away to the far end of the room so that the two women could talk in comparative privacy.

'Our situation's silly,' Makepeace said. 'I wanted you to know. You've had a settlement, and there'll be no more. You fight, I'll fight. The lawyers'll be the only ones to profit.' The sentences were lumpen, not the graceful phrases she'd rehearsed in her impatience to get here. 'Don't do it,' she pleaded. 'Let him be. He's been hurt enough. Let's all of us live in peace, I'm asking you.'

Catty told the room: 'Apparently I've hurt my husband enough. What a saintly savage it is—for a bigamist.'

She leaned forward. Her hair smelt of bluebells, her breath of alcohol. She whispered, 'Hurt him? I haven't even begun. I'm going to destroy him.' The pupils of her eyes were enormous, a night-hunting creature's. 'And you, my dear. *And* you.'

The gloves came off. 'We don't destroy easy,' Makepeace whispered back, 'we love each other.'

'You bitch,' hissed Catty.

The venom puffing from the woman's lips into Makepeace's nostrils was infectious. Irresistible to spit back, 'And I'm carrying his son.'

If she could have recalled the words, she would have. The little face close to hers withered. The effect was dreadful, like watching a healthy apple shrivel within seconds. 'Oh, don't,' Makepeace said. 'Don't.'

The man Conyers was beside them. He assisted Makepeace to her feet and hustled her to the front door. 'Have you a conveyance?'

She looked around and pointed. The cab had moved to the end of the street. Conyers hailed it, then went sideways down the steps, one hand held towards Makepeace to assist her to street level.

She heard him shout, 'No!'

A push against her back tumbled her down the steps.

As she lay in the mud, face up, she saw Catty Dapifer standing in the doorway, hands still outstretched, shaking. Then Conyers bent over her, all anxiety, and his face blocked her view. 'Are you hurt? Damn steps are lethal. Slipped on 'em meself only yesterday.' But the worry in his eyes, she could tell, was not for her.

For a moment Makepeace lay where she'd fallen, concentrating on an internal examination of baby Procrustes. He seemed to have survived; yes, she felt sick, but that was not from the fall, heavy though it had been. *She tried to kill the baby.*

Fanny and the footman were running towards her, Conyers was helping her up. Makepeace kept inclining her head to see round him to the figure in the doorway, still incredulous. *She tried to kill my baby.*

'What happened, missus?' Fanny and Tom were beside her, quivering with concern, listening to Conyers's explanation of 'accident, accident'.

Makepeace found herself in the cab, Conyers settling her cloak so that it didn't impede shutting the door. Their eyes met, his pleading, hers astounded. 'She *pushed* me,' Makepeace said.

'Very shaken,' he said, nodding to Fanny like a doctor to a presiding nurse, 'but she seems to have taken no harm. I'll have the steps seen to. Take her home quickly.'

When she confessed, on Dapifer's return to Grosvenor Square, to what she'd done, he could barely talk to her for rage.

She could hardly blame him. What she'd impulsively thought of as an attempt to protect him, present Catty with good New England common sense and stop her press campaign, now revealed itself to be a jumble of unworthy motives that had nearly brought Baby Procrustes to disaster. 'I'm truly sorry,' she said, and meant it.

'You flaunted yourself, didn't you? Trumpeted *our* happiness, *your* fecundity in her face. Knowing she has no children? Seems incapable of having any? What did you expect?'

She shouted, 'I didn't expect her to try and kill the baby!'

'And you,' he said quietly. 'Christ, she could have killed you.'

It was the ultimate reassurance. Makepeace crossed the room to him. Holding him, she felt an almost agonising contentment.

After a little, he said, 'I should have told you she was insane. You must understand that she can't help it. She needs protection from herself and I couldn't give it. God forgive me, I couldn't stand madness. It was cowardice, Procrustes, not kindness when I went to New England to divorce her. I wasn't sparing her, I was deserting.'

She couldn't follow him. She said, 'You *had* to leave her, she's wicked.'

He shook his head. He said, 'You realise, don't you, for all his faults Conyers is the better man?'

'He's a *bad* man. He betrayed you.'

'He loves that afflicted soul, poor devil that he is.'

'She ain't *afflicted*. She slept with your friend, she wants money for doing it and she tried to kill your baby. She's evil.'

'I don't believe in evil.'

'Yes, you do.' Makepeace was on home ground. '"He maketh his sun to rise on the evil and on the good." If there wasn't evil, we couldn't know the good. Simple. Come to bed.'

He wondered if she knew she was paraphrasing Milton. Probably not; it was her creed, the clarity of an uncluttered soul. She knew the good and held to it, *had* held to it, knowing it was to her disadvantage, when she rescued him not only from Boston harbour but from much else. For all her narrow, single-minded Puritanism, she was health, the only health he had. What would she say if he told her that he didn't believe in God either, but he trusted in the personal salvation Makepeace Burke Dapifer continued to offer him?

She'd be shocked, he thought. He took her to bed instead.

Grub Street was more than an unsavoury lane in an unsavoury area of London; it had become a swearword describing everything cheap and scurrilous in the writing profession. Originally a hiding place for seventeenth-century dissenters with their printing presses, over the previous hundred years it had become home to hacks, scandal-sellers, ballad-mongers, poets, political scribblers and dictionary compilers eking out their existence in the shabby upper rooms rented to them in return for their output by the booksellers who owned the shops below. It was also a battlefield for the irreverent and dispossessed versus the establishment, its gunfire the clack of presses in its basements.

This morning Makepeace didn't bother to knock on the decrepit door in one of Grub Street's alleys but, with Fanny, went straight in via the cellar and walked through to the winding staircase that climbed past the bookseller's apartment to the first floor. Here they knocked. Last time they'd walked in on Beasley in bed with a woman.

There was no reply today and, when they gave up and went in, no woman either. He was asleep, his bare backside protruding from frowsty bedcovers. Fanny lifted the blanket between finger and thumb and covered the protrusion before she and Makepeace started clearing up.

It was a largish room made claustrophobic by the number of books stacked in untidy piles against the walls, on the floor, on the window bench. Even if Beasley spent all his income on literature, which, to judge from the state of his clothes and person, he did, there was no accounting for the vastness of his library. The flyleaves Makepeace peeked at showed they were *ex libris* other people, probably stolen.

Once they'd pushed open the window from its worm-eaten frame, picked up and folded the clothes on the floor and cleared quills, paper and inkpots from the table, Makepeace set out some fresh bread and cheese and a can of steaming coffee she'd bought in Clare Market. 'Breakfast,' she said. 'Get up.'

The bed swore, a hand gestured towards Fanny: 'Want to fuck?'

'With *you*? When pigs fly.' She held out a shirt she'd laundered.

They averted their eyes as he squirmed, grumbling, out of bed, put on the shirt and struggled into a pair of breeches that Makepeace proffered sideways on a pair of tongs. Makepeace shook her head in wonderment at herself. Here was her *chosen* ally, in the fight against Catty.

After her disastrous foray to Bloomsbury, there had been no let-up in the ammunition Catty had supplied for *Picknicks* to fire at her.

> It has come to our ears that the female claiming to be the second wife of Sir Philip Dapifer was recently to be seen in Bloomsbury pleading with her predecessor not to pursue the case which cites her supposed marriage to Sir Philip as bigamous. Money was mentioned but the lady was ejected by Lady Dapifer's indignant footman.

Dapifer had refused to look at the piece, but if he chose to ignore it, Makepeace knew others did not. She became frightened by how vulnerable her husband's decency made him. He was the real target of the filth Catty was throwing and it was damaging not only his position in society but his health. She'd had to summon Dr Baines to him one evening when he'd come back short of breath after a difficult political meeting. Baines said it was exhaustion and recommended rest although, with the imminence of the Stamp Tax debate, there could be none.

Something had to be done. They could fight Catty through the courts, but by that time they would already be defeated; there wouldn't be a judge in England whose mind wouldn't already have been contaminated against them.

She'd unearthed the dog-eared card the man called John Beasley had given her in Hyde Park and sought him out. At first it was with the idea of finding the publisher of the tormenting *Picknicks* and either cajoling, threatening or bribing him into silence. Which, as Beasley said when she found him, showed how little she knew about the press. 'If there's someone as'll read it, there's someone as'll print it.'

'Who is it, then?'

He shrugged. 'Don't know.' He added, with meaning, 'Shit sticks if you don't fling it back.'

Her own sentiments exactly.

She and Beasley went into partnership. She saw no reason to tell Dapifer about it, though it made her uneasy to act behind his back.

John Beasley was everything that should disgust her: he was gauche, opinionated, morbid, rabidly anti-religious; yet she . . . *liked* wasn't the right word . . . felt friendship for him.

It was peculiar; when he wasn't exasperating her beyond bearing, she could confide in him as to nobody else and know he would keep the confidence. And he didn't like Catty Dapifer, neither her adultery—though despising the institution of marriage, he was censorious of those who betrayed it—nor her habit of aiming her carriage at pedestrians in the park. 'Nearly winged me once, arrogant bitch.'

'How'd you know who she was?' Makepeace had asked.

'Bigwigs ain't got a monopoly on who's who. Nor gossip neither.'

He picked up and sold his information in the political and literary coffee clubs. Somehow he'd inveigled himself into the world of the arts and boasted of his conversations with 'Sam Johnson' or 'Davey Garrick' or 'Josh Reynolds' or 'Ollie Goldsmith' or 'Charlie Fox'.

'This Josh . . .' she said wistfully.

'Reynolds.'

'Painter, you said. D'you think he'd teach *my* Josh?' Josh troubled Makepeace because she didn't know what to do about the child. The boy was gifted beyond his years in drawing and she was reluctant to betray his talent by subsuming it in domestic service. On the other hand, who'd ever heard of a black artist?

'Don't see why not.'

That was the lovely thing about John Beasley, he had no concept of limitation. Unexpected also in so loutish a young man was the delicacy with which he began conducting Makepeace's campaign, selling titbits of information to the more respectable organs that gazetted the comings and goings of society or cooed gossip into a thousand boudoirs.

> *London Magazine*: Sir Philip Dapifer and his New England bride are frequently to be seen in the company of the Marquis of

Rockingham. Lady Dapifer is a Bostonian and therefore particularly fitted to give her opinion and advice to his lordship on the American question.

'Lord's sake, don't put that in. It was a private conversation.'
'Well, *I* knew about it.'

The Ladies' Diary: It is forecast that the articulated hoop may have had its day; we happen to know that Madame Angloss, that most exclusive adviser to the *ton*, is dressing Lady Dapifer, wife to Sir Philip, more nearly to her natural and excellent figure.

Gradually, gently, Makepeace's image was rehabilitated from that of bigamous, low-class trollop to dignified second wife, the pure bosom on which Sir Philip Dapifer had lain his wronged head.

Beasley's vilification of Catty was less gentle:

The Coach Commissioners would do well to look to what use is made of their conveyances before licensing hackney coaches; we have heard of a liaison which took place in one such last Sunday between the Hon. Percy Cavendish and the former Lady Dapifer, divorced wife of Sir Philip, when the blinds were down. No doubt the undulating motion of the vehicle contributed greatly to enhance the pleasure of the critical moment . . .

Makepeace was horrified. 'You can't print this.'

'Why not? B*on ton*'ll love it. And it's true—the driver peeked. Don't look so mimsy; she'd have told the town crier if you'd done it.'

The thing was, she and Dapifer had. Beasley was right about the undulating motion of a coach. But we're married, she thought. Catty isn't even faithful to poor Conyers.

She felt her womb churn as if Baby Procrustes had flinched and she fell into a panic of disgust with herself, with Beasley, with a trade that paraded people's frailty for the delectation of others.

'I found out something else yesterday. Want to know who's feeding the poison to *Picknicks*?'

She was all attention. 'Yes.'

'Major Sidney Conyers, First Regiment of Foot Guards.'

She said dully, 'He was nice to me.'

'He was nice to Sir Pipwig an' all, weren't he? I tell you, he's a black-hearted bastard. His men fawn on him because he lets 'em loot. There's more than one highwayman carries a percentage of his takings back to Major Robbing Conyers and calls him "sir".'

'You're making it up,' Makepeace said. Conyers's class might sleep with other men's wives but it didn't go in for criminality.

'Am I? When are you going to learn about bigwigs? They're all robbers. Look at the enclosures. If Fanny here, or me, stole a sheep we'd be swinging in chains. The bigwigs steal a thousand acres and call it an Act of Parliament.' Beasley had become sullen. 'And if you want nice little pieces in the paper about your doings, you'll have to *do* something. What d'you want me to write? The Duchess of Dunghill's ball was graced by the absence of the lovely Lady Dapifer? You don't *go* anywhere.'

'Don't know why we bother with that little noserag,' Fanny said as they went home.

'I don't either.' She did really; her visits to Beasley were as much to ensure he stayed out of prison and had enough to eat as they were concerned with her campaign. And the little noserag was right: she *didn't* go anywhere. She preferred to shelter in company with which she felt confident. Blast, she thought, I've got to become one of the damn *ton*.

No need to blacken Catty's reputation—Catty could do that for herself—if she could enhance her own.

> *London Gazette*: Sir Philip and Lady Dapifer yesterday accompanied Lord Ffoulkes to the Royal Navy Hospital at Greenwich for the unveiling of a plaque to the young lord's late father, a patron of the hospital. Lieutenant Governor Boys was in attendance at the ceremony. Afterwards Sir Philip, who is Lord Ffoulkes's guardian, and Lady Dapifer, an accomplished oarswoman, took their charge rowing on the river.

Once they were out of sight, Dapifer took off his hat and held Andrew's for him as the child dropped the wreath onto the surface and stood watching until it passed out of sight beyond the river's bend. Then they rowed back, returned to the carriage and, with Tantaquidgeon standing on its backboard, took the road for Eton.

Holding Makepeace's hand, the boy was silent for most of the journey. She knew he was grateful to have said a personal goodbye to his father but, inevitably, he was suffering.

As they approached Windsor through a spring-scented dusk, he asked, 'May Tantaquidgeon take me in?'

Dapifer said, 'It was nice of Lieutenant Governor Boys to attend. Andrew, did your father ever tell you about him?'

'No.'

'When he was young he and seven others survived the sinking of the *Luxborough Galley* by eating the bodies of their shipmates.'

'Pip!' Makepeace remonstrated.

'Oh, *joy*,' Andrew said. 'A Red Indian and a cannibal all in one day. *Won't* the fellows be green?'

They watched him go through the school's arch, his legs trying to stretch to the pace of the tall Huron stalking beside him.

'Thought he needed cheering up,' Dapifer said smugly.

London Evening Post: Among those in the Dtrangers' Gallery for the House of Commons debate on the Stamp Tax were Sir Philip and Lady Dapifer . . .

Ladies' Diary: We glimpsed Lady Dapifer among the crowd in the Strangers' Gallery and attribute much sense to her for not indulging the current fashion for high heads which would have obscured the view of those behind her . . .

The carriage took them back through the night from Westminster to Grosvenor Square with Susan, exhilarated by the debate, shouting, 'We won! We won! We won!' over a clamour of church bells ringing out the news that the Stamp Act was repealed.

Makepeace turned to Dapifer and mouthed, 'Well done, my boy.'

In anticipation, she'd ordered Mrs Francanelli to prepare a celebratory dinner. Once they'd sat down, she lifted her glass to her husband. 'To Liberty and all them as sail in her.'

Dapifer didn't respond. 'I don't think so,' he said. 'What you heard tonight was the repeal of the Stamp Act. What you didn't hear was the reading of the Declaratory Bill yesterday.'

'Bad?' asked Makepeace, watching him.

'Bad.' He leaned back in his chair, closed his eyes and chanted, like a schoolchild repeating a primer: '" . . . The King's majesty, Lords and Commons etc, to have full power and authority to make laws and statutes of sufficient force and validity to bind the colonies and people of America subjects of the crown of Great Britain in all cases whatsoever."'

He opened his eyes on the silent room. 'Yes, I know. Rockingham couldn't have pushed through the repeal otherwise. The oligarchs had to save face. No, more than save face, save *themselves*. Allow the colonies to have a say in what laws are passed and our own people at home will shout, "No taxation without representation." Wilkes already is.'

Sam Adams knew, she thought. There'll be no liberty unless there's war.

London Magazine: Lord Rockingham's musical evening to celebrate the birth of the late Mr George Handel commanded a large audience among whom their Graces of Grafton and Portland, Sir Philip and Lady Dapifer . . .

In the early days of their marriage, Dapifer had arranged for Charles Burney, a doctor of music and a friend of his, to try to bridge what he called 'the chasm between my wife and the great composers'. It hadn't worked. Makepeace was tone deaf.

Tonight she sat in clanging boredom, watching a tiny spider weave a web on the towering hair of the Duchess of Portland in front of her. If this were a dance it would be different: she enjoyed dancing. She could keep to a rhythm even if she couldn't hold a tune.

Thanks to the example of the Marquis of Rockingham, invitations were now being sent to Grosvenor Square. It couldn't be said that the nobility clasped Makepeace to its bosom, however. Catty might be scandalous but she was still *Us*. Makepeace wasn't even English *Them*. The more rigid Whigs looked askance at Rockingham for shepherding this redheaded American into their society. (Reference was always made to her hair, as if it were an affront, a revolutionary flag.) Where would his mania for reform take him next? However, he *was* Prime Minister and Sir Philip's family *had* come over with the Conqueror, so . . . Very gradually, Makepeace was being absorbed into the fashionable world.

Something marvellous was happening, the noise was over, people were clapping. The Duchess of Portland turned round: 'My dears, was not that sublime? Is not the players' execution perfect?'

'Is that the end?' muttered Makepeace.

'No. This is an interval.'

'Oh, *Lord*.'

> *The Old Maid*: A little bird has chirruped in our ear that Lady Dapifer is to be in the audience at Goodman's Fields tomorrow night to watch her brother make his acting debut.

This was better than the opera. Less exalted, more shameful—*hokey*, what would her mother have said?—but jolly. She stopped laughing long enough to gasp, 'I didn't know King Lear had funny dogs.'

'I don't think Shakespeare did either,' Dapifer said grimly.

For this, his first performance, Aaron was playing a knight attendant on Cordelia. He had five lines in Act I, Scene IV. It may not have helped that Makepeace clapped his entrance, a solitary firecracker of sound echoing round the auditorium before Dapifer could grab her hands.

'"Where's my fool, ho?"' Lear asked him. '"I think the world's asleep. How now! Where's that mongrel?"'

Silence. Aaron stared at the audience, the limelight emphasising his ghastly pallor. The audience stared back.

'"How now!"' repeated King Lear, '"where's that mongrel?"'

There was an audible hiss from the prompt corner: '*He says, my lord, your daughter is not well.*'

Further silence broken by some booing.

'I *expect*,' said King Lear, 'he reports that my daughter is not well. "Why came not the slave back to me, when I called him?"'

'What?' said King Lear, sweating as the booing began. 'Thou whisperest that he would not?'

Eventually, the Earl of Kent got Aaron off by grabbing an arm and dragging him. After the performance they found him in the green room, still vomiting.

King Lear, who owned the company, reassured an anxious Makepeace that Aaron's career in the theatre was safe. 'No, no, dear lady, I prophesy a successful future for your brother. Stage fright afflicts the best of us.'

Makepeace was grateful. 'Oh, and I liked the jugglers and I'm glad the play ended so happy. I was feared it wouldn't.'

King Lear bowed. 'Madam, we aim to please.'

Makepeace had neither the art nor the inclination deliberately to mould herself to the set she was now in, but, inevitably, contact with its pumice began to smooth her edges so that she fitted better.

Her coiffure rose as her Puritanism declined. Unconsciously, her accent modified and her grammar improved. Fewer pennies were given to street beggars; she rarely saw any as she was borne by sedan chair to society functions. She and Dapifer entertained.

On the last occasion that she risked being seen in the area of Grub Street, John Beasley accused her of joining 'the fucking bigwigs'. They quarrelled. Anyway, she now had no need of him; the fashionable press had taken her up—America was news—and gave her publicity that had its own impetus. Such bile as Catty and Conyers introduced to the scandal sheets became stale and was overridden by the more outré doings of the Duchess of Newcastle.

Lady Judd was one of those who bowed to the inevitable. Living next door, it was impossible not to see the quality of the visitors now being ushered into Dapifer House. In any case, the woman had rescued a Judd child in danger of falling from the tree that overhung the Dapifer garden. 'Climbed the branches like a monkey, my dear, despite her condition,' Lady Judd told her friends. 'And Sir Benjamin dotes on her . . .'

Most men did. Her pregnancy was late in becoming apparent but its bloom suited her; she had become beautiful. Those who sat next to her at dinners found her conversation sometimes startling but generally more entertaining than that of the usual run of females. Not exactly *comme il faut*, of course, but perhaps Pip Dapifer hadn't done so badly for himself second time around.

She got on well with Sir Benjamin Judd. He was occasionally pompous but, like herself, an outsider. That Makepeace didn't hide the fact she'd been a tavern-keeper delighted him. 'Business, that's what makes this owld world turn. Yow and me, we understand that.'

He put her up for the ladies' section of his club, Almack's, the gaming establishment in St James's.

At first she refused. 'Don't approve of gambling, Sir Ben.'

'Noither do I, Lady Dapifer, noither do I. But yow don't go for the play, yow go to keep up with the new politics and such. Bright young woman like yow should know who's who, what's what.'

Surprisingly, Dapifer agreed with Sir Benjamin. 'Since you're embarking on the high life, you may as well join a club and Almack's is a respectable Whig stronghold. Lady Rockingham's a member of the ladies' section, I believe.'

> *Town and Country Magazine*: Lady Dapifer is the latest recruit of the many-headed hydra that is St James's. She has been elected a member to Almack's, known for its depravity in permitting gaming to both sexes.

Makepeace was not so far gone in high living that she didn't hear the moan from her mother's grave as she and Dapifer attended their first function together at the club.

'I shan't play, Mother.'

'Thy father said the same.'

Almack's was unique among gaming clubs, not only for having a ladies' section in the first place, but in its balloting system: men voted for or against the women who were put up for membership, women for or against the men. It was made obvious fairly quickly to Makepeace that, had each sex voted for its own, she would have been blackballed.

She and Lady Judd were visiting the ladies' 'retiring room', a carpeted chamber with pier-glasses, dressing tables and discreet, curtained stools of easement. A small group of women were already in there, conversing in tones more generally used to strike terror into foxes in the next county. Makepeace recognised the type: elderly Whig autocrats, Catty supporters. Twittering, Lady Judd tried to introduce her to the Duchess of Barnet. 'Your Grace, I don't think you've met—'

She was dismissed. 'I do not recognise *usurpers*.'

Makepeace gritted her teeth. Lady Rockingham came hurrying out of one of the closets to the rescue. 'They'll be calling supper, ladies.'

Makepeace turned to go but was hailed back by Lady Brandon, another of the coterie. 'You,' she brayed, '*I* wouldn't have voted for you. I don't believe in elevating colonials.'

Too much. Makepeace nodded to her over her shoulder. 'I wouldn't have voted for you either. Only way we colonials elevate old witches is by hanging 'em.'

'I gather blood's been spilt in the ladies' room,' Dapifer said, taking her into supper.

'Where do they get their manners—the hogsty?'

Makepeace prepared herself for battles ahead—and not just with the old guard. Through the dining-room door she had glimpsed gaming tables for the first time. She had not intended to enter the salon; she would stand aloof. 'I do not play.'

But there was a smell. She'd never smelt it before but somebody had. Ancestral addiction. Oh God, she was her father's daughter.

It was impossible to remain in the dining room after supper; the men had reached the port, politics and vulgarity stage; they wanted women gone. She left Dapifer to it and followed Lady Judd into the salon, trying to make her walk casual and less like an iron filing drawn to a magnet.

It was hazard that drew her, raw gambling. Lady Judd took two minutes to explain it. Makepeace understood within one.

It was the biggest table in the room. The air round it vibrated with concentration.

Dapifer was next to her. 'I *said*, are you all right?'

'Yes.'

'Grafton and I are going to take a turn round the park. Do you want to take the carriage and go home?'

'No, I'll wait for you.'

He turned her face to his. 'You look like Odysseus tied to the mast. Blow me down, Procrustes, *you want to play.*'

She said, 'I don't play.' When he'd gone, she retied herself to the mast.

Around midnight, there was a rowdy entrance by a young man bringing with him the scent of alcohol—and Catty Dapifer. The two of them began circulating the room noisily. The first thing Makepeace had done before agreeing to join the club was to make sure that Catty hadn't. This was planned humiliation. Withdraw? Makepeace thought. No, by the Lord. I ran from Boston. Here's where I stand.

A charming voice said, 'Oh my goodness, there's my husband's Indian. What *is* it doing here?'

A mumble from William Macall, the owner of Almack's.

The voice again. 'But I *am* a member, Mr Macall. It said so in the papers. "Lady Dapifer elected to Almack's," it said. How *nice*, I thought.'

Another low mumble from Macall.

'*Dear* Mr Macall, you are permitting squaws to play, but not respectable wives? Then I shall circulate. Come with me, Henry.'

The young man said, 'Goin' to try my luck here, Catty.'

'Very well. Now, where *is* that husband of mine?' She moved off, to the applause and embraces of Lady Brandon and the Duchess of Barnet.

The boy she'd called Henry was arguing with the club-owner. Macall was on firmer ground now. 'I'm no saying ye're not entitled to play, Mr Headington, I'm saying ye *should* not. I understand ye've already lost too much tonight elsewhere.'

'Got the stake here.' Headington waved a piece of paper. 'Deed of property. Good as guineas any day.'

'Only coin of the realm at Almack's tonight, I fear.'

'But Lady Fortune's relented, I can feel the warmth of her smile.' Headington began to go round the hazard players, pushing the document at them. 'Worth it. Thousand or more acres. Fowl an' fish an' . . . oh, all sortsa things. Scenery. Who'll sport me a monkey on it?'

There was a general shaking of heads. 'Go home, Henry.'

One of the players said, 'Where is it?'

'North'mberland.' Headington waved his arm towards the window as if it were somewhere in the region of Highgate.

There was general laughter. 'A thousand acres of damn all. Suggest you go and live on it, Henry. Healthier than Mayfair.'

Desperately, the young man staggered towards Makepeace. 'You've a kind face, ma'am. You'll sport me a miserable monkey, eh? Here's m'security. Nice little property?'

Close to, he radiated an ill health caused by neglect. He vibrated as if from fever and his eyes were terrified.

'You go home,' said Makepeace gently. 'Have a nice sleep.'

'No, no. M'luck's turned, ma'am. Jus' a monkey.'

'A monkey' was one of the few pieces of slang Boston and London had in common. Five hundred pounds.

She was shaking her head when a pretty voice called out, 'Don't bargain with a Yankee, Henry. Americans won't even pay their taxes.' Catty's eyes were sapphire chips. A challenge, pure and simple.

Through the cackling of the old guard, Makepeace heard a voice say, 'I'll play you for it.' It was hers.

Headington brightened. 'My land against your monkey?'

Catty applied the goad. 'It's my husband's money at risk. Do he and

I want a piece of Northumberland heath, I wonder?'

'Seventy guineas,' said Makepeace desperately. It was all she had left from saving Dapifer's life. 'My own money. I earned it.'

'I expect she did, darlings,' Catty announced, 'in a tavern.'

More laughter. People were leaving other tables and closing in.

'Are you satisfied by this, Sir Pip?' Macall asked.

Dapifer had come through the crowd. He put his arm around Makepeace. 'Of course. It's my wife's own money and honestly gained, I'm proud to say.' Quietly he said, 'Don't do this, Procrustes. The lad's possessed. He's been wagering property all over London.'

'I can't back out now.' Headington was an inconsequence. She was duelling with Catty.

'Seventy guineas it is, then.' Henry Headington would have played for buttons as long as he could play.

Immediately it became An Event with Procedures. The table was cleared of all other bets. A lawyer was brought from the dining room to draw up a promissory note for Makepeace in the event that she lost. She signed it with her maiden name to show that it would be paid with her personal money. A deed of transference of Headington's property from him to her, in the event that *he* lost, was also drawn up. Again, she signed with 'Makepeace Burke, formerly of Boston'.

The Earl of Orme said, 'I shall be groom-porter for this throw. Does either caster object? Call your main, Lady Dapifer.' The box holding the dice was passed to her. She could call five, six, seven, eight or nine. Her mind went blank. She could hear the dice vibrating in the box as she held it. The only number in her head was that of Creation's days. *Lord, forgive me.* 'Seven.'

Headington called five. Should either of them throw the number they'd called they'd 'nicked' it and won outright. Makepeace had two chances of winning; if she threw eleven it also 'nicked' it.

Makepeace cast her dice. A three and a two. 'Five to seven' called the Earl of Orme. From this point on if she threw a seven she'd lose, five being her number to win.

Headington threw. Four and three. 'Seven to five.' Now the odds were in his favour; there were three ways of throwing a seven and only two of throwing five.

It don't matter, Makepeace tried telling herself, I can afford to lose. And saw Catty's eyes. *No, I can't.* She threw again. Eight.

'She lost count of the throws. Dapifer told her later there were twenty-three. Tension and temperature rose, so did the cheers—and side bets. Spots came and went on the baize like an errant disease.

The dice rolled and stopped. One of the little squares on the table showed a four, the other a one. Confused, Makepeace stared at them; *had* that been her throw? She looked over to Headington and saw the ravaged face assume peace. Had *he* won? But the noise had ceased. People were turning away from table. Catty had gone.

Headington moved towards her. 'It seems America's not to be beaten.' He held out the deed and its transference.

She was reluctant to take them. 'I'm sorry.'

'For this relief, much thanks.' His voice was kinder than any she'd heard that night. He took her hand and closed it over the papers. 'You must promise me not to be sorry.'

They heard next morning that he went back to the Mayfair house he'd gambled away earlier that day, thanked its servants, walked into his study, closed the door and shot himself.

With a blotched, desperate note, Makepeace sent the Northumberland deed back to his lawyer, begging him to return it to whomsoever inherited his estate. A letter from Lord Braybourne, Headington's next of kin, returned it to her.

Madam, you are distinguished in being the only creditor of my unfortunate young cousin to cancel one of his debts. I cannot allow that this, the last and least of the properties he gambled away—one, moreover, that was fairly won—should place me under the burden of so rare a generosity. Luckily, I have no need of it. Here it is back again.

From that day on she kept the deed in her pocket wherever she went, in the way that a medieval sinner wore a hair shirt to remind himself of his need for salvation. As things turned out, it was to be hers.

IN JULY the Marquis of Rockingham lost office and was replaced as Prime Minister by the Duke of Grafton who, in turn, appointed as his Chancellor Charles Townshend, a man whose solution to the American problem was to impose more customs duties.

It was a relief to leave London. Makepeace and Dapifer repaired with young Andrew Ffoulkes to Hertfordshire for the rest of the summer. The weather was not good. There was trouble getting in the hay.

It can't be said that Makepeace laid Headington's ghost to rest. *For this relief, much thanks*; the words haunted her. There was much to do, however, accompanying the villagers to St Alban's Fair; St John's Day, dressing the apple trees with ribbons; cricket: Dapifers v. Tewinge, young Josh the highest scoring batsman; Lammas and well-dressing.

On St Swithin's Day it rained and therefore, they told her, it would continue to do so for the next forty days. She wasn't to remember whether it did or didn't, only that the month passed in a sort of self-imposed, pleasing bustle of cleaning and tidying that Betty called 'gettin' the nest ready for the egg'.

She was becoming big now, adopting a waddle that made Dapifer laugh. She took gentle rides in the trap to pay courtesy calls through a landscape teeming with men mowing and women gathering sheaves. Dapifer drove a wagon back and forth between the field and the yard where Andrew and Josh were being taught the art of rick-building. Despite the weather, all corn was in by the beginning of September.

The letter came two days later.

Robert brought it to them at breakfast, fanning his nose with it and sniffing. 'That nice Mr Little brought it up. He called in at Mrs Yates's this morning.' Mrs Yates kept the shop on the Great North Road a mile and a half away where local letters and parcels were deposited by the passing Royal Mail coach. 'And we know who it's from, don't we?'

The letter smelt of bluebells, was unsigned and very short: *Pip, dear hart, I am in Town this month. Please recieve me that we may discuss matters.*

'She wants you to go to London?'

'I may as well. It's time to return Andrew to school in any case.' There was a groan from behind a platter piled with kidneys and kedgeree. 'And I can bring Baines back with me.'

Makepeace had been content to let Betty attend at Baby Procrustes's birth but Dapifer wouldn't rest unless Dr Baines was standing by.

'What's she want, d'you think?'

'Terms, I imagine.'

'Don't give her any. You'll be back for Harvest Home?' she asked anxiously. It was the biggest festival of the year. Next Monday the household of Dapifers, the village and people from outlying farms would attend church and then a feast in the Great Barn afterwards.

'What's today? Tuesday? If we set off now I can be back on Saturday. Pack your traps, Andrew.'

Andrew said to Makepeace, 'Can't I stay for the feast?'

'I wish you could.' The two of them had become very close. 'But you'll be back in a month. Remind Pip to ask your headmaster for leave of absence for the christening.'

'I'll take Robert with me,' Dapifer said. 'Tantaquidgeon can stay here.'

She kissed him and Andrew, told Robert to look after them, and stood waving as the coach rocked down the yellowing chestnut avenue.

That was Tuesday. Dapifer had hoped to return on Saturday night but Makepeace was not worried when he didn't. He had a lot to do in the time; she had a great deal to do herself. The church and Great Barn must be decorated, chutneys made, fruit preserved, apples stored . . .

She was more concerned when he hadn't arrived by Sunday night but allowed herself to be reassured. Bad day for travelling, Sunday. He'd be back for Harvest Home. But on Monday afternoon, restless, she decided to take a stroll and meet the coach returning as it surely must. As she set off down the avenue, she heard the pad of moccasined feet behind her. Betty wasn't letting her go alone; she'd sent Tantaquidgeon.

The village street was quiet. Dust and the sound of flails came from the threshing floors, the smell of cooking apples and spice from the open doors of the cottages. Old Mrs Nash sat on her threshold making corn dollies. 'Don't you go far now, missus. That looks like rain.'

Any minute she'd see the coach roof in the distance . . . round the next bend . . . the next. She waddled on.

By the time she emerged from Dapifers Lane into the Great North Road the first drops of rain were hitting its surface. Southwards lay the hill down which Dapifer's coach would be coming. Makepeace walked towards it, making for Mrs Yates's shop. 'I'm waiting for Sir Pip to come back from London, Mrs Yates. Can I watch for him here?'

Having offered Makepeace a cup of herbal tea and seen that she was in no mood for conversation, Mrs Yates said, 'In the middle of making coughdrops I was. I'll get back to 'em if 'ee don't mind.'

The front door had to be shut against the rain that slanted past the window, blurring Makepeace's view of the hill. She shivered. An ache was developing in her back.

'There now,' said Mrs Yates. 'Forget my own head next. There was a letter came Saturday and I meant to send it up but I been that busy . . .'

My dear Lady Dapifer,

I beg you to remember your condition and not to be overly anxious but you should know that Sir Pip has been taken ill. In the event that it has slipped the mind of those looking after him to inform you, I thought it best to write. A doctor has been called and all is being done for him. Your friend and neighbour, Emily Judd

The date was Friday's.

Get to him, get to him. Board a coach here? No. No, no, no, *think*. The stage wouldn't pass until evening. Back to the house. Get the trap, Peter Little would drive her, or one of the men. Get to him.

Mrs Yates was hanging onto her arm. 'You're never goin' out in this, missus?'

She threw the woman off and lumbered into the deserted road, Tantaquidgeon behind her.

And *now* the coach was coming. Unmistakably, the Dapifer coach with Thompson driving. She sobbed with relief; he was all right.

Thompson saw her and the horses slithered to a halt in spraying mud. Two riders in military, rain-blackened cloaks drew their mounts up on either side. She began picking her way through the mud.

A head peered out of the coach window and said something she couldn't catch over the noise of the rain. One of the horsemen saluted and then called to Thompson, 'You heard the major. Drive on.'

The reins were shaken. She saw Thompson's face, wet, beseeching, turned to hers, as the coach went past her.

Two more outriders accompanied the conveyance that had been held up behind the coach. It was a funeral cart drawn by four black-plumed horses. She didn't move. It wasn't him.

The cortège turned left, into Dapifers Lane.

She said quite brightly, 'Well, what's all *that* about, I wonder?' And began to run.

Peter Little, coming to find her in the trap, met her at the bridge. 'Oh dear God, are you all right?'

Tantaquidgeon was helping her along as she struggled to walk through a contraction. 'Get me home.'

'Lady Dapifer . . .'

'It isn't him,' she said.

'We don't know who it is, they've shut the gates.' He turned the trap with difficulty. Leaves driven by the rain plastered themselves against her face as they went up the hill. Half the village stood by the gates in groups hunched over lanterns.

The world had come loose. No moment flowed into another; instead static, vividly drawn tableaux presented themselves and were washed away by the rain to make way for the next.

An outline had Fanny's shape. 'Oh, missus, they say he's dead.'

Josh knuckling tears from his eyes.

Another shape enfolded her and spoke in Betty's voice. 'You gotta be strong girl, an' mind that babby. They turfed us out.'

The gates were high; she had never seen them closed before, their wrought iron was angular and coldly wet against her hands. One of the coach's outriders stood behind them.

'Let me in. I'm Lady Dapifer, I live here.'

'Sorry, miss. No admittance.' A neutral voice, not unkind.

'Let me in.' She broke. '*Pip*. I'm here, Pip.' Once she'd begun shouting for him she couldn't stop. 'Pip, they're not letting me in.'

A light sprang up in the churchyard on the hill. The soldier turned to somebody she couldn't see. 'Better fetch the major.'

Someone behind her put an arm across her shoulders. She shook it off, rattling the gates, shrieking like an imprisoned animal.

Conyers was at the gate with two more soldiers. 'This is unseemly, madam. I must ask you to desist and go away.'

She didn't understand. 'This man won't let me in.'

He gestured to the soldier with the lantern to raise it so that its light shone on his face. He shouted, 'People of Dapifers, I regret to inform you that Sir Philip died three days ago in London. His wife was with him. We are about to bury him.'

Somebody screamed. A man's voice yelled, 'We're comin' in. We needs to see 'un. Why you stoppin' us?'

'I am Major Sidney Conyers, Lady Dapifer's champion. On her authority I am seizing this property and all Sir Pip's properties back to her, his lawful wife. There will be a magistrate here in the morning: don't make it necessary for him to read the Riot Act.' The strain went out of Conyers's face and it became kindly. 'Go home, good people. Mourn our dear Sir Philip as I shall. Let his lady bury him in peace.'

Peter Little called out, 'This isn't right, Major,' and somebody else said uncertainly, 'No, it ain't. You open they gates. Let's rush 'em, lads.'

But words of power had been spoken in an educated voice. Lawful. Magistrate. Major. Riot Act. Order. Authority. The lantern gleamed on bayonets. Conyers nodded and went away.

Nobody rushed the gates. Only a mud-spattered, hysterical woman went on shaking them, hour after hour. People buzzed around her, trying to draw her away. She clung on to the bars like a monkey.

From the house came a file of glow-worms. The file reached the avenue. Not glow-worms, but a train of flares and lanterns; people in black. Heading for the church. Clustering in the graveyard.

She began screaming, pulling at the gate, vomiting sound, commanding, begging, only let me see him. It's not him. You're burying him alive. Let me save him. I saved him before. It's not him.

The lights re-formed into their file to crawl back up the hill until the house swallowed them, one by one, and there was nothing.

They raised Makepeace out of the mud but couldn't dislodge her hands from the ironwork. Eventually, when they saw that the baby was coming, they forced her fingers back and carried her away. Part of her, the best of her, stayed at the gate.

Baby Procrustes was born an hour later in Peter Little's house. Makepeace bore the labour almost without interest, as if it were merely a physical manifestation of the greater agony. Anyway, it was a girl.

'Where is she?'

Betty walked with him along the village street. The weather had cleared but underfoot it remained muddy. In the fields seagulls followed the ploughs like a ragged train of lace blowing in the breeze. *Something* should have stopped, Aaron thought. Everywhere there was occupation, and people avoiding his eye.

They reached the vast, iron embroideries that were the gates to Dapifer House. A figure sat there, its head drooped into its lap like an exhausted beggar. Fanny Cobb stood helplessly beside it.

'Three days, Aaron,' Betty sobbed. 'She keep comin' back.'

'Makepeace? *Makepeace?*' Aaron threw himself on the gates and rattled them. 'Open up.'

A soldier ambled out of a makeshift sentry box. 'What now?'

'I'm Lady Dapifer's brother. Open these gates at once.'

'Go home,' said the soldier wearily. 'And tell the Indian if he tries to get her in round the back again, we'll shoot the bugger.'

'It's my sister's house, there's a law against this.'

'Take her home, son,' the soldier said gently. 'She's ill.'

At his side, Betty said, 'Ain't no good, Aaron, we tried.'

Aaron knelt down and smoothed the hair back from his sister's face. Was this broken thing Makepeace, his surrogate mother, arbiter, lifelong prop? 'Come away, 'Peace. Just for now.'

'Aaron?'

'I'm here, 'Peace. I'm here now.'

'Pip's in there,' she said, 'but they won't let me go to him.'

'We'll make them, 'Peace. I promise.'

Next day, taking Peter Little's advice and his horse, he set off to appeal to the lord lieutenant of Hertfordshire. 'Civil matter,' the lord lieutenant told him. 'Nothing I can do.' He was acquainted with the situation through his reading of the newspapers and knew that the late Sir Philip Dapifer's second marriage was questionable. The first Lady Dapifer 'may well be repossessin' property that was rightfully hers in the first place. Get your sister a lawyer and fight it out in the courts.'

Sir Toby Tyler, MP, pronounced himself equally hamstrung. 'Matter for the courts, my boy. Inform me if there is anything I can do.' It was a phrase Aaron was to become sick of. 'Anything', he noticed, did not extend to taking Makepeace and her child into his home nor prosecuting their cause.

Back at Peter Little's house, Mrs Little opened the door to him. 'Peter's been called to the big house,' she said, 'but that Robert is here. Perhaps he can persuade her poor Sir Pip is really dead.'

Aaron followed her into her scrubbed, sparse little parlour. Dapifer's valet was kneeling, weeping into Makepeace's skirt. Makepeace's eyes were directed out of the window. 'They killed him,' she said.

Despairingly, Robert looked up. 'Oh, tell her,' he said. 'We weren't *well*. We looked poorly by the time we reached London. I said to him: "You're not well, my dear. Let *me* take Lord Ffoulkes back to school," but, oh no, we had to stir ourselves and do it. Then *they* came. Thursday, that was. In the major comes *and* her, bold as a miller's shirt.'

Robert sat up, wiping his eyes on Makepeace's petticoat. 'I was at the door. Not to make out the words, but they weren't going to stop me listening. Talk, talk, talk, her voice mostly, sometimes the major's, ours once or twice, very quiet. And then *crash*. And her scream. I ran in. We were on the floor, bless him, breathing like . . . well, *snoring* really.'

'They killed him,' said Makepeace.

Almost regretfully, the valet said, 'They weren't nowhere near him.'

'Didn't have to be,' Betty said. 'They bothered him to death.'

Outside the wavered, greenish glass of the parlour window, a thrush was singing in an apple tree, punctuating the stresses of the valet's falsetto as it recounted the death of a beloved.

At first, he said, Dapifer's repetition of 'Heart, heart' had been received as an indication of where the pain lay. Only Robert recognised that his master was demanding to be taken to Hertfordshire. 'It was "Hert" and "Crust" over and over. We meant *Procrustes*. He wanted *you*.'

The man turned to Aaron. 'I *said*. Shall we send for her? I said. But nothing was done. Anyway, she couldn't have got there in time.'

A doctor resident on the other side of the square, had been called in. Dapifer was carried to his bed, leeches had been applied. Catty had been hysterical and had confined herself to another room. 'But I wasn't going to leave him. I never let go of his dear hand.'

Everything had been provided for the patient's relief. 'But you could see it wasn't going to be any good. Our breathing . . . oh bless us.' The noise of it had filled every room, Robert said. It had gone on grinding, on and on like a millwheel, all night until—he'd lost track of time—the house was suddenly silent.

So, now, was the Littles' parlour.

It hadn't seemed unreasonable, Robert said after a while, to take the body back to Hertfordshire for burial. It was the Dapifer ancestral home. '*She* was there.' He nodded his head towards Makepeace. And to have an escort of Conyers's soldiers seemed only proper.

Once at Dapifers, he'd stayed with the coffin like a dog at its dead master's side, followed it to the graveyard, heard the stone grate back over the tomb . . . The song of the thrush in the apple tree mingled with Robert's weeping.

From upstairs, where Fanny was looking after the baby, came the sound of crying. 'Time for that chil's feed,' said Betty.

Once she'd taken Makepeace upstairs and seen the baby begin sucking, Betty left them both to Fanny and joined the two men and Mrs Little in the garden. 'Mebbe we can shift her now,' Betty said. 'Where we goin' to go, Aaron? We cain't stay here.'

'London. Her lawyer.'

'When do we set off?' Robert asked. At Betty's and Aaron's stares, he said, 'Well, I ain't staying with *them*, am I? She's got the right of it that far—they done him in.' Tears began again.

Aaron warmed to him; but it was going to be hard to support his sister and the others, let alone take on another mouth to feed. He said so, though he was sorry; behind the irritating posturing lay a breaking, loyal heart and a rare sense of honour. He nodded towards the big house. 'Keep you on, will they?'

Robert gave a dreary shrug. 'Expect so. I used to do her hair.'

'Stay with 'em.' Aaron took his limp hand. 'We need someone behind enemy lines.'

'A *spy*.' He was cheered. 'My dear, you shall know what I know as soon as I know it. I'll get a black cloak. We can use a *code*.'

They watched him prance along the village street. 'He look like a titmouse strayed into a farmyard,' Betty said, wiping her eyes.

Peter Little came slouching back. He could hardly bear to tell them. The call to the big house had been to inform him that if 'the troublemakers' were not promptly evicted from his house, indeed from the village, he and his family would be. He said, 'They're maintaining the will that left everything to the first Lady Dapifer is the only one valid because she's Sir Pip's only wife. It'll be a matter for the civil courts.'

Betty patted his bowed shoulder. 'Ain't your fault, you got to think for your childer.'

They couldn't have stayed in the house any longer, anyway; four people, having learned separately of Dapifer's death from the *London Gazette*, immediately and coincidentally boarded the same coach to Hertfordshire, and the arrival that night of Lord Ffoulkes, truanting from school, a distraught Susan Brewer, Dr Baines offering medical help and, astonishingly, John Beasley, added to the overcrowding.

At last Betty managed to strip Makepeace of the dress she'd worn since Dapifer's body had been brought home. 'You got to look decent tomorrow, no matter what,' she said firmly. 'We gettin' that chil' named afore we take the coach for London. An' we callin' her Philippa after her pa.'

There was a long silence. 'If you say so.'

Betty sagged with relief. Until now Dapifers had been the only place that held validity for Makepeace. Wicked as anything else Catty and Conyers had perpetrated against her, Betty knew, was the deprivation of her husband's death. Without watching life depart or taking part in the obsequies, for her, it was as if he'd merely sauntered off into the mist.

She took the soiled dress down to the washtub. There were some neatly rolled documents in the pocket let into the skirt. She had neither time nor light to read the densely written pages and put the roll into the holdall that, along with a rush basket and baby clothes, they were having to borrow from the Littles.

The next morning, at the hasty christening in a Hertford side chapel, the priest protested, 'All of you. Him too?'

'He's a baptised Christian,' Aaron said. 'All of us.'

Betty, Mrs Little, Susan Brewer and Fanny Cobb were pronounced godmothers to Philippa Dapifer. The ceremony also gave her seven godfathers: an estate steward, an American uncle, a small lord of the realm, an equally small black boy, a Scottish doctor, a Red Indian and a hack scribbler who didn't believe in any of it.

'**O**h yes,' Mr Hackbutt said, 'he changed his will right enough. "To my beloved wife, formerly Makepeace Burke of Boston . . ." But we have to prove that she *is* his wife. Did you safeguard his deed box? The divorce decree's in it, and the ship's marriage certificate, I saw them myself."

'Grosvenor Square,' said Makepeace wearily. 'Box in his office.'

'I suggest you go and get it this minute, before our friends return from Hertfordshire and destroy its contents.'

At the door, he held Aaron back and handed him a letter. 'Young man, I would spare your poor sister this for fear of distressing her further but she must be apprised of it sooner or later.'

The letter was from Cresswell and Partit, Solicitors. An injunction was being taken out by Major Sidney Conyers against Makepeace Burke to prevent her from making contact in any way with Lord Ffoulkes.

'They *can't* do that. She loves that boy, he loves her.'

'I fear they can,' Mr Hackbutt told him. 'The late Lord Ffoulkes appointed his two greatest friends to be his son's guardians in the event of his death. One was Sir Philip, the other Major Conyers. It seems our good major has just reminded himself that he is now in sole charge of a minor with a fortune.'

Aaron handed back the letter. 'There's nothing they won't take away from her, is there?'

At Grosvenor Square's Dapifer House the door was opened by a woman whose time had come. 'Yes?'

'Let us in, Mis' Peplow.'

'I take my orders from Lady Dapifer,' said Mrs Peplow, smiling.

The closing door wedged on Betty's boot. The tussle ended with the housekeeper pinned to the wall by a black fist round her neck. 'We's goin' to the master's office,' Betty explained. 'You arguin'?'

A blink from Mrs Peplow's popping eyes indicated that she was not, but as they crossed the hall they heard her scream, 'Too late!'

She was right. Dapifer's tall escritoire was empty, his deed box no longer stood on its shelf. Money, houses, clothes, status: everything Dapifer had given Makepeace had been taken away in one expert, audacious move. She had nowhere to turn. They'd broken her.

'Time to go, 'Peace,' Aaron said.

Mrs Peplow's triumphant vituperation followed them as they left Dapifer House for the last time.

Chapter Ten

PHILIPPA DAPIFER MADE her stage debut aged six and a half months in a barn at Stickney in Lincolnshire. She played Moses; she was very good.

The wind from the North Sea was moaning like a bassoon through the hayloft, a suitably mournful accompaniment to Pharaoh's daughter's soliloquy in the barn below. Draught guttered the candles nailed into the earth floor for footlights and shifted the distant turrets of Pharaoh's palace which, last week, had been the spires of Canterbury Cathedral. They could only afford one backdrop.

The hen they'd tried to dislodge from the rafters during rehearsal started to squawk, inciting a wag in the audience—there was always one—to call out, 'That's another dang female wants to lay a egg.'

Peg Devereux knew when she was losing an audience and cut to the last of her speech. 'But soft!' she exclaimed. 'What is this that floats so gently down the Nile?"

Peg glared at Makepeace, hidden in the prompt corner. Makepeace roused herself, pulled, and a rush basket slid into the stage area, causing gasps at the magic of its entrance.

'But, soft!' exclaimed Peg again. 'What is this that floats so gently down the Nile? An offering to the river god?'

'Danged if I know,' the wag said, genuinely interested.

Peg knelt and lifted out the basket's contents.

There was a coo from the audience. 'That's a real babby, look.'

It had been a physical risk to go on the road as early in the year as March, when carts got bogged down in mud and actors died from exposure, but Aaron hoped that an untried travelling theatre company might survive if it could reach places where other companies had never been. 'Picture an East Anglian winter,' he'd pleaded to Betty. 'Wouldn't you lay out good money on some drama after months of looking at sheep?'

She was reluctant. 'We ain't had enough drama?'

But *something* had to be done; the landlord of the two Holborn rooms they all shared was becoming restive for his rent. She and Fanny and Makepeace were taking in ironing in order to eke out Aaron's salary from the theatre, but sometimes there wasn't enough money to light a fire to heat the iron with.

'And it'll give 'Peace an interest,' Aaron said.

'Maybe.' Nothing else had, not even the baby. Betty said, 'Wish I knew what that bitch-whore said to her.'

Carrying home some washing, Betty had seen the Dapifer carriage drawing away along Holborn from the front door leading to their rooms and had run after it, hurling mud and abuse. Then she'd raced back and up the stairs. 'How'd she find us? What she say?'

'Nothing.' Makepeace was sitting on a stool, perfectly still.

Whatever else Catty had done, she'd scattered some coppers on the floor for Makepeace to pick up; they were still there. The old Makepeace would have rammed them down her throat.

So Betty had said, yes, they would join Aaron's touring company.

'But we ain't *actin*', we ain't fallen that far.'

The money for three carts and the mules to draw them came from Susan Brewer, who'd been saving the tips given her by Madame Angloss's aristocratic clients. 'Oh, Lord's sakes,' she said, when Aaron worried about taking it, 'Pip helped *me* enough.'

She'd had the opportunity denied to the rest of them of watching the reception given to Makepeace's downfall by the best drawing rooms. Mainly it had been one of amusement and a vague relief. An interloper had been taught a lesson, the old order restored.

'Just you make a fortune,' Susan said, 'so that we can all go back to Boston where we belong. Aaron, these people are *foul*. For two pins, I'd come with you.'

But the prospective touring company had too many non-professionals on its books already. Its actor-manager was looking for performers with theatrical experience—and desperation. He didn't need to look far.

Peg Devereux joined because she was thirty-seven and saw the chance in a ramshackle company like Aaron's to continue playing the romantic lead. Aaron welcomed her, partly because she was a good actress but mostly because her lover, Frederick Tortini, was a talented musician and he came with her.

Tom Capper was a comedian of genius, who could roll an audience on the floor with one twitch of his eyebrow. The difficulty, Aaron found, was to stop him doing his own floor-rolling in the nearest ale house.

At first it didn't occur to Aaron to ask Mr and Mrs Hartley Witney to join him; they were too grand and, well, too old. Between them they'd appeared with everybody who was anybody in the established theatre. But, it transpired, the established theatre had asked them to retire.

'It'll be hard,' Aaron said doubtfully, when they applied to him.

'We have supped too long from the fleshpots of Egypt, my dear boy,' Hartley Witney said. 'It is time for us to take our art to the untaught.'

Or, as Penthesilea Witney put it, 'We'd rather drop in harness than be put out to grass.'

Mr Burke's Touring Company was complete.

Before it set out, John Beasley shambled into the Holborn attic and looked at Betty. 'Where's that youngling of yours? He still want to paint?'

'How you know that?' Betty was defensive, she found her son's love of art mystifying and a touch effeminate.

'*She* told me.' He nodded towards Makepeace at the ironing table. 'There's a place going in Josh Reynolds's house. Might suit him.'

'Who he?'

'He's a painter.'

'He earn money for that?'

'A hundred guineas for a full-length portrait.'

A whistle escaped Betty's teeth. 'He goin' to teach the boy? Or do he just want a little black servant?'

'His sister does. She keeps house for him. But Reynolds says he'll let the boy mix paint, do jobs around the studio.'

It was a job at least. Josh was found, washed, brushed and the three of them went off to Leicester Fields, Betty suspecting every step of the way that her son was about to be plunged into a pool of homosexuality.

She came back reassured. Mr Reynolds had been charming—in a manly way. He hadn't seemed surprised that a black child should be interested in art. 'See him sniff the paints for their bouquet? He may be a natural, ma'am. If he shows promise, I shall bring him on.'

It was wonderful yet heartbreaking. Makepeace managed to say, 'Certain this is what you want, Josh? We can't be with you for a while.'

He nodded through tears. 'I want it.'

As she held him, Makepeace thought, He's being brave. He don't want to be a burden on us.

The next day the new company was gathering in Holborn when another young boy presented himself. '*There* you are. I've had the devil's own job finding you.' Lord Ffoulkes's round, freckled face was aggrieved and desperate. 'I've run away from school. I'm coming with you.'

Gently, Makepeace kissed him goodbye and walked away from him. As she climbed the stairs to the attic she heard Aaron begin the explanation: 'Andrew, you can't. The injunction—' She shut the door to keep the voices out, to stop hurt from piercing the dullness. Don't feel.

Betty came up, sobbing, 'First his pa, then Sir Pip, now you. Ain't nothin' those whoresons'll spare that boy.'

'Has he gone?'

Betty rubbed the window. 'He goin'. He cryin' but he goin'.'

Makepeace picked up her daughter and looked round the attic. 'We're off, then.'

'Betty turned on her. '*When* you goin' to get mad?' But she had to follow Makepeace down the stairs unanswered.

Aaron had been right. Avoiding urban centres like Norwich, where there were established theatres, they took themselves to the barns, inns and booths of small towns and villages. The people of rural Norfolk, and then of Lincolnshire, had come in droves—or at least small flocks—lured by Aaron's playbills which, no matter what the play, always promised an endangered virgin.

Everybody had to hand out playbills, but letting Tom Capper deliver on his own was not efficient. After three successive days on which he was brought back, comatose and in the cart of a concerned, admiring labourer, Aaron was forced to send Tantaquidgeon with him as his sobriety-enforcer. The sight of a six-foot Red Indian in a market square intrigued the local populace as much as the posters did.

'Your amiable friend is a phenomenon to these poor bucolics,' Hartley Witney pointed out. 'Use him.'

They already used him as cart-loader, scene-shifter and mule-driver. However, the next night, Tantaquidgeon was given a spear to carry during the last act of *Amanta in the West Indies*. Unmoving, unspeaking, he nevertheless attracted hoots of admiration. After that the bills for every play, whether set in Verona or Scotland, featured 'that Illustrious Noble Savage, Chief Hassan, grandson to famed Pocahontas'.

But the greatest home-grown phenomenon was Fanny Cobb. The whiff of make-up sticks came to the girl's nostrils like the scent of ocean to a stranded seal. She badgered the cast until Penthesilea Witney, always kind, taught her Polly's songs from *The Beggar's Opera*.

Fanny's voice was pleasant enough but . . . 'I want you to hear her,' Penthesilea told Aaron. Fanny was not consciously seductive; merely by opening her mouth the girl released a contagious joyousness that was as sexual as it was unaware.

'God bless us,' said Aaron with feeling.

The next night Fanny was the musical entre'acte. 'She'll bring the magistrates on us,' Peg Devereux said jealously.

'She'll bring the house down first.'

She was singing again, now, in order to cover an unplanned hiatus in *The Pharaoh's Daughter* caused by Tom Capper's disappearance to the Red Lion down the lane. Aaron and Tantaquidgeon had gone to fetch him. The audience, apparently, was finding no incongruity in the sudden leap from biblical drama to Cockney street songs just as, on Capper's return, they would accept cruel Pharaoh's comic knockabout with his clown. All part of the magic.

And it *was* magic, Makepeace could see that. The elderly Hartley Witneys, hastily reshuffling the sequence of the play; Fanny singing; Aaron tearing his hair out and loving it; Capper reducing his audience to helplessness all magical. She just got into a cart, stayed in it, got out, moving on strings, a wooden thing among the living.

'*Prompt*.'

Peg Devereux was glaring again. They had reached Act III without the prompter noticing. In the wings Moses began to whimper. Makepeace handed the script to Fred Tortini and carried the basket through to the green room, a flapping tent attached to the barn's side door.

Betty was counting the night's takings. 'Two pounds, four shilling an' sixpence ha'penny, two hens, a basket of bread, clutch of eggs an' a pot of somethin' as looks like someone been sick in it.'

'Very good,' said Makepeace politely.

'Ain't bad. We all eat tomorrow, any rate.' She produced a small jar from the region of her bosom where it had been kept warm. Makepeace began spooning its contents into Philippa's mouth.

'How'd she do as Moses?'

'Very well.'

'Very *well*.' The magic of theatre escaped Betty. 'Half a year old an' *actin'*. What'd Sir Pip think, his chil' raised with painted Jezebels?' She didn't approve of Peg Devereux either.

'I don't know what else to do.'

It was no use for Betty to employ the child's vulnerability in order to provoke her into a reaction, a plan or anger—she was incapable of those things. The only vulnerable sound in the world was a man's voice calling for his wife as he died among those who wanted him dead.

The odd thing was that her mind couldn't yet accuse Catty or Conyers. The real guilt was within her. God had presented her with the loveliest of His gifts and she had not protected it. And sometimes she blamed him for his complicity in abandoning her to this awful place.

Mr Burke's Touring Company made its way slowly into Yorkshire, keeping ahead of its rivals by going always northwards so that it seemed to be keeping pace with winter while at the same time promising spring to snow-fatigued villages. At Thornton-le-Dale, as she got out of her cart, Makepeace stumbled and couldn't get up again.

The company extended its stay—'By Popular Demand!'—until she was over the pneumonia and audiences reduced to a trickle. But she was still too weak to travel.

'We'll have to go on, that's all the money we've got.' Aaron pressed what there was into Betty's hand. 'We'll be at Fylingdale and then Whitby. Somebody's sure to give you a lift.'

Betty watched them go from the inn's upper window then turned on the figure in the bed. 'You goin' to live.'

'I suppose so.'

'Ain't a question. I'm tellin' you. We ain't goin' on like this.'

She told Aaron the same when they caught up with the company. He was busy and irritated. The Whitby justice of the peace, having Puritan objections to actors, had invoked the 1737 Licensing Act which made strolling companies illegal and refused them permission to perform. Aaron was having to turn the entire script of *Pharaoh's Daughter* into vaguely rhyming couplets, insert some songs and call it a 'burletta'. Burlettas were not classified as drama and could be played anywhere.

It was difficult for him to comprehend that a way of life he found all-consuming was in fact helping to keep Makepeace in her limbo. Privately, he was beginning to think that it didn't matter what course was chosen for Makepeace; she was too broken.

Betty knew she wasn't. 'She need to catch up with herself. She need time to get over the grievin' an' take in what those shites done to her. *Then* she get mad. *Then* she do somethin'.'

'What? *What* can she do?' Aaron was stung by his own failure to avenge his sister. His request to Conyers to meet him in a duel had been dismissed with a note: *Major Conyers is obliged to Mr Burke but would point out that, for their sake, he does not accept a challenge from his inferiors.*

Betty was steadfast. 'Maybe she set herself up. I found this.'

This had inveigled itself behind a rip in the lining of the bulging holdall they had borrowed from Peter Little, stuffed away by Betty and then forgotten in the haste of the eviction from Hertfordshire.

'I asked her what is it an' she don't remember, then she say it jus' property an' throw it away, like she don't *want* to remember.'

'*Property?*'

Betty held out the squashed documents. 'You look 'em over, Aaron.'

He took them to the window. '"Manor of Raby in the County of Northumberland . . . held in fee simple . . . messuage"—hell and high water, Betty, that's a dwelling house—"fishing rights, brew-house, forest . . ." This is an estate!'

'We can sell it?'

'She can't live there, for sure. It's in Northumberland.' Aaron, once a Bostonian, was now a Londoner, a townsman heart and soul. 'That's about as far north as you can go without painting yourself with woad.'

'You sure she own it?'

'Seems to. There's a deed of transference from the owner to Makepeace Burke that looks legal enough. Wonder why she used her maiden name? Should buy her a nice little place in Chelsea.'

Or a tavern on the river, not too far from Josh. Betty's imagination was soaring. 'We better go see this Raby. Quick.'

'**C**an a step doon the lonnon passin' the stob an' ye're hyem,' the wagoner said. 'Aa'd tyek ye but Aa'm queer.' He flicked his whip and the wagon lumbered away northwards.

'What he say?'

'I don't know. Maybe Tantaquidgeon scared him.'

To the east, the land petered out in sand-hills and sea; but the wagoner's whip had indicated a track that led west, into moorland deserted by everything but sheep. 'Well, let's git.' Betty was regretting bitterly her insistence that they investigate the Raby estate. Her image of a manor house had shrunk to a shepherd's hut—if they were lucky. Yet she still held to the belief that the *motive* behind this expedition was good. The bustle of other people's activity left Makepeace rudderless; she must be forced to take the tiller again. The discovery that she had something to sell whereby this could be achieved had seemed God-sent—but now didn't. Who'd want to buy bare moorland?

Newcastle upon Tyne had proved to be a town of unexpected prosperity, but the further north they went the greater sense they had of approaching the space at the end of the world.

Should've waited for Aaron to come with us, Betty told herself. However, Newcastle had been avid for entertainment and it would not have done to interrupt the company's run.

So here they were, three of them with a child, presumably already on Raby land. They hustled on in failing light as it began to rain. Betty and Makepeace were stumbling now. They kept their eyes on Tantaquidgeon's feather floating ahead, trusting to his cat's eyes.

He stopped. They'd breasted a hill. Below them, in a dip, was a light. Praise the Lord. They went down towards it, slithering on the muddy incline. Not a shepherd's hut but an ugly house, its shape wetly black against the lesser darkness of the moor. A glimmer from a downstairs window showed a yard, dilapidated outhouses, more mud and a woodpile. They picked their way through. Betty rapped on the window.

There was movement, the glow faded from the window, more movement and a man's voice, 'Wha's aboot this sneck?' A door to their right scraped against flooring as it opened. 'It's daft to be out on such a neet.' A furious-looking man stood in the doorway. As his rush light illuminated Makepeace's face beneath her dripping hood, the anger faded. After a moment, he said, 'Howay, pet. Coom in.'

He cut short Betty's apologies and explanations and hurried them in to a room that was dark except for a small coal fire. He busied himself lighting candles. 'Thought you might be the gaugers.' He caught Betty's look of incomprehension. 'The excise, pet. There's no peace from the sods wi' candles dutiable.'

He was a grim-looking man, of medium height, though his width of chest and shoulder made him seem squat, like a pugilist—an impression enforced by a powerful neck and a broken nose. He had black eyebrows and hair, grizzled at the sides and cut brutally short.

The man introduced himself. 'Andra Hedley, the factor of this place. Gi' us those wet clothes.'

The divestment of their cloaks revealed Philippa. He knelt down to her. 'What cheer, wheen-love. Hoongry? Shall us see what's in the yettlins?' He held out his hand; Philippa took it. They could hear him talking to her as he lifted her down the passage.

Betty nodded at Tantaquidgeon to go after them. It was an automatic precaution, she wasn't concerned; the man exuded power enough to split rock, but not the sort dangerous to little girls. On receiving them his Northumbrian dialect had ameliorated; he'd greeted Philippa with concern; he was offering food.

'A Christian,' Betty said, taking off her boots. She noticed that, as she did the same, Makepeace picked up the book the man had been reading. It was *Gulliver's Travels*.

Philippa marched in, chattering baby gobbledegook and holding spoons, followed by the men with wooden bowls and a cooking pot that Hedley hung over the fire. 'Carlins,' he said. 'Grey peas.'

It was only courteous to state their business before they accepted his meal, however unappetising. As Makepeace wasn't saying anything, Betty asked, 'This Raby we're at?'

When he nodded, she brought the documents out of the holdall. He took the papers and held them close to a candle for examination.

It was difficult to tell how old he was, anything from thirty-five upwards. The hands holding the papers were crisscrossed with little blue scars; there was another across his flattened nose.

'I've been expecting these. I was sent copies from London.' He looked up. 'Mr Burke, where is he? A hard man to find.'

'*Mister* Burke?' said Betty. '*That's* Makepeace Burke. There ain't no mister.'

He went still. 'Female.'

'Yes.'

'Bought the place from the Headingtons.'

'Yes.' She looked at Makepeace through Hedley's eyes and saw a figure resembling not so much an estate owner as a woman who sold pegs door-to-door. 'She sort of acquired it.'

He asked flatly, 'She's not rich?'

Betty was getting tired of it. 'We left the jewels and gold coach at the crossroads.'

He nodded. Then he walked out of the room. They heard the bang of the front door. Betty hurried to the window, Makepeace with her. He was standing in the rain, his face lifted to a sky he was threatening with his fists. His mouth was open and glinting like a howling wolf's.

When he eventually returned to the room, he was carrying a jug and beakers. He served them 'Nettle beer.' He slopped the contents of the cauldron into bowls and handed them round. 'Eat,' he said. Anger radiated out of him as if from a furnace but he was controlling it.

The food was surprisingly good. The beer wasn't.

Makepeace broke the silence. 'What's wrong with me being a woman, may I ask?' It was the first time she'd spoken since entering the house and her first question since Dapifer's death. Betty sat up.

'Nothing, pet,' Hedley said bitterly. 'You've the requisites as far as I can see. But I'd have liked you wealthy. I've been waiting for rich Mr Burke for over twelvemonth. Now, who comes tapping at my window? A benighted female.' He crashed his fist against the wall. 'And both of us sitting on a treasure house wi' no cash to turn the key.'

'Treasure house?' asked Makepeace.

'Coal, pet.' He put his face in his hands. 'Just coal.'

'Oh, coal.' The word 'treasure' had conjured sunken galleons, a miser's hidden hoard, gold from an ancient burial mound.

'Coal,' he said, lifting his head, amazed at her tone. 'That in yon fire. Stuff as smelts iron and steel, as powers the blast furnaces, as'll take us to the machine age and free men fra drudgery . . .' He regarded their incomprehension. 'God save us the ignorance.' He grabbed a lump of coal and pressed it into Makepeace's hand. 'How many ton o' coal were dug from the northeast last year, tell me that?'

She shook her head.

'Two million, give or take. Two *million* ton. Can tha take in the size of it? You *southerners*'—a dirty word—'thinks that England's wealth is corn? Wool? Na, it's coal.' Hedley swivelled on the stool to face Betty, who was still struggling to multiply the price of a ton of coal in London by two million. 'An' that's without wor new steam pumps. Ah tell thee, who's got coal's got riches an' power an', better, he's got the future. Ah could be the new Prometheus, an' what am Ah? Bloody Tantalus. We're standin' on the sod and can't reach it.'

Silence fell over the room as if a high wind had suddenly stopped blowing. 'Howay,' he said wearily, 'no use gollarin' at the moon. Tha's not to blame. I'll light you to your beds.'

Makepeace was turning the coal in her hand so that its facets caught the light, like a black diamond. 'Why can't we?'

'Eh? Equipment, pet. Pump engines, picks, wagons, rails, props. Men to dig, ponies to drag. Outlay of thousands o' pounds before the gain of ha'pence.'

As he took up a candle, Makepeace, still sitting, said, 'Suppose I'd had money and could've got the coal out, it would've been my profit, not yours. How would you benefit?'

He looked back at her, grinning, suddenly vulpine. 'Half, pet. I'm the only one knows where it is.'

'Do you believe him?'

'Nyumwhaa?' Betty woke up. Her body told her it was the middle of the night. Moonlight showed Makepeace at the window.

'Do you believe him?'

Betty yawned. 'I believe he believe it. What you doin', girl?'

Makepeace was regarding her hand, where moonlight put a sheen on a piece of coal. 'Know what I'd do with power?'

'How 'bout sleepin'?'

'I'd crucify them.'

Betty was suddenly chilled. She'd wanted Makepeace angry, but this was too matter-of-fact, too quiet; this was decay. She heaved herself out of bed. 'You don't want to worry 'bout them no more,' she said. 'Di'n't the Lord say He goin' to deal out vengeance?'

'He won't,' Makepeace said. 'He doesn't. He just keeps letting them crucify His son.'

Betty put her arms around her. 'You git back to bed, chil', give that baby a cuddle.'

She was embracing marble. It said, 'I'm going to crucify them. As sure as Jesus gave His blood for me, they're going to shed theirs, every last drop, for Philip Dapifer.'

Makepeace slept late next morning. The room was empty, a small dint in the pillow next to her where her child had lain. It was a cupboard bed, of surprising beauty inside where the panels were carved with festoons of leaves and apples. At one end, shelves held the Bible, Shakespeare, a grammar and a dictionary, the library of a man educating himself; but the greater section was taken up with homemade folders of canvas, their titles neatly inked: 'Coke-smelting', 'Puddling and Rolling', 'Steam Atmospheric Engines', 'Circulation of Air'.

She washed with water from a ewer on the windowsill. It was a lovely morning. The view of the yard below was still unprepossessing but beyond it the hills were a palette of gentle colours and the air smelt of grass, like spring. But it was no longer spring, it was autumn.

Philippa, who was being led round the yard on a donkey by the man Hedley, caught sight of her and waved. Awkwardly, Makepeace waved back. In the bad place she had been occupying, Philippa had demanded an energy and attention she'd found difficult to give. The little girl mostly went to Betty when she was troubled, instinctively avoiding the invisible fence of grief that surrounded her mother. And Makepeace did not know how to bridge it.

She'd be a year old now.

Twelve months. How had she survived them? Such laceration, she'd had to crawl into the deepest part of her soul to withstand the agony. Something, God she supposed, had been stitching the wounds, but so haphazardly that the result was a limping freak in permanent pain.

With survival, if it could be called survival, the outside world had crashed in and brought with it this flooding hatred.

It was almost amusing, Makepeace thought, that what Catty and Conyers must see as the deepest injury they'd inflicted on her was, in fact, the least. They would be rejoicing at stealing Dapifer's wealth, his status, his lands, but they could have had them without trouble if they'd only allowed her to attend him while he died. They had been incapable of even that grace.

She would kill them for it one day. But the reason she would make them suffer before they died, see them chomped alive from the feet up like fledglings being eaten by a hedgehog, was for the malice that separated her from Andrew Ffoulkes, not caring how they hurt the boy as long as they hurt her.

And for the visit to the attic room in Holborn. '*What did she say?*' Betty had asked and asked. The thing was, she'd said nothing, just stood in the doorway and smiled: at the dingy room, at the grate's two pieces of coal, at the wounded thing in the middle of it.

And one day, when *you're* in the last extremity, I shall stand in your doorway. And I'll be smiling.

She picked up the piece of coal from the sill and looked down again at the man who'd given it to her. He was kindly enough, for all his anger. In effect, this was his house; he'd surrendered it to them last night: Headington House itself was a ruin, he'd said. He'd gone off to sleep in his workshop at what he called the but 'n' bens along the track.

At her approach he swung Philippa down from his shoulders.

'About this coal . . .' she said.

They went indoors for the discussion. He set the chair for her and took the stool. 'You'd best sell,' he said. 'It's what I advised yon Mr Headington.' He had the estate's books and accounts ready to show her, all meticulously kept. Raby had been a prosperous manor but, he said, had suffered a hundred years of neglect. To the Headingtons Northumberland had always been here-be-dragons land; they preferred London. They'd been fortunate in having an honest factor—Andra Hedley's grandfather, a man with a head for business, who'd begged his employers to speculate in order to accumulate. 'He found 'em coal. Would they put money in it? "Just keep up the rents, Mr Hedley."' He glared at Makepeace as if it were her fault. 'We dug what we could and the main seam was there, ready as a lass on a Saturday night, but she wouldn't wait for ever and she didn't.'

Makepeace shifted. Coal was not a substance she was acquainted with. 'Can't you just find another seam?' she asked.

Hedley lowered his head and drummed his fist on his forehead. After a minute he looked up. 'Get your boots on.'

They set out along a continuation of last night's track. As Tantaquidgeon followed, Hedley asked, 'Is that lad mum fra choice?'

'Wounded,' Makepeace said shortly. 'The talking bit of his brain got hacked away by another tribe.'

'How old is he?'

She shrugged. 'About five.'

'Pity,' Hedley said. He paused for a moment. 'What're you to be called? Mrs Burke? Lady Dapifer? What?'

Betty *had* been busy. Makepeace was at a loss; she couldn't answer him because she truly didn't know.

Going upwards, the track became a green lane sunk between beeches that diffused the sun into penny-sized dapples. A path to the right led to a row of cottages but they kept straight on.

At the top of the hill two gates marked an overgrown drive to a ruin. 'Headington House,' Hedley said as they went by.

They came out into moorland where sheep pulled at the thin grass in soft, dry rasps, unalarmed by intrusion. Butterflies bounced along with them. Peregrines winnowed the air before disappearing in a stoop to kill; some red deer posed as if for their portrait.

Hedley walked in silence and with a roll of the shoulders as if he were breasting a heavy sea. Makepeace wondered if he'd been born angry or had anger thrust upon him, as hatred had been thrust on her.

They'd negotiated a valley and come to the top when he pointed. And there it was in the distance, a black tangle of chimneys, frames, wheels and huts. They walked towards it. Nettles grew round the buildings; machinery rusted quietly in the sun. Weeds were beginning to forgive a slag mound and covering it in a haze of green.

Hedley removed boarding from under a rusted crane to reveal a great hole in the ground. 'Here's the main shaft.' A stone was pressed into Makepeace's hand. 'Chuck it doon.'

She leaned over the hole and let the stone drop. After what seemed a long wait she heard a tiny splash. Hedley said, 'That's watter. *Watter*. She drowned her bloody self when the roof came in.'

The shaft had been dug on his grandfather's initiative, he said, with the Headingtons reluctantly paying for only minimal equipment. After the roof fell in they'd refused to provide any at all. 'A decent pump, one decent bloody steam pump and we'd still have her dry, but Headington would only afford us a horse gin.'

Still standing on the edge of the shaft, Makepeace was given a brief history of coal and the vast fortunes that had been made from it. Newcastle and its industries—salt, glass, brewing, brick-making, the metal trades, shipping—had been built on it and were growing fast.

Makepeace peered again. 'There's still coal down there?'

'Think on a wall,' he said. 'Bloody eighteen yard of coalface. That's what my father and me saw down there. I been down pits twenty-seven year an' never glimpsed richer. An' then dust started tricklin' over wor heads an' we knew she was comin' in. The quicker the dust trickles, the faster you run. We bloody ran. Down comes the roof behind us. How we got out wi' wor lives is a bloody miracle.' His voice changed into that of a lover mooning over an unattainable mistress. 'She's under rock and water but she's still there. Come on, pet, we'll go down.'

They moved away from the pithead and walked down the hill to another entrance to the mine: a narrow cave overhung by ferns. Hedley brought out various items from the bulging pockets of his coat: a tinder-box, candles and a cap of quilted leather he told her to put on. For a moment, as she took off her linen cap, the sun on her hair made him blink. 'That'd set off fire-damp,' he said and led the way. Almost immediately, the entrance became a tunnel little over four feet high, sloping downwards so that they both had to stoop.

Hedley paused, looking back. 'What's doing?'

She turned to see that Tantaquidgeon wasn't following. It was so unusual, she went back. 'What's the matter?'

There was no expression on the Indian's face, there never was but, looking at it, she saw the deep creases carved into the bronze of his skin. He's got old, she thought, and I haven't noticed. Under her gaze he folded his arms and turned away.

'We all have wor demons,' Hedley said. 'Mebbe his lies underground.'

Perhaps it did. She turned and left him, feeling naked.

The tunnel sloped downwards, turned, flattened and sloped again. The place was a labyrinth; she lost her sense of direction. As they went deeper they were passing among small pillars, four-cornered piers of jet that glistened wetly. 'Is this coal?' she called.

'Aye. Keeps the roof up.'

After a while he stopped before a black and motionless pool of water. 'Flood,' he said. 'Same watter as at the bottom of the shaft.'

There was a niche in one of the walls with a bench fixed across it. He told her to sit. She was in his classroom. 'See, pet,' he began, 'the earth doesn't appreciate being violated, she'll keep her coal if she can . . .'

'She', apparently, had terrible ways of killing the human moles who tried to rob her, sometimes crushing them, sometimes flooding their tunnels to drown them. There was a noxious fume called 'choke-damp' that took miners' breath and lives, and 'fire-damp' which caused explosions so strong it could blow men's bodies hundreds of feet up vertical shafts into the open air.

'Wor Peter were killed like that,' he said heavily, 'me brother.'

She wasn't ready for other people's tragedies. 'How d'you know the wall of coal you and your father saw doesn't run out further on?'

He grunted, amused. 'I saw it. She's there, I *smelt* her.'

He stretched and stood up. 'One more thing. Folk that send men down mines do it lightly. They need to know what light is—*and* dark. Don't be feored, I'm dousing the candle for a minute.'

Black. A presence that pressed upon the eyelids; the coffin lid coming down, the withdrawal of self, of hope, of God. In that moment she knew what death actually was.

She lost Dapifer then. *Is this where you are, Pip? Is this what you know?* But he didn't know anything; he was in eternal insentience.

There was the scrape of a tinderbox and a tiny waver of light as the candle lit. Hedley started to speak, then went to his knees beside her. 'I'm sorry, pet, I'm a clown. You seemed unafeored . . .'

She thumped on his shoulder with her fist. 'He was the most alive person I ever knew, oh *God*, and they sent him into . . . there isn't a God, I saw it, just nothingness.' The loneliness was intolerable.

He sat down, one arm around her so that she could weep onto his jacket. It smelt of coal dust and iron.

'Obliteration,' he said, after a bit. 'Whiles I thought the same.'

When her weeping grew less fierce, he withdrew his arm and produced a kerchief. 'But see, bonny lass,' he said, 'the candle lit up again. Persephone comes yearly out the shadows and you'll do the same. Give us your hand and I'll take you home.' With her hand in one of his, the other holding the candle, he shuffled with her out of the tunnel.

Air, birdsong and the smell of bracken blasted themselves at her and she put back her head, letting sunlight wash through her. Then she was hurt by her body's surrender to physical contentment as if, like a child, it had not been paying attention to the grown-up business of mental agony.

She noticed Hedley walk up to Tantaquidgeon and talk to him. She experienced a sudden nausea at the intimacy he and she had shared. She'd exposed her soul, her *husband*, to a damn quarryman.

Anyway, it was her job to comfort Tantaquidgeon, not his.

'Anybody could get the coal out,' she said nastily. 'They wouldn't need you.'

'They could try, pet,' he admitted, 'but they wouldn't find her, they'd need to know where she lies.'

She took a last look around, trying to imagine the maze beneath her feet. Damn the man, he was right.

As she began to trail after him on the path back, common sense and the sweetness of being above ground gradually brought her balance back. The lesson had been well learned; she'd absorbed more knowledge about the working of mines by actually being in one than if she'd attended fifty lectures. She called out to him, 'How much money would it need to get the mine producing?'

'Ten thousand pound,' he called back. 'At least.'

When Hedley left her at the door of the ugly house, she was too preoccupied to say goodbye.

'Wife died givin' birth,' Betty said, serving rabbit stew. 'Only got the one and had him eddicated. The boy's gone for a lawyer in Newcastle. Andra said he din't want his chil' down a pit draggin' coal wagons at eight year old, like he was. Sent down to join his pa, Andra was, when work run out here. It's his brother give us the coneys. One got killed in the pit, this 'un's Jamie, lives in one o' the but 'n' bens down the track, got two childer.' Betty, also, had been absorbing local knowledge.

'What sort of man d'you reckon him, Bet? Clever? Or mad?'

Betty raised her eyebrows. 'Bit o' both, mebbe.'

The scales of Makepeace's opinion were out of level all night, first on one side, then the other. The wall he and his father had seen might be just that: a freak seam of coal behind which was just more rock. But *if* it didn't run out, *if* it went on to form the equation: wealth equals power equals ability to harm . . . what then?

It all depended on the person of Andra Hedley. Prophet or crackpot? Even supposing she could procure the £10,000, he would have to be her security; she had no other. Another look at Hedley might make up her mind. Next morning, she went up the track and took the turning off it that led to the but 'n' bens, which turned out to be a row of two-roomed cottages. Most were deserted but two at least were neatly kept. Hens pecked at feed a woman was scattering outside her front door. She nodded good morning at Makepeace. 'Andra?'

'How d'you do. Yes.'

'Plodgin' wi' his fire engines, end o' raa.' She indicated the last cottage.

Smoke issued in strong, regular puffs from the cottage's open door and windows. Makepeace could hear clanking and the wheeze of giant breathing. She approached carefully—into wet heat. It wasn't smoke, it was steam. Peering through it, she saw a brass cylinder on top of a washing boiler on top of a fierce fire in a bucket, the whole thing topped by a movable beam with two vertical arms going up and down.

She waited. In all the information he'd given her yesterday, there'd been mention of the names Savery and Newcomen, two gods who had converted fire to the pumping of water out of mines and had thereby supplanted the antiquated horse-drawn gin-mill. The contraption before her, she supposed, was one such engine.

She was reminded of Boston's shipyards and odd little men, like this one, who built model hulls in their parlour in order to make a marginal improvement on them; who obstinately refused to accept things as they were but had a vision of things as they could be; men who drove their wives mad and the world forward.

Eventually, the boiler ran out of steam and the contraption shuddered to a halt. The figure of Andra Hedley came like a ghost out of the steam. 'I'll find us the money, Mr Hedley,' she told him. She had, she realised, made up her mind some time before. What else was there to do?

Chapter Eleven

IN ORDER TO RAISE the £10,000, Makepeace decided to approach Philip Dapifer's richest and closest friends. She felt no qualms about playing on their sympathy and conscience. Investing in her mine would be recompense for having allowed a woman Dapifer loathed to disinherit both his child and the woman he'd loved.

Luckily for Makepeace, the time was right for investment. There was an excitement now, almost amounting to panic, which possessed men who saw that Britain was entering a new era. Because Dapifer had shown no interest in the coming of the mechanical age, Makepeace hadn't either. But the men she was to visit during that winter of 1767, asking them almost literally for money to burn, knew better. The new Jerusalem could only be built on coal.

They might have initially granted Makepeace a hearing through guilt or compassion, but it's doubtful whether they'd have given her anything more if it hadn't been for Andra Hedley. She very nearly didn't take him with her. They were seriously at odds: Makepeace wanted a controlling interest in the company to be formed if they found coal; Hedley had refused. 'Fifty-fifty or nothing, pet.'

'I own the damn land,' she said.

'And I'll be getting the coal out of it.'

His experience of coal-owners had not been happy; all of them 'pornicious sods' who treated their miners no better than rats and paid them crumbs for doing the most dangerous job in the world. Few collieries gave sufficient compensation for injury or death incurred in an accident, some gave none at all. In order to earn a living wage for the family, wives and daughters had to join their men underground and drag the baskets from the coalface to the surface. 'And I'm not having that in any pit of mine.' Hedley's colliery was going to treat its men and women as human beings should be treated.

He refused to believe that Makepeace wouldn't tolerate inhumanity either. He saw her as a representative of the ruling class. She might call herself Mrs Burke—the title she'd opted for—but in truth she was Lady Dapifer and *ipso facto* a persecutor of the labouring poor. All government, aristocracy, landowners and new industrialists were in a conspiracy to maintain a cheap work force.

The first visit to Raby by Aaron, who brought Fanny with him from Newcastle where their run was being extended by genuine public demand, had merely confirmed Hedley's view that here was a family with social pretensions. Introducing her brother to him, Makepeace saw that the two men were inimical. Against Hedley, whose idea of elegance was a clean shirt, Aaron looked every inch an actor, clothes a little too highly coloured, heels a little too high, gestures too grandiloquent.

Hedley mistook Aaron's bafflement at the mining process as belonging to a man who despised those who got their hands dirty.

'He's worse than John Beasley,' Makepeace fulminated to Betty. 'Thinks he's the only radical in the business. A pretty penny I'll get out of Rockingham and the others with him in tow. He's so damn rude.'

'Clever an' all,' Betty pointed out.

There was that. According to him, his adaptation of the Newcomen engine made it a more efficient pump. Furthermore, that swarthy head of his boiled with ideas for improvements to mining techniques. If potential investors could disregard how uncouth he was, she might yet get her money. So, yes, she would take him but, first, she gave him a lecture on behaviour. 'The men we're going to see won't lend us a farthing if you talk to them like a damn Leveller.'

He looked her straight in the eye. 'Credit me with sense, pet.'

'And don't call me "pet".'

She had to hope he would behave himself but, as they stood side by side in the glory that was Wentworth House, waiting to be shown in to the presence of the Marquis of Rockingham, Hedley still looked as if she'd brought him along to do the plumbing.

Rockingham came to them in the hall, almost bounding. This eager courtesy from such a magnate to one poor woman was either guilt on his part or, possibly, because he was a very nice man. She didn't care either way; she merely wanted his money.

'My *dear* Lady Dapifer, I cannot tell you the relief of hearing you announced . . .' But he continued to do so, detailing the enquiries he'd made for her, his worry, his distress over Dapifer's death.

You could have found me if you'd wanted to, she thought. Unsmiling, she introduced Hedley. 'It's a matter of business, my lord.'

Rockingham ushered them towards his library. He looked much older now that he was out of office. His liberal attitude to America had earned him the King's particular dislike, and Pitt had refused to cooperate with him in keeping the administration alive. He's missing Pip, Makepeace thought. Pip was the one who kept them all together.

Makepeace began by reminding Rockingham that his wife had been present at Almack's on the night of the wager between her and Headington, then she explained what she'd found at Raby.

Immediately she mentioned the word 'coal' Rockingham's expression sharpened. Where had she seen the look before? *Pioneering!* Good Lord, it was the same gleam that had been in the eyes of her father and other men setting out to explore the American wilderness.

He'd turned his attention to Hedley, asking sharp questions, listening carefully to equally sharp Northumbrian answers. How thick was the seam? Hard coal, was it? How deep? Watching them, Makepeace saw a new thing: two people from the two most distant ends of society bridging what had previously been unbridgeable. Here was the new age.

Hedley was drawing on a fine linen napkin. Makepeace heard Rockingham ask, 'Rectangular corves?' and Hedley say, 'Wheeled, d'you see. Save emptying, put 'em straight on rails. We'd stop fouling with conductors braged on opposite sides of wor shaft . . .'

Makepeace intervened. She had no idea what braged conductors were but there was no need to make Rockingham a present of them. 'No need to waste his lordship's time on details, Mr Hedley.'

Rockingham was wily. He took his guests on a carriage tour, and found an opportunity to speak first to one, then the other, alone.

He and she were by themselves in a rose garden when he gently offered to buy Raby outright at a price which, invested, would see her comfortable for the rest of her days. 'Coal production is a hard taskmaster,' he said, 'even supposing your pit proves profitable.'

Then why d'you want it? She didn't even consider the offer. He might be being kind, paying his dues to Dapifer's memory, but she didn't want comfort, she wanted to slake her hatred in blood and for that she needed vaster wealth than he could give her. Besides, how else was she to fill these leftover days of her life? Needlework?

'I have time to kill,' she said, and was struck by her unconscious *double entendre*. She smiled.

In the end she settled for a straight loan of £5,000. 'It's a long-term investment,' she warned Rockingham.

'I know,' he said, 'but if I'm a judge of Mr Hedley, it is a secure one.'

On the way back to the inn, she passed on the compliment. 'Rockingham thinks you're clever.'

'I am,' he said smugly. 'Yon's a canny lad. Asked me to work for him.'

So this was the world of business, was it? You couldn't trust anybody. 'The shite,' she said.

At his foundry in Birmingham, Sir Benjamin Judd was less amiable towards Makepeace than he'd been in Grosvenor Square. 'Yow seem to have landed on your feet, any road. Well, I'll lend you a shilling or two for old times' sake . . .'

'Lord Rockingham's investing five thousand pounds,' she said.

'Is he? *Is* he now? Aye, but hard coal's no use to me, my furnaces need coke . . . Any road, where's your security?'

Makepeace said, 'My security is my business partner. Talk to him.'

Sitting quietly in the background while Sir Benjamin and his foundry manager questioned Hedley, she watched the miracle happen again. Hedging it around with repayment requirements and eventual interest at three per cent, Sir Benjamin raised his offer to £3,000.

Makepeace took it, without thanks.

In Hertfordshire, she called on Sir Toby Tyler, MP, and let Hedley work the oracle once more—to the tune of £2,000.

It had been amazingly easy.

Hedley took the next stage back to Newcastle. Makepeace stayed on; she had duties in the South. She wouldn't go near her old home but she received two people from it at the White Hart in Hertford: Peter Little, its steward, and Robert French, now Conyers's valet.

Loyalty to his present employer prevented Peter Little from saying too much about what was happening at the big house. It had been another bad harvest. No, the . . . um . . . lady of the manor had not been at Harvest Supper; she'd stayed in London.

Makepeace filled in the gaps. With its foundation-head gone, the village of Dapifers was neglected; Catty was not a woman to leave the London season to attend a ceremony in a country orchard; nor was Conyers a man to toss corn-sheaves onto wagons. Who, if anybody, put flowers on Dapifer's grave? *I will, Pip. One of these days.*

But, of course, Robert had, on the anniversary of Dapifer's death. 'Nobody else there. Just a quiet little moment twixt him and me. The major looked at me very old-fashioned when I got back, I can tell you.'

'Why does he keep you on?' Makepeace wanted to know.

Robert surprised her. 'Because he wants everything that was Sir Pip's. That's what he's doing, you know, living his life for him. I think it's sending him mad.' In his high, mannered voice, Robert drew sketches of Hogarthian horror: Conyers's languid ease of manner and frantic lapses; the quarrels with Catty that went through a cycle of screams, blows and eventual reconciliation in violent sex.

'Are they going to enclose?' she asked him.

'Peter Little wants it, but I *don't* think we've got the money.'

'They've got all mine,' said Makepeace grimly.

'And are *spending* it, my dear. Paying off debts, clothes, pretty new jewels, gambling, entertainments in town—then there's the wedding . . .' Robert cocked an eye. 'You know we're getting married?'

'Not before time.' She hurried him on to what was important. 'Robert, how's Andrew?'

'Ah, *well*, Lord Ffoulkes is a disappointment. We've tried buying the boy's affection, we've positively *rained* gifts, but the little serpent's tooth lacks gratitude. Didn't want to come down for Christmas.'

'You'll tell me if they hurt him. In any way.'

'Of *course*.' Robert began crying. 'Didn't we love that boy?'

'Can you get a message to him for me?'

In London Makepeace stayed with Susan Brewer in the pleasant Clerkenwell apartment she was renting in Theobald's Road from a Jewish family, relatives of Madame Angloss.

'I didn't know Madame Angloss was a Jewess.'

'I didn't either,' Susan said, 'not 'til I gave her notice—'

'You've left Madame Angloss?'

'Stop interrupting. I've left her in one way, not another—well, it became impossible. Catty was everywhere, being *hideously* amusing about American taste. If I saw her again I'd have stuck the scissors in her.'

'Oh, Susan.' Makepeace was conscience-stricken; immersed by the tidal wave of Dapifer's death, she'd ignored the difficulty others might be experiencing in its undertow.

'It's all right, Makepeace, really. Madame Angloss understood; she said she knew what it was to hear one's race belittled in the mouths of vulgar English *aristos*. She put me in touch with Mr and Mrs Franco, who own this house, and you'll never guess what I'm doing . . .'

Susan produced a hat such as the second Lady Dapifer in her heyday would have killed for. It was straw, tip-tilted back and front, it was blond, it was springtime.

Makepeace snatched it. 'You designed this?'

'Good, isn't it? I call it the Philippa. I sent a consignment to Auntie that sold out in a week. Mr Franco says . . .'

Makepeace was standing in shock at the looking-glass. 'I'm too old for it. God, Susan, I'm *old*.' Something had happened to her face. It was not just haunted, it was haunt*ing*.

Wearily, she took the hat off. 'What were you saying?'

Susan's voice became very gentle: 'They . . . the Jews, Mr Franco says they're grateful to Sir Pip. When he was a young man, at the time of the "Jew Bill", something about giving them more rights, Pip was lobbying to get it made law. It didn't get passed but . . . they loved him for it.'

The loss filled the room; Dapifer was everywhere in it, gloomy, funny, valuable. After a while Makepeace said, 'They've got to pay for him, Susan, I can't live if they don't.'

And Susan said, 'He didn't have a price.'

John Beasley turned up uninvited because bailiffs were after him.

'What have you done this time?'

He'd drawn a cartoon for *Town and Country Magazine*, showing a man and a woman driving off in a coach, leaving its occupants, a mother and her baby, shivering in the snow. The name of Dapifer was writ large on the coach door. 'Conyers didn't like it,' Beasley said. 'Took out injunctions against me and *Town and Country*. Too late, though, it'd got round most of the clubs. Now the bastard's trying to sue us for libel.'

'We'll see about that.' Makepeace took the matter up with Mr Hackbutt when she went to consult him in Lincoln's Inn Fields.

'Ah yes, your friend Mr Beasley, a young man sailing *very* close to the wind,' he said. 'However, in this case I doubt if Major Conyers will proceed with the libel prosecution. A scrawl in a scandal rag is one thing, evidence produced in court another. Evicting a recently bereaved widow and child from their home is not an act to rehabilitate him and his fiancée in the minds of respectable people, and respectability appears to be what they are after.'

He had bad news. Chafing at the delay in receiving a copy of the divorce papers from Boston, Mr Hackbutt had written again. 'I have just received a reply to tell me that such confirmation was destroyed during the rioting.' He gave his desk a blow with his fist. 'The Boston court registrar of those days kept papers in his *house*, if you'll credit it, and the damn building was burned down with them in it.'

Makepeace said nothing; there was nothing to say. The stars in their courses were fighting for Catty.

Mr Hackbutt got up to thump his client encouragingly on her back. 'Now, now, we'll not give up. I have hounds in America even now approaching the judges who heard the case. We'll have their affidavit in time and then it's "Tally-ho", eh?'

'I'm tally-hoing now.' Makepeace told him about Raby and brought out the proposed partnership agreement that had been drawn up in Newcastle for Andra Hedley by his son.

Master Oliver Hedley had proved to be a newly qualified young lawyer, *very* young, but tall and graceful. He'd suggested Makepeace take the draft to her own lawyer. 'I shan't sign it,' Makepeace had told him. 'I want a controlling interest. It's *my* land, *my* coal.'

Master Oliver had smiled politely. 'But if you'll forgive me, ma'am, Dadda says "Find it".'

Mr Hackbutt took the document to the window. 'It's a workmanlike agreement as far as it goes, but I cannot advise fifty per cent—such an arrangement invariably leads to stalemate.'

'That's what I thought,' Makepeace said, 'but it's him got us the money, not me. I'm going to sign.'

On Makepeace's last night at Theobald's Road, those who had loved Dapifer and his second wife gathered round Susan Brewer's dinner table for what was, though none of them said so, a delayed wake. Alexander

Baines came to join John Beasley and so did Aaron; Mr Burke's Company had returned to London for a winter season after its triumphant tour of the provinces.

Dr Baines was another who'd been caught up in the undertow of Dapifer's death. Catty had spread word around town that he was an incompetent doctor who'd ignored Dapifer's dangerous condition. It was taking time for his practice to recover.

The two boys, Josh and Andrew Ffoulkes, arrived together into a riotous welcome. Lord Ffoulkes was having his portrait painted by Joshua Reynolds in order to keep in touch with his friend.

'Are you all right?' Makepeace asked.

He passed most holidays on his Kent estates with his servants, with whom he was happy enough. 'I don't like visiting *them* much,' he said of Catty and Conyers. 'They're very excitable, you know . . .' It was a gentleman's languid condemnation such as Dapifer might have used and it brought tears to Makepeace's eyes. 'I miss you,' he said.

'I miss you too.' She turned to Josh. 'Are *you* all right?' She hated the fact that Betty's son was in livery like any other negro servant.

'Fine, I'm doin' fine,' he said staunchly.

She didn't want them brave. Not yet, not yet.

They were all happier once they'd crammed themselves around Susan's small dining table, as if they'd formed a protective circle against the dark. Makepeace felt how precious it was, this unbreakable circlet of ill-matched friendships, how freeing to be given this little holiday from hate to play with them. It didn't stop her getting up before dawn the next morning and catching the stagecoach back to her coal mine.

THEY BOUGHT A NEWCOMEN engine and housed it, suitably adapted, in the flooded shaft—the one Hedley imaginatively called Shaft A. The machine clunked and after every clunk came the bronchial wheeze as water was raised to a wooden soakaway that ran to a stream and from there to the sea. Another shaft—Shaft B—was sunk. Then a ventilation shaft, to let out the gas that had been accumulating in the mine since it was abandoned. Tunnels had to be safely propped with timber; doors constructed to encourage draught along the tunnels; rails laid; wagons purchased; the staith (a pier) built at the sea's edge from which coal could be lowered into the keels (boats) to sail it to the great collier fleet on the Tyne for delivery to London. Miners hired . . .

'We're not going to have enough damn money,' screeched Makepeace, keeping the books in the Factor's House parlour.

'Have to get more then, pet,' Hedley said, and went back to work.

Spring came and went in hard work and expense.

One day in June, with the sun so hot that the arc of moorland around them stood to rigid attention, Makepeace suddenly raised her head from the accounts. The noise of the pump had changed.

'Come *on*.' Makepeace took Philippa's hand, Betty took the other, and between them they swung the child out of the yard towards the mine with Tantaquidgeon behind. Jamie Hedley, his wife Ginny, two children and a dog joined them, running down the track from the but 'n' bens.

Hedley was standing by his engine shaft, shrugging as if it were nothing. 'She's dry,' was all he said. But Makepeace knew him now, could sense the triumph in the very stance of his body.

They shook hands. '*Now* do we get coal?'

'Got to clear the fall first, pet,' he said. 'Where's that dog?'

'Here, Andra. Stray,' Jamie told Makepeace. The dog was wearing a harness with a pocket which held a candle.

Women and children followed the men to the new wheelhouse at Shaft B where a large basket hung from a windlass over the platform beneath which was the pit. Hedley swung the basket to the shaft platform. 'In you get, pet.' He lifted the dog in and got in himself. When Jamie tried to climb in with him, his brother pushed him away. 'Who's going to man the bloody wheel?'

The windlass shrieked. Makepeace, leaning over the safety rail, watched the basket and its cargo descend at speed until it was lost in the darkness. 'What's he going to do?'

'Test for fire-damp.'

A ratchet had stopped the windlass of its own accord. Jamie pulled on a lever, his eyes on the swinging chain. 'Howay wi' 'em, Ginny.'

His wife began shooing everyone out of the shed, leading them down the hill to sit on the grass in a dip out of sight of the mine. 'Reet, bairns, who'll get most dayseyes and pittlybeds?'

As the children ran to pick flowers, Betty said, 'Why the dog?'

'Carries the candle aheed on a long lead. She drops deed or blows up, you've found fire-damp.' Ginny wiped sweat off her forehead.

'What happens then?'

'Get another bloody dog.' Makepeace noticed her hands trembling.

'Look, Mam.' Philippa showered daisies and dandelions into Makepeace's lap.

'Lovely, pet. Stay here a bit.' She got up and walked up the hill to the wheelhouse. Jamie Hedley was by the wheel, watching the motionless chain. 'Howay, bonny lass,' he said, not moving, 'a fireball could blow us all into eternity.'

'You go then,' she said.

'He's me brother.'

'It's my coal.'

She sat down with her back against the rail and thought of him following the dog and knowing, however long the lead between, that if it came across a large enough concentration of the silent enemy the flame would ignite it, them, the whole damn mine.

Jamie was watching her. 'You and Andra sparkin', pet?'

'Sparking?'

'Lovers.'

'No, we're *not.*'

He nodded and turned his attention back to the rope.

Years went by. At last the chain jerked. Jamie shouted: 'He's hoom! She's clear!'

Later, back at her office, she and Hedley argued. He wanted to hire miners right away.

'If we're just clearing the fall, we don't need skilled men yet,' Makepeace pointed out. 'We can shift it ourselves with a few others. We'll hire women to pull the corves, they're cheaper.'

He pounded on the table. 'Didn't I tell you no women down pit?'

'And didn't I tell you we're running out of *money*?' she screamed back.

She knew she was right; there was still horrific expense to be laid out when they reached coal; even now she would have to go cap in hand for more investment. To tempt skilled miners away from other collieries would mean building accommodation for them and their families. And Hedley, damn him, wanted ponies to drag the corves of coal to the surface, not women, which meant more outlay, stables, feed . . .

She shouted at him. He shouted at her. Betty came in with a tray of nettle beer to say they'd woken Philippa. 'Quit cussin'. You forgittin' tomorrer's Sunday?' There was to be a church outing next day and she was looking forward to it.

When Betty had gone, Makepeace went to the window and threw the contents of her tankard outside. 'I can't drink this piss.'

'You don't like nettle beor?' Hedley was amazed.

'No.'

'I wor brought up on it,' he said.

'You can tell.'

She hadn't seen him laugh before; it was a loud surprise.

'Fifty-fifty, bonny lass,' he said, back in a good temper. 'We'll use women to clear the fall, temporary like, but it's men for the coal and paid enough to keep their wives at home where they should be.'

Where they should be . . . She had the sense to say 'Done.'

The next morning, dressed in their Sunday best, the two households headed to a large, flat expanse of grass on the edge of the sea.

'Why aren't we going there?' Makepeace asked, pointing at the church.

'Priest lives in Morpeth,' Jamie told her. 'Don't coom often. Anyway, he cast us out, divvn't he, Andra?'

They were Methodists and had been ever since John Wesley had come to the northeast to spread his message of Christ's love to its unlettered masses in the 1740s. The Hedleys had been taken to hear him as boys by their grandfather. 'We saw the light,' Hedley said.

They were still seeing it. The field already held three or four hundred people with others still threading in. Only seagulls and whistling redshanks bobbing along the shore vied with the preacher's voice, except for the occasional shout of 'Je-sus' from Tantaquidgeon, for whom it seemed to reawaken memories of the Boston meeting house. Whoever the preacher was, his message of a simpler Christianity was familiar to Makepeace as well. 'Though good works alone cannot save us, we may assure ourselves that without good works we have not the necessary faith, for good works are the evidence of our faith.'

Makepeace looked along the kneeling row to the profiles of Andra and Jamie Hedley, so similar in outline—does mining *demand* a broken nose?—so different in expression: Jamie's amiable; Andra's grim.

That's what he wants from my coal mine, she decided. It's his good work. Well, Lord, let it be that. But let it be *my* salvation too.

After the service there was chatter and exchange of news by people. Andra went off to the village to see if he could recruit corve-draggers from among its fishwives. Makepeace and the others settled themselves on a strip of blond sand to eat their provisions, paddle and build sandcastles with the children. Now that she had leisure, Makepeace tried to make friends with Ginny Hedley, but there was a reserve, sometimes amounting to covert scorn, which suggested that, like her brother-in-law, she regarded Makepeace as an escaped member of the ruling class come down in the world to exploit and then desert them.

'What's Ginny short for?' Makepeace asked.

'Ginny.'

I'll show *her*.

Further along the beach a group of village women sat apart by upturned boats, threading mussels on catch lines ready for the men to take to sea next day. Makepeace produced a ha'penny from her pocket and pointed at a rowing boat . . .

The sea trip was a success as far as the children and Jamie Hedley were concerned. 'This is grand. Where'd tha learn to row, pet?'

'Ran a waterfront inn. Kept lobster pots.'

Ginny showed no sign of being impressed; to hell with her, Makepeace thought. It was balm to be on the water again, she hadn't realised how much she'd missed the sea.

They arrived back to return the boat to its owners, sunburnt and happy. Hedley was waiting for them on the beach.

'She's a good waterfront lass,' Jamie told him. 'Owned an inn wi' lobsters. Rows like a bloody mermaid.'

Hedley looked at Makepeace as she tucked her untidy hair back into her cap. 'Aye, a woman of surprises,' he said.

Appraising the village women who reported for work next day, Makepeace saw that the fishing trade used all its able-bodied, male and female. The women gathered here at the pithead were the leftovers: the too old, the too young, the weak in head and body.

To her surprise, Ginny Hedley was among them. 'Left the bairns with Betty,' she said shortly.

Makepeace had hoped for ten workers at least. Winnowing out the obviously unfit, she was left with Ginny and four others—and one of those only because the girl had pleaded. 'Ah'm stronger'n Ah look, missus, and me mam's sick, please, missus.'

'What's your name?'

'Hildy, missus.'

'How old are you, Hildy?'

'Twelve, missus.'

Ten, more like. 'I suppose you'll have to do. And God dammit, I'll have to come with you.' She rolled up her sleeves and saw that Ginny was smirking. *The cow doesn't think I can do it.* She clapped one of the hard leather caps Hedley had provided onto her head and got into the corve that would take them down the shaft. 'This way, ladies.'

They got used to work underground, though for the first week

Makepeace seriously thought death would be the happier option. It was hot, limestone dust choked nostrils and throat, a filled wagon was so heavy it was immovable until the women learned the trick of setting it sliding over the rails. Their backs ached, their thirst was terrible; they were in the mine by five in the morning and finished at four in the afternoon when the men did, rising up into daylight, grey and blinking. But they were proud of what they did. It became a matter of honour, and not just for the farthing they earned by every load they carried, to work faster—and a matter of shame to show weakness. The donkey had to carry little Hildy back to her village at the end of the day, the other women holding onto her so that she didn't fall off from fatigue, but she was at the pithead every morning ready to begin again. Along with Andra, Jamie and the others—like Wullie Fergusson, Hedley's first mentor in the mining trade whom Andra had introduced with pride as 'my marra', the accolade pitmen accorded to those with whom they worked side by side—men in a skilled and invaluable job, they were inspired to an almost fanatical loyalty to one another by their shared danger underground and the incomprehension they faced above it.

It was always noisy from the *hit-hit* of the picks, trundling wagons, shouts of conversation or instruction. When the silence came, it was eerie. 'What's happened?'

'We're through, pet!'

'*Through*?' Makepeace hurried along to the right-hand tunnel and walked down it. There was nobody at the face, she was looking at a wall. Then she saw that she was in a cross-piece like the head of a hammer. '*Hedley*?' She turned left, into the bigger arm of the cross-piece.

His voice said, 'Howay, she's not right propped yet.'

Damned if she howayed; it was her coal. 'Where is it?'

'Look, woman.' He was impatient, studying the roof.

Straight in front was the wall of coal Hedley and his father had uncovered all those years ago. She'd missed it because it sucked in light and was only apparent in contrast to the reflective stone around it. 'It's good, is it?'

'It's grand if this roof stays up.' He was nervous. 'What's that?'

She heard it, a creak like the swing of a badly hung door. Dust fell from the roof further along. 'Out, pet,' he said, pushing her ahead. She stumbled, then he suddenly pulled her back—and the roof fell in.

Noise and shock took away her sense. Thundering angular boulders filled her view. Dust hit her in a wave so she had to close her eyes.

When she opened them, she was in a room of which one side was a heap of jagged rock from floor to ceiling. Detritus was filling its gaps, hissing like a viper. Hedley's voice, steady now, said,'It's all right, pet. It's not a bad one. Wullie'll get us out. Won't take long.'

She tried to copy him. 'Have we got air?'

'Aye, there's always air.' He kept talking—they were rich; this fall was nothing; he explained the science of falls; made plans—as if they were in the parlour at the Factor's House instead of a small cell made of rock and coal. 'You're all right, bonny lass. Wullie'll get us out.'

She was, but only because he was with her; without him she would have been scrabbling like a rat, squeaking, pleading to get out.

They both saw the dust falling, heard the massive crack above their heads. Their eyes met.

He leaped at her and the weight of his body pushed hers into a cavity in the wall. All light went out. The fall came at them like a thousand-strong cavalry charge. She felt Hedley groan as he was slammed closer against her by rock that tumbled on and on and on, an insane living thing walling them up. Gradually it settled itself, then it was quiet.

Her back was pressed hard against rock. Hedley's body was so tight against hers it held her suspended on tiptoe; he was panting with pain. There was only darkness. 'All . . . right, pet.' His breath coming and going on her skin. 'They'll . . . ah. . . get us out.'

Entombed, getting smaller, God oh God oh God, not like this.

'*Stop* it.' Through the blackness and compression, not a voice, a jagged hook of sound. 'Breathe, you . . . silly bitch.'

'I can'tIcan'tIcan't.'

'Breathe.' He was her lungs. Her mind kept sliding so he nailed it to himself, whispering like a lover, terrible things. For hours. 'Breathe, fuck you . . .' It wasn't bad, this end of the fall, hear him? Yes. Wullie'd come, they'd clear it, hear him? Yes. You'll not die, I'll not let you go. Hear him? Yes. Any moment they'd hear the picks. Hear them? Yes.

And then she did. A needle of sound so far away, so ineffectual, the panic began again.

'*Stop* it. Breathe.'

She felt his muscles make a gigantic move to free his arm, causing him to grunt with pain. His hand was against one side of her face, his thumb smoothing her cheek. 'Good lass.'

Life oozed back and with it lust, blood-red, wriggling, salt desire. She felt a hard swell against her pelvis and if she could have inveigled herself onto this new hook she would have. I want, I want. I want *him* . . .

The hit of the picks was nearer; somebody was shouting.

Another effort from him: 'Here, Wullie.' There was a vibration in the chest against hers; God, was he laughing? Or dying?

Dead weight on her now, the life had gone out of him and she was shouting for the rescuers.

Somewhere there was light. When they got through and lifted him away from her, they got blood on their hands.

Jamie's voice: 'God Jesus, Wullie, is he deed?'

'Not him.' They threaded him like a baby through the hole they'd made to where other hands took him and put him on a stretcher, then they came for Makepeace. 'All right now, pet.'

'Will he be all right, Wullie?'

He grinned. 'Andra?' She'd asked a silly question, but when she wanted to follow the stretcher, he held her back.

Jamie stayed with them so she knew it was serious. 'See, lass,' he said, gently, 'he heard the first fall an' down he coom, we tried holdin' the sod back but it were like hinderin' a bull . . . He were goin' to get to you no matter—an' the second fall tuk him.'

Who? Hedley had been with her. She didn't know what they were blethering about until they led her to the side of the tunnel and light from the candle that Jamie held fell on a broken white feather.

They'd cleared the rock off him and straightened him out. He was alive still, breathing fast and shallow.

'No,' she said, 'oh no.' She went to her knees and put her arm under Tantaquidgeon's head to raise it. 'No.'

'Don't shift him, lass,' Wullie said. 'Let him go easy.'

'*No.*'

The Indian's eyes were wandering; she cupped her hands round his face so that they could find hers. 'Don't go.' Her tears were plopping onto her fingers. 'What would I do without you?' Terror was making her mouth into ugly shapes; his was as firm as ever and she tried to smile at him. 'Don't be brave, does it hurt? Stay. Oh, *no*.'

Beside her Wullie said, 'The Lord's ma shepherd, He teks care o' me. Ah lie in pastures of tranquillity . . .'

'*NO*.' She watched the light recede from the dark eyes as if they were too tired to hold it.

' . . . for His namesake the paths of righteousness Ah tread wi' soul restored, nor could care less when Deeth his shadows ower the valley crowds . . .'

'He's gone, pet,' Jamie said.

'Heor in the midst of dangers Ah thrive, me table strewn wi' plenty. As Ah live, me cup runs ower wi' its thankfulness that all me days your love each hour will bless . . .'

She leaned down so that her cheek was against the poor chest.

Quietly, Wullie Fergusson finished his psalm. 'Me hairt 'n' mind ruled by a peace divine. For goodness, grace 'n' mercy will be mine, An' when my spirit flights to thee, wi' ye Ah'll dwell through all eternity.'

Tantaquidgeon was buried in the graveyard next to the ruins of Headington House. Makepeace and Betty had wrapped him in the dragon-embroidered wall hanging that Dapifer had given him. They'd brushed his hair so that it shone like a rook's wing, splinted the broken eagle's feather and stitched it on a new band to put round his head.

Even if they could have afforded a coffin, she wouldn't have put him in one, so Jamie and the hewers laid him on a wooden stretcher and carried him up the track on their shoulders.

Makepeace wouldn't allow the body put into the grave until the service was over. Better to have left him in a tree in the open air than in a hole in the ground, the only thing he'd ever been afraid of. In the end she couldn't speak the word so it was Wullie who covered the face and gave the order for the stretcher to be lowered. Philippa and the two other children scattered flowers over it.

Hedley was there, against doctor's orders. As Betty and Makepeace went by him he said, 'I'm sorry, pet.'

'Thank you,' Makepeace said. She paused. 'I'm going to London to raise more money, as we discussed. When I've done that I'll set up in Newcastle for a while, to get the business going. You can contact me through your son. I won't be living back here.'

She nodded to him and went on down the hill.

It was perfectly clear. She had betrayed her husband and his cause in lusting after that man and she had been punished by the death of her oldest friend. She must not be deflected again.

Chapter Thirteen

WITH 20,000 BUSY SOULS constricted by walls that had been built to contain 4,000, Newcastle upon Tyne bulged out of its seven medieval gates like flesh wobbling through rips in a too-tight corset. It smelt of lime from its kilns, salt from its pans and the sea, and sewage from the common midden of Dog Loup Stairs. But it nursed a product and ideas that, it knew, would change everything: landscape, thinking, ways of living. The future streamed from Tyneside, not just to London but Europe, Scandinavia and Russia, while the town itself waited for the rest of the world to catch up.

It was dirty, it was undemocratic, it was an anachronism, it was wonderful. And it was male.

'Item six,' said the secretary, 'a plea by Mrs Burke of Raby for permission to use the Tyne for shipment of her coals.'

'The vicar of Bray's got nowt on Newcastle,' Hedley had once told Makepeace. 'But you want to ship from the Tyne, you get the hostmen's permission.' The hostmen were kings of the coal trade, men who had fought for monopoly of their river for centuries against kings, the Bishop of Durham, Oliver Cromwell, Stuarts and Parliament, when necessary changing tactics, sides and religion to do it.

His son Oliver now produced a lump of coal and placed it on the polished conference table in the magnificent fifteenth-century hall. 'Honourable sirs, Ah am Mrs Burke's spokesman in this matter. Ah represent her, the landowner, an' t'partnership she's formed with me father, Mr Andra Hedley, to mine the coal. If tha'd care to examine this piece, gentlemen, tha'll find it of foremost quality.'

He'd broadened his accent, Makepeace noticed. He'd told her to let him do the talking; he didn't think women were allowed to speak in the hostmen's court.

'No precedent for females usin' Tyne, 'cept to do their laundry,' one of the men said, looking straight ahead. Alderman Sir somebody.

'Ah think th'all find exceptions, sirs,' Oliver said; he'd anticipated the difficulty and done his research. 'Early 1600s, Mrs Dorothy Lawson of St Anthony's—'

'She were eccentric,' said the first hostman, 'but there weren't nothin' foreign about Dot Lawson.'

'Aye, salt of earth, old Dot. Proper Tynesider. I remember we gave her a municipal funeral.'

'An' she were elderly. A respectable married woman.'

Now we're getting to it.

'Mrs Burke is a respectable widow,' protested Oliver.

'How'd she come by Raby then?' There was a sudden burst of viciousness. 'Ah heard she got it throwin' dice.'

'Aye, who were her husband?'

Makepeace had taken enough. She leaned forward and put her hands on the table. 'He's dead, that respectable enough for you?'

Oliver put a warning hand on her arm. 'Mrs Burke's an American, sirs—'

'I surely am. It's my land fair and square. There's a grand seam there and I want it shipped—from the Tyne if I can, but if necessary I'll bring keels up from Ipswich to my own waterfront and ship the damn coal from there.' She'd been doing research of her own. 'Do you gentlemen want my revenues or not?'

She heard Oliver issue a long sigh and slump in defeat. But the atmosphere had altered.

'American,' a hostman said sadly.

'Boston, Ah wouldn't wonder.'

'Red-haired.'

They'd placed her. As a good-looking woman trying to compete on their territory she was nothing, an amateur, she could use the Tyne when it—and hell—froze. But as an eccentric with some knowledge of the game they played, she might make a worthy successor to the formidable Dot Lawson . . . 'Pass bloody loomp along table then.'

You frauds, she thought. They could speak genteel English when they had to. They sent their sons to Eton, and there were as many titles around this table as there were in the Cabinet. When did you hypocrites last go down a coal mine?

In that she did the hostmen of Newcastle an injustice. They might send their sons to Eton but they married them to the daughters of families like their own, the aristocracy which made the land work, not the one that merely took its rents. And they knew coal, had known it for 500 years.

'Ah hear Hedley's usin' rectangular corves,' one said.

'What's that he's done wi' the Newcomen?'

So they'd been aware of her and the activities at Raby all along.

She heard Oliver plunge into the opening they'd given him, explaining his father's improvements and inventions and offering them free to the local collieries should the honourable gentlemen see fit to include Raby among Tyne users.

Makepeace and Hedley had argued about that. 'Let them invent their own braged conductors,' she'd said, 'or use 'em under patent.' But Hedley had borne her down; if his work made life easier and safer for miners, he worn't bloody standin' in the way.

No horse sense, that man, she thought, and battled with a treacherous languor in her body as she thought it.

The negotiations went on for some time; Oliver fought valiantly. At last. 'Howay,' said Alderman Sir somebody, 'mebbies we'll give Mrs

Burke a temporary licence but coal's for them as understands it. There's been a fair number o' Southerners cumen and gannin on Tyne and they usual end up drownin' in it.'

I can swim, you buggers. But she said, 'Thank you, gentlemen.'

Outside on the steps, Hedley's son picked her up and swung her round. 'You'll get a metropolitan funeral yet.'

She grinned back at him. 'Let tha and me go lay some flowers on Dot Lawson's grave, pet.'

At first Makepeace rented a tiny office in Merchants Court on the quay so that she could keep an eye on the keelmen and what they did with her coal. Oliver virtually abandoned his practice and worked with her, partly to protect her decency and even more because there was so much to do. Again for respectability's sake, she took on her former marra, young Hildy, as attendant and maid—a good attendant, terrible maid.

She went back to Raby as often as she could; Betty and Philippa were there. But of necessity her visits were short and infrequent.

She made sure her discussions with Andra Hedley were even shorter and more infrequent. In any case, he was as busy as she was and virtually lived at the pithead. With both of them stressed and exhausted, their meetings were edged with temper.

It seemed to her he was dismissive of how difficult it was to be a woman negotiating with men. 'You've no idea of my problems.'

'I've got my own.'

To make the point, he walked her round the pithead, pointing out engines that broke down, ventilation doors that warped, the damage to the staith by a violent wave.

All she saw was money draining out. More investment had been needed; this time she'd raised it in London, from Susan's willing Jews. 'Oh, Mr Hedley,' she said wearily, 'what are we doing here?'

His arm shifted as if he would put it round her but instead he smiled. 'We're having the time o' wor lives, pet,' he said.

The next year Raby went into full production. The year after it sank another shaft and began tunnelling under the seashore. A steady river of coal began an uninterrupted journey down the wagonways to the staith, to the Tyne, to the Thames, into the voracious fires and furnaces of London. And as coal flowed out, money began to flow in.

Aaron heard his sister's voice first.

' . . . ye knacky-kneed donnart, ballast tha bloody keel wi' this muck again an; Ah'll skelp yer arse . . .'

She was standing on the deck of a moored boat, shaking her fist at a coal-pigmented seaman. Men loading nearby had stopped work and, as Aaron opened his mouth to call her, one of them nudged him. 'Whisht, sor, when the missus's seein' reed 'tis a privorlege t'hear her.'

She waved her fist one last time under the seaman's nose, turned and strode down the gangplank.

'Hello, Mrs Burke,' Aaron said.

She flung herself on him. 'When did you arrive?' Among the detritus of the quay he stood out slim and sleek—like a clean young carrot, she thought. She tucked her arm under his. 'Come to the office while I finish.' The dockers whistled at them as they went off and she grinned at them. 'Howay, ye whaups, he's me brothor.'

'I see you speak the language.'

'Only one they understand.'

The brass plaque on the door in Merchants Court read simply: BURKE AND HEDLEY. Inside the offices clerks were busy writing at high desks and stood up politely as Makepeace entered.

'You look well,' she said.

'So do you, but what on earth are you wearing?' She was in widow's weeds of differing black, her hair entirely hidden by a scarf underneath a battered, greenly aged tricorn.

She looked down at herself. 'It's not Madame Angloss exactly, but . . . well, I'm playing a *character*, I'm not supposed to be fashionable.'

'You're not supposed to be an eyesore. Haven't you anything else?'

He hustled her to Middle Street to buy her a made-up bodice and skirt to go with the lawn shawl he'd bought her from Dublin, where his company had been playing to packed houses.

She loved his poise. Mr Burke's Touring Company was gaining a reputation for excellence and had staged a private performance of Goldsmith's *The Good-Natured Man* before Their Majesties.

When she'd dressed in her new clothes, they went to dine at the Pilgrim's Inn. She took pains to introduce him to its landlord as 'my brother'. 'Can't afford gossip,' she said, 'not in Newcastle.'

Aaron was relieved to find that she had at least not cut herself off from London. Andrew Ffoulkes visited on his way to friends in Edinburgh, so did Dr Baines. She was in touch with Susan through the Jews. Her most surprising visitor, she told him, had been John Beasley. She'd taken him to Raby and watched in amazement as he and Hedley became friends. 'Of all men I can't think of two more different,' she said. 'But they've come to some arrangement to get Mr Hedley's rectangular corves and braged conductors registered with the Patent Office, though they're both very rude about the place. Beasley says they're "inefficient fuckers" and Hedley says they're "porvorse sods".'

Aaron saw her delight and saw, too, that she forced herself away from it. She began to talk of coal.

'We've paid off the original debt,' she said. 'Now we can pick and choose our investors—we have to fight 'em off.'

'Are you making a personal profit, though?'

'A lot,' she said, 'I just don't have time to count it.'

'So isn't it time you came back?' he said. 'You're Lady Dapifer, not Mrs Burke. God, it distresses me to see you standing on a coal barge, swearing like a fishwife *and* dressed like one. *She* was in the audience the other day. Mrs Conyers as is. We were doing *Cleone*. Blasted harpy chatted to her friends through the whole damned performance.'

'I don't suppose *she* looked an eyesore, did she?'

'No,' he said, grimly, 'she didn't. She . . . glowed.'

Makepeace said. 'I happen to know she's glowing on borrowed money. I have it in hand, Aaron.'

'Oh, 'Peace, it isn't the getting back at them so much, it's knowing what Pip would say to you having to live and work in this squalor. It's what he took you away from . . .'

She was grateful to see his tears. There were few to cry for her husband nowadays. 'You loved him, didn't you?'

'I've never met anyone better.'

'Nor have I.'

The next day they set off early in her carriage to see Betty and Philippa. They passed by a small village where the sound of chanting came from a schoolhouse and washing was spread on bushes nearby. 'They have to watch the wind,' she said. 'If it changes they run out and put it in another field or it gets covered with coal soot.'

Further up, the landscape became a mass of chimneys, wheels, blackened buildings and rails. Mountains of slag rose out of the earth to disfigure it. It seemed to Aaron that everything he saw moved, made a noise and was filthy. One hut was disgorging a band of fiends from hell: black shapes with gleaming white eyes and teeth. 'Night shift,' Makepeace said. 'Wha' cheor, lads.'

'Mornin', missus.'

There were imps among the fiends. 'We don't use as many boys as other pits,' his sister said. 'Mr Hedley won't have it. Ponies do the pulling. Much more costly, of course, but he doesn't care for that.'

There was something in her voice that Aaron couldn't analyse.

He was relieved when she turned the trap and the two of them were trotted away, even more relieved to find that Headington House was being rebuilt for her. After a rapturous reunion with Betty in the kitchen, brother and sister walked across the moor to meet Philippa from school. 'Hasn't she got a governess?' Aaron asked.

'Mr Hedley found an excellent teacher for the school,' she said, 'so she goes there. She seems to have brains, she's very mathematical.'

'What about her music? Dancing? Elocution?'

'Oh, well,' she said, 'I'll see to that when I have time.'

Three children were approaching chattering in Northumbrian dialect. One, the neatest of the three, had shoes but they were laced together over her shoulder. She ran towards him. 'Uncle Aaron!'

She introduced her companions nicely enough: 'This is Polly, this is John. Polly, John, my uncle Aaron.'

'Ginny and Jamie's children,' said Makepeace. 'They're in the Factor's House now.'

Philippa exclaimed, 'Mam, Johnny says there's greet monsters doon the lonnen, wi' reet sharp teeth an' warts, but tha's blaa, in't it, Mam?'

'Blaa,' Makepeace nodded. 'Howay now, pet. We'll be in when we've said hello to Tantaquidgeon.'

Aaron kept his silence until after the visit to the grave but then he took his sister's arm. 'Makepeace, what are you *doing*?'

'What?'

'Leave aside that you're content to live as a vagabond, you cannot, you can *not* bring up Philippa like . . . some gypsy whelp.'

She looked up at him. 'Is it the shoes? We went without shoes . . .'

'Yes, we did. But she's not the child of a shiftless, drunken Irishman, she's the daughter of Sir Philip Dapifer. Look at her . . . *hear* her, for the sake of God! Are you so occupied steeping yourself in this northern sinkhole that you haven't noticed what she's become? Walking along just now I couldn't tell her from the pit brats.'

'There's *time*, Aaron,' Makepeace protested. 'When I—'

'You haven't got time—you keep telling me. What is she now? Five? Nearly six? And I wouldn't dare lead her into a decent drawing room.'

At the shock on his sister's face, he sat down beside her and took her hand. 'I'm sorry, my dear, but you must see. Who's she to marry? Some miner? You say she's clever but that's not good enough, she must be cultured. Pip was the most cultured man I ever knew. What would he say to what you're doing to his child? What would he say to *me* for letting you do it? Dear God, he'd think I'd betrayed him.'

It was as if he'd taken a broom to her mind and swept away everything except memories. *Procrustes?* It was her husband's voice.

'Makepeace?' It was Aaron's.

She turned to her brother. 'You're right,' she said. 'But you haven't betrayed him. I have.'

Hedley caught up with her as she climbed the hill to her apartment, her boots slipping on the cobbles. The rain found its way down the hill's depressions in grey, vitreous-looking rivulets.

'I want to talk to you, lass.'

'I'm tired,' she protested.

'You'll be tireder when I've finished.'

A side door led to the staircase to her rooms. Upstairs smelt damp. She put a candle on the mantelshelf. 'There's no food.'

'Drink'll do.'

By the time she'd found the brandy and glasses, he'd taken off his sopping cloak and hat and was lighting the fire. 'Where's Hildy?'

'I sent her home for a day or two. Her mother's ill again.' She braced herself. 'What do you want?'

'Sit down.' He set two chairs by the fire facing each other. Brusque movements indicative of anger. 'Betty says you're taking her and the bairn away to live in London.'

'Yes.'

He sat back in his chair. 'Why?'

'It's time Philippa took up her position as her father's daughter. I can afford it now.'

'Isn't she her father's daughter at Raby?'

Makepeace sidestepped. 'Anyway, I have business in London.'

'Would that be wor famous revenge? John Beasley told us.'

She tried to become angry. 'It's none of your business.'

'Mebbies not, but young Philippa is. I've affection for that bonny lass and she's affection for me. That apart, she's warm and bound in a tight community. What for d'you want to take her from it?'

Now she was angry. She leaned forward. '*You're* not her father.'

He leaned too. '*Damnation*,' he shouted, '*but Ah'm the next best thing*.'

Makepeace got up and went to the window to a view of the wet, grey, descending roofs of the hill. Well, she thought drearily, it's going to be easy to leave. She heard him say gently, 'I'm the next best thing, pet. We've been that busy, the day never came. But it's come now. I need you to make an honest man o' me.'

'*What*?' she screeched.

'I've been compromised, pet.' He sounded aggrieved. 'Down in t'pit, when roof caved in. You took advantage of me.'

She said warily, 'I don't know what you're talking about.'

'Yes, you do. Very compromising position, forced against a female body. Not the plainest I've ever seen, neither. Let's face it, bonny lass, it was a matter of who came first, bloody rescuers or you and me.'

She bit her lip, trying not to laugh, then she gave way.

He grinned back. The candlestick fell over and went out as he lunged for her. 'Where's bloody bedroom?'

Here was greed, violent and no holds barred. No flight to the stars but a desperate, grinding wrestle in sexual mud, go on, go on, until its groaning conclusion with both of them winners.

Peace fell on them like the rain on the window. She lay with her nose buried in his chest, breathing him in, wondering where she was, when it was. She was suffused with physical gratitude.

He said something. Dreamily, she cupped her hands round his face and moved her lips across his. 'What?'

'I was hungry for you.'

'I don't feel guilt for this, I was starving too, Andra Hedley.'

He sounded surprised. 'Guilt never entered my mind.'

She looked down at their entangled legs. 'It'd enter a lot of people's if they saw us now.'

'Porvorse sods,' he said. 'No idea of ecstasy.'

She settled her head into his shoulder and wrapped her arms round him; he was luxury, satisfaction, humour. 'I think I was shipwrecked,' she said. 'Struggling to stay afloat for years, and you're the island I've bumped into in the night, all warm and dark and safe . . .'

'An island,' he said. 'But you get off 'em eventually.'

She said, 'I've *got* to go to London, Andra, I've a score to settle.'

'Tell us.'

She told him everything. Here was mental release after the physical: an orgasm of pain and wrongs, explanation, confession.

'I've been watching them these years.' She told him about Robert as well. 'When I go to London he keeps me up with what they're doing. He makes it . . . vivid. It's like sitting in the dark at a theatre watching clowns on the stage. You wonder at them: so evil and at the same time so bloody *silly*. They've no conception of earning, or even paying their way. He owes his bootmaker nine hundred-odd pounds. Nearly a *thousand pounds*, just on boots. He'll ruin the man. Money spurts out of their fingers like taps: gambling, entertaining, doing nothing valuable. Everything's impermanent with them, as if they haven't long to live.'

'No bairns?' he asked.

'No bairns. She's barren. You could be sorry for them; sometimes I almost am, and then I think, That's Philippa's money, you're not sorry for her. They wouldn't even let me in to bury him. Oh God, Andra, they wouldn't let me say goodbye.'

He held her until she'd cried herself into a hiccupping stillness.

'Clay, pet,' he said. 'They've come from clay and they'll return to it.'

'Indeed they will.' She sat up, sniffing and wiping her nose on the back of her hand. 'And I'm sending 'em. That's what I've been doing: buying their debts. Susan's Jew's been collecting them for me. Nearly every penny of my profit's gone on financing Mr and Mrs Conyers—and at a very pretty interest. Next year, oh-ho, *next* year the price of coal goes up and so does mine.' She curled her hand into a fist. '*Then* I've got them. *Then* I send in the bailiffs. The Fleet, I think—King's Bench is for gentry. The Fleet'll hurt. Did you know that when you can't pay you need permission from every single one of your creditors to get out of debtors' prison? One creditor to say no, one creditor to keep them in for life. Just one.'

'You,' he said.

'Me.'

He watched her watching her own fingers gripe, stretching and clawing like a cat's. 'Know what I'll do then? I'll dress in my very, very bloody best and I'll walk into that prison, just to the door, and I'll stand there and smile at her. And then I'll walk away.'

'Smile,' he repeated flatly.

'She smiled at me once.'

'You've gone to a lot o' work for one smile, lass.'

'A lot.'

'And a lot of blaa,' he said. 'You'd have done it anyway. I saw it. One sniff o' that coal and you woke to what you are: as good a businessman as ever came over the Atlantic. No need to make that trash the excuse, pet. Leave 'em to the hell they've made for their own selves. You and me, bonny lass, the earners and makers, we're blessed wi' building things that matter.' He reached for her. 'Furthermore, you've breasts a man could drown his soul in.'

'Oh,' she said, 'oh, *Andra*.'

When she woke up, the window had gained light, though rain still pattered softly against the glass. 'It's morning,' she said, stretching. 'What?' He was muttering something.

He yawned. 'I said you'll have to marry me now.'

Makepeace sat up. 'Marry? I can't *marry*.'

'Have to, pet. I've been led astray.'

She peered at him closely. She saw a curly-headed man with grey beginning in his hair, a blue cut across his broken nose. *Have to, pet.* It panicked her. I can't marry you. I don't belong to you. I'm an independent woman. What she spent her money on, how she earned it—if she earned any at all—these things would be at this man's command.

She looked around, desperate, and her husband came into the room, not vulnerable as he'd been these past years, not the victim who'd died calling for her. Here was the essential Dapifer: laconic, elegant, amused and suddenly so vivid she could smell his skin.

And here she was, nauseatingly naked in a bed with a man marked by coal. Hurriedly, she got up and wrapped herself in a petticoat. In a rush she said, 'I'm marrying nobody.' It was only fair to tell him; she had slept with him, after all, *and* enjoyed it, God help her. 'We're partners, Mr Hedley, that must be enough for us.'

He stroked his chin. It rasped. 'Partners,' he said.

'Yes.'

'Still going to London?'

'Yes.'

'And you and me, what o' that?'

She said timidly, because there were long years of starvation ahead: 'I'll keep the rooms on. I'll have to come back now and then—I'm not leaving the business.' She couldn't rule out hunger.

'By *Christ*,' he said slowly. 'What do you think o' me?'

'I think highly of you, I truly do. Don't look at me like that.'

He said, 'You've lived too long among gentry, pet. What am I? Some prick-peddler coming round to render his bloody services?'

'No, I . . .Oh, go away.'

'I'm a marryin' man, lass, what's wrong wi' that?'

'Nothing. You see . . .' She grimaced at him, baring her teeth. 'I've a duty to my husband. He was a very special man.'

'I heard. But I'm special too, pet. And *he's* dead.'

She didn't say anything. She watched him pulling on his clothes. For the first time she saw the scars on his back where his body had protected hers from the roof fall.

At the door to the stairs he looked back. 'Tha's to be pitied, missus. We could have had wor bit share o' happiness, thee and me.'

She heard him go down the stairs, heard the side door slam.

After a long while she raised her head. The ghost that came this time was female. It stood exquisitely in the doorway and smiled at her.

Makepeace welcomed it like an old friend. 'Howay, wor Catty.'

He was wrong. This had been her purpose: the downfall of this woman. She just hadn't been attending to it properly.

Chapter Fourteen

AS PART OF LONDON'S TWELFTH NIGHT celebrations in 1772, a concert was held at Drury Lane Theatre to benefit the Foundlings' Hospital. The audience included royalty, peers and distinguished commoners, among them that well-known couple about town Major and Mrs Conyers.

One of the dramatic offerings was a burletta, *The Pillar of Fire*. It told the story of a kindly, mythical king, Philippus, whose wife, Katerina, betrays him with his brother, Sidneus, and plots his overthrow. This achieved, and with the King dead, the evil couple banish his second, faithful wife and her child to starve on a barren island.

Mercifully, because it wasn't very good, the burletta was short and doubtless would have remained in the common memory for no longer than it took to perform if it hadn't been for three events.

One was that, during the first scene, Major and Mrs Conyers angrily left the theatre. The second was that, at the burletta's close, its cast lined up on the stage to bow to a private box in which sat a woman with red hair. Thirdly, one of the burletta's songs, which was sung in her famous Cockney style by Miss Fanny Cobb, became popular. It was called 'Playing with Fire' and its chorus ran: 'Them as filch what they ain't earned/shall have their naughty fingers burned.' Not deathless lyrics, perhaps, but the tune was catchy and it hymned the fate of all dispossessed: the Enclosure Acts were creating a lot of those. Overnight, it was being sung in taverns and whistled everywhere on the streets.

Following an appeal by Major Conyers to the Lord Chamberlain, wrath was called down on the heads of the actors responsible but, since they had departed for a tour of Ireland immediately the curtain fell at Drury Lane, it missed. The burletta was banned.

The song, however, proved harder to suppress, and those who heard it were reminded by some well-placed articles in the scandal sheets that it referred to the forgotten plight of a real woman. 'Where is she now, that unhappy lady? Has she returned to haunt her persecutors?' For it was being rumoured that a certain Mrs Burke, a wealthy widow, had lately been seen in London and that she bore a remarkable resemblance to the person who had once described herself as Lady Dapifer.

The house near Hatton Garden had a dusty front door behind which was a spartan office. Both were deceptive. Makepeace was led up a tiny, creaking flight of stairs to a room warm with the wealth that a man of Mr Franco's race and occupation dare not display to the outside world.

'How is Miss Susan?' asked Mr Franco.

'Very well.'

'The hat trade, that goes well too?'

'We're now selling to Russia.'

Mr Franco pretended to hit his forehead with the heel of his hand. 'I should not have let Miss Susan go. But what can a poor man do against you?'

Makepeace smiled. 'You're not doing so badly, Mr Franco.'

Mr Franco consulted a file of papers. 'I was summoned to Grosvenor Square again, Mrs Burke.'

'Good. How much this time?'

'Fourteen thousand. I gather the lady and gentleman have been once more unlucky at Mr Almack's gaming tables.'

Makepeace shook her head. 'What security did they offer this time?'

'Some forest in Kent.' Mr Franco scanned his papers again. 'Yes, yes, Barton Wood. Five hundred and forty-two acres of prime oak. Good security—the navy is always eager for oak.'

'Barton Wood? Are you sure?'

'Here is the valuation. As always, I temporise. I must consult my hard-hearted associate before I can advance more, I tell them. The major called me a reptile in his light-hearted way. Do you agree the loan?'

'Not this time, no. May I borrow that valuation?'

Mr Franco raised his eyebrows. 'You know something? Very well. Then they are nearly done. You should soon be in a position to execute a warrant for their arrest. There are promissory notes too,' he added. 'Most bills find their way to us reptiles sooner or later. These as well?'

'If you please, Mr Franco.'

'Also, you remember, you asked me to keep an eye open for those of other ladies and gentlemen. Now, where . . . ?'

The column of names on the page he handed over was a long one. Half the English gentry was exposed on it as being in debt.

Before he showed her out, Mr Franco asked, 'You are well guarded as you go abroad, Mrs Burke?'

'Why?'

Mr Franco shrugged. 'Major Conyers is a good soldier and therefore a bad man . . . The word among my people is that your presence in town annoys him.'

While she waited for Robert in the upstairs room of The Spaniards, Makepeace asked for paper, ink and pen.

Dear Mr Hackbutt [she wrote],
Today a money-lender showed me this valuation (enclosed) on a property offered to him as security on a loan by Major Conyers. I believe it to be part of the inheritance of Lord Ffoulkes. Andrew is travelling in Italy and cannot have given his permission. Send it to Lord Ffoulkes' lawyers and tell them what is toward.
Yours respectfully, Makepeace Dapifer

There was a quick triple knock on the door and then two slower ones. Makepeace sighed. 'Come in.'

A muffled figure slouched in, crossed to the window and pulled the shutters to. He's probably got a dagger as well, Makepeace thought, but it cost little enough to indulge Robert's affection for subterfuge.

He ate the meal she'd ordered for him ravenously. 'No food at home,' he said, 'and nothing to eat it off, neither. Our bootmaker finally lost his patience and sent in the bums. They took the silver plate in payment.'

Philippa's silver plate.

'What we'll pawn next I don't know because the place is completely *stripped.* We'd like to sell Hertfordshire but it's mortgaged to the hilt.'

'I know,' Makepeace said.

Robert eyed her over his plate. 'Oh-ho, *you've* got it, have you, little sly boots? If I were *us*, I'd flee the country, but we still think we can recoup with a lucky win at the tables.'

It astounded her that her enemies looked to gambling, which had been their downfall, for their salvation. A disease, she could only suppose.

'*She's* going to Almack's again tonight,' Robert said, 'some little do of Lady Brandon's.'

'I know. Macall told me.' The Scotsman was now one of her investors.

Robert was quick. 'Are you planning something?'

'I might be.'

'You be careful. I know you think I've got a bee in my bonnet, but you're *haunting* them and that's dangerous. The other morning he heard the coalman whistling "Playing with Fire". Well, *out* comes the riding whip, *out* comes the major—still in his *nightcap*—and gives the poor fellow such a lashing as I feared would *kill* him.' Robert shook his head. 'I wish you'd make your move, I really do, and put us out of our misery.'

As he swung his cloak around him before setting out into the night, he said gently, 'Don't be too hard on them.'

She was incredulous. 'Hard on them? Hard on *them*?'

'I know. They're awful, awful. But she's deranged. Did I tell you about the dog?'

'That dog's watching me, Siddy.'

'Darling, how can she be?'

'She's got the squaw's eyes, Siddy.'

'No, my dear. The red-headed bitch has blue eyes, Bracken's are brown.'

'She's watching me, Siddy.'

And two days later: *'What the hell's that noise?'*

'I think it's the dog, Major. Madam's got it in there with her.'

'I don't know what she'd done to the poor creature, he wouldn't let us see,' Robert said, 'but he buried it that afternoon.'

'And you don't want me to be hard on her? She's *evil*.'

Robert shook his head. 'Mad and getting madder. Sir Pip understood.'

As her carriage took her home, Makepeace nursed a headache and a longing for Newcastle, that smoke-grimed repository of everything clean. Oh God, I just want to *be* there.

'We're home, ma'am.'

'Thank you, Sanders. I shall need you again tonight with the coach.'

It was a nice house, in the highest and most prestigious part of Highgate. She'd bought it, complete with furniture and servants, from Lord Braybourne's widow after his death. Lady Braybourne had returned to her native Ireland immediately after the sale so society had not yet become aware that Makepeace was living in it.

As she passed the footman, she said, 'Tell Hildy to lay out the gold satin, if you please.'

She went through to the Grand Saloon. Susan and Betty sat by the window in a concentration of candles, Susan doing her embroidery, Betty knitting. 'Is Philippa in bed?'

'She got tired waitin',' Betty said.

'There were things to do.' The more she entangled Catty and Conyers in her web the less inclined she felt to talk about it. She added, 'And I've got to go out again later on.'

Betty sucked her teeth.

Susan followed her up to her room and stood at the door, her hands pleating her skirt. 'I think it's time I went home to see Auntie.'

Makepeace looked up. '*Boston*, do you mean?'

'Yes. She isn't getting any younger and I can help with her business.'

Oh damn, this was going to require manipulation. 'My dear, what would I do without you? What would *Philippa* do without you?'

And, actually, what would you do without Philippa? she thought. It had been a happy arrangement to buy this house for them all and, while she was in Newcastle, to leave her daughter in the care of Susan and Betty. The child was the apple of Susan's eye and she devoted a good deal more time in attending to Philippa than she did to creating hats.

Miss Brewer looked shifty, then squared her shoulders. 'I was wondering, Makepeace, if you might allow Philippa to come with me—just for a visit.' At Makepeace's look she said, 'Well, sakes, she *is* half an American.'

Makepeace was astonished and amused. 'Susan, it's good of you, but I really think Philippa's visit to the Americas must wait 'til I have time to go with her.' She went back to her dressing.

'When's *that* going to be?' But it was a rhetorical question.

Some members are paying their gambling bills even if Catty isn't, Makepeace thought as she went up Almack's staircase. The club looked even more luxurious than it had. She proceeded along the gallery to the open door of a smaller room. The footman on its threshold bowed. 'May I announce you, ma'am?'

'Lady Dapifer,' Makepeace said.

He turned. 'La-*dee* Dapifer.'

Immediate silence. Every head in the room turned to her like a field of sunflowers. She let them look; she was in splendour and knew it—gold suited her. After a moment she heard Catty's voice. 'It's the squaw, my dears. I thought it was dead but I see they've gilded it.'

Given the circumstances, Makepeace thought she did well.

Another footman came hurrying over. 'I'm sorry, madam, but Lady Brandon says this reception is by invitation only.'

'I know,' Makepeace said. She put a piece of paper in his hand. 'This is my invitation.'

Lady Brandon advanced on her. 'What does this mean?'

'It's a bill, madam, a note promising to pay, one of several signed by you which I have bought from those to whom you owe money. I can show the others to your husband if you'd prefer.'

Catty danced up. 'Is it being a nuisance, Prissie? Dispose of it.'

The rouge on Lady Brandon's cheeks formed garish circles against skin that had turned grey.

'Prissie? What is it?' Lady Brandon remained silent. 'Prissie!' Catty turned to Makepeace almost in appeal. 'What are you *doing*?'

'Being invited to play,' Makepeace said. 'Aren't I, Lady Brandon?'

She watched Catty's hands scrabble at her friend's sleeve. *Do you see them? Did you see hands clawing at closed gates?*

'She's got to go, Prissie. Send her *away*.' It was a plea.

Lady Brandon opened her mouth, then closed it.

'I see,' Catty said. Makepeace was surprised at her sudden control—until she saw her eyes. 'You will pay, you know.'

'I already have.'

Lady Brandon's hand came out as Catty swept past her out of the door, and then fell back to her side. Makepeace waited until the sound of clicking heels had faded before she said, 'Thank you, Lady Brandon, but I'm afraid I must refuse. I don't gamble.'

On the way back to Highgate in the coach, she took in deep breaths of satisfaction. The memory of that little skirmish could be laid away with battle honours.

She was pleased to see that there was still light in the Grand Saloon. Betty had waited up for her. 'Wait 'til I tell you—' she said.

'I'm a-goin' with Susan,' Betty said.

'What?'

'Boston. I'm goin' home.'

It developed into the worst quarrel they'd ever had.

'How *can* you be lonely? You've got Susan and Philippa. You see Josh nearly every week; Aaron's not far away.'

Betty's lower lip protruded dangerously. 'Don't like it here.'

'For God's sake.' Makepeace reined in her temper. 'This is your home. I'd be lost without you, you're my mainstay. And you're Philippa's.'

'That chil' need to come with us, she ain't happy here neither.'

'Of course she is. It's everything Pip would have wanted for her. Dammit, you didn't like it when we were hauling her around in a basket with Aaron's troupe. I suppose you think she was better off at Raby?' It had taken long enough to rid the child of her Northumbrian accent.

'She surely was. An' you too. Should've married Andra.'

'Don't you dare say that to me. Marry a . . . a fellow like that? Don't you remember who I *was* married to?' They were shrieking now.

'You 'memberin' he's dead? Sir Pip's dead?'

'Not to me.'

'Then he oughta be.'

'You bitch, you *bitch*. Get out of my sight.'

Betty lumbered from the room.

It took a long time for Makepeace's hands to stop shaking. She felt ill; they'd never rowed like this never. Betty ain't lonely, how can she be lonely? She's too bloody old to cross the Atlantic and she knows it. What she wants is me to give it up . . . stupid old baggage . . . *now we're almost there*. Wallowing, Makepeace thought of what it had cost her to reach this position. She hadn't done it by sitting at home to keep company with a fat old black woman.

Oh, *Betty*.

She left the saloon and went up to Betty's bedroom. It was unlit. A bulky shape sat slumped in a gilded chair by the open window.

'Don't leave me, Bet.' She knelt down and rested her forehead on the old woman's knees.

'Ain't me as is leavin'.'

'We're so close, almost *there*. I've nearly got 'em, girl.'

'You ain't doin' this for him. You ain't even doin' it for you. You like one of them pit wagons, the rails is there an' you jus' runnin' away on 'em. You likely crush your own child while you doin' it. Not me, you ain't crushin' me too. Susan goes, I go.'

The argument went on for an hour, gently on Makepeace's part, obdurately on Betty's. Only once did her voice waver. 'I miss that smelly ol' Indian.'

'So do I. Oh, so do I.' All the time.

She evoked every memory she could bear to, every cause of gratitude for both of them; she piped but Betty would not dance.

'Susan goes, I go.' It was her final word.

In bed that night, it came to Makepeace that Betty was passing the judgment of Solomon on Philippa. You love this child enough to give up your revenge for her? Or do I cut her in half?

For Philippa would be cut in half by Betty's departure. Without that big, black buoy, the one fixture to which she had always been attached, she would be lost and unhappy—like I'd have been at her age, Makepeace thought, if the blasted woman hadn't been there.

Which could Philippa least afford to lose? Betty the constant? Or a mother who was travelling elsewhere for eight-tenths of her time? Do I love my daughter enough to abandon everything I've strived for these last years and be a better companion and mother to her?

She heard her groan break the silence of the room. 'Lord forgive me, I don't.' It was, literally, a physical impossibility; she would be eaten away by a disease called unfinished business.

Next morning, she called her daughter into the saloon. 'Now, Philippa, I don't know if your Aunt Susan has told you, but she intends to go to America for a visit to her relatives. She wants to know if you would like to go with her.'

Makepeace watched her daughter consider. The child had her father's long face and sallow skin, without in any other way resembling him. Her habitual expression possessed none of the mock-gloom and humour that had made Philip Dapifer so attractive; it was merely grave. She looked like a small, studious camel.

'Would you be coming too, Mama?'

'No. I have things to do in England. I must go up North again soon.'

Was the girl disappointed? It was difficult to tell. Oh God, she's guarded—so young and guarded. My fault, I uprooted her.

Makepeace became irritated. Wasn't I bloody uprooted? I'd been dragged over half America by the time I was her age—*and* lost my mother. Didn't do me any harm; she's got nothing to complain about.

The thing was, Philippa did not complain. Makepeace said gently, 'Betty thinks she would like to go with Auntie Susan.' Was it panic, that shift of the child's eyes? Makepeace added, 'But I don't think she means it. If you'd like to stay here, I'm sure she'd stay too.'

'Are you going to be busy again, Mama?'

'Only for a little while longer.'

'Could I go on with my mathematics?'

Makepeace blinked. 'I'm sure you can.'

'Could I see the Roaring Meg?'

What *had* Betty been telling her? 'If Auntie Susan thinks it suitable.'

'I think I should like to go. Just for a visit.'

Don't go. Stay here. 'Are you sure?'

'Yes.'

Is this how she feels every time I leave *her*? Awkwardly, Makepeace reached for her daughter. 'I'll come and fetch you back, you know. If you like America, we might even stay there together.'

The small body resisted. It was the worst moment of the interview; Philippa didn't believe her.

The fact that Philippa was prepared to go wasn't the end of the battle. Betty no more wanted to return to America than visit the moon; her strategy was to make Makepeace give up her career of avenging angel; Makepeace's was for Betty to capitulate and stay in England.

It was Josh who called the bluff of them both. He turned up one morning having walked from Leicester Fields. 'I've run away.' His face was set—he had become handsome. 'I ain't saying Sir Josh ain't a great man in his way, but it's *his* way. "Got to do it like this, not like that." Mam, there's a thousand ways of painting, and he won't let us try any of 'em. I'm a-goin' to work my passage to Boston. Ain't no Royal Academy in America to tell a man how an' what to paint.'

Two combatants looked past him at each other in despair. Now Betty would be forced to leave. She must go with Josh; separation from her son at her time of life could be permanent. The very thing neither wanted had been taken out of their hands to become a reality.

In a fury that she had to do it at all, Makepeace began making the arrangements. The ship that would take them was to be the *Lord Percy*, the same frigate that had carried them all to England seven years before. Makepeace had been corresponding with Captain Strang. In September, subject to wind and tide, the *Percy* would dock at Deptford after an Atlantic crossing, bringing the papers Mr Hackbutt needed to begin the case against Catty. *Lord Percy* was a sound craft, her captain trustworthy; Makepeace could take possession of the papers and wish her people Godspeed at the same time.

The drive to Deptford was awful. Josh chattered brightly, Susan and Makepeace tried to, Betty and Philippa didn't say a word.

The *Lord Percy* was anchored in midstream. Captain Strang gave her assurance that Boston was safe along with her documents. 'No, no, ma'am,' he said, 'all's quiet. Your compatriots are once again loyal subjects of King George, more loyal than those at home if what I hear about Mr Wilkes and his supporters be true.'

The goodbyes were stiff. As she held Philippa, Makepeace felt the child's hands tighten around her neck and then make the effort to let go. The little face was expressionless and Makepeace didn't know if the gesture indicated grief or whether it was being interpreted as such by her own agony.

Susan said carefully, 'I love her like my own but I know she's yours. I'll keep her safe for you.'

'My dear, I know you will. I don't deserve you, either of you.' She had neglected them both.

The knowledge that she had failed all of them in different ways, even Josh—she should have enquired into his disillusion earlier—was too overwhelming to be borne and she took the coward's way out, not even waiting to see the pinnace reach the ship.

'London,' she told Sanders. 'Straight to Lincoln's Inn Fields.'

Mr Hackbutt sorted through the documents. 'Marriage certificate from the ship, properly signed and sealed, excellent, excellent. Sir Pip's decree—I have to say, Lady Dapifer, that with your fellow countrymen behaving themselves there has never been a better time to ask their lordships to recognise an American divorce. In the meantime, I informed Lord Ffoulkes's lawyers about Barton Wood. They were as appalled as myself and have informed Major Conyers that any further attempt to defraud will result in prosecution. I did not tell them whence my information came and we can only hope the major does not guess. You are tweaking his nose, Lady Dapifer, and he is a dangerous man.'

'I'm a dangerous woman, Mr Hackbutt.'

The lawyer nodded; she could see he didn't like her as much as he once had. Nobody does, she thought. 'Have you made out the other documents I asked you for?'

He counted them into her hand. 'And here's your opening salvo: a warrant ready for your signature. It can be executed at a moment's notice, the bailiffs are standing by.'

The thought of returning to a house empty of everyone but servants was daunting. She needed a friend to talk to; where was the nearest of the few she had left? 'Grub Street, Sanders.'

'You going armed?' Beasley asked.

'As a matter of fact, I am.' Makepeace balanced a gun case on her knee. The two weapons inside were smaller than the average duelling pistol, chased and inlaid with ivory. 'Nice, aren't they? Watch out, they're loaded!'

Beasley, a self-acknowledged coward, hastily put the guns back. 'You do realise you've become insane. You're a hundred times richer than they are, you're hounding them into Bedlam. Ain't your revenge wreaked yet?'

'There've only been little wreaks so far.'

'What are you going to do after the final wreak?'

'Smile.'

'Smile at what?' Beasley leaned forward and poked his finger at her. 'There won't be anything there, woman. Madam Midnight's gone, your kid's gone, Susan, Josh . . . Aaron's had to run for it to Ireland. That's nearly all of us. You're scorching your own earth, you madwoman.'

She'd let down her guard, exposed her triumph, thinking she could relax with a friend. She began gathering her wraps. Her head was aching. She said, 'Your breath stinks.'

He sat back, nursing his knee. 'Andra's in town, did you know?'

Makepeace closed her gun case carefully. 'How is Mr Hedley?'

That was the trouble with Beasley, he clawed like an animal and then, as you bled, came a reminder of what a true ally he was.

'Another bugger intent on suicide, like you,' Beasley told her. 'Nearly blew himself up the other day experimenting with fire-damp. I've put him in touch with a couple of chemists I know. What's the matter?'

Blast him. She wiped her hands hard down her skirt to get rid of their sudden perspiration. 'It's just that it's . . . a terrible thing, fire-damp. A spark can set it off. I was in Newcastle when the pit at Gerrards blew up, ten miles away. Thirty-five killed.'

She hadn't known any of them but she knew people like them—Wullie Fergusson, Jamie—and had grieved for the loss of such men. Hedley *had* known them, most of them. Of course he'd be experimenting. Of course it was suicide. *Blast him*. And it probably would.

'I introduced him to Johnson as well,' he said, altering course.

'And what did Dr Johnson think of Mr Hedley?' asked Makepeace.

Beasley crunched himself up like a bear and lowered his voice an octave: '"Andra Hedley is an ingenious, hard-working descendant of *homo sapiens*." He liked him.'

'Well, I must be going. I've some wreaking to do.'

Beasley didn't move from his stool; he let people see themselves out. 'From the look of you, you could do with a bit of ingenious hard-working *homo sapiens* yourself. When'd you last have a fuck?'

'Oh, shut up,' Makepeace said, and went.

It was late. Beyond Grub Street, the alleys were empty, enabling Sanders to take short cuts. They'd reached the deserted space of Clare Market when Makepeace heard a clatter of hoofs approaching fast on the coach's right-hand side. She saw a pistol barrel appear at her window and then a flame as whoever held the gun pulled its trigger.

Chapter Fifteen

WHAT SAVED MAKEPEACE'S LIFE was her headache.

She'd taken off her hat to ease the constriction on her forehead and hung it on the seat opposite hers. It was of undyed straw and its pallor, in the darkness, misled the attacker into thinking he fired into a face: the bullet smashed through the middle of its crown.

She sat and stared at it. Somebody was shaking her arm: Sanders, his mouth making shapes but no sound.

'What?' she asked and couldn't hear her own voice either. The report of the pistol had been literally deafening.

He pointed behind him, his thick gesticulating hands indicating her assailant had gone that way and should he go after him?

She forced a 'No'. There was no point, the attacker was on horseback and a mile away by now. She was too frightened to face the journey through darkness to the lonely house in Highgate. Probably Sanders was as well, poor man. Where then? She needed a brandy and a friend as she'd never needed either. 'Back,' she told Sanders, exaggeratedly formulating her mouth. 'G-rub S-t-reet.'

Sanders supported her up Beasley's staircase. She was seated on one of the stools by the unlit fire. Beasley was actually lighting it. Unheard of. A dirty glass containing brandy was in her hand.

Now Beasley was shouting at her, his voice reaching her from a muffled distance. 'Where's the bloody warrant?'

'What?'

'The warrant for the Conyers's arrest. For debt.'

She pointed to her reticule. He found the document, laid it on her knee and presented her with a quill and inkpot.

He wants me to sign it.

Shock made her slow, she just stared at the pen.

'Oh, for Christ's sake,' he shouted, 'he tried to kill you.'

She signed, with difficulty, on the line left for the complainant, and he snatched it from her. 'Sanders'll take me to the magistrates, we'll set on the bailiffs immediate.' He was miming as he shouted. 'Stay here. I'll put a couple of men downstairs to guard you.'

She nodded. The men left. Makepeace huddled over the fire, unable to get warm or stop shaking. *He tried to kill me.* She shook so hard she had to hold her glass with two hands to stop it slopping. *I want Betty*.

But you let her go. And Susan. And Philippa. And Josh. Aaron's gone, Andrew . . . She'd allowed all the people whom she loved, and who loved her, to slip away.

She clutched at anger. I was *right* to go for revenge. God damn their two souls to hell, look what they did to me, to us; they wouldn't stop even at murder. Oh please, the scales *had* to be balanced.

And now they had been. She took in a deep breath, then another swig of brandy. If Beasley and the warrant did their job, Major and Mrs Conyers were even at this moment being hustled into the closed cart that would take them to the Fleet Prison.

And there they would stay. *For the rest of their lives.*

She had spent hours envisaging their years of hopelessness and now, to regain a sense of control, she did it again. Conyers's hair was greyed; wrinkles glazed Catty's face. She watched them wither into dust like two forgotten apples in a store cupboard.

And they'd know how hopeless it was. From the first, they would know. She'd ordered the dress she would wear to the prison from Madame Angloss. She'd decided on primrose: Catty had worn primrose in Grosvenor Square at their first encounter.

The times, thinking about it, her mouth had curved into the smile that would pronounce their life sentence. They would see the exaction she was making for Dapifer, for Philippa, for humiliation, poverty, pain. She curved it again. Payment in full.

Oh yes, she was in control now. She was the victor.

Now she became fully awake and found herself cold. This was victory, was it? Alone, drinking inferior brandy in a dreary room?

Beasley and Sanders were away some hours. For Makepeace the time was spent in travelling the landscape of her life from the harsh spring of a Boston shoreline into the summer of Dapifer country and on to this chilly, urban winter in which she found herself.

You're scorching your own earth, you madwoman.

You ain't doin' this for him. You ain't even doin' it for you. You like one of them pit wagons, the rails is there an' you jus' runnin' away on 'em.

And truest signpost of all: *You'd have done it anyway. I saw it. One sniff o' that coal and you woke to what you are: as good a businessman as ever came over the Atlantic.* Hedley was right. The years in Northumberland had been the time of her life. Not because she'd made money with which to destroy two souls, not at all; that had merely been the goad, almost the excuse to do what Makepeace Burke was good at doing.

As Lady Dapifer she'd been blessed with an exceptional husband but she hadn't suited his life nor had his suited her. The year she'd spent in society had been astonishing, but only because she'd spent it with him; after a while the endless round of entertainment would have palled.

They had loved each other. In one way she had been good for him, but not, perhaps, good enough; he had suffered continual pinpricks from those who'd disliked her. She'd been his health, he'd said, but in the end she hadn't been able to invest him with enough to stay alive.

Oh Pip. My dear. You married a square peg that didn't fit into anything so well as the shaft of a Northumberland coal mine.

There, at least, was achievement. Whatever else she had or hadn't done, enabling Raby to become a working colliery, creating employment for one hundred men, making a village where their families could live in dignity, was a labour she could show to St Peter with pride.

When John Beasley came back, it was to a woman who'd drunk a lot of brandy and yet was more sober with self-knowledge than she'd ever been in her life. 'Is it done?'

'It's done.' He looked haggard. 'They're taking them to the Fleet. I didn't wait. She was screaming.'

'I'm going back to Newcastle tomorrow,' she said.

'You're going back to Highgate tonight,' he said, ushering her out of the door and down to the coach, 'and I'm damn well coming too. I'm not staying here. You realise that bastard must have been watching this place, waiting for you to leave. Suppose it was an assassin he'd hired—he might try again. Jesus, he could shoot *me* by mistake.'

And Makepeace laughed.

She woke up the next morning to be surprised at how assuaged she felt. Well, she'd escaped death and trampled her enemies underfoot—good reasons as any for a sense of peace. But it wasn't that alone; the battle of the past years hadn't just been with Catty and Conyers, it had been against herself. That, too, was over. At some point during the previous night she'd made terms with Makepeace Burke.

Mrs Burke, it turned out, was not a society woman, nor even a family woman. I'm a businesswoman, she thought. I'm the New Age.

There was movement and rustling in her dressing room. She pulled back the side curtains of the bed. 'What are you doing, Hildy?'

'Packin', missus. We're off hoom.'

So we are. She lay back.

She sat up. 'Last night . . . did I tell you to pack?'

'No, missus, tha was duzzy stannin' up. Tha jus' craaled to yer bed. It was Mr Beasley told me. He's doonstair havin' his breakfast. An', missus'—Hildy's pleased, narrow little face peered round the door—'there's a surprise wi' him.'

They'd finished breakfast by the time she swept into the dining room, looking her best. 'Good morning, John, Mr Hedley.'

They were both reading, Beasley a newspaper, leaning back in his chair, his boots on her delicate Irish tablecloth to show he was a true revolutionary, Andra pencilling notes in the margins of a learned-looking publication. He got up at her entrance, which Beasley did not, and then returned to his journal. 'Morning, missus.' He was as polite, even affable, as he always was nowadays when they met—nothing more.

Makepeace considered him. Despite better cloth and a smarter cut to his coat, he still looked like the man who'd come to do the plumbing.

'While I was risking my damn neck on your errands last night, I rousted Hedley out,' Beasley said. 'He'll travel back north with you.'

'Thank you, Mr Hedley. I have to make two calls in the City first, perhaps we could go on from there.'

'Where?' demanded Beasley.

'The Fleet.'

'God, Andra, she's going to smile. Lord save us from vengeful women.'

The Great Fire of London had destroyed the original Fleet prison but it had been such a profitable enterprise for the previous 500 years that its keepers had rebuilt the place virtually unchanged.

Up again went the long wall with its arched doorway and the grille through which prisoners could beg for alms from passers-by. Up again went four storeys of wards and cubicles for the better-off inmates. Down again went the cellar known as Bartholomew Fair, where those with no money at all lived—and died.

Common criminals incarcerated in it were either hanged, or released after serving their sentence. Debtors, on the other hand, the majority of the prison's population, were in for life unless their creditors relented. And for their sake there was one, delicate addition to the new Fleet: the figure 'nine' was placed above the entrance gates so that they could write and receive letters under the euphemism of '9 Fleet Market'.

Makepeace's coach drew up on the other side of the road and its three occupants peered across at the immense wall opposite.

Her business with Mr Hackbutt had taken longer than she'd expected; it would be late now before they reached Barnet.

'Howay,' wailed Hildy, 'I'm feored o' goin' in.'

'You're not coming,' Makepeace said.

'Best not go in alone,' Hedley said.

'Sanders is coming with me.'

A tipstaff took them to the office of Mr Amos Middleton, assistant keeper. 'Ah, yes, madam. They came in last night. A high-spirited couple, very debonair, very humorous.' So Catty had stopped screaming and put on a show. You had to admire her.

Makepeace told Mr Middleton what she wanted and signed several documents to effect it. It was an expensive procedure; virtually every activity in the Fleet had a price to be paid by inmates or their visitors, the money going into the pocket of Mr Middleton and his superiors.

There was a fee for being led along passages and climbing urine-scented stairs. 'Sixpence in advance is the usual, ma'am,' her turnkey escort told her. 'Shillin' if you want me to wait.'

'D'you charge for breathing?' Makepeace asked as she paid him.

'Air's free,' he said cheerfully. 'Diseases extra.'

Despite the law forbidding spirits to be sold in prisons, there was a taproom on both second and third floors. Vomit along the passageway outside suggested trade was brisk. There was a skittles alley, a food hall, a chapel where a wedding was in progress . . .

As they reached the top floor, the turnkey slapped his leg with his keys: 'Number Four, o' *course*. I remember *them*. Come in last night, lady pretty, gentleman humorous. Ordered visitin' cards to be printed immediate with this address. Got to admire 'em.'

Number Four was quiet, its door closed.

The turnkey raised a circular disc attached by a nail to the door and peered through the hole behind it, then nodded to Makepeace to take his place. 'Nice 'n' quiet.'

Conyers sat on the bare boards of a truckle bed, both arms round Catty who was leaning against his shoulder, her eyes closed. As Makepeace watched, he pulled a handkerchief from his pocket and wiped the spittle from her mouth. When he heard the door opening, he laid Catty gently on the bed. His face went blank on seeing Makepeace, then he smiled. 'I missed, did I?'

'You did.'

'Ah, well.' He sat himself on the edge of the bed so that Catty's head was hidden behind him.

Surprisingly, it *was* a nice room. The ceiling sloped down to enclose an open dormer window beyond which Makepeace could see the masts of small trading boats in the Fleet inlet. 'Close that window, will you?' Conyers said. 'It's chilly in here.'

Makepeace closed it. The turnkey brought her a stool and returned to join Sanders in the passage outside, leaving the door open.

Conyers brushed some dust off his knee. 'Well,' he said, 'that brings us to Plan Two. We sell Grosvenor Square.'

'No.' Makepeace reached into her reticule for her account book. 'You passed that alternative on . . . March the 22nd. The loans and interest overtook the value.'

'Nice house,' Conyers said persuasively.

'I know. I lived in it.'

'So you did. One forgets.'

She'd forgotten what a pleasant face Conyers had: trustworthy, not too handsome, not plain, very English. As much a mask, she thought, as the one he'd worn last night when he tried to kill her.

'Did you buy *all* the debts? Coal trade must be profitable.'

'Very.'

'That rather brings us to Plan Three: we recognise your marriage as legal.'

Makepeace shook her head. 'I'm advised I'll win the case anyway.'

Conyers examined his fingernails. 'Plan Four then.' He leaned forward suddenly; she smelt sweat. 'Cancel the debts, set my wife free and I confess—before witnesses—to attempting to murder you.'

It was love of a sort. Hadn't Dapifer once said Conyers was the better man? *No he ain't, Pip*. The man was acting, not for her, but to some unseen audience applauding in his mind: old schoolfellows, regimental officers, fellow gamblers, playing to a conception of honour that precluded the paying of bills and murder.

She shook her head. 'I doubt you'd hang and there'd be a term to your sentence. This way you're both in for life.'

She watched the long eyes flicker towards the doorway and assess the chances of gouging out her windpipe before Sanders and the turnkey could stop him, and saw the regretful rejection.

She said, 'That's what I *intended*.'

He leaped at the past tense. 'You changed your mind?'

She reached into her reticule for papers tied together with black ribbon. She took them with her to the window and pointed. 'Sooner or later,' she said, 'there will be a schooner in the Pool out there. Her captain will be handed some money you can survive on for a while when you reach your destination. *If* you two will be aboard her when she sets sail, and *if* you sign these papers now, I won't pursue the debt.'

'Where's she bound?'

'The Carolinas. Other criminals have prospered over there. I'm sure you will.'

'And what are the papers?'

They damned him. There was an acknowledgment that Major and Mrs Conyers owed Lady Dapifer, otherwise known as Mrs Makepeace Burke, the sum of £190,000 exclusive of interest, the debt to be pursued if they returned to England. Another acknowledgment by Major and Mrs Conyers that they had committed adultery while Mrs Conyers had been married to Sir Philip Dapifer and a recognition of Sir Philip's subsequent divorce. That Sir Philip's second marriage had been legal and that his daughter, Philippa, by this second marriage was therefore the true owner of all his estates.

The last document he balked at. 'I'm not signing this.' It was a confession that he had attempted to defraud his ward, Lord Ffoulkes, of moneys from the property known as Barton Wood. Odd, she thought, that he should bridle at the admission of a crime involving considerably less money and hurt than that committed against her and Philippa. But Andrew was of his own set; it was the one offence his audience would not forgive. He was blustering however; he had to sign.

'Do you intend to publish these?'

'Only if you come back.'

They waited for the turnkey to bring pen and ink. Conyers, showing agitation for the first time, left the bed to pace the room, leaving Catty exposed. Makepeace looked and then looked away. The woman's eyes were half open but fixed on a point in the ceiling; saliva came from the corner of her mouth.

Don't pity her; she didn't pity you. Yet to see the damn woman vulnerable was like watching a wolf limping.

She said gently, 'Let me get her a doctor.'

Conyers turned. 'How dare you,' he said. 'How *dare* you. She's merely tired. And you're not fit to lick her shoes.'

The turnkey came back and, with Sanders, witnessed Conyers's signatures. Makepeace put the papers in her reticule; they were as watertight as Mr Hackbutt had been able to make them in the time. She was also putting her trust in the two tipstaffs and Mr Hackbutt himself who were to take the transportees on board when the ship came, only leaving it themselves as it passed Tilbury for the open sea.

She'd promised herself she wouldn't say it but she did. 'Did you never wonder what happened to us? Did you care at *all*?'

He was calm again. He considered it. 'Do you know, I don't think I did. Somehow one doesn't attribute feelings of any depth to the lower classes. What made you change your mind?'

Mr Hackbutt had asked her the same question that very morning. Why had she decided to let her catch off the hook?

There'd been so many reasons. Because revenge was not, after all, a dish better eaten cold; it palled. Because she had lost so much in pursuing it. Because she had found a completion in herself that this diminished couple would never know. Because she knew what love was. Because Jesus would have forgiven them—and so would Pip Dapifer.

She searched now for explanations that would hurt—she wasn't that much of a Christian—while still being true. She shrugged and made for the door. 'Actually, you did me a good turn. If you hadn't robbed me, I'd never've found out how clever I was at making money.'

Did that sting? Well, here's another. 'And Pip found you pitiable. Even when he caught you swiving his wife, he pitied you both.'

'God,' he said, 'you're a barbarian, aren't you? Sheer gutterslush. What did he ever see in you?'

She whipped round. 'What did he ever see in you?'

He was shaking but he smiled. 'It's called style.'

'It's called shit,' she said and left.

Hedley was waiting for her in the street. 'Did you smile?'

'I meant to,' she said wearily. 'But there wasn't much to smile about.'

'Relieved at the thought of Carolina, were they?'

'Not much.' She blew out her cheeks. 'The money they've cost me. It'll be the most expensive voyage in history.' And not just the money, she thought. They've cost me everything. Or *I've* cost me everything.

A voice behind them said, 'We won't make Barnet 'less we go now, missus.'

'All right, Sanders. Just one more delay tomorrow.' To Hedley, she said, 'There's somebody I must say goodbye to.'

'As you please,' he said.

It was no better in the coach; he was pleasant and unapproachable, talking mostly in dialect to Hildy, who adored him.

'Tell me about your fire-damp experiments, Mr Hedley,' she said.

Immediately the coach interior became a Leyden jar of energy. If we'd got fire-damp in here, she thought, he'd explode it all by himself. As it did when he was in the grip of emotion, his speech became increasingly Northumbrian. 'There's a mystery to yon bloody gas and 'lessen we solve the sod it'll continue to slay good men.' He glared at Makepeace. 'An' bloody coal-owners are wussun useless: "Why fret, Andra? It's coal that matters, not the poer yakkors as hew it." Porvorse sods.'

It would have been useless to point out that *he* was a coal-owner; he could never ally himself with the overlords. *And that's why I love him.*

She said, 'You're bloody-minded enough to make a good American.'

He didn't rise to it; he wasn't going to ally himself with her either. 'I met another o' them, t'other day,' he said. 'Young Beasley introduced us. Benjamin Franklin. Know him?'

She shook her head.

They dined at Barnet, went to their separate beds and set off again next morning. At Hatfield, she told Sanders to stay on the Great North Road instead of making for Hertford. 'I'll tell you when to turn.'

Evening was drawing in; they were encountering wagons carrying corn, bales of straw and tired men and women. She realised with a shock that she had lost track of the seasons—in the years since Dapifer's death, she'd been too busy to relate that September to this.

The weather was more chilly, though drier, than it had been then; it looked as if it was another poor harvest. She thought, That'll put the price of coal up, and grimaced at herself for thinking it.

'Next turning left, Sanders.'

The lanes seemed narrower than she remembered, at some points brambles scratched the sides of the coach. This was neglect: they hadn't been trimming the hedges. By the time they'd gone through the splash and were heading uphill to the village, it was becoming difficult to see into the fields.

At the Littles' house she made the introductions then cut the family's welcome short. 'I've foreclosed on the place, Peter. I'm the new owner.' She was too strung up to give explanations. 'I'll leave my party here for a while if I may. Are the gates open?'

Without a look at Hedley, she set off along the village street. Peter walked with her, carrying keys and a lantern.

'What happened?' Some of the cottages were empty.

'They didn't have any interest in the place,' he said. 'Absent most of the time. Took the rents but didn't pay the wages. Freeholders have mostly gone—Edgar took his family to Birmingham to work in a factory. They'd have starved here else.'

'We'll enclose now,' she said. 'I want you to see to it.'

The gates were locked. She'd been dreading them. They'd lost their massivity and looked rusty. One squealed as Peter pushed it open.

'You go back now,' she said.

'You'll need the key.' He handed it to her; he knew where she was going. He paused. 'We keep it nice.'

'I knew you would.'

The elegant leaves of the sweet chestnuts showed pale in the light of the lantern as she made her way up the avenue to the churchyard. At the door of the vault she had to put the lantern on the ground and struggled with both hands to turn the huge key in its escutcheoned lock. She had to lean backwards to pull it open.

She picked up the lantern and went carefully down the steps. One relief: the place smelt merely of fungi. The candlelight fell on shelves filled with coffins; she raised the lantern up and down, looking.

They have taken my Lord, and I know not where they have laid him.

But, of course, it was the newest. She found it at the vault's far end. She'd been expecting—they'd had so little time. But this . . . oh God, they'd found some London undertaker to provide a monstrosity of lead funerary wreaths and eye-hiding cherubs to acquit their conscience and satisfy the audience they played to.

Did you laugh at it, Pip? Of course you did.

She put her fingers to her lips, kissed them, touched the plaque bearing the family motto . . . and waited. There were so many things to tell him and she couldn't think of any of them.

Beside her, the lantern guttered and went out, leaving her in the dark—though not the blackness she'd experienced in the Raby drift; the moon came and went. What had she expected? Confrontation? Reunion? Instead, she was sending love and gratitude into nothing—but not a vacuum, a *space*. He'd gone on to wherever he was going and left her to go on to wherever she wanted to go. '*Oh, Pip*,' she said.

A figure in the doorway interrupted the light from outside. 'Where are you? You all right? I were worried.'

She said, crying, 'He's gone, he's not here.'

'I am,' Hedley said. He came down the steps. 'Shall we go, pet?'

'Yes.'

Once outside, she took his arm. 'Do we *have* to be married?'

'I'm not fathering bastards, I can tell you that.'

She stopped. 'You want *children*?'

'My brains and my looks,' he said, 'they'll be grand. And we'll have young Philippa home. Ben Franklin reckons it's not so quiet over there as it looks. I told him: I know Americans, I said, red-haired, mule-headed, bound to cause trouble.'

'Porvorse sods,' she said happily.

DIANA NORMAN

At the age of twenty, Diana Norman was one of the youngest female journalists ever to be employed in Fleet Street and learned the hard way how to survive and prosper in a male-dominated society; a subject she has subsequently enjoyed pursuing in her historical biographies and novels. After working on the *Daily Herald*, later to become *The Sun*, for five years, she met and married film critic Barry Norman and had two daughters. At this point she started to write freelance articles for magazines. 'Luckily for me, *She* magazine commissioned me to write six pieces on "Women in History",' she told me. 'And the more I delved, the more I found these most astounding women and so the series continued for a couple of years.' One of the women she discovered was the first woman ever to win a seat in the House of Commons in 1918, Countess Markievicz, but as a Sinn Feinn candidate the countess refused to accept it. 'What annoys me,' Diana says, with passion, 'is that she has almost entirely faded from history and is only mentioned as a footnote to the fact that Lady Astor was the first woman to take her seat in the House.' Indeed, it is the injustice of history that riles Diana Norman. 'Just take Henry II. He was the best king this country ever had—gave us the jury system, Common Law, ruled an empire from Scotland to the Pyrenees—and all he is remembered for is bumping off Thomas à Becket, which Becket deserved, I must tell you. It

seems to me that throughout history the wrong people had the best PR.'

Her love of history and her need to 'get things right' means that Diana Norman painstakingly researches every historical detail, often reading four or five books just for one sentence. 'My first book about Henry II took me fifteen years to write and was received with great critical acclaim. Then I received a letter from an academic in which she wrote: "My dear, in one of your chapters a bucket clanks but there would have been no clanking buckets in the twelfth century." And she was right—they would have been made of wood.' Diana Norman smiles at me, resignedly. 'Oh, how I sometimes wish I had decided to write thrillers!'

Her research for *A Catch of Consequence* took her to Boston as well as to the depths of an eighteenth-century Northumberland coal mine. 'How on earth they got people to go down there, I don't know, what with the coal-dust and the fire-gas which would split them in two like herrings. In the mine we went down we crouched all the way and I can't tell you what the dark was like when the miner blew the candle out.'

Diana Norman has become so fond of her character, Makepeace Burke, that her next two novels will continue to feature her exploits, and those of her entourage. 'Having been a little involved in the Industrial Revolution, I thought I would now place her in both the American and French Revolutions. It is such a fascinating period of history, and a knowledge of history, you know, helps us to understand today's world a little better.'

Jane Eastgate

PICTURE CREDITS: COVER: Terry Husebye/Gettyone Stone. Susan Madison photograph, and page 161: © Jerry Bauer. Claire Calman photograph, and page 313 © Faye Norman. Diana Norman photograph, and page 479: © HarperCollins. TOUCHING THE SKY: pages 6 & 7: illustration by Claire Rankin. I LIKE IT LIKE THAT: pages 162 & 163: illustration by Kim Smith @ Eastwing. A CATCH OF CONSEQUENCE: pages 314 & 315: illustration by Kim McGillivray @ Debut Art.

Printed and bound by Maury Imprimeur SA, Malesherbes, France

601-018-1